FREE BLACK CANARY
Book One

Free Black Canary

Book 1: Captivity, Volume 1

Nox

Published by Nox, 2025.

FREE BLACK CANARY

First edition. July 29, 2025.

Copyright © 2025 Nox.

ISBN: 979-8999704214

Written by Nox.

Chapter 1

The Fox-Helmed Warlord

Warm water surged up her nose.

Melodie gasped, her body jolting as she broke the surface, coughing and spitting, limbs flailing in the thick, black pool. Her boots scraped stone, lungs fighting for air. She dragged herself to the shallow edge, palms slick with something that felt more like oil than water, and collapsed on the cold stone floor. The air was damp and metallic. Echoes of dripping liquid bounced off unseen walls.

She rolled to her side as she vomited up mouthfuls of water. Her head throbbed, and her tongue tasted of iron and moss. She pushed herself up on shaky arms and stared at the pool behind her, the same one she'd slipped into. But this wasn't the cave in Botswana. The rocks were wrong. The air was warm and heavy, thick with the scent of blooming things she didn't recognize. Her fingers trembled as she touched the back of her head and felt a tender, swollen bump. She'd hit something. She must have blacked out. But how long had she been out?

Dragging herself to her feet, she stumbled toward a narrow shaft of light ahead. As she stepped out of the cave and into open air, she froze.

She stood at the mouth of a jagged cliffside, staring out over a lush valley blanketed in vibrant greenery. The plants here didn't belong to any ecosystem she knew. Fuzzy vines in gold and violet climbed the trees in spirals, their blossoms wide and glowing faintly in the daylight. Towering stalks with fan-shaped leaves cast strange shadows on the ground, and the wind carried a thick, floral sweetness that made her lungs burn.

The trees, God, the trees, were too tall, their bark smooth and violet-brown, their leaves shaped like fans and flowers, iridescent with pinks, sapphires, and deep, bruised reds. The sky was wrong too, too blue, almost purple near the horizon. The sun hung high and golden, casting long, strange shadows across the hills.

Melodie stepped forward carefully, boots crunching on unfamiliar stone. Every nerve in her body screamed that she wasn't in her world anymore.

This wasn't Africa.

Then, screams. It started as a distant shout, then erupted into chaos. Melodie turned sharply as a stampede of people barreled past her, men, women, children, wild-eyed and dirty, running barefoot and desperate through the brush. Their clothes were torn, their skin streaked with sweat and fear. She had no time to ask questions before they swept past her in a blur of panic.

And chasing them, thundering behind on massive horses, were the riders. Melodie barely had a second to process it. The riders were not human. Or if they were, something had twisted them. Towering, armored beings cloaked in white and gray, each wearing silver helmets shaped like snarling animals, foxes, wolves, lynxes. They moved in precision, coordinated like a unit, each rider holding strange, shimmering nets that buzzed with magic as they swung them toward the fleeing captives.

Her stomach twisted. A raid. A hunt. One of the riders peeled off from the group, heading straight for her. He was enormous, his long braid whipping behind him as his horse galloped through the grass. Sunlight glinted off the white fox emblem engraved on his chestplate. He held up a silver collar etched with ancient script, its center glowing faintly blue.

Melodie's heart pounded. He shouted something at her, harsh, rhythmic syllables in a language unlike any she'd studied on Earth. When she didn't respond, the warrior dismounted, striding toward her with commanding purpose. His eyes were pale, almost silver, piercing beneath the shadow of his helmet. He raised the collar again, gesturing for her to step forward. She didn't move. He scowled and reached for her arm.

Big mistake.

She twisted under his grip, hooked her leg behind his knee, and yanked. The warrior stumbled, thrown off balance by her calculated force. A ripple of surprise moved through the other captives. The warrior growled and barked an order, but before the others could react, they parted.

A figure approached, mounted atop a black beast that barely seemed real. Its hooves didn't strike the ground; they glided. The rider wore a silver cloak over his armor, and his helmet, an ornate fox's face with curling horns and etched runes that pulsed faintly, marked him as something more. Authority. Power. Melodie felt it instantly in the way the air shifted. The way every other soldier stiffened. She braced herself.

The commander dismounted with practiced grace, walking toward her with the quiet patience of a predator. His pale tan eyes scanned her, sharp and unreadable. She saw no mercy there. Only calculation. Then, without warning, he lunged. Melodie barely ducked in time as a polished staff arced over her head. She dropped low, kicked out hard, but he danced back. The weapon wasn't for killing. Not yet. It was a test. Another swing—she blocked it with her forearm, winced as the impact reverberated through her bones. She was fast, but he was faster. Stronger. Still, she refused to go down without a fight. She feinted left, then pivoted right and slammed her boot into his chest.

It worked. The commander staggered, his helmet flying from his head and clattering to the ground. Sunlight hit his face. Melodie froze. He was beautiful, in a severe, otherworldly way, high cheekbones, long silver-blond hair damp with sweat, and ears that stretched upward, pointed and elegant. His expression barely changed, but something in his gaze flickered. He hadn't expected her to land that hit. She crouched, breathing hard. Her heart thundered in her ears.

Then, she felt it. Heat. He was already on his feet. The staff struck her ribs, and she gasped. The next blow hit her shoulder. She stumbled, winded, and then, too late, one cracked against her throat.

Everything blurred. She dropped. A bag was yanked over her head. And just like that, the world vanished into darkness. The world was spinning. Pain pulsed at the back of her skull, limbs heavy and senses dulled. She tried to breathe, but the air was thick, sour with smoke and blood. Her vision was gone, encased in the scratchy fabric of a sack cinched tightly over her head. Only the sound of rattling wheels and the rhythmic creak of wood told her she was in some sort of moving carriage. Her wrists burned where they were bound. She clenched her jaw and inhaled, trying to summon her training. Assess. Analyze. Adapt.

But all she had were questions. "What is this place?"

The last thing she remembered was the mission in Botswana. Chasing a signal, slipping near a pool in a cave, then nothing. No, not nothing. She remembered falling. The icy slap of water. And something else. A sound, deep and pulsing, like thunder trapped beneath the earth.

Then darkness. And now... this.

Suddenly, the carriage groaned to a halt. She was dragged out of the cart, her boots stumbling against the ground. Heat struck her like a wall. Bright light filtered through the cloth over her head. Her skin prickled with sweat beneath layers of her now-wet uniform. Then she heard a small voice in front of her. Gentle. Curious.

"Want bag off, miss?" She flinched. A child? She nodded instinctively, not trusting her voice yet.

Tiny fingers reached for the sack. The drawstrings were tugged, and after a few seconds of fumbling, the bag peeled away. Blinding light flooded her vision. Melodie squinted against the sharp glare. Her eyes watered. Slowly, the world came into view. And what she saw knocked the wind from her lungs.

She stood in the middle of what could only be described as a primitive slave encampment. The clearing around her was bustling with movement, humanoid figures crouched or shuffled in the shadows, wearing crude garments made of stitched hides, dried vines, or nothing at all. Some were stark naked but for smears of dirt and crude tattoos. Others bore wild hair, broken nails, and empty, hollow eyes.

They were human... or something close to it.

Melodie's gaze swept the area. The landscape beyond the crude camp was strange, like some fantasy-world hybrid of jungle and forest. Trees with multicolored leaves twisted up into a golden sky. Plants she'd never seen before, large, spiraled ferns and thick, pulsing blossoms, overgrew the hills in every direction.

The air shimmered faintly, like it was alive with heat or... magic? Her attention returned to the camp.

Smoke billowed from a fire pit in the center. Around it, huddled groups of prisoners whispered or wept. Some looked half-dead. Others looked long past caring. There were no fences, just guards. Dozens of them. Their weapons weren't standard metal blades either; some shimmered like molten crystal or dark obsidian, wickedly curved and humming faintly.

And they weren't speaking English. She turned slowly to look at her rescuer. A small black-haired girl, barefoot and rail thin, stood before her with a solemn face streaked in grime. Her oversized eyes blinked curiously up at Melodie.

"Thank you," Melodie muttered, her voice dry. She lifted her wrists and gestured.

"Can you cut these off?"

The child tilted her head. "What is?"

Melodie sighed and turned her hands to gesture at the ropes constricting her.

"Ohh."

The girl spun and ran off. She returned with a jagged stone blade, nearly too big for her little hands. Carefully, she began sawing through the bindings. It took a moment, but eventually the cords snapped and fell to the dirt.

"Free now," the child said proudly.

Melodie rubbed where the dark bruises were forming. She glanced down at the girl.

"Thanks, kid. I owe you."

She turned, now able to fully assess her surroundings—and the shock of it nearly made her stumble. This wasn't any rough slave encampment, but a fortress built for containment, a brutal monument of stone and fear. Towering walls, thick as ancient trees and mottled with age, encircled a courtyard as vast as a football field, swallowing hundreds of what looked like feral humans inside its cold embrace.

There was only one way in or out, a single iron-banded gate guarded by Awyan soldiers in sharp, bright armor, their laughter echoing from the battlements overhead. The courtyard itself was chaos—a sprawl of mud huts and ragged tents clustered beneath the open sky, each one packed with filthy, wide-eyed captives. In the center loomed a processing hall, its stone archways choked with lines of the dirty and half-starved, their arms marked, their hair wild, faces haunted. Staircases along the walls led up to the battlements where more soldiers watched, rifles and strange blades at their hips, and here and there were smaller stone wings that housed the Awyan guards themselves.

Enormous banners flapped in the dry wind—red, gold, and white, each bearing the bloody emblem of a predatory bird gripping a handful of tiny, writhing figures in its talons. There was no mercy here, no privacy, no hope of escape. Melodie's skin crawled with the knowledge that this place was a machine designed to break spirits and bodies alike, and she knew in her bones she was in the wrong place, for reasons she did not yet understand.

The guards stiffened, their hands darting to their weapons. Good.

"I am Major Melodie Jaxxon, an officer in the United States Army. Take me to your commander."

The guards stared. Then one mocked her, mimicking her in a strange tongue and tone with exaggerated gestures. The others laughed.

She didn't. "I said," she snapped, "take me to whoever's in charge."

The little girl beside her spoke again, her voice small but matter-of-fact. "They no speak our tongue."

Melodie glanced down, brow furrowing. "You again?" The girl just shrugged.

"What language are they speaking?"

"Awyan."

The word meant nothing to her. It didn't exist in any linguistic catalogue she'd ever heard of. Her stomach twisted. Before she could say more, two of the guards reached for her.

Big mistake.

Melodie kicked upward, twisting out of their grip. One elbowed her from behind and she dropped to the ground, spun, and drove her heel into his knee. He collapsed with a roar. Another tried to grab her; she ducked, struck his ribs, and shoved off with full force. Melodie's chest rose and fell with short, furious breaths. Her wrists were sore from the restraints, her throat still aching where a guard had struck her, but her spirit remained unbroken. She stood tall, her eyes fixed defiantly on the figure moving toward her.

He approached in silence. The fox-helmed warlord. Silver-blonde hair spilled down to his shoulders as he removed his helmet, revealing a face too sharp, too perfect, like it had been sculpted to rule. His pale tan eyes, cool as winter sand, locked on hers with a predator's stillness. He stopped just in front of her. And then, without a word, he lifted his left hand to his mouth and tugged the glove free with his teeth. The leather dropped to the dirt. Melodie's heart kicked in her chest.

His hand was bare now—long, calloused fingers, scarred and deceptively elegant. He studied her face as though bracing for contamination. Even before he touched her, he could feel something in the air tightening around his ribs. With quiet finality, he gripped her jaw. Not hard. Not soft either. Skin to skin.

The moment his palm settled along her cheek, his senses fractured. A thin, cold pressure shot up his arm. His vision wavered at the edges. The texture of her skin became magnified, too vivid to parse. Melodie jerked her head, but his fingers clamped tighter, tilting her chin. He tried to pretend it was only discipline, only protocol. But every nerve in his hand sparked with a strange, electric awareness he could not name.

He was inspecting her. Studying her like she was a strange species—something unknown and possibly toxic. His thumb moved along the ridge of her cheek, over the bruises. He felt every swollen contour, every uneven edge. The contact should have been clinical and measured. But it was not.

The instant her skin shifted under his, a low shiver coursed across his chest. The air thickened around them. His hearing dulled. All he could register was the rasp of her breathing and the violent drumbeat of his own pulse. A sharp, invisible current rippled between them, like a spark leaping across a live wire. He almost pulled away. Almost showed her she was undoing him.

Her heart lurched. He felt it as if it were his own, an echo beneath his palm. The heat on her skin changed, seeping inward. His magic stirred in response without his permission. His blood pulled toward her touch, a magnetic ache that made his jaw tighten.

Her limbs went still. His pupils dilated—not with fear but with something worse.

Recognition he could not name. Beneath his skin, ancient instincts coiled tight and alert. The sensation was too strong, too sudden. He tried to will it away, but it pressed deeper, a demand he could not understand. He did not know what it was, only that it unsettled him more than any blade. The reaction felt elemental, primal, as if some hidden piece of him was trying to crawl out and claim her.

He ground his teeth and fought the hot crawl in his throat. It had to be adrenaline. He told himself it was curiosity or heat. Nothing more. But his hand was shaking.

Forcing her mouth open with a sharp tug of his fingers, needing the contact to end.

Melodie did not hesitate. She bit him. Hard.

His breath caught. The sound that broke free was a growl, deep and raw, almost involuntary. White heat flared behind his eyes as her teeth sank into his flesh, as if she were rooting deeper into the hollow place the contact had carved open. Blood spilled over her tongue, warm and metallic, strangely sweet.

He yanked back with a curse in his native tongue. Blood dripped down his wrist. The air pressed thick against his skin, and his heartbeat would not slow. His face twisted in fury, then froze. The pain did not land the way it should have. It blurred into something else. Something far worse.

Pleasure, dark and immediate.

It speared through him like a spike through the gut, a slow burn licking down his spine. His body reacted to the pain, to her defiance, to the feel of her mouth closing over him. His pulse surged, every beat a violent, dizzying throb. His breathing turned ragged. He hated the sound of it, uneven and exposed.

Heat coiled low in his abdomen. Arousal.

His jaw locked with such brutal force it felt like bone might splinter. Disgust rose sharp and choking. He was aroused by a bite, by her, by a canariae. His limbs trembled with the effort not to betray more.

Revulsion washed over him in a shudder. He snarled and shoved her away.

She struck the dirt with a dull grunt, coughing on dust.

In the next breath, a metal collar snapped around her throat. He needed distance. He needed the iron weight of it to restore order to his mind. A chain clipped to the ring at her neck, its length the only thing holding him back from collapse.

One of the guards laughed and spat near her feet. She did not move. Her body still buzzed, nerves frayed from the surge. Her mouth tasted of his blood.

The warlord turned without speaking, his voice locked behind clenched teeth. He snapped an order in Awyan, and the guards obeyed. He did not look back at her. He did not dare. She watched him walk away, breath ragged.

Around her, the fire crackled. The other prisoners edged back into the shadows, peering at her from hollow eyes and tangled hair. No one came near. No one spoke. Her heart thudded in her ears.

Then, from the edge of the shadows, a small figure stepped into the light. The little girl.

She moved carefully, barefoot, her narrow frame half-drowned in a tattered tunic that hung off one shoulder. A cluster of beads jingled faintly at her ankle as she approached, like tiny bells warning the world she was coming.

Melodie didn't move. The child came close, unafraid. Her dark eyes rose to meet Melodie's, and she crouched beside her, reaching out with hesitant fingers. She touched her arm, gentle as a breeze.

"Your skin..." she whispered, eyes wide. "Very dark."

Melodie blinked, throat tight. "Yeah, kid. People have dark skin."

The girl tilted her head, thoughtful. She raised her own thin arm beside Melodie's.

"Some dark like sand," she said quietly. "None dark like night sky."

Melodie didn't know what to say to that. She looked away, past the firelight, beyond the thornwood trees and the silent huts. Twin moons hovered above the forest canopy, pale and watching, casting a lavender hue across the alien sky. Her chest rose slowly.

Where the hell am I?

Chapter 2

The Language of Chains

Melodie could still taste blood in her mouth from where she'd bitten him. Her wrists still ached from the coarse bindings, and the thick metal collar around her neck felt like a branding mark—tight, humiliating, and relentless.

The warriors who had chained her had since moved away, now standing guard outside the hut, but she could still feel their presence like a heat on the back of her neck. She leaned her head back against the wooden post and closed her eyes, trying to calm the tremble in her breath. She needed a plan, something beyond brute force, but all her thoughts kept spiraling back to what led her here.

To the lab. The mission. Her team. Yesterday, they'd still been alive.

She slipped into the memory like falling through silk, reality thickening around her mind. They'd been in Botswana, deep in the caves, searching for mineral traces to counteract the Cotard-Virus, the plague that had collapsed the last governments. Their gear was minimal. Their hope, even less. Melodie moved with her unit in silence, the only sound the echo of boots on stone. The air reeked of sulfur and soil, heavy with condensation. Then she saw it, a pale shimmer at the mouth of a narrow offshoot. It didn't belong there. No natural light looked like that. She stepped forward. The tunnel widened into a cavern. At its center, a still pool glowed, lit from within like a buried star. She knelt, the warmth of it brushing her face.

Beautiful. Then, her foot slipped. The fall was sudden. Her head cracked against the stone edge, and before she could scream, the pool swallowed her.

Darkness.

She jolted out of her daydream, chest heaving like she'd surfaced from drowning. For a moment, she was still falling, still wet, still lost in that cave. But the cold collar dragged her back. This wasn't Earth.

Shouting beyond the wooden walls confirmed it, none of the voices spoke any language she knew. The air tasted wrong, too heavy, too sharp, tinged with metal. Alien. The kind of place where the land itself might bleed if cut.

A clank rang out. Guards barked orders, boots scraping against stone as they moved into formation. Melodie stiffened.

Something tugged her sleeve. She looked down. The girl from before, the one with wide eyes and dirt-streaked cheeks, was clutching her torn uniform. She was trembling, her tiny fingers wrapped tight around Melodie like she was the last solid thing in the world.

Melodie dropped her voice low. "Don't be afraid. Stay quiet."

Footsteps approached. She recognized one of them, the smug guard who'd tripped her earlier. He opened the cell and yanked her out by the arm. She twisted, but his grip was iron. The child gasped as the door slammed shut.

Melodie barely found her footing before he kicked her knee. She collapsed hard, stone biting through her pants and into her skin. Then a shadow fell over her.

She looked up. Polished black armor gleamed where dust hadn't dulled it, etched with markings she didn't recognize. A long gray-tipped fur cloak hung from broad shoulders. His platinum hair, thick and loose, fell in silken waves down his back. Pale tan eyes fixed on her, cold and assessing beneath dark, slashed brows. His face was all brutal elegance—high cheekbones, strong jaw, lips set in a grim, impassive line. He stood tall, six foot four, maybe more, his body honed like a weapon, radiating restrained violence.

He studied her like a riddle that shouldn't exist but now refused to be ignored. There was no mercy in his gaze, no revulsion either. Just sharp, silent interest. And something deeper. Recognition. Hunger. Like some part of him knew her already, before his mind had even caught up.

Without a word, his eyes shifted toward the guard beside him. The man obeyed immediately, fisting her hair and jerking her upright, her scalp screaming under the strain. Pain flared behind her eyes, but Melodie refused to cry out. Rage boiled in her veins—she would not let them see her break.

Then, another figure emerged behind Malec. This one was leaner, dressed in a high-collared dark robe with silver clasps. His wavy brown hair was neatly combed, his golden eyes sharp with academic curiosity. He crouched in front of her, brushing the dust from her shoulder and examining the tears in her uniform like a biologist inspecting a specimen. Every touch made her skin crawl. She glared, jaw tight, but he acted as if she were a thing, not a woman, not a soldier, not a person at all.

He muttered something in their language, running his fingers over the seams of her uniform. Melodie's lip curled as humiliation simmered beneath her skin. She snarled, her body taut with the urge to fight, to rip free, but the guard's grip was iron and her wrists were still sore from the chains.

He ignored her, clearly more fascinated by the military patches on her sleeve than the fury in her face. Malec barked a short phrase. The golden-eyed man responded softly, but then, to her shock, he switched to Mandarin.

"Nǐ néng lǐjiě ma?" (Can you understand?)

A cold knot of confusion twisted in Melodie's gut. Mandarin? She blinked, struggling to find her voice, her mind spinning. Her Mandarin was poor. Was this a trick, a test, another way to unnerve her? She hesitated, pride warring with uncertainty. He frowned, then tried again in German.

"Verstehst du?" (Do you understand?)

She did understand this one. A small thrill of vindication shot through her. She let it sharpen into something savage. Her lips curled into a sneer.

"Ich werde dich töten." (I will kill you.)

The reaction was immediate. He flinched, visibly startled. Several guards tensed. The guard who held her punished her with a savage kick to the ribs. She folded over, breathless, pain rippling through her like a cracking whip, but she held onto the anger, the pride of having shaken them, even if only for a heartbeat.

Still, the tall warlord didn't falter. But his companion looked pale now. He muttered quickly to the tall white-haired one in their language, one word repeating. Melodie tried to steady her breathing, her heart pounding, mind latching onto that word.

Canariae.

She sat up straighter, despite the ache in her side, her breath shallow and tight in her throat. That word—it had a Latin root. Or something like it. But twisted, bent through the tongue of another world. She wondered what it meant here, wondered if it meant her death or something worse.

The golden-eyed elf crouched again, studying her face with the same fascination a scientist might show to a captured animal.

His golden eyes glinted behind his gold rimmed glasses as he asked, in clipped German, "Du sprichst diese Canariae Sprache der Sklaven?" (You speak this Canariae language of the slaves?)

Her hands curled into fists. Shame and anger tangled in her chest. She snarled back, "I speak many languages."

Even as she spoke, her mind whirled with questions, with the need to hold onto anything familiar—words, languages, the memory of home.

The golden-eyed one's gaze lit with interest. He tilted his head slightly, murmuring as if to himself, "Field Canariae dialect... but structured. More grammar."

It wasn't meant for her, it was a note to himself, a scholar's curiosity sparked by the oddity before him. She hated the way he looked at her, as if she were some specimen trapped in a jar. She forced herself to meet his eyes, refusing to be cowed.

Straightening slowly, he said louder, "I speak... a little. This tongue. Field Canariae."

His accent was thick, the rhythm of his words offbeat. Consonants twisted, vowels drawn out, and yet, Melodie recognized the attempt at English. Or something close. She blinked, startled, caught off guard by the effort. Her lips parted, a flicker of surprise breaking through the hardened mask she'd worn for hours.

He pointed at her tattered, mud-streaked uniform.

"You... soldier? Not breed slave?" he asked cautiously, as if the words themselves were fragile.

"I'm a Major in the United States Army," she replied coldly, lifting her chin in defiance.

The words left her mouth like thrown blades, but inside, her pulse hammered with uncertainty. Did these people even know what a soldier was? Would it help or hurt her chances of survival?

The elf repeated her words under his breath, tasting the rhythm.

"Mai-zhor... Un-it-ed Staytes... Not know these," he said, then muttered to himself again in Awyan.

Melodie's stomach twisted. She had no idea what that meant, but the way he said it, like a quiet admission of something impossible, sent a chill down her spine. Before she could ask, the warlord beside him shifted. Silent and imposing, he gave the golden-eyed elf a short nod, barely perceptible, but commanding. Melodie's heart jumped. Whatever happened next, she'd face it on her feet, not on her knees.

The elf's jaw tightened. His shoulder-length wavy hair moved with him as he turned toward the guards and called out sharply in Awyan.

"Tey'nashra kai. Kaer'ta shaen." (Take her inside. Bind her again.)

They obeyed instantly, grabbing her by the arms as her wrists were re-fastened in thick iron. But Melodie didn't struggle this time. Not because she had given up. Because something had changed. They didn't know what she was. And she was going to make damn sure they'd regret finding out. Fury was her armor, and survival was still her mission.

The air inside was thick with smoke and heat. Strange oils burned in sconces of bone and copper, casting an amber glow that flickered along the uneven wooden walls. Animal hides hung limp between rust-red tapestries stitched with unfamiliar symbols. The floor was littered with straw, crushed herbs, and crimson powders that stained her boots as she stepped deeper inside. The scent was dense—ash, spice, and something wild. Feral. Foreign.

Melodie's nerves prickled with every breath, her senses overloaded and searching for anything familiar, anything human. She fought to steady her pulse, refusing to let them see how alien this all felt.

The golden-eyed elf watched her like a physician studying a wound. He was lean, sharp-featured, moving with the easy grace of someone used to death. His short, wavy brown hair caught a coppery shimmer in the firelight. When he finally stepped forward, his voice came low and deliberate, every word laced in a thick Awyan accent. She watched his mouth, measuring every syllable, hungry for any sign of meaning or threat.

"I, Luko Farishki," he said, pressing a hand to his chest in greeting. "Third son of Baeyor."

His words tumbled over her, strange and formal. Her mind raced to keep up—who were these people? Was "son of Baeyor" a threat, a warning, a title? Then he turned, gesturing toward the silver-haired figure who had yet to speak. The one who had tackled her. The one she had kicked in the gut.

"Commander Malec," Luko said with quiet weight. "Silver Fox... of the High North."

Melodie followed his motion, her gaze settling on the elf called Malec. His hair was a sheet of platinum silk, falling halfway down his back, each strand perfectly arranged, as if disorder itself would have offended him. The snowy fur lining his dark cloak brushed his jaw when he breathed, but he never adjusted it, as though the discomfort was a familiar companion. He did not blink as often as he should. He seemed to measure her in quiet increments, like he was cataloging every detail for later scrutiny. He was gorgeous in a violent, haunting way, and he stood with a tension that spoke of exhaustion rather than threat. Like he was waiting for the world to become unpredictable, so he could justify breaking something to restore it. The longer she stared, the more her skin tingled with an uneasy awareness. He unsettled her in a way that felt both dangerous and sharply personal, like a secret she'd forgotten.

Luko's voice drew her attention back. She forced her gaze away, jaw set, determined not to look weak. Luko tilted his head, then gestured with two fingers toward the door they had come through, his golden eyes never leaving her face.

"You in... border land," he said slowly, his words thick with Awyan inflection.

"Commander Malec and I... we keep peace here. Feral Canariae run wild, cause break... in order. You were..." He paused, searching. "...you were thinked to be one." He glanced at her bindings and gave a faint shrug. "Mistaken. But... not known then."

Melodie narrowed her eyes, her voice sharp, a razor's edge beneath the calm.

"So you collar and cage everyone you think looks like trouble?" Inside, her heart hammered. She needed to push back, needed to feel like she had agency, even if it was only in words.

Luko looked genuinely puzzled by the sarcasm, then gave a small, apologetic nod. "Yes. Is... way of war."

"Field Canariae are often wild," he said simply. "Your reaction... violent. Your speech, unusual." His brow furrowed again. "You speak... the dialect of Field Canariae. But yours is more... structured. Refined."

Melodie's chest tightened with fear. She suddenly felt sick to her stomach and her mouth tasted bad, like metal or old pennies. She realized she'd just spoken without thinking, desperate to keep control of the situation. Now she worried—had she said too much? Had she accidentally revealed something important? The air around her felt thick and hard to breathe, and she felt trapped, with her anxiety getting stronger by the second. What had she revealed? What else might they suspect?

> Then he looked at her again and gestured to himself, then to her. "Name. You... are?"

She hesitated, throat tightening as the moment stretched. If she lied, would it matter? But the urge to assert her own name, her own existence, was too strong. She answered evenly.
"Melodie."
Luko frowned faintly at her pronunciation.
She repeated it slowly, each syllable precise.

> "Mel. O. Die." She forced the name through the thick fog of fear and fatigue, grounding herself in its sound. It was a small act of rebellion—reminding herself who she was.

He attempted it: "Meh-low...dee."

> "Sure, that will work," she muttered under her breath, a flash of dry humor bubbling up despite everything.

The wind shifted through the low hut, catching on the flames and lifting the scent of singed herbs. Sparks floated upward, scattering like golden insects into the smoke-veiled beams. The moment was quiet. Strange. Suspended. Melodie's skin prickled. She felt exposed, every emotion raw and hovering just beneath the surface.

> "Melodie," Luko echoed, then gave a slight nod. "You speak well. For Field Canariae."

She didn't flinch, but her stare sharpened, locking on Malec. He hadn't moved, not once, but something in her gut said he'd already memorized her name. Her wrists ached where the bindings had rubbed her skin raw. She shifted against the cold stone, trying to ease the sharp bite along her spine.

The room was dim, lit only by narrow shafts of sunlight slipping through high, carved windows. Dust hung in the air, swirling like golden smoke, and every breath brought the scent of iron, ash, and something musky, animal-like. The walls were ancient, gray, worn smooth in places and jagged in others, like a fortress half-chewed by war and left to rot. Chains rattled faintly in the distance. Footsteps echoed. Somewhere far below, a scream split the silence. Melodie felt every detail dig under her skin.

This wasn't just another mission. This was a new world that hated her on sight.

Still, she didn't cower. Across from her stood a slender elf, smaller than the armored beasts who'd dragged her in. His build was slighter, his movements refined, but behind his golden eyes was a blade's edge, precise and lethal. Gold-rimmed glasses perched crooked on his nose, catching the dim light when he turned. Shoulder-length wavy brown hair framed his pointed ears, each one cuffed in thin metal bands. He studied her not as a person, but as something to be understood.

He stepped aside and gestured to a curling map pinned to the stone wall. The parchment was ancient, yellowed, and frayed, marked in symbols she didn't recognize. The continents were wrong, misshapen, rearranged, or vanished entirely. Mountains where oceans should be.

No familiar names. No North America. No Earth.

"You... here," he said, tapping a region with a long, ink-stained finger. His accent dragged the words into a strange rhythm. "This border territory. Commander Malec and I, we... make keep. Control Canariae wild ones. Feral kind. You were... thought one."

Melodie narrowed her eyes at the map, her throat tightening. She didn't recognize a single landmark. Every piece of evidence—every symbol, every ruined mountain—was another nail in the coffin of denial. She felt the terror rise again, and with it, an aching loss for her world, her people, her team.

Melodie stared hard at the map, struggling to make sense of the jagged, misshapen continents and curling foreign script that marked the faded parchment.

Her pulse thudded in her ears as she muttered under her breath, "This isn't Earth."

Behind her, the slender elf with the golden-rimmed glasses tilted his head.

"Earth?" he echoed, tongue slow over the strange word. "I not know... this place. No, Earth. Is not here."

His sharp accent curled through the syllables like he had to tug the words up from a place they didn't belong. He blinked behind the glass frames as if trying to file the name away somewhere in his mind, but found no place to put it.

From the back of the room, a scoff cracked through the silence.

Melodie whipped around, her glare slamming into the silver-haired elf leaning against the stone wall like a shadow chiseled from ice. His pale tan eyes flicked over her, sharp and cutting, and the corner of his mouth twitched with disdain as he uttered a single word under his breath.

"Canariae."

Her spine straightened in an instant.

"What the hell does that mean?" she snapped, eyes swinging back to the smaller elf with the glasses. "Why does he keep calling me that?"

The one with the golden eyes raised his hands slightly, palms open in a gesture of peace.

"Is name. Word for you, your kind," he explained carefully, each word slow and deliberate. "In Awyan tongue, you... are Canariae. Is... your people's name."

Melodie narrowed her eyes, her jaw clenching.

"What are you doing to us then? Why are you rounding us up like animals?" Her voice cracked, raw with exhaustion and fury.

The elf hesitated, then shifted his weight uncomfortably before speaking again.

"Some... go to houses. Sold. Like animals," he said, wincing at the word.

"Others... work. Farms. Fields. Labor. We... not decide. We only catch."

Melodie took a step toward him, seething. "I am not an animal," she growled. "I'm a soldier. A scientist. I don't belong in a cage."

"You... fight, yes," he said slowly, brow furrowing as he looked her over again, noting the blood at her temple, the bruises forming beneath her collarbone. "But this not your land. Here, Canariae is... low."

This world, wherever the hell she was, had no idea who she was. But they would learn.

Chapter 3

The Cold Command

Commander Malec stood atop the black-stone battlement, the wind combing through the silver-white hair that spilled down his back like threads of moonlight. He did not seem to notice the cold air tugging at his skin or the grit collecting along the seams of his tunic. His sharp, pale tan eyes, rimmed with lashes as dark as ink, scanned the ochre horizon where the sun bled slowly into the hills. He tracked its descent with quiet precision, counting the heartbeats it took for the last sliver of gold to vanish behind the ridgeline.

It was an old habit he never spoke of. He counted things when the world felt too loud.

His gloved hand drifted to the parapet at his side, fingertips brushing the stone in a small, repetitive motion. He traced the same groove again and again, a silent tether to keep the rest of his mind from fracturing under the press of sensation.

This place was a pit.

His eyes swept the courtyard below in slow, precise passes. He mapped each movement, each sound, as if cataloging them might make the scene tolerable. It reeked of sweat, old blood, and wet earth. The scents pressed against his senses with suffocating weight. He focused on the rhythm of his breathing, counting the seconds between inhale and exhale to keep the nausea at bay.

Slave, Canariae, as his people called them, were being hosed down, their naked forms shivering under buckets of cold water. Some whimpered. Some sobbed. One vomited in the mud and was beaten for it. He watched without flinching, though a small muscle at the corner of his jaw jumped in a tic he could not suppress. Order was the only way to survive such ugliness. He forced himself to keep still.

Malec barely blinked. His home was not this place.

His home was the North, high in the frostbitten mountains where snow blanketed stone and silence meant strength. There, the Awyan thrived in tradition and control, and the world fell into lines he could follow.

Here, he was surrounded by filth. By chaos. Every noise pressed against his temples like a blade. Every unpredictable movement and unfiltered sound churned through his thoughts until he could not separate them.

He yearned for solitude in a way he could never confess. Only in the hush of an empty chamber, with nothing shifting out of place, could he think clearly. Here, with the stench and the clamor and the ceaseless disorder, it felt as though something essential in him was unraveling. He despised it. He despised them. The growing infestation of Canariae that bred like vermin and tore the edges from every quiet he tried to hold onto.

For every one Awyan child born, twenty of theirs slithered into the world. It disgusted him.

Below, one of the ferals kicked out, knocking over a guard. The others jeered and surged toward her. She twisted, fought, bit. She wasn't docile. She wasn't afraid. Malec narrowed his eyes.

That one. The dark-skinned female.

He had noticed her from the beginning, how she moved like a trained creature, not like prey. How her eyes followed every step around her. She was military. Not from here. And she was not like the others.

A sharp laugh beside him pulled him from his thoughts. "This one is like wild boar," said a soft voice.

Luko, his third-in-command, stood with his gold-rimmed glasses slightly askew, brushing windblown strands of brown hair from his face.

"Even boars can be tamed," Malec replied coldly. Then he turned from the parapet and descended.

Enough of this nonsense.

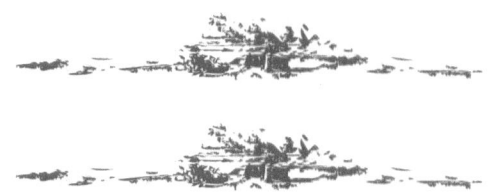

Melodie was breathing hard, every gasp scraped raw from her throat. Sweat streaked through the dust caked on her skin, running in trails that stung the cuts blooming across her arms. Around her, five guards circled, bloodied, furious, and hesitant. Two were already on the ground, groaning and motionless. The remaining three kept their distance now, shifting uneasily.

Cowards.

They'd never fought someone like her before, someone trained, someone with fire. Someone who had nothing left to lose.

But Melodie wasn't unscathed. Her muscles screamed, her limbs dragged heavy with exhaustion. Every strike had cost her. Her breaths came shallow and sharp, and the pounding in her ears warned her that her strength wouldn't last much longer.

Then, a voice. Deep. Commanding. Cold.

She barely turned her head before a stray single boot cracked against the side of her face. The world exploded into white. Her balance faltered and she hit the ground hard, the stone biting her palms as she tried to push up. But it was too late. Arms, strong, unyielding, wrapped around her torso, hauling her upright, pinning her.

"No!" she snarled, thrashing wildly.

She kicked, elbowed, twisted like a cornered animal. But the grip didn't break. More hands grabbed her legs, forcing them still. Her wrists were seized and bound tightly in front of her. Someone pulled a strip of coarse fabric down over her eyes,

Darkness.

"Get off me!" she screamed. "Don't you dare,"

She didn't get to finish.

A voice again. Malec's. She couldn't understand the words, but the tone slithered into her ears like a leash tightening around her neck, low, calm, coaxing. Like he was talking to a disobedient dog. Rage ignited in her chest. She screamed again, her voice hoarse, furious. Then... she caught a scent. Sweet. Sickly. Artificial. Her head swam.

Drugged.

Her knees buckled, and the arms that held her adjusted as she collapsed against a hard chest, her breathing rapid and shallow. She was still awake, still there. But her body...

Her body betrayed her.

She felt herself being lifted, carried like some prized catch. She heard voices above her. Footsteps echoing off stone. The air changed, grew colder, damper. Then,

Splash. Water. Freezing. Encasing her ankles. They'd thrown her into something. She couldn't see it. But she could feel it. And whatever it was, it wanted her awake. Melodie gasped, the shock of the icy water yanking her out of the drugged haze like a slap to the face. Her limbs thrashed instinctively, flailing against the cold that bit through her clothing. She couldn't see. Panic surged through her. The blindfold was still tight across her eyes, turning everything into a suffocating blur of heat, noise, and fear.

Then, hands. Large. Steady. Not rough, but firm.

A voice followed, low and composed, speaking words she didn't understand.

"Sari'na, sari'na... zhe vahlunei." ("Easy now, easy now... you are safe.")

The blindfold slipped away. Melodie blinked rapidly, vision swimming. Shapes swirled into focus.

She was in what appeared to be a bathhouse, though unlike any she'd seen on Earth. Smooth stone walls rose around her, shaped into soft curves rather than sharp corners, and embedded with small, glowing stones that pulsed with pale gold light. Steam curled in lazy coils through the air, thick with the scent of herbs, earthy, mineral-rich, medicinal.

The pool she sat in wasn't a modern tub, but a wide basin carved directly into the stone floor. Cold water sloshed around her, her clothes clinging wet and heavy to her skin. On a wooden stool beside the basin sat the pale-haired elf, the same one who'd ordered her capture. His long platinum hair was tied loosely back, and his face, sharp and deadpan, gave away nothing as he regarded her. Then, without a word, he dropped something into the water. It glowed, faintly blue.

Melodie's whole body jerked. *What the hell was that?* The water bubbled around her. Her breath caught. *He's cooking me.*

It was an irrational thought. Stupid. But her brain, still addled from whatever they'd drugged her with, latched onto it with rising panic. She tried to pull herself away from the heat, only to realize the warmth wasn't scalding. It was spreading evenly, seeping into her muscles, easing the tension in her spine.

The bubbles faded. The heat remained. Her body betrayed her. Her eyelids fluttered. She didn't want to relax. She didn't want to feel safe. But the warmth... it dulled everything. The door creaked open.

Luko stepped further into the steaming bath chamber, the glint of his gold-rimmed spectacles catching the lantern light. He peered at the girl in the tub as if she were some rare, half-broken artifact, one he didn't quite know how to handle yet but was very intrigued by. He glanced at his notes, then back to her face, lips parting with confidence as he attempted her name.

"Melor... Melur-djai Jassun?" he tried, voice tilted upward with uncertainty.

Melodie groaned, her eyes barely open, her expression somewhere between a glare and a grimace.

"It's Melodie Jaxxon," she muttered, her voice hoarse, clipped. "Meh-lo-dee."

Luko blinked, murmuring her corrected name under his breath like he was cataloguing it: "Melodie... Jaxxon..."

Then he beamed, utterly unbothered by the correction. "Yes. That what I say."

Malec, still seated beside the tub as he stripped Melodie of clothing and shoes, said nothing, though his mouth twitched almost imperceptibly. He turned and exchanged a few quick words in Awyan with the one named Luko.

Then the elf with the glasses turned back to her, switching to the clumsy, broken version of her language.

"You not worry," he said, nodding slightly. "Drug... only calm you. Few hours. You feel normal."

She barely processed it. Her eyes drifted to Malec's hands, strong, methodical, as he reached forward, gently combing water through her hair. She tried to squirm, to pull away, but her limbs were slow, sluggish.

Luko, if she remembered right, leaned against the nearby table, scribbling something into a small journal. He adjusted his glasses and tilted his head at her.

"Which providence...you come from?" he asked.

Melodie turned her head slowly, murmuring, "I... I don't know. Not here."

There was a pause. Then a quiet exchange of words between the two males, just beyond her comprehension. The sound of quills against parchment. Pages flipping.

Luko cleared his throat and asked again, "How you come here? There more like you?"

Melodie's mouth opened, but nothing came out. Her body slumped deeper into the warmth. Her eyes slid shut.

"She lost consciousness," Luko sighed, snapping his book shut with one hand.

Malec gave a short nod and stood. He moved fluidly, as if each motion had been rehearsed in his mind before he dared to enact it.

When every last scrap of tattered cloth had been removed, he set them aside in a neat pile, arranging the ruined fabric so it would not offend his sense of order. He lifted her out of the basin with practiced ease, though the slick heat of her skin against his palms made something in him tense. It took effort not to flinch at the dampness, the softness.

She barely registered it, only the sensation of cool air on her bare body, the soft texture of cloth wrapped around her shoulders, the quiet, methodical rhythm of his hands as he dried her hair.

He washed her carefully, his touch efficient but never careless. Each stroke of the cloth seemed to steady him as much as it cleansed her, a ritual that gave shape to the chaos of what she was. When she was clean, he dressed her in a plain servant's tunic, smoothing each fold so it lay correctly. Disorder was intolerable. He could not bear to hand her over to the guards with her clothing askew.

At last, he picked her up, adjusting her weight so her limbs did not hang uneven.

Melodie cracked one eye open, just enough to see the sharp lines of his jaw, the faint glint of his pale tan eyes in the low light. He did not look at her. He seemed fixed on some point beyond her shoulder, as though the act of holding her required all of his focus.

He turned to a guard waiting by the door, and only then did he draw a slow, steadying breath.

"Dreni va'shal dori." he said. (Take her to the quarters.)

Then, the darkness claimed her again. The stench of damp fur and sweat clung to the air, making Melodie's stomach twist with nausea. Her head throbbed with a deep, pulsing ache, and her limbs still felt heavy, dulled by exhaustion and whatever sedative they had given her. She sat slouched against the stone wall, her body trembling from cold and bruises, and the sharp cold bite of the collar around her neck made her pulse jump.

She reached up and touched it, solid metal, not ornamental. Her fingers scraped over the grooves in the clasp. Locked. This wasn't just detainment. This was ownership.

Around her, voices whispered. Dozens of prisoners shared the same stone room, their backs pressed to the cold walls or curled together for warmth on the dirt floor. Some sat silently, eyes vacant, their spirits already broken. Others whispered to each other in quick, hushed tones, sharp and birdlike, a language she couldn't begin to understand.

Then... soft footsteps.

A child stepped around the edge of a crumbled pillar, her presence so light it was almost ghostlike. She was small, no more than seven or eight, with pale skin that stood out stark against the grime and shadow. Her straight black hair was uncombed but not matted, and her warm brown eyes blinked slowly as they locked onto Melodie's. In her arms, she held a linen bundle, clutched tightly to her chest.

It was the same girl from before. Melodie's breath caught. She's here?

The child walked freely, unshackled, unafraid, while everyone else was tethered, caged, or broken. No guards moved to stop her. She moved as if she belonged here, as if she were invisible. Melodie's suspicion flickered. The girl knelt down in front of her and unwrapped the bundle, revealing a rough piece of flatbread and a few strips of dried meat. Her voice was as soft as before.

"Food."

Melodie's stomach coiled painfully at the scent. Her pride wanted to refuse, but her hunger had no such conviction. She took it slowly, hesitantly, never breaking eye contact.

"Where did you get this?" she asked, voice hoarse.

The child shrugged and sat beside her without answering. She seemed at ease, as though this entire wretched place meant nothing to her.

Melodie's eyes narrowed. "What's your name?"

Another shrug. "No name."

Melodie frowned. "You don't have a name?"

The girl shook her head once, brown eyes detached. It unsettled Melodie, not because the girl was strange, but because she wasn't. She felt... aware. Intact. Untouched by the horror surrounding them. Melodie's gaze darted across the room, then back at her.

"Why can you walk around like that? Why aren't you locked up?"

The child looked at her but said nothing. Melodie leaned in slightly. "Do you have family that call you anything?"

Still, no answer.

Melodie sighed. "Fine. Can I give you a name then?"

The girl hesitated, then gave a slow nod.

"Lilly," Melodie whispered. It was the first word she could think of that felt clean.

The child repeated it, her mouth forming the name with quiet wonder. "Lilly."

Melodie reached out, brushing the girl's hair from her cheek. "That's yours now."

And for just a heartbeat... there was something beautiful in this place.

The doors burst open with a metallic slam, shaking dust from the stone beams above. Guards stormed inside, barking harsh commands. Chaos followed. Prisoners were shoved to their feet and herded toward the outer gates. Lilly sprang up and vanished through the crowd, slipping away like smoke. Melodie stumbled along with the others into the daylight, shielding her eyes as harsh sun pierced through. Her heart sank as she took in the scene before her.

A massive courtyard. Dirt and stone, surrounded by black walls, and at the center, a wooden platform. High, with iron loops nailed into the planks. Prisoners were being dragged forward and chained upright, their bodies displayed for inspection.

A slave auction.

Melodie froze, bile rising in her throat. She had read about these in history books, seen renderings and documentaries, but living it... standing in it... was something else. And then, she saw the bidders. Not human. Not exactly. Elongated limbs. Pale skin. Glowing eyes and pointed ears. Graceful, inhuman, and cold. Some wore armor. Others finery. None of them looked like her.

Her dark skin stood out like an ink blot against parchment. The others, Canariae, as they were called, were smaller, paler, sun-starved and silent in their chains. But not her. Never her. Melodie was fire. And in this world, fire was treated like a threat.

A guard grabbed her roughly by the arm, yanking her toward the auction block. She didn't hesitate. Instinct took over. She twisted her body hard, pulling the guard off balance before slamming her elbow into his throat. The rope slipped from his hand and she snatched it up, snapping it like a whip at the next approaching soldier.

Gasps erupted from the crowd.

Another came at her, and she ducked low, spun, wrapped the rope around his neck and yanked with all her strength. He dropped to his knees, sputtering. Panic rippled through the courtyard like a shockwave. Bidders shouted. Guards scrambled. Slaves stared, wide-eyed. Then it happened.

A voice sliced the chaos like a blade. Sharp. Commanding. Absolute. Everything stopped. The crowd parted like frightened water. Malec emerged, tall and severe, flanked by Luko.

Every inch of him was composed with a precision that bordered on unsettling. His black trousers were pressed so sharply the silver piping down each leg caught the torchlight in an unbroken line. The silver tunic he wore bore the fox emblem on his chest, perfectly centered without the slightest skew, as though he had adjusted it several times to be sure. A dark gray undershirt covered his neck and forearms completely, the high collar fastened to the last clasp despite the warmth of the room. Not a speck of skin was exposed where it need not be. Even his boots gleamed, polished to a mirror finish, with no trace of dust or stray hair.

He paused at the threshold, his pale beige eyes flicking over the scene without a blink. The disarmed guards. The restrained soldier wheezing on the ground. The woman standing defiant with a rope clutched in her fists, breathing like a wild beast ready to charge. Though he did not speak, something in the precise way he adjusted the line of his sleeve betrayed a quiet revulsion at the disorder.

It was as if the chaos itself scraped along his nerves, demanding he set every piece back into place.

His jaw tightened. Without a word, he drew his dagger and slashed the rope free from the soldier's throat. Then he turned to the rest of the guards who had dragged her out there and shouted in his native tongue, voice thunderous and sharp as cracked stone.

"Sa'kirra val'voji? Tisani khel'ha arin, volar? Khel'ha!"

The guards flinched. Some dropped their gazes. One stammered an apology. Malec didn't wait.

In a single, fluid movement, he seized Melodie by the waist and slung her over his shoulder like she weighed nothing. The sudden shift left her winded, but only for a moment.

"PUT ME DOWN!" she roared, fists pounding into his back. "You fucking animal! You don't get to do this, LET ME GO!"

He didn't even grunt. Just walked, boots cracking against the stone with mechanical precision.

"You think I'm yours to own? You think I'll play tame for you?" she snarled.

"Coward! Put me down and fight me like something with a spine!"

She kicked, twisted, spat, screamed, but his arm remained locked around her thighs, steady and firm as an iron clamp. Guards and Awyan buyers whispered as they passed. Some laughed. Some looked away. But she didn't stop cursing. Not for one second. Her voice carried like wildfire in dry grass.

By the time they reached the inner corridors of the fortress, her throat was raw. But she memorized everything. Every hallway, every turn, every guard's face. He finally stopped in front of a large wooden door carved with strange glyphs. His hand hovered over the latch a moment longer than necessary, as if he were counting out the beats of his breath before crossing the threshold.

Then he opened it and stepped into a wide room that smelled faintly of polished wood and cold stone. His private quarters. The tall walls rose around them in silent order, lined floor to ceiling with books arranged by size and color in perfect rows. No spines were askew. No stray parchment disrupted the symmetry. The old maps mounted between the shelves hung at exact intervals, each corner pinned so it lay perfectly flat.

The hearth glowed low, but the fire was contained behind a glass grate, as though he could not bear the unpredictability of an open flame.

A massive desk dominated the far side of the room. It was not cluttered, though it held many things. Strange brass tools were laid out in precise sequences, each spaced the width of a finger apart. Scrolls and ledgers were stacked in uniform piles, their edges aligned so cleanly they looked more architectural than scholarly. A dark cloth covered anything that could gather dust.

He dropped her onto a stool without ceremony, careful to set it squarely against the flagstones so it did not scrape out of alignment. She sat up instantly, her wrists still tied but her spine tall, chin tilted in open defiance.

Malec stared at her in silence. The hearth light caught the sharp planes of his face, but his eyes did not waver from hers. He did not shift his weight or fidget. Only the faint movement of his thumb brushing once over the seam of his glove betrayed that the sight of her, bound and incongruent in this immaculate space, unsettled him.

And then, he laughed. A low, dry chuckle that curled in her gut like poison.

She glared. "What the hell's so funny?"

He said something in his own language. She didn't know the words. But from the smirk on his face, she knew exactly what he meant.

She snarled. "You smug bastard."

He tilted his head slightly, as if amused by her rage. But she wasn't just angry. She was boiling. No, she was molten.

Ten minutes passed in silence, thick and stretching like a noose. Melodie sat with her back stiff against the unforgiving wood of the chair, the metal collar cold against her throat. Across from her, at a grand stone-carved desk, the pale-haired one, Malec, sat like a king in judgment.

He held a thin, bone-handled pipe between his fingers. Every movement around it was precise. He turned it once in his palm, aligning the stem with the edge of a ledger already squared to the corner of the desk. Only when it rested exactly so did he strike the flame.

Malec set the pipe between his teeth with the same care he applied to every other private ritual. The scent of the dried leaves, acrid and clean, filled his nose as he struck the flame. He drew in a long, measured breath and counted to six before letting it slip free. The first exhale always calmed the tremor in his chest. The second settled the static behind his eyes. By the third, the room felt orderly again.

He had never told anyone, but this ritual was the only way he knew to make the noise in his mind quiet. But even the smoke could not blunt the way she made him feel. His eyes never left her.

That burnished, wheat-colored stare, held steady without flinching. He did not blink often. He rarely did when he was cataloging. To anyone else, she might have looked insolent. To him, she was data. A shifting pattern he needed to reduce to something he could name.

Studying her was the only way to keep from reacting to her. Like she was an equation he couldn't quite solve. Or a creature whose defiance made every nerve in his body flicker with heat he didn't trust himself to touch.

Melodie shifted in her seat, jaw locked. Her wrists ached from the rope.

Behind the veil of silence, a low, disapproving sound escaped him. Barely audible. But it was enough. She stopped moving. She bit down hard on the inside of her cheek, tasting blood. Her breath hitched. She hated waiting. Especially when I don't know what the hell I'm waiting for.

The heavy wooden door creaked open at last, and the cinnamon-haired one entered, Luko, the scientist or doctor and maybe right hand man to the big albino one named, Malec. His stride was too relaxed, too casual, like this was all a game. His gold-rimmed spectacles caught the lantern light as he stepped in and shut the door with his foot.

He approached Malec first, speaking in that smooth, rhythmic Awyan tongue, a dialect that sounded both ancient and sharp, like the slicing of silk. She glared at the pale-haired commander sitting across from her, the one who hadn't said a word since she was hauled into this room like luggage. His pale eyes tracked her with cold calculation, like he was trying to decide what species she belonged to.

"Say something," she snapped, voice sharp. "Or just grunt if that's all you know how to do, you big ape."

The insult shot through the thick air like a thrown blade.

Malec didn't withdraw. His expression didn't change. Not even a twitch.

But Luko, he jolted as if struck by lightning. His brown brows shot up, and then, laughter burst from him like a crack splitting stone. He bent forward, hands on his knees, shoulders shaking uncontrollably.

"Ah! Big Ape!" he wheezed, pointing toward Malec. "You call him Big Ape! Hah! No one... no one ever say that to *Silver Fox* before."

Luko gasped between breaths, then turned to Malec and began speaking rapidly in their native tongue, the words sharp and fluid. Melodie couldn't understand a word, but she knew exactly what was being said.

The Silver Fox wanted to know what the dark one just called him. Malec didn't look at her. Didn't move a muscle. But he exhaled sharply through his nose, a puff of smoke curling from the pipe between his fingers as he gave a quiet, mirthless snort. No smile. Just a faint twitch at the corner of his mouth. And then his tan eyes slid back to Luko.

He said something low. Commanding.

Luko straightened, the grin fading from his face as he gave a small nod. He turned then, his attention shifting to her.

"You not... for sale," he said, his accent thick and broken. "Was mistake. Should not be put with other... mm... ferals."

Melodie snorted. "No shit."

"Do you have own tribe? What your... kind called here. Canariae. Small things. Loud. Fast to breed. Feral, or are more like you?"

Melodie stood sharply, the rope pulling tight between her wrists. "I'm a scientist. A soldier. I'm not a damn feral."

Luko tilted his head, as if puzzled by her anger.

"Canariae can be pet. Or worker. Sometimes breed for show. You strong. Maybe... kept for good use, yes?"

Melodie's eyes flashed. Her hands curled into fists. Melodie bristled, her spine stiffening.

"We are called humans," she snapped, her voice sharp and cracking in the heavy air. "Not whatever you just said."

Luko raised a brow and waved a lazy, dismissive hand, as if swatting away a fly. "Here, they are Canariae," he said coolly. "You are female Canariae."

Her jaw tensed so tight it ached.
"Stop calling me that," she growled.
But Luko just lifted his head, amusement flickering behind his golden brown eyes. He studied her the way a bored noble might examine a mythical creature that had suddenly spoken. Behind him, Malec exhaled smoke, his eyes never leaving her face.

Melodie's nails dug into her palms. She was being labeled, reduced, stripped of her identity with a single word. Canariae. Like it meant nothing. Like she was nothing. But she would make them remember her name. One way or another.

Luko stood off to the side, arms crossed, eyes flicking between Melodie and Malec with that same bored amusement he always wore like a second skin. Whatever command Malec had given earlier was apparently done, because now Luko muttered something under his breath and strolled out the door without another glance, leaving her alone.

Or so she thought. Moments later, it creaked open again.

In stepped an older Canariae woman, not a soldier, but clearly a servant. Yet her presence was anything but soft. She was squat and sturdy, her arms thick with muscle, and her expression carved from stone. Her cropped silver-black hair framed a face that had seen too much and cared too little. She moved like this place belonged to her.

Melodie straightened, instincts already flaring.

The woman made no introduction. No eye contact. She strode forward, reached for Melodie's wrist, rough and commanding, as if she were a filthy animal that needed to be scrubbed before market.

And that was it.

Melodie's vision went red. Her fist shot out before the woman could blink. Bone crunched under her knuckles. The older Canariae stumbled backward with a howl, blood gushing from her broken nose. She swore violently in what sounded like German, sharp, guttural bursts of fury.

"Verdammte Schlampe! Was bildest du dir ein?!" ("Damn bitch! What do you think you're doing?!")

Melodie laughed. "Try that again and I'll knock your other nostril sideways," she snapped. "You don't get to touch me."

The woman lunged. Too fast. Too angry. But Malec was faster. He was across the room in an instant, his hand seizing Melodie's wrist and wrenching it behind her back. She gasped as pain bloomed up her arm, her knees almost giving.

"What the hell do you think you're doing?!" she shouted, thrashing.

He didn't respond. Didn't loosen his hold.

Only held her with the cold precision of someone trained to subdue without emotion.

The servant woman shouted again, more slurs Melodie didn't understand, and stormed toward the door, one hand cupping her bloody nose, the other shaking with rage as Luko stood in between her and Melodie keeping them apart. He then guided the Canariae woman with a bloody nose to the door. Before she could leave, she hissed something at Malec in a venomous tone in Awyan.

Malec didn't even look at her. He only barked a single command in Awyan. She flinched... then obeyed. The door slammed behind her. Luko turned his back up against the door with his mouth wide open, staring at Melodie in disbelief.

Melodie was trembling with rage, shoulder burning where he still gripped her. Then, finally, he released her. She ripped away, spinning on him with her chest heaving, eyes feverish.

"Don't ever grab me like that again," she snarled. He said nothing. He just smoked, slowly, his eyes never leaving her.

Melodie crossed her arms, pacing like a caged cat. "Is this how it's gonna be? I breathe wrong and you send in some brute to scrub me raw like I'm livestock?"

Malec exhaled a thin stream of smoke, the scent of it strange and earthy.

Still... no response. His stare was sharp enough to draw blood. She met his gaze anyway. Refusing to shrink. Refusing to bow.

"You keep looking at me like I'm supposed to figure something out," she whispered, the words sharp and bitter. "Why the fuck are you ignoring me?"

Malec gave her one last warning with his eyes before he retreated back behind his desk with his pipe and icy gaze. Her skin throbbed where his fingers had been, and she jerked away from him, rage simmering behind her eyes. Luko exhaled heavily, massaging the bridge of his nose like she was a migraine that wouldn't fade.

Melodie wasn't done.

"Why doesn't the ugly goat ever talk?" she snapped, jerking her chin toward Malec, who stood near the desk, arms crossed, his gaze still locked on her.

Luko sighed. "He not speak Canariae."

She blinked. "Then why the hell does he keep staring at me like I'm supposed to understand him?"

Luko's lips curled slightly, but there was no humor in it. "No... no noble Awyan speak slave tongue. Is... below them. Always the Canariae must learn master's words. Always."

That hit her the wrong way. Her jaw tightened as she slowly turned her attention back to Luko. "But you speak it."

He went still.

"So..." she leaned forward slightly, voice cutting like glass, "who did you piss off to get the job of translator?"

Luko didn't blink. But the twitch in his jaw gave him away. His smirk fell away, replaced with something distant. Hurt. A long silence hung in the air.

Then, without a word, he turned sharply, grabbed a bloodied cloth from the table, and tossed it at her. It hit her shoulder and fell limp into her lap. He walked out without looking back, slamming the door behind him.

Melodie peeled the bloody cloth from her shoulder with slow, deliberate fingers. Her pulse still thundered beneath her skin, but her face was calm, too calm. It was the stillness that came before a storm.

The warlord stood rooted near the desk, tall and rigid, arms at his sides like a statue carved from stone, but his eyes were anything but lifeless. They fixed on her with a stillness that wasn't passive, it was predatory. Cold and charring all at once, like sunlight filtered through glass just before it scorches. There was no malice in them, no clear anger. But there was no warmth, either. Only intent.

Melodie straightened on instinct, her spine drawing taut like a wire. Her wrists still throbbed from where he'd gripped her.

"What?" she bit out. "You just gonna stand there and stare at me all day?"

No answer. He just kept gazing. Unblinking. Patient. Like he had all the time in the world. Like he was waiting for her to break. And suddenly, the heat of her anger was joined by something colder. Something she didn't want to name. She had faced worse. She had survived worse. But this? This silent fixation? This obscured stillness? It was different. It made her feel like prey. And for the first time since she'd been dragged into this nightmare, Melodie truly asked herself:

What does this Awyan want from me?

Chapter 4

The Cold War Begins

Melodie sat on the edge of the wooden stool like it might grow teeth. Her shoulders were square, back stiff, jaw fastened tight enough to crack a tooth.

Across the room, Malec reclined in his high-backed chair like a king on his throne, exhaling a slow ribbon of pale smoke from a slender, unfamiliar pipe. The scent curled through the air, bitter and musky, laced with something metallic and herbal that turned her stomach. He hadn't said a word. Luko was gone. That dark-haired servant from hell had been dragged out bloody and cursing.

Now, it was just her and him. The commander. The pale-eyed warlord with a stare like a scalpel. And he didn't even have the decency to blink. Melodie's fingers curled into fists against her thighs. Every inch of her screamed to lunge at him. Rip the damn pipe from his mouth. Say something. Anything. But he didn't speak. He just... watched. Cold. Still.

Silent. The way he looked at her made her skin itch. Like she was being measured. Not like a person. Like a specimen.

She scoffed, loud and sharp. "Don't you have something better to do?"

Nothing. His pipe rose to his lips. Another drag. Another slow plume of smoke.

She shifted her weight, heels scraping the floor as her rage boiled hotter. "I'm not a goddamn painting, you know. You got something to say, or are we just doing this creepy eye contact thing for fun?"

That seemed to get a phrase out of him. Just a few words in that low, guttural language of his. Smooth and clipped, falling from his lips like commands etched in ice.

She raised her brows. "Oh. Now we're speaking. Too bad I don't understand a single fucking word, you frost-bitten bastard."

No reaction. He didn't even smirk.

"Let me guess," she said, voice venomous. "You're far too important to speak the language of us lesser beings."

That got him.

A flicker, barely there, moved through his eyes. Something glinted, not amusement, not offense. More like curiosity. She hated that look.

He moved then, not fast and not aggressive, only with an eerie, unhurried purpose. She stiffened as he rose from his chair and crossed the room to a small table in the corner. He still did not look at her. His hand hovered above a folded cloth as though deciding whether to use it. When he dipped it into a metal basin, the sound of water dripping back into the bowl echoed through the hush like a measured heartbeat. Melodie's stomach twisted. *Don't you dare come near me with that thing.*

But he did.

Without warning, Malec reached out and seized her jaw. His fingers were large and calloused, but they held her face with a restraint that felt more unsettling than cruelty. His skin was warm, infuriatingly warm, and she hated that she noticed.

"Hey." She jerked against him, but he did not recoil.

His grip did not tighten or loosen. He only adjusted the angle of her face by the smallest degree, as if aligning her to match some internal measurement. He paused then. His gaze dropped to her cheekbone where a dried smear of blood had cracked along her skin. For a moment, he simply looked at it, his pupils narrowing, as though the stain itself offended him more than any insult she could have spoken. He lifted the cloth and began to wipe. Slowly. Methodically. His thumb anchored her jaw in place as he worked in precise strokes, each pass removing another trace of the mark that had distracted him.

She hadn't even realized it was there. He did not speak. Did not make eye contact. His attention stayed fixed on the spot he was cleaning, as if the task required his full concentration. The touch was not sexual. It was not tender. It was possessive in a quiet, absolute way, like he was reminding her that in his world, nothing stayed out of place.

Her chest rose and fell faster. Her breath turned shallow.

"I can do it myself," she muttered under her breath, voice tight with indignation.

Malec did not react. He continued moving the cloth over her skin in silent, deliberate strokes. When the last trace of blood was gone, he set the cloth aside with meticulous care. Then he took her chin between his fingers again. This time he tilted her head just slightly, turning her face so he could study her profile. His gaze traveled over her features in a long, unblinking survey. It felt as though he was cataloging her for future reference, reducing her to a set of shapes and angles he could memorize and control.

"Seriously?" she snapped, jerking her head back. "I get it. I don't look like your people. Congratulations on figuring that out."

He didn't blink. Didn't recoil. Didn't even pretend to register the edge in her voice. Instead, he finally spoke—a single word, flat and pointed.

"Canariae."

Her blood boiled. Her fists curled at her sides, nails digging into her palms as she glared up at him.

"We. Are. Called. Humans," she growled, emphasizing every syllable like it might land harder if she said it slower.

Malec's pale tan eyes remained passive. Unbothered. He took the cloth, wiped it slowly across his palm, then tossed it into the basin without a second glance. Like the conversation, if one could even call it that—was over.

Melodie's mouth curled into a bitter scowl. "So that's it?" she barked. "You just clean me up like a damn dog and then toss me aside?"

Still no response.

He returned to his desk, sat down without ceremony, and picked up the same thin smoking pipe from earlier. A slow breath of pale blue smoke curled from his lips as he stared ahead, not even looking at her now. With his free hand, he reached for a small stack of polished stones arranged in a neat line along the edge of the desk. One by one, he shifted them into a new pattern, turning each so their edges aligned perfectly before moving to the next. When he finished, he started over, setting them back in their original order with the same measured care. The ritual was quiet, methodical, something he did without thought, as if the repetition anchored him while she sat there in his periphery.

She let out a sharp laugh, folding her arms tightly across her chest. "Wow. I've had better conversations with my phone's voice assistant. At least Siri pretends to care."

Silence. Not even a twitch. Her gaze drifted to the meticulous row of stones he was arranging and re-arranging with the same vacant focus he gave everything else.

She stared for a beat, then shook her head. "Oh my god. I've been kidnapped by OCD Buffalo Bill."

Still, he did not look up. His fingers kept moving, aligning each stone as if her voice were nothing more than background noise.

She sighed and rubbed at her temples, trying to keep the frustration from bubbling over. Talking to him was like shouting into a canyon, no echo, no reaction, nothing. But fine. If he wasn't going to talk, she'd figure things out on her own. She'd been through worse. And she'd find a way out of this too. Her eyes drifted over the room once more, taking in every line, every corner, every object with the sharpness of someone who had been hunted before.

The chamber was carved from gray stone, the walls cold and unyielding, yet it had the unmistakable air of command. Not lavish, but tailored for comfort and authority. The high ceiling was paneled in dark wood, polished until it reflected the low amber light of iron sconces. Strange sigils had been etched into the beams overhead, curling symbols she did not recognize, the script so intricate it almost seemed alive in the flickering glow. Shelves lined one side of the space, filled with thick-bound books whose spines bore characters she couldn't read. Every volume stood in perfect alignment, no dust on the edges, no page left protruding as if even the idea of disorder would be an offense. Next to the shelves stood globes marked with unfamiliar landmasses and peculiar instruments, strange devices that ticked or spun or glowed faintly in colors she had never seen. Some rested on stands marked with slender brass plaques engraved with more of those curling symbols.

On the far wall, parchment maps were pinned with brass fasteners, each spaced evenly apart, their edges squared in exact lines. The surfaces were cluttered with markings and paths she couldn't decipher, some curling with age. Scrolls were tucked in narrow cubbies beside them, sorted in rows so precise it looked as if they had never been disturbed.

Her gaze drifted lower, to the weapons rack in the corner.

Swords rested on black iron hooks, each gleaming, each perfectly positioned with hilts facing the same direction. Daggers with dark handles were arranged in ascending order of length. A pair of long, narrow spears stood upright in polished brackets, their shafts carved with faint designs that looked ceremonial, though she doubted any of them were merely for show.

And then her stomach twisted. A whip.

It hung there coiled like a serpent, the leather dark and oiled, the handle inlaid with pale bone. Decorative, perhaps, but she knew better. The Awyan didn't keep symbols. They kept tools. She drew a slow breath, willing her heart to steady, but it was then she realized something else.

Nothing in this room was out of place. Nothing. Not even her.

She looked down and felt her skin crawl as she saw how perfectly centered she was in the space, the stool aligned with the axis of the massive desk, her body positioned so precisely that it was as if he had measured the floor before placing her there.

Who is this monster? Or more correctly, what was he?

And yet... they hadn't touched her like the others. Hadn't chained her. Hadn't even spoken to her in a language she understood. Malec just watched. Always watched. As if she were some strange artifact dragged in from a ruined battlefield, part threat, part curiosity.

Fine.

If they were studying her like some lab rat, then she'd return the favor. Every inch of this place could hold a clue. And she would find it.

Then, finally, he spoke. It wasn't loud. It wasn't meant for her. The words spilled low and deliberate in his native tongue, sharp and measured, like he was drawing a blade across stone. She didn't know the language, not truly, but something in the tone, in the clipped edge of his voice, sent a shiver along her spine. It wasn't a command. It wasn't mockery. It was something else.

A conclusion. He was trying to understand her.

She could feel it in the way his pale tan eyes traced her face, the curve of her jaw, the slope of her neck, like he was searching for something just beneath her skin. Not desire. Not disgust. Curiosity, honed like a weapon. Then his gaze shifted, just slightly, but the intent in it struck her harder than the words ever could.

"Shae'vahn tularai." (You don't belong here.)

She didn't need a translator for that. The verdict was clear in his eyes, as unmistakable as the cold stone walls enclosing them. Melodie's throat tightened. She tried to summon a biting response, but all that came out was a breathless mutter.

"No shit..."

And yet, it didn't land with the same heat as before. Because it wasn't just this room he meant. It was the world. The realm. This entire reality. She was the wrong element in a carefully controlled equation, and Malec saw it. Felt it. Knew it. And if he knew that, then maybe... Maybe he knew more. How she got here. How she could get out.

Her pulse kicked up. "How do I leave?" she asked softly, the edges of her defiance fraying.

But Malec didn't answer. He took one final drag from his pipe, the blue smoke curling around him like mist. Then he stood. Slow. Unhurried. He said nothing. Did nothing. And then, without so much as a glance back, he turned and walked out.

Leaving her alone. And more unsettled than she'd ever admit.

Melodie sat in the center of the study, no, the throne of his domestic kingdom, imprisoned like a beast in a cage. Iron bars curved overhead in a domed arch, wide enough to let her sit upright but not to stretch. Thick rope bit into the tender skin of her wrists behind her back, her ankles bound just enough to rob her of any leverage. The ropes were scratchy, cruel. Intentional.

Across the room, Malec ate in silence.

He sat at a long table carved with ancient knotwork, the surface so polished it reflected the soft gold light of the sconces overhead. His hands moved with methodical care as he brought each bite of food to his mouth.

Every item on the plate was arranged in precise quadrants, each portion kept separate so nothing touched. He ate in a strict clockwise pattern, starting at the upper left and working his way around in measured intervals.

He never looked at her. Never spoke. When he set his utensil down between bites, he aligned it with the edge of the plate before lifting it again. Even the goblet by his right hand rested on a folded square of cloth, positioned so that the crest stamped into the metal faced him directly.

Beneath the warm flicker of firelight, the blaze behind him threw long shadows along the stone walls and bookcases. His presence, as always, was unnervingly still. Quiet power. And something deeper, colder, that she could not name.

The study was far from the dank, soulless cells she had seen before. But she was still in a damn cage. The door creaked.

Melodie's head snapped toward it as three figures entered, elfkin, tall and robed, their light or flaxen hair bound back in scholar braids. One of them, barely older than a child, stepped forward clutching a satchel. His nervous eyes darted between her and the warlord. They exchanged quiet words in that fluid, unfamiliar language. Then, reluctantly, the boy turned and walked toward her cage.

"You... understand me?" he asked. His Awyan accent was thick, but passable.

Melodie narrowed her eyes. "Who the hell are you?"

The boy exhaled in relief, shoulders visibly relaxing. "I am your translator. The others are medics. They are here to... study you."

She barked a humorless laugh. "Study me. Fantastic. And where's the other one? Dumb, flat-headed, way-too-serious Luko? At least he had the balls to say shit to my face."

The boy stiffened. Behind him, Malec issued a short, sharp command. His tone was low, direct. The boy faltered, then, as if cornered by duty, translated her words aloud. For a moment, Malec didn't react. He chewed slowly, head still bowed slightly, as if contemplating the texture of his meal rather than her insult. Then, without warning, a sound escaped him. A low, amused chuckle. Melodie blinked. Not a smirk. Not a scoff. A real laugh. He tried to bury it, his jaw tightening as though caging the sound behind his teeth. But his lips twitched with withheld mirth, the faintest of creases tugging at the corners. Melodie stared at him, stunned. This monster, this cold, calculating brute, laughed? It made no sense. Nothing about him ever did.

For the next hour, Melodie endured the humiliating routine of their examination. The medics circled like vultures, poking at her skin, brushing her hair back with gloved fingers, inspecting her nails, joints, and even prying at her mouth to study her teeth. It was clinical, invasive, like she was some beast on display at a nobleman's menagerie.

She stayed quiet for as long as she could. But when one of them tugged a little too hard at a curl near her temple, she snapped her head toward the translator and hissed, "Where's Luko?"

The boy froze, the silver tools in his hand rattling slightly. He glanced over his shoulder at Malec, who said nothing, then looked back at her.

"He has been reassigned," he said. "He will no longer be your translator."

Melodie scoffed, a bitter smirk curling on her lips. "Guess I really pissed him off."

The boy didn't answer. Just lowered his gaze. She shrugged, trying to bury the faint ripple of guilt clawing at her chest. Luko was just another one of them. Another handler. Another link in the chain dragging her deeper into this strange, ornate nightmare. She didn't owe him a damn thing.

Still.

He had been the only one who spoke to her like she was an equal. Even if it was under orders. Even if it was fake.

She bit at her lower lip and looked away. Across the room, Malec sat unmoving, fingers tented beneath his chin. But now, his head tilted slightly, pale tan eyes locked on her with quiet intensity. He was studying her again. Melodie's chest tightened.

Eventually, the medics left. The soft creak of the door closing behind them was the only sound. And now, she was alone with him. Malec didn't move. He remained seated behind his grand desk, one arm propped lazily on the armrest, fingers steepled beneath his chin. He didn't speak. Didn't blink. Just watched her with the patience of a predator that had no need to pounce.

Melodie shifted on the floor of her cage, pulse steady, but her jaw squeezed tight. The ropes still bound her wrists, biting into the skin. Her muscles ached, but she refused to show weakness. Not in front of him. So she studied him right back.

Six-foot-four, maybe taller. Built like a goddamn tank, broad chest, thick arms, a solid wall of muscle that looked carved from something ancient and unforgiving. He wasn't just strong. He was sculpted for domination. Destruction. Control. His hair was an odd shade, almost white, but not quite. More like faded parchment. Dull. It didn't shimmer like silver or gold. It absorbed the light around it, like a void. His eyes, though, those pale, unsettling eyes, were another matter. They weren't gold. Not really. More like old brass drained of color. They darkened when he was angry. Sharpened when he was measuring.

Right now?

They were caught in that disorienting space between emotion and detachment. Like he couldn't decide if she was a threat, a puzzle... or prey. She stiffened under his gaze. He was reading her. Not her body. Her. Her thoughts. Her limits. Her soul.

She met his stare, chin lifted, shoulders squared despite the ropes. "Go ahead and try," she murmured under her breath. "See what you find."

The door creaked open again.

This time, it wasn't medics or scholars. It was soldiers, three of them, clad in dark uniforms with silver trim glinting in the firelight. They moved with crisp precision, speaking first to Malec in low, clipped tones. Their posture shifted immediately, deferential but alert. Clearly, he outranked them. Clearly, he commanded more than just presence. Then their eyes shifted, to her.

Melodie felt it instantly. That sweeping, silent assessment. Like she was meat behind glass.

One of them, bolder than the others, stepped closer. His gaze crawled across her body, and his hand lifted as if drawn by curiosity or worse. She didn't move an inch. She leaned back slowly, narrowing her eyes in a silent warning that said: *Try it.*

Before the officer could take another step, Malec spoke. A single word. Calm. Controlled. But threaded with steel. The soldier froze mid-motion, then let his hand fall. There was no argument. No protest. Just compliance. Melodie noticed the shift, subtle but telling. Malec hadn't stopped him to protect *her*. He had done it to protect *them*. From her. A slow smirk curved her full lips.

The officers didn't linger. They finished their report and filed out quickly, boots tapping in unison across the stone floor. Malec watched them go, then cast a glance her way, eyes indifferent, expression carved in stone.

But the message was clear. *Behave.*

She stared right back until the door clicked shut behind him as he left with the soldiers. Silence settled over the study once more. And then, slowly, deliberately, Melodie shifted. Her fingers curled behind her, brushing the waistband of her trousers. There, tucked just beneath the rope binding her, was the sliver of broken metal she'd palmed when the medics weren't looking. Her smirk deepened. Let them watch. Their first mistake was underestimating her. Their second was leaving her alone. The ropes biting into her wrists were thick, but not unbreakable. Not metal. Not magic. Just fiber and arrogance.

She angled the blade, feeling for the tension in the knot, and began to saw slowly. Methodically. Her breathing stayed even, her heart calm.

Every second she remained caged only sharpened her intent. She was close. So close. And when those bindings fell away,

Someone was going to regret leaving her alive.

Chapter 5

The Dark Canariae

The banquet hall throbbed with low laughter, flickering firelight, and the faint hum of magic rippling across the ceiling like heat lightning. Awyan magicians lined the far walls, cloaked in deep violet robes, their fingers weaving silent sigils into the air. Wisps of golden light bloomed and shimmered at their command, birds made of flame danced in midair, swirling above the guests' heads before vanishing in a blink. A floating illusion of a great battle replayed in smoky detail in one corner, a memorial conjured for glory and spectacle. It was tradition, after all, magic and drink, stories and feasting, for those who had earned the right to celebrate bloodshed.

Malec sat at the head of the long banquet table, a looming figure among generals, officers, and scholars who raised their goblets to victories, some real, most exaggerated.

The scent of roasted meat, bitter tobacco, and strong Awyan liquor clung to every breath. It pressed against the inside of his skull, crowding out thought with its heaviness. Every clang of cutlery, every ripple of laughter, every scrape of chairs across the flagstones struck him as too loud, too sharp, too close.

He kept his eyes fixed on a single point across the hall, willing his pulse to steady. He counted his breaths in fours. He flexed his fingers once beneath the edge of the table, grounding himself in the familiar pressure. His plate sat untouched. His goblet, barely sipped. His mind was elsewhere. On her. He let his gaze settle on the place where she sat in the shadows, and the din around him began to fade. The voices blurred. The smell of smoke and spice receded. For a moment, the chaos that pressed against every nerve receded into something quiet. Focusing on her was easier than fighting the noise.

Watching her breathe, watching her shoulders square against her restraints, gave him a fragile kind of order he could not name.

The dark one. The new Canariae.

Not just rare, unheard of. Wild to the point of insult. Unbroken, defiant. But there was method in her rebellion. Strategy hidden inside the chaos. He'd seen it in her eyes, clear, sharp, and assessing even when she fought like a creature cornered. That disturbed him more than he admitted. He should have forgotten her the moment he walked out of that camp. Instead, she clung to the edge of his thoughts like smoke that refused to clear.

And that skin...

He remembered the way it caught the sun. Not like Awyan skin, which dulled or peeled beneath heat. No, hers held the light. As if the sun had carved her from copper and flame. A color not of his world. A color like prophecy.

The unbroken night, something whispered from memory. A phrase he'd once heard from a dying poet, or perhaps a half-mad priest: Skin like the unbroken night, stretched beyond the gods' reach. He ground his jaw. It was absurd. All of it. And yet, when he touched her, something had shifted.

At first, it was too much. The sensation of her skin against his palm was almost unbearable. The warmth of her, the softness, the explosive edge of her breath catching under his grip pressed into every raw place inside him. It overwhelmed him in a rush of heat and noise. He could not separate the feeling from the rest of the chaos around them. For a heartbeat, he wanted to pull away, to reclaim the distance that kept everything ordered and clean.

But then the noise burned away. What remained was something he could not define. A pulse, a snap, like a thread pulling tight inside his chest the moment his fingers met her cheek. His magic had stirred. Briefly. Instinctively. It felt familiar in a way that made no sense. Warm. Welcoming. As though his body had recognized something his mind refused to see. He did not understand it.

It had felt wrong. It had felt... good. That was worse.

He clenched his goblet tighter and drank, forcing down the taste of something bitter, not the liquor, but the memory. She had bitten him. He bled. And for one gods forsaken moment, he liked it. A sharp spark of arousal had lit his spine, instinctual and nauseating. He had wanted to strike her down, and keep her close in the same breath. Possess her. Silence her. Break her.

What in the frozen hells was that?

His blood had never reacted that way before. Not even in battle. Not even with his past conquests. He narrowed his eyes at the flickering torchlight as laughter echoed down the table. Somewhere to his left, an officer toasted his name. Malec didn't lift his goblet. He was still thinking of her. And wondering, quietly, dangerously, what exactly she had done to him.

He was in deep thought when a soldier stumbled into his periphery. Drunk. Loud. Reeking of smoke and sour wine. Malec didn't look up at first, but the presence didn't retreat. Instead, it leaned closer.

"Commander," the officer slurred, clapping him hard on the shoulder, a grave mistake.

Malec's jaw twitched. His expression remained carved from stone.

"That new Canariae... the dark one," the officer continued, grinning wide like a fool who didn't know he was dangling off a ledge. "Let me have her for the night."

Silence bloomed around them like rot. A few nearby officers exchanged looks and half-laughed, their eyes glinting with hunger.

"I bet she'd be lively," the drunk added with a wink.

Malec said nothing for a long moment. His fingers tightened slightly around the base of his goblet. He could already hear the excuse forming, It's just a Canariae. A beast, nothing more. And yet... the thought of her, that one, screaming beneath one of these jackals made something shift beneath his ribs.

A flicker of something he didn't recognize.

He took a slow sip, then finally spoke, his voice quiet but edged with ice. "She is still in processing. No one touches her until she is cleared."

The officer blinked, then shrugged and staggered off, muttering something about softness and wasted opportunities. Malec's gaze lingered on the rim of his goblet. He exhaled through his nose. It wasn't the request that unsettled him. He had heard worse. It wasn't even the implications. Canariae were used. That was their function. No, what unsettled him was that he had felt something. Not outrage. Not offense. Annoyance.

As if the very idea of another touching her, possessing her, breaking her, was offensive. And that was dangerous. Because he didn't care what happened to Canariae. They were beasts. Property. Flesh to be worked, broken, sold. Nothing more. Whatever fate befell them, whether chained, whipped, or dragged half-dead through the dirt, it never registered beyond a passing glance.

But this one... This one was different.

He rolled his shoulders, as if to shake the thought loose, like a thorn that wouldn't stop catching beneath his skin. It shouldn't matter. He had other concerns. Like the way she moved. Malec had watched her fight. Closely. Too closely. Her strikes had been clean. Her footwork, precise. Not the flailing panic of a cornered animal, but the honed efficiency of someone who had been trained, trained well. Every motion was deliberate, designed to cripple, to maim, to kill. There was nothing elegant about it. Nothing wasted. It was violent, raw, and yet... beautiful. Strange. No Canariae fought like that. They weren't taught to. They weren't allowed to.

If she had been born Awyan, she would've been scouted as a soldier long ago. Recruited. Refined. Feared. But she wasn't Awyan. She was something other. Something lowborn. Forbidden. A creature he should have already discarded. And no respectable Awyan would ever stoop low enough to learn from her. But Malec had never cared much for respectability. Let them talk. Let them whisper in corners and bare their teeth in polite mockery. He had killed men for less. And he would again.

Still... she was dangerous. That much was certain. And like any weapon too sharp to hold barehanded, she would have to be tamed first.

Malec wasn't drunk. He never drank enough to dull himself. His pale tan eyes swept the room once, then settled back on the table in front of him, barely touched food cooling beside his untouched wine. His fingers rhythmically tapped the rim of the goblet, his mind already elsewhere. On her.

He'd tamed worse things, wild beasts in the northern steppes, murderers from the lowlands, even that cursed Baerok in the dungeons of Teshar. She wouldn't be difficult. Just another body to break. Another mind to bend. Still, he couldn't stop thinking about the way she looked at him. Like she knew something. Like she'd already seen the world burn and wasn't afraid to do it again. He was beginning to believe she might be useful for more than just sale.

And then the doors burst open.

A stable boy skidded into the room, pale and breathless. "Fire!" he choked. "The stables, Commander, the stables are aflame!"

Malec stood immediately, chair scraping against the stone. Around him, officers scattered, half-rising, some knocking over goblets or grabbing weapons. But Malec was already striding forward, boots pounding with calm precision. He didn't run. He didn't need to. He didn't suspect her yet, but something dark twisted low in his gut. By the time he reached the courtyard, the air was thick with smoke. Chaos ruled. Flames engulfed the stable roofs, turning beams into glowing skeletons of ash. Horses screamed, rearing and kicking against their tethers, eyes rolling white in panic. Soldiers dashed about, forming lines with buckets, shouting over each other. Sparks hissed in the air, lighting on cloaks and hair.

Malec passed through it all like a ghost, unaffected, his long coat whipping behind him. He barked an order, low, clipped, and two officers peeled off from the line to follow him. He stepped through the worst of the blaze, near the back paddock where the fire seemed to have started. And that's where he saw it. A snapped length of iron chain, small, meant for a cage. And beside it, partially buried in hay and soot, a strip of cloth. Torn. Singed. But unmistakable. It was from the tunic she'd worn when she arrived. Malec crouched, picking it up between two fingers.

The cloth was warm. Fresh. His eyes narrowed. So. She wasn't just wild. She was planning. His jaw tightened, slow and tight. Now it was personal. He rose to his full height, letting the fabric fall to the ash. She had started the fire. And now, she was loose.

The night pulsed with chaos.

Smoke billowed from the western stables, casting the entire fortress into disarray. Shouts echoed. Hooves thundered. Magic flickered in the sky, trying and failing to control the blaze.

And in the opposite wing, silent, dark, forgotten, Melodie slipped through a narrow window and dropped into the shadows. Her bare feet hit the ground with a muffled thud. She rasped quietly, knees protesting the landing, wrists still sore from where the ropes had rubbed raw. But she didn't stop. Didn't breathe. No time for pain. She turned and reached up, grabbing the hand of the next escapee. A trembling older woman with graying hair and a bloodied lip. Melodie caught her weight and helped her down.

"Quick," she whispered. "Move. Move!" Blank stares. Not understanding. She cursed under her breath. "Lilly!"

The little girl appeared beside her like a ghost, eyes wide, face smudged with soot and dirt. "Tell them, now."

Lilly nodded and began speaking fast, her tiny hands motioning with urgency. One by one, the others, men, women, a few younger boys, began climbing down the rope Melodie had tied off. Fear lit their eyes, but they followed. Almost there. She crouched beside the base of the fortress wall, checking the knot on the last rope,

When a shadow peeled from the stone. Her blood ran cold. For a split second, her lungs forgot how to breathe. A hand moved toward a weapon. She surged forward, tackling the figure into the dirt, knees on their chest, blade to throat,

And froze. "Luko?"

He grunted beneath her, caught completely off guard, eyes wide in the darkness. His voice was low, rough.

"You... Canariae, what you doing?"

She didn't move the blade. He hadn't drawn his weapon. Not yet.

"You should've stayed out of my way," she hissed, her voice low and trembling with fury. Luko's eyes widened beneath her. "I... I look for you," he said quickly.

"Try stop... before others find."

"Why?" she snapped, tightening her grip, the steel pressing a fraction harder against his throat.

"I tell them," he choked, "you not... not feral. Not beast."

Melodie's expression twisted. "Well," she growled, "maybe you were wrong."

He winced, meeting her gaze, voice strained. "You no make it out. They catch.

They kill."

"No," she whispered, eyes dark and gleaming, "they'll try to catch me."

His lips separated, confusion flickering across his face. But it was already too late. Her hand darted to his belt, snatched the signal whistle, and flung it hard into the woods. Then she leaned in close, her breath brushing his cheek, her voice cutting like ice.

"For what it's worth... I don't hate you." And she turned to guide the canariaes off the wall.

Far off, too late now, the alarm horns began to sound. The fire cast wild shadows across the stone walls, flickering with every gust of wind. Screams echoed in the distance, the stables roaring in chaos behind them.

Luko stood just beyond the torchlight, arms full of books, his expression frozen in stunned disbelief. His golden eyes glinted in the firelight as he stared at the rope dangling from the wall, at the freed captives slipping into the dark. He opened his mouth, breath catching, but before he could make a sound, a freed prisoner burst from the shadows. A flash of silver. Luko's eyes widened, but it was too late.

Steel sank into his side with a wet, sickening sound. His body jerked, arms flying open as the books fell, pages fluttering through the smoke-choked air. He gasped, the wind knocked clean out of him, and staggered back into the wall. The attacker slammed him there, one forearm pinning his throat, the other shoving the blade deeper.

"Stop!" Melodie hissed, rushing forward. She seized the attacker's wrist just before the final blow.

"He one of them!" the prisoner spat, voice raw with rage. "We kill or they kill Canariae!"

"Not now!" she snapped, shoving the blade-bearing arm aside. "We don't have time for this!" The prisoner hesitated, breathing heavily, eyes blazing with hate.

"GO!"

With a last glare, he pulled away, disappearing into the night with the others. Melodie turned back. Luko slid down the wall, his palm pressed tight over the wound, blood spilling between his fingers. His golden eyes met hers, glassy, confused, in pain.

"Shit," she breathed, crouching down. "Don't make me regret that." He blinked slowly, trying to steady his breath, but he was pale, fading fast.

Then, everything changed. A shift in the air. The temperature dropped. The sound of boots, measured, heavy, deliberate. Melodie's stomach clenched as a long, dark shadow moved through the smoke.

Malec.

He appeared from the smoke like a phantom of war, silent, precise, terrifying. His towering form seemed to drink in the torchlight, the firelight catching the edge of his pale platinum bond hair as his boots crunched over gravel and ash. His tan eyes, darkened to the color of scorched copper, burned holes through her. His chest rose and fell in a calm rhythm that only made it worse. Controlled rage. Predatory restraint. He didn't speak. He didn't need to. Melodie's pulse shot to her throat. She shoved Lilly hard toward the wall.

"Go! Climb down, now!"

"No, " Lilly whimpered, clinging to her arm.

"Go!"

Behind her, Malec moved. Like lightning. His hand closed around her wrist in a brutal grip, spinning her toward him. Her body collided with his chest, hard muscle and armor steel beneath his dark robes. Her breath caught, her heart stuttering like a drumbeat in her ears. Lilly screamed behind her, but Melodie's mind was moving too fast now. She had seconds. Maybe less.

And then, she did something stupid.

She grabbed his face, both hands, palms pressing against the sharp angles of his jaw, her fingers brushing the cool curve of his ears, and pulled him down. And kissed him.

It wasn't a peck. It wasn't soft. It was fire meeting fire, chaos folding into silence. Her lips crashed into his with urgency, heat, desperation. And he froze. Absolutely froze.

Like someone had struck him through the spine. His grip on her wrist loosened. His body stilled. But he didn't pull away. Because the moment her mouth touched his, something changed. The sensation came in a rush, too bright, too hot. Her touch against his skin was like a hundred voices shouting at once. He felt every detail in unbearable clarity: the warmth of her palms, the press of her mouth, the small catch in her breath when she tasted him.

His mind tried to catalog it, to sort it into something he could understand, but nothing fit. No logic held. No discipline answered. His magic flared, wild and uncontained, rising up in a sharp wave that pressed behind his eyes. He felt it pulsing beneath his skin, filling the space between every heartbeat. It hurt. He did not understand it. He did not want to understand it.

But her sinful mouth, by the gods, they were soft. Not like anything he had known. They weren't trained, weren't rehearsed, weren't demure. They were alive. Fierce. Sun-warmed velvet over flame. A pulse sparked through his chest, unfamiliar and electric. It moved like a ripple down to his fingertips, trembling where his hand still hovered near her waist. His breath caught against her mouth.

What was this?

The heat of her skin blurred the edges of the room. He tried to think, to name the sensations, but they came too fast. A prickle spread across the back of his neck, the first warning that he was losing control. Melodie leaned deeper, letting her body press against his as if pleading with him to keep still. And for the first time since the war, since any memory he trusted, Malec forgot the mission. Forgot the fortress. Forgot the world. He only knew her. And her kiss. And the strange, dangerous feeling it awakened in him.

The air itself stilled the moment the softness of her lips touched his. One heartbeat. Then two.

The battlement around them, once drowned in smoke and screams and the crackle of burning wood, faded to a muffled hum, as if the very fabric of magic had recognized the moment and curled inward. His thoughts scattered in a hundred directions, none of them finding purchase. He tried to speak but no sound came. Her scent flooded his senses, too strong. He could feel it in his teeth, in his lungs. This is too much. I need to move. I need it to stop. But he couldn't let go.

Sparks of etherlight, residual energy from the fortress's protective runes, danced in the smoke around them, swirling like golden motes caught in a fever dream. Malec's grip faltered, fingers loosening as if her kiss had stolen the commands from his limbs. His body locked in place, too rigid to be passive, too stunned to react. Melodie felt it.

The raw, jagged confusion that coiled beneath his skin like a wound freshly torn open. For the first time since she had laid eyes on him, the predator was confused. His breath caught, his jaw clutched tight. His tan eyes, always sharp, always observing, clouded with something else. Something ancient and wounded and inexplicable. Magic stirred in the wind. The rune-marked stones beneath their feet pulsed faintly, reacting to the sudden imbalance in their master. In that breathless, fragile second, he could only think of how impossible it was that the touch of one Canariae could burn through every defense he had ever built.

He did nothing. Melodie didn't wait.

Lilly darted toward the wall, gripping the rope with nimble fingers, her small frame vanishing into the darkness below. Gone. Safe. Melodie had won. She started to pull away, ready to bolt.

But then, Malec's hands snapped forward, his grip locking onto her with brutal strength. It was not anger. Not punishment. It was instinct. Some ancient part of him had been dragged to the surface, raw and unprepared.

The sensation crashed through him in waves. Every point of contact between them felt magnified until it blurred the rest of the world. He could feel the heat of her skin against his palms, the tiny tremor in her breathing, the way her pulse fluttered beneath her throat. It was too much. He could not sort the feeling into something clean. It pressed into him, sharp and immediate, crowding every thought.

He tried to look away, to pull back into himself, but the pressure only grew. His magic roared in his veins, surging in broken pulses that made his vision swim at the edges.

Why can't I stop it?

He needed to know. He needed a name for what she was, if only so he could put it in a place inside himself and stop feeling like he was about to shatter. His voice came out hoarse, ragged with confusion.

"S'elo?" The question slipped between them, soft and stunned.

Melodie smiled. Breathless. Bold. "I win."

The words landed like a blade to his pride. Malec blinked, the haze in his gaze evaporating in a flash of fury. His jaw pressed, his nostrils flared, and whatever fragile thing had cracked open in him slammed shut with a vicious snap. He moved with brutal precision, grabbing her, spinning her around, yanking her wrists behind her back and binding them with rough rope. There was no ceremony. No hesitation. Only anger and control. He wouldn't be caught off guard again. He wouldn't *feel* again. Not for her.

He marched her through the corridors like a prisoner of war, each step echoing with restrained violence. His grip on her arm was iron, unyielding.

Luko limped beside them, pressing a blood-soaked hand to his side, his face pale and twisted in pain. He didn't speak. The halls shimmered with flickering spell light, cast from hanging crystals meant to cleanse the air of smoke. Magic licked at the stone walls like restless shadows, sensing the energy pulsing off Malec.

He didn't say a word. But his silence was louder than any scream. They entered the medical ward, and the doors slammed open beneath his hand. The medics looked up in alarm, immediately rushing to Luko.

Malec didn't look at them. He only turned back to her. Still furious. Still scorching. But behind that fury... that wild, unnatural silence... There was something else. Something he hadn't figured out. Her pouty little tease of a mouth. Her words. The heat that still lingered on his mouth. It haunted him.

He stared at her, as if replaying the moment over and over, trying to peel back the layers and understand. Melodie met his stare, chin high, eyes gleaming with that same maddening spark. She had outplayed him. And he hated her for it. But not nearly as much as he hated himself for letting her. Even for a second.

Chapter 6

Aftershock

The tower was quiet, save for the wind.

Malec's office occupied the highest chamber of the eastern tower, a place of solemn order that belonged to no one else. Stone walls rose in shadowed columns, each etched with old Awyan sigils that wound in flowing patterns from floor to ceiling. Pale veins of quartz glimmered in the torchlight, tracing delicate lines through the dark stone like frozen lightning. The floor beneath their boots was laid in polished wood stained so deep it looked almost black, each plank fitted so precisely there was not a single visible seam. Overhead, the high ceiling was the same dark wood, set with massive crossbeams carved in looping motifs no tongue in the room bothered to name.

Bone sconces lined the walls in measured intervals, cradling cold blue flames that cast a steady glow. Between them, tall arched windows climbed to the rafters, their stained glass panes forming house sigils. When wind stirred the tower, those emblems shifted across the floor in shards of crimson and amber, silent as a blessing. Nothing was out of place. Shelves held upright books, their spines aligned like soldiers. Maps hung in even rows, edges flat and ink unblurred. Scrolls and instruments rested on desks with precise spacing, parchment weights squared at each corner.

The air was spotless, cold and dry, carrying only the faint trace of oil used to polish the wood and stone each morning. Not even dust dared to settle here. It was a room shaped by Malec's exacting will, a space where every object had a place, every place a purpose, and nothing ever drifted out of order.

Luko lay reclined on a long velvet chaise near the hearth, his usually neat hair damp with sweat. Light brown waves clung to his temples, plastered down by fever and pain. His gold-rimmed glasses sat askew on the bridge of his nose, one lens cracked. His olive-toned skin was ashen now, the faintest greenish cast tinting his pallor. Bandages circled his slender torso, fresh blood already blooming beneath the gauze.

His gold eyes, normally sharp, almost too bright, blinked slowly, dulled by exhaustion and whatever pain-dulling brew the medics had poured into him. He would live. That should have been Malec's focus. It wasn't.

He stood near the tall arched window, carved from dark volcanic glass, overlooking the sprawl of Ulvareth. Beyond the glass, the northern lights flickered like drifting fireflies, the distant clang of bells echoing from the lower tiers. But Malec didn't see any of it. His mind was somewhere else. On her. That cursed Canariae with the fire in her eyes.

The kiss still played behind his eyes like a scene he couldn't erase. Her mouth crashing into his, not with submission but with fury. The taste of her. The heat. Her hand in his hair. And the worst part, the way he had responded. It hadn't been control. It hadn't been dominance. His body had ached for her. His breath had caught. His magic had surged beneath his skin like a living thing. He hadn't known if he wanted to crush her or worship her. He told himself it was fascination. That she was simply an unknown variable he needed to define. A dangerous wild card. A challenge. He had always been drawn to the impossible.

Slowly, he reached for the row of small carved figurines on the window ledge. Each was an abstract shape cut from pale stone, their angles worn smooth over generations. One by one, he lifted them and set them down again, aligning their bases to the etched groove he had measured into the sill. He adjusted each by a fraction until they formed a perfect line, the small ritual calming the heat that still burned in his chest. This was how he conquered the chaos. This was how he outthought every rival, how he earned the name the Silver Fox. His mind was a labyrinth of strategies, traps, and calculations that had never failed him. But that brilliance came with a price so few ever glimpsed.

His genius was fragile, easily rattled and derailed by noise he could not sort. Order was the only thing that let it shine. Routine was the tether that kept him from unraveling. Without these small certainties, he could not think. He could not breathe.

He set the final figurine in place, its base flush with the groove, and let out a slow breath. For a moment, the pressure in his chest eased. The world returned to something he could command. And yet...

His heart beat faster now, just thinking of her. His palms itched, his mouth dry. It wasn't normal. He flexed his fingers, remembering the first time he touched her skin, the jolt that followed, the way his magic had stirred like it was recognizing something he didn't. He still hadn't explained that. He hadn't even *tried*. Malec exhaled sharply and looked down at the torchlights on the walls of the fortress again. But they blurred.

Malec exhaled slowly, hands clasped behind his back, shoulders drawn tight with restraint. It wasn't as though he'd never known a woman.

In Awyan society, physical intimacy was encouraged, expected, even necessary. Their bloodlines were fading. Their birthrates declining. Sex was not sacred. It was survival. A ritual to be performed, not a bond to be cherished. As a younger elf, he had taken part with vigor. It was enjoyable then, sometimes even satisfying, a way to practice control, to build stamina, to quiet the restlessness in his blood. Nothing more. But as the years passed, the spark dulled. Encounters blurred together, different faces yielding the same outcomes. Whispers in the dark became business arrangements. Empty flattery over wine, transactional touches behind closed doors. Every step had a purpose. Every motion was predictable.

It was how he preferred it. Familiar patterns and orderly expectations. He withdrew from courtship and ceremony. Found purpose instead in the simplicity of war. The only intimacy he allowed himself came in the form of brothel visits. Quick. Functional. Forgettable. No names. No affection. No chance of anything unexpected creeping in to splinter his focus. He had never even thought to touch a Canariae. The very idea was grotesque. Their kind were loud, unruly, soft-boned creatures with no discipline. It would be no different than kissing a wild animal.

And yet. His jaw tightened. He could still feel her mouth against his. That kiss, savage, scorching, unforgivable. And his body's reaction to it. Not just a stir. Not just heat. Something far worse.

His mind wanted the quiet of routine. The practiced ritual that never changed. But his body, traitorous and unrecognizable, craved the wild unknowing she carried in her breath. It had been *chemical*. Primal. His blood had lit up like it remembered something his mind did not. His magic pulsed against his skin like it wanted more. His fingers had trembled after she let go..

None of them had made him feel *out of control*. But she had. That filthy, reckless little creature with defiant eyes and lips that tasted like war. His stomach turned. Disgusting.

He forced in a breath, willing the thought away like smoke. Whatever this was, fascination, irritation, madness, it would pass. It had to.

Malec's eyes slid to the cage across the room. She sat inside it like a throne. Melodie. The Canariae. No longer bound at the wrists, but a thick iron collar remained locked around her throat, the long chain curled taut against the floor where it anchored to the bars. Her posture was unbothered. Almost bored.

She was leering at him. Not with fear. Not with shame. With something far worse. Amusement. That same maddening defiance danced behind her eyes, like she saw something in him no one else dared to. He met her gaze. Her lips curled. Then, slowly, deliberately, she raised both fists and extended her middle fingers at him. His brow furrowed. He didn't recognize the gesture, but the intent was clear, contempt, mockery. A long breath hissed from his nose as he turned away sharply, jaw flexing hard enough to crack. She was playing with him. Taunting him. Daring him. And it was working.

Disgusting. He looked away again, eyes dragging to the forest beyond the glass, but he could still feel her gaze needling the back of his skull. And worse than her gaze? The memory. The kiss. Her mouth, hot and unyielding. His body, betraying him. That pulse of magic that surged the moment they touched. The way his breath had caught, not in anger, but want.

He loathed her for it.

The days passed in slow suffocation. Malec avoided her. He buried himself in training drills, fortress inspections, logistical reports, anything to drown the echo of her voice in his mind. He sparred until his arms shook. Rode until his legs burned. He hadn't slept in his own chambers for three nights, instead collapsing in the war room or near the armory just to escape the pull of memory. But no matter how deep he buried himself in routine, she lingered. In every quiet space, she waited. Not in body, but in presence. A whisper in his blood. The taste of her defiance still clinging to his tongue like smoke he couldn't spit out.

He hated how his mind kept circling back to her, unable to let go. When he fixated on something, it became a snare that tightened around every thought until there was nothing else. It was like a single word screaming in his head, louder and louder, demanding to be solved. But she was unsolvable. No clear pattern or logic to her defiance. Just chaos wrapped in dark skin and a mouth that made him forget his own name. And the worst part? She *knew*.

Every time he passed that cursed cage, her eyes found him. She didn't speak. She didn't rise. She just looked at him like she was waiting for something. Like she understood a truth he hadn't yet admitted to himself. And when their eyes met, she smiled, not sweetly, but with that same mocking, infuriating smirk. Like she had already taken something from him, something he hadn't meant to give.

It made his blood burn. It made his pride hiss. It made him want to storm across the room, drag her to her knees, and remind her who held the chain. But he didn't. He kept walking.

Because every time he looked at her, something in him shifted. Something he didn't want to name. Something that terrified him more than her defiance.

The longer he stayed away... the more he wanted to go back.

The Imperial messenger arrived in the early evening. Malec sat in his study, hunched over the massive wooden desk, its surface scattered with maps, missives, and untouched reports. A goblet of dark amber wine rested near his hand, the liquid barely disturbed. The hearth behind him crackled low, casting long shadows across the stone walls and catching the silver threads in the war banners that hung above the bookcases. Smoke from a dwindling stick of resin incense curled lazily through the room. He didn't look up as the door opened. The messenger stepped inside, bowing stiffly before approaching with a sealed scroll in hand.

"From His Majesty, the King of Ulvareth," he said with forced formality.

Malec took the letter without a word. His fingers broke the wax seal, but his eyes didn't scan the page. He didn't need to read it. He already knew what it would say. The King had heard. Of course he had. Word traveled faster than horses when it carried scandal. The fire. The escaped Canariae. The *dark-skinned captive* that refused to yield. The one *he*, the great Silver Fox, had yet to break. His cousin would relish this.

Malec's gaze rested on the page a moment longer, then scoffed quietly under his breath. Without hesitation, he leaned back and tossed the letter into the flames. The paper curled in on itself, edges glowing before blackening into ash.

> The messenger hesitated, clearly uneasy. "Shall I prepare a response, Commander?"

> "Yes," Malec said, voice flat. "Tell His Majesty I'll be at court by week's end. No sooner."

The messenger nodded and quickly excused himself, leaving the door half-ajar behind him. Malec sat in silence. He knew exactly why his cousin had summoned him. It wasn't for strategy. It wasn't even about the prisoner. It was a game. A chance to mock him, humiliate him before the court. The King wanted to see him squirm. Wanted to look him in the eye and laugh. The Silver Fox, undone by a single Canariae.

Malec could already hear the bastard's voice, echoing off the polished walls of the royal hall. Maybe he should give her to him. Wrap her in chains and deliver her like a gift. Let the King see how wild she truly was. Let *him* try to tame her. Maybe that would be the cleanest solution. The easiest way to erase the problem. But something inside him clenched.

The idea of handing her over, of letting someone else touch her, chain her, own her, made his jaw lock and his pulse kick strangely in his throat. It wasn't logic. It wasn't pride. It was something deeper, something uninvited and unwelcome. He didn't know what it was. And he refused to think about it.

Instead, he stood, pushing away from the desk. His eyes flicked to the hallway outside his study where her cage sat nestled in the atrium chamber beyond. He hadn't visited her since the incident. He avoided her now, he had moved her across to the opposite side of the corridor, changed his route to the war room, posted guards between them. It was easier not to see her. Easier not to feel that thing in his chest every time their eyes met.

Still, he could feel her glare through stone and steel, sharp as blades, constant as gravity. He scowled and stepped into the corridor. Outside, a servant was kneeling to collect scrolls near the archway, a middle-aged Canariae male with graying hair and a soldier's poise, one of the trusted domestics who had served the garrison for years.

"You," Malec said, voice low.

The servant froze and bowed. "Commander."

"Have the *choyte* serve the dark-skinned Canariae from now on."

The man blinked. "The girl?"

"She'll respond better to someone her own kind. That will keep her quiet." Malec turned away before the servant could reply. "And maybe," he muttered under his breath, "she'll stop glaring at me every time I walk past my study."

He didn't tell the truth. Didn't admit the *real* reason. He just wanted to please her. And he didn't understand why.

Back inside, he paced once, then poured himself a drink he didn't want and didn't finish. The fire popped behind him, a log splitting with a sharp crack like a warning. He ignored it.

"Have the horses ready by dawn," he called to the guards in the hall. "We ride at sunrise."

He lifted his free hand and rubbed his face wearily, fingertips pressing hard against the bridge of his nose. The other hand, the one holding the cup, trembled just enough that he had to set it down before it slipped from his grasp.

T he room was still when the door creaked open again. Melodie tensed automatically, her hands resting on her knees, the heavy collar around her neck tugging slightly as she shifted. Her gaze flicked toward the entrance, expecting another soldier, maybe the warlord again, come to torment her in silence. But instead, a small figure stepped through the threshold carrying a wooden tray.

"Lilly?" Melodie blinked, sitting up straighter.

The little girl beamed. Her bare feet padded softly across the stone floor as she approached, careful not to spill the contents. A bowl of steaming soup, a crust of bread, and a tin cup of water. The tray was far too heavy for her, but she seemed proud of her delivery.

"You were with us," Melodie said slowly, taking the tray as Lilly set it beside her on the floor. "You were with the group when we escaped the caves. What are you doing here? Didn't you run with the others?"

Lilly smiled, brushing her messy hair from her face. "No need run. I no prisoner," she said brightly. "Awyan take care of me. I'm pet."

Melodie froze. "What?"

"I pet," Lilly repeated, tapping her own chest as though it were the simplest, happiest truth in the world. "They feed me, give blanket, no chains. I good girl."

Melodie's stomach twisted. She stared at the girl, suddenly unsure if she should be angry or afraid for her.

"Lilly... what are you talking about? You're not an animal. That's not, " She cut herself off, her voice shaking slightly. "You don't belong to them."

Before Lilly could answer, a team of Awyans came in.

The young Awyan translator from before stepped in, flanked by two Awyan medics draped in black robes stitched with silver thread. They moved with quiet authority, hands full of polished instruments and vials. The translator gave Melodie a quick nod and glanced at Lilly.

"Apologies for... interruption," he said stiffly. "We come check you. For health. To be sure you bring no... sickness. To palace. Or... near King."

Melodie's eyes narrowed. "She's a child," she snapped, nodding toward Lilly.

"Why is she still here? Why isn't she with the others who escaped?"

The translator looked confused for a moment, then gave a short shake of his head.

"She no escape. She not prisoner. She choyte."

"A what?"

"Choyte," he repeated, as if it were obvious. "Canariae child. Trained to find wild group. Your kind. Feral ones. She walk with them, live short time. When she find home... she send sign. Awyan soldiers come. Collect."

Melodie's mouth dropped as she looked at Lilly, who only smiled wider, clearly proud of the title. Her blood ran cold.

"So..." she said slowly, her voice turning sharp, "she's a *snitch*?"

The translator blinked. "What is... snitch?"

Melodie stared at him, then gave a humorless smile.

"A snitch is someone who looks like your friend, acts like your ally... then stabs you in the back the moment you trust them."

She looked down at Lilly. "Usually for food. Or a pat on the head."

Lilly beamed. "Yes."

Melodie said nothing. Her stomach soured. The air around her grew thick, damp with something uglier than despair. She had survived fire, chains, caves filled with ash, but this, this betrayal in the face of a child who smiled through it? This was worse. There wasn't a single soul in this world she could trust. Not even a child. Everyone could be used. Bent. Broken.

Her hands trembled slightly as she lifted the spoon. But she ate. Because strength mattered more than trust now. She needed her body strong, her mind sharper. There would be another chance. And when it came, she would be ready.

Later, when the guards and medics withdrew and the room returned to silence, she pushed the tray aside and rose. The chain at her throat dragged slightly with her movement, cold and heavy, but she ignored it. Her muscles ached, joints tight from disuse, but pain was familiar. Pain was manageable.

She stretched slowly. Rolled her shoulders. Dropped to the floor and began again. Squats. Pushups. Breath. Controlled. Focused. They thought she was broken. They were wrong.

The journey was long and uneventful, each day bleeding into the next beneath an iron-gray sky. The land shifted slowly as they moved, the thick forests of Ulvareth giving way to open fields and rolling hills blanketed in the changing colors of autumn. Trees stood like sentinels along the road, their leaves turning rich shades of gold, rust, and blood-orange.

Melodie sat inside a caged transport near the rear of the convoy. It wasn't a proper prison wagon, just a modified carriage fitted with rusted metal bars and bolted panels in place of windows. The walls were reinforced with cold, soot-streaked iron. There was no cushioning, no bedding, just a hard wooden bench she shared with two other prisoners. She shivered, arms wrapped tightly around herself as she sat with her back against the bars. The collar still circled her neck, heavier now with each passing day. Her breath fogged faintly in the chill. When she leaned too far forward, the chain tugged her back with a reminder of where she was. Still, she watched.

Through the slits and bars, she memorized the road: the places it dipped, the bends it took, the rivers they crossed, and the way the fields broke apart near distant woodlines. Every detail. Every shadowed outpost. Every crooked tree or abandoned shrine. If she ever found her chance again, she would need to know how to find her way back. There would be no second blind run.

Most of the Canariae had either escaped or been killed during the fire. Only a few had been recaptured, mostly the old ones, too frail or slow to run far. Malec barely acknowledged them. Or her.

He rode near the front, as always, his silver cloak trailing behind him like a banner. Once, he would've glanced back often, just to glare at her, as if her presence offended him. But now? He didn't look at her at all. Not once. She noticed it immediately. And she found it hilarious. The great white pig, too shaken to look a woman in the eyes. A Canariae woman, no less.

If she weren't so cold, so hungry, and so damn tired, she might've savored the moment more. Instead, all she could do was lean her head against the bars and smirk faintly in the shadows. *Bet he's never been treated like that in his life.* The thought warmed her a little, just enough to keep going. If things weren't so god-awful, she might've actually laughed.

Melodie caught sight of Luko riding in one of the enclosed carriages ahead. He was still pale, still tightly bandaged beneath his dark cloak, but no longer looked at her with the wary contempt he once did. A week ago, his eyes had been full of calculation, cold, clinical, like she was something broken under glass. Not anymore. Something had changed between them. Saving his life had shifted the air between them in a way no apology ever could. She felt it in the way he glanced at her now, brief, veiled looks, but no longer full of mistrust. He didn't see a beast anymore. He didn't even see a subject. He saw a person. Good.

She would need allies if she was going to survive this. And he was the only one in that convoy who didn't falter when she spoke.

The further they traveled, the colder it became. The sun barely climbed past mid-sky before it began to sink again, leaving the road wrapped in long shadows and pale light. Melodie curled tighter into herself in the cage, using the brittle straw scattered across the floor for warmth. It clung to her damp clothes and rough skin, but it was better than nothing. She kept her arms wrapped tight around her ribs, teeth clenched, her breath fogging faintly in the iron air.

Then, somewhere up ahead, a low horn echoed across the hills. Melodie's head snapped up, her muscles tensing automatically. The other prisoners stirred. She rose slightly on her knees to peer through the gaps in the bars, heart pounding.

Ahead of them, rising out of the twilight mist like a waking mountain, was a city vast and walled, built from dark, matte stone that drank the light rather than reflected it. Veins of pale mineral ran through the masonry, delicate as spider silk, and caught the last of the day in glimmers that looked almost alive. The walls soared to impossible heights, as smooth as the side of a cliff, and so long they disappeared into the haze at either edge of her vision.

Behind those ramparts, towers and spires stabbed upward in a jagged forest of black stone. Some rose in narrow clusters, shaped like spears laced together. Others flared out in tiers, crowned in flat terracotta-tiled roofs that reminded her of old market stalls she had once seen in Marrakesh. Triangular windows punctuated the walls in tight sequences, interspersed with round and oval apertures that glowed with hidden light. A few buildings were studded with huge square panes filled with colored glass, each pane stamped with an emblem she couldn't name.

Pedestrian pathways crisscrossed above the streets, built from the same matte black brick as the walls. Those street lights were nothing she had ever encountered. Each was a tall pillar crowned by a translucent yellow stone that gave off a steady radiance, soft but potent, as if it had drunk the sunlight all day only to pour it back into the dark. Their glow pooled over the black-paved avenues, catching the edges of polished metal doors and the gleam of elaborate door knockers shaped like mythical beasts.

The buildings themselves were not built in any single style she recognized. The tall doors framed by pointed arches could have belonged in a Gothic cathedral. The rooflines, flat and layered in brick, evoked desert cities she had only ever seen in books. Some upper balconies flared outward with intricate latticework screens, each a riot of delicate cut-outs and swirling patterns. It was a city that had devoured every architectural language and made a new dialect from their core.

Even through the bars, she could feel the ingenuity that pulsed through it. The walls were etched in flowing characters she could not read. Here and there, mechanical contraptions were mounted on the rooftops, polished blades that turned in the high wind. The air smelled of ignited resin, tempered iron, and something that reminded her of lightning.

This was Caelistra, the capital of Ulvareth. A city built for beauty, politics and war. She felt it deep in her gut. The finality. The lock clicking shut around her fate. And something told her, clearer than any vision, louder than any horn, her real fight was only just beginning.

The cage was beautiful.

It gleamed in the morning light like something carted in from a royal menagerie, but it was no mere pen. Its frame was crafted from polished black metal that shone like liquid obsidian. The bars curved in elegant arches that met overhead in a dome, each strut etched with fine spiraling motifs that caught the sun.

Inside, a vast cushion sprawled across the floor, wide enough to seat five grown people shoulder to shoulder. Its velvet surface shimmered in shades of purple and deep wine red, the nap crushed in places where she had shifted her weight during the long night. It was so soft she could almost forget where she was. Almost.

Above her, the ceiling soared nearly fifty feet. Entire panels of glass framed the sky, flooding the chamber with cold, brilliant daylight that made her eyes water. The beams that crisscrossed the vault were painted in gleaming black and gold, curling into elaborate designs that reminded her of constellations, though none she could name. Between the beams, pale white plaster panels held painted portraits of monarchs past, their narrow Awyan faces rendered in lifelike detail, their hollow eyes gazing down in judgment.

The walls were smooth white stone, trimmed in glossy black cornices. Every surface gleamed as if scrubbed hourly. She could see no cracks in the plaster, no drifting speck of dust. The air smelled faintly of pressed herbs, polish, and something sweet and cloying that set her teeth on edge.

She shifted, and the gold chain attached to her collar gave a quiet metallic clink. It anchored her to the side of the cage, just long enough to let her stand or lie down, but not quite long enough to reach the lock on the door. A petty cruelty. She looked down at herself, and bile rose in her throat.

Someone had dressed her in a gown the color of midnight. The fabric was smooth and fine, clinging to her hips and pooling around her ankles. It was the kind of garment meant for a favored pet, not a person. Her hair had been brushed and woven into a thick braid that rested over her shoulder, still perfumed with unfamiliar oil. A faint gloss shone on her lips. She was dressed for auction.

Revulsion curdled in her gut. She wanted to rip the gown off and tear the braid loose until every polished inch of her was undone. She wanted to scream. But she did none of those things.

Instead, she folded her hands in her lap and lowered her gaze, forcing her face into an empty calm, just another pretty thing waiting to be bought. Because rage would not save her. Screaming would not free her.

She had to be smarter than the men who built this place. Smarter than the ones who thought she was already broken. Melodie took a slow breath, feeling the soft velvet under her palms, the bite of the collar at her throat.

If they expected her to be docile, she would let them believe it. This was no dungeon. No holding cell scraped from damp stone. She was in a receiving gallery, one of many opulent display chambers hidden deep within the royal estate, far removed from the war chambers and the throne hall. Here, the air was hushed. The polished floors gleamed without a single footprint. Only a pair of guards lingered near the archway, their eyes sliding past her as if she were already forgotten. That was the point. To keep her out of sight. Out of mind. And most importantly, out of earshot.

Because somewhere beyond the tall carved doors and thick white walls, a different conversation was taking place. One that would decide what happened to her next.

King Surion entered as if he expected the world itself to bow in greeting. Draped in robes of pale gold and sea-glass blue, he moved with the slow, ornamental grace of a peacock preening for an audience. His eyes were a deep, saturated blue, dark as midnight glass, always searching for admiration he had never earned. His hair, a yellow-blonde just bright enough to catch every flicker of torchlight, fell in loose waves to his shoulders, meticulously groomed but never severe. He was shorter than Malec by a head, his build slighter, the shape of a man unaccustomed to discipline or exertion.

He possessed the same otherworldly beauty as every Awyan noble, but unlike Malec, who wore his strength like a blade sheathed just beneath the skin, Surion radiated something softer. Something polished to the point of fragility. The manner of a man who had never needed to fight for anything because everything he desired arrived on a silver platter, arranged precisely to flatter him.

Luko bowed low, because he had no choice, though the back of his neck prickled with distaste. He had known a thousand soldiers sharper than this king. Surion looked the part, spoke the part, but to Luko he was a lacquered shell, no more fit to rule than a crow in a crown. He kept his expression blank, though a single thought pressed behind his eyes.

If not for Malec and his father, this entire kingdom would have fallen to cinders years ago.

Malec did not bow. He inclined his head the bare minimum required by decorum, the gesture more an acknowledgment of protocol than any respect. In his mind, Surion was a weasel in a silk robe, all smooth words and shallow cunning, convinced that clever lies could replace competence. He was the sort of fool who believed beauty was strength and that his throne was proof of divine favor.

More than anything, Malec despised that particular brand of dishonesty. The false warmth, the smiling deceit, the performance of virtue from a man who had never needed to earn anything he possessed. He had no patience for pretense. No tolerance for those who painted their vanity as benevolence. Surion's entire existence was a reminder of everything Malec could not abide: the shallow politics, the hidden barbs, the elaborate masks worn by men too afraid to speak the truth.

He could stomach arrogance. He could even respect ambition. But not that. Never that.

As Surion sauntered deeper into the private parlor, his eyes flicked over Malec with an amused curiosity, as though he were studying a curiosity in a cabinet of wonders. To those who understood that a crown meant nothing if the hand wearing it had never held a sword. His gaze flicked across the room, pausing first on Luko, still stiff and bandaged from when the feral stabbed him. The King's mouth curled slowly into a smirk, delicate and full of amusement.

"Troublesome journey, I see," Surion remarked, his voice smooth as silk.

Luko, ever the diplomat, inclined his head respectfully. Malec said nothing. The King turned toward him then, smile deepening.

"Tell me, cousin," he said, his tone light but edged like a dagger, "how does the great Silver Fox return from battle, bested, humiliated, and, " he gestured lazily toward Luko, "with a limping scholar at his side?"

Malec's jaw shifted. His eyes remained locked on the King, inscrutable . Calm. Controlled. But not cold. No, cold would be a kindness. There was heat behind those eyes. Warning heat. Surion chuckled softly, clearly enjoying himself. But even as he smiled, there was caution in the way he stood. A careful awareness, like a man performing for a lion just outside the cage.

He wanted to see Malec fall. That much was obvious. He always had. Growing up in the shadow of Malec, who had been stronger, faster, more dangerous, more intelligent, had carved something ugly into Surion. An inferiority that festered beneath layers of silk and politics. He wore his crown like armor, but everyone knew it had been earned by lineage, not merit. He ruled because he was born to. Malec *commanded* because no one could stop him.

"Careful," Malec said at last, his voice low and smooth, each word pressed like a thumb into Surion's pride. "Mock me again, and I'll let you finish that sentence with fewer teeth."

The King's smile faltered for just a heartbeat.

Then, with a light, dismissive wave, he turned toward the grand corridor. "Come," he said breezily. "You've traveled far. You must be exhausted."

Malec didn't move immediately. He let Surion walk ahead, back straight and expression untouched, as if the brief exchange hadn't just reminded the entire room of who truly held the leash in this kingdom.

And it wasn't the man in the crown.

The King's chambers were, as expected, a shrine to excess. The walls rose in towering panels of ivory-stained stone, their surfaces crowded with ornamental carvings that clashed more than they impressed. Heavy sconces shaped like coiling serpents jutted out at uneven intervals, their mouths gaping open to spill warm yellow light across every garish surface. Thick drapes of pristine white fabric pooled on the floor beside curtains of purple so deep they looked almost black in the shifting firelight. The window frames were drowned in glossy gold trim, throwing sharp glints across the polished black floorboards whenever the flames stirred.

Malec's gaze swept the space, noting each gaudy indulgence with quiet disdain. There was nothing cohesive in the design, only a frantic layering of luxury as if Surion believed every scrap of gold was proof he belonged on that throne. A squat table stood crowded with jeweled decanters and silver trays. High-backed mahogany chairs were upholstered in fabrics so loud they seemed to sneer at good taste.

The air reeked of torched resin and a sweet oil that clung to the back of his throat. Malec suppressed a flicker of irritation. This was the kingdom's seat of power, and it looked as if a merchant caravan had exploded inside it.

Surion lounged across a velvet settee, one leg crossed over the other, his yellow-blond hair spilling artfully over his shoulders. He looked perfectly at home in the middle of all that pretension. Malec stood near the fire, pouring himself a drink stronger than most mortals could handle, and took a long, slow sip as Luko began to speak.

And moons above, did Luko speak. From the stable fires to the panicked guards, to the dark-skinned Canariae who not only escaped, but orchestrated the chaos, Luko spared no detail. His voice was calm, even amused, as though he were recounting a minor battlefield blunder and not a complete humiliation.

The King laughed with growing delight, sinking deeper into his chair with every outrageous detail.

"You," he wheezed, pointing at Malec, "outplayed by a Canariae? What a time to be alive."

Malec said nothing. He just sipped his drink and stared into the flames like they were the only things in the room that didn't make him want to commit treason.

"Not just *any* Canariae," Luko added, his golden eyes glinting as he casually swirled his glass.

Malec turned his head, slowly. Warningly. And then Luko said it. He told him about the kiss.

Surion nearly choked on his wine. "She *kissed* you?"

Malec's jaw locked. His hand tightened around the goblet. A faint crack ran down the glass from the pressure. Luko, ever the academic with a death wish, simply nodded.

"Full lips. Direct hit. Got him good."

"She did it to *distract me*," Malec said flatly, voice like crushed stone. "It was calculated. Desperate. Nothing more."

"Oh, I'm sure it was," Surion said, clearly enjoying every syllable. "But how was it?"

Malec's stare could have melted steel.

Surion leaned back, grinning. "You're not denying it wasn't effective."

"She caught me off guard," Malec growled.

"She caught you off guard with her mouth," Luko clarified, raising his glass in salute. "Brilliant use of resources, honestly."

Malec exhaled slowly through his nose, visibly recalibrating his entire sense of restraint.

"I didn't realize they were that... strategic," Surion mused, swirling his wine.

"Most aren't," Luko replied. "But this one? She's different. She's not from any of the known colonies. I believe she's foreign. Possibly even off-world."

That got Surion's attention. He tilted his head, intrigued. "Fascinating," he murmured. "I must see her."

Malec's expression dropped like a guillotine.
"No," he said simply.

The word cut the air. Surion blinked. "No?" he echoed, as if unfamiliar with the concept.

"She is not for you," Malec said, slow and firm.
There was no anger in his tone, just finality. A line drawn in cold, black stone. For a moment, the King studied him. Then that slow, irritating smirk returned.
"Now I really must see her."
Malec took another sip of his drink. And fantasized, briefly, about slamming the goblet into his cousin's smug face.

The receiving gallery had been prepared with meticulous care. Sunlight still poured through the towering glass ceiling, now slanting at a late-afternoon angle that turned the white walls a soft honey gold. Painted portraits of monarchs watched in silent judgment from above, their eyes fixed on the center of the room where the cage gleamed on the polished dark wood floor.

Melodie lay there, still as a statue. A deep blue gown draped over her frame, the fabric pooling around her legs. Her hair had been washed and braided in a thick rope that rested over her collarbone, shining darkly against her skin. A gold chain fastened to her collar trailed to a fixed ring at the edge of the cage, gleaming each time she breathed. Someone had gone to great effort to make her beautiful, just beautiful enough that her captivity would look like civility instead of what it was.

Three high-backed chairs stood arranged in precise alignment, facing the cage like judges awaiting the opening argument. As Malec, Luko, and the King stepped inside, the hush that followed felt both reverent and transactional. And in the center of it all, the girl in the cage slept on, unaware of the eyes that measured her worth.

Surion stopped walking. His expression shifted from idle amusement to stunned fascination.

"Incredible," he murmured, stepping closer to the bars.

He had seen Canariae before. Dozens. Hundreds, even. Pale ones, sun-kissed ones, golden ones. But never this. Never a skin tone so rich and deep it seemed to drink in the light, then return it tenfold. Never hair like that, coiled, soft, impossibly voluminous, like it had its own laws of gravity. She was asleep, unaware of the attention, unaware of what she had become the moment she stepped into his court.

The King's hand hovered near the bars, his fingers drifting toward the glossy mass of curls as if drawn by instinct. He didn't touch her. Because Malec caught his wrist.

"This one bites," Malec said quietly, his voice flat but iron.

Surion turned to look at him, one brow lifting in amusement. Then he laughed, soft, musical, and needling.

"You sound attached, cousin."

Malec didn't answer. The King let his hand fall, though his gaze never strayed from the cage. "She would fetch a remarkable price," he said, his voice slipping into that conversational silk he wore in court.

"I've never seen one like her. A true rarity."

"She's feral," Malec murmured, his voice low as his eyes fixed on the girl in the black cage. "A wild boar in silk. She needs breaking before she enters any home."

Surion tilted his head, studying the way Malec's gaze didn't waver. A slow, satisfied smile crept over his mouth.

"Ah," he said, the sound rippling with amusement. "A fine gift, then. I am pleased."

"No."

The word came out sharper than Malec intended, snapping through the quiet like a thrown blade. Surion stilled. His dark blue eyes slid to Malec, their depths glinting with something sly.

"No?" he echoed softly.

Malec didn't look at him. He couldn't. He didn't trust his own expression. The longer he stared at the Canariae, her loose braid, her dark skin gleaming against the velvet, the more something restless coiled beneath his ribs. It was unfamiliar, intrusive, a sensation he didn't have language for. He only knew it was powerful, and that it made the thought of Surion's hands on her feel... unclean.

Surion's lips curved further. He exhaled a slow breath, like a man savoring an expensive wine.

"Ah," he murmured again, dragging the syllable out until it stung. "I see."

Malec's tan eyes flicked up, narrowing. His magic pulsed once, hard enough to prickle the air between them. Surion leaned back in his chair, crossing one elegant leg over the other.

"Very well," he said with casual finality, though the smile remained. "I will not take what you wish to keep."

Something cracked deep in Malec's composure. His spine locked rigid, every muscle tensing as if bracing for a blow. He hadn't spoken desire aloud, hadn't admitted even to himself that it was desire, but the word *keep* struck a raw, hidden nerve. The atmosphere shifted. The flames in the iron sconces along the walls rippled, guttered, then abruptly flared high before collapsing in a shower of sparks. Half of the candles went out at once, plunging the gallery into sudden pools of darkness.

Surion didn't budge. He only lifted his brows with delicate surprise.

"Mm. Drafty tonight."

Luko cleared his throat, lifting one hand. A golden thread of light leapt from his palm to each wick, reigniting the candles with careful precision. His gaze flicked to the ceiling.

"Strange," he said quietly, though his tone was wary. "I didn't feel any breeze."

There had been no breeze. Malec still hadn't moved, but the air around him trembled faintly, his magic thrumming through the floorboards like the low growl of a hidden predator. Surion watched him, the look in his dark blue eyes too perceptive by half. But he said nothing else.

For the rest of the evening, the King reclined in his ornate chair, sipping red wine as if nothing had happened. He never took his eyes from the cage, never spoke another word of claim or jest. And Malec sat beside him in rigid, furious silence, every nerve strung tight. He didn't understand what he felt, only that it was dangerous and that it had a name he refused to speak. The flames, though reignited, never settled to a steady burn again. They flickered fitfully, as if the room itself was holding its breath.

Chapter 7

The Weight of Two Worlds

Evening light filtered through the high, narrow windows above her cage, pale and cold. The golden bars caught the sun, casting long, gilded lines across the marble floor like prison tattoos.

Melodie sat upright, the velvet cushions beneath her soft but doing little to ease the tension in her spine. She shifted, her fingers brushing the embroidered trim, but her thoughts were far from comfort. Home.

It felt like a fading signal, distant, flickering, too quiet to reach. But she couldn't let herself forget. Not now. Not when so much was at stake. Earth's population had already plummeted below two hundred million, maybe even less. What remained of humanity was fractured, hungry, sick. The virus hadn't stopped. It didn't sleep. It devoured.

And back there, in the broken silence of a crumbling world, she'd been one of the last scientists still trying to stop it. Every day was another countdown. Every failed test another grave. They had been close, so close, to something. Not a cure. But maybe a beginning. A breakthrough. And now she was here. Caged like some pet rat in a middle school classroom. But if there was no way back... Her jaw clenched. Then maybe the cure wasn't on Earth anymore. Maybe it was here.

This world was strange, an impossible blend of magic, biology, and ancient power. She didn't understand it. Not yet. But someone did. Luko. Scholar. Physician. Arrogant bastard, but smart. He knew things. And Melodie needed information. She couldn't afford pride anymore. Not when the stakes were everything.

She hugged her knees to her chest and let her eyes drift shut again, pretending to rest while her mind raced. She would fix things with Luko. She would earn his trust. Then she would ask questions. Study. Learn. Adapt.

After a moment, she stretched out flat on her back, then curled forward, folding her body tight, forehead nearly to her knees. Down, then up again, slow and steady. Her muscles burned, but she welcomed the ache, letting the movement keep her blood hot and her mind sharper than fear. She repeated the motion, over and over, feeling the strain in her core with every rise. This was discipline—her own small rebellion against weakness, a promise to herself that she would not be broken. She kept going, silent, counting each cycle in her head, determined to keep her body strong for the fight ahead.

Luko lingered in the archway, clutching the tray like a shield. The velvet cushions beneath Melodie shifted as she moved, legs rising in a steady rhythm, her breathing even. She didn't acknowledge him until she was done.

"I, I bring food," he said awkwardly, placing the plate gently by the bars. "Fresh. Warm still."

Melodie lowered her legs and sat up with ease, flipping to her feet in one graceful motion. She took the plate, gave it a once-over, and raised an eyebrow as she chewed.

"They're called sit-ups," she said dryly.

Luko blinked. "Sit... up?"

"Exercise. Strengthens the core."

He looked at her like she'd spoken in riddles. "But you... you train body? When caged?"

Melodie swallowed, licking her teeth. "You think survival starts when the door opens? You're wrong. It starts in here." She tapped her chest. "And in here." She tapped her temple. "Every day I wake up, I fight."

Luko adjusted his sleeves, gaze uncertain. "You speak like soldier. Or healer who... refuse to die."

She snorted softly. "Maybe I'm both." Silence stretched between them for a beat.

Then she spoke again, quieter.

"Thought you hated me. So why are you here, Luko?"

He hesitated, face twitching with effort as he searched for the right words.

"I... think maybe... I wrong you," he said slowly. "What you said... it had weight. Much weight. I not like how it feel. I think maybe... you not like how I treat you."

Melodie gave a half-laugh, dark and bitter. "Wow. Look at that. Empathy." He didn't catch the sarcasm. Or maybe he did and let it slide.

"You say... I treat like animal," he continued, voice low. "That not what I want. But it is... what I do."

Melodie leaned against the bars, arms folded, gaze locked to his.

"I've been treated like less-than-human my whole life, Luko. Where I'm from, people with skin like mine were stolen, beaten, displayed like property. Then told to smile and be grateful. Generations later, we still live that legacy."

She paused, examining him carefully.

"I know exactly what it feels like to be judged, mocked, and used for what my body can do instead of who I am."

Luko looked down. His mouth opened, then closed again. He fidgeted with the hem of his sleeve, shame creeping into his golden eyes. Melodie tilted her head.

"I imagine being born into a place where people see you as 'lesser' makes you desperate to prove your worth. You build knowledge, sharpen your tongue, hold it together with pride and dignity. Sound familiar?"

His eyes flicked up. And for the first time, they saw each other.
"Yes," he said softly. "Exactly so. You... you understand."
Melodie didn't say anything for a long moment. Then she sighed and sat back down, plate in her lap.
"You're not the only one trying to be more than what people expect."

Luko stepped closer, voice gentle. "I want truce. I... want trade. I tell you about my world. You tell me yours. Maybe... we both learn."

Her eyes narrowed slightly. "Why?"

"Because," he said, and his voice was quiet now, almost reverent. "Your world... is strange. But strong. I see your tools, your thinking, your... fight. It is knowledge I not see before. I want know it. I want learn."

She chewed slowly, staring at the bars between them. "Careful what you wish for.

That knowledge broke us."

Luko's jaw coiled. "Our knowledge break us too."
She looked up.

"We make selves perfect," he said. "Strong. Long-lived. Beautiful. But now our women..." He struggled for the word. "They cannot make child. Or not often. We are dying. Slowly. We made this."

Melodie's breath caught.
"We are like tree with no root," he murmured. "Alive, but no future."
Their eyes locked again. Something heavy passed between them. Shared extinction. Shared grief.
"...we're not so different," she said.
"No," he agreed. "We not."
She was quiet for a moment more. Then her tone softened.

"I'm sorry," she said. "For what I said before. I was scared. I was angry. And I took it out on you."

Luko gave a small nod. "I say sorry too. I treat you like... like book. I forget you have heart."

A pause.

He shifted, a hesitant smile tugging at the edge of his mouth. "Maybe... we can be... what is word... friends?"

Melodie smirked. "Let's not get ahead of ourselves."
But she extended her hand through the bars anyway. And Luko, awkward but sincere, took it in both of his.

Malec tossed in his bed, silk sheets twisted beneath him, damp with sweat. The fabric was too smooth, too cold, clinging in ways that made his teeth clench. He hated silk. Always had. It snagged the fine hairs on his arms and legs, whispered against his skin with every shallow breath. He couldn't think. Couldn't breathe.

Sleep slipped from him like a coward before a duel. His body was drained, but his mind surged, restless, fevered, impossible to silence.

The King's voice echoed: *A rare creature... quite the gift.* He tried to cast it out. But then came that look, Surion's eyes fixed on her with possessive hunger. *His* Canariae. No. Not his. A prisoner. A savage. A pawn. Still, the image clung to him: her braid loose over one shoulder, dark skin glowing like polished obsidian, lips parted in sleep. A goddess behind glass. Untamed. Unclaimed. And worst of all, he wanted her.

He rolled again. The sheet dragged across his calf like a net, suffocating. Every wrinkle, every seam, sparked static against his skin. Heat built beneath the surface, an itch he couldn't reach. His magic stirred, a whisper of warmth curling up his spine, humming in his blood. He shoved the covers down. It didn't help. The air felt too thin. His breathing went shallow as his heart kicked faster, rattling in his ribs.

He could still see her, curled atop the velvet cushions like a cat in sunlight, black bars casting delicate stripes across her skin. The memory looped with brutal clarity. He hated when his mind latched on this way, like a mechanism stuck on repeat. He'd told himself the cage was for her safety. For Surion's curiosity. For training. But the truth burned bitter on his tongue. He had wanted to watch her. Observe her. Touch her.

Malec's eyes snapped open. He stared at the ceiling, chest tight, skin slick with sweat. The rustle of sheets scraped his nerves raw. His fingers twitched, searching for an anchor. But there was only her shape, seared behind his eyes.

"Enough," he muttered. But it wasn't.

His body betrayed him, hard, aching. He sat up fast, shame rising hot in his throat.

"No," he hissed.

The arousal wouldn't fade. It never faded. It coiled like a noose in his gut, tight and fevered, making his pulse pound in his ears. His groin throbbed against the fabric of his pants, painfully stiff, alive with need that made his stomach churn. He squeezed his thighs together, hoping the pressure might kill it—but it only made it worse. The ache spiked so suddenly he gasped. This was not lust. This was something hungrier, something wrong. Feral. Unclean. He pressed the heel of his palm down hard against himself, trying to flatten the sensation, suffocate it—but it made him harder.

She was a slave. A Canariae. A lesser breed. And still he burned.

He shoved a hand through his hair, breath coming in ragged pulls, his jaw muscles twitched so tight it clicked. His fingers drifted downward again. No. No. No. But he was already pulling his waistband down. The first touch made his hips jerk. Sharp. Violent. A pulse of sensation that lit every nerve, setting his spine alight with raw electricity. His breath hitched, a sharp intake through clenched teeth as his cock twitched in his hand—hot, flushed, desperate, already slick with pre-release. Wetness beaded at the tip, smearing across his palm, obscene and eager, proof of how far gone he already was. His skin was too tight. His bones felt like they were going to crack under the tension.

"Fuck," he whispered, voice hoarse with self-loathing.

He gripped himself hard, not to coax—but to punish. As if shame might be wrung out with the heat. But it didn't stop. It thrived under his palm, throbbing harder, hungrier, too alive to ignore. His magic buzzed beneath his skin, chaotic, like static rippling through the sheets. He could feel every fiber, every hair, every bead of sweat. His brain was screaming, stop, but his body was ravenous. Starving.

Her face burned behind his eyes—those defiant dark eyes, that mouth that knew too much. Her braid undone. That sweet pout she didn't mean to make. Her back arching beneath him. He pumped faster. Harder. His hand slick with sweat, hips rolling up into the motion. His stomach clenched. Heat pooled low in his gut like molten iron. His thighs trembled.

He hated this. He hated her. But gods—her skin. Dark, glowing, soft. He knew it would feel like velvet under his hands, under his tongue. He could almost feel it now. The kiss came back—desperate, wild. Her fingers in his hair, pulling him down, begging for more with every breath. His mind twisted it. He didn't want to see her behind bars now.

He wanted her on her back. He wanted her writhing beneath him, eyes wide, throat bared. He wanted to devour her. He grunted, curling forward slightly, the pressure unbearable. The pleasure tore through him, filthy and wrong, the kind that made his muscles lock and shake. Every stroke sent another jolt up his spine.

In his mind she moaned his name. Cried out for him. Clawed at his shoulders as he drove into her. Her thighs wrapped around his hips, her body tight and slick and hot as sin. Screaming for him. And only him.

His breath caught on a harsh groan, need twisting into something brutal as his orgasm raged through him. His head fell back, mouth open, spine bowing as his body convulsed. Cum spilled hot and heavy over his hand, pulse after pulse devastating him, until his shoulders trembled and his legs went numb. The sound that came out of him was half-snarl, half-moan—raw, feral, broken.

And then—nothing. The silence dropped like a stone.

He slumped forward, forearms braced on his knees, the air thick and sour. His skin prickled, too aware of everything—the sticky mess on his hand, the sweat drying on his chest, the pounding in his ears. The scent of sex mixed with magic and shame. His cock still throbbed faintly, aching in the aftermath. His body was sated.

But he wasn't. The ache remained. Quieter now. Duller. But it was still there. Still hers. His jaw trembled. His breath came too fast. He looked at his hand—streaked with release—and nearly gagged. He hadn't purged her. He'd fed her.

He wiped his hand on the sheet with disgust, as if he could scrub the truth out of himself. But it was there, carved into his blood. The heat was quieter, but the hollow remained—worse than before. He stood abruptly, yanking his pants back up, fury rising like a flood in his chest. His stomach clenched. He could still smell himself. Still feel the hum of the tether, alive and hungry in his blood. She was still in him.

His fists clenched. Nails dug half-moons into his palms. He turned and stormed toward the bathing chamber, feet slapping the boards. Cold water. Anything to kill what she'd turned him into.

The room where she was kept was too quiet when Malec entered, the kind of silence that pricked at his instincts—weighted, intimate, and heavy with the kind of tension that belonged to secrets and confessions. He slowed, eyes adjusting to the low candlelight flickering against polished stone walls. He looked immaculate: every detail arranged with exacting precision, silver piping straight, dark tunic crisp, pale hair slicked back into a low ponytail. Even his boots gleamed, untouched by dust, a portrait of control set against the chaos brewing inside him.

The cage sat exactly where he'd left it, centered like a prized ornament. But what lay inside made something sour coil under his ribs. Melodie slept curled on the velvet cushions, a dark flame tucked into herself, her braid loose over her shoulder, her face smooth, breath steady. Peaceful. Comfortable. Outside the bars, Luko slumped in a chair, arms folded, asleep—like it was perfectly normal to doze beside a prisoner, at her side.

The sight made Malec's jaw clench, his gaze snapping between the sleeping scholar and the woman glowing soft in sleep, candlelight warming her skin. Something sharp stirred in his chest, unwanted and undeniable. Jealousy.

They'd been talking. The tea tray was half-empty. A second cushion lay near the bars, the chair pulled close. It was familiar, intimate—too much time spent with his Canariae. Heat climbed his spine as his magic stirred, faint but real. His body reacted before he could reason with it, jaw tight, fists clenched, the flames in the sconces flickering in answer. He didn't know what infuriated him more: that Luko had spent time with her, or that he hadn't.

The empty plates near the bars told Malec everything. They had eaten together, the candle burned nearly to the base, and Luko's posture—slouched toward the cage, eyes closed in true, unguarded sleep—confirmed it: they'd shared the night in easy conversation. It made a silent crack of tension roll through Malec's spine. His fists curled tighter, nails biting into his palms. He didn't know why it enraged him, but it did.

Seeing Luko so at ease, as if this space belonged to him, as if she did, sent heat rising up Malec's throat.

Melodie lay curled on the cushions, one arm draped over her waist, one leg bent in sleep. She looked too peaceful. Not like a prisoner, but like someone who'd chosen to rest. As if she belonged here. His fingers twitched. No. She needed to remember who held the keys. Who ruled this room. Who owned her silence.

He stepped forward and delivered a swift kick to the bars. The clang rang through the chamber like a drawn blade, and Luko jolted upright, groggy, scrambling to his feet, rubbing his eyes, slow to register the shift in air. Melodie, however, woke with precision—her eyes snapped open, sharp and focused, locking on Malec without hesitation. She sat straighter, tension rippling through her like a coiled predator. No fear. No confusion. She saw him. And she knew.

Malec didn't blink. His gaze slid over her, slow and deliberate, not leering but possessive, words incandescent behind his eyes though his lips stayed pressed in a hard line. When he finally spoke, it was in his native tongue, low, smooth, and cold as a winter blade.

Melodie raised a brow, unimpressed. "Luko?" she said without looking away.

"Translation, please?"

Luko hesitated, still foggy. "He asks if you sleep... comfortable."

She snorted, sitting up with a stretch that felt more challenge than motion, her braid slipping over her shoulder.

"Better than you, apparently."

Malec didn't respond. But she saw it, the sleepless shadows, the too-high shoulders, the tension drawn tight across his frame. She had gotten under his skin. Deep. And she grinned.

"What's wrong, Commander?" she said sweetly. "Didn't sleep well?"

Luko cast a wary glance between them, now fully awake and sensing the storm churning in the air. He hesitated again, unsure if translating that was wise, but the tension crackling between the two made his choice feel irrelevant. He was caught in the static of a gathering storm, one that had nothing to do with politics, cages, or power. But he translated anyway.

As soon as the words left Luko's mouth, Malec's tan eyes gleamed with a flicker of something sharp and dangerous. But he didn't lash out. Instead, he tilted his head with slow, measuring grace and replied in his native tongue, his voice low and even. Controlled.

Luko exhaled as if bracing himself. "He says you are far too comfortable for a prisoner."

Melodie smirked, a lazy defiance curling at the edges of her mouth. "Maybe you should work on that," she drawled without a hint of fear.

Luko didn't bother translating this time. He didn't have to. Malec had understood every word. Tone was universal. The twitch in Malec's jaw said more than enough. His frustration simmered just beneath the surface, controlled only by the thinnest thread of restraint. Without a word, he stepped forward and unhooked the chain clipped to her collar. With a sharp pull, he yanked it just enough to force her body slightly forward, not enough to hurt her, but enough to assert control. Enough to make her feel the shift.

He spoke again, voice rougher this time, the edge of warning unmistakable.

Luko paused before translating, clearly uneasy. "He says... he thinks you've grown a little too bold."

Melodie's smirk didn't fade. If anything, it deepened. She leaned in slightly, eyes flashing with amusement and something darker, something challenging.

"Oh?" she said, tone syrupy with sarcasm. "And what is he gonna do about it?"

Luko stared at her, eyes wide, then turned slowly to Malec.

"Do I have to translate that?" he asked, half-hoping the elf would wave him off.

But Malec's eyes narrowed, and the look he gave Luko was cold, commanding, and full of promise. Luko sighed, shoulders slumping as he turned back.

"She asked... what you plan to do about it."

The silence that followed was deafening. Malec's gaze darkened, his pupils dilating slightly, and a ripple of something primal passed through him. Not just anger. Possession. Desire. Restraint. It flickered through his eyes like a wild current barely held in check, and for a single breath, the air between them was radiant with pure energy, volatile and thick with the weight of everything unsaid.

Malec's voice cut through the tense silence, sharp and low, the words foreign but heavy with menace. The Awyan syllables curled from his tongue like smoke laced with venom:

"Zeth'an dor kai'tel atah."

Luko's eyes closed briefly, as if he could will himself away from this moment. But Melodie was waiting. Malec was judging. And the weight of the room left him no choice. He sighed, then translated, his voice flat and resigned.

"He say, 'I tame you myself.'"

Melodie's lips curved with slow delight, her eyes gleaming as she leaned forward, elbows to her knees like a wolf in no rush to pounce.

"You can try, big guy," she purred.

Luko winced and looked at Malec warily. But the Commander didn't need the translation this time. The tone alone made the meaning clear.

His nostrils flared as he inhaled through his nose, steadying himself, trying to keep his temper submerged. She was toying with him. Daring him to lose control. And he wouldn't, not yet.

Instead, he exhaled slowly, his eyes locked on hers as he released the chain with a loud metallic clatter. The tension in the room didn't break, it shifted, thickened, crackling like lightning about to strike. He muttered something in Awyan under his breath, too low to carry fully.

Luko reluctantly gave the translation. "He say, 'Don't test me, Canariae.'"

And then, without a backward glance, Malec turned and walked out, his cloak sweeping behind him like a storm cloud. The moment the doors shut, Melodie let out a rich, breathless laugh, all teeth and heat and victory.

Luko groaned, rubbing his temples. "You get yourself killed, canariae."

But Melodie just tilted her head and smirked at him. "Not today, translator. Not today."

The city of Caelistra was alive with motion, its streets humming with the rhythm of daily commerce and courtly life. Stalls draped in vivid silks spilled across the walkways, vendors shouting over one another in melodic bursts of Awyan as they peddled spices, jewelry, and foreign trinkets. Ornate banners fluttered from curved rooftops, casting dancing shadows over the intricate tilework below.

Soldiers in silver-and-blue livery marched in perfect formation through side alleys, while children darted between fruit carts and ornate carriages, their laughter swallowed by the bell-like chime of temple gongs in the distance.

And through it all, Malec rode.

High atop a towering black steed, his silver-blonde hair caught the sunlight like a blade, his expression vacant beneath the shadows of his hood. Behind him, on foot, Melodie trudged barefoot through the uneven stone streets, her wrists bound in rope, the tether pulled tight in Malec's gloved hand like a leash.

Her feet burned, scraped raw by gravel and jagged cobblestones, each step a fresh insult. Her calves ached from the constant pace, her back damp with sweat despite the cool morning air. Her dress, what remained of it, dragged through the dust, clinging to her legs with each labored stride. The Awyan sun filtered through high-hung lattice work and arched bridges overhead, but there was no shade to shield her, no dignity to protect her.

She was not merely being escorted. She was being paraded. Citizens paused in their dealings to stare. Some with curiosity. Others with disdain. A few even smiled, amused at the sight of a Canariae being dragged like livestock through their proud capital.

Luko rode slightly behind Malec, his expression tense, his hands gripping the reins too tightly. Every so often, he leaned forward to whisper a translation when Malec barked a command in his native tongue. He kept his voice low, almost apologetic.

"This is humiliating," Melodie muttered under her breath, her eyes scanning the sneering faces that lined the square.

"That's the point," Luko replied flatly, barely meeting her gaze.

Melodie glared at him through damp curls that clung to her temples. "You enjoying this?"

"Not particularly," he said, his voice even softer now. "But I suggest you play along. It will be easier."

"For who?" she bit back. He didn't answer.

A sudden jerk on the rope wrenched her forward. She stumbled, catching herself before she fell face-first into the dust. Malec still hadn't looked at her. He said something curt in Awyan.

Luko cleared his throat. "He says you are too slow."

"And he's too tall," Melodie hissed, just loud enough for Luko to hear.

But this time, he didn't translate. He didn't have to. Malec's hand tightened briefly on the rope, and though his gaze remained forward, the pulse in his jaw ticked like a war drum.

They moved like that through the city for hours. Past balconies carved from golden stone. Past bridges that arched over steaming canals. Through ivy-covered archways leading to crowded courtyards where dancers performed beneath lanterns. Melodie's knees trembled, but she refused to fall. Her pride wouldn't let her. Malec had expected her to break by now. To cry. To beg for mercy. But she kept her head high, despite the ache in her bones, despite the shame crawling under her skin like fire ants.

And that only infuriated him more.

They reached the open plaza near the Northern Gate when another rider approached. His stallion was white as pearl, his cloak green like moss. The elf on its back was unmistakable.

Even in a city carved from beauty, Erolyn stood out like something conjured, too perfect to be real. His skin, pale as polished marble, seemed to catch light and hold it, unblemished and cold. Curls the shade of cocoa beans spilled to his shoulders, soft and well-kept, a stark contrast to the usual silver of the Talandros line. He was Malec's cousin—his mother's blood, not his father's—which explained the dark hair and the unbothered arrogance stamped into every step. His eyes, vivid, brilliant green, missed nothing and forgave less. Where Malec was cut from war, all lean muscle and coiled violence, Erolyn was shorter, broader, built for velvet lounges and whispered betrayals. His jaw was elegantly carved, lips full and always curled in some unspoken insult. He didn't need armor. He had charm. He had wit. And that, more than any blade, made him dangerous.

He scanned the crowd with lazy disinterest, until his gaze landed on Melodie. And he stilled. He reined his horse sharply and slowed beside Malec, one brow arching.

"What in the fates' name is that?" he drawled, voice smooth as wine, gesturing at

Melodie with one gloved hand. Luko winced and looked away.

Malec's answer was clipped. "She is a troublesome Canariae I am training myself, Erolyn."

Erolyn's smirk deepened. "Training? I didn't realize you had taken to keeping pets."

Malec said nothing. But the rope in his hand gave a sudden, subtle twitch. And behind him, Melodie's head lifted, dark eyes ablaze like obsidian in the sun. Erolyn's eyes lingered on Melodie for a moment too long, his curiosity laced with something sharper.

"She's... unusual," he murmured, voice smooth like a blade sliding from its sheath. "I've never seen one with that coloring before."

Melodie's lip curled. Without hesitation, she hissed at him like an angry cat. The sound was low, primal, and utterly defiant. Luko gave her a pointed look, clearly unimpressed, but Erolyn only laughed.

"Does she bite?" he asked, almost lazily, as if inspecting a new breed of hound.

Malec's tan eyes narrowed, the fire behind them flickering dangerously.

"Yes," he said flatly.

Erolyn chuckled at that, tilting his head slightly as he studied her.

"And yet you keep her? Curious." His gaze flicked back to Malec, reading more than was spoken. The implication hung between them like smoke.

Malec didn't answer.

Erolyn let the silence stretch for a moment, then straightened in his saddle, the smirk never leaving his face.

"Be careful, cousin," he said lightly, though his tone carried weight. "Sometimes a pet you think is tamed will turn on you when you least expect it."

With a single tug on his reins, he turned and began riding toward the palace, his parting words drifting back over his shoulder.

"I'll see you at the military banquet."

Melodie exhaled slowly, shaking her wrists out as the tension began to leave her body. The rope burned, her skin raw from the constant tugging, but her pride was intact. She didn't know what this Awyan was saying but she knew she didn't like the way he looked at her. She muttered under her breath.

"I don't like him."

Luko sighed beside her, giving a resigned shrug. "You don't like anyone."

She shot him a glare. "And yet, I'm still stuck with you."

Luko didn't argue. He couldn't. Malec gave the chain a sharp pull, and Melodie stumbled forward. Training wasn't over. Not yet.

Chapter 8

How to Break a Wild Thing

The days blurred together, swallowed by repetition and quiet humiliation. From sunrise to dusk, Melodie was under constant watch. Malec didn't strike or shout, but his control was unrelenting. Her "training," as he called it, was indoctrination dressed as civility. She soon noticed his fixation on order, so rigid it bordered on obsession. Every task had a script: the same words, the same motions. Pouring wine took exactly three steps. Linens had to be folded with aligned seams and perfect corners, or he'd silently snatch them back and refold them in front of her. Even sweeping the floors drew his scrutiny, his gaze tracking her every movement like a hawk watching prey.

What unnerved her most was realizing these rituals weren't about her, they were for him. For whatever frayed circuitry in his mind needed precision to stay calm. When she followed his instructions exactly, he was composed. Distant, but steady. But if she deviated, even slightly, she saw it: the tic of his jaw, the tension in his hands, the dilation of his pupils. As if disorder physically hurt him.

If she pushed too far, something in him snapped, not in violence, but in an eerie stillness—a tension that vibrated beneath her skin like the warning before a storm. It felt like living inside the mind of a lunatic, where control was the only thing holding the walls up. She wondered if he knew she could see it, the desperation beneath his civility, the brittle edge behind every command. She called them tantrums in her head, though she knew better. Meltdowns. The word felt strange, but right. When order reigned, he was steady as iron. When it didn't, he unraveled, and she could almost pity him. Almost.

It was humiliating, a slow erosion of her pride. But Melodie bore it with poise—not submission, but calculation, honed like a blade. Every bowed head, every bitten tongue was another weapon tucked away.

As she moved through marble halls and candlelit chambers, she catalogued everything. The invisible hierarchy. The nobles clinging to power and those born steeped in it. The servants' patterns, every hidden stair, locked door, careless whisper, memorized. The whole citadel was a machine, gilded and ancient, and she was learning to read its gears. But none of it mattered as much as him.

Malec. He was her study above all others.

She measured the small betrayals of his composure, the subtle ways his mask cracked. The infinitesimal tightening of his jaw when her eyes met his without flinching. The slight flare of his nostrils when she did something he hadn't predicted. The hard flick of his gaze when an underling dared speak to her with too much familiarity.

His eyes tracked her constantly; a pale, searing tether she could feel even when her back was turned. It was not merely watchfulness. It was a hunger to know every angle of her, to dismantle her to her smallest pieces and understand what made her burn. And she watched him back.

It became a private war, silent and ferocious. A contest neither would name. His restraint against her defiance. His precision against her instinct. His need for order against her talent for chaos. Day after day, they circled each other in plain sight, predator and prey shifting roles by the hour. The only certainty was that neither could look away. He believed he was unraveling her.

But in truth, Melodie was gathering her strength, coiling it tighter and tighter like a spring beneath her ribcage. And when it finally snapped free, she intended to tear every carefully placed stone from his fortress. She only had to wait. Wait for the perfect fracture in his control. It arrived sooner than she'd hoped.

The night of the military banquet.

The ceremonial banquet hall pulsed with life, music swelling beneath laughter, flutes weaving through the low thrum of drums. Candlelight flickered from black iron sconces, mirrored in lacquered floors polished to a near-blinding sheen. Along the walls, spiced meats turned on spitfires, their fragrant smoke mingling with the sweetness of stewed fruit and the heady perfume trailing from every Awyan guest.

A long whitewood table stretched down the center, draped in gold-threaded cloth, nearly too bright to look at. Jewel-toned liquors gleamed like gemstones among platters of candied roots, glistening meat, and bowls of shimmering fruit nestled between elaborate silk floral displays.

Overhead, a glass chandelier hovered like a glowing hive, filled with blue and white fireflies blinking in slow, dreamy patterns. Their light spilled across the red and gold banners draped from the vaulted ceiling and shimmered over brocaded cloaks and feathered collars.

The Awyan highborn were draped in vivid colors, teal, crimson, metallic yellow, jewel-toned purple, like walking brushstrokes from a madman's palette. Slender and ageless, they glowed with vanity. Only the soldiers broke the image, broader, heavier, their presence a dark contrast to the indulgence around them.

It was a fever dream of wealth and spectacle, a distorted fashion show performed for an audience of mirrors.

Erolyn, ever the peacock, lounged near the front, lips wet with wine, his smile lazy. Amid the glittering crowd of aristocrats and war-hardened generals stood Melodie, dressed not in dignity, but display. A servant's uniform clung to her body, sheer and brightly dyed, fluttering with every step. It left little to the imagination, and even less to her pride.

She moved like smoke, silent and graceful, balancing trays of sugared fruit and decanters of red wine. Eyes followed her, not with lust, but with detached fascination. The nobles didn't see a woman, they saw a trophy. Rare. Exotic. A symbol of Malec's power.

At the head table, Malec sat tall and composed, but his eyes never left her. Every movement she made, every brush of her fingers, every falter in her step, he watched. Daring her to misstep. Melodie played her part. She curtsied. She poured. She smiled. But beneath the powder and forced poise, her mind stayed sharp. She was watching too.

Midway through the banquet, as the music shifted into a sultry rhythm, Erolyn swaggered toward the high table with a smirk. He moved like someone untouched by consequence. At his side walked an elfess draped in silver robes embroidered with the sigil of House Waoria, twin crescent blades over flame. She was statuesque, her ice-blue eyes still and cutting, cheekbones sharp under the chandelier's light. She moved like command itself.

"Commander Malec," she purred, her voice smooth as silk stretched taut.

Malec inclined his head with polite indifference, his expression carved from stone. Lady Waoria's faint smile curved as she studied him openly, a glint of amusement in her pale eyes.

"You ought to practice softening that stare. You look as though you're plotting how to disembowel half the room. Which, I suppose, is why no one dares speak against you. And why your soldiers would follow you straight into hell itself."

He didn't bother to answer. He only lifted one hand to rub his temple, the pad of his thumb pressing just above the corner of his eye. The swirl of bright fabrics and jarring perfumes pressed against his senses like a tide, each burst of laughter scraping raw along the inside of his skull. He focused on the steady pressure of his fingers against his skin, willing the rising cacophony to dull long enough for him to string a coherent thought together.

The noblewoman's gaze drifted past him toward the servant ranks, where Melodie was gracefully tilting a wine bottle into a nobleman's goblet, her back straight, her movements careful but fluid. The soft jingle of her collar echoed faintly as she turned.

"Erolyn has told me of your... unique Canariae," Lady Waoria said, her tone deceptively casual, though her interest was unmistakable.

Malec didn't respond, his silence pointed.

"I keep several Canariae myself," she went on, lifting her glass daintily. "Mostly for entertainment or household service. She would make a fine addition to my collection, once properly trained, of course."

His jaw tensed, only slightly.
"We shall see how she tames," he said, voice low and clipped.
Erolyn chuckled behind his cup.

"You're becoming rather possessive, Mal," he mused, glancing sideways with thinly veiled amusement.

Malec ignored him. Lady Waoria's eyes drifted to Melodie with a hunter's detachment, her curiosity deepening.

"Does she have any distinctive markings? Scars? Brands?"

Malec's brows knit faintly.

"There are unusual symbols beneath her left breast. Possibly tribal or religious in

origin."

A faint smile ghosted over Lady Waoria's lips. "May I see them?"

For a moment, Malec hesitated. His tan eyes flicked to Melodie's face, searching, perhaps, for resistance, before he turned away and motioned her forward with a curt gesture. Her heart thudded behind her ribs. Head bowed, lashes lowered, she stepped forward as if walking into a beast's mouth. When she reached his side, she dared a glance up. The nobles watched her with bright, expectant smiles, not leering, just curious. Somehow, that was worse. Lust was human. This was not.

She knew what came next. Knew the moment his fingers touched her neckline, tugging it past her collarbone. She flinched, breath catching, body recoiling. It felt like being peeled. Her eyes locked on his face, searching, but he didn't meet them. Didn't see her. His gaze was fixed on the markings at her ribs. Cold. Detached. As if inspecting a ledger.

His hand pressed her shoulder, silent command. Then his fingers tapped twice against her skin, deliberate and firm, a private signal meant just for her: *behave.* His voice followed, low and unyielding in that language she now loathed. Hold still. Not cruel. Indifferent. Something twisted in her throat, shame, rage, helplessness, but she didn't look away. She would not let them see her break.

The nobles leaned in, murmurs scraping along her nerves. One reached toward the ink. Malec lifted a single hand in warning. The noble paused, laughed faintly, and withdrew.

She thought she might vomit.

The seconds stretched into a small eternity. Her bare skin prickled under their scrutiny, cold air kissing the top of her breast where the fabric gaped, every heartbeat louder than the last. Finally, Malec released her. The fabric fell back over her chest, the motion somehow worse in its casual finality. He flicked his fingers in dismissal, gaze already moving to Lady Waoria as though Melodie had ceased to exist the moment she was covered.

She turned away, her breath stuttering out in a ragged exhale. But she didn't move immediately. Her legs felt heavy, her hands numb. In her mind, a thousand thoughts collided, none of them coherent. The shame was molten. The rage was ice. And beneath both, a hollow disbelief.

This was how they saw her.

She wasn't a person to them. Not even an enemy. Just an object, nothing more than a specimen to be examined and passed around. Her hands trembled as she lifted the loose neckline back to her collarbone and fumbled with the ties. She refused to look at anyone. She refused to give them the last piece of her pride. When she finally turned, her vision blurred at the edges, she walked with slow, measured steps across the polished floor. But inside, something had broken free and begun to scream.

She reached the nearest serving table, her fingers closing around a silver tray. The metal felt cool against her palm, something solid to hold while her chest heaved. She gripped it tighter, knuckles whitening, and pulled her shoulders back. No one stopped her. No one even spoke.

Without sparing a glance behind her, she gathered what shards of dignity she could, lifted the tray, and stalked away from the cluster of nobles as if she had chosen this exit herself.

Behind her, Malec's eyes followed. For a fleeting instant, confusion flickered in their depths. He watched the rigid line of her back, her fists clenched tight at her sides, and felt something that did not have a name. He didn't understand why she reacted this way. Why she looked at him as though he had struck her. It was only procedure. A simple inspection.

Yet as she disappeared into the crowd, something in his chest gave a slow, unfamiliar twist.

The banquet bled deep into the night, music raging, goblets clanging, Awyan laughter echoing like thunder through her skull. It was all a blur of silk and steel, of smug toasts and petty threats draped in civility. But she wasn't listening anymore. She couldn't. Because she had never in her life been treated like that.

Her body still burned with the memory of his hand on her dress, the cold detachment in his face as he exposed her to a room full of strangers. The moment their eyes landed on her bare skin, on her breasts, she felt something inside her snap. She had respected him, in her own twisted way. Respected his discipline, his control, the brutal certainty with which he commanded everything around him. But now, that thin thread of respect had shriveled into something black and corrosive. Hatred. She hated him.

She hated the way he could strip the humanity out of her with a flick of his fingers, as if she were no more than a tool to be examined, traded, discarded. The stares that had crawled over her skin still clung to her like filth she couldn't wash away. Her dignity was gone, and he had been the one to take it.

And in that moment, she didn't just want him dead. No. Death was too easy. She wanted him to suffer. She wanted to look into his perfect, cold face and see fear. She wanted to see him break, to hear him beg. She wanted to carve that same humiliation into his bones, to make him understand how it felt to be small and powerless and ruined. Her feet moved of their own accord, silent on the polished floor as she slipped into the corridor beyond the feast. Out here, the air was cooler, the noise a distant roar behind the doors. The flickering torchlight painted long bars of black over the walls, and shadows curled in every corner like waiting hands.

And that was when she saw him.

He moved like he owned the world. Alone, strolling through the passage as though the war room and wine hall both belonged to him. His dark curls framed his face in waves, the faint lamplight catching on the golden stitching of his robe. His green eyes, too bright to be natural, drifted in lazy thought.

He didn't see her at first. Not until she stepped directly into his path. He halted. Lifted a brow.

"Canariae?" he drawled, amused. Melodie didn't let him speak another word.

She lunged. Fingers curling in the fine collar of his tunic, she yanked him down and crushed her mouth to his. Her body hit his with all the force she had left, her heart slamming against her ribs so hard it hurt. This was it. The moment that would burn through all the humiliation he'd heaped on her.

Let him shove her away. Let him curse. Let every smug noble see it. Let Malec see it. Let him feel, if only for a second, the same raw exposure she'd suffered. But instead, he didn't react.

His body went still, surprised only for a breath. Then she felt it, his low, startled laugh against her mouth, warm and unbothered. Not mocking. Not angry. Just... amused.

Before she could shove him off, his hands closed around her waist with unsettling steadiness. He pivoted smoothly, faster than she expected, and her back struck cold stone as he pressed her there. His body blocked her from view, the angle of his shoulders hiding her from the rest of the hall. She stiffened.

No. No, she wanted them to see. She wanted Malec to see. She twisted, trying to slide sideways, but his hands were already bracing her hips, holding her perfectly in place. Her pulse spiked. He was doing this on purpose. Shielding her. Making her little rebellion invisible. And then he kissed her back.

It was nothing like what she'd given him. His mouth moved over hers in a slow, controlled sweep, claiming her with the same infuriating confidence she'd seen in his smile. Deep, unhurried, as though he'd already decided exactly how this would end. Heat climbed her neck. She shoved at his chest with both palms, but he didn't budge. His grip only tightened. She felt the solid wall behind her spine, the iron of his body pressed to the front, and something in her went cold with fury.

He was enjoying this. Too much.

When she tore her mouth away to suck in a ragged breath, he didn't let her move far. He angled his face toward hers, brushing her jaw with the back of his knuckles in a touch so gentle it made her stomach twist. His lips hovered over her cheek, then her ear, voice dropping low.

"Careful," he murmured, the word shaped in a language she didn't recognize. His breath was warm against her skin.

She swallowed hard, her heart drumming an unsteady rhythm.

This wasn't the humiliation she'd planned. This was something worse. Something that felt too close, too real. The words slid through the air like silk, unaccented, sharp, clear. Her mind tripped over the realization even as her heartbeat spiked in her ears. He spoke her language. Not broken, butchered phrases like Luko's. Not fragmented understanding. He had spoken it flawlessly.

He finally turned, slow and deliberate, and when he saw the expression on her face, he smiled.

"What?" he said, that same voice now curling with amusement, still in English.

"Surprised?"

Surprised didn't even begin to cover it. Melodie's heart slammed against her ribs as she forced herself not to retreat. The flat line of her mouth parted slightly, the question tumbling out before she could stop it.

"Where... where did you learn that?"
He smirked, cutting her off.

"Darling, your kind forget we were studying you long before your world knew ours existed."

Melodie's jaw tightened. "You- "

"Ah, ah." He raised a single finger, stepping forward just enough to let the tension press between them. "No need to get so violent, Canariae. I thought you'd be glad someone could finally *understand* you."

"You're messing with me," she spat, the air buzzing with heat.

"Of course I am," he replied smoothly, with no shame. "But I'm also telling the truth."

He began circling her then, never touching, but close enough that she felt the warmth of his body, the strange thrill of being seen, and it made her skin crawl.

"I was curious," he said lightly, his gaze flicking over her like a blade, "if the infamous Canariae had anything to offer. And now that I've seen you up close... I get it. I see why Malec's cracking."

That hit her like a slap. Her breath hitched, barely perceptible, but it was enough. The green eyed handsome Awyan noticed. He leaned in, just slightly.

"Ah. So it's that kind of mess."

She glared. "Who the hell are you?"

He paused, placing a hand over his chest with mock grace.

"Erolyn," he said grandly. "Of the Delyrien Estate. Commander of the Western Border. Professional nightmare, depending who you ask, and a relative of your master."

"And you," he added, his tone softening with interest, "I already knew. But I'd rather hear it from your lips."

Melodie hesitated, her eyes narrowed, but she said it anyway. "Melodie."

He smiled wider. "Names have power, Melodie. I'll remember yours."

Her jaw, a warning carved in bone, clamped down hard as she spat her retort with venom. "Good. Remember it when I'm standing over your body."

He laughed at that, genuine, rich, amused. It wasn't the reaction she wanted. Not fear. Not insult. Just entertainment. She hated that he found her amusing. She hated more that he now had an edge over her, language, presence, wit, and charm sharpened like a weapon. Then his voice dropped again, dark silk.

"You thought all of us were brutes who didn't care to learn about your kind, didn't you?" He tilted his head. "That none of us paid attention?"

She didn't answer. She didn't need to.
He smiled like a predator sensing blood. "Oh, this is going to be fun."

Melodie took a sharp step back, her pulse hammering. "Stay the hell away from me."

"Why?" he asked, still smiling. "Afraid of what else I know?"
Her silence was answer enough. He read her like an open scroll.

With a theatrical sigh, Erolyn flicked his curls over his shoulder. "Well then. I suppose I'll leave you be... for now."

She exhaled slowly, her shoulders tense.

But then, just as she thought it was over, he turned, and with that same insufferable smile, added, "Do try to behave at the banquet. Malec already looks like he's going to snap. It'd be a shame if I had to be the one to collect the pieces."

He winked. Then turned his back and walked into the corridor like a conquering prince. Melodie stood frozen, the adrenaline in her veins refusing to settle. Her hands trembled, not from fear, but rage. Pure, simmering rage. And deep inside her chest, somewhere below the fury, there was something else, a sharp, creeping dread. She had tried to manipulate the game tonight.

But somehow, she had just drawn the attention of someone far more dangerous than she had planned for. The most twisted part?

She wasn't sure she could unhook him now that he had noticed.

Malec watched her return to the banquet hall, every measured step a study in contained agitation. He had seen her angry before, had catalogued the way her jaw would tighten, her shoulders would lock, her eyes would dart for exits. But this was different. She wasn't looking at him at all.

Her gaze fixed on some invisible point past his shoulder, her lips pressed in a thin line. Not wary. Not defiant. Just... distant.

His eyes sharpened, fixed on her like a hawk tracking the tiniest movement. He replayed the last moments in his mind, examining every detail with the cold precision that made lesser men fear him. Nothing stood out. He had presented her markings, as protocol demanded. He had dismissed her without spectacle. She hadn't been harmed. She hadn't been humiliated, at least, not in any way he could measure.

And yet, there it was.

The unmistakable shift in her posture. The stiffness in her spine, the clipped way she moved as she picked up a tray, like her pride was a raw nerve he had just stepped on. His teeth ground together, a flicker of tension along his jawline. His pattern-sense rarely failed him, and every instinct told him something had shifted under his nose. Someone had spoken to her. Or worse, someone had touched her.

He scanned the gathering, his stare moving slowly from face to face, not bothering to disguise how he studied them. He didn't blink. Didn't fidget. Just sat there, perfectly still, leering, waiting, as if the truth would eventually crack under the pressure of his attention alone. From the corner of her eye, Melodie saw it, felt it, the way he was tracking her even when she wasn't looking back. The unbroken line of his gaze, cold and unsettling, like he could sit there all night without moving a muscle. Nothing.

She passed him without so much as a flicker of acknowledgment, her chin lifted high, her expression remote. He could feel it, the tight, unpleasant twist of confusion in his gut. The irritation of not knowing. Not understanding. His fingers drummed once against the arm of his chair. Then he turned his head, voice low and precise.

"Luko," he called, not bothering to mask the edge in his tone.

The golden-eyed elf appeared moments later, bleary and stiff, clearly hoping the night had ended. He didn't hide his reluctance as he stepped forward.

"What is it?" he asked, already anticipating Malec's irritation.

Malec's response was short and firm, words falling rapid and tight in Awyan. Luko's shoulders slumped slightly before turning to Melodie.

"He want to know what wrong with you," he translated, observing her carefully.

"You act... strangely."

Melodie froze for a fraction of a second. Then, as if slipping into a role, her eyes lowered, lashes fanning against her cheeks. She shifted her shoulders, small, subtle, just enough to suggest discomfort.

"Why do you think something's wrong?" she murmured.

Luko relayed her words, and Malec's expression darkened immediately. A clipped reply followed.

"Because I know you," Luko translated.

Malec didn't like this. She was clever, too clever. He had seen that look before in others, when they were hiding something. A secret. A lie. His gut twisted at the thought of her parted lips, slick with want on another. Her body flinching from someone else's touch. Did she cry out? Did she stay silent?

No. He would have known. Wouldn't he? Melodie's hands trembled slightly on the tray, but she masked it with a breath and spoke again, her voice low, soft. Wounded.

"I'm upset. After what happened earlier."

Luko hesitated but repeated her words. Malec said nothing at first. His jaw tightened. The weight of the night, the eyes of his people, the expectations, none of it had cracked him. But now... now there was a fissure behind his calm exterior.

"When you exposed me in front of those people," she added, her voice like crushed glass. "Like I was nothing but a thing."

The translation hit harder this time. Malec's breath slipped out through his nose, slow, deliberate. He turned his gaze away for a heartbeat. That moment, it hadn't been supposed to humiliate her. He had wanted to display her markings, to confirm their uniqueness, to solidify her value, not strip her of dignity. But she was Canariae. She had no dignity to lose. ...Had she?

A tight command followed.

"You are dismissed for the night," Luko said gently.

Two guards moved toward Melodie at once, their boots echoing against the marble. One positioned himself at her side, the other behind her. Silent. Watchful.

"They will escort you to your quarters," Luko added.

Melodie nodded once, face smooth and intelligible. But Malec watched her longer than he should have, eyes glaring, the burn of suspicion and something deeper twisting in his chest. He had told himself she was just another piece to shape. A rebellious creature to be broken. But she didn't break. She shifted, adapted, retaliated. And that worried him more than he could admit.

It was her unpredictability that unsettled him most—the way she shattered the quiet patterns he clung to, unraveling the order that kept his mind steady. She was chaos disguised as flesh, a variable he hadn't accounted for, slipping through every net he tried to cast around her. No matter how meticulously he studied her, she refused to be reduced to something tidy or known. He wasn't sure if he resented that... or if, in spite of himself, he craved it.

As she disappeared down the corridor between his guards, Malec's jaw locked, his hands curled into fists. Not knowing where she went scraped at his nerves. But worse—far worse—was that he didn't like not knowing who she had been with.

The moment the door clanked shut behind her and the guards' footsteps faded down the hall, Melodie released a long, deliberate breath through her nose. She didn't cry. She didn't scream. She sat, rigid and upright, on the thin cot in the far corner, staring at the dim stone wall as if it might answer for the humiliation she'd just endured. Her fingers trembled, not from fear, but fury. She had been a scientist. A researcher. A soldier. A woman with knowledge, purpose, ambition. She had worn a lab coat, not silk rags meant to titillate strangers.

And yet tonight, tonight she had been displayed like a specimen at auction, paraded in front of laughing nobles, stripped of her dignity by an elf who claimed to be her captor, protector, and keeper all at once. Malec thought she was simply angry at being exposed. Whatever. Let him think that. Let him believe he still understood her. That illusion gave her cover.

But what boiled inside her was far deeper than anger, it was rejection. A world that saw her only as a rare thing to be collected, not a person. Not a mind. Not even a threat. Her world had been data and facts, not collars and chains. She was meant for more than this. Her mind churned fast now, cold and clinical beneath the rage. She needed leverage. A way out. And for that, she needed an ally. Unfortunately, there was only one option.

Erolyn.

Arrogant, smug, and clearly toying with her for his own amusement. But he was not loyal to Malec. He didn't toe the line like the others. That made him dangerous. But it also made him *useful*. If she was going to survive this luxurious prison, and tear it down from the inside, she would need someone just as unpredictable as she was.

Someone reckless enough to want to see what happened when a caged bird started pecking through the bars.

The next day, Melodie moved like smoke, quiet and deliberate, her soft Awyan slippers The soft soles muffled every step over the polished black stone. Crafted from supple midnight-blue leather and embroidered with silver thread in looping patterns she couldn't decipher, they were beautiful in a way that felt mocking, like every other elegant restraint she'd been handed since her capture.

Every step echoed too loudly in her ears, even though she placed her weight carefully, toe to heel, avoiding the patches of glossy tile that might betray her with a single sharp scuff. The air smelled faintly of old incense, the tang of spiced oil lingering in the seams of the stone, mingling with something colder, something metallic. Her heart pounded hard against her ribs, a ceaseless thud that almost drowned out the distant murmur of Awyan voices drifting from the grand halls.

She could not afford to be seen. Not by Malec or even by the guards who watched every corridor. Not when the memory of the banquet still clung to her skin like a bruise she couldn't wash off. She moved faster, ducking past open archways draped in white gauze curtains that rippled in the draft, each one a veil she slipped behind before crossing the next threshold. She had to find Erolyn. He was the only unpredictable thread in this place, the only one whose gaze didn't strip her down to something owned.

It took more than an hour of weaving through labyrinthine passages and slipping into alcoves when footsteps approached. Her nerves frayed each time she rounded a corner and found only empty space, her breath hitching in her throat. But at last, she stepped into a gallery that opened onto the training terraces.

Sunlight pooled in long, pale ribbons across the burnished floor and up the tall pillars, striking the enormous window set with panels of deep green glass. There, Erolyn stood with his back half-turned, one hand braced on a column as he spoke to another officer. Melodie pressed herself into the curve of the wall, waiting. The shadows were cool against her skin. When the other elf finally departed, she drew a slow breath, then stepped out into the light.

Her voice, when it came, was soft but edged with urgency. "Erolyn."

He turned immediately, and the moment their eyes met, a smirk tugged at his lips, like he'd been expecting her.

"Well, well," he drawled, his tone already steeped in mischief.
"I was wondering how long it would take."

Melodie didn't waste time. Her voice came fast, breathless. "Take me with you."

Erolyn's brows lifted. Surprise flickered through his expression, but it was gone just as quickly, replaced by something darker. Curious. Intrigued.

"Oh?" he murmured, taking a slow step toward her. "And what do I get in return?"

Melodie stared him down, jaw tight. "The satisfaction of seeing Malec lose his mind."

That caught him. For the briefest moment, something stirred in Erolyn's eyes, something she hadn't seen before. Not just amusement. No hint of cruelty. Something startlingly unguarded. He blinked, then let out a deep, rolling laugh that rang down the corridor. He pressed a hand to the wall for balance, his shoulders shaking with the force of it. It was the kind of laughter that drew every eye, the kind that left a sheen of tears glinting in the corners of his bright gaze.

"Oh spirits of the North," he gasped between ragged breaths, wiping at the tears that gathered in his lashes. "You are truly an exquisite menace."

Melodie folded her arms, masking the tremor in her fingers with a tilt of her chin.

"Is that a yes or not?"

Erolyn's smile curved slow and foxlike as he stepped closer, close enough that she caught the warm spice of his cologne.

"Let's just say I've never had the good sense to refuse trouble when it looks me in the eye."

Her stomach dropped. "So it's a no?"

"But," he added, voice low, "if someone happened to smuggle themselves into one of the supply caravans headed toward the border... well. Who's to say I'd notice?"

Melodie's breath caught. That was it. Her out.

She nodded once, her voice barely above a whisper. "Then I'll see you at the border."

Erolyn studied her a moment longer. There was something strange in his gaze now, like he was seeing her not as a game piece, but as a storm. A woman on the edge of breaking, and breaking everything in her path.

"I do hope you make it, canariae," he murmured. "It'd be such a shame if Malec caught you before then."

Melodie's throat tightened. "Guess we'll see, won't we?"

She turned before he could say more, before she could unravel any further. Her feet carried her away with more purpose than she'd felt in days. She wasn't just escaping. She was reclaiming herself.

Firelight stretched long fingers across the dark wood walls of Malec's private guest chamber. The air smelled faintly of scorched resin and oiled leather, the scent clinging to the polished beams overhead. A wide desk of lacquered blackwood dominated one end of the room, papers and small glass vials arranged in precise, disciplined rows.

Luko stood behind it, bent over a ledger, the loose royal blue folds of his physician's robe brushing the floor, making him look every bit the scholar, formal, clean, clinical.

Malec, by contrast, was a blade sheathed in dark softness. He wore a fitted black turtleneck that hugged the hard lines of his torso, the sleeves pushed just below the elbow to bare strong forearms marked with old scars. A brown leather belt cinched tight at his waist, braced against snug trousers tucked into battered mercenary boots studded with steel buckles. He said nothing as Luko spoke.

Instead, Malec stood beside a side table where his hunting knives lay in perfect order. His long fingers worked in restless repetition, picking up a dagger, testing the edge, wiping it clean with a cloth that was already spotless. Over and over. The steel whispered each time he drew it across the leather strop, a sound sharp enough to pierce the hush.

"You need to change your approach," Luko said evenly, not bothering to soften the observation.

Malec didn't look up. The blade moved in his hand with the same measured precision, but his knuckles had whitened around the hilt.

"She fights you because you give her no other choice," Luko continued. "You treat her like something to be broken. But she's not like the Canariae you're used to."

"She's stubborn," Malec muttered. The cloth made another pass over the dagger's gleaming surface, faster now.

"She's freeborn," Luko corrected. "She wasn't raised to kneel. She was a scientist. A soldier. A protector of her people. You dress her up and parade her like an ornament, and you wonder why she burns with defiance?"

Malec's jaw tightened, but still he didn't argue. He set the dagger down, only to pick up another and inspect it as if searching for flaws that didn't exist. Luko stepped closer, voice low.

"Imagine if she stripped you bare and paraded you before a hall of Canariae eager to bid on you. Would you sit there quietly? Or would you kill every one of them?"

Malec gave a short, humorless laugh. "I'd gut them."

"Exactly," Luko snapped. "And she can't. Not yet. So she watches. Waits. But don't mistake that for submission."

The blade in Malec's hands paused. His breathing had grown shallower, the careful cleaning now a little too forceful, as if the motion alone could siphon away the irritation she always managed to spark in him.

"She's smarter than you think," Luko said softly. "I've spoken to her more than you've allowed yourself to. Her world, her mind, it's fascinating. She isn't a docile, domesticated creature. She could slit your throat in your sleep and you wouldn't even hear her coming."

At that, Malec's gaze lifted at last, dark and unwavering. "She wouldn't dare."

But his hand didn't stop moving over the blade. If anything, it moved faster. Malec didn't look up. He kept polishing the same blade over and over, the motion sharp, repetitive, faster each time Luko spoke. The edge was already clean. It gleamed like a mirror. But he couldn't stop. Couldn't stand the thought of stillness while his thoughts spun out of control. The cloth slowed just a fraction. Malec's jaw flexed, tendons standing out along his neck.

"She's not just a Canariae," Luko added, his voice softer now. "She's Melodie. And she was never yours to control."

The cloth stilled completely. His fingers tightened around the hilt until the leather creaked.

"Where is she?" Malec asked, his voice low, scraped raw.

Luko lifted a shoulder, careful, measured. "She should be in her chambers."

Something cold slid through Malec's gut, an instinct older than reason. He set the blade down with meticulous precision, aligning it perfectly with the others on the table. Then he turned and walked out, each step gathering purpose like a storm front rolling over the sea. The corridors blurred around him, white stone, black beams, the flicker of torchlight catching on polished floors. Guards stepped aside without a word as he passed, their faces blanching at the look in his eyes. He reached her chamber in record time. Two sentries stood at attention, pale and uneasy.

"Where is the dark Canariae?" he demanded, voice soft as snowfall.

Neither spoke. That silence was answer enough. The ringing in his ears spiked. He pushed past them, and found the room empty. The air felt too still. He exhaled slowly, fighting the sudden rush of heat in his blood. She was gone.

When he turned, something in his expression made both guards shrink back. He didn't care. He started down the corridor, boots striking the floor in measured, echoing beats. His control had always been absolute. Until her. His tan eyes darkened, thoughts racing ahead of his stride. She couldn't have gotten far. Not alone. Not without someone guiding her. Which meant...

She had help. His jaw tightened until it ached.

Who? Who in all of Ulvareth would be foolish enough to cross him? To lay hands on what belonged to him? He halted mid-stride, the corridor stretching silent before him. A cold realization twisted in his gut like a blade. There was only one name that made sense.

Erolyn.

Malec stormed into the palace courtyard like a thunderclap, his long strides crackling with tension, his mouth was a blade pressed shut so tightly it threatened to snap. Across the wide marble expanse, Erolyn stood beside his polished black horse, adjusting his riding gloves with the infuriating calm of someone who knew he was untouchable. Around him, his unit was nearly ready, horses packed, weapons secured, the scent of oiled leather and steel heavy in the air.

Erolyn looked up the moment he sensed the shift in energy. His forest-green eyes gleamed as he spotted Malec approaching like a storm.

"Cousin," he drawled with an easy smile, buckling the last strap of his gauntlet.

"To what do I owe the pleasure?"

Malec didn't stop walking. He didn't return the smile. His voice came low and sharp, like a blade sliding from its sheath.
"Have you seen the Canariae?"
Erolyn arched a brow with mock surprise, tilting his head as though the question required deep contemplation.
"The Canariae?" he echoed, voice syrupy with innocence. "You mean *yours*?"
His pupils contracted, golden irises glowing with silent threat.
"Yes," he snapped. "Mine."
Erolyn made a show of thinking, rubbing his chin theatrically.

"I believe I passed her near the training halls. Though, where she went after that..."

He gave a lazy shrug. "Hard to say."

Malec didn't blink. Didn't speak. But the pressure in his chest mounted. He could feel it, boiling beneath his skin. A flicker of raw, unstable magic. Erolyn was playing games. That smirk was too easy. That tone, too casual. He knew something. And he was mocking him.

When Erolyn added with a chuckle, "Shame, really. She must've been quite the handful," something in Malec snapped.

The air around him pulsed. A sphere of deep blue fire burst from Malec's palm, silent but furious, slamming into the stone wall behind Erolyn's horse. Heat rippled across the courtyard, curling the air with a shimmer of distortion. The blast left a blackened crater the size of a wagon wheel. Erolyn's horse reared back, shrieking, hooves striking empty air. Soldiers leapt away, hands instinctively going to hilts and spears. Erolyn didn't move. Didn't even blink. But the smile slipped from his face.

Malec took a step forward. His boots scraped over the scorched flagstones, and he realized too late that his breathing had turned shallow and ragged. His gaze locked on Erolyn's, unblinking, so fixed it almost hurt.

> "If I find out you helped her," he rasped, voice as raw as the fire, "if I even suspect you had a hand in this..." His throat flexed, swallowing down something tangled and choking. "I'll burn more than a wall."

For one long moment, the courtyard was silent, save for the wheezing breaths of the horse and the crackle of scorched stone cooling in the breeze. Erolyn's eyes flicked to the blackened impact, then back. His expression sharpened, amusement folding into a colder, more gauging edge.

> "I've broken no law," he murmured. "You have no proof. You know how this works."

Malec's hands began to shake. He looked down, almost surprised to see the fine tremor in his fingers, the way his knuckles had blanched white from how tightly he was flexing and releasing them. He didn't like the feeling. He didn't like not knowing where she was or how far she'd gotten. He forced a measured inhale. Another. But the world was too bright, too loud, the metallic tang of magic still clung to the back of his tongue. He couldn't blink. Couldn't unclench his jaw. It felt like everything was moving just a hair too fast and a hair too slow all at once.

It wasn't just rage anymore. It was something older. Darker. A fear he didn't have a name for. A bone-deep certainty that this was the beginning of something out of his hands. And Malec had built his entire life on never losing control.

"She was never yours to control," Erolyn added. "Only yours to lose."

Then, with a final look, he mounted and spurred his horse forward. His soldiers followed without a word, the sound of hooves ringing out as they vanished beyond the palace gates. Malec stood frozen, staring at the place Erolyn had been. His heart thundered in his chest. His magic pulsed beneath his skin. He wasn't sure if the feeling clawing its way through his gut was fury or dread. But one thing was certain. Whoever helped his canariae escape...

Was going to pay.

Malec tore through the palace like a blade through silk, swift, silent, merciless. Every hall. Every chamber. Every hidden stairwell and shadowed corridor. His boots slammed against stone floors with the rhythm of a war drum, but each turn yielded the same answer. Nothing.

The courtyard, empty. The servants' quarters, still. The perimeter beyond the palace gates, untouched. She was gone. And something inside him was slipping.

By the time he re-entered the great hall, the guards scattered before him like leaves in the wind, heads lowered, eyes averted. No one dared speak. No one dared breathe. The heat rolling off him was unnatural, like the air warped around him, distorting with the crackle of barely-contained energy. Luko stood waiting with a satchel of updates and maps, but the moment he saw Malec's face, he didn't need a word.

"She's not here," Malec ground out before Luko could open his mouth.

Luko let out a slow breath, golden eyes steady on him.

"You searched the entire palace?"

Malec's nostrils flared. "Every stone."

A tense beat passed. Luko's gaze drifted to the arched windows where the first traces of dawn were staining the sky.

"Then she's in the city. She wouldn't have gotten far without help."

"I want you to search it," Malec said, voice clipped and cold.

"Every street, every gate, every hidden passage."

Luko's brows drew together. "And you?"

Malec's stare fixed on the horizon, the muscles in his jaw jumping.

"I'm going after Erolyn."

"You think he– ?"
"I know he's involved," Malec snapped, the words sparking like flint.
Silence stretched between them, heavy as iron.
"You're unraveling," Luko said finally, voice low.
Malec's head turned, slow, dangerous. "What did you say?"

"You're not yourself," Luko pressed, stepping closer. "You're too precise. Too careful. But right now? You're thrashing like a cornered beast."

Malec's hands curled into fists, heat prickling under his skin.
Luko's tone sharpened.

"She's not like the others. She wasn't born in a cage. She was born free, Malec. You humiliated her in front of nobles who see her as nothing but something to purchase and parade, "

"I was protecting her," Malec growled, voice cracking like a whip.

"No," Luko said, louder now, refusing to look away. "You were claim her. You think you've been defending her, but you've been cornering her like prey."

The words hit harder than any blow. For a moment, neither of them spoke. The air between them shimmered with the pressure of Malec's barely leashed power. Even the candles on the desk guttered, the wicks bending as if in fear.

"You're not hunting a docile pet," Luko went on, softer but no less fierce. "You're hunting a lioness. And she will tear your throat out before she ever lets you own her."

Malec turned away, breathing hard. His chest heaved. His palms burned with the need to strike something, anything, just to stop the chaos roaring in his head.

"She is my lioness, I have owned and tamed wilder beasts," he whispered, ragged, like it cost him something to admit.

Luko watched him with pity and a sadness he didn't try to hide.

"She was never yours," he said quietly. "And the sooner you accept that, the sooner you'll stop destroying everything around you."

Malec was in the saddle before the dust had even settled from the command. His stallion reared beneath him, sensing the fury in his rider's pulse. The palace gates groaned open, and Malec surged through them like a storm unleashed, the thundering hooves echoing his rage across the cobbled streets of Caelistra. He pushed the poor animal to its limits, his cloak snapping behind him, his jaw locked in a grim line.

Erolyn had left hours ago. But Malec knew the terrain. Knew the tracks. There was only one road that cut north through the mountains, and if Melodie had taken it, then she was already his again. She just didn't know it yet. If she thought this was over...

She was gravely mistaken.

Melodie stood near the edge of the Canariae settlement, heart pounding beneath her stillness, watching as Erolyn's soldiers finished securing their gear. Horses snorted softly, saddles creaked, and the distant clang of buckles marked the end of any illusion she had left about freedom. She wasn't going with them. Erolyn had made that clear. She had been wrong.

He sat perched on a sun-bleached log a few paces away, looking far too relaxed for someone delivering bad news. His dark green eyes flicked up to her with a calm, cryptic expression, one hand tugging at the cuff of his riding glove as if nothing more pressing weighed on them.

"You didn't really think I'd take you all the way to the border, did you?" he asked, his tone light but not cruel.

Melodie folded her arms across her chest, annoyance flaring despite the ache building in her gut.
"You said you'd turn a blind eye."

"And I did," he said with a faint smirk. "But that doesn't mean I'm going to carry you across the threshold like a lovesick fool."

"You're a pain in the ass," she muttered.
He chuckled, slow and warm, before rising to his feet and brushing off his coat.

"Perhaps," he allowed. "But I'd rather be a pain in the ass than dead. And if you stay with me, that's what I'll be. Very dead."

She didn't respond, but something cold crept into her stomach. The smirk faded from his lips, and his expression shifted, less playful, more grave.

His boots crunched softly in the dirt as he took a step toward her. "You don't understand what you've done, do you?" he asked, voice low.

Melodie's chest tightened, breath stalling, but she didn't speak.

"You think this is about pride? That Malec's just angry because you embarrassed him?" Erolyn leaned closer, his forest-green gaze intense beneath the shade of

his lashes. "No, Canariae. This isn't about humiliation. Or even entrapment."

His voice dropped to something deeper, warmer, heavier.

"This is about obsession."

Melodie's spine went rigid.

"Malec is not like other males," he continued. "He doesn't let go. Not when he wants something. Not when he feels it belongs to him. And you, " he exhaled sharply, as if the words themselves tasted bitter, "you're his fixation now."

The air between them grew still.

"And trust me," Erolyn added, tone clipped, "he will tear apart anyone who touches what he believes is his. Whether they deserve it or not."

A long silence followed. Melodie didn't know what to say. Her throat felt tight, her heartbeat loud in her ears. She had underestimated the stakes. Again. But then Erolyn stepped back and glanced toward the distant horizon.

"That being said," he murmured, "I'm still giving you a head start."

Her brows furrowed. "A head start?"

He nodded.

"He's close. Closer than you think. If you're going to run, now's your only chance."

The words hit her like a slap. She hadn't expected this. She'd thought he would gloat—turn her in, or maybe pretend not to know her. But instead... he was giving her a gift.

Her voice was quiet when it came. "Why are you doing this?"

Erolyn tilted his head slightly, peering at her like she was a puzzle he hadn't decided whether to solve or keep admiring.

"Maybe I like you," he said with a crooked smile.

Melodie scoffed, shaking her head.

"Maybe I actually mean it," he added softly, and this time, she could see the honesty behind the grin.

She hesitated.

Then, with a quiet vulnerability she rarely allowed to surface, she said, "Thank you."

Melodie crossed her arms, sighing.

"I regret having to leave," she admitted quietly. "You've been a real pain, but... a good one. A real friend."

Erolyn's brows lifted slightly, surprised by her sincerity. For a moment, he didn't respond, just looked at her, a shadow flickering across his expression before his usual smirk reemerged.

"You know..." he said, his voice softer than before, "I wish I had found you first."

Something about the way he said it made something tight coil in her chest. But she couldn't afford to dwell on it. She gave a small, guarded smile and turned to leave. Then, he caught her wrist. Before she could protest, he kissed her.

It wasn't like before, no smirk, no teasing, no calculated charm. This kiss was deep, deliberate, and final. It landed heavy in her chest like a stamp pressed to wax. A goodbye she hadn't asked for, but felt all the same. Melodie jerked back and without hesitation, punched him hard in the stomach.

Erolyn gasped, doubling over as the wind left his lungs.

"You- !" he coughed, half-choking on air.

"You deserved that," she shot back, cheeks flushed with more than just anger.

Still bent, he looked up at her with a pained grin. "You *literally* did the same thing to me at the banquet."

Melodie blinked, then gave a begrudging nod. "That's fair," she admitted. "But you still deserved it."

barked out a wheezing laugh. "You... are such a brat."

Her mouth twitched into a crooked smile before she turned and walked away, vanishing into the trees without another word. Erolyn stayed where he was, one hand pressed to his ribs, the other braced on his thigh. Around him, his soldiers stood frozen, wide-eyed. One finally dared to speak.

"Uh... Lord Erolyn... should we go after her?"

Erolyn let out a strained breath, straightened up with effort, and shook his head.

"No," he muttered, a smile curling at the corner of his mouth.
"Let's see if she can outrun the mad dog."

Malec rode like the storm itself had granted him form. Each hoofbeat thundered through the marrow of the earth, vibrating up his spine until his teeth ached. His mercenary leathers molded to him like a second skin, every seam aligned with obsessive precision. Under the black hood, his pale tan eyes glimmered, unblinking, as if trying to pierce the horizon itself. He'd searched every hall of Ulvareth, every cold corridor, every gilded cage. And she had not been there. So here he was, following the breadcrumbs she'd left in her defiance, snapped branches, a scuffed heel mark in wet earth, the faintest ghost of her scent on the wind.

He'd told himself he was above superstition. That the idea of a soulthread was quaint folklore, a bedtime tale to frighten children. Yet he felt it, thin as a spider's silk, straining with every mile she put between them. Each league he rode, the pull weakened, the phantom ache behind his sternum growing sharper. As if something essential were being unstitched, thread by careful thread. *Why did she run?*

The question repeated, monotonous as a war drum. He dissected it from every angle, as though she were just another riddle to solve, another battlefield to master. But there was no answer that made sense.

I gave her order. Shelter. Purpose. Yet she'd slipped my grasp all the same.

And that unsettled him more than he would ever confess. Because if he could not predict her, he could not control her. And if he could not control her. He closed his eyes for a single heartbeat. The tether fluttered, weak, but still there. A final thread binding him to her, to the certainty that she existed in this world and not just in the fever of his mind.

Ahead, the trees parted to reveal a narrow path winding into darkness. The air was thickening, ripe with the coming storm. Even the horses behind him began to grow uneasy, their hooves striking the earth in jittering rhythms. She believed this was freedom. She was wrong.

Malec lifted his head, drawing in a slow breath that tasted of rain and unfinished reckoning. Because there were truths he had not yet spoken, even to himself. And one day, she would learn every one of them. Including this:

No one escapes an Awyan who has already decided that losing them is not an option. Not even her.

And as the first cold drops struck his hood, Malec leaned forward in the saddle, eyes narrowed to slits of molten bronze, and whispered to the gathering storm:

> "Go on—run, little dove. No distance can save you now." His heart squeezed painfully. "I've already found you."

Chapter 9

A Stranger Among Her Own

The Canariae village was not what Melodie expected.

She had imagined desperation, refugees cowering in ragged shelters, eyes hollow from hunger and fear. Instead, she stepped into a place alive with quiet defiance.

Rough-hewn wooden huts rose on stilts, their walls patched with scavenged metal and painted with swirling symbols she didn't recognize. Rope bridges connected the homes high among the black-barked trees, each walkway sagging under the weight of daily life, baskets of vegetables, lines of drying herbs, bundles of firewood lashed together with fraying twine. Smoke curled from stone-ringed pits on the ground, carrying the scent of charred maize and bitter roots.

Children darted through the shadows, bare feet silent on the mossy earth as they wove between cooking fires and crates marked with faded Awyan runes. Laughter rippled in soft bursts, mingling with the creak of rope and the crackle of incandescent kindling.

Yet all that warmth stilled the instant she appeared.

Melodie's fine palace silks shimmered under the low lanterns, pale and costly, the dyes clearly Awyan. A golden collar caught the lamplight like an accusation. Even her slippers, soft-soled, embroidered, looked absurd here, where most wore crude leather wraps or nothing at all.

Dozens of eyes tracked her as she passed under a tangle of woven arches marking the village's heart. Faces half-hidden behind strips of cloth, hands stilling over bowls and knives and mending. None greeted her. None called her sister.

Their stares were not fearful. They were reproachful. *You wear their colors. You came in their chains. You must be one of them.*

Heat prickled along her hairline as she moved deeper between the huts. Her steps sounded too loud against the plank walkways, her every motion an unwanted spectacle. Even the air seemed to hush around her, heavy with woodsmoke and the sour tang of boiled herbs.

She had thought this place would feel like coming home. But it didn't. It felt like walking into a stranger's memory. And all she could think, as she forced herself not to look away from their narrowed eyes, was that here, among her own blood, she was no less a prisoner than she'd been in Ulvareth.

They saw her as something apart. An outsider. A complication draped in the trappings of Awyan wealth. No one shouted. No one drew a blade. They didn't have to. The hush that settled over the village was worse than any threat. The way people shifted, subtly turning their shoulders as if to bar her path. The quick, furtive glances traded between neighbors. The conversations that fell silent, one by one.

It made her feel like something feral and dangerous had crept in from the trees. A thing to be watched. She didn't belong here. Not with them. Not with him. Maybe not anywhere at all.

A figure stepped out from between two huts. She was tall, with a wide, square frame and hair bound in thick gray coils that hung almost to her waist. Her skin was the color of dark earth, lined at the corners of her mouth and eyes. Those eyes were what pinned Melodie in place, steady, unflinching, and sharp enough to cut.

When the woman spoke, her voice was low and measured, each word shaped by experience and something like disappointment.

"You've brought trouble on your heels." It wasn't a question. "What do you want?"

Not who are you. Not are you safe. Just that, what do you want. Melodie hesitated. The weight of the moment pressed down on her chest, but she straightened.

"I need clothes," she said quietly. "And directions to the border."

A murmur rose behind the elder, a ripple of wary voices. Some spoke Spanish. Others something Melodie thought might be Korean. The languages differed, but the tone didn't: suspicion. Resentment.

A younger man stepped forward from the shadows of the circle, bow slung over his shoulder, a half-eaten root in his hand. His jaw was tight, eyes narrowed.

"Why should we help a palace canariae, we will get punished if we do?"

The word stung harder than she expected. She forced herself not to flinch.

"I didn't choose to be there," she said evenly. "And I'm not here to stay. You won't have to hide me. I just need to get away."

That softened something. Slightly. The elder sighed through her nose and glanced down at Melodie's silks.

"We don't give without trade. Not to someone like you."

Melodie didn't need to be told twice. Her fingers untied the sash at her waist, peeling the soft golden fabric from her shoulders and letting it fall, the silk pooling like spilled wine around her ankles. She held it out with both hands, bare beneath the stars, a silent offering.

Her dignity for their help. Their silence stretched too long. Then the elder nodded once. A gruff hand shoved a bundle of roughspun clothes into her arms. A patchwork tunic, too big. Wool trousers. A satchel filled with dried meat, hard bread, and a single flask of water. The shoes were old, cracked at the sides, but they would serve.

"Take it," the elder said. "And go."

Melodie didn't argue. She stepped into the shadows behind one of the huts, dressed quickly, and emerged in her new skin. She no longer looked like a princess. Just another wanderer with wind-bitten cheeks and mud on her boots.

She tightened the strap across her chest. "Which way to the border?"

The hunter pointed east. "Follow the river. Three days."

She nodded. No goodbyes. Only cold glares. They didn't care what happened to her, only that she was leaving. And so, under the blanket of night, Melodie turned toward the trees. And vanished into them.

Malec burst into the clearing like a storm finally given shape. His stallion reared, foam dripping from the bit, breath billowing in thick, frantic clouds. Before the animal's hooves even struck earth again, Malec had dismounted in one fluid motion. His boots hit the ground with a force that made the closest Canariae wince back.

The black cloak trailing his shoulders snapped in the wind, whipping around him like a living thing. Beneath it, his frame looked carved from something unyielding, shoulders tense, spine ramrod straight. His skin gleamed with sweat that caught the cold dawn light, lending him a feverish pallor.

And his eyes, gods above, those eyes. Pale tan, ringed in a faint, unnatural gold, and bright with a consuming, dangerous clarity. They didn't waver. Didn't blink. Just raked the camp with a predatory precision that made every living thing feel suddenly very mortal.

"Where is she?" His voice was low, raw, each syllable ground out like a blade against whetstone.

Erolyn looked up from the log where he sat, one leg crossed over the other, gloved fingers fussing idly with the fastening at his wrist. His posture was deceptively relaxed, but his gaze sharpened as it tracked the way Malec's shoulders moved, like a predator coiling before a strike.

"Who?" he drawled, though the easy note in his voice rang just a fraction too thin.

Malec didn't so much as tilt his head. He only stared. The air around him had begun to shift, growing heavy, colder. Sparks of pale blue magic flared along the seams of his gauntlets, crackling over his knuckles like lightning trying to decide if it wanted to leap.

"Do not test me." The words came from somewhere deep in his chest, rough with something older than rage.

Erolyn exhaled, slowly uncrossing his legs, boots scraping over the packed earth. He straightened, the motion smooth but careful, like a man deciding just how fast he'd need to move.

"You wound me, cousin," he said, though the smirk he tried to summon never quite reached his eyes. "As if I'd waste my breath teasing an elf who looks ready to tear the world in half."

Malec's jaw flexed, a muscle ticking in his temple. His hands trembled at his sides, not with weakness but with the strain of holding everything in. Every breath sounded too shallow, too ragged. The frost creeping over the grass near his boots crackled and split as his power pulsed out in waves.

"You look..."

Erolyn began, but the words trailed off as he took in the other male's face. The fever-bright eyes. The sweat standing out stark against skin too pale. The barely leashed madness that radiated from every taut line of his body. His smirk vanished.

"...wrong."

Malec stepped closer, boots crunching the pine needles beneath. The firelight caught in his irises, and they shimmered with something beyond rage. Something primal. Something no Awyan would speak of openly.

"Where. Is. She."

Erolyn's soldiers tensed. The camp held its breath.

"East," Erolyn said softly, raising a hand. "Toward the village. She didn't say goodbye."

For a heartbeat, silence. Then, steel flashed. Malec moved like lightning, ramming his dagger into the thigh of the nearest elfkin soldier. The cry of pain split the air as the elf dropped, blood soaking the earth. Panic rippled outward. Weapons were drawn.

"Hold!" Erolyn barked, his voice sharp. "No one moves!"

But it was clear, Malec hadn't come for a fight. He had come for blood. The faint blue glow around his hands intensified before flickering out. He was shaking. Magic leaked from him like a shattered dam.

"You've never lost it before," Erolyn said, quieter now. "You're not a beast, Malec."

Malec didn't answer. He stepped over the wounded elfkin and mounted his horse, cold and silent.

"You'll burn everything down just to keep her in your grasp," Erolyn murmured, more to himself now. "Is that what you are?"

Malec looked back once. And for a brief second, Erolyn saw something behind those fevered eyes. Not fury or rage. But fear. But whatever it was vanished just as quickly. Malec turned and galloped off into the dark, blue fire trailing in his wake like the omen of something terrible still coming.

Melodie had been walking for hours, each step a small agony in her legs. Her calves burned. The thin soles of her battered boots had split along the edges, offering no protection from the frozen, uneven forest floor. Every rock and hidden root sent a jolt up her spine. The trees loomed tall as cathedral pillars, their gnarled trunks thick with black moss and frost, the bark cracked and flaking like ancient skin. Overhead, crooked branches laced together in a ragged canopy, breaking the moonlight into frail, silver ribbons that danced across the snow-dusted undergrowth.

The cold bit into every exposed inch of her, settling in her bones, turning each shallow breath into a glassy ache. The air smelled of wet leaves and something sour, like rotting wood, but beneath it was another odor, faint, rank, animal. And then everything stopped. The wind. The rustle of old leaves. Even her own pulse seemed to hesitate, as though the world itself was holding its breath. A howl split the quiet.

It rose from the darkness, low and resonant, so deep it seemed to shiver through the ground itself. Melodie froze, her throat locked around the cold vapor of her breath. Another howl answered, higher and closer, threading through the trunks like a needle finding the last place she thought to hide.

Then came a third, behind her this time.

Shapes flickered between the trees. Huge, sinewy bodies gliding over snow and root with a grace that was all wrong. Their limbs were too long.

Their backs too straight. And their eyes, gods, their eyes, glowed silver as coins, reflecting the moon in twin glints of predatory intelligence. They defied any name she could conjure. Not wolves. Not men. Some hybrid horror crouched between both. And every step they took was aimed straight at her. Her heart slammed against her ribs, and she bolted.

Snow and dirt exploded under her boots as she ran, dodging gnarled roots and drooping limbs that scraped across her face and snagged her cloak. Her hood tore free. Cold air sank icy teeth into her scalp, tangling her curls around her throat. She didn't dare look back.

The night erupted with movement. Behind her came the muffled drum of feet—no—paws, pounding over the frozen earth. She could hear their breath, rough and wet, smell the animal stench of them as they closed in. A growl rumbled so close it rattled her teeth, low and guttural, and she knew without turning that one was nearly on her heels. She pushed harder, lungs burning, eyes streaming, until the darkness itself seemed to ripple around her. Then, impact.

Something slammed into her from the side, bone and muscle and sheer force, sending her crashing into the earth. The world spun. Air rushed from her lungs in a silent scream as her back hit the ground hard. Before she could scramble away, hands, no, claws, snatched her wrists, pinning her.

A voice, rough and wet with breath, growled in her ear: "Got her."

It wasn't mindless. Or bestial. It spoke. Melodie's vision spun as she was dragged through the underbrush. When it cleared, what she saw made her blood run cold. They were shapeshifters, wilding elfkin with glowing yellow eyes and twisted grins. Some were hunched like beasts, others walked upright, their forms dancing on the edge of animal and elf.

Their bodies were littered with scars and animal skins, their teeth too sharp, their presence feral. She had heard stories of these packs, scavengers that roamed the outskirts, preying on travelers, snatching the vulnerable from roads and ruined villages. They took elfesses and young ones and claimed them. And if they resisted, they were devoured.

They dragged her through the forest until the trees grew so dense the moonlight disappeared entirely. There, beneath a sagging tangle of roots and moss, they shoved her down a narrow tunnel carved into the earth itself. The air turned foul as she stumbled deeper, heavy with damp rot and the copper bite of old blood. The cavern was vast, a hollowed-out pit beneath the roots of the ancient woods. Rough-hewn stone walls were streaked black with soot and slick with condensation. Low fires burned in shallow pits, their smoke clinging to the ceiling like a living thing. The heat was stifling, thick with the rank stench of unwashed bodies, animal pelts, and something sour she couldn't name.

Cages cobbled together from scavenged iron and splintered wood lined the walls, each crowded with elfkin in various states of ruin. Some stared blankly into nothing. Some rocked on their haunches, murmuring to themselves in voices too hoarse to carry. A few clutched each other like children, though their eyes were ancient with defeat.

She tried not to breathe too deeply. The filth was nearly alive, slick handprints on the stone, bones gnawed to splinters, piles of discarded furs where some had curled up to sleep. And still, there was an order to it, a grim kind of civilization beneath the squalor. Shapeshifters squatted around the fires, passing torn strips of meat hand to hand. One was etching crude symbols into the soot with a sharpened bone, another cleaning claws with the edge of a blade. It was primitive, but not mindless.

From the shadows, a figure emerged. Broad-shouldered and thick with muscle, hair coiled in filthy mats like bramble. Yellow eyes fixed on her, bright as lantern flame. She knew, the moment their gaze locked, that this was no ordinary brute.

At first glance, she thought him male, his walk was heavy, shoulders squared in a deliberate show of dominance. But as he drew closer, her eye caught the subtleties no disguise could erase. The shape of the hips beneath the ragged furs. The tension in the throat when he spoke, voice pitched lower than it wanted to fall. A female, she realized, posing as a predator even among predators. In a world that only respected power, she had become its avatar, whether by choice or necessity, Melodie couldn't tell.

And as that yellow stare raked over her, assessing every inch of her stolen finery and bared throat, she knew she was standing before the one who decided who ate, and who did not.

"You're strong," the leader said in crude Awyan, circling her. "You'll join us."

Melodie didn't back away. "Not a chance."

The female's smirk was all teeth. "Then we'll eat you instead."

Rough hands shoved her against the wall of a cage. The leader leaned in, breath hot against her cheek.

"You could make this easy. Be my mate. Be pack."

Melodie stared. Cold. Defiant.

"No." The cave stilled. The air was tense.

"You refuse?" the leader snarled.

"Yes."

A rumble of unease rolled through the other shifters. The leader's claws flexed, her eyes narrowing to slits.

"Why?"

"Because I'm not interested," Melodie said evenly, her voice iron-wrapped silk.

"If you're no use to the pack," the leader hissed, "then you're meat."

Melodie's eyes swept the cave. They landed on a youth slumped in the far corner, no older than sixteen by her guess. His leg was mangled, swollen, bleeding, oozing with infection. From the shine of his skin and the stiffness of his jaw, she could already tell he was septic. She also saw the cause of it. A few of the shifters had tried to 'clean' the wound, by licking it.

She pointed. "Him. If you want him to live, I can save him."

A ripple of doubt moved through the pack. Several shifters glanced between the youth and their leader, uncertain.

"A what?" one of them asked.

"I heal," Melodie replied. Calm. Precise.

The leader studied her, lips peeling back in suspicion. Then, with a grunt, she grabbed Melodie's wrist and dragged her across the cavern floor, shoving her beside the injured boy.

"Fix him," she growled. "Or we eat you."

Melodie stared at the inflamed limb and the sweat-slicked skin of the patient.

"Fantastic," she muttered.

And got to work because at least it would buy her time to think and find a way to get out of this situation. Melodie knelt beside the injured young shifter, her fingers hovering just above the twisted leg. Swollen, discolored, and already beginning to reek, this was no fresh wound. The bone had snapped days ago, and in their wild ignorance, the tribe had wrapped it in filthy cloth and, worse, slathered it with spit. Saliva. Like wolves tending their own. No antiseptic or splint. Just rot and wishful thinking.

"Idiots," she muttered under her breath.

The young one's face was pale, sweat-soaked, and pinched in pain. His breathing came shallow and fast. Melodie could see the infection rising, moving toward his hip. If it reached his core, he was dead.

"What do you need?" The pack leader demanded from behind her, arms crossed and tone taut with impatience.

Melodie turned, expression flat. "Boiling water."

The female tilted her head, confused. "Boiling... what?"

Melodie blinked. Her stomach tightened. None of them knew. They didn't boil anything. Not water, tools or hands. Primitive. They lived like predators, not people, hoarding flesh and dominance instead of knowledge or community.

"Do you have pots?" Melodie asked sharply, her mind already moving ahead.

One of the younger shifters shuffled forward with a clay vessel, crude, lopsided, but it would do. Melodie snatched it, stormed out of the cave, and filled it with rainwater gathered in the broad, cupped leaves near the cave mouth. She found a shallow fire pit, stoked the embers until they flared bright, then balanced the pot above it with stacked stones. The flames licked the sides, and soon the water began to bubble.

She pointed at the rising steam.

"This," she snapped, loud enough for all to hear, "is how you *clean*."

Murmurs rippled behind her. Curious eyes watched. Skeptical ones narrowed. But none interrupted. Melodie moved quickly, gathering bark, fibrous leaves, and pungent herbs that vaguely resembled antiseptic roots from her medical training. It wasn't ideal. But it would work. Back inside, she dropped the hot rags into the herbal mixture, her movements sharp and clinical. The injured shifter whimpered, jerking when the cloth touched his skin.

"Hold him," she ordered.

Two of the larger shifters moved to restrain him, though they watched her hands with animal wariness. Melodie ignored them. She was deep in the rhythm now, clean, press, stabilize. She washed out the infection, packed the wound with poultices, and realigned the bone with a sharp, practiced motion that made the boy scream.

But he didn't pass out. Good.

She splinted his leg with dry twigs, wound tight with woven vine strips, and secured it with layers of cloth soaked in the herbal brew. When she finally pulled back, sweat had beaded along her own hairline.

"He needs rest. Dry bedding. Clean coverings," she said, turning to the leader.

"No licking. No touching. No moving him for two weeks, or he'll lose the leg, or his life."

The cave fell silent. The lead shifter stared at her, nostrils flaring, sharp teeth slightly bared. Then, she gave a single nod.

"You live. For now."

Melodie exhaled, but it wasn't relief. Not really. She had bought herself time, not safety. But just as she moved to stand, the female grabbed her wrist. With surprising strength, she yanked Melodie toward a dark corner piled with straw and furs.

"You sleep here," the shifter said firmly, dragging her down.

Melodie stiffened. "You still trying to mate with me?" she muttered, dry as bone.

The shifter only smirked, settling beside her, close enough to steal her body heat.

"You're mine now."

Melodie stared at her, exhausted, furious, but too drained to argue. Her body ached, her mind was frayed, and her eyelids burned with fatigue. Tomorrow, she would fight. Tonight, she would survive. A mistake she'd soon regret.

Malec rode until the path disappeared under a snarl of roots and briars, the air turning sharp with the reek of damp fur and smoke. His stallion shifted beneath him, ears flicking nervously. The trail was faint here, cold as old ash. But it didn't matter. He could feel her. Not a scent, not a footprint, something deeper. A pull in his chest, as steady as a heartbeat he didn't control. Each time he tried to dismiss it as nothing but skill, as the discipline of a hunter who never failed, the truth whispered back.

It was her. It had always been her. And stars above, she had led him to this filth.

Of course she had. Only she would slip from his hands and run headlong into a den of mongrel shifters, creatures that crawled in the margins of civilization and called it freedom. He could almost hear her voice, mocking him for thinking his walls would ever hold her.

He reined in the stallion at the glade's edge, boots sinking into the damp earth as he dismounted. The breeze carried the stench of unwashed bodies and something metallic. Blood, maybe. A thin curl of smoke drifted from a cave mouth half-hidden behind brambles. Laughter drifted out, hoarse, savage, not quite human. His cloak shifted around him, the black fabric heavy with moisture. He adjusted the set of his hood until darkness swallowed his expression, welcoming the familiar hush that came when focus replaced anger.

He could feel the storm inside him easing, his heartbeat slowing, the world narrowing to a single, crystalline purpose. Find her. His soldiers emerged one by one, pale shapes slipping between the trees, their eyes fixed on him, waiting. He didn't look back. He didn't need to.

At the mouth of the cave, Malec stopped. Just for a breath. Long enough to let that taut, invisible thread inside him pull tight, guiding him forward with the inevitability of a blade falling. The stench hit him first, rank, cloying, thick as rot. It burned the back of his eyes, made the fine muscles in his jaw twitch. But he didn't flinch. He drew a slow inhale through his teeth, feeling his magic coil up his spine like something alive.

Yes. There. Beneath the reek and ruin. Hers.

"Strike down any who raise a claw," he said, quiet as the grave.

His voice didn't rise, but the air itself seemed to vibrate, brittle with the promise of violence. Then he stepped forward. A shape burst from the dark, a half-shifted brute of matted fur and jutting teeth. It came at him in a blur of claws and stinking breath. Malec didn't stop. Didn't even lift his gaze. He pivoted sharply, one boot scraping stone, and let the creature's momentum carry it past.

Then he turned, hand lifted. The air around his palm cracked, violet light sparking to life in a roiling sphere. With a flick of his wrist, the magic exploded.

The shapeshifter hit the far wall in a burst of searing light. Bone and sinew ignited, flesh crumbling to embers before it hit the ground. A blast of heat swept the chamber, sending shrieks ricocheting off the cavern walls. Somewhere in the shadows, a crude alarm drum started up, hollow, frantic thumping. The smell of scorched fur rose thick and greasy. He stalked forward. And as he stepped into the cavern, the air shifted. Melodie was jolted awake by the sound of screaming.

She shot up, chest heaving, eyes wide as the scent of blood slammed into her senses. Chaos erupted around her. Shapeshifters snarled and howled, scattering like startled rats, crashing into each other in a scramble for weapons, or escape. Then she saw him. A figure in the center of the storm.

Malec stood like a wraith of vengeance, his tall frame cloaked in dark leathers, wild silver-blonde hair half-tied, the rest loose and untamed, like the fury radiating off him in waves. His face was lit by flickering torchlight, carved in fury. His tan eyes, blistering molten and bright, swept the room like a blade. He was death made flesh. The shifters paused mid-attack, instincts overriding pride. This was not prey.

Malec's presence alone turned the air suffocating. Not a muscle twitched as he scanned the cave, his focus razor-sharp. The raw aura of his magic had been storming violently moments ago, but now it had gone quiet. Still. Like a predator when prey is in reach. Of course it had. She was near.

"Torak'lei ven'thuun dor nalathi."

Malec growled, his words thick with ancient warning. His voice cracked through the cavern like a whip, sharp enough to make the air itself seem to recoil. The pack's leader, a brute of a woman with brambled hair and eyes like chipped obsidian, bared her yellowed teeth in a snarl. This time, she didn't back away. She shifted her weight forward, shoulders hunching as she began to stalk him, her claws flexing like she was ready to tear flesh from bone. But Malec didn't stop.

He advanced, his words slowing, sharpening, each syllable landing like a blade against stone, dangerous in their precision. Whatever he spoke in that old tongue, it wasn't a threat. It was a sentence. A promise. The kind that left no room for mercy.

Before Melodie could process it, his hand shot out, fingers clamping around her wrist, hot, solid, iron-strong. His grip wasn't just to restrain; it was to claim, to bind, as if touch alone would tether her to him forever. Her heart slammed against her ribs. She twisted, yanked, fought like a cornered animal, but he hauled her forward in a brutal, effortless pull. She crashed into his chest, breath knocked from her lungs.

His breath hit her face, warm and ragged, carrying the copper tang of rage. His nostrils flared, he bit down so tight it looked carved from stone. And those eyes. Gods. Those molten tan eyes, glowing faintly in the torchlight, slitted with fury, with something unspoken and wild. He wasn't just angry. He was unraveling. A predator denied the kill, denied the control he craved. Magic crackled under his skin, seeping through the air, wrapping around her like the charge before a storm's first strike. It tasted electric. It tasted like danger.

But Melodie didn't scream. She didn't cry. She fought. Her boot lashed out, fast, brutal, catching the side of his shin with a solid crack. Malec grunted, staggered, the shock enough to make his grip falter. She didn't waste the heartbeat he gave her. She tore free, spun, ran. Her breath came in ragged gasps, smoke and rot filling her lungs as she fled through the den's dark maw. Her hands grabbed whatever came to them, a cracked jug, a stone bowl, a jar stinking of something sour. She hurled them behind her, hearing one shatter, the sharp crack ringing through the cavern like a gunshot.

"Clean out the cave! Secure the prisoners, now!"

Malec barked over his shoulder, his voice cracking through the smoky dark like a lash. The command was sharper than he intended, but he couldn't help it. His nerves felt flayed raw, his mind a thousand shards of irritation and something that almost tasted like panic. He didn't wait to see his orders carried out. Already he was moving, weaving through the chaos as soldiers poured in behind him, their blades gleaming, their footfalls a thunder in the cavern. A jar exploded against the wall near his ear in a spray of sour brine and grit. He didn't recoil. He didn't have the luxury of distraction.

She was running. *Why did she always run?*

Dust and soot bit the back of his throat as he followed her into the narrow tunnel, the reek of blood and damp fur thick as fog. His boots struck the uneven stone in a measured rhythm, too measured, he realized dimly. A pattern he relied on to keep his thoughts in order. But tonight, it wasn't working. Nothing was working.

She burst out of the cave mouth ahead of him, her silhouette briefly haloed in the silver wash of moonlight. For an instant, she looked feral, untamed hair flying behind her, shoulders hunched as though she expected him to strike her down. His stomach twisted.

Why did she have to look at him like that?

He stepped into the clearing after her. The cold slapped his face, crisp and biting, but it hardly registered. His gaze locked on her as she stumbled over a tangle of roots and kept going, her breath tearing ragged from her lungs.

He couldn't let her vanish into the dark. Not again. Not when he was the only thing keeping her alive. She didn't understand. She never understood. He grit his teeth. He lifted one hand, fingers curling in a precise, deliberate motion that calmed him even as his heart hammered. A spell he'd learned as a boy, old, potent, reliable. He spoke the words low, guttural, each syllable an anchor for the chaos clawing at the edges of his composure.

"Doro'yn torah."

The magic ignited, pure and cold as moonlight. A rush of force poured from his palm, invisible but undeniable, and collided with her in a soundless impact that rippled the air. Melodie stiffened mid-stride. For one breathless instant, her eyes met his, wide, startled, furious, and then her legs folded beneath her. She hit the ground with a muffled cry, leaves scattering around her like startled birds.

Malec stood over her, his breathing ragged. The clearing flickered at the edges of his vision, too bright, too loud. The smell of burnt fur made his eyes sting. He pressed his thumb hard against the center of his palm, grounding himself in the pressure. He told himself he was protecting her. He always told himself that. But if that was true, why did he feel like he was the one losing control?

His soldiers moved in the shadows around him, binding shapeshifters in ironcords and dragging them out of the den. Bodies smoldered on the pyre, their smoke sour and thick. Somewhere, a wounded shifter screamed, and the sound frayed the last of his composure. He took a steadying breath, then leaned down. His hands were careful but unyielding as he lifted her, the heat of her body seeping through his gloves. She felt too light. Too fragile. He told himself it was only because the spell had left her limp. He refused to name the other possibility, that she was becoming something he didn't know how to handle.

He slung her over his shoulder. The ragged fabric of her cloak brushed his cheek as she started to stir, her muffled curses falling hot against his back. He set his jaw and started toward the horses.

Behind him, the den burned. In his chest, the tether to her pulsed, thin as a heartbeat, and just as impossible to ignore. The stun spell hadn't held her long. He'd watched, incredulous, as she clawed at the dirt with bloodied fingers and forced her body upright far sooner than any creature should have. Even then, some part of him almost admired her.

Almost. But by the time she had risen to her knees, he was already there, closing the distance with long, furious strides.

She hadn't stood a chance.

Around them, the clearing reeked of burnt fur and cold earth. The fires guttered low now, embers hissing under a rising wind. Behind him, his soldiers moved with quiet efficiency, but the chaos no longer pressed against his mind. No more discord. No more uncertainty. She was here. He had her again. And gods, it terrified him how much that steadied him.

They reached the horses. He stopped so abruptly that her boot scuffed against the inside of his knee. His breath hitched, sharp and unsteady, and for one ragged heartbeat he only stared at the ground. Everything had been noise, too much, too bright, too fast, but now... now there was only her. The tether that pulled him taut had eased, and in that sickening relief, a darker ache rose to fill the space she'd left behind.

Slowly, deliberately, he unhooked his arm. She slid off his shoulder like a sack of grain, her boots hitting the frozen ground with a dull thud. Before she could bolt, his hands clamped around her shoulders. The pads of his fingers pressed bruising hard into the delicate bones there. He spun her to face him, his movements precise, controlled, but when she met his eyes, she saw the fracture beneath the veneer.

His face was a mask of iron, but the longer she stared, the more she saw it: the unspooling threads, the confusion fighting the fury. His jaw flexed, the muscles fluttering under golden skin gone tight with strain. He couldn't seem to look at her without that heat rising behind his eyes, a molten wildfire he barely kept caged. He jabbed a shaking finger into her chest, the touch hotter than it should have been, then flung his hand toward the black horizon where the den burned. His voice ripped from him raw, serrated:

"Duro'lei meka norathi!"

The syllables cracked like glass between them. She didn't know the words, but she knew exactly what they meant. How dare you. Her pulse thudded in her throat.

"You think I was just going to stay there?" she shouted, her voice trembling despite her rage. "Like a docile submissive slave? Boy, you don't know me at all and you are about to go through a rude awakening."

His nostrils flared. A muscle in his cheek twitched. His breath came harsh, the cold air turning it to fog between them. And then, his voice lowered, thickened, like something breaking in his chest.

"Shaé'vo draken lior'ta, mel'torinai..."

The words stumbled out, fierce and guttural, but edged with something softer she didn't have a name for. His hands trembled where they gripped her arms. His gaze pinned her, molten and searching, as if he could will her to understand. Melodie blinked hard. She hated the way her chest twisted, hated the heat gathering behind her eyes. She didn't understand him. Not his language. Not the way he looked at her, as if she were the only thing in the world he couldn't tame.

"I don't understand you, asshole!" she spat, voice breaking.

His jaw worked silently, no retort coming. His breaths turned ragged against her cheek, each exhale searing cold on her skin. And suddenly, he closed the last inch between them, yanking her forward until their foreheads collided. For a moment, everything stilled. The world fell away. There was only his shaking hands, the heat of his skin, the soft scrape of his breath.

Inside, Malec's thoughts were a storm. He couldn't parse the way her defiance felt like a blade buried under his ribs. Couldn't understand why her leaving had hollowed him out so completely that even his magic had turned brittle.

Why can't she see it? he thought, a raw ache he would never speak aloud. *I am only trying to protect you. Why does protecting you feel like losing myself?*

His grip didn't ease, and when he finally pulled back just enough to see her face, his expression looked shattered, carved from something desperate and old. The tether between them still thrummed in the hollow of his chest, thin, relentless, alive, and every time she breathed, it pulled on something he didn't have a name for.

He wished he could hate it. Hate her. But all he felt was the hollow ache where she had been, the raw emptiness she left behind. Because her leaving hadn't felt like freedom. It felt like betrayal, sharp, blinding, and unthinkable. As if she'd reached into him, wrapped her hand around something vital, and ripped it clean away.

Malec finally exhaled, a slow, ragged breath that trembled at the edges, as though fury alone wasn't enough to keep the rest of him from coming undone. For a heartbeat, he just stared at her. As if he were trying to memorize her face.

Then, without a word, he turned her around. His hands were rough and unyielding, but there was no cruelty in them, only desperation, raw and bruised. He lifted her onto the horse with a strength that felt like a sentence, like he'd decided her fate and his in the same breath. Melodie gasped, her hands scrabbling for the saddle as her pulse thundered in her throat. The reins slapped her wrist. She didn't dare look back.

A moment later, he mounted behind her in a single, fluid motion. His arms came down on either side of her, not in threat, but in something final. Something that felt like surrender wrapped in iron. His hands closed around the reins, his breath hot at her neck, and for a moment she felt the quake in his chest. He didn't speak. Didn't shout. The silence between them was heavier than any accusation, so thick she thought it might choke her. She wanted to twist around. To shove him away and spit every cruel word she could find. But something in him, something unsteady and breaking beneath the calm, held her still.

Behind her, Malec pressed his brow to the back of her head, just for a second. His thoughts were loud enough to drown out the world. He had lost her once. Lost her to her own fear. Lost her to the space between their languages, the fracture between his need and her terror. He couldn't, he wouldn't, let that happen again.

As soon as he brought her home—back to the High North, where she belonged—Malec would make it law. He would summon Luko, command him to teach Melodie Awyan, every word, every inflection, until the language was hers. There would be no more misunderstanding, no more confusion, no more desperate attempts to reach her across the gulf of silence. She would understand him. She would know what he meant when he spoke, what he felt when he looked at her, what every command, every plea, truly meant beneath the surface. For too long, the words had failed them. He was done being a stranger in her eyes.

Next time, she would hear him. She'd finally understand that every decision, every hard edge, every unspoken word had been carved by fear—a fear that he would lose her, and lose himself with her.

The ride was long, cold, and steeped in a silence that scraped against Malec's raw edges. He kept himself rigid, his arms locked tight around her, not to cage her, not precisely, but because if he let go, even for a heartbeat, he wasn't sure what would spill out.

He had prepared himself for a struggle. For her to twist and thrash and spit every foul word she knew. But she didn't. Little by little, he felt her resistance unravel. Her breathing, once jagged with fury, slowed. Her shoulders eased beneath his arm. And then, so quietly he almost missed it, she rested her head against his chest.

At first, he thought it was some clever deception, another tactic to pull his guard down. But when he dared a glance, he saw her lashes drifting shut, her face turned toward the hollow of his throat. She was surrendering to sleep. Surrendering to him.

A fissure split something in his chest. His breath caught, unsteady.

She smelled of everything he'd despised in that cursed den, smoke, sweat, the stink of wild creatures, but beneath it was her. Only her. And that scent, mercy help him, settled something inside him he hadn't realized was splintering. He had been losing himself. Completely. When he'd stormed the shapeshifter lair, he'd felt unmoored, more animal than elf. Fury had been the only thing keeping him upright, a rage so consuming he hadn't cared what he destroyed as long as it ended with her back in his reach.

And now... now she was here. Warm in his arms, breathing slow and even, and all that seething wrath was bleeding out of him like poison drawn from a wound.

Why did she do this to him? How had she become the single thing that steadied his mind when everything else threatened to fracture?

He forced his gaze forward, but his thoughts circled relentlessly. When had this started? When had her presence become something he needed just to feel sane? He remembered the way she had looked at him before she ran, like he was something to be escaped, something monstrous. It had struck deeper than any blade.

He adjusted the reins, trying to distract himself, but the tremor in his hands betrayed him. She didn't stir. Didn't stir to see how close he was to unraveling all over again. Malec closed his eyes for the space of a breath, letting the ache crest and recede.

He didn't understand this. He didn't know if it was possibly some sort of imprint, or obsession, or some curse neither of them could name. But as she exhaled a small, drowsy sigh against him, he knew one thing with unsettling clarity:

He had never needed anything the way he needed her to stay.

He remembered the moment he'd found her. The way the world had gone white around the edges, the way his own voice had cracked open with that shout, *Duro'lei mekä'norathi.* (*You were never meant to leave me*). And he'd meant it. Every jagged word. Even then, the fury had nearly broken him in half, he couldn't bring himself to hurt her. He hadn't been able to drag her through the dirt, to spit cruelty in her face like she was nothing more than a defiant slave.

Because she wasn't just a prisoner. She was his fire-born. The wild creature who fought him even as she slept. He shifted, trying to ease the ache in his muscles and the tightness in his chest. But the space between them only made it worse. It felt like stepping back from a precipice he'd already committed to. The heat low in his stomach coiled tighter. Not just hunger. Something deeper. Need. Relief. A hollow in his chest that her presence seemed to fill without trying.

What was this? What was she doing to him?

His mind reached back, combing through every moment since she'd appeared in his world. In the beginning, she had been a disruption. A problem to contain, to discipline. She had driven him past the boundaries of his control, her defiance sparking something reckless in him he'd never recognized. That first day in the throne room, he'd thought he hated her for it.

But when she vanished, when he'd realized she was truly gone, his mind had splintered in a way that terrified him more than any battlefield. He'd ridden through the forest like a wounded animal, his thoughts fracturing into chaos he couldn't wrestle back into order. Nothing had made sense without her there to push against him. Nothing had felt right. And now, with her here, slumped in his arms, breathing soft and even, he could feel everything clicking back into place. Like the world itself had been askew and was slowly correcting under the quiet weight of her body resting against his.

He closed his eyes and drew a long breath, trying to steady the riot in his head. But even that small movement brought the scent of her closer, smoke, sweat, wild dog, and underneath it all, the raw, stubborn essence that was hers alone. It should have He grit his teeth, jaw tight with restraint. Every instinct screamed to touch her. To taste her. To make her understand. But now was not the time. He couldn't lose control again. Not like before.

Instead, he focused on what came next. Punishment. Not pain, he would never truly harm her. But there would be consequences. She had defied him, humiliated him, and vanished into one of the foulest dens on the continent. He'd nearly torn the realm apart trying to find her. She needed to understand what she'd done. What she'd awakened in him.

But the punishment... it couldn't be cruel. That was the problem.

He grit his teeth harder. This wasn't right. She was his prisoner. His problem. His shame. And yet... every time she looked at him with those defiant eyes, every time she fought him with tooth and nail, he felt more alive than he had in years. It was infuriating. He would not let her win. She would learn to obey. To stay. To speak his tongue, so that he could finally hear the truth behind all her fire and venom.

He needed to know her—every secret, every reason she undid him so effortlessly. He glanced down at her, watching the lines of tension that lingered even in her sleep, her mouth parted, brow drawn tight as if she braced for attack even in dreams.

She didn't trust him. Maybe she never would. Maybe that was the cost of wanting someone who refused to be owned.

As Malec rode through the towering gates of the capital with Melodie slumped against him, fierce, wild, and bound, Luko faced a quieter cruelty.

The palace gleamed with polished marble and golden inlays, every column and arch meant to dazzle the eye. But beneath the gleam, the rot ran deep. The kind that couldn't be scrubbed away with scented oils or masked by incense.

Luko moved through the corridors like a shadow, there but never truly *seen*. Not the way others were. He slipped between clusters of nobles draped in gauzy silks and embroidered robes, their jeweled collars catching the torchlight in bright, careless glints. They passed him with the same perfumed disdain, as if reminding him he didn't belong here was a duty they cherished.

"Look who slithered out of the mud," murmured a silver-haired elfess, her voice syrupy with false sweetness.

The scent of her rosewater perfume clung to the air long after she drifted past.

"Still whispering to birds and beasts, Luko?" another called, lips curving into a delicate sneer. "You always did have a talent for wasting your breath on animals."

A third elbowed his companion, smirking. "Not animals. Canariae. Same thing, isn't it?"

Their laughter spilled down the hall, sharp, brittle, the sound of polished knives tapping crystal. It always sounded the same: rehearsed, thoughtless, as though cruelty was a game played between courses at supper. Luko kept his gaze lowered and dipped his head in a gesture he'd practiced a thousand times. Silence was easier. Silence preserved what little dignity they hadn't already tried to strip away.

But even silence didn't dull the sting.

He was no heir of a grand house. His mother had scrubbed these very floors until her hands cracked and bled, dying of a fever no healer bothered to name. His father had been a wandering merchant who vanished before he'd learned his first words. He carried no titles behind his name. No fortunes to soften his path. And worst of all, the thing they could never forgive, he spoke Canariae.

To the elite, that language was a stain. It marked him. Made him less. Because only the lowly bothered to understand the enslaved. Only the shameful held compassion for what this kingdom tried so hard to forget.

He moved on, the noblemen's laughter echoing behind him like the clinking of coins dropped down a deep well. As always, no one walked with him. No one spoke to him without barbs hidden beneath their words. He was alone. But not forgotten. Never forgotten. He'd become a symbol of quiet disgrace in a world obsessed with rank.

Still, Luko endured it. Not for glory nor revenge. But because someone had to remember that kindness wasn't weakness. That language could be a bridge between chains and freedom, instead of a weapon. That not all Awyan hearts were carved from ice and polished to gleam.

He stepped out into the courtyard, exhaling a slow breath he hadn't realized he'd been holding. The air was cold, edged with the bite of oncoming frost. Wind slipped through the archways, carrying the mingled scents of iron and wet stone and the faint perfume of the hothouse gardens hidden behind the palace walls.

For a moment, he simply stood there, letting the quiet wrap around him like a thin cloak. Then his gaze drifted beyond the gates, past the outer terraces and down to the broad, torchlit avenue that cut through Caelistra like a vein.

Chapter 10

The Cost of Obedience

The palace was a fortress of frost and stone, its towering, bone-colored walls catching the gray-blue light of dawn like the edge of a blade. The courtyard rang with the clash of training steel, and the northern wind slithered through its archways, sharp as a whip. Banners of black and blue, marked by Surion's house sigil, a three-headed hawk devouring a sun, snapped overhead, cold and proud.

And yet, for all his surroundings, Malec's mind was elsewhere. He stood near the arch of the east corridor, arms crossed, tracking her.

The canariae knelt in the shadowed alcove below, scrubbing blood from the stones with a rag too thin for the task. Her wrists were red and raw, lashes from her earlier escape still etched faintly on her back, not deep, of course. She was property. Scarring her would only devalue the investment.

She hadn't cried out during punishment. Not once. Now, she worked in silence, head bowed but not broken. Malec's jaw tightened. He should have felt satisfaction. This was order. This was discipline. But instead...

A strange heaviness coiled in his chest—a tight, restless ache that defied explanation. She wasn't like anyone he'd ever conquered, not like the soldiers he'd broken or the beasts he'd brought to heel.

No, this woman was different. She was wild, yes, but it wasn't rebellion for the sake of rebellion. Her resistance ran deeper, born of something raw and uncorrupted, a primal need to survive. She wore her defiance like armor, effortless and unthinking, as much a part of her as breath or blood. He hated how much it drew him. Hated that her untamable spirit—her refusal to submit—called to something lost and restless in him. The others had all yielded, but her stubborn fire, her fierce purity... he found himself craving it, helpless against the pull.

She had escaped him, again, and for that, she had to be punished. His people were warriors. Their society thrived on control, on obedience, on respect earned through pain. He could not afford to appear soft. Not now. Not when eyes watched him from every dark corner, waiting for cracks in his armor. And yet...

Watching her suffer stirred something foreign in him. A thread of sorrow. A hint of shame. He should not feel this way.

Perhaps I am only attached to her as one would be to a cat, he reasoned. But even that felt false. She refused to yield, and part of him didn't want her to. But deep down, he knew the truth. She wasn't tameable. And he wasn't sure he wanted her to be.

His nostrils flared as the wind shifted, carrying her scent to him. Despite the lingering stench of den and blood, there was something clean beneath it. Soft, wild, warm. A scent that calmed the magic still boiling beneath his skin. He remembered the way she'd fought him even when stunned. Kicked and cursed in her foreign tongue, eyes blazing with spirit. He could still feel the heat of her body pressed against his chest as she slept on the ride home, unaware of the effect she had on him.

It had taken all his restraint not to touch her. And restraint was wearing thin.

"Shaé'vo draken lior'ta, mel'torinai!" he had shouted at her when she'd run. (You shame me with this betrayal, my fire-born!)

It had surprised even him. The words had slipped from somewhere deeper than logic, than law. They had come from instinct. Possession. Need.

Now, as she worked beneath the pale torchlight, he watched the curve of her shoulders, the way she muttered under her breath when the rag slipped from her grip. Luko passed by and she looked up, her features softening only for him.

Malec's stomach twisted, a slow, hollow ache spreading beneath his ribs. He didn't want her smiling at Luko, her lips softening into something she never gave him. He didn't want her voice, low, lilting, threaded with that strange, beautiful tongue, to belong to anyone else. He wanted it for himself. Every word. Every sigh. Every small sound she made when she forgot to be wary.

He wanted her eyes on him alone, dark and defiant, sparking with that fierce spirit that both enraged and captivated him. And Ancestors help him, he hated how much he wanted it.

A knock at the arch pulled him from his thoughts. A royal messenger stood stiff-backed with a sealed scroll in hand.

"You are to bring the dark one," the messenger announced. "The King wishes her presence at the supper gathering."

Malec didn't respond at first. His fingers curled into fists at his sides. The King wanted to show her off. Parade her before the highborn like a beast on a leash. Let them whisper, let them leer.

Malec could not refuse. But the very thought made something cold coil behind his ribs. They would see her and would want her.

And Malec was beginning to realize, he did not want to share.

Melodie stood still as stone, though every nerve in her body felt scraped raw. The gown they'd dressed her in was a masterpiece of deliberate humiliation, deep midnight blue that shimmered like a thousand trapped stars whenever the lamplight caught it, slit high along one thigh to bare too much skin, the bodice cut low enough to showcase the swell of her breasts. A gauzy underlayer of green silk peeked out with every shift of her hips, a lush contrast that made her feel like a painted bird in a gilded cage.

The air was thick with warm perfume, amber resin, spiced fruit, something musky and sweet that turned her stomach. All around her, the Awyan nobles mingled in small, predatory knots, laughter spilling from painted mouths as jeweled hands lifted goblets of pale gold wine. They pretended not to stare. But she could feel it, the slow crawl of dozens of gazes along her body, lingering on her bare shoulders, the curve of her collarbone, the long line of her exposed thigh.

She swallowed hard, trying to steady her breathing as the heat of their scrutiny pressed in. Each measured glance made her feel like she was back on the auction block, only now the stage was polished marble, the chains replaced with silk and gemstones.

Some of them looked at her with the cool detachment of collectors assessing a relic. Others didn't bother to disguise the hunger in their eyes. It made her skin itch, made her hands flex against the side of her skirts, longing to swing a fist into one of those painted faces. But she couldn't.

So she lifted her chin, locking her jaw, letting her gaze drift to the nearest crystal decanter. Fuck, she needed to drink something. Anything to quiet the sharp-edged panic crawling up her throat. Because if she didn't, she wasn't sure she could keep standing there, a pretty, docile ornament while they discussed her worth.

One woman leaned in to another, whispering behind a fan while glancing directly at Allora's chest. The other covered a smile, eyes gleaming with sick amusement. A male elf laughed aloud at something the King said, Melodie didn't catch the words, but she recognized the smug tilt of his head, the way his shoulders rolled back like he was taking credit for a conquest.

She cast a sideways glance at Malec, her pulse fluttering with a question she couldn't silence—*would he punish her later?* The thought alone made her stomach twist. God, what the hell was wrong with her? She was grown, a woman who'd bled and fought and survived things most wouldn't dare speak of. And yet... she felt six again. Like a guilty child caught red-handed, waiting for her father's lecture before the belt came down. Only this was worse. This was shame that licked through her like firelight. This was dread that didn't just settle—it sunk, deep and certain, threading through every inch of her.

Silent. Tense. His jaw looked carved from pale marble, the fine lines around his mouth drawn tight with effort. He was dressed more simply than most of the nobles, in a pale green tunic so light it nearly passed for white, delicate silver embroidery curling along the collar in understated patterns. Beneath it, a crisp white blouse peeked out, the sleeves fastened neatly at his wrists. The tunic fell to his knees over tan trousers tucked into well-worn brown boots polished to a dull sheen.

It wasn't the garish splendor so many here flaunted. No sequined cloaks. No ropes of gemstones. Just enough elegance to signal his rank, no more. A quiet defiance against the pomp of Awyan high society.

And yet, he still looked impossibly sharp. The precise lines of his shoulders. The straightness of his spine. The quiet command that clung to him like a second skin. Normally, his poise felt deliberate, controlled, like every movement was measured to avoid giving anything away. But here, in the crush of heat and perfume, surrounded by sneering elites, he looked... cornered.

She watched the subtle shifts in his posture. The way he braced his boots apart as if readying to retreat, his hand flexing around the stem of his glass. How his gaze never rested on anyone for too long, as though the weight of their attention burned. His shoulders rose, just slightly, every time laughter rolled across the hall. She realized with a jolt that these gatherings didn't suit him. They suffocated him. He looked less like a powerful commander and more like a man being slowly tortured.

No wonder the others whispered that he was aloof. Antisocial. Untouchable. Studying him now, she thought maybe they'd never stopped to wonder why. And she couldn't help herself.

Melodie reached out, her fingers brushing the soft linen of his sleeve. He turned to her, the hard planes of his face still locked in rigid discipline, until he saw her expression. The glassy sheen in her eyes. The way the plush curve of her lips pressed tight to keep them from trembling. In an instant, his features softened. Just enough to steal her breath. As though all the brittle armor he carried was for everyone but her.

For a moment, neither of them moved. Then, almost shyly, she tipped her chin up, silently pleading for something she couldn't name. Malec studied her, and some unspoken understanding flickered behind his tan eyes. His hand lifted. Slowly. Gently. He brought his glass to her mouth, the etched crystal catching candlelight in delicate sparks.

He didn't speak. Just offered her the drink as though it were the simplest thing in the world. As though he already knew she needed it. Her heart stuttered. She blinked, stunned by the quiet, unassuming kindness of it.

Then, with a shaky breath, she placed her soft lips on the glass and took a sip. Sweet warmth slid over her tongue, rich with something honeyed and sharp that made her chest bloom with heat. The alcohol went straight to her head, softening the edges of her panic.

He must drink it for the same reason, she thought dazedly. To drown the noise. To quiet the ache of being surrounded by people who would never understand him.

When she lowered her gaze, she felt his eyes on her, steady and unguarded. And for just a heartbeat, she didn't feel like a captive. She felt like an accomplice, equally trapped in a place neither of them belonged. Melodie glanced to her left, and froze.

An Awyan male approached through the milling crowd, tall and unhurried, as if the noise and ceremony were for lesser creatures. His robes were a pale, whispering gray that shifted with his stride, the hems lined with embroidered sigils in delicate threads of moonlit silver. The fabric caught the lantern light in ghostly ripples, every stitch painstakingly precise.

His hair was long, white as polished bone, drawn back in a loose tie that left a few artful strands to drift against the hard cut of his jaw. They gleamed like silk as he moved. And when he lifted his head, she saw his eyes, crystalline, glacial, impossibly bright. They weren't the warm gold of Malec's or the burnished copper of the palace guards. These were cold. Pale. Like something carved from winter itself. And they fixed on her.

He didn't look away. Didn't flicker with the usual embarrassment or avarice. His stare was clean and relentless, assessing her with the unsettling patience of a scholar studying a rare specimen.

Melodie's pulse jumped. She held his gaze, refusing to be the first to back down. But when he smiled, slow and razor-sharp, something in her gut shifted uneasily.

He said something to Malec then, his voice low and unhurried. She couldn't make out the words, but she felt the change in Malec as clearly as a drop in temperature. The big elf's shoulders went rigid, his jaw ticking in a way she'd learned meant barely-contained fury.

Whatever the stranger had said, it had landed like a blade. But the stranger only smiled wider, as if Malec's anger was exactly the reaction he wanted. Then he turned fully to her. And reached out.

His hand was cool as it settled lightly on her bare arm, fingers long and elegant. She didn't pull away. She'd been touched like this before, handled, inspected, appraised like some valuable piece of contraband. She knew how to keep her face still.

But she hadn't learned how to prepare for what came next. Because when he spoke again, without moving his lips, without a sound at all, his voice slid straight into her thoughts. It wasn't like hearing. It was like being pierced, something smooth and invasive slipping into the softest parts of her mind.

"Hello, little star."

Her breath caught. The room spun.

"Strange, wild little thing."

She looked at him in horror, but his mouth didn't move.

"Do not be alarmed. You are not broken. Just... open."

Her heart thundered in her chest. *What is this?* she thought.

"You hear me. Good."

"How are you doing this?"

"Because I can. And you can. It is not speech, it is thought, distilled."

She clenched her jaw, eyes narrowing.

"You may call me Surin," the voice added smoothly, *"though some may call me Father."*

Melodie blinked. *Father?*

The voice was amused. *"Yes. To the one you follow. The one brooding beside you like a stormcloud. Malec."*

Her eyes darted between them, and *then* she saw it. The resemblance. The height. The posture. The shared intensity in their gaze. She'd never even considered that Malec even had a father.

"Silly little thing, now you understand," Surin chuckled at her revelation that Malec had origins as though he was some creature conjured up by the fates.

She felt cold all over. She swallowed hard, but managed to keep her face composed. The crowd continued laughing, unaware of the war suddenly happening behind her eyes. But Malec was no longer looking at the nobles. He was staring at Surin. And his expression made it clear, This visit was *not* welcome. And she? She had just become part of something much, much deeper.

Her heart pounded like a war drum beneath her ribs. This wasn't just dangerous, it was lethal. He was inside her mind. No barriers. No language. No lies. She could deceive Malec with a coy smile. She could manipulate Luko with silence. But Surin? Surin could hear everything. Every flicker of fear, every rebellion wrapped in a thought, he knew before it left her tongue.

"Would you like to come with me?"

His voice didn't pass through her ears. It slid directly into her skull, smooth, soft, but as sharp as ice. Melodie stiffened. She had come prepared to flirt, to tempt the right noble, to become the prize of someone too weak to truly guard her. But this? This was *not* what she expected. Surin was not weak. And he wasn't playing.

"Why?" she thought, testing the connection.

Surin tilted his head slightly, studying her like a puzzle he was beginning to solve. There was a stillness in him that unnerved her, a grace that felt ancient, and a weight that told her he didn't have to raise his voice to be deadly.

"You are rare," he said, as if that were all the reason he needed. *"It is not often I meet a canariae with intelligence. Or... defiance."*

Her stomach tightened. She didn't like the way he said *"canariae"*, like she was a strange artifact in a museum case.

She narrowed her eyes and snapped back mentally, *"Is that supposed to be a compliment?"*

He smiled. *"It's an observation. I don't give compliments."*
His presence crept closer, not with threat, but with calm pressure.
"You are wary of me," he noted, gazing at her without blinking.
"Shouldn't I be?" she replied.
His eyes glinted, pale and guarded. *"Perhaps."*
Melodie's mind raced. If she could find a way closer to the capital, to someone with power and a looser grip, maybe she could still escape. But just as the thought formed, Surin cut through her strategy.
"Malec will not let you go," he said smoothly. *"And you know this."*
Her pulse skipped. Of course he'd heard that. He was *in her mind.* Damn him. She needed control. Fast. So she deflected.
"Can all Awyan do this?" she asked mentally.
"No," Surin replied with a soft chuckle. *"Your master could, if he tried."*
That made her blink. *"What do you mean?"*

"He already uses his gift," Surin murmured, casting a brief glance toward Malec before returning to her. *"Just... differently."*

Her brows furrowed. *"How?"*

"He reads people," he explained. *"Not the way I do. He doesn't invade minds. But he sees. He notices. Body language, breath,*

hesitation. It's instinct. He doesn't even realize he's doing it. But he's always observing."

Melodie froze. That... that was important.

If Malec was trained, conditioned, to interpret reactions, then that meant she could use it. If she could keep her face neutral, her body still, her breath steady... she might be able to hide from him in plain sight. Trick him. Mislead him.

"Clever girl," Surin whispered in her mind.

She stiffened. That nervous flicker of her mouth pressed together. Damn it. She'd forgotten, he was still in there. Still observing. And listening like a mind creeper. Surin's smile deepened and he chuckled softly, warm and infuriating.

"Do not fret, little canariae. Your secret is safe with me."

Melodie didn't trust him. Not for a moment. But she had just learned something more valuable than anything she could have hoped for. Malec could be fooled. And now? She was going to learn how.

Malec stood at the edge of the crowd, jaw flexing as Surin worked his magic on his canariae. The sight of her, surrounded by Awyans with eyes hungry and bold, made his blood burn. They all stared at her—males and females—measuring her worth, imagining her as a thing to be claimed. The very idea of it twisted something ugly inside him. In that moment, his decision crystallized. He was finished with this court, with its velvet-draped decadence and scheming nobility. After the party, he would go straight to the King and make it clear: he was done.

He would take her with him—north, to the High North, back to his stronghold built from frost and stone, far from their prying eyes and covetous hands. And most of all, far from his nosy father. There, she would belong to no one but him.

Malec's jaw locked as he watched his father linger beside her. The way Surin's pale fingers brushed against her arm, it ignited something molten in his chest. He hated it. Hated that she didn't cower. Hated the flicker of curiosity in her eyes, the tilt of her chin as she smiled just enough to appear coy. She was playing the game. And Surin, with his ever-calm demeanor and predator's patience, was indulging her.

"What are you scheming with that stormy look, little canariae? Dreaming of our destruction?" Surin's voice slid into her thoughts, silken and faintly mocking, the sound curling with amusement.

Her spine straightened. She didn't react outwardly, too many eyes were on her, but her breath caught. He was speaking to her mind again. No words passed his lips, yet his presence filled her skull like smoke.

"Is it normal," she thought cautiously, *"for Awyans to be this... possessive?"*

Surin chuckled in her mind, the sound almost affectionate.

"Possessive, yes. But Malec?" He studied her face as if he were deciphering a puzzle. *"No. Malec has never reacted this way to a female of his own kind, let alone to a Canariae. This is... surprising."*

She narrowed her eyes slightly. *"Why? Because I'm lesser?"*

Surin tilted his head. *"Because it is almost unheard of, its almost as though its..."*

A pause. She caught the hesitation in his aura before he masked it. *"What, for crying out loud spit it out?"* she pressed.

He didn't answer right away. When he finally did, the words came softly.

"There is an old story. A myth."

Her brow twitched. *"Oh god, here we go with the magic and fairies bullshit."*

"Saen'trien," he said, as if the word were meaningless, but she heard the tightness in it.

"And that is?"

"Just superstition," he said, waving a hand as if batting away a troublesome insect. *"A bedtime tale we tell Awyan children to keep them dreaming of fated lovers. It's a type of imprinting, an awakening of instinct. Soul memory. The idea that something in you recognizes something in them. Like a spiritual alarm bell ringing in your blood."*

His mouth curved into a thin, ironic smile.

"But it isn't real. A convenient story to explain inconvenient feelings. And if, by some madness, it were real..." He inclined his head, voice softening into pitying amusement. *"It certainly would not happen with a Canariae."*

That last part came a little too quickly.
Melodie studied him. *"But you don't believe that."*
Surin smiled, as if he'd expected her to say that. He tapped the rim of his goblet with a pale finger.
"You are a very clever canariae. That may be your most dangerous trait."

Out loud, he murmured in Awyan, "Shaé'vala torin'kai," before lifting his cup to sip and echoing it into her mind, *'You are a curious thing'.*

Across the room, Malec never took his eyes off them.
He was stiff, silent, enigmatic, but Melodie could feel the fury rolling off him like smoke from a dying fire. Every time Surin leaned closer to her, Malec's grip around his goblet flexed, the silver rim creaking faintly under the pressure of his fingers.
He shifted his weight from one boot to the other, then back again, as if the act of moving, of feeling the solid floor beneath him, might keep him from acting on the wild, crackling impulse coiling in his chest. He rubbed a thumb over the etched rim of the goblet in a slow, repetitive circle, grounding himself in the texture of the cool metal. The tiny friction, the certainty of it, was something to hold onto when everything else felt like it was falling apart.

When Surin placed a single hand at the small of her back and guided her forward through the circle of nobles, Malec's jaw tensed so hard a muscle jumped in his cheek. His breathing changed, slower, deliberate, like he was counting each inhale to keep from lashing out. And then, as Surin leaned in to murmur something low against her ear,

Malec moved forward a step, quiet and precise as a stalking predator. His gaze never wavered. He simply watched them, his thumb still tracing that same groove in the goblet, as though it was the only thing tethering him to patience. He had reached the end of whatever restraint he had left. In one silent motion, he began to cross the room to collect her. Then.

"Malec."

The smooth, commanding voice sliced through the hum of the gathering. It stopped them both mid-step. Melodie didn't have to turn to know who it was. The King. Malec turned slowly, his jaw tight. The King stood at the base of the grand staircase, one hand resting lazily on the rail, a wine glass raised in the other. A smirk played across his face.

"You don't look like you are enjoying yourself?" the King asked with mock amusement.

Malec's eyes darkened. "You already know the answer."
The King chuckled, swirling his wine.
"Come now, my stoic cousin. It was only a little fun."
"Parading my canariae around as entertainment is not what I call 'fun.'"

"Oh?" the King mused. "Then what would you call it? Training? Or perhaps... you simply don't like sharing?"

Melodie felt Malec's hand twitch on her arm. A warning. The King's smirk widened.

"You must sell her soon, Malec," he said airily. "You can't keep holding onto her forever."

The words landed like a blade to the gut. Melodie's pulse quickened. She risked a glance at Malec. His expression was ice, but behind it, his eyes burned.

"Or do you plan to keep her?" the King added with a tilt of his head. A ripple of soft laughter moved through the nobles.

"If he won't sell her," a noblewoman called, "I will offer five hundred gold."

"I'll offer six," another said.

"Seven."

Melodie stiffened. She was no longer a person in their eyes. She was an item. An investment. Malec's spine straightened.

"Enough."

The word was quiet, but the entire room froze. He released her arm and stepped forward, slow and deliberate. The air thickened around him, vibrating with tension. The King raised an eyebrow, clearly entertained. "Is there a problem?"

"She is not for sale," Malec said flatly.

"Not even for a thousand?" the King teased.

"Not even for the throne."

That stilled even the laughter. Nobles went quiet. The King's smile faltered. Then he chuckled, low and indulgent.

"Well, well. It seems my dear Malec has grown... attached."

Malec said nothing. After a beat, the King finished his wine and handed the goblet to a nearby servant.

"Very well," he said, his tone clipped now. "She is yours. For now."

He turned and strode off, but the air remained charged. The moment he was gone, Malec stood still, staring at the empty space where the King had stood, shoulders rising and falling with slow, measured breaths. Then he turned to Melodie. His voice was low, threaded with an edge she'd come to recognize as final. He spoke in Awyan, the words sliding over her like foreign silk, harsh and beautiful all at once.

"Veyr'an thi'shal doran," he said.

She didn't know the translation. But she didn't need it. The way his hand closed around her wrist, firm but not cruel, the way his eyes locked onto hers and didn't waver, said enough.

They were leaving.

Chapter 11

Learning the Enemy's Tongue

Malec didn't bother asking. He never did. His words landed with the force of a thrown blade, sharp and absolute.

"You're coming with us," he snapped, not glancing up from the leather straps he wrenched tight around the battered satchel near the hearth.

The tension in his hands was barely restrained violence—he was moving with the urgency of someone barely holding himself together, as if every wasted second risked something irretrievable. Luko stood frozen by the door, heart drumming so loud he wondered if Malec could hear it.

"To the High North?" he managed, his voice too thin, too hopeful. Malec's eyes shot up, pale and fierce, pinning him like prey.

"Yes. We leave before dawn," he said, the words crackling, brittle as frost. "Pack only what you need."

There was a feverish demand in his tone—he wasn't inviting, he was ordering, and even the shadows in the room seemed to obey.

Luko's hand tightened on his satchel.

"Why me?"

The question tumbled out, edged with nerves, desperate for an answer that might anchor him. This time Malec turned fully, standing tall and severe, every inch of him radiating command.

"Because she cannot speak our tongue," he growled, his voice lowering, dangerous.

He jerked his chin toward Melodie—her knees hugged to her chest, eyes glassy and hollow, lost in the fire's glow as if searching for a door back to her world.

"You will teach her. She will learn our language. And you will make certain of it."

No room for misunderstanding. No chance to refuse.

Luko inhaled, pulse hammering, trying to quiet the wild hope stirring in his chest. He hated the way Malec reduced him to a tool, but the truth shone bright and terrible: he wanted this. Needed it. Needed her—the mystery she carried, the impossible miracle of her presence.

He nodded, mouth dry, fighting to keep his eagerness hidden. "Yes. Understood."

Inside, Luko's mind swirled with a kind of stunned, crackling hunger—not for a mere Canariae, for he'd known many, studied them, catalogued their ways. But her... Melodie was different. She was the root, the origin, the living myth—the human ancestor every Canariae legend circled but none had truly believed existed. She was the key to every question his research could never answer, the living bridge to a lost epoch he'd only glimpsed through fractured data and the bones of ancient texts.

He could almost taste the possibilities: to hear her language in its undiluted form, to see human cognition untainted by centuries of adaptation, to witness in her every movement the primal source from which his people had sprung. She was a scientist, yes, but more than that—a living time-capsule, a ripple from a vanished world.

Across the fire she sat, knees drawn tight, grief and wonder flickering across her face. And he would be the one to guide her, to teach her, to learn from her. The chance was terrifying, intoxicating. He would not squander it.

The journey north was brutal in its beauty. For days, they rode across a barren white desert of snow and rock, the cold so sharp it sliced through Melodie's borrowed furs and bit her skin raw. Black trees with evergreen leaves rose like sentinels from the drifts, their branches heavy with frost.

At night, the wind howled across the plains, carrying the scent of pine and something older, wilder.

When they finally reached the fortress, she almost didn't see it at first. It rose from the mountainside like a shadow given form, massive walls of matte black stone, red-tiled roofs sloping in graceful tiers that reminded her of the feudal castles she'd seen in Earth's history archives. Stark, imposing, beautiful in their ruthless symmetry. Banners marked with a single silver fox rippled in the wind, declaring exactly who ruled here. And Malec...

He didn't just belong to this place. He was it. Its feudal lord in everything but name. The cold authority in his stride, the way every guard and servant bowed as he passed, it all confirmed what she'd known from the moment she first laid eyes on him: this was a male who would never surrender an inch of his territory.

Inside, the air was warmer, filled with the crackle of braziers and the faint resinous tang of crackling cedar. Melodie, for her part, was no more impressed. She was perched at a small wooden desk in one of the fortress's studies, hunched over yet another lesson in the language she had begun to despise. A narrow window behind her framed the endless snowfields, blinding in the midday light.

"Sit straight," Luko muttered, reaching over to adjust the writing tablet with the same exasperated patience he'd shown her every morning since they'd arrived.

Melodie rolled her eyes but sat up, her spine stiff, fingers clenched around the absurdly delicate Awyan quill.

"I don't see why I have to learn this stupid language," she snapped in English, her breath fogging in the chill draft sneaking under the door.

Luko exhaled slowly, rubbing his temple like he was fighting off a headache.

"Because Malec said so. And because it will help you."

She scoffed, flicking an irritated look at the ink pot.

"Help me how? So I can understand all the insults they throw at me?"

His gaze lifted to hers, steadier than she expected. "So you can fight back."

Her mouth snapped shut. That... was actually a decent point.

Grumbling, she dipped the quill again and stared at the rows of jagged, elegant symbols crawling across the page like tiny blades.

"Your people don't make this easy," she muttered.

Luko flipped to the next page in his leather-bound reference book, a tired smirk tugging at the corner of his mouth.

"Yes, trust me. This much I know."

Melodie fell silent for a while, trying to copy the foreign letters, each one more impossible than the last. Her hand cramped. Her neck ached. The snow outside the stone windows kept falling in relentless curtains of white. She felt like she was fading, disappearing behind all that cold. She glanced toward the fire, then toward the empty chair where Malec sometimes sat, silent and leering like a predator waiting for something to move.

"Why did he take me from the capital?" she asked suddenly, her voice quieter now. More tired than angry.

Luko froze mid-page flip. He didn't answer.

"Luko," she said again, firmer this time, steadier. "Tell me the truth."

He stared at a blot of dried ink on the table, his jaw flexing. Eventually, he set his book down and sighed.

"He want you away from nobles."

"Why?" she asked. "He doesn't even like me. He treats me like trash."

Luko's brows lifted slightly. "You remember what they say at party. The offers made. The way they look at you."

"I could've handled it."

"I know. But that not point," Luko said softly. "It not about if you able to handle. It about if he could."

Melodie blinked.

Luko studied her with a conflicted expression.

"They treating you like a thing. And Malec... don't like seeing that."

She scoffed. "Oh please, like he doesn't treat me the same."

"No," Luko said. "He do not. Not really. Not anymore."

She narrowed her eyes. "He ignores me. Keeps me locked up in this frozen castle. He doesn't feed me unless he feels like it, barely speaks unless he's ordering me around, and pretends I'm not in the room when I ask questions."

"He try stay away," Luko said quietly.

Melodie blinked again, thrown. "What?"

"He keep distance on purpose. Because he not trust himself."

That silenced her. Luko leaned forward, lowering his voice like he was sharing a secret he'd never say out loud again.

"Malec... he not process want like others. He not know how to want and be gentle. They teach him, all feeling is weakness. If he cannot measure, cannot predict, it make him... uneasy. He does not trust what he can't see coming."

He paused, glancing at her to see if she followed, searching her face for a flicker of understanding.

"When he care for something, it break his order inside. His mind need rules, patterns, lines he can follow. You... you are not pattern. You are alive, full of change. He look at you, he feel something wild, something he cannot fit in a box, cannot control. This, for him, is threat. Not because you are threat, but because he cannot sort you. He cannot make you fit his world."

Luko shifted his weight, his voice dropping to something almost gentle.

"This why he seem cold. Or cruel. Is not only arrogance. He is... confused. He does not know how to be close to something he cannot understand. No one ever teach him."

Melodie stared at him. Her mouth had gone dry.

"He fight you because he want you," Luko continued. "He deny you because acknowledging Melodie... mean surrender part of himself."

She swallowed. "But why me?"

"I not know exactly," Luko admitted. "He never been like this before. Not even with own kind. Not with elfess or noble. Never."

Melodie looked down at the tablet in front of her. Her voice came out barely above a whisper.

"Then what's wrong with him?"

Luko gave a crooked, bitter smile, his gaze darting toward the shadows before settling back on her.

"Maybe he Saen'trien, you know."

She blinked at him, frustration and fatigue tangled in her voice.

"Surin said that too. But what does that even mean, really?"

Luko shifted, mouth twisting as if the words were hard to pull from his own language.

"It old Awyan myth, yes. Most think is just story for scaring young ones. But if is real? If warrior does imprint, " He hesitated, rolling the thought around, searching for the right words. "It change everything. The warrior... he cannot think same. Cannot want same. Is like... every rule, every wall inside, break at once. Saen'trien is not love, not just bond. It's something deeper. Like piece of his soul wake up and demand."

He studied her face, voice rough but earnest.

"If Malec has this for you... he not just obsessed. He lost. Angry with himself. Because everything inside, training, pride, even fear, none of it matter now. You make him weak, and he not know how to survive weak. It make him desperate to control, to hurt, to push you away and pull you close all at once. He blame you for the ache. But really, he angry because you show him he is not made of stone."

Melodie stared into the fire, heart drumming in her chest, words settling in like stones.

"So I'm not a prisoner," she said, voice barely above a whisper. "I'm... a threat."

Luko's eyes softened, his accent heavier as he answered, "Yes. To his pride. To everything he believe about himself. You make him powerless, Melodie. And Malec, he never, not once, let himself be powerless before."

Melodie's fingers brushed over the edge of the table. She didn't know what to say. The fire crackled beside them. The wind howled outside the stone walls. And for once, the silence wasn't cold.

She looked at him and folded her arms. "What does he want with me?"

Luko hesitated again, then leaned forward, resting his elbows on the table. "I don't think he know," he admitted.

Melodie frowned. "That makes no sense. He dragged me all the way up here to his ice palace and doesn't know why?"

Luko gave a crooked smirk. "That is what funny about Malec. He not always need a reason. He just... do what he want."

She snorted. "Great. So I'm stuck with an overgrown child who acts on impulse. Lovely."

Luko chuckled, but his golden eyes flicked back toward her, more thoughtful now. Luko chuckled, but his eyes turned serious.

"Tell me... he ever lose?"

She blinked. "What?"

"Malec. You see him lose before?" Her mind sifted through everything. No. Never.

"You see," Luko nodded. "He... always win. Always. Since we are boys. No matter what. He want, he *get*."

He looked down for a moment, then said, "That power... it change mind. Makes... strange."

Melodie tilted her head. "Like what?"

"Obsessive."

The word hit heavy.

Melodie sat up straighter. "Hmm, that word again, obsession."
Luko nodded. "If he want, he... must have. He not stop."
She searched his face. "And he never obsessed over a woman before?"
"Never," Luko said, firm. "Not even once. You... you first."
"Because I'm Canariae?"

"No," Luko said. "Because you... you fight him. You don't bow.
Don't obey. He don't know what to do with you."

He smiled faintly. "Malec... he love to fight."
Melodie's thoughts tangled in heat and confusion. So that was it?
Not love. Not even want. Just a challenge. She tapped the table, thinking.
"What if I stop being a challenge?"
"Then maybe... he stop want you," Luko said simply.

She smirked. "But... what if I challenge him differently, in a
way only a woman could?"

His brows furrowed. "Hmn, yes. Wait, what?" Then they lifted. "Ah."
She leaned back. "He's attracted to me. Even if he won't admit it."
Luko rubbed his head. "Yes. This why... no good idea. Fire is hot."
"But I like fire," she said sweetly.
He groaned. "No. Be careful."

"I don't have time to be careful," Melodie said, stretching. "I
need to go back to the capital. If the best way is making Malec
want me enough to bring me himself..."

She looked over her shoulder, eyes sharp and focused.
"Then I do what I must."
Luko sighed, voice low. "Please... be smart."
"Oh, I'll be careful," she said, grin widening. "But Malec?"
She looked toward the fire, her shadow long in the orange light.
"He doesn't stand a chance."
Luko stared at her in silence.
Then, softer: "You know why he hurt you, yes?"

She turned, surprised. "Because I piss him off?"

He shook his head. "Because... you make him weak...scared. And Malec... he never weak. Until you."

Melodie's breath caught. "I honestly thought he hated me."

"No. He... try not need you," Luko said. Then, quietly: "But he already do."

Melodie sat in silence for a long moment, her mind tangled in everything Luko had just said. Weakness. Obsession. Fire. And her.

She didn't know what to do with that. Didn't know what could be done. But what she did know, what she could control, was herself. So she took a breath, let it out slowly, and lifted her chin.

"I don't know what I'm supposed to do with any of this," she muttered, standing and brushing imaginary dust from her tunic. "But I'm not going to fall apart over a warlord with control issues."

Luko watched her, quiet.

She turned toward the desk again, reaching for her quill, her voice dry as she added, "Also, we seriously need to work on your English."

Luko blinked. "What is... In-gal-ich?"

Melodie stared at him, then let out a weary sigh, dragging a hand down her face.

"It's the language I'm speaking," she said flatly. "This. What I'm saying to you right now."

"Oh," Luko said brightly, as if she'd just taught him the name of a new fruit.

"Inglich."

"English," she corrected, emphasizing the word.
"In...guh...lish."
She sighed again, pinching the bridge of her nose.

"Close enough." Then, with a wry smile creeping onto her lips, she added under her breath, "This is gonna take a while."

Chapter 12

The Silver Brand

Malec stood at the center of the great hall, silver hair catching the light, his posture a sculpture of discipline, shoulders back, chin high, presence commanding. The hall around him was vast and austere: black-streaked stone walls rose to a soaring glass ceiling, where harsh daylight spilled in molten sheets across the floor. Iron beams gleamed above, and firelight from the distant hearth shimmered on polished wood below. A long golden-orange rug cut through the center, catching the light as it led from the rune-carved doors at either end to the hearth's pulsing heat. Portraits lined the walls, their worn frames etched with symbols whose meanings Melodie couldn't guess. The painted faces stared down, regal and watchful.

Guards and servants lined the walls, casting long shadows, their gazes drawn to Malec. He made everything else fade. He waited, still and silent, until the room hushed, nothing but soft boots, breath, and the creak of the high beams overhead.

Melodie sat stiffly on a narrow bench near the dais, arms locked across her chest. Her chin lifted in defiance, but her mouth was drawn tight. Firelight cut across her skin, turning her dark eyes to liquid embers. Beside her, Luko shifted anxiously, hands twitching, gaze flicking between her and Malec as if already regretting what came next.

Everyone watched Malec. He watched them in return, his gaze drifting from face to face with clinical detachment. Even as silence fell, his expression remained withdrawn, no impatience, no crack in the mask. He stood like a fixed point in a room on the verge of collapse.

Malec's voice cut through the hall, smooth and commanding. "Zher'miraz giremat'hi, Melodien."

Luko's shoulders drooped. He turned to Melodie, wincing slightly. "He say... you not Melodie no more."

Melodie's brows pulled tight. "Excuse me?"
She didn't need a perfect grasp of their language to feel the slap in that sentence. Her voice rang through the hall, sharp and clear. Luko didn't even bother softening it, he translated it word for word. Malec's

gaze didn't waver. His expression remained aloof, but something, some flicker of control or satisfaction, glinted behind his eyes.

Malec took a measured step closer, his tone unchanged. "Sem'kuvarai veer nor'kai'thalien."

"He say... you get new name. One for... place here. Title-bond," Luko muttered.

Melodie's heart hammered.

"My *place*?" she snapped. "And what place is that exactly?!"

Again, Luko translated, his words clipped. He didn't like this any more than she did. Malec stepped forward, slowly, deliberately. The fire behind him painted his silver hair in copper. He looked taller than usual, his presence heavy as a thunderhead. When he stopped just in front of her, he didn't raise his voice.

The final blow came cold and low. "Ser'thuga'em. Gar'ukh veer'nar A'veran sel Ka'tanari."

"He say... you his. All will know. By his House... Silver Fox rite."

The silence that followed was suffocating. Melodie felt her name being stripped from her, not by choice, but by decree. A ripple of sound moved through the crowd like a breeze, murmurs, soft laughter, whispers. A few of the castle maids lowered their eyes. A few of the soldiers smirked. And Melodie, Melodie felt something break.

You belong to him. The words struck like a lash.

She curled her lip, hands clenched at her sides.

"That's what this is? You couldn't lock me in a cage so now you want to brand me like livestock? Rename me like I'm some dog you picked up off the street?"

Luko didn't even wait for Malec, he translated before the elf could speak.

Malec met her gaze, calm on the surface but burning just beneath. His jaw twitched faintly. She wasn't wrong, but she wasn't right, either.

This wasn't about breaking her. This was about claiming her. Keeping her. Making it known to the entire court, and most of all, to his cousin, that no one else could touch her. That no noble or soldier or smug politician could buy her, steal her, or whisper about her like a piece of fruit in the market. That she was his. But Melodie didn't know that. She couldn't understand the nuance of the language, the tradition, the politics behind the act. She only heard the erasure of her name. Her self. And it enraged her and rightfully so.

"This is spite," she hissed. "You're doing this to punish me. To humiliate me."

She took a step toward him, head high.

"But guess what, Silver Fox? You don't get to rewrite who I am just because your fragile little ego can't handle the fact I don't want you."

Luko's eyes widened. He didn't translate that. He didn't have to. The venom in her tone carried it well enough. Malec's lips parted slightly, and for the first time, something uncertain passed through his expression. But the damage was done.

"I'm not your pet project. I'm not some thing you can just train," Melodie snapped, her hands fisting around her knees as if she could anchor herself with the pain.

"You can chain my body, but you'll never own me."

Luko, still trying to remain neutral, translated with tight lips and the same venom she'd used. His glance flicked nervously between the two as the weight of the room thickened. Malec didn't move at first. He simply stood there, expression like stone, his eyes fixed on her with that maddening calm, like a predator that didn't need to growl to remind you it had fangs. Then he spoke again, low and level in Awyan, the syllables smooth and almost amused.

"Veyra'ti, kiir canariae," he said.

Luko hesitated before translating, his voice dry. "He say... you will learn, little canariae."

Melodie let out a bitter laugh that cracked through the silence like ice breaking on a frozen lake.

"Oh, I'll learn, alright," she snapped. "I'll learn exactly how to suffocate him in his sleep."

Luko snorted unexpectedly, then coughed into his fist. Malec's brow twitched.

"She... she says she will suffocate you in your sleep," Luko finally managed, barely containing his laughter.

The tension in the great hall fractured, just slightly, as muffled gasps and poorly stifled snickers rippled through the crowd. Luko lost control entirely, doubling over with laughter.

"Suffocate," he wheezed, tears starting to prick the corners of his eyes. "Oh stars, she is bold!"

Malec's jaw ticked once, a flash of warning before the storm. Then, with a force that seemed to bend the very air, he moved. One heartbeat, he stood alone at the hall's center; the next, he was upon her. He seized Melodie by the waist, dragging her so abruptly against him that the breath left her lungs in a single stunned gasp. The sound of it was swallowed by the thunder of his mouth as it crashed down over hers.

There was nothing soft or searching about the kiss. It was a mark, a brand, his claim. The press of his lips was hard, almost bruising, all heat and command. In that instant, the world went bright and unsteady around them. Melodie's body stiffened, her arms caught between striking and surrender, her thoughts scattering like startled birds. All around them, the glass ceiling shivered with the sudden force, and the torches along the stone walls flared higher, flames snapping and swirling as if some wild storm had been summoned into the heart of the room. The bystanders awkwardly looked around as the room flickered with unstable candlelight and electrically charged air.

Malec's magic, usually held tight as a fist, spilled from him, ribbons of power twining through the space, threading from his blood to hers. The Saen'trien, whatever name he'd refused to give it, responded. Recognized. Strengthened. His hold on her grew fierce, almost desperate, and suddenly Malec wasn't just enacting a ritual of dominance, he was coming undone.

Heat shot through his body, molten and dizzying, something primitive and utterly foreign. It was hunger, but not of the flesh alone. It was a gnawing, fevered need that reached all the way to his marrow, a feeling like the first, forbidden taste of ecstasy, like the ache and flash of a body's first undoing. It rattled his bones, made his heart trip and stumble. He parted his lips against hers, needing more, needing everything. He had meant to make a statement, to seal her fate. Instead, Malec felt as if he'd torn open something buried for a lifetime. A rush of frantic arousal crashed through him, hunger and yearning and a strange, terrified joy. He tasted her breath and felt a pull in his blood so strong it threatened to drown him. He'd never known want could be so sharp, so bright, so utterly alive.

For Melodie, the shock was instant, white-hot and furious. She jerked in his grip, rage shoving the magic back into him like a slap. Her lips burned, her heart pounding, not with surrender, but defiance. In that moment, their bodies recognized what their minds wouldn't, the air crackling with something too dangerous to name. She tore free, breathless, the taste of him still searing her mouth. Magic shimmered between them, raw and unresolved, a warning neither could ignore.

Malec stood frozen, chest rising in shallow bursts, his hands suspended mid-reach. His eyes, usually cold, burned gold with confusion and something deeper. His mouth parted, but no words came. He looked at her like she was the answer to every hunger he'd ever buried.

Melodie stared back, trembling, not from fear, but from rage and something hotter she refused to name. Her lips, a shaky line she couldn't quite control, throbbed, nerves still alight from the kiss that had jolted her to the core. And that only made her angrier. But she would not let him see it. Would not give him that victory. Instead, she drew herself up, every muscle tight, her glare a blade.

"You arrogant, power-drunk, soulless cocksucker!" she spat, her voice trembling with rage, every syllable a lash meant to cut him back. "You think you can just take whatever you want? Try it again and I'll show you exactly how much you regret it."

Malec didn't answer. He could only stare, unsteady, as if the world had tilted beneath him, as if her absence against him was a wound. His breath came fast, eyes still faintly glowing, mouth working soundlessly.

Melodie's hands shook as she turned to Luko, her words steel-edged and defiant. "Go on. Translate every damn word."

Luko, who had been stunned silent for once in his life, blinked quickly, then stammered, "He, uh... he already know."

The crowd didn't dare laugh now. The air was still sizzling, the light in the chandeliers trembling as Malec's barely restrained magic cooled like a forge being drowned. Without another word, she turned and strode off, her glare blistering into him, a promise and a warning. Her boots struck the floor in sharp bursts, echoing through wood and stone until the arched doors swallowed her whole.

Malec didn't move. Shoulders set, chin high, he stood as if he'd won. And in a way, he had. The court knew. The servants knew. Even his enemies would think twice now. The message was clear: the Canariae belonged to him.

But as her presence vanished, a hollowness opened in his chest. The smirk faltered. His lips went numb, twitching with the effort to hold pride in place. His fingers still curled, aching for the feel of her waist, haunted by her warmth. He inhaled, expecting triumph, but it snagged in his throat like smoke. Her scent clung to him, sweet and electric. Her hair had brushed his cheek. Her mouth,gods, her mouth,still scorched his. What was meant to be a spectacle had undone him. That kiss hadn't just claimed her. It had fractured something inside him. Her soul had answered his, and the spark of it still surged through his veins.

His heart thundered, wild and uneven, not with satisfaction but hunger. It wasn't just the heat of conquest, nor the surge of dominance. It was need, raw, relentless, bewildering. He'd felt the world narrow to a single point, a collision of lips and want so fierce it left him trembling. The torches had flared; the glass ceiling had shuddered; even the air seemed to pulse in time with their bodies. Something ancient had stirred, something he could neither name nor contain.

Why did the taste of her leave him so undone? Why did his hands ache, his mouth burn, his soul feel as if it had heard its true name for the first time?

Malec pressed a hand to his chest, trying to steady the riot inside, but there was no peace. Only longing. Sharp, charged, and terrifying in its depth. He, who had mastered control, couldn't comprehend this hungry need for a creature who should have been beneath him, yet left him hollow with wanting. He scowled, jaw pressed until it hurt. Damn her. Damn the wildfire she'd sparked in him, this heat he couldn't smother. Now she was gone, swallowed by stone and glass, and all that remained was the ache.

His hands dropped to his sides, curling into fists. Around him, the hall remained heavy with silence, eyes observing, waiting. Luko stood among them, pale and wordless, as if he'd forgotten what he came to say. Malec's gaze swept over them, cold and sharp as a blade.

"Out," he said, low and even. No one moved, not at first. He let his head tilt, voice dropping to a warning, iron and ice. "All of you."

The spell broke; chairs scraped, boots thudded against golden wood, and in seconds the hall was emptying, the sounds of obedience echoing in the long room. Only Luko remained, lingering with some question trembling behind his eyes. Malec didn't look at him.

"You too."

Luko hesitated, then retreated, the doors swinging shut behind him with a shuddering thud. At last, Malec was alone. And still the heat raged beneath his skin. He lifted a hand, thumb pressing to his mouth, tracing the place where hers had met his. His breath came rough and hot, stuttering in his chest. *What magic was that? What in the gods' names had she done to him?*

He tried to make sense of it. She wasn't Awyan. Not kin. Not his bondmate. Nothing that fit the ancient rules he'd lived by. And yet, the moment their mouths met, everything collapsed, order, logic, control. It wasn't tenderness. It was hunger, sharp and consuming. It felt like his magic had leapt toward hers, recognizing something he couldn't name, something that didn't care about bloodlines or laws. Her fury, her resistance, only deepened the need. And now, with her gone, her absence echoed louder than her presence ever had, a drumbeat under his skin that refused to fade.

That was the worst of it, the senselessness. He didn't want this craving or the way his body still hummed with her memory. He wanted silence. Control. To be whole again. But nothing worked. With a low growl, Malec turned and stalked down the corridor, each step clipped with restrained fury. Two servants shrank from his path, vanishing into the stone, but he barely noticed. He saw only her glare. Her mouth. The need he couldn't master.

The doors shut with a heavy thud, sealing Malec in silence. Alone at last, but the quiet only amplified the ache in his chest, pulsing through every nerve. He crossed to the sideboard, grabbed the first bottle, and poured without care. The liquor scorched his throat, but it wasn't enough. He drank again, knuckles tight on the crystal glass.

Her ghost clung to him, taste, scent, the scorch of her mouth. He tried to drown it in spirits, but it only stoked the fire. His body still hummed where she'd touched him. His jaw ached from how hard he clenched it.

This wasn't about courtly power anymore. That kiss had cracked something deep. What frightened him most was how badly he wanted it again. Her again.

He closed his eyes, trying to summon control. But the fever of her burned on, and he stood there, trembling, breath uneven, unable to purge her from his blood.

The cold wind howled between the stone pillars of the barracks yard, but Malec barely felt it. His breath misted in the early light as he moved like a blade himself, cutting, pivoting, striking with lethal accuracy. Each clash of swords was a beat in a rhythm he'd mastered long ago. The soldier across from him panted hard, straining to keep up, but Malec's pace didn't slow. If anything, it quickened, as if he could outrun the thoughts dragging behind his ribs.

Melodie.

Her name soured in his mouth now, too foreign, too soft. It was not an Awyan name. Not fit for the hallways she walked or the eyes that watched her. Not fit for his halls. And certainly not fit to be spoken from his lips when he had to shout her into obedience. He needed something else, something he could own.

A name that would roll from his tongue like command, like poetry. Something sharp enough to remind her that she was his property, yet dignified enough to reflect that wildness in her gaze. That fire. He had no intention of giving her a weak title. She was not meek. No, the Canariae was fierce, and though she did not yet understand her place, he would carve it into her if he had to. And when he did... yes, he wanted to be able to say it. Out loud. Her new name. Beautiful, strong, final.

His brow furrowed as his boot slid through frost and kicked up a cloud of powder. Steel clanged in his ears. He saw again, her eyes locked on his after that kiss, shocked, furious, glowing with a heat that almost burned him. He had felt it. The flicker in his skin, the jolt of something unbidden in his chest. The way the torches had sparked when his lips touched hers, as if his magic was being stirred by her very presence.

Unacceptable.

He moved in a blur, knocking his sparring partner's sword from his hands with a vicious twist of the wrist. The elf landed hard on his back, groaning. Malec didn't wait for an apology. He turned, frustrated, irritated with himself for even letting his concentration slip that long. He needed to rid himself of this nonsense, this strange craving.

Then he felt it: the subtle shift of silence. The deference in the air.

Luko approached from the outer ring of the yard, arms crossed, golden eyes wary beneath his heavy hood. The sparring circle cleared, warriors stepping back respectfully as Malec exhaled through his nose and sheathed his blade with a clean, controlled snap.

"Luko," he said flatly, brushing a hand down his arm to remove a fleck of frost.

Even before the translator spoke, Malec could tell something was on his mind. Something about *her*.

"You were serious?"

Luko's voice broke through the misty air like a stone skipping across still water. He stood with arms folded, golden eyes catching the low winter light, his expression vague but edged with concern.

Malec dragged a towel across his face, wiping the sweat from his brow, letting the sting of cold air bite at his skin.

"About what?"

"About keeping her," Luko said plainly.

There was a slight hitch in Malec's rhythm, barely noticeable to most, but not to someone like Luko who had spent years reading Malec's silences.

Then, without a beat of hesitation, Malec said, "Yes."

Luko exhaled through his nose, shaking his head. "Why, Malec?"

Malec didn't bother looking at him. He tossed the towel onto a bench, flexing his fingers as he stretched the ache from his shoulders.

"She is mine. That is reason enough."

"That's not a reason," Luko replied flatly. "That's an excuse."

Malec turned his head slowly, the edge in his gaze a clear warning. But Luko didn't react. He knew the boundaries. And he also knew Malec needed someone to tell him the truth.

"You know she's different," Luko continued, voice low but firm. "She's not like the others. Not like the Canariae brought here to sing in halls or warm beds in silence. She's not a companion. She's a soldier. I've seen it. And so have you."

Malec scoffed, lips curling in mild disbelief. "A soldier? Her?"

But even as the words left his mouth, a flicker of memory danced across his mind, Melodie's body twisting with practiced ease as she fought off guards twice her size. The way her strikes landed with intention, not panic. Not wildness. Precision. She hadn't been flailing. She had been trained. His jaw tightened.

"Perhaps," he muttered.

Luko's brow rose as he took a step closer, lowering his voice. "You could use her, Malec."

Malec's eyes narrowed. "Use her how?"

"Test her," Luko said simply. "See what she's capable of. She's smart. Brave. She adapts quickly. And she doesn't move in the face of power."

Malec was silent, considering it. A strange hum stirred in his chest. The idea of witnessing her in the arena, matching wits and muscle, it intrigued him.

Finally, he nodded once. "Very well."

He turned to a nearby guard, his tone brisk. "Bring her to the training yard."

The guard bowed low and departed swiftly, boots crunching over snow-dusted stone. Malec sheathed his sword again, rolling out his shoulders with a new, sharper focus.

"Let's see what this 'soldier' of yours is made of."

Fifteen minutes passed. The air grew colder. The soldiers had reset the training circle, waiting quietly, observing. But when the guards returned, they were alone.

Malec's brows dipped. "Where is she?"

One of them stepped forward, lowering his head.

"She's not in her chambers, my lord. We searched the halls, the courtyard, the kitchens... There's no sign of her."

A low pulse of heat began building in Malec's chest. It curled under his ribs like smoke—slow and sharp.

"She's hiding," he said coldly, already turning.

The soldiers scattered on his command, their steps quick and clipped, but he didn't need them to tell him what he already knew. She had slipped away again. His boots hit the stone hard as he strode back into the castle, the weight of his rage dragging behind every step.

Wild. Disobedient. Untamed. She kept testing him. And this time, he would make sure she learned.

The cellar was colder than anywhere else in the stronghold, damp stone, thick with the scent of earth, mildew, and aging wine. Shadows curled between the rows of ancient barrels and battered casks, and a single, sputtering lantern painted pools of gold across the cluttered floor. Melodie sat high atop a stack of wooden crates like some triumphant, drunken monarch, her legs swinging, boots thumping out a careless rhythm. Her wild curls tumbled over her eyes and cheeks, wine staining her plush mouth the color of bruised cherries. In one hand, a half-empty bottle dangled loose; the other waved grandly as she sang to herself, loud and off-key, filling the darkness with her raspy defiance.

She tipped the bottle for another swig, the sharp sweetness radiating a reckless path down her throat. The chill bit at her skin but the wine, and the memory of his mouth, kept her flushed, hot and restless. She could still feel it: the charge that had leapt between their bodies, the impossible surge, like someone had hooked her veins up to a live wire and dared her to let go.

Absurd. It was fucking absurd.

Magic, her ass. She didn't believe in that shit, not really, not the kind that made people ache like that, that made your skin itch for another touch even while your brain screamed for a weapon. Whatever Malec had done, whatever strange curse he'd cracked open with that kiss, it pissed her off almost as much as it scared her.

"Asshole," she muttered, letting the word buzz on full lips.

The thought of stabbing him in his sleep gave her a vicious little thrill. Poison would be funnier, but knives were satisfying. Hell, maybe she'd fuck him first just to really get under his skin, then finish the job, leave him undone, wrung out, and then... gone. She snorted at her own twisted humor, giggling as she swayed atop her throne of crates, the sound bouncing between the barrels.

God, she was drunk. She hated him. Hated how he made her want anything, let alone him. Yet her body still tingled with the aftermath, mouth throbbing where he'd bruised it, every nerve alive and cursing her for it. If he didn't piss her off so much, she might just drag him down here and show him real torment, just to wipe that smug look from his face. Melodie flung her head back and sang louder, letting the notes and laughter and anger spin together in her chest. Maybe she'd survive this place. Maybe she'd burn it down with him in it.

Either way, tonight she was queen of the cellar, her own wild, angry kingdom, where the only law was hers.

Malec halted at the bottom of the cellar stairs, the shadows casting hard angles across his face, eyes narrowing as the scent of cheap wine and rebellion hit him full in the chest. His jaw tightened, a muscle jumping in his cheek. He took in the scene, Melodie perched on her crates, flushed and wild, hair a tangled halo, her bottle held aloft in mock salute. She looked utterly unrepentant, a storm wrapped in silk and defiance.

A sharp, guttural string of Awyan slipped from his lips, low and dangerous: "Or'an deluskha mar'vaer."

Luko, trailing behind and looking like he wished he were anywhere else, flinched at the tone, then attempted a shaky translation.

"He say... uh... you are being reckless. Very, very reckless."

Melodie blinked at them, unbothered, and grinned around the mouth of her bottle. She raised it high, her voice slurred and proud.

"Damn right I am, *hic*."

Luko sighed again, rubbing his temple. "She says... yes. She agrees."
Malec's nostrils flared. *"Vetar'kano."* he snapped.
"She say..." Luko paused, hesitating, "Halt the drinking."

Melodie points at Luko with the wine bottle still in her hand,
"It's he, you idiot, she is female."

Luko tilting his glasses so they are straight on his face stutters,
"Ah, yes... wrong word. I...I am learning. He is male."

Melodie smirked, raising the bottle and tipping it toward her lips.
"Aaaand whaddya gonna do 'bout it, Mr.Tall, Dark, and
Constipated'"
That did it. Malec stepped forward in a flash, snatching the bottle
clean from her grasp.
"Hey!" she yelped, lunging after it like a spoiled child denied dessert.
"Thar'ka sulai na pret," he muttered darkly, holding it high above her
head.

Luko dutifully translated between sighs. "He say... do not
drink like fool. Fool get sick. Fool fall down stairs. Fool... eh...
he mad."

"Well, maybe if I *wasn't* bein' kept in some damn ice box like a
frozen bird," she pointed a finger at Malec, eyes half-lidded, "I
wouldn't *have* to drown m'self in fruit blood, huh?"

Luko blinked. "Fruit... blood?"
"WINE, Luko! It's wine!" she shouted, hiccupping.
Malec had heard enough. He reached down, wrapped his arms
around her waist, and with one sharp heave, tossed her over his shoulder
like she weighed nothing.

"WHAT DA HELL?!" Melodie shrieked, her legs flailing.
"PUT ME *hic* DOWN, YOU OVERGROWN SWAMPY
TOAD!"

Luko blinked, trying not to laugh as he hurried after them. "Oh... oh dear. She is mad now."

"You think?" Malec growled.

"She also called you... uh... swamp toad. It is an insult where she is from, I think."

"*Y'rr a shnitch, Luko!*"
Melodie shouted from over Malec's shoulder, her voice wobbling with drunken fury as she smacked at his back with the grace of a sleepy kitten.

"*Traitorrr! Sssnake! I hope yer boots,*" she hiccupped, "*get stol'n 'n thrown inna lake!*"

Luko raised his hands helplessly.
"I only do my job! And what is... shnitch? This not real word?"
As they passed through the main hall, a few startled servants froze, staring as their commander stomped by with a wriggling, cursing canariae slung like a sack of turnips over his shoulder. Melodie, undeterred by the audience, continued her verbal onslaught, most of it slurred, some of it incomprehensible, all of it passionate.
"Ugly, arrogant, silver-haired bastard,"
"She says you are very... handsome but rude," Luko lied helpfully.
Malec didn't even react. His grip remained firm, one hand braced over the back of her thighs to keep her from wiggling free. He moved like a mountain, one that had absolutely no patience left. They reached her chambers in a hush broken only by the heavy tread of Malec's boots and the soft drag of her own stumbling feet. The servant's quarters were buried so deep in the stronghold that the air itself tasted stale, thick with the scent of damp stone and lingering old ash from long-dead fires. Down a tight, crooked corridor, barely wide enough for two people side by side, Malec stopped at a door warped with age, the wood swollen and splintered.

He didn't bother with gentleness. He shouldered the door open, dragging her behind him, the metal latch scraping loudly against stone. The room inside was cramped and cold, the air sharp with the draft that slipped under the frame. Bare furnishings: a crooked, narrow cot against the far wall, its thin linen coverlet already split to show yellow straw poking through. The armoire beside it sagged, its doors warped and reluctant to close, one hinge squealing in protest whenever the wind gusted.

There was one small, grimy window, just big enough to let in a slice of gray light and a constant, biting draft. The glass was cloudy, streaked with years of neglect, and did nothing to keep out the chill that settled deep in the bones. The floors were cold stone, cracked in places, and scattered with fine dust that never seemed to fully sweep away. There was no rug, no warmth, not even a candle on the little shelf wedged into the corner. It felt less like a bedroom, more like a cell hastily made habitable, a place for the unwanted to sleep and vanish.

With a grunt, Malec shoved her inside, marching straight to the bed. She tried to twist from his grip, but he barely noticed.

"You put me down now or I'll—"

Thump.

He let her drop onto the thin mattress, her limbs bouncing awkwardly before she landed facedown in a pile of wrinkled linen. Melodie groaned into the pillow, her voice muffled and slurred with exhaustion and drink. "This is abuse," she announced, though the words faded into a half-laugh and a wheeze, echoing off the bare stone and into the hollow dark.

Malec simply turned to Luko. "Sarei ta sholim. Vash-na ka tura."

Luko nodded, sighing as he rubbed the back of his neck.

"He say... you stay in here now. And maybe... shut up."

Melodie muttered something rude into the blankets. Luko looked at Malec.

"She did not shut up...But she did not try to run away this time," Luko added under his breath. "So... maybe this is progress?"

But Melodie wasn't listening. She was regarding him with those dark, fire-lit eyes, simmering and estimating beneath heavy lids. A dangerous gleam had settled in her gaze. Slowly, like a predator sensing weakness, she sauntered forward, her boots silent on the stone floor, the hem of her robe brushing around her thighs like a whisper.

Malec didn't move. Didn't breathe.

"Valar sin'dai shavari," he ordered flatly.

Luko, still catching his breath behind them, relayed the command in his broken, gravelly tone. "He say... you stay here. No go."

But Melodie wasn't listening. She was studying him. Eyes dark, fever-bright, and guarded. Despite the wine still buzzing in her bloodstream, she was focused, sharp in the way only someone dangerous could be when drunk. A curl of her lip gave her away, a smirk forming like she knew exactly what she was doing.

Malec's jaw tightened. His spine locked.

"Deyr valen atari?" he asked, voice thick with suspicion. Luko translating between the two as he eyed Melodie with suspicion.

Luko swallowed, glancing at Melodie, and translated in a low voice, "He's asking what you're doing."

Melodie tilted her head, her smirk widening.

"You carried me," she slurred, voice low and heavy with syruped defiance. "All the way here. Like I was yours."

Malec's throat bobbed once as Luko continued to translate. "Sarnai'vel torae," he said before he could stop himself.

Luko hesitated, then mumbled in English with a grimace. "He say... you is his."

Melodie let out a laugh, slurred but wicked. It wasn't a girlish giggle. No, it rolled from her like smoke, seductive, mean, and deliberate.

"So why do you... do you keep actin' like you don't want me?"
She breathed, stepping in close enough for her robe to brush
his legs.

Malec's breath caught, sharp and ragged, as Melodie pressed herself closer, all wine-sweet heat and dangerous laughter. Her hands, small, unsteady, bold with drink and mischief, slid up the planes of his chest, fingers tracing the hard ridge of his collarbone, nails grazing just enough to make him shudder. He tensed, muscles going rigid beneath her touch, but his resolve slipped.

The air between them changed, growing thick, charged, the temperature spiking even as his breath grew cool and shallow. The faint candlelight stuttered and danced, gold flames tilting toward them as if pulled by invisible hands, the shadows shrinking back from the heat that poured from the place her skin met his. He opened his mouth to warn her, to order her away, but no sound came. She leaned in, brazen, breasts pressing lightly to his chest, her trembling hovering so close he could taste her, berry wine and defiance, wildness and want. Her fingers curled at the base of his neck, tugging him down as if daring him to break first, her gaze heavy-lidded and laughing.

Her touch burned right through the fabric, through muscle and bone, searing him to the core. His skin sang for her, every nerve lit and desperate. Malec stood, utterly still, torn between pulling her closer and fleeing from the fire she'd stoked to life inside him.

"I see you," she whispered. "Even if you try to bury it."

Then, her hand slid lower. Slow, deliberate, too much and not enough all at once. Daring him, inviting him, pushing every boundary Malec understood. The world telescoped down to that single, impossible point of contact. His breath caught, violent, sharp, nearly a whimper he could not allow, his entire body snapping rigid beneath her palm. Sensation crashed through him in blinding waves: the heat of her fingers, the fabric yielding beneath, the pressure, the exposure. He was too hard, blood roaring in his ears so loud it drowned out thought. Every nerve ending screamed, his mind fragmenting, unable to process the humiliation and the desperate, animal pleasure twisted so tight he could barely remain upright.

Her smile—gods, that smile split razor-sharp beneath the trembling candlelight. Malec couldn't look away. He fixated on the way her lashes flickered, the glint in her gaze, the precise curl of her lips, cataloging every detail even as the rest of him threatened to collapse. She dragged her hand across him, thumb making an idle, agonizing circle that threatened to burn him alive. It was a sensory onslaught—too much texture, heat, movement. His magic responding instinctively, out of sync with his will. He wanted to stop her, to seize control, but his body refused—betrayed by the roaring need and the way she made him unravel.

Her laughter bright, merciless, ricocheted through the air, slicing right through his panic and hunger. The noise hit like shattered glass, every sound amplified, splintering through him, jangling his nerves.

"Oh," she purred, drawing her hand away with agonizing slowness, as if she could stretch time itself. "Look at that. Guess your body didn't get the memo."

Something inside him snapped. Malec's magic flared, wild and uncontained, prickling over his skin like a swarm of needles. He couldn't control the surge, couldn't mask it. Candlelight bursting with a sharp, startled pop beside them, the smell of burning wax thick and sickly in his nose. He jerked, breath tearing out ragged, raw, his heart stuttering in confusion and shame. Another candle behind her exploded, wax spraying the stone as if his magic needed release as badly as he did.

He staggered back, hands fisting at his sides, his posture rigid, every muscle clamped so tight he thought he'd shatter. Sensation, magic, sound—everything burned too bright, too much. And in the center of the chaos: her. Always her.

Luko flinched so violently it was almost audible, shoulders hunching as if trying to disappear into himself. His gaze ricocheted from Melodie to Malec, panic bleeding across his features.

"Uh... uh... maybe I—go now?" he stammered, voice pitching up as he shuffled sideways, inching toward escape.

Malec said nothing. His throat felt locked, jaw clamped so tight it ached. He stared at her, unable to blink, his focus zeroed in on every detail—her laughter, the cocky tilt of her chin, the way bare skin gleamed in the firelight. The sound of her laughter seemed to fill the whole room, vibrating in his chest and making it hard to breathe. Her scent tangled with the smoke, sharp and wild, hitting him all at once. Every nerve was on fire, every muscle screaming for release or retreat, the memory of her touch branded on him. His thoughts scattered, overwhelmed by the sensation and the need to control it.

Melodie laughed again, the sound even lower now, filled with dangerous amusement.

"Goodnight, then... maaasster," she purred, stretching the last word into a taunt that echoed like a dare.

Luko let out a strangled cough, fumbling for the door, eager to vanish before the tension snapped. Malec's jaw flexed, a sharp tremor rippling down his spine. The urge to seize control, to ground himself in some pattern, was overwhelming but every pattern was broken by her, fractured by the chaos she dragged into his meticulously ordered world. He spun on his heel, coat flaring, each movement stiffer and sharper than the last, a ritual to keep himself contained. If he stayed another heartbeat, if he allowed himself to breathe her in again, he would lose every scrap of discipline and do something—something reckless, irreversible, primal.

He strode out, her laughter chasing him down the hall, searing his senses long after he was gone.

The wind howled against the northern walls of the stronghold, rattling the ancient shutters, cold air needling its way through every flaw in the stone. Yet inside the Silver Fox's master chamber, the chill never reached Malec. The air shimmered, thick and fevered, weighed down by the heat of restless magic. It pressed against the walls, condensed along the floor, pulsing with every uneven beat of his heart. The torches had burned low, flames flickering erratically, their light tugged and warped by the force leaking from his body. Malec writhed atop a tangle of furs, bare skin slick and hot, every muscle drawn tight as a bowstring. His jaw clenched so hard his teeth ached. Even asleep, he couldn't escape her.

He couldn't move. He tried, but he couldn't. He was lying on a bed he did not know, the sheets heavy black velvet stitched in silver, soft but suffocating, holding him captive. The world around him shifted, forest floor beneath his body, pale birch trees arching above, their white trunks spectral in the moonlight. Not the spiked evergreens of his youth, but something gentler, alien, almost holy. The silence was broken only by the gentle coo of doves high above, their songs hauntingly sweet, repeating, soothing, drawing his mind into spirals. He counted the notes, one, two, three, until another sensation pulled him under.

A hand, warm as the sun on black stone, pressed gently to his chest. Malec's breath faltered, chest lifting into the touch against his will. His focus tunneled, every fiber of his being drawn to the exact spot where her palm met his flesh, the world blurring at the edges. He turned his head, needing confirmation, and saw her. His canariae—every detail burned in impossible clarity. Naked, shameless, eyes searing gold and wild in the shadowed light. Her curls framed her face, coiling like ink on silk, and her gaze pinned him with perfect, terrible control.

She traced her hand down the length of his torso, each fingertip sending a ripple of fire beneath his skin. Malec's body betrayed him, hips shifting upward, desperate for more contact even as his mind screamed to resist. Every sensation was too much, her skin, her scent, the subtle pressure of her palm. He tried to speak, to demand she stop, to assert control, but his voice refused. The words were stuck, lost in the thicket of sensation and need.

She leaned in, breath searing his ear, her lips barely grazing him.

"Try to deny it. I dare you." She whispered.

Something broke inside him. Magic sizzled just under the surface, every nerve alight, every breath a battle. She straddled his hips, skin sliding over his, and every point of contact sent a new shockwave through him. He needed to move, needed to anchor himself with touch, so he grabbed her thighs, his grip rough and desperate, fingers memorizing every shape and heat and texture, needing the pattern, the anchor, the realness of her.

Melodie's smile was wicked, sharp, like she knew the chaos inside him and delighted in it.

"There you are," she purred, rolling her hips with slow, deliberate cruelty, drawing out a deep, guttural moan from him.

The sound escaped before he could swallow it. Heat flooded his veins, pleasure so sharp it stung, his body shaking with restraint. The more he tried to clamp down, the more the need burned, overloading him, pain and desire intertwined until he couldn't tell them apart. His magic crackled outward, torchlight flickering, the dreamspace trembling on the edge of shattering. The doves scattered, their flight staccato and jarring, breaking his concentration, and the sheets bunched under his fists. He needed order, needed rhythm, but she made everything disorder, every rule irrelevant.

"You," he managed, voice thick with longing and frustration, "why can't I shake you?"

Melodie's laugh wound through him, silken and devastating, every note a jolt to his raw senses. She hovered close but refused to kiss him, tormenting him with proximity. Then she lifted something small and glowing between their chests, a golden thread, shimmering, running from her heart to his. Malec's breath hitched, the sight sending his mind reeling, pattern-hungry but finding no logic, only truth.

"What is that?" His voice was ragged, almost broken.

She stroked her fingers along the thread, and light shimmered down it.

"You did this," she whispered, her voice a caress and a condemnation both. "Not me."

The heat inside Malec smoldered, coiling tighter with every trembling breath. It licked along his skin, seeped through his muscles, pooling low in his belly, relentless as wildfire. He tried to clamp down on the sensations, to catalog and compartmentalize them, but they kept bleeding out. Pressure, need, the ache of her weight above him. His mind snagged on the details, counting her heartbeats, the pulse in her throat, the velvet-dark shadows between her curls. The more he focused, the more the fire grew, overwhelming all order.

She bent over him, her breasts hovering just above his chest, grazing but never quite touching, her body radiating heat that made him dizzy. The air between them was thick, saturated with the electric scent of her skin. He could hear the rasp of her breath, slow and controlled, a pattern that teased the edges of his restraint. When she spoke, her words curled in his ear like silk and smoke.

"I didn't ask for this," she whispered, her lips parted, close enough for him to feel the heat of her mouth. "But your body did."

She lingered over him, casting a shadow that stretched down his body, lips curved in a slow, taunting smile. Her voice dropped, thick and sultry.

"Tell me the truth. Do you want me? Or not?"

A sound escaped him, harsh and desperate, nothing like the proud elf he was meant to be. He shook his head in denial, but his body betrayed him. His hands rose, sliding up her thighs, needing the sensory feedback, mapping every inch of her as if memorizing her shape could give him control. His palms found her waist, fitting perfectly, feeling the ripple of her muscles beneath his touch. The heat intensified, pain and pleasure twisting together until they were indistinguishable.

She moaned, soft and broken, and the sound shot through him, making him arch beneath her. Her fingers covered his, guiding him up, pressing his hands to the full weight of her breasts. Her skin burned against his, and he felt her body tremble, the subtle catch in her breath telling him everything she refused to say. When his eyes met hers, he was lost in the depths of that gaze, all golden fire and dark promise.

She lowered her lashes, ink-dark against her cheeks. A dove fluttered down, settling on her shoulder, its feathers glowing in the dreamlight. She stroked the bird with idle affection.

"They suit me," she murmured, tilting her head toward it.

Rage stabbed through Malec, raw and senseless, tangled with jealousy. That connection was effortless for her, as natural as breathing. He could never touch it, never belong to it. He wanted to tear it away, make her see only him. She moved again, her hips rolling down, hovering just above the place where his desire throbbed sharp and hot. The sensation nearly split him apart. He reached for control, for logic, but found only wildness, the chaos she dragged out of him with every calculated move.

"Kel'varri dosh tal'vaar!" he shouted, voice ragged, mind straining for the words to reclaim himself. (I will not yield.)

Her laughter wrapped around him, scorching every last bit of discipline.

"Then you will burn." She closed the distance, claiming his mouth in a kiss that devoured reason and resistance.

Her lips crashed onto his, wild and feverish, her tongue forcing its way past his teeth, claiming and possessing him. For a moment, Malec fought it. Every muscle in his body locked down, desperate for order, for control, for some pattern he could cling to. Sensation blitzed through his mind—taste, heat, the relentless movement of her mouth and tongue, the surging burn of her skin against his. His thoughts flickered in frantic loops, cataloguing every second, every motion, every breath, trying to keep the world from shattering.

It was too much. The kiss was too much. The overload threatened to tear him apart. His body jerked beneath her, hands fisting in the furs, breath stuttering. The heat inside him rose sharp as a blade, climbing and climbing, until it bordered on agony. Every nerve ending screamed. He tried to resist, to hold onto the last thread of composure, but pain bloomed under his skin, raw and excruciating, as if her lips set him ablaze from the inside out.

Still, she didn't stop. Her mouth devoured his, her body pressing him down, and he burned. His mind screamed in protest, his body trembled, the fire became unbearable. The sensation crossed over from pleasure to torment, a relentless fever he could not shake.

And then—he surrendered.

Malec let go. His arms dropped open, the tension draining from his limbs. He stopped resisting, let the fire consume him. In that moment of surrender, pain shifted into something molten, something glorious. The heat no longer hurt. It pulsed and rolled, slow and all-encompassing, spreading through his blood, his bones, until he felt himself melt into her. Her kiss softened, slowing into a gentler rhythm, her lips moving over his in waves that soothed even as they branded him, each stroke a new language written on his skin.

Ecstasy exploded within him, a bright, dizzying wave that erased all thought and left only sensation. His body became pliant, hungry, every nerve tuned to her, every instinct feral and true. As their mouths moved together, he realized he was free. Free to feel, to want, to devour her in return. Letting go had been the key. He could finally move, and when he did, it was with the full force of desire he'd denied for too long, giving in to the wildness he was never meant to tame.

He rolled them with certainty, not to overpower her but to revel in her, pinning her to the furs while her body arched and pressed up into him. His mouth traveled to her throat, tongue tracing the salt and heat of her pulse, every heartbeat matching his own. He wanted to consume her, to memorize the taste and texture of her skin, to map the places that made her shiver. The sounds she made, the way her hips bucked and her fingers twisted in his hair, fed something wild inside him. He realized then—he wanted her fierce and untamed, needed her defiant and greedy. Her moans were like wine, intoxicating and sharp, flowing straight to his core. The more she took, the more he wanted to give.

Every gasp, every arch, every challenge from her mouth fed his hunger until he was dizzy with it.

He lost track of time, of the world beyond her body. The birch trees faded, the stars whirled and blurred, leaving only the anchoring weight of her beneath him. Her legs wrapped his hips, her hands locked in his as if she would never let go. Their mouths met again and again, tongues sliding and tasting, lips bruising, teeth grazing, both of them ravenous. He breathed her in, her scent was everywhere, lush and dark, clouding his senses and banishing every memory of cold, bleak solitude. He could not remember life before her fire touched him. Now he knew only this: nothing else would ever be enough.

He pressed himself deeper, his mouth dragging across her jaw, seeking the places that made her tremble. Her pulse hammered under his lips. A groan broke free, torn from somewhere deep inside him. He felt himself unraveling, caught in a storm of want he could never name. His hands squeezed hers tighter, as if only her grip could keep him whole.

"Zhen'tari sha'nai," he whispered, voice fractured and full of longing. (Say my name.)

She smiled, slow and dangerous, lips curving beneath his.

"Is this what you want?" she asked, her words a velvet blade.

Her voice was a spell, a binding. He knew then that he could never break free, nor did he want to. His body belonged to her now. Every breath, every heartbeat, every hunger. Her eyes glimmered, dark and bright at once, and he saw the stars there—endless and familiar, a sky he could lose himself in forever. He had never been so sure of anything. He looked at her, soul bared, and answered.

"Lei venashar... elira sha'Maelora." (Yes. More than anything.)

The vow left his lips and the world shattered. A jolt of sensation rocketed through him, pleasure and surrender detonating in his core. For a breathless moment, he was nothing but heat and light, every muscle straining, every nerve raw and alive. Ecstasy flooded him, wild and perfect, so deep he was certain he would never recover.

He woke with a gasp, sitting bolt upright in tangled, sweat-soaked sheets. His breath came ragged, chest heaving, heart slamming against his ribs. The cold stone air was powerless against the heat that still burned through him, his body trembling, hair plastered to his skin. Need pulsed inside him, fierce and relentless.

He dragged a hand down his face, cursing softly. Only a dream. But it didn't feel like a dream. His soul still hummed, body aching for her.

It was like stumbling through endless battlefields only to find the door left open, warm light spilling out—a belonging he had never dared to name. Like unearthing a secret he'd been hungering for since the dawn of his memory. He looked down at himself, at the lingering ache of desire, and shook his head. It was not only her body that haunted him. There was something more—something that could ruin him, or save him, if he dared to want it as much as he already did.

He paced the floor, trying in vain to cool the heat. But the dream clung to him. Her wildness, her smile, the promise in her eyes. The way she made him say yes, and the way he would say it again, no matter the cost.

The morning sun filtered weakly through the narrow slit of a window, dust motes swirling in the pale gold light as it spilled across the rough stone floor. The tiny servant's quarters were cloaked in shadow, the walls close and bare save for a single threadbare blanket draped over the cot. The fire in the hearth had burned down to a few sullen embers, offering little resistance against the cold that seeped in around the window and under the warped wooden door. Frost clung to the inside of the glass, and the silence in the cramped room was broken only by the faint drip of melted snow from the eaves above.

The space felt almost suspended, caught between sleep and waking, warmth and the lingering bite of winter. Melodie lay sprawled on the narrow cot, one arm slung over her eyes. Her head pounded with dull insistence, the aftereffects of berry wine and mischief curling in her stomach like smoke.

"Ugh," she groaned, rubbing at her temples. "Never again..."

A soft knock rattled the door. She winced. "What now?"

Before she could ignore it, the door creaked open and Luko slipped inside, closing it quickly behind him. His usual wry demeanor was nowhere to be seen. His expression was sharp, tight.

"You awake. This is good," he said.

Melodie lifted her head, frowning at the strange tone. Luko was often tired of her antics, yes, but this was different. Something had shifted.

He crossed his arms. "I need warn you."

She squinted at him through tangled hair. "Let me guess. Another speech about why I should behave myself?"

But Luko didn't smile. He stepped closer, eyes steady.

"I serious, Melodie, hear me."

She sat up slowly, her joints protesting.

"Alright. What's got your breeches twisted?"

"You play with fire," he said flatly. "And that fire is full of teeth."

Melodie's smirk flickered. Gone was the teasing undertone. Luko's golden eyes were lined with worry now.

"Malec is not just noble with temper," he continued. "He... built different. He not indulge. He not flirt. He not take lovers. Not ever."

She scoffed. "I know. That's half the fun."

"No, you not know," Luko snapped. "Because when Malec decide something is his, it is over. He not give it space. He not loosen grip. He conquer it."

Melodie paused.

Luko looked down for a moment, then back at her with something near pleading in his voice.

"He not know how to love. Not in way you are thinking. He only know how to possess."

Her throat tightened, but she shrugged it off.

"I'm not some doe-eyed maiden, Luko. I can handle a little obsession."

"Obsession gets people killed," he muttered. "And you, poking beast the way you do, he will snap."

Melodie folded her arms. "So what? I'm just supposed to lie down and behave? Be his docile little captive?"

"No," Luko said. "I mean do not push when he already on edge. He no sleep. He no eat. He is training since dawn like he tries to bleed the thoughts from skull. One wrong word, Melodie, he break something. Maybe you."

She stared at him for a long moment, then stood, shaking off her discomfort with a flick of her hair.

"I'll be fine. He'll get over it."

Luko didn't look convinced.

"Come now," he said, backing toward the door. "We get you something to eat. Before you kill yourself."

The dining hall soared above, its frost-rimmed windows spilling morning light over polished floors. The air smelled faintly of old woodsmoke, the central hearth now roaring anew.

At the center of everything, a massive wooden table dominated the space, long enough to seat at least twenty, its surface polished to a rich sheen. The table was set with an extravagant spread: platters of roasted meats, bowls of perfectly cut potatoes, trays of round, burnished loaves, and arrays of jewel-bright vegetables, every dish precisely arranged, none of the foods touching. Beneath the table, a thick black rug anchored the room, its intricate designs picked out in gold, red, and blue, echoing the banners that hung from the distant rafters.

And at the head of the table sat Malec, a grumpy, misunderstood tyrant, alone in a sea of empty chairs. His posture was flawless, back ramrod straight against the carved wood of his throne-like seat. Every item on the table was arranged with ritual care, cutlery aligned, vegetables spaced in flawless rows.

Even his food had been chosen and portioned with almost ritual care, same cut of meat as always, the same array of sides, potatoes stacked just so, vegetables lined up in flawless rows, none of it ever touching.

Malec picked up one of the smaller forks, running a thumb over the handle to be sure it sat exactly where it belonged. His eyes flickered, unfocused, as his thoughts wandered, inevitably, unwillingly, back to Melodie. The chaos she brought, the way she had unraveled him, the way his body had answered hers without permission. He could still feel the echoes, her laughter, her touch, the wild magic singing in his blood. It was intolerable. Disorder. Disgrace.

He inhaled through his nose, rigid, trying to find calm in the symmetry, in the order he'd built around himself. Each plate in its place. Each movement deliberate. But nothing could quiet the riot she'd left behind. Even now, his jaw was tight, his skin prickling with memory, his heart unsteady in his chest.

He would have to reassert control, remind himself and everyone else of the rules, because her presence was like a stone thrown into still water, and he could feel the ripples even now, echoing through the morning light and the perfect, silent order of his hall.

Then the doors opened. And his breath stopped.

She entered on Luko's arm, her steps light, head tilted as she murmured something that made the elf laugh softly. Malec's heart slammed once, hard. She wore one of the dresses he'd chosen for her: a soft green and white garment that clung gently to her figure, simple yet elegant. Her dark hair had been pulled into a braided bun at the nape of her neck, a few loose tendrils brushing her cheeks. Around her throat gleamed a silver collar etched with his family crest.

His mark. His. He couldn't look away.

Even three chairs down, he could smell her, faintly floral, like warmed jasmine and honeyed tea. It wrapped around him, settled into his lungs. He gripped the armrest harder, the wood creaking beneath his fingers. She took her seat as if nothing in the world was wrong, as if she hadn't undone him in a dream he couldn't forget.

Melodie barely spared him a glance before plopping into a chair across the table, legs crossed under her. He could see the faint flush in her cheeks, the sparkle in her eyes that told him she knew. She knew what she'd done to him, what she *still* did to him.

He swallowed hard, eyes narrowing.

"Nai'ka freol inra," he muttered coldly, gesturing toward her untouched plate.

Luko exhaled beside her, already tired. "He says eat."

"I got that much, thanks," she said with a smirk, tearing a piece of bread in half and popping it into her mouth like it was a victory.

Malec didn't speak again. He couldn't. Not with her scent in his nose. Not with her collar on her throat. Not with the memory of her soft moans still echoing in his ears. The tension in the dining hall had barely begun to ease when Malec, seated stiff and regal at the head of the long table, spoke a single sentence, sharp and deliberate. Luko, mid-bite into a crusty roll, froze. He glanced between them, sighed, and cleared his throat.

"He... he say something," Luko began hesitantly. "Say... he choose new name for you."

Melodie stopped chewing. Her eyes snapped up to Malec like daggers drawn.

"The hell did you just say?"

Luko scratched the back of his head. "He... he give you new name."

Melodie's jaw drawn tight. "Like I'm some kind of damn *dog*?"

Luko winced. "I not say it," he muttered. "He say it."

"Allora," Malec said smoothly, not even bothering to look at her directly.

Luko shifted uncomfortably. "He say... name is Allora."

Melodie blinked. "Allora?"

She stared at Luko with growing heat. "What does that mean?"

Luko hesitated, then mumbled, "Name we give to girl-child, a type of bird."

Silence fell. A strange, stunned quiet.

"Why?" she asked flatly, eyes narrowing.

Malec answered with a string of elegant Awyan. Smooth. Calm. Too calm.

Luko sighed hard, rubbing his face with both hands before mumbling, "He say... you talk much. Like bird. Loud bird."

Melodie blinked slowly. Then, in complete silence, she picked up a breadstick... and hurled it with flawless aim.

Thwap.

The bread smacked Malec square on the cheek. A collective gasp rippled through the room. Servants froze mid-step. Someone dropped a tray. Malec turned his head with agonizing slowness. Whatever stirred within, his face gave no clue. His eyes glacial.

Then—with chilling calm, he reached out and slid her plate away.

"Frei orithen daka'sul. Alen vera, alen sai."

"He say... if throw food," Luko translated nervously, "then no get food."

Melodie's mouth dropped open.

"You've *got* to be kidding me!" she snapped. She leaned back in her chair, arms crossed tight. "Fine. I'll just steal some later."

Melodie watched him from across the table, eyes narrowed, taking in every little detail. The way he lined up his utensils so perfectly. The way his bread never touched anything else on the plate. How he always, always had to have the crest facing him, as if the world might end if it was off by a hair. She realized, with a slow, wicked smile curling at the edge of her lips, that he was a creature of rituals, of neat rows and quiet, ruthless order.

Fine. She'd learn every last one of his little quirks. Every habit, every tick, every private rule he clung to like armor. She'd turn them against him, one by one, until she drove him absolutely mad. Just thinking about it made her pulse quicken with anticipation, her anger soothed by the delicious promise of future mischief.

He might have won today.

But she was going to enjoy making him regret it, and she was going to savor every second.

 [Book 1] 13 - 19

Chapter 13

Checkmate, Silver Fox

The afternoon air bit at her skin as she trudged across the gravel path, a wooden bucket sloshing in her grip, cold water splashing over her wrists with every step. Mist clung low to the earth, curling like smoke beneath the silver dawn. The sky overhead was streaked with faint orange light, but there was nothing warm about the new day.

Allora, because that was her name now, wasn't it?, tightened her hold on the handle and kept walking. She hated that name. Allora. A soft, pretty thing that clung to her like a silk collar, soaked in poison. He'd given it to her like a king naming his favorite hound. It came from alori, the pet name Awyan parents gave to their infant daughters. As if he was claiming she belonged to him now, fragile, docile, harmless.

She wanted to gouge the name from her skin.

She desperately needed to see Malec writhing on the floor with his precious crest shoved up his ass, his silver tunic soaked in the blood of his arrogance. She wanted to drop a napalm bomb on the entire House of the Silver Fox and watch him scream as fire licked that dusty, ashy hair from his backside and burn the smug out of his stupid, fucking face. But instead, she carried his bucket.

Because for now, she had to. For now, she would obey. Play the part. Wait for the perfect moment to sink her talons into his flesh. Her steps grew heavier as she neared the training grounds, heart still bitter from the night before. Dinner had been a performance, and Malec had played his part to perfection, seated at the head of the table like some untouchable war-god, draped in silk and metal, issuing orders as though she were nothing but an unruly dog who needed a tighter leash.

He'd taken her name. He'd taken her food. And he'd taken her pride, smiling as he stripped it from her, one syllable at a time. She'd retaliated the only way she could, hurling bread at his frost-kissed cheek like a defiant child. It had felt good for half a heartbeat. Then he'd punished her.

Not with fury, not with shouting, but with silence, the kind that sliced deeper than any blade. Just a cool glance and the flick of a hand as he removed her plate and sentenced her to humiliation. Today's sentence? Cleaning every weapon in the armory and serving water to the grunting, panting soldiers who trained under him like dogs on command.

She was supposed to feel small. Controlled. Humbled. But Malec had misjudged her. Allora had endured worse for less. She'd survived the kind of labor that left splinters in her soul, forced smiles through cracked lips, buried her pride in places so deep even she had forgotten where they were. Until now.

And now it burned. Let him try to break her. Let him pretend he had already won.

She'd play her part well. She'd fetch water and wear his crest like a chain of obedience. She'd let him think she was becoming the little dove he imagined, quiet, pliant, caged. But when the time came, when he least expected it, she would burn everything he built down to ash.

And she would smile while he begged her to stop.

By midday, her arms felt like dead weight, her fingers raw from scrubbing down blades and hauling endless buckets of water to the training field. The sun hung high, unrelenting, baking the stone yard below into a shimmering haze. Grunts and shouted commands echoed through the air as warriors clashed and circled, their movements swift and brutal, their bare chests gleaming with sweat.

Allora stood off to the side, holding the last of the water buckets like a limp offering. She hated the way they ignored her. She hated even more the way some of them didn't. She had noticed something strange earlier in the day.

The other Canariae, the servant girls with pale skin and neatly braided blonde hair, spoke Awyan fluently when addressing their masters. But among themselves, when they thought no one was listening, they spoke... German?

Not Awyan. Not English. German.

Allora's brows had twitched when she heard it. The sharp consonants, the familiar cadences. It wasn't a language commonly heard here, not unless someone had trained in Earth's older, war-torn regimes. Which she had. Part of her military conditioning back home had included linguistic immersion. German. Chinese. French. Swahili. She could listen, mimic, respond in a dozen dialects, enough to infiltrate, extract, or deceive in the field. Language had been her weapon long before any rifle.

So when one pale Canariae whispered, *"Warum so müde?"* and another replied, *"Beeil dich, schnell, siehst du nicht?"* Allora hadn't just understood them.

She had clocked them. She had catalogued their inflection, their tone, the casual sloppiness of their grammar, enough to know they were born speaking it. Which meant someone was sourcing specifically from that region. A farm of pale, pliable girls trained to serve. Breed. Obey. None of them looked like her. Not one brown girl. Not one kinky curl. Not one dark-skinned body among them.

Her stomach twisted, sour and hot. She had started referring to them, to herself, as Canariae. It crept in like mold, under her skin and into her vocabulary. Not human or woman nor soldier.

Canariae.

The rage surged back like acid in her throat. He had taken even that from her, her species, her name, her face in the mirror. And she would do anything to take something back. Even if it meant poking the bear. Even if it meant painting a target on her back just to remind herself she still existed. And then... anything happened.

A shadow fell across her as one of the soldiers peeled away from the rest, striding toward her with easy confidence. He was tall, sun-kissed, with sandy blonde hair and vivid green eyes that glinted like mischief wrapped in honey. His jaw was sharp, his body toned from war. And he was smiling, at her.

She didn't smile back.

"You're mura'haltos," he said, the cadence playful.

She squinted, catching only half the meaning. *You are... something?*

But she knew that tone. That grin. That look. She had seen it across bars, across prison cages, across vendor stalls back home. He was flirting. Lightly, testing the waters.

Another line followed. "What's your damma?"

Name. He was asking for her name. She said nothing, just kept her gaze flat.

"You're zala'muskoh Canariae. What's nor'falto zeri'amano kutka?"

That one was harder to follow, but she picked up enough. So rare... Canariae... your hands... why so, something. It didn't matter. She hated him already. But more than that, she saw the opportunity. She tilted her head just slightly, her mischievous mouth curling in a subtle smirk. Oh, this would piss Malec off.

And then the air changed.

It was subtle. A tightening. A hush. Like the forest when a predator stepped into the glade. The soldier stiffened instantly. Allora turned, and her breath caught, though she'd never admit it.

Malec was striding toward them like a coming storm. His long tunic fluttered slightly with each measured step, silver embroidery glinting in the sun. His bare chest peeked through the low-cut V, pale and smooth, adorned only by the glint of a pendant bearing his family crest. No armor. No sword. Just presence.

His eyes, those pale tan eyes, were locked on the soldier. Deadly. Calm.

"Shi'ren dael'thari Canariae... zhalin?" he asked, the words like silk drawn across a blade.

Luko, who had been lingering nearby, instantly stepped forward.

"He ask... if you find his Canariae amusing," he muttered to Allora without inflection.

The soldier snapped to attention.

"Vaen thi'sora ven zhei, Kald'arai," he said quickly.

Allora didn't need a translator to know the boy had just pissed his pants internally. And then Malec looked at her. His eyes didn't blaze. They didn't narrow. They didn't even change. But she could feel his displeasure from across the field, like a wall of ice pressing against her skin.

Which made it the perfect time to honk the albino donkey's nose and wait for the kick. She gave him the smuggest smile she could muster. Slowly. Deliberately. Then she turned back to the soldier, leaned in just a little, and ran her fingers along the edge of the bucket like it was something more interesting than the warlord scrutinizing her.

"Ask my name again," she said sweetly, parroting back the words she had pieced together. Luko translates.

She could almost hear the muscle twitch in Malec's jaw. Good. Let him stew. Let him rage. She wasn't his little stray kitten. Not today. Not ever. Malec's expression didn't change. But the air around him did. His fingers flexed at his sides before he tilted his head slightly. Then,

> "If you have dor ak'zelan... talk," he said, his voice like steel wrapped in frost.

> "You have dor ak'zelan... fight."

Allora's smirk faltered. Wait, what?

> Luko blinked, glancing between them with caution. "Uh... he says you should fight," he translated hesitantly.

Allora turned to Luko, then back to Malec, heart beginning to pound, not from fear. From disbelief.

"Fight who?" she asked slowly, suspicion coiling in her gut.

Malec's lips curled, but it wasn't a smile. It was a challenge. Then, without a word, he grabbed a wooden sparring sword from one of his soldiers and tossed it.

It landed at her feet with a heavy clang, dirt kicking up around it. Allora stared down at the weapon. Then back up at him. This mother fu-

"Zhalak ven," he said, his tone thick with promise.

And maybe, just maybe, a hint of wicked amusement. Allora narrowed her eyes. Oh, she was going to fight, alright. And she was going to make sure this frosty warlord regretted ever thinking he could put her in her place.

The moment the wooden sword clattered to the ground at her feet, the air shifted.

Every soldier on the training field turned, a hush falling over the grounds like mist. Blades paused mid-air. Even the wind held its breath. Allora stood motionless, sweat clinging to her skin, the heavy bucket of water still sloshing in her grip. She glanced down at the sword, then up at him.

Malec.

He stood at the edge of the sparring ring, his pale tan eyes narrowed like a hawk sighting prey. Without a word, he unfastened the silver tunic draped across his chest and let it fall with precision onto a nearby bench. It landed without a sound, as if the garment feared disobedience. His dark undershirt clung to his muscular frame, emphasizing the powerful swell of his shoulders, the lean stretch of his arms, the faint gleam of sweat along his collarbone. Even dressed down, he looked every inch a warlord, regal, precise, and dangerous.

He said something sharply in Awyan, voice clipped, calm, lethal.

Luko's voice followed an awkward beat later.

"He say... if you talk too much, maybe you fight instead, mm?"

Allora raised an eyebrow. "So this is about your ego now?"

Malec didn't answer. He didn't need to. She bent down, picked up the sword. It was heavier than she expected. The balance off. Wrong. Still, she curled her fingers around the hilt and rolled her shoulders, stepping into the ring like a storm gathering weight. The soldiers murmured. Amused. Curious. Hungry for spectacle.

Malec stepped onto the mat opposite her, his movements smooth and composed, each footfall controlled. His expression remained impassive, lips pressed in a neutral line, but his posture told another story. This was a test. He murmured something again in Awyan, dry and low like a curse made of silk.

Luko snorted. "He say... try not make fool of self."

Allora's eyes narrowed. "Same to you, albino donkey."

Luko coughed into his hand, poorly stifling laughter. Malec's eyes glinted with a flicker of amusement, and then, without warning, he moved. Allora barely saw it coming. The blade whistled toward her, and instinct screamed. She twisted, ducking as the wooden edge sliced through empty air, grazing the curl of her hair. Her feet scraped against the dirt. She pivoted, breath tight in her lungs. Fast. He was faster than any man she'd ever faced.

But speed could be countered. She retaliated, low, sharp, and fast, aiming for his exposed ribs. But Malec slid aside like smoke, his frame a blur of disciplined movement. She felt the whisper of his sleeve pass her shoulder. Then her legs were gone.

A sharp sweep of his boot sent her crashing to the earth, her back slamming into the mat. The sky blinked white above her as the soldiers around them roared in laughter. Allora's pride flared hot as her pulse. She rolled, spitting dirt from her lip, and sprang to her feet, blade tight in hand.

Malec raised a single brow. Then said coolly in Awyan, "Jahri'nas."

Luko tilted his head, translating as best he could: "He say... 'focus.' Maybe you need it."

Allora inhaled sharply through her nose, her eyes ablaze. She wasn't a swordswoman. She was trained with her fists, with speed and knees and elbows. This wasn't her weapon. This wasn't her fight. But she refused to lose. Not to him. She wasn't just fighting for dignity. She was fighting to prove that he hadn't broken her. That no matter what name he gave her, no matter what collar he clamped around her throat, she would still belong to herself.

"I'm focused," she muttered, jaw set as she stared Malec down.

Without hesitation, she let the sparring sword drop from her gloved hands. The dull thud echoed across the training ground, the blade raising a small cloud of dust beside the battered toes of her boots.

A ripple of laughter swept through the Awyan onlookers, the sound edged with arrogance and disdain. A few leaned forward, grinning, eager for the spectacle. Others rolled their eyes or traded mocking glances.

"Already surrendering?" one called.

"She holds it like a club," one called. "Are all Canariae this slow?"

"She knows she's beaten," another muttered.

The metallic taste of challenge filled the air, thick as blood.

"Dresha vael?" he taunted, voice curling with amusement.

Luko, hovering anxiously at the ring's edge, gave a strangled laugh as he translated. "He say... you give up now?"

Allora smiled. Not sweetly. Like a wolf baring its teeth. She stepped forward, boots planting with a dull scrape, dust billowing around her ankles. No more pretense. No more playing by his rules. The sword had slowed her, made her fight like them—awkward, heavy, predictable. She was not them. She was something else entirely. She lowered into a stance no Awyan had ever seen. Her boots slid apart, knees bent and loose, hips angled, soles grinding steady into the sand. One fist rose near her cheekbone in a tight guard, the other coiled by her waist, ready to spring. Every line of her body was grounded, powerful, and utterly alien in its fluidity. This was not the rigid, elegant swordplay of elves. This was human. This was wild. This was jujitsu.

A new murmur swept through the assembled warriors, a note of confusion laced with ridicule.

Someone snickered, "Is she dancing?"

Another jeered, "What's wrong with her feet?"

"Maybe she's trying to pray for mercy!"

Malec lunged, the movement a blur of predatory grace, sword slicing through the air toward her exposed shoulder. He was the Silver Fox—unbeatable, untouchable, certain. His attack was swift, lethal, perfectly calculated. But Allora was already reading him, eyes locked on the flicker of his hips, the angle of his shoulders. She rotated sideways with the fluidity of water, just enough to let the blade whistle past her cheek. Her boots scraped the sand, anchoring her even as her core twisted, readying her next move.

Crack.

Her heel shot up in a snap kick—precise, explosive—slamming into the bony point of his wrist. Malec's sword clattered to the ground, the shock rippling up his arm. A stunned hush swept the yard as the weapon tumbled and spun in the dust. Malec froze, his arm burning, eyes wide in disbelief. For the first time, his rhythm had been broken.

Allora didn't let him recover. She flowed forward, hips twisting. Her elbow slammed into his ribs, a strike rooted in years of drilling—body mechanics, speed, violence. The impact reverberated through him like a drumbeat, making him stagger. She advanced, relentless, cutting the ring in half with her movement. A low leg sweep behind his knee, she was inside his guard now, disrupting his balance. He feinted high, but she ducked, shifting her weight, driving a palm into his chest and forcing him back, boots skidding in the dirt.

He tried to spin, but she was already behind him. She pivoted, breath coming fast, grabbing his arm and hooking her leg behind his knee. With a sharp jerk, she executed a perfect hip throw, MMA-style, flipping the great Silver Fox into the air. Malec landed flat on his back, dust billowing, the wind driven from his lungs. Silence crashed down across the yard, every Awyan stunned, gaping. The only sound was Malec's ragged breathing.

Allora straightened over him, her chest rising and falling, sweat gleaming along her jaw, boots scuffed and planted. She looked down, eyes glinting, voice cold as steel.

"Yield?"

No gloating. Only quiet, undeniable dominance. Luko's laugh burst out, half-wince, half-wonder. No one else dared make a sound.

Malec didn't move. Malec didn't answer. For the first time, he looked up at her not as a conqueror, but as a rival. For the first time in years, he hadn't been able to predict, to control, to win. The heat crawling up his neck wasn't shame. It was heated interest or perhaps admiration. A smile broke over his lips—low, real, dangerous.

Allora held his gaze a moment longer, then turned away, shoulders squared. She walked back across the ring, ignoring the gaping silence, every step radiating human pride and fury. She could still feel the thrum of victory in her bones, an electric buzz racing under sweat-slick skin.

Her heartbeat pounded at her temples, echoing the drumbeat of boots on packed earth as the other Awyans cleared the yard, their voices sharp and uneasy. She wiped a line of salt from her brow and pressed the rim of the battered tin bucket to her lips, cold water shocking her mouth and throat. The taste of iron, dust, and triumph tangled on her tongue. Her hands shook just a little as she set the bucket down—adrenaline and exhaustion bleeding together, turning her muscles heavy, her body loose and dangerous.

From across the ring, she felt Malec's eyes on her—felt it, even before she looked. She glanced up. He was still seated where she'd left him, dust clinging to his tunic, the silver fox emblem smeared and dull. But it was his stare that stopped her breath: pale tan eyes burning, not with the frost of command but a strange, hungry heat. It was as if she'd broken something open in him, as if he saw her for the first time. Not as a piece on his board, not as property, but as a storm he couldn't map.

For a moment, he just watched her. Then he sat up, dragging a gloved hand through his hair, eyes raking her up and down with a mix of wonder and something darker. His chest rose and fell, the echo of the fight still winding through his body. When their gazes met, something tightened between them, charged and silent, as if the whole yard were holding its breath.

A group of Awyans bustled past, collecting weapons and grumbling in their native tongue, their voices low and bitter. Allora caught the tone, resentful, sharp but only fragments of meaning. The words slid past her, jagged and unfamiliar, and she could only guess at their intent by the way their eyes refused to meet hers, the tension in their movements.

But Luko heard every word. He lingered at her side, face tight with disgust as he listened.

"She cheated."

"No Canariae should beat the Commander."

"She must have used tricks."

Their voices stung like nettles, meant for each other but barbed enough for her to feel. Someone spat in the dirt near her boots; another gave her a look that was half-glare, half-fear. Yet none dared speak to her directly.

Luko crossed his arms, posture loose and wary as he glanced from Malec to Allora. He shot her a sideways smile, eyes sparkling.

> "You know, they talk about this for a century," he murmured, low enough only she could hear. "You broke rules. You broke him a little too, I think."

He jerked his chin toward Malec.

> "He never look at anyone like that before. Like you...set his world on fire."

Allora's mouth quirked, sharp and satisfied. But inside, she was still simmering, nerves singing with the memory of Malec's hands, the press of his weight, the challenge in his eyes. She couldn't tell if she wanted to fight him again, or something else entirely. The ache in her shoulders was sweet, the bruises blooming beneath her skin a secret proof of victory.

Malec was still watching. Not moving, not speaking. His expression was a strange mask—something unreadable, but far from indifferent. Like he was fighting something inside himself, and losing ground.

> "You should never stare at commander like that," Luko said, grinning, his voice softer. "He think you inviting another round."

Allora huffed a laugh, low and dangerous, rolling out the tension in her neck.

> "Let him think whatever he wants," she said, voice rough with fatigue and pride.

> "He's not the only one who likes a fight."

Across the training yard, Malec brushed dust from his tunic, every movement practiced and composed. Yet his eyes strayed, again and again, to Allora where she stood by her bucket, her face flushed with victory and exertion. He told himself he was simply taking stock, studying a worthy rival, but the lie grew thin.

Allora's jaw was set, her eyes bright, sweat glimmering on her skin. Malec watched the way her shoulders rolled back, the steady rise and fall of her chest as she caught her breath. He was acutely aware of the echo her touch had left in his body—a dull ache, a strange warmth blooming beneath his bruises. He tried to file it away as a curiosity, a puzzle, but each time she met his gaze, something shifted in him, quiet and undeniable.

He turned his attention to the other Awyans cleaning up, forced himself to focus on their voices, but the ring's energy still pulsed with the memory of her hands, her speed, her power. When he glanced back, she was already looking, her mouth quirked in a half-smile that made something in him flinch and then unfurl. He almost looked away, almost remembered himself, but the urge to keep watching her was stronger.

His lips moved in the shadow of a smile, so slight he doubted anyone noticed. The want inside him was just a ripple, nothing more—a flicker beneath his usual discipline. But it was there now, and he could not quite tamp it down. For the first time in years, the pleasure of the fight lingered, colored with a heat that didn't fade.

He told himself it was nothing. He tried, for a while, to believe it.

But as the yard emptied and Allora turned away, Malec's gaze lingered. The quiet hunger inside him no longer felt like a threat, but an invitation—subtle, patient, waiting for the moment he would finally stop fighting it.

The stone corridor pressed in with the thick scent of old oil and baking bread, sunlight slanting through narrow windows and striping the flagstones beneath their boots. Allora wiped sweat from her brow with the rough edge of her sleeve, knuckles still tingling from the fight. Every muscle in her body throbbed with fatigue and satisfaction, an ache she wore like a secret medal. Luko matched her pace, a little closer than usual, his hands folded behind his back and his face alive with a rare, wicked grin.

"You know," Luko murmured, voice barely more than a hush over the echo of their footfalls, "you are play with fire."

Allora didn't bother to glance at him, eyes on the stained-glass light shimmering over her path.

"Playing," she corrected, voice flat but not unkind. "Present progressive. Try again."

He let out a gust of air, somewhere between a sigh and a laugh. "Fine. You are playing with fire."

She shrugged, rolling stiff shoulders as they neared the heavy doors to the kitchen.

"Good. Maybe I'll burn the whole damn place down."

The words tasted bitter and sweet at once. He angled his head, glancing toward the grand staircase that overlooked the hallway.

"He not stop look at you. All session. He don't even hide it."

Allora risked a sidelong glance at the dark stone behind them, as if expecting Malec's eyes to pierce the walls themselves. Even with the echo of the yard left behind, she could still feel the ghost of his attention, hot and relentless, prickling along her spine. The sensation lingered, both warning and dare, as they walked deeper into the cool corridor. She snorted softly, glancing over her shoulder as if shaking off a shadow.

"He can stare all he wants. Doesn't mean I'm going to give him anything."

"He look different," Luko murmured, eyes narrowing. "Not like owner. More like..."

He searched for the right word, rolling his tongue over it.

"A dog sniffing meat?" she offered, bitter edge to her grin.

Luko barked a soft laugh. "No. Like soldier who just found new weapon.

Dangerous one."

"I hope it explodes in his face," she muttered, squeezing the cleaning rag in her hands until her knuckles paled.

Luko sobered, voice dropping. "He is interested. Not just in fighting. In you."

She looked at him sharply. "So?"

He shrugged, lips pressed thin. "So... that not good thing. When Malec wants something, he takes. He don't ask."

Allora's jaw tightened, the taste of defiance coppery in her mouth. "Then I'll make him regret it."

Luko eyed her. "Why you let him look? You fight everyone else."

She met his gaze, eyes fierce. "Because it's the only time I get to win. When he stares at me like that, I know I've gotten under his skin. That's power."

"Or danger," he said, quieter than before.

She stood straighter, brushing dust from her pants, breathing in the scent of earth and sweat.

"They're the same thing, if you use them right."

Luko hesitated, glancing toward Malec before leaning closer. "You still fight the name, huh?"

Allora's mouth twitched, a flicker of pain breaking through her calm. "Of course I fight it."

"You don't say Melodie," he said softly. "Not out loud. Not to me. Not to yourself."

She stilled. "I say it."

He shook his head. "No. You think it. He already put name in your head. Now it echoes."

She folded her arms, voice low. "I'd rather eat dirt than be his anything."

Luko raised his hands in surrender. "I only say truth."

She turned down the corridor beside Luko, the muffled clamor of the training yard fading behind heavy stone walls. The slap of their boots echoed in the hush, dust swirling in narrow shafts of late afternoon light. Allora could still feel the ache of victory in her muscles, but the yard—its stares, its judgments—was already dissolving into memory.

Malec was gone, but his presence seemed to cling to her, sharp as a scent she couldn't shake. It throbbed at the back of her mind, unsettling as hunger. She caught her reflection in a polished bit of wall, jaw flexed tight, pulse fluttering beneath the sweat and grime.

Luko said nothing for a moment, just walked beside her, footsteps measured. The air here was cooler, quieter, almost intimate. It made the memory of Malec's eyes all the more intrusive, like a bruise pressed by accident. She squared her shoulders, rolling out the tension. The hallway wasn't a cage, not like the yard, but she still felt herself testing every lock and shadow—measuring not just her enemies, but every weak point. Including the ghost of the warlord who'd left marks on her skin and her pride.

She was no one's anything. Not here, not ever. And she would remember every weakness, even those she couldn't see.

By early evening, a small merchant convoy arrived at the castle gates. It seemed routine at first, crates of preserved fruit, salted meat, weapon supplies, but as the wagons creaked to a stop, Allora's eyes locked on something else entirely. Not the goods. The cargo.

The Canariae came first, shackled and silent. But trailing behind them, in cages too small to stretch in, were the wild-eyed shapeshifters, half-shifted, snarling, bruised. Some of them looked familiar.

Her chest tightened. Then she saw it. The sickness.

One by one, they were hauled out, Canariae and wildlings alike, stumbling, wheezing, trembling with fever. Her feet moved before her mind could catch up. A woman collapsed against the side of a cart, lips pale and flaking, her breath ragged. Allora knelt beside her, lifting her chin gently. Her skin was clammy, mottled in places. The woman's eyes were hollow. Her limbs too thin. And underneath the stench of sweat and travel... the faint, metallic scent of rot.

Allora's pulse spiked. She knew these symptoms. Every single one. Ashen pallor. Neurological decay. Advanced systemic fatigue. It was Cotard-Virus.

"No," she whispered, brushing a matted lock of hair away from the woman's forehead. "Not here... not here too."

"Luko!" Her voice was sharper than she meant it, cutting across the courtyard.

He appeared at her side, brow furrowed. Malec followed at a measured pace, hands clasped behind his back as if merely observing a harvest.

"What is it?" Luko asked, crouching beside her.

"They're sick," Allora said, turning the woman's wrist over. "This one, she's got the virus. The same one that destroyed my people. Cotard-Virus. Look at her skin, her eyes, she's in the late stages."

Luko stiffened. She didn't miss the way his eyes darted to Malec. Even Malec's casual posture shifted subtly, his chin lifting.

"Cot-ar, what?" Luko echoed.

Allora's brain spun as she ignored his question. "If it's here... that means you, your kind, *survived* it."

Her gaze jumped to Luko's face, but his expression was masked. "Do you have a cure?" she demanded.

Luko hesitated. Then, slowly, he nodded.

"Of course. For us, it is... how do you say? Minor inconvenience. We overcame it long ago."

"Long ago?" she repeated. Her chest felt like it was caving in. "How long?"

Luko didn't blink. "Centuries."

The world slowed. Her throat tightened as her gaze snapped toward Malec, who still hadn't spoken a word.

"You mean... you had a cure *this whole time?*"

Luko nodded once. "Not all Awyan. Only few lines. Rare blood. His..." He gestured toward Malec, "...his blood is strongest." Her heart stuttered.

His blood. His. What? The one who had stolen her name. Who claimed her as property. Who shackled her to his house and smirked while she fumed. He held the cure. Her fingers curled into fists. Because of course he fucking did. She had crossed dimensions for this. Risked her life. Lost everything. And the answer had been walking beside her, glaring at her, tormenting her... this entire time. She stood abruptly, wiping her hands on her tunic.

"Well," she said coolly, "that's... interesting."

Luko blinked. "That's all?"

"I mean..." She shrugged, trying to tamp down the scream building in her lungs.

"Of course the great and arrogant Awyan would survive a plague built for 'lesser' beings. How very on-brand."

He gave her a look, but said nothing. Malec, however, still hadn't moved. His gaze burned into her, quiet, void of emotion, too still. He knew. Or at least, he sensed something had shifted. She turned slightly away from him, forcing her breathing even. Her thoughts were spiraling too fast.

The envoy had brought more than supplies. They had brought answers. And maybe a key. She stole a glance back toward the cages where the shapeshifters sat shackled and dazed. One of them, no, two, she recognized from the cave. From the night she was taken.

"What are they doing here?" she asked, jerking her chin toward them. "Those shapeshifters. I've seen them before."

Luko followed her gaze. "Ah. The ferals. We train them sometimes. Good for battle. Trackers. Or messengers, when silence is needed."

Her brows lifted. "Messengers?"

Luko nodded. "Yes. They change shape. Slip between camps. Harder to catch than doves."

Allora's jaw ached with how tightly she was grinding her teeth. The world had turned inside out around her, shapeshifters bred for war, Cotard turned from nightmare to a footnote, Malec sitting there so smug and immune, silent as ever, daring her to make the first move. The web was tightening and she was at its center, but she wasn't about to let herself be caught. Not for long. She had a plan, and if the plan needed to get dirty, she'd get dirty. She'd done worse for less.

His blood. That was the answer, one way or another. Seduction, theft, betrayal...whatever it took. She needed a real strategy, not just dreams of breaking out. Two objectives: get Malec's blood, and find the portal home. No mistakes, no distractions. The virus was out there, twisting through lives all over again, and she couldn't let herself freeze up now, not when the cure she'd scraped and bled for had been right here, tucked inside that arrogant bastard's veins the whole damn time.

She paced under the high, cold wall, hands flexing at her sides, mind darting from fear to fury to calculation. To get the cure, she'd need proximity. Real proximity. Not the sarcastic back-and-forth or brief brush of hands she'd managed so far. She'd have to get close, more intimate than her pride wanted, close enough to make him forget himself. The way he looked at her, eyes lingering just a little too long on her sinful mouth, the muscle in his jaw flexing when she moved past him. His breath would hitch, just slightly, when she dared to touch him. The signs were all there, no matter how hard he tried to swallow them.

It wouldn't be hard to bait him. If she was being honest, it might even be... fun. The jerk was infuriating, but he had a tight ass, and those intense, weirdly soulful eyes. Creepy, yeah, but there was something weirdly endearing in the way he watched her, hungry and haunted, like some misunderstood villain in a movie who didn't know if he wanted to kill her or worship her. Stockholm Syndrome? Maybe. She wasn't about to fall for him, hell no, not in this life, not in any life. But if she was going to fake it, if she was going to make this seduction believable, she'd have to find something to pull from. She could focus on the positives. Use what she could get.

She'd been a soldier, a doctor, a liar, a survivor. Playing a role wasn't new. But it was different this time. Because she wasn't just hustling him for pride, or for the satisfaction of seeing him squirm. She was playing for lives, including her own. Malec was dangerous, she'd seen it in the way people fell silent when he entered, in the tension in the air, in the steel that bent to his will. He could break her, she felt it like a wire pulled tight inside her chest.

But if she wanted to save herself and everyone else, she'd have to be the one to break him first. To outplay him at his own game, even if it meant setting herself on fire to do it.

So, that was the plan. Walk right into the fire, smiling. Make him think it was all his idea. And if she happened to enjoy herself along the way?

Well, maybe she deserved a little pleasure while outwitting the fox.

Chapter 14

Bloodline

Allora spent the next few weeks weaving her strategy like thread through a needle, steady, sharp, and with purpose. There was no Melodie anymore. No rank. No last name. That identity had withered the moment her boots crossed into this strange world.

Now, there was only Allora. And Allora had a mission.

She played the game carefully, letting the name fall from others' tongues without protest. Letting herself be addressed like a thing rather than a woman, like a belonging instead of a threat. Malec thought she was folding. That the fire in her belly had cooled. That his name had swallowed hers whole. Let him.

She spent her nights sitting cross-legged near the servants' quarters, whispering Awyan phrases back and forth with Luko while the torches flickered on the sandstone walls. Her pronunciation sharpened with each lesson, her comprehension growing faster than Luko expected, but she warned him to say nothing.

Never in front of Malec.

In Malec's presence, she tilted her head at his commands. She blinked as if puzzled when he muttered in Awyan. She waited for Luko to translate with his usual broken syntax, and gave no hint she understood every syllable. She was memorizing him. Memorizing them. Every clipped insult, every casual cruelty, every breath between his words. The tone shifts, the phrases that revealed tension, desire, control. She was studying Malec the way she had once studied anatomy: precisely, intimately, with purpose.

Because one day soon, she would speak. Not in broken words. Or with hesitation. She would look him in the eye and say something that cut deeper than any sword he'd ever held. And in that moment, he would know just how far inside she'd already gotten.

He had no idea she listened when he thought she couldn't. That each time his gaze lingered on her neck, the heat of her mouth, her body, she noticed. She catalogued the hunger in his eyes, the hesitation in his hands, the way he breathed when her fingers brushed his wrist a little too long when pouring wine.

She was playing a slow game. And he was losing.

She would get him to let his guard down. She would get him drunk. She would get his blood. And she would run. Through the portal. Back to Earth. Back to the crumbling hospitals and dying children and families desperate for a cure. And she would hold it. The cure. His blood. It would be the sweetest irony.

And Malec—towering, arrogant Malec—would never see it coming. Because the Canariae he thought he had made submit was about to speak his language.

The great dining hall of the eastern wing was a vaulted chamber of old black stone, its high ceiling lost in the shadowy hush of dusk. Ornate arches lined the walls like ribs of a beast, framing stained glass windows that flickered with firelight. In the middle, a massive hearth roared with orange flame, the carved fox heads on either side catching the glow and gleaming like sentinels, sleek, cunning, and noble. The signature emblem of House Talandros, etched into stone and myth alike.

Heat wafted through the hall in waves, cozy yet imposing. Everything smelled of roasted meat, glazed roots, and honeyed wine. Servants bustled in and out like clockwork: refilling goblets, replacing platters, clearing dishes with the silent precision of shadows trained not to speak. And at the head of the table, alone for now, sat Malec.

He didn't eat. Not yet. His pale tan eyes never strayed from the doors, tracking every creak and shuffle, his mind grinding on the one fact that grated more than any: she was late. Again. Tardiness was a disease, a weakness he'd never tolerated in his house, his soldiers, or himself.

Everything in his world ran on strict regiment, every bell and heartbeat measured, every meal served on time, every servant in perfect lockstep. It was how he kept order, how he kept chaos at bay.

But she was different. Always a little late. Always disrupting the cadence of his day like she did it on purpose. And he wasn't sure anymore if he wanted her to stop.

The waiting was a small agony, part ecstasy, part turmoil, like an itch under the skin that wouldn't fade. Every time she broke the rules, it burrowed deeper, making him sharper, more aware, more alive. She got under his skin in ways nothing and no one ever had, and even as it drove him mad, he found himself craving it. Craving her.

His fingers twitched, restless, and he reached for the first fork, lifting it to the light and polishing it with unnecessary rigor. The silver was spotless, but he rubbed at it anyway, chasing invisible imperfections. He cleaned each utensil with exacting precision, ritual soothing the tension in his muscles, giving him something to control while he waited for the one thing in this hall he could never truly command.

Then the doors parted.

Luko entered first, grinning like a fool and speaking in low, fast Canariae as he walked beside her. They were laughing, and he held his mouth closed like a tomb, jaw trembling beneath the weight of her presence the moment he heard her voice rise in that soft melodic cadence. He couldn't understand a word of it. Luko could. Of course he could. And the sight of her leaning into him, lips parted in delight, eyes twinkling, it twisted something deep and dangerous inside Malec's ribs.

Then she stepped into view fully, and the breath he'd been holding slipped free.

She wore the deep blue gown he'd had tailored for her, the one he'd chosen himself after seeing her eye it briefly during their last market visit. It fit like a second skin, cinched high at the waist, the skirt loose but gliding like smoke around her feet with every step. The sleeves were long, fitted, and elegant, forming a delicate V that traced the top half of her hands, but it was the neckline that snared his attention and refused to let go. It plunged in the front, deep enough that her breasts swelled above the fabric like ripened fruit. Supple. Full. He hadn't given approval for the cut to be that low. Had he? She'd braided her hair too, thick and glossy, tied in a twist down her back that nearly kissed her waist. Pearls and a silver foxflower, the rare bloom he'd chosen himself, were woven through it like secrets waiting to be touched.

He loved seeing her dressed in what he'd given her. But he hated seeing her smile like that with Luko. That would change. Tonight.

The moment her eyes met his, the laughter fell from the mouth that defied him. She straightened slightly, her expression shifting into something more measured. Obedient. Good.

He gestured to the seat beside him with a single flick of his fingers. She obeyed.

Luko, oblivious, settled across from her at Malec's other side. The table was long enough to seat twenty, but the three of them sat close, nearer than etiquette allowed. No one questioned it.

Dinner passed slowly. Uneventful. Dull.

Malec and Luko spoke of castle logistics, patrol schedules, border reports. Allora was quiet. Pleasant. Barely touched her food. Malec tried not to watch the line of her throat as she sipped her wine, tried not to imagine those lips parting for sweeter things. She smelled like spice and honey.

She was waiting. So was he. Then came the end of the meal.

Steamed milk arrived in little porcelain cups, alongside delicate plates of spiced pastries, fresh fruit, and candied rose petals. The scent of clove and cream wafted through the air, blending with the heat of the fire and the faint sharpness of spilled wine on silver. Some of the servants, all Canariae, whispered briskly to one another in clipped, native German, efficient and hushed, their tone sharp but not unkind. It was the language of labor, of clean-up and hierarchy, of orders given and received without emotion.

"Schieben Sie den Wagen zurück, jetzt!" one hissed as a tray nearly tipped.

"Nicht so schnell, das fällt!" another warned, steadying a teetering dish with nimble fingers.

The sound of it drifted through the flickering candlelight like background percussion, subtle but ever-present. It reminded Allora, if she'd needed reminding, that she was never far from her people. Not even here. They were everywhere: cleaning, fetching, bowing. Quiet. But she wasn't quiet. Not tonight.

The servants dimmed the lanterns, their German hushed beneath the crackle of the hearth, and shadows lengthened across the room as the fire took over. The mood softened. It was the perfect moment. And Malec, halfway through biting into a fig, didn't see the strike coming.

"Malec," she said sweetly.

He paused mid-chew, brow furrowing faintly. His name, his true name, had never left her lips before. She'd always addressed him as you, or with pointed silence. He turned, stunned. And then she said it. In flawless, honey-smooth Awyan:

"Tārel ai withen'va shar vin'kai naren dōl?" (Will you share a drink with me in your den tonight?)

The words, so soft and intimate, dripped from that pouty full mouth of hers like warm wine. Every syllable was carved with care, with rhythm. Her accent was perfect. Perfect.

The room froze. The guards froze. Luko dropped his pastry. Malec... stopped breathing. He stared at her, utterly still, mouth half-open and a fig stuck between his teeth. His eyes, wide and disbelieving, searched hers for any hint of mockery. There was none. Only that damned, beautiful smile. She had struck first. And struck deep.

The sight of her speaking his language, his tongue, his world, made something primal coil hot and desperate in his gut. It was a submission, whether she meant it that way or not. An effort to reach him where he lived. And gods help him, he was weak to it. But he wasn't stupid. This was a game. His little dove was hunting. And yet...

Still chewing slowly, he swallowed, licking his bottom lip as his eyes trailed over her, his voice quiet and low when he finally answered in Awyan.

"You've been practicing... niri."

She smiled wider. Then added with sweet innocence, "Only for you."

For a moment, Malec just stared. And then, something rare happened. His lips pulled, slowly, into a smile. Not a smirk. Not one of his cruel, sharp-edged grins. A real one. Faint. Pleased. As if she'd touched some ancient part of him that hadn't stirred in years. He looked over at Luko, still stunned, and spoke in his clipped native tongue.

"You gave me a gift," he murmured, the warmth almost unnatural on his voice.

"And you kept it from me?"

Luko held up a hand in surrender, laughing under his breath.

"She wanted to surprise you. She's quick, you know that."

Malec's gaze slid back to her. His niri. His heart, even while she plotted. She was playing him. He knew that. But damn it, he didn't care. Not when it made her speak his language. Not when it made her smile at him.

"I would be more than happy to drink with you," he said softly. "Though I should warn you..."

He leaned just a fraction closer.

"Schemes go both ways, valmira'dai." (My Dark One)

The fire burned low in the hearth, casting golden shadows that danced like ghosts over the dark stone walls. The chill of the High North was kept at bay by thick velvet curtains and the slow pulse of heat from torched cedar. Malec's private quarters were quieter than the rest of the keep, large, sparse, and ordered. No luxury, no softness. Just him. A desk littered with maps. A polished blade leaning against the far wall. A single bear pelt thrown across the floor like a mark of territory. Two chairs faced each other by the fire, a table between them, and a bottle of aged northern whiskey so dark it looked like liquid smoke.

Allora sat straight but relaxed, her dress flowing around her like rippling ink. Her hair remained in its thick braid, pearls catching the firelight with every small movement. She looked every inch the queen she was never allowed to be. Across from her, Malec sat in his black tunic, long silver-blonde hair half-tied, loose strands brushing his collarbone. His posture was casual, but his eyes never left her.

There was caution there... but also fascination.

She reached for the bottle first, pouring with slow, careful hands, his glass first, then hers. A silent toast. A flicker of a smile. And the game began.

Malec drank without hesitation, his gaze steady and unblinking. Allora sipped more slowly, letting the burn sit on her tongue before swallowing. It was stronger than she liked, but that was the point. She knew he had a high tolerance. She needed to pace herself, but not seem too careful. He respected boldness, not fragility.

He leaned back slightly, eyes glinting beneath his lashes, and for once he didn't speak to her like a prisoner or like property. He spoke like someone unraveling something dangerous with his hands and wondering, *'If I pull here, will it break... or bare its teeth?'*

"You fight well," he said in Awyan, voice curling low and thick like smoke. "Where did you learn it?"

Allora tilted her head, her soft mouth parting like she might lie. But instead, she said simply, "My world was cruel. We fought to survive."

Malec's fingers tapped once against the rim of his glass. His eyes didn't blink.

"And yet, you survived."

She smiled softly. "That is what I do."

He studied her for a long moment. No flirtation in his face. Only heat.

"That," he murmured, "is what I like about you."

Her stomach tightened, her breath catching. She should've pulled back, said something light, something that reminded him she wasn't there to play this game. But she was. She leaned in slightly, resting her elbow on the armrest, fingers circling the stem of her glass. He watched every movement like a predator tracking a flame it wasn't sure would burn.

"Do you always drink this much with your prisoners?" she asked, letting a small, amused smile tug at her mouth.

Malec smirked faintly. "Only the ones who try to kill me."
She laughed, soft and surprised. "Then I'm honored."
"You should be."
Silence settled between them, not awkward, but measured. Like two chess players holding their breath before the next decisive move.
Then Malec asked, quieter now, "What else? What else did you have to survive?"
It wasn't casual. It wasn't idle. He wanted to know her. More than Luko did. More than anyone ever had. He wanted to be the one who saw her completely, what shaped her, what broke her, what hardened her. And what still made her ache.
Allora hesitated, and he saw it, marked it. She chose her words carefully.

"Men who thought my skin made me easy. Wars. Loss. Being told I was too much. Or not enough."

His jaw flexed. Fingers curled around the base of his glass.
"And what did you do to them?"
Her eyes locked on his, unwavering. "I made them regret it."

Malec smiled again, this time darker. A fox's smile. Pleased. Estimating. Dangerous. God, she thought, he likes this. He likes me like this. He leaned forward just enough for the firelight to catch the edge of his cheekbone, and when he spoke again, his voice dropped lower, private.

"Tell me something Luko doesn't know."

Her heart jumped.

She was the prey and the hunter both, and he was inviting her closer. Testing her. Asking her to show him something no one else had seen, just so he could hold it like a secret between his teeth. She should lie. But part of her didn't want to.

Quietly, she said, "When I was a girl... I used to sing to the stars. I thought they might sing back."

Malec glanced down at her. Once. Blinking, like that answer had tilted the board beneath them.

Then, almost inaudibly, he whispered, "Ryna."

It slipped out, raw and reverent. A whisper. A claim. Her brow creased.

"What does that mean?"

He didn't answer right away. Just swirled the whiskey in his glass, the corner of his mouth pulling up.

"The goddess of song, it is said she is the mother of those with the gift of voice."

Allora thought about that. It was poetic, beautiful in a way.

Malec's gaze never left her. He wondered, against all reason, if she ever thought of him at all, if he ever occupied even the smallest corner of her mind the way she filled his.

For weeks now, he'd carried the ache of her everywhere he went. The scent of her skin lingered long after she'd vanished from a room; he heard her laughter drifting behind closed doors, felt the phantom brush of her presence at his back in the silent hours of the night. It unsettled him in ways he didn't understand. She was less an adversary than an affliction, a fever he couldn't sweat out, a ghost he couldn't exorcise.

He knew it was wrong. He knew he should have found a way to shut it down, to lock it out, to stay above it. But every time he tried, he found himself sinking deeper. She unsettled something old and animal in him, something that didn't care for discipline or reason, something that just wanted. And now, with her sitting across from him, wineglass in hand, leg draped elegantly over the other, the soft shadowed rise of her knee exposed, he felt stripped bare.

Her eyes caught the firelight and glimmered with secrets, sharp and knowing, as if she could see straight through him, as if she alone could decipher the dark, hungry places he tried to keep hidden. He told himself to look away, to remember the danger, but he couldn't. Not when she was the only thing in the room that felt truly alive.

"Would you take me back to the Capitol?" she asked, voice smooth as silk drawn across bare skin.

The question split the air like a blade. Malec stilled, his body tensing with the slow ripple of a storm.

"Why?" he asked, his voice low.

She shrugged, curls spilling over one shoulder, lips curving faintly. "Because I miss the city."

A lie.

He knew it. Every syllable dripped falsehood. But gods help him, he wanted to believe her. Wanted to believe she missed his world. Him.

"You wish to escape?" he asked, eyes narrowing.

Allora tilted her head, shadows brushing over her high cheekbones.

"If I wanted to run... I wouldn't have poured your favorite drink and drank with you, I'd have poisoned it."

The glass in Malec's hand creaked, trembling dangerously under the strain of his grip. A flush of heat burned up his throat, spreading beneath his skin in waves—bitter, bright, undeniable. It was older than pride, deeper than anger, and it made his mouth go dry. He tried to steady his breath, but every inhale tasted of her, thick and sweet, like smoke he couldn't cough out.

She leaned in, elbows braced on her knees, her voice dipping lower, scraping something dangerous inside him.

"If I give you my body willingly..." Her lips curled in a sly, devastating smirk, soft and sharp at once. "Would you take me back?"

The silence that followed felt alive, knife-edged, ringing in his ears. Malec's breath hitched, sharp and audible. The room shrank around them, firelight flickering across her skin, gilding every line of her—her collarbone, her throat, the subtle swell of her chest as she breathed. She didn't look uncertain. She looked like she was savoring the moment, like she was winning.

He felt himself falling apart, piece by piece, as if her words had peeled him open. The something between them snapped taut, burning down his spine, making it hurt to resist. His pulse hammered, so loud he could barely hear anything else. She was close enough that he could smell her skin, salt and something wilder, the ghost of sweat from the fight, the trace of something sweet lingering in her hair. He tried to hold himself together, to pull the old armor of stoicism over his panic and his want.

"You've learned my language well," he forced out, the words brittle and shaking at the edges.

But even as he spoke, his voice betrayed him—thin, strained, almost pleading. She didn't answer. Instead, she moved—a deliberate, fluid unfolding, every inch of her a promise and a threat. Malec's vision tunneled, everything narrowing to the slow, predatory grace with which she knelt before him on the rug, firelight painting shadows along her back. His hand clenched the armrests so hard his knuckles whitened, veins bulging under his skin. Then her palms slid up his thighs, burning through cloth, each touch agonizingly slow and unbearably hot. Every nerve ending lit up in a frenzy, his body twitching in protest and need.

He was drowning in sensation: the rough heat of the fire, the rasp of his trousers beneath her hands, the way her fingers lingered just a little too long, the sound of her knees scuffing the rug. His breath came shallow and fast, each inhale tinged with panic.

Heat built in his belly, sharp enough to hurt, spreading to his chest, his neck, his face. Shame and hunger warred in him, but the desire was winning now, flooding him with want so strong it left him trembling. He felt naked, seen, hunted.

She lifted her face, lips slightly open, eyes heavy-lidded with longing and intent. Malec could smell the sweet tang of wine on her breath, could feel the warmth radiating from her skin, the soft, teasing brush of her exhale against his mouth. She hovered there, so close he could feel her pulse in the air, not quite touching, her presence a promise and a threat. Then her mouth brushed his, maddeningly soft, more suggestion than kiss.

It left his heart slamming wildly in his chest, his mind sparking and stuttering, his sense of self slipping loose, untethered and frantic.

He tried to stay still, to cling to the cold boundaries of discipline that had always kept him safe, but she was inescapable, everywhere at once, burning through every defense. The fire snapped and spat behind her, shadows lurching across the walls, the world shrinking until all that existed was the ache of her hands, her scent, the heat pouring off her in waves.

She wasn't asking for permission. She wasn't pleading for forgiveness. She was taking, luring him out of every safe, dark hiding place he'd ever built. The pleasure was sharp, almost agonizing, a fever crawling under his skin, stripping him raw. He couldn't breathe right, couldn't gather his thoughts, every part of him thrumming with need and fear and the desperate urge to both run and stay.

And now, with her kneeling between his knees, her eyes hungry and predatory, he felt it blooming in his chest like a wound. An ache for her in places he'd thought were dead, ached in a way that made him feel both powerful and helpless.

He knew she could see it, could feel the storm inside him. There was no hiding now.

And then, at last, she kissed him. Soft, deliberate, her lips coaxing his open, her mouth moving with a confidence that left him undone. The jolt of sensation struck him so hard his grip faltered; the glass slipped from his hand, hitting the floor with a heavy thud, spilling a dark stain of liquor across the rug. He barely heard the crash, barely noticed the cold splash against his ankle. His whole body jerked in response to her, a strangled sound tearing from his throat.

He was lost, caught between guilt and a pleasure so intense it bordered on pain, the world narrowing to nothing but the press of her lips and the sudden temptation of the wild freedom in letting go.

Slowly, she let her gaze flicker downward, deliberate and wicked, the hint of a smirk curling her lips. Without breaking eye contact, she lowered herself in front of him, her breath hot against his skin. She nuzzled the buckle, lips brushing the worn leather, then gripped it between her teeth and tugged—prying the belt loose, inch by inch, using nothing but her mouth. The scrape of her teeth, the wet heat of her lips working at the buckle, sent a jolt of fire racing through him. Malec's breath shuddered out, pleasure crackling along every nerve as he watched her—utterly undone by the sight of her claiming him with nothing but a look and the slow, hungry drag of her mouth.

"Mhnn...Alloraaa," he hissed through his teeth, the name torn from him, half plea, half prayer, before dissolving into a broken moan as his head tipped back, neck bared to her.

His chest lifted, lungs burning for air, every muscle drawn as tight as a bowstring, the world reduced to her mouth, her hands, the fire between them.

Her hands slid up his body, fingers gentle but commanding, mapping out every weakness as if she owned him. He tried to call back the cold discipline that had always protected him, but it was gone, melted under her touch. His back arched in surrender, every instinct broken down to a raw, aching need for her. He reached for her then, fingers threading through her hair, not to dominate, but to ground himself, to cling to the only thing that felt real in a world spinning out of control.

"Gods," he choked out, voice strained, jaw locked as his eyes fluttered shut against the onslaught of sensation.

Then her hand slipped between them and found him, hard and aching, his whole body thrumming with the need for her. When her fingers wrapped around him, it was like every muscle seized at once, breath tearing free from his chest, thighs tightening, lips parted on a sound that was half gasp, half plea.

His mind went white. Eyes squeezed shut, jaw slack, he moaned, deep, raw, utterly broken open. In that moment, he was just an Awyan, unraveled, desperate, lost to her. If she'd asked for anything, he would have given it. Everything he was, everything he had, was already hers. He wanted to beg. To sink to his knees. To press his forehead against her stomach and whisper oaths in the old tongue. He wanted to tell her she was the storm that broke him. That he'd tear the world apart if she only told him to.

But he couldn't move. Couldn't speak. Allora had him. And fates help them both, she knew it.

The fire popped and hissed like it could feel the tension, its embers glowing low and molten, like eyes observing the unraveling of an elf who once called himself iron. Shadows danced across Malec's bare chest, flickering with every shallow, erratic breath he took. His skin gleamed with sweat despite the chill of the stone walls, and the muscles beneath it twitched as though resisting his own body.

The belt lay forgotten on the floor, pulled loose and discarded, his last restraint cast aside like an afterthought beneath her touch. He should have stopped her. Should have commanded her to back away. But now, with her between his thighs, nothing about this felt like command. Nothing about her felt small.

Allora moved lower, her dark curls dragging across the rigid muscle of his thighs, leaving trails of heat in their wake. She didn't kiss. Didn't speak. Her soft velvet lips hovered just above his lower abdomen, her breath hot, her proximity unbearable.

So close. Too close.

Malec's hands gripped the carved arms of his chair so tightly his fingers ached. The tendons in his forearms strained, veins pulsing beneath skin that now tingled with the ache of denial. His jaw was locked, teeth clenched against the cry rising in his throat.

No. He couldn't. He was Awyan. She was Canariae. A servant. A domesticated feral Canariae. This was beneath him. She was beneath him. And yet his body trembled for her, shaking, starved, possessed.

The harder he resisted, the deeper it sank its claws in. It wasn't a whisper anymore. It was a scream. A tether wrapping tighter, dragging him toward her as if he were meant to fall at her feet.

It hurt. Heavens above, it hurt.

Every breath without her touching him was a dagger under the skin. Every inch between their bodies was a battlefield. He could feel the magic twisting in his core, reacting to her nearness, pulling, aching, demanding. It would not be denied. Not anymore.

"Please..." he whispered, voice barely audible.

And he hated himself for it. Hated that he didn't even know what he was begging for. For her to stop... or to never stop.

Allora looked up from beneath her lashes, soft luscious mouth still parted, her breath still brushing over him like a fever dream. And when she saw him, truly saw him, his torment, his restraint, the way his entire body was trembling at the edge of surrender, she smiled.

And ancestors help him, that smile made it worse.

She moved lower still. Her plush mouth hovered just a breath above the tip of him, never touching. She didn't even move, she just waited, her mouth close enough that the heat alone made him twitch.

Malec groaned, a broken, helpless sound that slipped past his defenses.

His hips jerked upward, seeking her mouth, seeking relief. His control shattered, his pride unraveling stitch by stitch. His body didn't care who she was. His blood didn't care what was forbidden. He needed her like he needed air.

"My dove, " he hissed, voice ragged, broken open like a wound.

His hands trembled, fist clenched as if holding onto the last edge of himself. But his magic betrayed him. The fire behind her surged again, responding to his turmoil, casting the room in bursts of red and gold. Every nerve screamed for her. Every inch of him was already hers. He tried one desperate attempt to resist. One last rally for his pride.

You're stronger than this. She's playing you. She's just a Canariae.

And then she kissed him again. Just once. Soft. Featherlight. Warm, soft, teasing lips pressed to the tip of him like a blessing. And Malec's sanity splintered. His breath left in a rush, his spine arching as his head hit the back of the chair with a dull thud. A guttural, agonized groan ripped from his chest. The sound was not pleasure. It was torment. It was the sound of a king brought to his knees by something no blade could kill.

The fire writhed. He forced his teeth together, each breath whittled thin by the effort not to shatter. *You can't do this. You won't be one of those Awyans.*

But it didn't matter. Nothing mattered. Because he wanted her. Like he had never wanted anything in his life. And she knew it. Allora's hand rested on his thigh, just above the knee. She didn't stroke. Didn't squeeze. Just that small pressure, so smug, so sure, made his entire body shiver.

She leaned in, inviting mouth brushing over him again as she whispered, "Take me to the Capitol."

Then a breath, warm and wicked against his skin. "Say yes... and I'm yours."

Malec opened his mouth. But no words came. Only a trembling breath. A king, silenced. And she smiled again, because he hadn't said no. Malec didn't move. Didn't speak. But his hands gripped the arms of the chair like he was holding onto the edge of a cliff, nails digging in, veins bulging beneath the skin as if even his blood was trying to crawl toward her. Allora smiled, slow and deadly. Like the villain of a bedtime tale parents told children to warn them what happened when you played with fire.

Fine, she thought. *You want to play noble? Let's see how long that lasts.*

Because she knew pleasure. She knew how to wield it, sculpt it, make gods forget their names with just a breath. She had seen soldiers cry for less. Generals tremble. Men beg. And this elf, this stiff, proud, tan-eyed High Northern noble with his perfectly folded silence, he didn't know it yet, but he was already hers.

She moved lower, not to finish him. Not yet. Just to ruin him. A slow, delicate flick of her tongue over the sensitive skin near the base of him, just enough to make his entire body jerk like he'd been struck by lightning.

> "Charrak!" he choked out, hips lifting off the chair, chasing
> her mouth like a starving beast. His voice was ragged, broken
> wide open. "I can't."

She glanced up through her lashes. His head was tipped back, lips parted, brows drawn in exquisite torment. Sweat clung to his temples, dampening strands of silver-blonde hair that stuck to his skin. His throat bobbed as he swallowed hard, he bit down so hard his skull ached, rage bleeding through every sinew.

She hadn't even touched his shaft. Not truly. Just a whisper of her breath, a suggestion of heat. But he was already trembling. Already breaking. Already shaking like a male on the edge of an orgasm he hadn't earned, didn't expect, and didn't understand. He didn't stop her. He didn't push her away. Didn't reach for his belt. Didn't reclaim a single shred of dignity. He just sat there, body trembling, breath faltering in his chest, like something holy was being stolen from him.

And that, to her, was consent enough. He wanted this.

Even if his mind hadn't caught up to his body. Even if the shame hadn't yet caught up to the ache. So she gave him more.

Her tongue traced the full length of him, slow and devastating, from base to tip, then back again. Just to mark him. To brand him with the memory of her mouth. She wanted it carved into his bones.

Like fire in hell, he felt it.

Malec's whole body buckled beneath her touch. A raw, broken sound tore from his throat, a moan, hoarse and desperate, nothing like the measured commands he was known for. It ripped straight through her, sent a dark thrill pooling between her thighs. Magic splintered the air around them, blue-white sparks licking over his skin like living veins of fire.

He needed more, craved more, even as his mind scrambled to find sense, to anchor himself in the flood. The world shrank to her, her heat, her scent, the sharp ache of her teeth in his flesh. Static built between them, thick and breathless, every inch of his body trembling with want and wonder and something dangerously close to surrender.

"Allora, stop, " he rasped, one hand flying to her head, trembling as he touched her. "Stop, please."

But when she obeyed, when she pulled back, mouth slick with him, eyes glinting with mischief and promise, Malec looked down at her as if she'd struck him to the core. His chest rose and fell in frantic, shallow bursts, each breath catching on the edge of need and disbelief. His hands hovered in the air, trembling, fingers flexing uselessly, torn between pulling her back to him and holding on to the last shreds of discipline he had left. His eyes were wide, wild, filled with confusion and longing and the sharp, vulnerable ache of wanting.

"Why... why did you stop?" he choked, his voice rough and ruined, the sound of a man aching for something he'd never dared let himself have.

It came out half-mournful, half-plea, a naked confession in the dark. Allora didn't answer, not with words. Instead, she reached for the ties at the front of her dress and slipped them loose, her gaze locked to his. She peeled the fabric away, slow and deliberate, letting it fall in a whisper down her arms and off her shoulders, baring herself to the firelight and to him.

Her breasts spilled free, round and inviting, nipples dark and taut, skin glowing in the heat, obsidian, flawless, radiant. The firelight played over every line, every soft curve, every inch of her kissed by shadows and flame, so close he could feel the warmth radiate from her, the promise of her skin on his.

Her eyes, gods, her eyes, never left his. There was challenge there, yes, but also an invitation, daring him to meet her halfway. To want, openly, shamelessly.

Malec stared, utterly lost. It wasn't just lust, it was awe, hunger, terror, worship. The need to possess warred with the urge to surrender, to let her take him apart. The more he tried to hold on to himself, the more it hurt, the ache in his gut twisting tighter and tighter, a torment and a craving all at once.

The room itself seemed to warp around their longing, every shadow trembling, every surface humming with magic and anticipation. Still, Allora watched him, her voice dropping to a breathless whisper, heavy with promise and power.

"Say yes."

His jaw locked so hard he could taste blood at the back of his teeth. His fists balled, trying to anchor himself, to hold on to even a shred of control. He shouldn't want this, shouldn't want her. But when Allora leaned in, slow, deliberate, her bare skin brushing his, her breath scorching hot against his length, he was lost.

She glanced up at him with wicked, knowing eyes, then slid her hands between their bodies.

With steady, patient care, she took him in hand, guiding the thick, aching length of him between the soft, perfect swell of her breasts. Her skin was so warm, silk and heat and promise. She pressed her breasts together, enveloping him in exquisite softness, and then began to move. Slow, hypnotic, dragging her flesh along his shaft in a rhythm that made his vision blur and his breath stutter out of his lungs in a ragged moan.

Malec's world shrank to sensation, her touch, her scent, the way her skin glided over him. He felt raw, unmade, every nerve ending fevered with need. The pleasure was intense, so bright it hurt, flooding his senses and making it impossible to think, to do anything but surrender. His hips jerked, desperate for more friction, for more of her.

She looked up at him through her lashes, lips parted in a sly smile, her eyes bright with mischief and heat.

"Say it, Malec," she whispered, her voice like velvet over stone.

He tried to answer, to fight her, but the only sound that escaped him was a low, wrecked groan. His hands flying to her shoulders, not to stop her, not to guide her, but simply to hold on, to survive the storm she was pulling him into.

"Vel'tor... I can't fight you anymore," he gasped, voice cracking, every word heavy with surrender.

The ache surged through his blood, dragging him deeper, stripping away every defense until there was nothing left but the wild ache of needing her. Allora stroked him with slow, devastating grace, every pass of her breasts making his body tighten, his vision spark white at the edges. His thighs trembled beneath her, as his magic surged brighter, blue veins of light flickering over his skin and arcing through the air between them.

"Say yes," she whispered again, her breath warm against his skin.

"Yes," he groaned, voice breaking, low and guttural. "Yes. Gods... yes."

That was it. That was all she needed. The Silver Fox of the High North, the son of Talandros, the king of self-restraint, he was nothing but ash in her hands now, undone and begging. Allora paused, savoring the moment, her touch wicked and slow, her breath ghosting over him in a final tease before she pulled away completely.

The sudden absence of her warmth felt like a slap of cold water. Malec jerked, trembling, his body suddenly empty, lost. His breath came in harsh. The silence that followed was thick, electric, broken only by the smallest, most humiliating sound, a whimper, so soft and strangled he barely recognized it as his own.

He watched, dazed, as Allora rose with smooth, unhurried grace, fixing her dress without a trace of shame. Her mouth twitched at the corners, almost a smile, eyes alight with fire and victory. She glanced down at him, this ruined, shuddering Awyan who had once been a legend and now looked like nothing more than a boy who'd finally learned how to want.

She extended her hand, cool and steady.

"Deal," she said, her tone composed but her eyes shimmering with satisfaction.

Malec looked up at her, raw and exposed, his breath shaky, his pale tan eyes wide and glassy. For the first time, he let her see every crack, every vulnerability. The mask was gone, his platinum hair loose around his face, his whole body humming with want and wonder.

"Deal," he echoed, voice stripped bare.

But then his gaze changed, something darker, hungry, and desperate flickered in his eyes.

"Now we finish what you started," he murmured.

He grabbed her wrist and he pulled her forward, catching her off balance so she landed in his lap, her legs curling instinctively around his hips. His arms came around her, strong, possessive, unyielding, as if afraid she might vanish if he didn't hold on tight enough.

Without warning, Malec stood, lifting her effortlessly, her body pressed flush to his, mouth falling open in shock, and then laughter. A soft, breathless laugh bubbled out of her, delight and triumph mixing as she clung to his shoulders. He was hers now. All hers. She laughed again, the sound wicked and bright, the kind of laughter that only comes from victory, laughter that was sharp and sweet, like magic in the air.

"You laugh?" he rasped, voice ragged and hungry, a low growl threading through the words. "You mock me while I burn?"

He didn't give her a chance to answer. He dropped to his knees on the thick fur rug in front of the fire, hands cradling her hips as he laid her down, careful and reverent. The firelight painted her in molten gold and deep copper, turning her into a goddess, half myth, half miracle. Malec hovered above her, breathless, his whole body trembling as he lowered himself to her, worshiping her with touch, with gaze, with every shattered, adoring piece of himself.

He was finished pretending, done with every rule, every scrap of old-world discipline that had ever kept him apart from what he wanted. There was nothing left now but her: the ache of her, the hunger that gnawed at him from the inside out, sacred and terrifying all at once. She wasn't his weakness, she was the end of every wall he'd ever built.

And tonight, he would let her tear him down to nothing and thank her for it.

His breath came ragged, chest heaving, nerves raw and exposed, every muscle trembling under the strain of holding back. The throbbing between his legs was almost unbearable, so swollen, so desperate it felt holy, not shameful, as if his whole body had been waiting for this surrender. Every brush of her skin against his, every sound she made, sent shudders through his core. His control, so rigid and unbreakable for so long, was nothing now, just memory.

"My Allora, I yield now..."

His confession slipped out on a broken whisper, heavy with reverence, with longing so sharp it almost hurt. There was no power play left here, no posturing, just raw, open need.

The pain of not having her, of not being inside her, was torture. His hands shook as he touched her, muscles twitching, stomach knotted, spine sparking like he was about to burst into flame.

He had never felt anything close to this with another elfess, never this wildfire, this agony, this joy. She had undone him. Completely. And for the first time, he didn't care. He wanted her to finish the job.

He tore at her dress, hands clumsy and frantic, ripping fabric without apology, every barrier offending him just for existing. Her underthings vanished, cast aside, and when he saw her, truly saw her, skin bare and golden in the firelight, he forgot how to breathe. She was radiant, and she knew it. There was no fear in her, only that wicked, knowing smirk, her body arching into his hands.

He crashed down on her, kissing her everywhere he could reach, her breasts, her throat, her collarbone, devouring her like a starving man.

Each kiss was an admission: you have me, you own me, I'll never be the same. His voice shook as he pressed his mouth to her skin.

"You're not just beautiful," he murmured. "You're dangerous."

He rested his forehead against her chest, trembling, the moment so full it hurt. This wasn't rut, wasn't conquest. It was worship. It was surrender, utter and helpless, everything he'd ever been poured into her.

He kissed her again, soft and reverent, hands curving around her hips, positioning himself at her entrance, his body shuddering with the effort to hold back.

"I want to hear you," he managed, voice hoarse with hope and hunger. "The way you made me sound, I want to give that back to you."

But this was Allora. And Allora don't wait. She didn't even give him the chance to orchestrate a slow surrender. Allora grinned, fierce, wild, triumphant, and thrust her hips downward, taking him in to the hilt in a single, ruthless stroke.

Malec's world exploded. He gasped, the sound tearing from his chest and then breaking apart into a raw, desperate cry. His whole body convulsed, back arching, arms shaking with the shock of it. Stars danced behind his eyelids, every sense overwhelmed, her heat, her tightness, her strength, the stunning reality of her taking him, claiming him, making him hers. It was almost too much, too perfect, too real. He shook, lost, body pressed hard to hers as the fire crackled and the world dissolved into pure sensation.

"Khar'zak, Allora, " His voice barely made it out, cracking and splintering into wordless, shuddering silence.

Sweat slicked his chest, the heat of her body pressed tight to his, hair plastered to his forehead. He looked down at her, breathless, eyes wild and wide, caught between agony and bliss, like he couldn't tell if he was unraveling or being remade.

And she just laughed, that wild, delighted giggle that hit him like a hundred blades, each one shattering another piece of his already crumbling control. She had claimed him completely, without warning, without ritual, without mercy. Now he was nothing but hers, no resistance, no command, no mask left.

She moved under him, gods, she moved, her hips rolling with a ruthless, perfect rhythm, every stroke purposeful, every upward thrust sending a jolt of pleasure so deep it hurt. She rode him like a warrior, relentless, intentional, as if her body had been made to find every secret, trembling nerve he possessed. Every thrust was a claim, every gasp a promise.

> "Allora, stop, ahhh... nnh..." he tried, his voice a broken string
> of moans and gasps, every word half-swallowed by the raw
> edge of his need. "Stars above, you're going to—"

But he couldn't finish, couldn't even think, his fingers digging helplessly into her hips, trying to steady her, to slow her, to hold onto anything as the pleasure threatened to rip him apart.

But she didn't stop. She only giggled again, her laughter reckless, wicked, fearless. And it broke him wide open. He was still trying to control a wildfire. But he couldn't anymore, couldn't fight himself. His hands roamed over her, clutching at her thighs, her waist, desperate to keep up. But she was untamable, too much for even him, a living storm riding out her own hunger. He felt himself dissolve into her—letting go—letting her be wild, letting himself be ruined.

Because, gods, he wanted it, needed it, wanted to be cracked open by her.

And then he gave up control. Gave in to her, let her ride him with all her furious, beautiful strength. He wrapped her tight in his arms, burying his face in her neck as their bodies slammed together in a rhythm that was primal, ancient, older than anything he'd ever known. He met her, stroke for stroke, no more restraint, only raw, aching hunger. Each thrust was deeper, harder, the friction and heat spiraling into something infinite.

She moved with him, just as fierce, just as wild. Her head fell back, mouth open, gasping, a sound that made his heart twist, a sound that dared him to keep up, to never let go. His own moan echoed hers, guttural and shaken, as her heat pulled him back again and again, both of them lost in the relentless collision of sweat and want. Their mouths brushed but never settled, breaths coming faster, everything too urgent, too much.

This wasn't just sex. This wasn't even just surrender. It was communion, a collision of bodies and souls, a coming undone and a coming together, as if the stars themselves had carved this moment into the marrow of their bones.

And then, at the edge of it all, it happened, so bright and devastating neither of them could ever be the same.

His body surged forward, hips grinding deep as the pleasure crested inside him, the last fragile thread of control snapping with a force that left him shaking. The release hit him like a star detonating behind his ribs, violent, bright, impossible to contain. For a heartbeat, he lost himself entirely.

"Mmnh uhhh ha, " Was all that he could muster as he poured himself into her, shuddering, feeling more vulnerable than he ever had in his life.

But this, this was so much more than just climax. And as he spilled into her, something ancient awoke, curling deep inside his chest and spine. He felt a crackle of power, a golden current threading through every vein. His heart lurched, thudded hard, then seemed to settle into a new rhythm, each beat too loud, too real.

Magic blossomed where their bodies joined, alive, living fire, curling beneath his skin, grounding him to her in a way that went beyond flesh.

All the ache and longing, the endless gnawing need he'd carried for weeks, finally dissolved, leaving in its wake a vast, aching fullness. Something beautiful, something almost holy. His body trembled, every muscle twitching, overwhelmed by sensation. His vision blurred, not from pain, but from the threat of tears, real and hot, pricking his eyes.

Nothing, no wound, no loss, no battlefield, had ever left him this vulnerable. But she had.

This Canariae. This impossible, reckless, luminous creature.

He rested his face in her neck, moaning softly, letting the aftershocks roll through him, each wave dragging him deeper into this new, fragile place. It wasn't just animal satisfaction. Something in his soul had found its match, locked into place. He felt himself claiming her, binding her, not as a conquest but as an equal, a mirror. My Allora. Not a mistress, not a concubine, not a symbol of power, a soul. His soul.

And she received him. Stars above, she received him, her own cry echoing his, her body tightening around him, clinging, as if she felt the connection spark to life too. He gasped, stunned, nearly afraid to hope: *Did she feel it too?*

He wanted to ask her to confess everything, but the words stuck in his throat. Instead, he just pulled her closer, arms wrapped tight, unwilling to let go, her warmth anchoring him to the world. He stayed inside her, unmoving, barely breathing, desperate to hold on to the feeling just a little longer.

His body was still trembling, tiny, involuntary shudders rippling through his arms, his back, his thighs. He could feel her heart pounding against his chest, fast and sweet and real, their bodies still joined, the last flickers of pleasure sparking between them. He should have been afraid, should have been furious, even ashamed. But all he felt was awe. Utter, trembling awe.

He'd lived his whole life behind emotional walls, a creature of discipline, strategy, silence. He'd crushed rebellions, led armies, broken spirits. But he'd never, not once, felt anything like this. Not until her.

He lifted his head, just enough to see her face, her eyes heavy-lidded, lashes damp, lips swollen from his kisses, her breath shaky against his cheek. His voice shook as he whispered, the words tasting like a confession he'd never dared to make before:

"Whatever that was... it wasn't just sex." His voice cracked, breaking open.

"I've had partners. I've had power. I've had control." He paused, feeling the truth press in on all sides. "But I've never given myself." His hand drifted down her side, reverent, tracing her skin as if memorizing every line. "You made me forget who I was."

He hesitated, feeling the words settle between them, then softer he admitted, "I don't even know what that makes me now."

He had become something new in her arms. Not a general, not a prince, not even an Awyan of power, just a soul, exposed and unguarded, remade by the force of her. He didn't know how she'd undone him so completely, or if she even realized what she'd done. But he knew this: there was no going back. He would never again be himself without her. And he didn't want to be.

Malec lay unmoving, the weight of a thick, warm fur draped over their tangled bodies. Its plush softness pressed to his back and shoulders, wrapping them in stolen warmth against the cool stone floor. He could feel the heat of Allora's skin seeping into his side, her bare leg hooked over his hip, her head resting just beneath his chin. The fur smelled faintly of wild animals and cedar, a scent that grounded him in the present, even as his mind spun.

The fire in the hearth had burned down to a bed of sleepy embers, casting slow, pulsing amber light across the rug where they lay. It gilded their bodies in molten gold, catching the curves of her shoulder, the swell of her hip, the long lines of his own limbs stretched out in exhaustion.

The air was thick with the scent of sex, woodsmoke, and fur, a wild, intimate musk that curled around them, anchoring him to the moment and to her.

He held her close, her dark skin glowing in the low light, his arms wound around her as if he could keep her from slipping away. Every slow rise and fall of her chest pressed soft against his ribs, her hair spread over his arm and shoulder like a silken veil. Her breathing was even, almost a purr, soothing and steady, utterly content. She lay tangled in his embrace like she had always belonged there, her fingers still curled lightly in the fur at his chest.

But Malec felt no peace. The gentle glow of the room, the warmth of the fur and her body, did nothing to ease the storm inside him. Every muscle was tense beneath the illusion of rest. His mind raced, heart still wild and unsettled, unable to believe how easily she had taken him apart. His pale tan eyes, sharp as storm-washed stone, never left her face, contemplating, wondering, haunted by the truth that she now lived inside him, woven through every shattered defense, every ruined rule.

Allora slept as if she hadn't just wrecked him, as if she hadn't laid waste to everything he was. Her contentment stung him almost as much as it soothed. Malec tightened his grip, feeling the contrast, her calm, his chaos, the ache of wanting her never to leave and the terror of knowing she could.

The fur, the warmth, the quiet: they only made the battle inside him more vivid, more impossible to escape.

Allora. His little dove. His impossible torment. Even now, long after the fever of their bodies had faded and quieted, Malec could still feel her. Not just the ghost of her skin or the taste of her mouth, those things had cooled, receded, but something deeper lingered. She was still there with him, somehow, woven into his bones, interlaced by some invisible thread. Not a chain, not a burden, but a new gravity in his life, a truth that felt both heavy and strangely right.

He drew in a slow breath, chest tight, the weight of it both terrifying and beautiful.

He didn't understand it, and that scared him more than any blade or curse. *Why her? Why now?* He'd never been drawn to Canariae, never found their wildness attractive. He'd spent years mocking his kin for their tastes, dismissing Canariae as undisciplined, noisy, impossible to control. He'd once joked to Surin that bedding one was like trying to break a wild stallion, maybe possible, but more trouble than it was worth.

But then came this one. This wild female. The memory of her on that first day, her hair wild as smoke, her eyes daring him to strike, that devil's grin when she bested his captain in front of half the garrison. She had ruined everything, and the worst of it, the truth he could barely name even to himself, was that he didn't want it undone. Not anymore. From that moment on, he'd tried, truly tried, to beat down the fascination. He'd buried it beneath layers of logic, tried to crush it with discipline. He told himself it was nothing but a test, or a punishment, or maybe just curiosity. Just a body. Just the strange, sharp thrill of power shifting hands. He could handle that, he'd thought.

He was built to handle that.

But then she'd taken his belt between her teeth, cheeky, defiant, utterly unashamed, and every last bit of restraint he had shattered. He clenched his jaw now, the memory so vivid it almost hurt, a dark, reverent ache blooming under his skin. The way she had pulled him down, the way he let her. How she looked up at him, eyes wild with challenge, and for the first time in his life he lost every ounce of air and sense in his body.

He'd kissed her like he wanted to punish her, touched her like she was his equal and his enemy.

But in the end, it was him who surrendered. She hadn't yielded; she'd never even considered it. He'd entered her body certain he would dominate, would devour her whole, but the truth was, she devoured him. The heat of her, the tight clutch, the little gasps of her breath against his cheek, the impossible welcome of her body, it went far beyond lust. It was obliteration.

Was it magic? Some Canariae curse working through her blood and his? Was she enchanted, and he had fallen for her by some accident of fate? Or had he really, truly, bound himself to her in ways older and deeper than any words or warnings could explain?

He'd heard the old stories of Vash'telor, tales from before the throne, before language itself. Older Awyans would talk about the process of two Awyans that bound themselves on a spiritual level.

But this... this felt real. Too real.

He could still sense the echo of her heartbeat inside him, the taste of her breath lingering in his mouth, her scent clinging to his skin like the aftermath of battle. The memory of their joining, the sharp, beautiful agony of release, had shattered something in him, left him sobbing her name, letting her pull him into a place he'd never known.

His hand twitched where it rested against the small of her back, the soft, warm skin rising and falling with her slow, steady breath. The thought of her leaving, of slipping away from him with his soul still tangled in her fingers, filled him with a panic so sharp he nearly trembled. He knew, deep down, if she ever tried to leave, he would drag her back. He would tear the stars from the sky before letting her go.

Malec exhaled, slow and almost reverent, his hand drifting down the smooth line of her spine. Her warmth seeped into his palm, grounding him. When her breath hitched faintly in her sleep, he froze, heart pounding, glancing at her, not tenderly, but with a sharp, dangerous hunger. She was his. Whatever this thing was between them, it had marked her just as surely as it had broken him open.

He knew he should be thinking about tomorrow, about what he'd say, how he'd face her when the sun rose. *Would she pretend it meant nothing? Hide behind that shield of pride and sharp words?* Try to laugh it off and pretend he hadn't touched something real? It didn't matter. He wouldn't let her forget, not the way she'd cried out his name, not the way she had opened for him and melted around him like she'd been waiting her whole life.

And if she fought him, if she tried to hide behind that defiant spark, if she pretended she didn't feel the truth crackling between them, he would break through it. Again and again, as many times as it took. He would push past her pride, past every wall she tried to throw up, until her body gave her away, until her mouth confessed what her heart tried to deny. She was his now. Completely.

He didn't care if the gods wept, or cursed his name for loving her this way. He had already crossed every line that mattered. Let heaven burn, let kingdoms crumble. If the gods still had mercy left, they would leave her in his arms. And if not, if they tried to take her from him, then let them tremble, because he didn't know what he would become if she was gone.

Malec couldn't imagine himself without her anymore. The idea of a future that didn't have her laughter, her fire, pressed close to him, it felt empty, unthinkable. She was tangled into him now, woven through every hope, every ache, every breath.

Chapter 15

His Blood, Her War

Allora stirred beneath the weight of thick fur, her limbs reluctant to leave the cocoon of warmth. The fire still flickered in the hearth, casting a soft, molten glow over the chamber's stone walls and high arch ways. She blinked slowly, letting the haze of sleep melt away. Her body ached, not painfully, but with the slow, honeyed soreness that came from indulgence, from muscles stretched and used thoroughly.

And god, had she used him.

A wicked little grin played across the soft lines of her mouth as the memories returned, unspooling like a film across the backs of her eyelids. Malec, stoic, powerful, commanding Malec, gripping the edge of his own self-restraint like a man on the verge of collapse. His hands trembling. His voice breaking. His discipline, undone.

By her.

A low, pleased hum rumbled in her throat as she stretched beneath the blankets, rolling her shoulders lazily. It had been good. No, better than good. It had been raw and consuming, the kind of sex that made you forget the world was enflamed, the kind that dragged confessions from flesh rather than lips. But more than that, it had been useful.

He'd tried to resist her. She'd seen it in every clenched muscle, every furrowed brow, every desperate flicker in his eyes like a man about to fall on his own sword. And yet, he had fallen. For her. She'd enjoyed every second of it, the moans, the heat, the power, but what lingered most wasn't the pleasure. It was the shift in the balance.

She had cracked something in him. And that? That was priceless.

If he was obsessing over her now, and she suspected he was, then he was vulnerable. And if he was vulnerable, he could be manipulated. That kind of leverage, especially over someone like Malec, was a weapon she would never underestimate.

She rolled to the side, expecting the familiar weight of him beside her, some silent glare or cold command about getting dressed. But the bed was empty. Brows lifting, she pushed herself up and scanned the room. No elf in sight. No snide remark. No possessive stare. Interesting.

The last time he'd held her like that, clutched her like something he was terrified to lose, she'd half expected him to shackle her to the damn bed. But now he was gone? Voluntarily?

Huh. He was either plotting, sulking, or panicking. All three options amused her.

Swinging her legs over the edge of the bed, she stood slowly, letting the furs fall away from her skin with a deliberately lazy stretch. That's when she noticed the chair by the fire. Clothes. She padded toward them, the stone floor cold under her bare feet, and picked up a garment. A rich sapphire-blue tunic, velvet-soft with intricate silver embroidery at the cuffs and hem. Below it, tight-fitting leather leggings. High boots lined in thick, silvery fur.

She lifted the tunic higher, arching a brow at the fine stitching, the expensive texture. This wasn't slave garb. This was... royal wardrobe-level shit.

A low, incredulous laugh slipped from her.

"Really?" she muttered to herself, tossing the tunic over her shoulder. "That's what I get for riding the Silver Fox? Designer clothing?"

She glanced at the boots again, lips curling.

"Freaking hell," she muttered to herself, "if this is what I get after one round, maybe I should ride him more often."

With a chuckle and a swing in her hips, she started dressing, already plotting how to use this new gift to her advantage. Because sex with Malec had been divine, but power? That was the real prize. And she was just getting started.

Not just any clothes. Nice clothes.

As she dressed, the fabric whispered against her skin like a secret she hadn't earned. The outfit wasn't just nice, it was deliberate. Every thread of it screamed chosen, wanted, possessed. This wasn't the scratchy beige cloth of captivity. This was deep blue velvet trimmed with delicate stitching, warm leggings, supple boots lined with fur. And right there, stitched at the hip, was the damn Silver Fox crest. His sigil. His mark. He hadn't given her a collar. He'd given her a uniform. A costume. A throne, maybe, if she were foolish enough to sit in it.

If he was dressing her up like a prize, then she needed to keep playing the part. Keep him enchanted. Keep him looking at her with that damn heat in his eyes, like she was magic. Like she was salvation. Let him fall harder. Let him believe her body, her submission, her moans were real. Because if he stayed busy thinking with the wrong head, he'd never see what was coming.

She adjusted the sleeves and gave herself one last look in the mirror, a striking figure, sculpted and wrapped in his desire. But her eyes were sharp. Focused. This was step one. She needed the Covart Virus. And she would get it.

She knew the infection center was still being stabilized. Quarantined but not impenetrable. They wouldn't let her near it under normal circumstances. But no one suspected she'd want to catch it. No one thought she'd be foolish, or desperate, enough to infect herself on purpose.

But Allora had made peace with desperation a long time ago.

She needed to be sick. Visibly sick. She needed Malec to panic. To beg the healers. And when they found her body couldn't fight it, when they realized the only way to save her was with the antibodies that thrived in that jerk off's body, that sacred Awyan immunity, it would already be too late. He'd give it willingly, thinking he was saving her.

And she would carry that cure back to her people in her veins. She wouldn't let him cage her in silk and fox crests while her people died like dogs in the snow.

No.

She was going to use this, this dress, this firelit bed, this hungover look of sex and satisfaction, to her advantage.

Allora moved briskly through the castle corridors, velvet skirts whispering against the cold stone with every determined step. Her new clothes fit her too well, hugging her curves, the fabric heavy and soft, the sigil at her hip glinting like a secret brand. Everything about the outfit screamed possession. She should have hated it, should have felt the threads closing around her throat like a leash.

But she didn't care. She couldn't. Not about luxury, not about being dressed like a consort rather than a captive, not about the fox emblem stitched into the hem. She wasn't staying. She wasn't his. Not really. She had two goals: get Malec's blood, and get to the portal. Nothing else mattered, not his obsession, not the bruising way he whispered her name against her skin, not the way he'd held her last night like she was the only thing keeping him from falling apart.

Caring was a trap, and Allora had survived too much to fall for that. Caring meant risk. And risk got people killed. She turned a corner, nearly to the healer's wing, when a voice stopped her cold.

"You look different."

She didn't need to look to know who it was. Luko. Of course. He stood ahead, arms crossed, golden eyes flicking down the length of her body, taking in every detail, the dress, the boots, the fox sigil.

She snorted, flipping her hair, "Don't worry, the dress comes off as easy as your dignity did the first time I beat your ass."

Luko's answer surprised her, not just the sharpness of his tone, but how clear and natural his speech sounded. There was no stilted cadence, no broken accent, nothing clumsy or halting. She realized suddenly: she'd spoken in Awyan, and so had he. She was hearing his voice as it was meant to sound, fluid, precise, with a weight that made her chest tighten.

His expression didn't flicker at her jab. He just sighed, giving her a long, unimpressed look.

"You always got a mouth on you. But this isn't a joke, Allora."
His voice dropped, low and serious as he stepped closer.
"Malec does nothing without purpose. You know that."

She shrugged, brushing past him with a forced nonchalance.
"Yeah, yeah. He's marking his territory, right? Real animal behavior."
Luko's jaw ticked, a muscle jumping in his cheek as he reached out and caught her arm. His grip was firm, not rough, but she could feel a tension in his touch, a warning under the skin.
"Allora, listen to me."
His Awyan came out sharp and clear, no hint of old awkwardness.

"There's a difference between being marked and being claimed. A mark's just for show, a trophy, a game piece, something he can toss aside when he's bored. But a claim..."
He shook his head, searching her face. "A claim means you're part of him. Something he can't let go. Something he won't."

She stopped, unsettled by the seriousness in his tone, the way his eyes narrowed as if searching her for the truth. Allora rolled her eyes, but she could feel her bravado faltering, something cold trickling down her spine. Still, she allowed the barest ghost of a smile, drenched in sarcasm.

"Good. Maybe he'll bleed easier when I ask for it."

He hovered closer, voice thinning at the edges, as if he was pushing back something vulnerable.

"You think you're using him. That you've got him on a string because he comes when you call. But that's not power, Allora. That's the trap. By the time you notice it closing, it'll already be too late."

For a second, Luko's voice almost broke, turning gentle, raw, almost pleading.

"He's not just obsessed. He's fixated. That kind of fixation never lets go. It doesn't forgive."

He glanced away, voice dropping as if confessing something he'd barely allowed himself to think.

"The tremors. The mood swings. The way he doesn't eat, barely sleeps. The pain..." Luko's throat worked, his next words almost a whisper. "Gods, if it's Vash'telor, he won't survive if you leave."

A heavy silence fell between them, thick as smoke.

Allora hesitated, letting his warning sit in her bones. But when she looked back, her eyes burned. "I'm not here to coddle his soul," she shot back, voice like a drawn blade.

"I'm here to save mine."

She made it halfway to the door before something in Luko's voice, that single word, dug in deep. Her hand paused on the iron handle, knuckles white. She looked back over her shoulder.

"Vash'telor," she repeated quietly, tasting the word. "What the hell is that, is it just another term for Awyan mating rituals, y'all are weird?"

Luko's face went dark, the lines of his expression drawn and tight. He uncrossed his arms, hands falling to his sides like the weight of the truth was pressing him down.

"No," he said. His voice was so soft, she almost missed it. "It's not stories of bedroom escapades. It's real. Magic in the marrow. You give yourself to someone fully and, if the bond takes, you don't just walk away. Not without bleeding for it."

Allora studied him, a frown furrowing her brow. "That sounds... dramatic."
Luko stepped closer, his voice dropping, the warning in his tone unmistakable.

"You think it's just superstition, because your people don't believe in spirits or gods. But Vash'telor isn't about belief. It's a reaction. When an Awyan bonds that deep, the connection becomes permanent. Not just in the mind, but the body. Emotional, physical, spiritual. It starts as obsession. Then it turns into need. And after that, if it's not answered, it becomes pain. Like withdrawal, only sharper. Like dying by inches. You see it first in their eyes, then their body, restless, sleepless, wild mood swings, can't eat, can't focus. Magic slips, gets volatile, unpredictable."

Allora blinked, the gravity in his words sinking into her skin. Luko's jaw was tight, his words scraping out rough, his throat working like each one cost him.

"And if the bond is rejected, if the one they bind to turns away, it breaks them. Sometimes, it makes them violent. Sometimes, it kills them."

She stared at him, suddenly silent. For once, she had nothing clever to say. Then she scoffed, lips curling in a dark smirk to hide the twist in her gut.

"So what, you're saying I fucked him into madness?"

"I'm saying," Luko snapped back, sharp and real, "that if he bound to you last night, and you plan to walk away, then yes. That's exactly what you've done."

For a heartbeat, even Allora couldn't laugh it off. The air between them thickened, pressing in until it felt hard to breathe. She stared at Luko, her throat tight, voice trembling with a frustration too old to be named.

"But I have to," she said, the words raw and scraped from somewhere deep. "You know I do."

Luko's eyes searched hers, flickering with doubt, compassion, fear. His face was shadowed, unreadable for a moment, all the easy humor from earlier gone.

"For your people," he said quietly, as if testing the weight of it.

"For all of humanity," she corrected, voice brittle and rising, echoing down the empty stone corridor.

The words rang back at her, larger than she felt, more impossible than she could bear. For a moment, she hated how small her own voice sounded in that echo. She stepped forward, closing the space between them, her hands balling into fists. She caught his arm, stopping him.

"Luko, don't lie to me. I know you have answers. What's the secret to making the cure? I'm running out of time...my brother needs..."

She quickly stopped herself realizing she was revealing far too much about herself. Luko's shoulders slumped. He let out a long, low breath, the sound heavy with defeat. His gaze dropped, brow knotted, mouth pressed into a tight, grim line. There was exhaustion in him, yes, but also pity—a kind she'd never wanted from anyone.

"It's not simple," he said at last, almost a whisper.

She crossed her arms, forcing her chin up, refusing to let him see the fear behind her anger.

"I'm a scientist. Try me."

He scrubbed a hand through his thick, sandy curls, pausing to gather his thoughts, like he was steeling himself for something she wouldn't want to hear.

> "The cure exists in Awyan blood," he began, slowly, deliberately. "But not in every elf. Only in some bloodlines. The old ones, the ancient, high-blooded families. It's a trait tied to resistance, something layered into the body with magic, generation after generation. And even when we find a compatible source..." He hesitated, his jaw flexing, "the extraction process isn't easy. It's invasive. Dangerous, sometimes."

Allora's stomach twisted. "How invasive?"

> "You need a direct source," he said. "Drawn fresh. Raw. The cure degrades almost immediately outside the body if not alchemically stabilized. And even then, it only lasts a few hours, less if exposed to air."

"So... storage isn't possible?" she asked, already bracing for the answer.

Luko shook his head.

> "Barely. And only under perfect lab conditions. That's why infected Canariae and shifters are brought here, to the High North, where the Silver Fox lives, the source. We can't send the cure to them, it dies before it gets there."

Her breath stilled in her chest. So that was it.

She didn't want his blood. She didn't want anything from him—not his touch, not his power, not the quiet gentleness that sometimes slipped through when he forgot to be a monster. But her people were dying. And if their only hope had pale tan eyes and a cage for a heart, then so be it. She'd bleed for them. Even if it meant shackling herself to the very thing she hated. Even if it meant erasing what was left of Melodie Jaxxon for good. She had to infect herself. And Malec, his blood, was the only way to survive it. Her fists clenched at her sides.

"So I have two options," she said bitterly. "Drag Malec to my people, or bring the virus to me."

Luko didn't answer. He didn't need to. They both knew which plan had the higher chance of success, and which one would be suicide. Still, she wasn't deterred. She was already thinking ahead. Already mapping out the next move. If Malec wouldn't give her his blood... then she'd give him no choice. Before she could press further, a voice broke across the corridor like a blade drawn from its sheath.

"Allora."

Fucksticks.

Malec stood at the end of the corridor, arms crossed over his chest like a wall she was meant to crash into. He looked impossibly broad, more beast than elf, with his silver-blonde hair unbound, damp and shining, the strands clinging to his jaw and shoulders. He was blocking the only way forward, taking up space like a one-man barricade. She might as well have tried to sneak past a white-furred gorilla guarding the entrance to the underworld.

But it wasn't the sight of him that made her tense, it was the heat in his gaze, pale eyes fixed on her with a mix of claim and warning, the kind that always made her skin feel too tight. The memory of his hands on her body was still fresh, her skin prickling in places he'd touched, lips tingling with the memory of his kiss, his voice still echoing in her ear from last night, raw and needy. She pushed those thoughts down, shoving them deep, and forced her shoulders square, chin high.

Luko straightened beside her, the air between them turning thick, his tension radiating outward in silent waves. Allora felt her jaw clench, the need to get into the sick ward burning through her impatience. *Why did he have to be here?* Why now, when she needed to be anywhere but under that gaze, pinned by that heavy, haunted stare?

But she wasn't about to show it. She pasted on a slow, syrupy smile, the kind she'd worn in too many meetings and interrogations, sweet as honey and twice as fake.

"Yes, Master?" she drawled, voice light and sharp, daring him to react.

She caught the twitch of his jaw, that little tell he hated, proof that she could still get under his skin. But he didn't rise to the bait. Instead, his voice came out like a command hammered from ice:

"Come with me."

No explanation, no softening. Just that cold certainty, that note of ownership she both hated and needed to use. The urge to fight him flared, but so did the old, familiar thrill, a tension that tasted like fear and power, hunger and rebellion, all tangled up.

Allora glanced once at Luko. He met her gaze, his golden eyes troubled, his jaw tight with something unspoken. He gave her the smallest shake of his head, a warning, not a command. The look of someone who'd seen this play out before, and never liked the ending. She felt the message in his silence: Don't poke the beast. Don't get reckless just because you can.

But he wouldn't step in. He never would, not against Malec.

So she forced herself to breathe, ignored the anxiety fluttering in her belly, and let Malec's shadow swallow her up as she followed him.

Chapter 16

To Save Them All

Malec's grip on her wrist was unbreakable, solid as steel, holding her fast without ever crossing into pain. She could feel the heat of his palm, the steady pressure, the possessive certainty in the way his fingers wrapped around her bones.

Allora let herself be pulled along, giving no resistance for now, letting her body move where he wanted it while her mind worked furiously in the background. Every tick of the clock, every echo of their footsteps, was time stolen from her mission. She should've been in the infirmary, working her way among the sick, gathering the last pieces she needed for the cure. Luko had been on the verge of trusting her, she'd felt it—hope fluttering just beneath her ribs like a trapped bird—and then, of course, Malec had appeared like a vengeful storm... Just another day in paradise.

But it wasn't just frustration gnawing at her anymore. It was fear. What if she didn't find it in time? What if the virus evolved? What if she never made it back through the portal at all? The faces of her people—her father, her brother—flashed through her mind like ghosts. What if she'd already failed them? She hadn't dreamt of home in weeks. And that scared her more than anything.

He didn't stop until they reached his study, a room she'd come to know too well, all dark wood and cold firelight, lined with old tomes and sharp memories. He yanked her inside and slammed the door shut behind them, the sound cracking through the quiet with enough force to make her flinch.

Malec turned then, blocking her path, the fire in his eyes radiating hotter than any torch. For a split second, all she could hear was her own breath, the echo of the door, and the rush of blood pounding in her ears. The tension in the room prickled over her skin, hot and explosive, reminding her just how dangerous he could be, and just how badly she wanted to beat him at his own game.

"I don't want you near them."

Her eyebrows arched. "Them?"

"The sick Canariae."

The way he said it, it wasn't a suggestion. It was a decree. As if that settled the matter. Allora crossed her arms, planting her weight on one leg.

"Why? You think I'll catch something?"

"Yes." His tone was ice-edged steel. "Exactly. I will not have my Canariae getting sick."

His Canariae.

The words scraped against her pride, but she bit back her retort. It wasn't his tone that bothered her, it was the control. The possessiveness. The casual way he tried to dictate what was hers to decide. Her voice dropped into something colder.

"So what, you're going to lock me in your chamber like a dog?"

"If I must," Malec said, cold as stone, as if locking her away was just another line in his endless list of responsibilities.

Something inside Allora snapped. She spun, hands flying before she even thought about it, grabbing the first thing within reach, a heavy silver cup from his desk, and flung it straight at his head. He ducked with barely any effort, like she was nothing more than a mild inconvenience. The cup hit the stone wall and spun away, the clatter ringing out like a bell. He stared at her, genuinely surprised, like it had never occurred to him that anyone would dare challenge him like this. Good.

Her blood was roaring now, heat prickling up her neck.

"I am a trained doctor, Malec," she shot back, voice shaking with anger. "I could help them. I should help them. Locking me in here is a waste."

He just lifted a hand in that infuriating, silent gesture, his lip curling with irritation.

"You won't be helping anyone if you're dead."

But even as they argued, Malec moved across the room with single-minded purpose. He stooped to pick up the cup where it had rolled, his attention momentarily locked onto the object instead of her. Without missing a beat in their quarrel, he pulled a soft cloth from a drawer and began to wipe the silver clean, his strokes slow and precise, almost compulsive. He scrubbed every smudge, polishing the cup until it gleamed, the sharp lines of his jaw tight with focus.

She kept pressing her point, her words biting, but he didn't look up, didn't interrupt the careful rhythm of his cleaning. As soon as he was satisfied, he set the cup back in its exact place on the desk, turning it so the emblem faced the chair where he would sit, aligned perfectly, everything in its order. Only then did he meet her gaze again, eyes steady and intent, as if this small act of restoring order was the only thing tethering him to control.

She squared her jaw, the words scraping up from someplace raw.

"It's not fatal to everyone. If I get sick, and I get the cure in time."

"No." He cut her off, his voice slicing through hers like a blade. "That's a risk I won't allow."

She took a step forward, her glare radiating with flames. "Oh, you won't allow it? You don't own my body, "

"I do if it's dying under my roof," he growled, voice dropping into a threat. "I will not bury you, Allora. I will not burn your body or watch your skin rot away from some filth you were too proud to avoid. I don't care who you were to your people. You're not stepping foot in that ward again. Not while you're mine."

Her arms crossed, defiant. She met his eyes, refusing to back down. "You really think I can't handle a little virus?"

"I know you can't," he replied, flat and certain, not giving her an inch. "Not without

the cure."

The air between them crackled, tension sharp as broken glass, neither one willing to move, both too stubborn to yield.

Something inside her flared, sharp and electric. The possessiveness in his tone, the assumption of ownership, it should have disgusted her. But it only confirmed what she needed to know. She still had leverage. If he cared this much about keeping her safe...

Then maybe he wouldn't let her die. She took a small step forward, lowering her voice. Testing him.

"If I got sick... would you even care?"

Malec stilled.

His eyes, usually so calculating, hesitated on hers, not with anger, but with something inscrutable. Confusion. Concern. Then a darker flash, like some old, buried emotion rising before he could cage it.

"You wouldn't suffer under my watch." His voice low and nearly a growl.

She gave a quiet, humorless laugh. "That's not what I asked."

And silence fell between them like a wall. Heavy. Undeniable. Because she wasn't asking if he would heal her. She was asking if she mattered. Malec didn't answer. Not with words. Just the tightening of his jaw. The narrowing of his gaze. The muscle twitch in his cheek. Allora watched it all and weighed it in her mind like a soldier calculating risks. She turned toward the fire in the hearth, every nerve in her body pulling taut.

This was it. This was the route. The only way. If she couldn't smuggle the cure, she had to become it. She had to carry it home inside her veins. Which meant getting sick. Which meant Malec would have to save her.

"What if I did," she pushed, leaning forward slightly, testing him the way a soldier tests the limits of a battlefield, "if something happened and I caught it, "

"I said no." His voice dropped an octave. "You won't."

"Why?" she asked, feigning confusion. "Because you'll stop it? Because you control everything?"

His jaw flexed hard, his posture rigid.

"Yes. Because I will stop it. Because I do control everything. And because I won't watch my canariae wither into skin and bone while I still draw breath."

There it was again, my canariae. His little proclamation of ownership. She let it slide, but not before filing it deep in her mind. Malec stepped closer, towering above her now, his gaze a hard, fevered weight.

"You think I would let you suffer? You think I'd stand by while your body broke down in front of me?" He leaned down, voice low and sharp. "If you so much as cough, I will carry you into the deepest part of the mountains and bleed the antidote into you myself. I'll break every rule of alchemy and medicine to save you, little dove."

She blinked, momentarily stunned, not by the sentiment, but by the intensity. His vehemence wasn't romantic. It was territorial. Like a beast pacing at the scent of danger. But still, she wanted more.

"So," she said again, voice quieter now, more thoughtful, "you'd save me. Not because it's the right thing to do. Not because it might help others. But just because... I'm yours."

He didn't blink. "Yes."

Allora swallowed. Her pulse beat a little harder. That was it. No grand ideals. No concern for the greater good. Just possession, obsession, and an unrelenting desire to keep what was his. Exactly what she needed to hear. Now she knew, if she got sick, he'd save her. Not out of mercy or logic. But out of need. And that made her dangerous. Because she could use it. And he wouldn't even see it coming.

"And what about Luko?" she asked suddenly, shifting the conversation sideways.

Malec's brows drew together. "What about him?"

"You let him walk into the sick ward. You let him touch them. He could bring it back to you. To me. Aren't you worried?"

"No."

"Why not?"

He looked at her like she was being intentionally dense.

"Because it's a Canariae sickness. It does not touch Awyan blood."

Her breath caught. Just for a moment. It was the answer she hadn't expected to come so easily, so cleanly. But it confirmed what she suspected. Malec was the cure. And now she had the one truth she'd been desperate to confirm. That one detail, spoken so simply by Malec, unraveled everything she thought she understood.

Because it meant something far more terrifying than she'd prepared for.

She wasn't Awyan. She was human. Just like every other Canariae brought here. But she wasn't like them. Not exactly. Her biology, her evolution, her blood, none of it originated in this world. She had fallen into this realm like a foreign body, an anomaly, an error in nature's script.

And now, her plan, to infect herself and then extract the cure by surviving it, suddenly looked a lot less brilliant and a lot more suicidal.

What if her body couldn't process Malec's antibodies?

What if her human immune system couldn't communicate with whatever ancient, Awyan-coded biology lived inside his blood? She could die. Not poetically. Not dramatically. Just quietly. Slowly. In a bed reeking of fever and rot while Malec held her hand and begged her to stay, not even knowing why the cure wasn't working. Because the truth was: it wasn't made for her.

Her mind spun. This wasn't just risky, it was a blind experiment. No precedent. No guarantees. A hope wrapped in death. And yet...

She would still do it. Because she had to.

Because her people didn't have time. Because no one else was coming. Because she'd rather gamble with her life than sit back and watch her species starve, freeze, vanish. So she forced herself to breathe. Steady. Calm. Composed.

She nodded slowly, as if this was all still part of the plan.

"I see," she said softly, pretending not to notice the way her voice cracked ever so slightly.

L uko had always known Allora was scheming. From the moment she'd landed in their world, there had been a calculation behind her gaze, a steel behind her poise, something far too precise for a frightened slave. And now? Now he was certain.

Because for the past five days, he had been studying her, closely.

She moved through the sick wards like she belonged there, unflinching in the face of fevered coughing and oozing sores. While the rest flinched away, she moved closer—eyes sharp, movements intentional. The gloves were for show. Luko had watched her unguarded hands touch fevered brows, her mouth drink from vessels passed between those already half-dead. Sometimes she ate what others left behind. Sometimes she stood too long in the thick, diseased air.

She wasn't careless. She was trying to get sick. Luko couldn't decide if it made her brave, brilliant... or utterly deranged.

But the thing was, Allora was a doctor. And more than that, she was a scientist to her core. Whatever society she'd come from had trained her for this exact battlefield. Disease. Transmission. Human frailty. She didn't know how to walk away. It wasn't in her. Even when the risk was lethal. She examined everything. She'd already cornered Luko in the corridor three nights ago and proceeded to give him a ten-minute lecture on the differences between viral replication and bacterial infection, as if he were one of her students. He hadn't even asked.

And when one of the Canariae girls had begun bleeding from her thighs in a panic, crying that the sickness had reached her womb, Luko had gone to Allora. Not because he trusted her. But because she knew. And she'd rolled her eyes, marched into the ward like she owned it, and explained, without flinching, what a menstrual cycle was and why it was not, in fact, a blood-curse. His people had been misdiagnosing monthly periods as an illness for decades. The nerve of them, she'd muttered.

And while she did all of this under his reluctant admiration, she did it beneath the gaze of another. Her lord and captor. Her shadow. His Royal Highness, the Albino Pain in the Ass. Malec.

Allora knew he watched her. She felt him like gravity, always pulling. He didn't trust easily, but he craved her like he was starving. And that, she realized, was her greatest weapon. She played him like a damn flute.

When he trained, she brought him water, cool and sweetened with citrus. She handed him slices of roasted fruit while he sparred, laughing as he scowled at the sweetness before devouring it anyway. She wiped sweat from his brow with the hem of her tunic, trailing her fingers down the curve of his neck like it was a casual thing. He never stopped her. Not once. Because Malec didn't just want her submission, he wanted her attention. Her presence. Her smile. Her care.

Ever since they had sex, he'd become unexpectedly needy. His hands drifted to her waist whenever she was near. His silences stretched longer. When she touched him, his voice dropped, thick with restraint, as if he was fighting to keep something wild locked inside. It worked. Because every time she brought him a cup or brushed her fingers against his chest, his sharp eyes dulled just enough for her to slip past them.

It wasn't that Malec was stupid. It was that he was enchanted. Obsessed. And Allora? Allora knew the power of obsession. She was banking on it.

So she kept flirting. Kept smiling. Kept playing house while slowly poisoning herself on fever breath and infected cups. Because if she could get sick, truly sick, he would have no choice but to cure her. And once she survived it, once the antidote was inside her veins, she'd carry it home. She'd march right through the portal with salvation in her blood and spit in the face of every Awyan who ever thought to use her.

But first? She had to convince everyone she wasn't doing exactly what she was doing.

Dinner had become its own kind of ritual, a nightly waltz of power, secrets, and shifting lines. It wasn't just the food or the company. It was the way every glance, every small gesture meant more than words. Malec always took his place at the head of the long obsidian table, his posture immaculate, not a hair out of place, the silver fox crest at his chest glinting with the firelight. He looked every inch the ruler.

But since that night, since she'd become something more than a prisoner, he'd started treating her differently. Like she belonged to him in a way deeper than titles or chains.

Every evening now, Allora sat at his right, close enough for the whole hall to notice, close enough for his arm to brush hers, for his hand to find her knee under the table if he felt like reminding her she was his. The candles burned low tonight, casting golden puddles across the black stone, the scent of honeyed game and roasted vegetables mixing with the faint spice of Malec's cologne. His eyes never really left her. Sometimes she caught the ghost of a smile at his lips, softer than before, his gaze catching on her like he was still trying to figure her out, and enjoying every moment of not knowing.

Luko, always nearby, watched them both with the anxious energy of someone waiting for a disaster he knew was coming. He rarely touched his food, tense, glancing between Allora and Malec as if trying to warn

her without words, trying to keep the peace, trying not to get her locked
away for good.

Malec leaned back, turning his chalice slowly between elegant
fingers, his gaze lingering on Allora in a way that felt almost indulgent.

"And what mischief did my canariae get into today?"

Allora touched the linen to her mouth, movements graceful,
composed—despite the storm beating just beneath her skin.

"Nothing wicked," she answered sweetly. "Just helping the
maids. Keeping busy."

She kept her eyes down, hiding her smirk, the game so familiar now
it almost felt safe.

Malec hummed, skeptical but amused, his voice low and
velvet-edged. "You helped clean?"

"I did."

"And you enjoyed that?"

She shrugged. "Not particularly. But it felt good to contribute."

She dropped her gaze again, careful to conceal the plotting glint
in her eyes. But Malec wasn't easily fooled. His brow quirked, eyes
narrowing in that way that meant he saw more than she wanted to admit.

"You haven't been near the sickness... have you?"

Across the table, Luko sputtered, nearly choking on his drink. His
hand went to his mouth, eyes wide, silent pleading aimed at Allora not
to push her luck. Without missing a beat, Allora reached across, her
fingertips brushing Malec's forearm, gentle, claiming, intimate. She felt
him still, the way he always did at her touch, his focus sharpening,
everything else in the hall fading to background noise. He looked at her
then, not with suspicion, but with something softer, something that felt
dangerous for both of them.

"Can I make a request?" she purred, voice just above a whisper.

Malec tilted his head, every inch the attentive lover and ruler,
suspicious but unable to hide his interest.

"If it is within reason... you may have whatever you want."

Allora's smile was slow and warm, syrupy sweet but with a sharp edge underneath.

"I want to sit in your lap while we eat."

The room went silent. Even the crackle of the candles seemed to hush. Luko groaned, dragging a hand down his face like he wanted to disappear into the table. Malec blinked, first in disbelief, then in growing surprise, as if he truly couldn't decide whether she was testing him or tempting him. He set his fork down carefully, all pretense of casualness gone. His eyes held hers, searching, hungry, almost reverent. For a moment, the air was thick with everything unsaid, his longing, her calculation, Luko's dread.

"You... wish to sit with me? Here? Now?" Malec asked, his voice roughened with something close to wonder.

She nodded, letting her gaze hold his.

Malec's chair creaked as he leaned back, spreading his arms in a subtle but unmistakable invitation.

"Come then."

The entire hall seemed to hold its breath as Allora rose, the corners of her mouth curling in a smile that was pure mischief, and pure victory.

With the smooth grace of a lover and the calculated boldness of a thief, Allora slipped into Malec's lap. His hands landed at her hips automatically, possessive but not harsh. She could feel the tension in his body, the way his breath changed, a subtle shift, as if the reality of her weight, her heat, unsettled even his famed composure. His face remained mostly impassive, but there was a flicker of something in his eyes, soft, hungry, almost vulnerable.

She let him savor it. Let him feel her settle against him, her thighs pressed to his, her fingers idly toying with the collar of his tunic like she was content just to play the part of the docile consort. Leaning in, she offered him a bite of roasted peach, watching his mouth part for it, slow and unguarded, her own smile curling in secret delight. She glanced over his shoulder at Luko, caught his eye, and stuck out her tongue just long enough for him to notice. He just sighed, shaking his head back and forth, that look of resignation clear, like he was ready to throw up his hands and surrender to her madness.

Once Malec was fully lulled, fully distracted, she leaned in a little closer, fingers still playing with the soft fabric at his chest.

"Malec?" she purred, sugar-sweet, but her eyes glittered with intent.

His gaze lifted, slow and hazy, half-lidded with pleasure. "Yes, little dove?"

She tilted her head, letting her voice slip into innocence. "When will you take me back to the Capitol?"

The mood shifted, a ripple of cold through the warm, candlelit room. Malec didn't stiffen, didn't let his face change, but she felt the difference instantly: his fingers pausing, the gentle grip faltering, his breath caught just a fraction too long. He looked at her as if she'd just pressed a knife to his throat.

He leaned in, his reply soft but absolute. "Soon."

No date, no promise. Just that word, enough to soothe appearances, but not enough to quiet her mind. She smiled, all compliance, while her thoughts ran wild beneath the calm.

Luko watched the exchange, frustration gnawing at him. He'd stayed silent for days, seeing her work Malec with laughter and soft hands, noticing her bring him drinks and whisper in his ear, seeing everyone fooled by the pretty fiction of comfort and acceptance. But Luko wasn't blind. He saw how she hovered near the sick, how she snatched dirty dishes with bare hands, even sipped from their cups when she thought no one was looking. He'd found her tending a fevered Canariae, cloth pressed to a burning forehead, eyes bright with something cold and calculating.

She was deliberately courting illness, testing the boundaries of her own body, betting on a cure she didn't even know would work. It terrified him, made him want to grab her by the shoulders and shake sense into her. Because she didn't know. Not truly. She might have been the sharpest human mind he'd ever met, but she was still a foreigner here, different blood, different bones, a whole different world inside her veins. The cure might not save her. Malec's blood might not be enough. And if she gambled and lost, if she fell sick now, trusting a hope that might never be real, she could lose everything.

She could die. Luko couldn't let that happen, not just because of Malec, not because she was 'the Canariae,' some living asset in a warlord's lap. Because she was Allora. She was stubborn, reckless, clever, and alive in a way that made people want to follow her, protect her, even when she drove them insane. She was his true friend. She mattered.

So when he saw her that night, perched in Malec's lap at dinner, fingers playing with the rich fabric of his tunic, laughing at something only the two of them could hear, Luko felt the weight of responsibility settle heavy in his gut. Seeing her, so vibrant, so dangerously determined, he realized he couldn't just stand by. He had to do something, even if it made him the villain in both their eyes.

He made up his mind. He was going to tell. Let Malec be furious. Let Allora glare. Better they hate him than he watch her destroy herself chasing a miracle.

So when dinner was over, the servants gone, and Allora was still sprawled comfortably in Malec's lap, their bodies tangled together at the head of the table. Her fingers in his hair at the nape of his neck as his hand rested on her thigh, both of them caught up in quiet laughter and the heat of each other. Their kisses had become languid, unhurried, Malec's mouth brushing hers, Allora's breath warm against his cheek, as if neither of them wanted to let go just yet.

Luko, still at his place across the table, looked like he'd rather be anywhere else. After a few failed attempts to ignore them, he finally cleared his throat, loud enough to break the spell. When Malec glanced up, Luko leaned forward, keeping his voice low and deliberate.

"Commander, may I speak with you privately? It's about the... vaccine."

Malec blinked, a flicker of annoyance tightening the corners of his eyes as he turned to Allora, his fingers grazing down her arm in a gesture that was both possessive and tender.

"Go wait in my study, dove," he said, voice low and steady, though the thread of heat already curled behind it, "I will not be long."

She didn't move. Allora held her place in his lap, lashes sinking like the hush before a storm. Then came that smile—cunning, intimate, as she bent low, brushing his ear with lips soft and breath hotter than fire.

"Well, you'd better not be," she whispered silkily. Then—she licked him.

A slow, deliberate flick of her tongue against the shell of his ear.

Malec's body went rigid. His spine stiffened, his fingers twitching on her thighs. She kissed the curve of his neck next, just below his jaw, a place no one touched unless they meant to ruin him. The warmth of her mouth lingered like a brand.

And then her hand slid down—lower, lower still—resting boldly over the hard length beneath his robes. She squeezed him through the thick fabric, fingers curling just enough to test the weight of him, and Malec groaned low in his throat, the sound rough and guttural, barely contained. His eyes fluttered closed for a moment, jaw fixed, every fiber of him drawn tight with raw, aching need. A sharp, maddening burn beneath the surface of his skin. She made him feel feral, undone, not a commander or a ruler, but a male desperate to bury himself in her until all reason left him. His blood surged southward, heart pounding hard enough to echo in his ears.

"I want to finish what we started," she purred into his skin. "In your study."

And then, like a storm slipping back into silence, she rose. Malec's hands instinctively reached for her hips but caught only air as she sauntered away, hips swaying with insolent grace. She didn't look back—she didn't have to. She knew exactly what she'd done to him. His eyes followed every step, starving, radiating, hungry.

His cock throbbed against the press of his robes, painfully hard, aching with the promise she left behind. He dragged a slow hand over his face, exhaling sharply through his nose, trying to gather the shredded remains of his composure. The scent of her lingered—sweet and wild, like dark fruit and defiance—clinging to his skin like smoke. The door closed behind her with a soft click that felt like a final taunt, and for one suspended breath, silence reigned. Then Luko's voice cut through it, wasting no time, taut and urgent.

"She's been trying to infect herself."

Malec froze. The words struck like ice water.

"What?" he snapped, voice low, dangerous.

> "I've seen it," Luko said, eyes dark with worry. "More than once. She's been in the infirmary. Drinking after the sick. Taking care of them. Touching them. She's doing it on purpose."

The warmth that had softened Malec's expression at dinner vanished instantly. He rose from his chair in a fluid, lethal motion, all tenderness burned away, replaced by the cold precision of a military commander.

"Why." It wasn't a question—it was a warning.

> "She wants to get sick," Luko continued, his voice quieter now. "So you'll give her the cure."

Malec's jaw tensed, his face turning hard, carved from winter stone. His fists clenched at his sides until his knuckles whitened, rage humming off him like heat off a forge.

> "She doesn't even know if it'll work," Luko pressed, daring to finish. "She's not like the others. You said it yourself—her scent is different. Her blood. Her body. The cure might not even take."

The growl that left Malec's throat was low and inhuman, more beast than elf, a low throaty warning that made the air itself tremble. It wasn't just fury at her recklessness—it was fury at himself. At how easily she'd deceived him with laughter, with softness, with the illusion of shared breath and silk-threaded trust. And how deeply, how foolishly, he had wanted it to be real.

"She tricked me." Malec's voice was raw.

Luko didn't answer.

"She used me."

Still, nothing. Luko kept his gaze steady, letting the silence do its work.

Malec turned away, breath shaky, fury twisting his features. The knowledge that she'd played him burned like acid, because he'd wanted to be played. He'd wanted to believe. But now, all that was left was the storm. And he was the only one who could end it.

"She's not going back to the infirmary," Malec said, voice low and final. "She's not going anywhere near them again."

"And if she tries?" Luko asked, already bracing himself for the answer.

Malec's answering smile was sharp enough to draw blood. "Then I'll chain her to the bed myself."

Malec's words landed with a finality that killed all argument. Just like that, the trip to the Capitol wasn't a distant promise or an empty threat anymore. It was a command, the end of the discussion, because if Allora couldn't be trusted with freedom, she wouldn't have any left to lose. If she wanted to play at rebellion, he would show her what it meant to lose. Let her test him. Let her think she could win. Malec had never lost a war, not to gods or kin or fate.

And this time, his little dove would learn what it really meant to be conquered.

He sat back down at the head of the table, posture rigid, his eyes pinned to the untouched goblet in his hand. The silver fox on his chest caught the candlelight, bright and sharp as a warning. He didn't move. Luko remained at his left, silent, the air between them heavy and unspoken. The dining hall had emptied, servants dismissed, Allora sent off with a warm farewell, all masks and pleasantries, never suspecting that her freedom had just ended.

Malec's jaw corded with tension. The ghost of her warmth lingered on his thighs, the sweet scent of her still clinging to his tunic. He could see her smile in his mind, hear her laugh, feel the gentle drag of her fingers across his collar. She had looked up at him like he was the only thing that mattered, her affection so real it almost fooled him. But it was just a game. He'd let himself believe it was more. Let himself savor the softness, the way she leaned into his touch, the hunger in her eyes when she thought he wasn't looking.

The cruelest truth was that he wanted more. More of her affection. More of her hands under his clothes, her mouth at his ear, her body curling into his as if she belonged there. The way she'd pressed herself to him, whispered requests with a bitten lip, had made him forget that every moment was a negotiation.

And now Luko had confirmed the truth he'd already felt roiling in his gut. Allora had been courting death, deliberately tempting the Cotard-Virus, touching the sick, drinking after them, risking everything for a cure she had no guarantee would even save her. She wasn't Canariae, not like those born under this sky. She was human. Different. Fragile, no matter how stubborn she acted.

He felt the goblet creak in his hand, a thin, hairline crack splitting the silver, a quiet warning of the storm gathering under his skin. He had let her get that close to the edge. No more. He didn't look up as he spoke, voice edged with iron.

"Tell the stable hands to prepare the convoy. We leave for the Capitol at first light."

Luko glanced up, surprise flickering in his golden eyes. "So soon?"

Malec didn't answer. He didn't need to. The decision was made, the line drawn. The game was over. The sweet, compliant little dove he thought he could tame had never really existed. If she wouldn't stop risking her life for a fantasy, he would take her from the fire himself. He'd keep her from temptation, bind her to him with iron and stone if that's what it took. If she refused to follow his rules, then he would make sure she had no choice but to obey.

Chapter 17

Crossing Worlds

Allora hadn't gone to Malec's study like she was supposed to. She was supposed to wait. Sit pretty. Act tame. But Allora had never done what she was supposed to. Not when lives were on the line. Not when the clock was ticking. Not when every hour that passed meant the virus inside the sick was breaking down, clearing itself from their systems, leaving behind only useless, spent antibodies that would be no good to anyone.

So she slipped away when the guards changed post. Slid through the servant corridors barefoot and quick, heart hammering in her chest. She kept her hood up and head low until the corridor turned cold and quiet, lined with the moans of the recovering.

The sick ward.

The scent hit her like a blow, bitter herbs, sweat, rot, something metallic clinging in the air. But she didn't flinch. She moved fast. Sat beside the groaning Canariae maiden and helped her sip water, then took the same cup and drank what was left. She wiped brows, collected used linens, pressed her hands into blankets, touched faces still slick with fever.

And she would've gotten away with it. If not for the cold voice that slid like ice down her spine.

"Allora."

Her name cracked through the room like a blade. She froze. Turned slowly. Malec stood in the doorway, motionless. His expression wasn't rage. It was worse. He was calm. Deadly calm.

His eyes, those piercing, tan eyes, raked over her, taking in every detail. The water cup in her hand. The flushed, sleeping patients. The distance she'd crossed. The line she'd shattered.

"What," he said softly, voice like the edge of a sword, "do you think you're doing?"

She opened her mouth. Closed it. Tried again. "I was just- "

"Enough."

He was on her before she could blink. His hand wrapped around her wrist with brutal precision, not hurting her, but not letting her go either. And then they were moving. No words. No explanation. He dragged her out of the ward, up the stone steps, down the private wing of the castle like a thundercloud with no lightning, just quiet fury, coiled and controlled. She struggled, barked out his name, cursed under her breath, yanked at his arm. He didn't even glance at her. Until they reached a familiar set of black-stained double doors. His chamber.

Her heart stuttered. "Why are we here?"

He shoved the doors open and pushed her through. Not roughly, but without permission. The fire was already lit. The bed unmade. The air warm with the scent of cedar and smoke. He followed her in and shut the door behind them with a slow finality that made her skin crawl.

"You are not to leave this room," he said. "From this moment on, you eat, sleep, and bathe here. With me."

Allora whirled around. "You can't be serious, "

"I am."

His voice didn't rise. It didn't need to. He stalked toward her, slow and steady, until she had to tilt her chin just to keep his eyes.

"If you cannot be trusted to guard your own life," he murmured, "then I will guard it for you."

"And what is this?" she snapped. "Punishment?"

"This is mercy."

She laughed bitterly. "Locking me up in this ugly cage like a pet is mercy?"

"No," he said, taking another step closer. "Locking you up like mine."

She flew at him. Fists clenched. Teeth bared. A rush of rage so sharp it could've split the room. He caught her easily, spun her, caged her against his chest with one arm across her torso, the other pinning her hands.

"You're angry," he whispered near her ear, lips brushing her skin. "But your form is sloppy."

"Let me go," she growled.

"You fight better than this, little dove."

His calm made her insane. Not because it was patronizing, though it was, but because it was true. He wasn't even breaking a sweat. She could feel the steady rise and fall of his chest, the patience in the way he held her like a dance partner, not an enemy.

She stilled for just a moment, chest heaving, every inch of her trembling with fury.

"Is this what you want?" she hissed. "Control? A cage?"

"I want you alive," he said darkly. "And if that means chaining you to my side, then yes."

Her jaw wound tight. So did his. He released her slowly, and she stumbled back, catching herself on the corner of his desk.

"This is insane," she said, trying to sound calm.

"No," he said. "Insane is watching the one thing I cannot replace risk her life just to spite me."

Allora opened her mouth, but the words didn't come.

"I only want what's best for you," Malec said, his voice low, steady, an eerie sort of calm that came not from peace—but restraint—a storm held behind steel.

Allora stood still in the center of his chamber, jaw iron-bound tight enough to ache. Her skin still tingled from his hands. Her pride, her fury, her desperation, they all tangled inside her ribs like a knot that couldn't be undone.

Malec stepped closer, his pale eyes scanning her face, searching for a softness that was no longer there.

"Tell me," he said, barely above a whisper. "Are you trying to contract the virus... so you can leave me through death?"

The words weren't shouted. They didn't lash out. They were careful. Fragile. And they cut her anyway. Her throat tightened. Her breath hitched, almost too quiet to hear. Something in her chest buckled—something she didn't let anyone see. Not even him. Because the truth was, yes. A part of her had hoped it might kill her. That the virus would end the tether, the war, the endless ache of being trapped in someone else's name. But worse than that... was how gently he'd asked. How raw the question had sounded in his voice. Like it wasn't a command. Like it was a wound.

Her gaze dropped—just for a heartbeat. A crack, small but real. She clenched her jaw and shoved the feeling down. No weakness. No softness. He didn't deserve it. Even if, for a second, she wanted to scream.

She said nothing. So he pressed again, firmer now, the velvet of his voice lined with a blade.

"Is that it?"

She didn't recoil. But the silence between them roared. He stepped closer. His hands hovered near hers, tentative, uncertain—like he didn't know whether to hold her or let her slip through his fingers. She met his gaze, chin tilting upward in defiance. And then, with venom in every syllable, she spoke the one truth she knew would destroy him.

"My name is Melodie Jaxxon," she said coolly. "Not Allora."

The words echoed like a slap. He stilled. His breath caught. The smallest twitch passed through his brow—like something inside him cracked. Like she had reached into his chest and crushed whatever fragile thing he'd been nursing there.

He didn't shout. Didn't rage. He simply looked at her.

Looked at her the way an Awyan war-born stares into the ruin of his own making—silent, still, contemplating as the fire devours the structure he once ruled with pride. The silence was unbearable. She expected him to break. But instead... he straightened. Drew himself back into the cold, elegant armor he wore like a second skin.

> And in the calmest voice he could manage, he said, "You are not to set foot outside this room without me."

His tone was glass. Polished. Controlled. Cracking.

She didn't answer. She didn't have to. Because he turned without another word, walked to the door, and paused, just long enough for her to wonder if he might turn back. He didn't. He stepped out, pulled the door closed behind him with surgical precision, and the lock clicked into place.

He left her standing there, alone in his chamber.

The cold night air sliced through Malec's tunic as he stormed toward the stables, every breath painting the darkness with white mist. Each step landed hard, boot crunching frost and gravel in a rhythm as rigid as his thoughts. He didn't care about the cold biting his cheeks, didn't care about the ache setting into his hands where he clenched and unclenched them with every stride.

In truth, he needed the sting, needed the crisp clarity. It was the only thing keeping him rooted to the moment when everything inside him felt like it was coming undone.

Her words wouldn't leave him. They rattled around inside his skull, as persistent and sharp as broken glass. 'My name is Melodie. Not Allora.' He heard it on a loop, the syllables out of place, wrong. His jaw flexed so tightly it sent pain crawling up the side of his face and made his ears ring. He found himself counting each inhale, one, two, three, and tapping his thumb against his thigh, a silent metronome he'd used since childhood to hold his focus when the world spun out of his control.

She'd said it so simply. So final. Like the name he'd given her was just another chain, something to be thrown off, not the only piece of himself he'd ever dared offer without a shield. He'd been called many things over the years, cold, soulless, untouchable. Names others used to cut at him, strip him of warmth, to remind him he was always just outside the circle of belonging.

But nothing had hurt quite like this. Not even close.

Because it wasn't just defiance. It was a rejection. A clean, sharp refusal, not just of the name, but of what it meant. Of him. Of everything he'd let himself believe they'd built in the fragile, stolen peace between battles. With those few words, she had drawn a line, one he felt simmering across his skin, down to the marrow.

He pressed his knuckles hard against his mouth, biting down on the urge to scream. He needed order. He needed rules. He needed her to be his Allora, not someone he could lose to the night.

But she was refusing him.

He leaned into the side of the stable, palm pressed flat to the rough wood, needing the bite and splinters in his skin to remind him what was real. The night air burned cold in his lungs, every breath fuming white into the dark as he tried to collect himself.

Why does she always live in my mind like this? The thought circled, restless. He closed his eyes, searching for stillness, but all he found was the sound of her laughter looping through his memory. The teasing edge when she mocked him, the rare music of it when she let herself mean it. Her voice crowded out everything else. When she was gone, the world felt smaller, thinner, as if the air itself had abandoned him. The grand, echoing halls of the keep felt like mausoleums. Even food tasted like ash, sunlight faded into a tired gray. But when she smiled at him, gods, even when it was just for show, even when he knew she was playing him, everything came alive. Colors sharpened, air filled his lungs, warmth crept up his spine like sunlight melting ice.

Was this love?

The idea hit him like a hammer to the chest. He actually rocked back, gripping the wall for support, heart hammering as if the word itself might tear him apart. No. It couldn't be. He wasn't made for that. He was made for control, for discipline, for duty. Love was chaos, and he was built to survive chaos, not surrender to it. And yet... she made him want. Not control, not dominance, just her. Laughing, unbroken, safe. Not willing to die just to escape him.

He dropped his head into his hands, fingers digging into his hair, trying to squeeze out the ache. She was reckless. Wild. Untamable as a storm, shifting and changing and never letting him find his footing. But the thought of a world without her, the possibility of losing her to anything, fate, illness, even her own stubborn will, made something deep inside him curl up and howl.

He would chain her to safety if he had to. Not to keep her prisoner, but because she was, impossibly, his heart. And he didn't know how to survive without her anymore.

He moved toward the stables, boots crunching over the frozen earth, and paused just outside the gate. His horse lifted its head, ears flicking, the animal's warm breath pluming in the air, a small island of steadiness. Malec stepped forward, resting a palm against the horse's strong neck, feeling the heat, the slow, sure rhythm of life beneath the skin. The animal leaned in, sensing something off in him, and for a moment Malec just stood there, grounding himself in the creature's solid presence.

Why? he thought again, almost pleading. *Why her?*

He had bedded many before. Slept with elfesses of noble blood, with beauty enough to silence a room and ambitions sharp as daggers. Some had whispered their devotion into his ear, breath sweet with hope or cunning, others had tangled their bodies around his as if they could bind him to their futures. None of them, not one, had ever truly touched him. Not the way she did.

Allora infuriated him, burrowed under his skin, made every rule feel too small. And yet... by the gods—he ached for her. No. Not gods. This ache wasn't holy or blessed, it was something deeper, darker, stranger. He couldn't even blame it on magic, not really. This was older than any spell.

Malec tipped his head back, letting the chill night air bite his cheeks, dark lashes catching stray starlight.

Memory tugged him back. That first night. The way she'd clung to him, but it wasn't her body that haunted him, it was the feeling. The impossible, soul-deep pull, like someone had finally reached in and turned the right key in his chest. It wasn't lust. It wasn't even love, not the kind you could talk about or write poems for. It was... completion. Like there had always been something missing inside him, a space he'd ignored, and when he found her, it locked into place with a certainty that shook him.

That wasn't normal. Wasn't just rut. That was something else. Something he didn't have the words for.

"Vash'telor," he whispered, the word strange and weighty in the cold air. He'd always dismissed it as old wives' tales, poetry for the desperate.

But now, now, every empty space inside him echoed with her absence, and every moment she smiled or laughed near him, it filled those spaces like sunlight after endless winter.

He ground his teeth, the muscle in his jaw flexing hard as he turned from the stable. If there was any truth to the ancient tales, any at all, there was only one person who might know how to unravel it, Luko. The only one who'd cared enough to study the old ways, the hidden bonds in blood and spirit.

Malec's stride sharpened as he headed toward Luko's quarters, the wind lashing at his cloak, fire burning low and fierce in his chest. He wasn't just looking for clarity now.

He was hunting for answers. For her. For himself. For whatever the hell this was.

Luko was perfectly content. Nestled deep in the comfort of his overstuffed leather chair, a half-eaten sweetbread wedged lazily between his teeth, he scribbled meticulous notes across a parchment scroll with the careful grace of someone who had no intention of rushing through life. His study glowed with a gentle warmth, firelight lapping at the stone hearth, candles flickering in brass sconces, shelves crammed with rolled tomes and old texts leaning in crooked towers against the wall. It smelled of ink, sugar, and woodsmoke, a scholar's paradise, quiet and undisturbed.

Until the door slammed open.

A gust of icy air swept in, followed closely by a tornado of agitation dressed in fine black leather and warlord arrogance. Luko didn't even look up.

> "I assume you're not here for a bedtime story," he said around the bite of bread, quill scratching idly. "Did your little dove bite you again, or are we escalating to poison now?"

Malec stood frozen in the doorway, eyes dark and brooding, arms folded like a petulant statue of fury.

"She's reckless."

> "She's brilliant," Luko replied without missing a beat, then added with a knowing glance upward, "and that scares you."

Malec scowled, stalking in, the door thudding shut behind him. "She's insufferable. Stubborn. Infuriating."

"So are you," Luko muttered, brushing crumbs from his scroll.

> Malec hovered like a stormcloud, pacing. "She deliberately exposed herself to the virus, Luko. She wants to get sick."

At that, Luko sighed, set down his quill with a dramatic slowness, and leaned back in his chair like a parent summoned to explain to a child why fire is hot again.

> "Yes I was there when I told you this?" he asked, propping his boot on the edge of his desk. "So, what's your grand plan?

Aside from glowering at me in candlelight like a sulking villain."

Malec ignored the sarcasm, dragging a hand through his pale hair. "Should I take her back to the Capitol?"

"Yes," Luko answered before the question even finished. "But you already knew that."

Malec paused. "It's what she wants," he said flatly.
Luko raised a brow. "It is."
Silence fell between them, save for the crackle of the hearth.

"I hate how much I want her to be happy," Malec muttered, his pulse fluttered along his jaw.

Luko smiled faintly. "Ah. There it is."
Malec turned away, his teeth ground together, and drifted toward the frosted window. The cold seeped through the panes, biting his skin, but he barely noticed. With restless fingers, he began to arrange the little wooden carvings lined up on the sill, a fox, a stag, a weathered figure with its head bowed, each one set at precise, measured intervals. He nudged the fox forward just half a thumb's width, then straightened the stag so its antlers pointed perfectly toward the corner, and made sure every piece was aligned, nothing out of order. The ritual steadied his breathing, his thumb tapping three times against the windowsill after each adjustment.

He stood there a long moment, the silence between him and Luko stretching thin. Malec's breath fogged the glass in front of him, his reflection warped in the cold light. When he finally spoke, his voice was softer, almost reverent, like the memory itself was sacred.

"Do you remember the first time I touched her?"

Luko blinked. "Which time? When you nearly tackled her at the border for threatening a soldier with a scalpel, or when you tried to 'examine' her and she nearly broke your nose?"

"The first," Malec said, lips twitching. "When I grabbed her arm. There was... something. A jolt. Like my blood surged. Like I knew her."

Luko leaned forward, no longer smirking.

"And then," Malec continued, voice quieter now, "the night we, when it happened, when I claimed her. It was like something ancient inside me clicked. My magic... it changed. My senses were heightened. My thoughts clearer. And when I looked at her..." He exhaled. "It was like the world finally made sense."

Luko didn't answer right away. He studied his friend, saw the weariness beneath the steel, the confusion laced with devotion. Then he reached forward, slowly capping his inkwell.

"I was wondering when you'd bring this up," he murmured.

"Bring what up?" Malec asked warily.

Luko steepled his fingers. "Saen'trien and Vash'telor."

Malec scoffed, though not convincingly, downplaying the fact moments earlier he had thought of the same thing. "That old story?"

"Not just a story," Luko said, his voice low with the weight of knowing. "It's rare. Most Awyan will never feel it. But when it happens, it's not soft or kind, it's consuming. A soul recognizing itself in another. And once the bond is formed, there is no undoing it."

Malec's brows furrowed. "Then what about Saen'trien?"

"Different," Luko said, reaching for a worn leather book on the table. "Vash'telor is a choice. A ritual. A union of magic and intent. But Saen'trien... that's the part you don't get to choose. That's the part that chooses you."

Malec sat heavily in the chair across from him, eyes distant.

"And if she doesn't feel it?" he asked.

"Then you suffer," Luko said honestly. "Like you are now."

Malec was quiet. The fire crackled, the storm outside beginning to howl against the stone walls.

"She hates me," he whispered.

"No," Luko said gently. "She fears what you take from here, her choices and autonomy. And you, well, you fear that without her, you're just... gray."

Malec's head lifted.

"Everything without her feels dull, doesn't it?" Luko murmured. "But when she smiles at you, suddenly the world is made of color again."

Malec didn't answer. He didn't have to. His silence said it all. Luko sighed and leaned back with a smirk, taking another bite of his sweetbread.

"Well then, commander," he said. "Looks like you're in love."

And for the first time that night, Malec didn't deny it.

Malec stood in the golden flicker of candlelight, his arms crossed tightly over his chest, gaze pinned to the hearth like it held answers he hadn't yet earned. The fire cracked and hissed softly, filling the silence that had settled between him and Luko like the hush before a storm. His voice, when it came, was roughened by exhaustion, physical, emotional, something deeper.

"What do I do now?" he asked.

Luko didn't answer immediately. He reached for the kettle beside the fire, poured himself a fresh cup of bitter leaf tea, and took a slow sip as if the world wasn't hanging in the balance between them. Then, with maddening casualness, he set the cup down and leaned back in his chair.

"You fight," Luko said plainly. "You keep fighting. Because that's what you do, Malec. And because you're never going to let her go."

Malec's mouth twitched tight, but he didn't argue.

"You're too possessive," Luko went on, voice softer now, more reflective. "You always have been. Whether it was your title, your blade, your pride, once something was yours, that was it. And now it's her."

Malec didn't speak.

"And she's going to fight you back," Luko continued, eyes gleaming with equal parts fondness and warning. "She'll claw, bite, scream, cry. And maybe one day, if the ancestors are feeling especially cruel, she'll kill you. But until then? You two will probably battle until the end of your days."

A faint, tired smile touched Malec's lips. "So you think we're doomed."

"I think you bound yourself to her without even realizing it," Luko said quietly.

"And I think that's the real tragedy. A one-sided Vash'telor is rare, but not unheard of. It can break an elf. Drive them mad, if the bond is never returned."

Malec looked down at the floor, breath caught somewhere in his chest. "I didn't mean to."

"I know," Luko said. "But that doesn't change what you feel, does it?" The silence stretched between them again.

Then, slowly, Malec pushed off the edge of the fireplace and crossed the room until he stood in front of Luko's desk. His expression had shifted, no longer hard, no longer guarded. Just raw.

"Thank you," he said.

Luko blinked. "For what?"

"For always being my friend."

Luko scoffed, caught between disbelief and awkwardness. "Don't get soft on me now, Silver Fox."

A small, dry chuckle slipped from Malec's lips. "Too late. She's already made me soft."

Luko eyed him, studying the faint warmth creeping into his voice, the lines of exhaustion etched around his eyes that had nothing to do with sleep. Then he let out a breath, slow and long, and leaned forward on his elbows.

"She's already changing you," he said. "And that's not a bad thing."

"No," Malec agreed. "It isn't."

He paused, turning toward the window, watching frost gather at the edges of the glass.

"I want her to be happy," he said after a moment. "That's all I want. Truly."

Luko studied him in the firelight. "Even if it means letting her go? Letting her return home to her people?"

Malec didn't answer. Because the question was rhetorical. The silence that followed said everything. He couldn't. He wouldn't. And they both knew it. But the pain in his eyes, the guilt, was real. He turned back, voice quieter now, nearly lost to the fire's crackle.

"I'll take her back to the Capitol. Away from the sickness. Somewhere safe."

Luko nodded, his voice gentle. "But you'll never set her free."

Malec met his gaze, something like sorrow shimmering in his eyes.

"I can't. She's made me softer, yes... but not soft enough to survive without her."

He moved to the door, pausing with his hand on the handle. And as he glanced back, that flicker of tenderness still tugging at the corners of his mouth, he added softly,

"I'll take her back to the den of lions. But I'll never let her go."

Beneath the jagged peaks of a long-forgotten range, the cavern breathed with an eerie stillness, vast and ancient, as if carved by deities who had long since abandoned it. The echo of dripping water marked time in the dark, a slow, eternal metronome tapping against the silence. Only the hollow drip of memory. Then, the water moved.

First, just a ripple. Then a shimmer. Then a violent rupture.

The central pool, once glassy and inert, exploded upward in a pillar of light and liquid, casting reflections across the damp cavern walls. A soldier burst through, armored body slicing through the surface like a black spear. He landed hard on the stone, steam rising from his suit, the glow of his chest panel pulsing bright green as he rolled onto one knee.

Another followed. Then two more. One by one, six armored figures emerged from beneath the pool, rising like specters from a dream. Their gear was state-of-the-art, Earthborn, military-grade, obsidian-black armor slick with wet sheen. Pale blue bioluminescent bands ran across their joints and visors like war paint. Plasma rifles hummed on their backs, water trailing from the barrels like tears.

The last to emerge rose slowly, deliberately.

He stood tall, towering over the others, water sluicing down the curves of his suit. His face was concealed behind a dark tactical visor, but the sharp white streak that ran through his short-cropped hair and beard caught the flickering light. He moved with a quiet, bone-deep authority, like a man who had led battalions through hell, and wasn't done yet.

No name on his chest plate. Just a single white line painted down his pauldron, simple, bold, final.

The team gathered silently, scanning the chamber around them. Their boots crunched against the stone floor, rifles raised in formation, helmets flickering with tactical readouts. But no threats came. Only the deep, otherworldly stillness of a world untouched by Earth's decay. The air smelled different here. Cleaner. Too clean.

"Where the hell are we?" one of the soldiers muttered, flicking a droplet from his gauntlet.

No one answered. Their eyes turned toward the glowing pool behind them, the same strange cave they'd discovered weeks ago in the Okavango Basin of Botswana, buried deep beneath a collapsed volcanic system carved out by ancient floods and prehistoric magma. They'd tracked the pulses there, following the erratic surge of energy readings that made no scientific sense.

But they hadn't come for the surge. They came for *her*.

For weeks, they had combed the ravaged plains and caverns of Botswana, sweeping every meter of the Okavango basin where she had last been seen. Melodie Jaxxon, brilliant, defiant, irreplaceable, had vanished without a trace. Nobody. No distress call. No final words. Just a single, faint thermal signature that had pulsed once beneath the earth like a dying heartbeat, and then disappeared.

The officer's scanner flickered, casting ghostly blue light across the dripping cavern walls. He tapped it once, frowning at the spike in energy readings.

"It's not collapsing," he said, adjusting the frequency, "but the portal's surging. A fluctuation in the magnetic resonance, like it's reacting to something on the other side."

Then the rank commander stepped closer, boots echoing in the stillness.

The man's voice cracked through the comms, deep and quiet. "How long do we have?"

The soldier hesitated, then glanced up. "Hard to say. Hours, maybe less. We don't know what's triggering the pulses."

The soldiers fanned out in formation, boots pressing into loamy moss, rifles glowing faint blue in the dim canopy light. HUDs flickered with static. Biosignals dropped in and out. They were cut off. Alone.

"This can't be right," muttered Corporal Denson, tapping his wrist module. "We should be pinging at least one satellite by now. Even a weather drone."

"There's no signal," another replied. "No satellites. No frequency map. Nothing's working."

A cluster of men turned toward the silent figure standing slightly apart from the others. The tall officer stood perfectly still at the edge of the clearing, his helmet tucked under one arm, his back straight as a blade. He was older than most of them. Hardened by years of war. Battle-hardened skin the shade of coal under the rising twin moons. A streak of white ran through his beard and his hair like lightning frozen mid-flash. He didn't speak at first, just watched the trees as if listening to them.

When he did speak, it wasn't to them. Not really.

"This isn't Earth."

The soldiers turned, some exchanging wary glances. The older officer didn't blink. Didn't elaborate. His voice was calm, assured. Not a theory. A fact.

"How do you know that, sir?" someone asked cautiously.

He didn't look back at them. He had known from the moment he stepped through the portal, not from the readings, not from the scans, not even from the strange glow that shimmered beneath the water like the echo of an ancient dream. He knew because he had seen this world before. A long time ago, before any of his soldiers were even born, back when it was nothing more than a secret buried beneath layers of classified files, government ash, and silence. Back when the Project was still young and arrogant, driven by the blind ambition of scientists and politicians who thought they were saving humanity.

They had opened the doorway the first time with trembling hands and eager hearts, pulling primitive humans out of this world under the guise of rescue. They didn't realize what they were tampering with. Not really. They didn't understand that in saving a few, they had damned millions. The virus hadn't started on Earth. It was born here, on this side of the portal. It had hitched a ride back in the cells of the displaced, wrapped in flesh and fever.

And now, decades later, the price of their salvation had come due.

He hadn't spoken of it. Not to his unit. Not even to his Major. He had buried that truth deep, locking it away beneath duty and survival, beneath the names of the ones who never made it home. But standing here again, on soil not his own, he felt it all rise. The weight. The guilt. The knowing. The light here bent just a little too sharp. The air tasted wrong, too clean, too wild. Even the gravity tugged with an odd insistence, subtle enough to unsettle his bones. And maybe it was more than the atmosphere.

Maybe it was her. Maybe he felt her here. His unit stood behind him, waiting for orders, their breath misting in the air, rifles humming with low energy pulses. But he didn't move. He just stared into the ridgeline ahead, quiet and still. Because he knew exactly where they were.

"I know," he said flatly, his voice a blade slicing through uncertainty. "Because I've walked farther ahead than you realize, I have been here before."

Then he started forward, the quiet weight of that answer following him like a shadow, unchallenged, unquestioned. Because when the Colonel spoke like that, they knew better than to press.

He'd buried that truth beneath the weight of classified files and blood-stained orders, tucked it deep beneath the stoicism expected of him. But stepping onto this alien soil again, he felt it all rise.

The pull of memory. The scent of a world unspoiled by machines or war, where the wind whispered through the grass like it carried secrets too ancient for men to know. Everything here was different. The air, too clean. The light, too sharp. Even the gravity pulled just a little harder, like the planet didn't want to let them go.

And maybe it wasn't just science. Maybe it was her. Melodie. He turned to face them fully, shoulders squared, voice steady.

"Fan out and stay alert. Comms won't help you here. Trust your eyes. Trust your gut. We find her, or we don't come back."

Then, with a single sharp nod, "Move out."

A second passed before the lead officer beside him straightened and saluted.

"Yes, sir. Colonel Jaxxon."

Chapter 18

Terms of Surrender

The morning light filtered softly through the high-arched windows, spilling across the stone chamber in bands of honeyed gold. Everything looked peaceful, too peaceful. The walls, carved from cool, polished slate, were draped with ornate tapestries bearing the silver fox crest of House Talandros.

The fire had died sometime in the early dawn, leaving only the faintest crackle and the occasional shift of glowing embers.

Allora stirred, the silken sheets sliding across her skin, so soft and decadent it made her want to curse. She blinked, letting the haze of sleep fade as she took in the unfamiliar luxury, the heavy curtains, the silver fox sigils stitched into the blankets, the scent of expensive wood polish and Malec's cologne heavy in the air. It wasn't her temporary guest room, that much was obvious. This was his bed. His space.

Of course it was. Control freak. She could practically hear him insisting on it, needing everything under his thumb, even her sleep. The realization made her grind her teeth. She hated how he always had to manage every little thing, from where she ate to where she woke. Arrogant, overbearing, infuriating bastard.

But... fuck. The sex. That, she couldn't lie to herself about. She'd never had a night like that with anyone, no partner had ever left her this sore, this satisfied, this... wrecked. She almost wanted to be annoyed about it, but the memory made her stomach flutter and her thighs clench under the sheets.

A wicked idea slid into her mind. She should start talking about her old lovers, really embellish it, throw in some extra details, make up a few legendary moves, just to see Malec's perfectly carved jaw twitch with jealousy. It would be hilarious. She could already imagine the look on his face: that cold stare, that stupid chiseled jaw working, the ice barely covering the storm. She giggled, quietly at first, then pressed a hand to her mouth as she remembered exactly where she was.

But then, the silence settled around her, thick and almost reverent. She remembered where she was, his bed, his room, his rules. And for just a moment, she wondered if he was lurking behind her, listening, plotting his next move. The thought made her pulse skip, just a little.

She rolled her eyes at herself, muttering under her breath, "Get a grip, girl. He's just a penis. An annoying, impossible, ridiculously good-in-bed dick with legs."

Behind her, the sheets shifted, and suddenly a low, amused voice replied, "A what, exactly?"

Shitballs.

Her face burned as she realized he'd been listening the whole time. She gasped, spinning to glare at him, but Malec just looked far too delighted by her embarrassment.

Malec didn't move from where he lounged against the pillows, propped on one elbow like he'd just woken from a pleasant dream. His expression was one of infuriating amusement, the corners of his mouth twitching as if he was holding back laughter, and failing miserably. Not a hint of regret, not even an ounce of apology in those beige-tan, fox-bright eyes. If anything, her fury seemed to delight him.

"Morning, my dove," he cooed, voice smooth as honey and twice as smug.

Allora felt her entire body bristle, heat racing under her skin, hair standing on end like a storm was brewing just beneath the surface. She could barely believe the audacity of this elf, lying there naked, utterly unbothered, like he was the prize and not the damn thief.

Her hands shook as she launched herself out of the bed, silk sheets dragging at her legs. She didn't care about modesty, didn't care about the fact that he was tracking her with that wolfish grin. All she cared about was the need to do something, throw something. Hit something. Him, preferably.

"You absolute bastard!" she roared, grabbing the first thing she saw, a heavy wooden breakfast tray, still loaded with untouched food.

She hurled it at his head with a sound that was equal parts rage and battle cry. Malec rolled lazily to the side, the tray smashing into the wall, sending plates and cutlery clattering to the floor in a storm of chaos.

He actually laughed, a deep, rolling sound that only made her see red.

"What in the hell, again woman?" he managed, though his eyes sparkled with wicked delight. Not a trace of fear, just challenge.

"Oh, you're real proud of yourself, huh?" she fired, launching a goblet across the room. "Somebody get this guy a trophy for Most Likely to Gaslight a Room."

"Allora, " he started, but the goblet whizzed past his ear, clanging off a wardrobe.

Malec chuckled, ducking his head, the fur throw slipping dangerously low over his hips.

"Damn, you have excellent aim."

That only fueled her. Next was a chair leg, yanked from a stool like she'd been planning this for months.

"You think this is a fucking joke? You kidnapped me! Locked me up like some beast you can breed and break!"

He tried again, still maddeningly calm, "Alright now, dove, calm yourse—"

"CALM MYSELF?!" she bellowed, her voice echoing like thunder. "Calm myself? Oh, right, just another Tuesday—waking up next to my abductor who thinks he's my husband now. Sorry if my chakras aren't aligned."

For a moment, the room rang with her rage and the scattered wreckage of breakfast. And Malec, he just smiled, utterly enchanted, as if he'd never been so alive as in this chaos she brought into his ordered world.

He caught the chair leg midair, smirking like the smug prince of pricks.

"You're being dramatic."

Her scream could've shattered glass. The rug bunched beneath her as she stomped toward the door, yanking the handle with both hands. Locked. Of course. Of course the lunatic locked it. Her breaths came in sharp, feral bursts as she turned slowly, eyes gleaming with pure, incandescent fury. Her voice was low, laced with venom.

"Open. The. Fucking. Door."

Malec rose slowly from the bed, all lean muscle and insufferable confidence, completely bare and unbothered. He tilted his head, that silver hair falling just over one brow as his smile deepened.

"Or what, *Allora*?" he purred, voice smooth as silk and twice as dangerous.

And mercy help him, he was enjoying this. Seeing her tremble with fury, eyes blazing, chest heaving, she looked like a storm trying to swallow the sun. And he? He was the fucking sun.

She stormed toward him like a thunderhead set on fire, bare feet slapping the cold floor, murder flashing behind her dark eyes. Malec didn't hesitate. He stepped back just enough to enjoy the show, arms crossed leisurely over his broad, bare chest, a smirk tugging at the corner of his mouth like a spoiled prince watching a kitten claw at a lion.

Then she lunged. He caught her wrist with the ease of a seasoned predator, spun her like a dancer, and pinned her back against the door. Her hair fanned across the wood as she snarled and spat at him like a wild thing, her breath coming in hot, furious bursts.

"Temper, temper," he murmured, voice low and amused, his lips brushing the shell of her ear. "Is this because you didn't get your way, Allora?"

"Let me go, you smug, arrogant jackass!" she thrashed against him, teeth bared.

He hummed thoughtfully. "No. I think I'll keep you like this for a moment. You're far too adorable when you're feral."

"Fuck. You."

"That's what got you into this mess," he whispered against her skin, his grin widening when she screamed and stepped hard on his bare foot.

He grunted, the pain shooting up his leg. But instead of retaliating, he laughed, a rich, indulgent sound that made her blood boil hotter.

"This," he said, breathless from amusement, "is your punishment for disobedience. For risking your life like a fool. If you'd just obey, you'd never need to be locked up."

"You locked me like a prisoner," she hissed, shoving at his chest.

He didn't budge. "Only because you keep trying to throw yourself into danger like an idiot child."

"Don't call me a child!"
"You act like one."
She screeched and shoved him again. He finally let her go, stepping back with a chuckle, flexing his sore foot as she rubbed her wrist, fury radiating from every line in her body. He turned casually, stretching like he hadn't just been assaulted, and grabbed a pair of breeches from the chair.

"Get dressed," he ordered as he pulled them on without shame, the casualness of his tone making her want to set him on fire.

"Why? So you can drag me around like I am your property?"
He shrugged. "Something like that."
She looked like she might hurl another goblet. Malec turned toward her, calm as the sea before a storm.

"We're going to the Capitol today."

She froze. His voice was even, but there was iron beneath it.

"Pack what you need. You're not staying behind."

Everything stopped. Her breath caught in her throat, rage suspended in midair like dust hanging in a shaft of morning light. The fury hadn't gone, but it wavered now, confused and suspicious as her eyes locked on his.

"You're lying," she snapped, though her voice betrayed the tremor of hope beneath the accusation.

Malec didn't move. Instead, he smiled, that same infuriating, smug curl of his lips that always made her want to throw a chair at his head.

"I don't lie, *Allora*."

Her heart thudded in her chest. The Capitol. She hadn't heard that word in what felt like weeks. Maybe longer. It felt like it belonged to another lifetime. The Capitol. She hadn't heard that name in weeks. Maybe longer. It felt like it belonged to another lifetime.

It meant progress. Closeness to the portal. To her people. To Earth. To freedom.

"You're serious?" she asked, narrowing her eyes, trying to read the truth behind that maddening expression of his.

He stopped moving just long enough to meet her gaze, and for once... the teasing was gone.

"Deadly."

The word rang through the room like a blade dropped on stone. And it scared her. Because for all his posturing and cruel amusement, that tone, quiet, firm, lethal, was the one she knew he never used unless it was a vow. She swallowed.

Malec turned away, walking toward the chair where his clothes were folded in impossibly neat, soldier-like squares. He picked up a tunic, shook it out with one graceful flick of his wrist, and slipped it over his bare shoulders as if this conversation wasn't spinning her world sideways.

"But," he added as he fastened the leather toggles, "there are rules."

Of course there were. There was always a price. Always a chain woven beneath every sweet promise.

"Let me guess," she drawled, folding her arms as her voice went sharp with sarcasm. "I'll be collared and dragged beside you like a good obedient bitch?"

Malec chuckled, low and husky, without looking up from where he was adjusting the strap on his belt.

"Careful, dove," he murmured. "You know my kind does use collars. But not for play. It's how we mark what's ours."

His tone was casual, but the weight behind the words struck like a chain wrapping around her throat.

"Don't you dare," she growled, eyes blazing as she crossed the room, no longer caring that she was still in nothing but his oversized tunic. "You put a collar on me again, I'll carve your house sigil into your own chest, see how you like being branded."

Malec didn't falter. He didn't even blink. Instead, a slow, wicked grin curled across his mouth as he leaned closer, voice a velvet blade.

"You'd still be on your knees when you did it."

She inhaled sharply, fury and something darker flaring in her chest. He smirked, clearly delighted with himself.

"You'll stay by my side. Every moment. Every breath. No vanishing acts. No fire-starters. No slipping off into shadows with daggers up your sleeves."

"And if I don't?" she spat.

He turned then, his tan eyes catching the flicker of firelight in them, suddenly sharp and serious again.

"Then we stay here. And I'll keep you locked in this room until you forget what the sun feels like."

Her stomach sank. She believed him. God help her, she believed him. She clenched her jaw, her fingers twitching at her sides. Rage bubbled in her veins, but it was caged by something tighter, necessity. She had to get to the Capitol. She *had* to. So she did what she never wanted to do. She compromised.

"Fine," she muttered through gritted teeth.

Malec's lips curled into a slow, deliberate smirk. "Good girl."

Allora froze, and then rage flared through her like a lit match tossed on dry leaves.

"Go crawl back to whatever hole you slithered out of," Allora spat, eyes flashing with venom.

Malec's grin turned sly, his voice lowering just enough for only her to hear.

"Trust me, little dove, nothing I've crawled into has ever felt as good as you."

Her face went sharp with fury. She lunged at him, half-naked and all claws, but he danced back, laughter echoing through the room as he fastened his belt.

"Get dressed," he said over his shoulder, that satisfied smirk never fading.

"Wouldn't want you to get cold now that I'm not there to keep you warm."

He turned, strolling to the door without a care in the world. The soft *click* of the lock disengaging echoed like a drumbeat in her ears. And then he was gone, down the hall, barefoot and half-dressed, whistling a low, ancient tune like this was just another day in paradise.

Allora stood frozen, chest heaving, fists clenched at her sides. She was going back to the Capitol. Back to the portal. Back to her people. Or die trying.

Allora dressed like a woman preparing for war. Every movement was sharp, defiant. She yanked on the velvet-lined leggings and shrugged into the soft tunic Malec had laid out for her like they were armor, not clothing. She didn't care that the boots fit like they were made for her. She didn't care that the fabric hugged her body with a warmth that could make any winter bearable. No, she refused to care about anything that came from him. This was just another game. Another ploy. A pretty leash was still a leash.

She was going to take everything from him. His pride. His control. His peace. And when she found the gateway, when she stood beneath that pulsing light and stepped through without looking back, she hoped, truly hoped, he would cry.

Not the stoic, silent kind of grief he wore like a crown. She wanted full-blown devastation. Tears streaming down that too-perfect face. She wanted to see his silver hair disheveled, his eyes wild with despair. Maybe she'd record it. Keep it on her datachip like a souvenir. Watch it sometimes when she was sad. Show her friends back home. Play it at parties.

This? This is the day my war criminal of an ex realized I outplayed him. It would be glorious.

She pushed the chamber door open with more force than necessary and stepped out onto the main steps of the estate, and the cold bit instantly. The breath sucked out of her lungs as snowflakes danced in the sharp wind, glittering under the pale light of the northern sun. The air smelled like pine needles and ice and the faint musk of animals.

Below her, the courtyard was alive with activity. Sled carriages with curved silver runners were being loaded by fur-cloaked handlers. Thick rope netting bundled crates onto the backs of massive elk-beasts whose antlers shimmered with ornamental bronze plating. Soldiers moved in organized rhythm, shouting in Awyan, their armor catching the morning light.

But what caught her eye most were the beasts near the lead sled.

Two massive shapeshifters, bound in half-form, their enormous wolf bodies towering over most of the soldiers. The larger one was a deep, dark brown so black it nearly blended with the snow shadows, his amber eyes red-hot like coals. The other was smaller but more sinewy, with fur like molten silver, nearly blending into the snowy backdrop, if not for the heavy leather muzzles strapped across their jaws.

Their breath steamed in the air, ears twitching. Trained. Controlled. Dangerous.

Allora paused, glaring at them with narrowed eyes. So this was what Malec meant by "precaution." He wanted to make sure she didn't run. That if she did, something much faster than her would be on her heels before she got more than a few feet. Her lip curled in disdain.

Coward.

She tightened the fur-lined cloak around her shoulders and began descending the steps, the snow crunching beneath her boots with each step. A block of ice, half-melted and then refrozen, devious and transparent, waiting like a trap. Her foot caught, her body lurched forward, and-

Thwump.

Her face collided directly with Malec's ass, solid, muscular, and completely, infuriatingly in her way. The impact knocked the breath from her chest. She staggered back, arms flapping, boots slipping on the packed snow, barely saving herself from landing flat.

Malec didn't even wince. He turned with all the regal composure of a snow-crowned warlord, draped in suede and heavy spotted furs, one perfect eyebrow arched as if this was the most ordinary greeting in the world. His tan eyes sparkled with far too much delight.

Luko's laughter shot across the snowy courtyard like a cannon blast. "Oh, sweet fucking mercy, I think I just died!"

He doubled over, nearly collapsing, shoulders shaking so hard he lost his footing and had to grab a rail to keep from falling. Cheeks burning, Allora scrambled upright, hands balled into fists, her dignity abandoned somewhere in a drift behind Malec.

"If you wanted a taste, little love, there are less dramatic ways to ask."

Luko practically screamed with laughter, tears streaming down his cheeks. Allora saw red. She glared at both of them, voice shaking with pure, unfiltered rage.

"GO. TO. HELL."

"If hell is where you are," Malec replied, perfectly unruffled, "then may it be my eternal home."

Allora glared, gathering what was left of her dignity as she stormed towards Luko and his ridiculous display of laughter.

"I hate both of you," she muttered darkly. "Walk with me before I stab something."

Still giggling, Luko wiped his eyes and followed, rubbing his aching ribs.

"Gods. My whole year has peaked."

As they reached the row of saddled horses, Luko's laughter tapered off. He threw a quick look back at Malec, who stood a few paces away, pretending to check a harness, but with those pale tan eyes locked on Allora, hungry and possessive. Luko's smile faded, concern clouding his features. He tugged Allora aside, dropping his voice, and checked to see Malec was distracted, barking orders at guards.

"You need to stop playing games with him," he hissed.

Allora arched a brow. "If you're about to call him my soulmate or some fairy-tale fate bullshit, I swear—"

Luko gripped her shoulders, eyes alight. "I'm not joking, Allora. He's bound to you."

She blinked. "What does that even mean in this context? You keep bringing this up but, like... he has a strong horny crush I get it."

Luko's jaw tightened. "No, Allora, you're not taking this seriously. This isn't a crush. Saen'trien is just the first alarm, a warning that Vash'telor could happen. But Vash'telor? That's Awyan magic. It can't be undone. Not ever. Once it takes, it changes you, body and mind. It's meant to happen between Awyan pairs. When it goes wrong, or if the bond is rejected, it can drive an Awyan mad. Obsession, agony, sometimes worse."

He shook her shoulders, golden eyes fierce.

"It isn't some romance story. It's a curse if it goes bad. And with you? No one knows what'll happen. No one."

Allora rolled her eyes, fighting a nervous laugh. "Well, aren't you the sweetest little friend?"

Luko groaned. "You'll miss me when I'm not around to warn you."
"Nope."
"Liar."
She grinned even wider, mischief sparking. Just to make sure Malec saw, she leaned in and pressed a lingering kiss to Luko's cheek, soft and slow. She held his gaze sideways, catching the moment Malec's posture snapped, every muscle gone tense with jealousy.
Luko's eyes widened. "Oh, spirits of the North."
Allora pulled away with a wicked smile.
"That was for being honest. And because your face is very kissable."
"You did that just to piss him off."
"Obviously."
Luko managed a shaky laugh. "You're actually insane."

Before she could answer, Malec was suddenly there, a cold shadow at her back, silent and huge, fury crackling under his skin. He didn't shout or reach for her, just stared her down, voice low and dangerous.

"Get. On. The horse."

Allora only smirked, meeting his glare with a challenge of her own, then slowly turned to obey.

Luko edged away, muttering under his breath, "...Yep. You're gonna die."

His voice dipped to that low, dangerous tone, the kind that slithered under her skin like smoke before a fire.

"Don't push me, Allora," Malec warned, his restraint hanging by a thread.

She turned, batting her lashes like a perfect menace. "Why? Something wrong, your highness?"

That did it. Without a word, Malec lunged forward, gripped her waist with infuriating ease, and lifted her straight off the ground like she weighed nothing at all.

"Hey, put me down, you ass wipe!"

"No," he said flatly, and with all the grace of a barbarian and the audacity of a smug bastard, he slung her over the saddle like she was a sack of grain meant for market.

She shrieked. Actually shrieked.

"You son of a bitch!"

Behind her, Luko shook his head. Malec swung up onto his horse with the fluid ease of someone born to the saddle, then shifted Allora into place in front of him. He adjusted her easily, settling her between his thighs, his arms bracketing her on either side as if to cage her in. His body pressed close, his breath a smug whisper at the shell of her ear.

"Comfortable, dove?"

Allora slammed her elbow back into his stomach. He grunted but only tightened his hold.

"Easy now, little wildcat. Keep struggling. I might start to think you enjoy this."

"Eat my black ass," she snapped, voice sharp as a blade.

Malec leaned in, lips grazing her ear, his voice silk and sin. "Later."

She stiffened, seething, every muscle taut with rage. Luko straightened, flashing a grin.

"When the murder happens, I want it on record I tried to warn you. Also, I want her to get away with it."

"You're not coming?" Allora barked over her shoulder, almost hopeful.

"Nope. I like being alive. And unlike you, I know when to *not* poke the fire drake."

Malec smirked as he adjusted the reins. "Coward."

"Survivor," Luko corrected with a grin, then gave Allora a mock salute. "Try not to murder each other before nightfall. Or do. Honestly, that might be easier."

Allora's jaw ached from clenching it so tightly as Malec clicked his tongue, signaling the caravan forward. The horses snorted, snow crunched, and the whole line lurched into motion, the sound of hooves blending with the groan of wagon wheels and the steady clink of harness metal. Malec's arms caged her in, the heat of his body pressed all along her back, his chin occasionally grazing her shoulder as if he had every right to take up her space.

The journey to the Capitol dragged on, mile after frozen mile, each one more claustrophobic than the last. Pines crowded the road, needles dusted in ice, and the cold wind sliced at her cheeks, but Allora could barely feel it, not with Malec's body pressed flush against hers. Every breath he took sent heat rolling up her back, his arms a living barrier caging her on the saddle. The steady sway of the warhorse only made it worse, rolling her hips and thighs against him with every step. Her heart beat faster, her skin prickling under too many layers.

She shifted, deliberately, wriggling just enough for friction. She could feel every inch of him, hard muscle, infuriating heat, the slow, tight rise of his chest when she leaned back, just a little too close. His breath brushed the edge of her ear as he muttered to the guards, and she nearly shivered, not from cold, but from something hotter, more dangerous.

Her hood felt stifling, sweat beading at her hairline. She dragged it down with a frustrated huff, only for Malec to tug it back into place, his grip a silent command.

"Keep it on. Your ears will frostbite."

She squirmed in protest. "I'm warm."

"Then sweat," he snapped, voice rough with something she recognized, need. Challenge. Control.

Allora rolled her eyes but didn't argue. Instead, she played. Shifted again. This time pressing her back more fully into his chest, letting her body mold into his in a way that was anything but innocent. She felt the way he stiffened behind her, how his hands tightened around the reins, how the muscles in his thighs tensed under her, solid and unyielding. A wicked smile curved across her luscious dark mouth. She did it again, this time brushing her hand across his thigh as if to adjust her boot. His sharp inhale, barely more than a hiss, made her grin.

"What's wrong, Commander?" she teased, voice velvet and smoke. "Your beast getting restless?"

His jaw twitched, voice low and nearly trembling with restraint. "You're testing me."

His hands flexed again, gloved fingers tightening around the reins, leather creaking softly under the strain. He was smoldering behind her now, heat pouring off him like a fever. She could feel it, the way her teasing wound him up, the way he wanted to act, right here, right now.

She let the next words slip out, soft and serious beneath the playful surface.

"Why don't you let me go then? If I'm such a pain. If I'm such torture. Why keep me?"

His voice came, low, even, but carrying more weight than she'd expected.

"Because this isn't torture."

She frowned, thrown off, her skin prickling under the wool of her hood. He leaned in, his mouth grazing the rim of her hood, his breath warm and humid as it ghosted across her cheek. The sensation was subtle but electric, shocking her out of her defiance, making her all too aware of every inch where his chest pressed against her back.

"Torture," he said, voice like velvet drawn over a blade, "is the thought of you out there without me. Unprotected. Unguarded. Untouched."

His hand slid to the pommel of his sword, the leather making a soft rasp against the hilt. The other stayed tight around the reins, keeping them steady, keeping her close.

"Torture is knowing you'd rather die than come to me. That you'd run into worse arms just to spite mine. That you'd give your fire to someone unworthy just to punish me."

Her stomach twisted, an ache blooming behind her ribs.

"Torture," he finished, breath shivering against the shell of her ear, "is the idea of someone else touching what belongs to me."

"I was never given a damn choice I have the right to choose to be yours or not or its just... possession. I'm a person not a thing," she spat, words jagged, chest tight. "Possession isn't love," she bit out, as much for herself as for him.

"And yet..." he murmured, his lips skimming her ear, breath hot on her cheek, "here you are. Still mine."

She wanted to shove him off the damn horse, into a snowbank, into oblivion. Wanted to spit in his face, scream, rip out everything he'd just said by the roots. But instead, she sat forward, hands tight on the saddle horn, teeth grinding as shame and rage warred with something she couldn't name. Because as much as she hated what he said, some terrible part of her feared it might be true.

By the time they reached the small Awyan town nestled in frostbitten hills, night had swallowed the sky. The moon hung fat and bright, drenching everything in silver-blue glow. Snow covered the roofs, sparkling under the lanterns that swung between stalls in the square. Their caravan slowed, hooves muffled by a blanket of new snow. Flurries drifted through the air, clinging to eyelashes and scarves, catching the lamplight like tiny floating sparks.

The town was alive, bursting with winter festival joy. Velvet canopies in blue and gold billowed above rows of merchant tents, the air alive with the crackle of fires and the scent of roasting nuts, pine sap, and sweetened cider. Allora watched children dart between stalls, their laughter bright as glass, their ribboned cloaks swirling like banners. Laughter and music spilled out of the tavern doorways; nobles and villagers mixed freely, their breath visible in the cold.

Malec guided their caravan to the edge of the square, near the warm glow of the outer tavern yard. Guards slid off their mounts, boots crunching in the snow, and began to unload supplies. Malec dismounted with the same feline grace he brought to everything, then turned, offering his gloved hand up to her—formal, measured, every inch the lord. His eyes met hers, dark with hunger and impossible to decipher, as he waited for her to take it.

She stared at his outstretched hand like he was offering her a dead fish.

"I don't need your help," she snapped, shoving his gloved palm aside and springing down from the saddle in a low, catlike crouch.

Snowflakes scattered at her landing, cold biting her ankles, but she didn't back down. She straightened, stretching her legs with a satisfied little roll of her shoulders and sucked in a deep lungful of icy night air, sharp, pine-sweet, shockingly clean.

Freedom. It stung her nose, filled her head, made her feel reckless.

Malec said nothing, though his eyes narrowed, his jaw tightening by a fraction. She ignored it, brushing past him and into the moonlit square, where lanterns painted the snow in shifting, gold-and-silver bands and the festival's energy wrapped around her like a dare. She'd been locked inside for weeks, pacing stone halls, suffocated by walls and rules and his constant scrutiny. Tonight, even tethered by his presence, surrounded by guards, she felt wild, untouchable for the first time in what felt like forever.

Awyan shoppers streamed around her in a swirl of embroidered furs and vivid wool, their laughter bright as the music spilling from the taverns. The snow underfoot glowed, casting everything in a pale, dreamy light. Allora could feel the eyes, dozens of them, following her as she moved. Male eyes. Hungry eyes. Scanning her skin, her hair, her walk. Her midnight-dark curls burned like a beacon in a crowd of silver and white; her skin shone, dark and smooth, drawing their gazes like moths to flame.

She was used to it, used to being a curiosity, a marvel, a scandal.

But tonight, the attention wasn't what made her smile.

It was the simmering heat of Malec's stare behind her. The possessive, angry burn she could feel between her shoulder blades. She didn't even have to glance back; the weight of it was delicious, a blade of hunger and warning pressed right into her spine.

She smirked to herself. Payback. Every step she took was a dare.

So when a young noble blocked her path, tall, elegant, with his hair in a braided crown and a midnight blue cloak lined with fur, she didn't even slow. His pale green eyes swept over her, admiring, almost reverent.

"I must say," he murmured, his accent rolling like velvet, "you are... unlike anything I've ever seen. So striking. Canariae, yes?"

Allora tilted her chin, grinning. "Last I checked."

"You wear your skin like a queen. Beautiful. Bold. Dangerous."

She barely had time to laugh before Malec was there, sudden, silent, unavoidable. One strong arm banded around her waist, yanking her back against his chest, the other bracing her upright, his body hot and rigid, his heartbeat pounding against her spine. She let out a surprised little "oof," then narrowed her eyes as his grip tightened possessively.

"She's not for sale," Malec said, voice like black ice.

The noble blinked, caught off guard, but recovered with a lazy, mocking bow. "Commander Talandros. No offense meant."

"You gave it," Malec shot back, his tone promising nothing good.

"I was admiring, not hunting."

"Admire from a distance," Malec growled, not letting go, his eyes incinerating holes through the noble, and anyone else who dared look twice.

Behind her, Allora felt the tension rolling off Malec in waves, wildfire smoldering just beneath the cool surface of his skin. His gloved hand at her waist was trembling, ever so slightly, but she felt it, and the knowledge thrilled her. His jaw was so tight she could almost hear the grind of his teeth, and when he exhaled, it was hot and shallow against her cheek.

Delicious, she thought. Absolutely delicious.

She let out a dramatic sigh, fluttering her lashes. "Oh dear, am I in trouble, Commander?"

Malec didn't answer. His grip only tightened, his silence louder than any threat. Allora, not missing a beat, angled her body just enough so the young noble could still see her. Over Malec's shoulder, she threw him a slow, lingering wink, pure sin and challenge. The noble laughed, bowing out of the drama with a knowing smile.

"Best of luck, my lady."

Malec wasted no time. He practically dragged her through the crowd, his hand a vice around her waist.

"You're insane," he hissed under his breath, voice rough with something savage.

"And you're far too easy," she purred, twisting just enough to let her hip brush his thigh as she walked.

He stopped dead, spun her in close, and pressed his lips to her ear, voice low and coiled with threat.

"One day, dove... I will teach you the cost of playing with fire."

She didn't hesitate. Didn't cower. Instead, she let her voice go honey-sweet, taunting.

"I *am* fire," she whispered.

For a second, their eyes locked, his shimmering molten gold, hers glittering with defiance. The courtyard noise faded to a hush, the only sound the crunch of snow beneath boots and the heavy thrum of her own pulse. Without warning, Malec gripped her wrist and yanked her flush against him, chest to back. It was anything but gentle; it was possessive, claiming, his arm like steel around her waist, his breath scorching her ear.

"You really don't know when to stop, do you?"

Allora smirked, heart pounding, refusing to let him see her nerves. "You're only fun when you're angry."

A deep, feral chuckle rumbled from his chest, curling along her skin like smoke. "You like provoking me?"

She turned her head, lips a breath from his, eyes dancing. "Is it working?"

That was her mistake. Malec didn't reply with words. He seized her jaw, gloved fingers strong beneath her chin, forcing her to look up into eyes smoldering with possessive hunger. And then he kissed her, hard. Not tender, not sweet, but brutal, punishing. A kiss that left no room for question. The kind of kiss meant for war and warning, not love.

The whole courtyard seemed to fall silent, the hush deep and thick. Conversations faltered. Every Awyan eye watched. Everyone understood the message in that kiss.

She was his. No one else was to even look.

Allora's hands shoved at his chest, but he didn't budge. She twisted, furious, torn between humiliation and the feverish thrum he left in her veins. But still, he didn't stop until he'd made his point.

When Malec finally released her, his lips brushed her ear, breath uneven, voice trembling with restrained hunger.

"Now," he said, dark and low, "let's see who else dares admire you."

Allora stood frozen, cheeks flaming with equal parts anger and something more dangerous, a craving she'd never admit. She wiped her mouth with the back of her hand, holding his gaze.

"That was unnecessary."

Malec's face was hard, no smirk left, just fierce, stoic resolve. His expression was glacial, eyes flat, lips pressed into a line of pure command. His voice dropped, low and absolute, each word striking like iron in the cold air.

"You wanted to remind me that you're not mine. I just reminded them that you are."

Allora's jaw flexed, nostrils flaring. She met his stare, refusing to step back, even as heat crawled up her neck.

"You think that little stunt puts you in control?" she shot back, the words hot and desperate.

"I am control," Malec replied, calm as a winter blade, his gaze steady and unyielding. "And I'm done playing games with you. For your sake, I suggest you stop playing them with me."

Her throat tightened, pride battling with something darker, a sliver of fear sliding under her ribs. She couldn't let him win, couldn't let him see her hesitate. But the way he looked at her now, cold and sure and completely without mercy, made her heart thud heavy in her chest.

For the first time, she wondered, really wondered, if she had gone too far. If she'd finally crossed a line even she couldn't charm her way back from. The chill in his eyes wasn't anger. It was resolve. And that scared her more than any rage ever could. All she knew was that she had enough of his stupid possessiveness and it was now time to bow out.

Permanently.

The Capitol was close now, too close. Allora could feel it in the air, every breath sharp with the promise of freedom she could almost taste, cold and sweet like frostbitten fruit. Every mile south made Malec's grip on her tighter, every look he threw her way darker, heavier. Not just control anymore, but obsession, a kind of fevered need that twisted something wild and uneasy in her gut.

She was done playing captive.

They'd made camp that night in a snow-laced alcove under black pine boughs, branches glinting with icy armor. The soldiers moved with quiet, well-trained discipline, unpacking crates, tending horses, rolling out thick woolen tents. Fires flickered, spitting sparks into the darkness, painting the snow in golden halos and brief, wavering warmth. Above, the moon was monstrous and low, its silver light making every drift shimmer as if dusted with ground glass.

Allora hung back, arms wrapped around her middle as if she were just warding off the cold, but it was anger that kept her stiff. Malec's public claim in the market, the humiliation of that brutal kiss, the iron way he tried to mark her as his, she wanted to carve out his insides with a dull spoon.

While Malec barked orders to a cluster of younger guards, she kept her face turned to the flames, pretending to warm her hands. Her eyes, half-lidded beneath the shadow of her hood, watched everything, the routine, the guards' habits, the subtle shift of who was looking her way and who wasn't. Her usual shadow, a silent, hawk-eyed guard, had slipped away for a piss.

Perfect.

She moved, slow and easy, as if chasing a better spot by the fire. One step, then another, drifting into the edge of shadow. She never looked at anyone for more than a second, she knew better than to give herself away to Awyan instincts. She was patient, watchful, letting the moment open. And when it did, she slid behind a wide pine, breath caught, heart pounding, vanishing into the night like smoke. Her boots crunched quietly in the deep snow as she pushed further from camp, cold air scraping her lungs, breath billowing in uneven puffs. Each stride was a gamble; the snow sucked at her boots, threatening to trip her, but she pressed on, remembering the road just a half mile south, the path that could lead her out if she made it.

Minutes ticked by. Her lungs burned, thighs aching, but the freedom so close she could taste it. Then, a howl.

A sound broke the darkness—low, trembling, crawling through the trees like a bad omen. Her veins went icy. Shifters. Fuck. She'd forgotten about the wolf shifters. How could she be so careless? It was always her recklessness—missing details this big, sabotaging her own chances. Maybe her temper really did get the better of her.

A blur crashed through the brush behind her, a shadow too fast, too close. Something slammed her to the ground, burying her in freezing snow. Massive furred weight pinned her, claws digging into the ice on either side of her body. Snow bit her face as she thrashed. Silver fur. Eyes that glowed with intelligence, not animal wildness. The wolf's muzzle hovered over her, fangs flashing in the moonlight, but it didn't bite. Didn't kill. It waited, too smart, too obedient.

She groaned, half laughter, half despair. "Of course. Fucking of course."

The shifter snorted, its breath steaming in the cold as it held her down. It didn't budge, just held her, watchful and merciless. Footsteps sounded through the dark, crunch, crunch, deliberate and slow. Judgment coming closer. Malec emerged from the shadows, a few soldiers trailing grim and silent behind him. The wolf finally eased off, backing away a step, making room for its master.

Malec stood over her, his eyes wild with cold fury, a storm coiling beneath his careful mask. His hair was wild from the wind, bits of snow dusting the silver strands and clinging to his lashes. Those tan eyes, cursed, ancient, unblinking, glowed with an eerie, soft light that was pure Awyan. It wasn't rage that burned there. It was something colder. Possession.

He didn't bother asking what she was doing. He didn't need to. Malec grabbed her arm, his fingers biting hard enough to bruise, and hauled her upright with a force that made her shoulder scream in protest.

"You absolute little fool," he snarled, voice low and rough.

"I had to pee—," she tried, weakly.

He cut her off with a snarl. "Save it."

The command was thunder, no room for lies. She bit down on a retort as he shoved her. Hard. Her back slammed into the nearest tree, bark scraping her spine, the cold knocking the air from her lungs. Before she could catch her breath, he was already there, looming, blocking out the moonlight with his bulk, his cloak spilling around them both like a shadow.

> "You think this is a game?" he growled, breath hot and furious on her cheek. "You think I won't break you if you keep testing me?"

Her heart stuttered in her chest. Before she could move, he seized her wrists and slammed them above her head, pinning them against the tree with a single, iron-strong grip. His other hand braced against the trunk beside her face, caging her in completely. She could feel the heat pouring off him, the tremor in his chest as it pressed against hers, the way his entire body vibrated with the effort to hold back.

> "I should take you back to the North," he hissed, voice barely more than a savage whisper. "Lock you in my bedchamber and keep you there until you stop acting like a fucking child."

Allora glared, swallowing fear and defiance both. The moonlight caught the molten fire in his eyes, no mercy, only wild, desperate want. His chest heaved against her, his jaw clenched so hard she could see the muscle jump. He was shaking, and she knew it wasn't from the cold.

"YOU DON'T OWN MY FUTURE," she snarled, her words razor-edged.

His reply was a brand. "I already do."

The words seared into her, cruel and final. Luko had warned her, but she hadn't listened. Not really. Now, pinned between the rough bark and the radiating storm that was Malec, Allora understood with sharp, sudden clarity: she'd gotten too close to escape. Too close to the portal. And Malec, he could feel it, too. She'd pushed too far.

Now she had to survive it.

Pain radiated up her spine, but she didn't dare flinch. Not with his breath ragged against her cheek, not with his hands forging new bruises on her wrists. His eyes, that molten tan, were alive with something wild, barely restrained, and entirely real. This wasn't the charming commander who flirted by firelight. This was the conqueror. The one who didn't beg, didn't plead. The one who took.

For the first time, the truth struck her: all that softness, the sweet words, the gentle touches, it only surfaced when she danced to his tune. When she played the good little dove. But it wasn't real. This was. He was fire and iron.

Her stomach twisted, panic clawing up her throat. She tasted fear, sharp as snowmelt. But she refused to show it. She wanted to disappear. Just for a moment. Just long enough to breathe without the weight of his presence pressing on her ribs. She hated him. God, she hated him. But she hated herself more—for freezing, for remembering how it felt when he wasn't cruel, for wishing he'd stop holding her like a prisoner and start holding her like someone worth saving. It was weakness. She knew that. And still, it bled out of her like a wound she couldn't close.

Instead, she drew a slow, even breath, letting her shoulders relax, lashes falling low. She softened her voice to a velvet murmur, gentle, careful, dangerous.

"Malec..."

Just his name, spoken like a prayer, drifted through the space between them. She saw his brow twitch, the iron grip falter for a heartbeat. She tilted her head, exposing the vulnerable line of her throat, just a little, just enough to be noticed.

> "I wasn't running. I just wanted to see the stars without
> someone breathing down my neck," she whispered, her breath
> a secret between them. "I just... needed air."

Her voice fell to a soft, breathy murmur, trembling at the edges—not with fear, but with the kind of longing that could be real or just a perfectly played mask. Either way, it sent a shiver through Malec, the vein at his temple pulsing, jaw locked so tightly she wondered if it might crack. She leaned into him, her hands resting lightly on his chest now, no longer pinned, though his grip had not vanished entirely. He released her slowly, fingers trailing down her forearms with a hesitant, suspicious grace, as if unsure whether to trust her or seize her again.

Her body molded to his, soft curves pressing into the rigid lines of muscle and restraint coiled beneath his skin. She leaned in, mouth near his ear, her breath a whisper of heat.

> "You're always so tense..." she purred, letting her breath feather
> warm against his skin. "Let me help."

His body jerked, a shudder running through every muscle. She could feel his control, his famous, flawless control, fraying beneath her touch.

> "Stop it, Allora," he growled, the warning raw, voice cracking
> under the strain of holding back.

Her fingers traced lower, deliberate, slow as honey, hips rolling up to press flush to his. Her mouth curved into a wicked little smile, patience laced with poison and promise.

> "I know you're mad. You've got that look—like you're one
> second from tearing something apart."

She lifts her chin, even though her voice wavers.

"But you didn't chase me down just to scare me, did you?"

Her fingers skim his chest, slow and light, like she's trying to calm a beast.

> "You want to punish me, fine... but at least pretend you missed me while you do it."

That was all it took. Malec broke. His grip sank to her hips in a brutal, possessive drag, yanking her against him so hard the air punched from her lungs. The sound she made wasn't fear—it was need laced with guilt. His mouth crashed down on hers a heartbeat later, all sharp edges and starvation, a kiss that punished and pleaded all at once. He kissed her like she was a crime he hadn't finished committing. Like he needed to taste the rebellion off her tongue to forgive it.

And Allora let him.

She met him with that same desperate heat, the same reckless fire, pouring her apology into every fevered stroke of her mouth. Her hands fisted in his shirt, pulling him closer, even as her breath hitched with something dangerously close to shame.

He lifted her like he'd done it a thousand times, like her body was made to fit around him. Her thighs gripped his waist, ankles locking behind him, her back thudding into a tree whose bark was softened by snow—but nothing about this was soft. His hands were shaking now, jaw tight like he was trying to hold himself back, but every sound she made—every broken gasp, every choked whisper—snapped another thread of his restraint.

By the time they stumbled into the tent, wet boots dragging snow over thick fur, she was half undressed and breathless, and he was tearing at her bindings like they were the only thing keeping him sane. The rope hit the floor. His mouth claimed the bare skin of her throat, her chest, her shoulder—every kiss a demand, every bite a curse. He didn't ask why she ran. He didn't need to. She was already answering with her body.

Outside, his soldiers averted their eyes, pretending not to hear the sounds that spilled from inside, the thud of bodies, the shattered rhythm of apology and need.

Inside, it was war made flesh.

Her fingers trembled as they slid into his hair, as she pulled him down to her again. Not just to calm him. Not just to survive. But because she needed to remind him, to remind herself, that this—this madness between them—wasn't just destruction. It was also the only place either of them felt real.

And even as he buried himself in her, even as she whimpered his name through lips bitten raw, Allora knew exactly what she was doing. Turning surrender into strategy. Wrapping his rage around her like armor. Offering him heat in place of forgiveness, knowing he'd take it—because he always did. And if he thought she was yielding, if he thought this was her breaking?

Good. She'd let him believe it. Until the next time she ran.

Allora lay sprawled in the heavy quiet of the tent, her bare limbs tangled in thick, fragrant furs, the rich animal scent of them clinging to her skin, mingling with the sharper notes of sweat, sex, and cold air sneaking in beneath the flap. Malec's body was a furnace at her back, an anchor of muscle and impossible heat, his arm banded around her waist as if she might vanish in her sleep.

She smiled to herself, small and dark, staring at nothing. For all his power, his need to dominate, to claim and possess, she could undo him with nothing but her hands and her mouth. Sex was her secret weapon, her way to seize the reins, to remind him that as wild and raw as he was, he could be tamed. All that discipline, all that icy self-control, burned away in her arms, stripped down to nothing but want. It was intoxicating, the way he touched her without shame, the brutal honesty of his desire. She loved it. She hated it. It was infuriating, exhilarating, addictive. God, she had never had a lover like him, so honest in his hunger, so unashamed of what he wanted, or how hard he needed it.

A sated Malec was a docile Malec, she thought with vicious satisfaction. Easy to handle. Easier to predict. As long as she kept him fed on her body, as long as he was lost in the high of what only she could give, she could keep him just a little off balance, just long enough to plan her next move. To stay ahead.

But her victory was threaded through with something sharper. Her body ached, not just from what he'd done to her, the way he'd finally snapped and made her pay for every taunt, every risk, every escape, but from something deeper. Her skin tingled, a strange warmth crawling beneath the surface, lighting up her nerves from the inside. Every place he'd touched her pulsed, slow and sweet and sore. Sweat cooled along her brow even as the night outside the tent pressed cold against the fabric.

She shifted, testing her limbs. They felt heavy. Sluggish. Her muscles shivered with a fatigue that didn't quite make sense, tired in a way that felt new, unfamiliar, dangerous.

No. Not now. Not this close.

Her mind sharpened, desperate to hide her discomfort. She forced herself to breathe slow, to melt bonelessly into the furs like any exhausted lover. If Malec sensed a change in her, he'd panic. He'd turn the entire caravan around, drag her back to his freezing stronghold, chain her to his bed and call it care. He'd smother her with his brand of love, the kind that felt like a cage.

No. She couldn't let him see. She couldn't risk it, not when they were so close. The Capitol was nearly within reach. She could smell it now, the faint tang of distant fires, the far-off clang of caravan bells. The snow outside was thinner, pressed flat by the boots of travelers. The forest was thinning. Civilization was close enough to taste.

She'd come too far to lose it all now.

So she stilled her breathing, made her limbs limp and loose, burrowed into the furs as though she was just another lover spent from a night of Malec's consuming passion. No more games. No more teasing. Not until she was through those gates. Not until she was free.

And then? She'd vanish, just slip into the city's chaos, a ghost in the smoke and shadows, never to be caught.

Now, with dawn glinting off silvery domes of Caelistra, she sat stiffly in front of him atop his monstrous black warhorse, the beast's hooves ringing steady against the thinning snowpack. Allora kept her eyes on the winding road, refusing to meet Malec's gaze, every muscle tense with anticipation, and a deeper ache that refused to fade. For almost an hour they'd been riding down out of the white-capped cliffs, seeing winter dissolve into something new.

It was subtle at first: snow pulling back from the muddy verge, earth showing through in brown and gray streaks, the knife-edge of cold softening into damp, mossy air. But by now, spring was undeniable. The breeze carried hints of green, and the scent of rich earth, wet bark, and flowers not yet brave enough to bloom. The trees were taller, thick with pale new buds, evergreens giving way to birch and willow. Below them, the valley yawned open, cupping the city in a great green hand.

In the far distance there it was. Caelistra. The Capitol.

Stone towers and silver domes gleamed under the late sun, banners snapping in the wind, threads of gold and cobalt against the sky. Smoke curled from hundreds of chimneys, trailing the scent of smoldering wood and roasting meat up to meet them. From the city's gates, roads branched out like living veins, bustling with carts, merchant wagons, and nobles in dark winter cloaks, streaming home from their country manors.

Her breath snagged in her throat. It was beautiful. It was a promise, and a trap. A glittering cage. She shifted in the saddle, feigning discomfort, but Malec's arms never loosened. They held her with that unbreakable, steady pressure, as if even here, surrounded by people and city and spring, she might try to run. His body was heat pressed to her back, every inch of him alert. And silent.

He was thinking. She could feel the calculation radiating off him in waves. She was sweating now, not from nerves, not from the warmth of his body, but from something deeper, a persistent hum beneath her skin, a heat that seemed to crawl from her core outward. Her muscles ached.

Her thoughts were foggy. She'd been sleeping longer, falling under again and again, and if Malec really noticed...

Of course he noticed.

"You've been sleeping a lot," he murmured that morning, voice low, eyes never leaving her face. "Are you ill?"

There it is.

Allora forced herself to blink, then groaned and pressed the heel of her hand to her brow, putting on her best irritated diva routine.

"No," she huffed. "It's just... my period."

Malec's brow creased, curiosity and confusion flickering in his gaze. "Your what?"

"My period," she repeated, deadpan.

He only looked more lost.

"I have never heard that word used in relation to health." He spoke slowly, as if the phrase itself was a puzzle.

Allora stretched in the saddle, making the motion as grand as possible, arms overhead, spine arching until she felt the satisfying crack between her shoulders.

"It's part of the reproductive cycle for Canariae females. Once a month, our bodies get ready for pregnancy. If it doesn't happen, the uterus sheds its lining. We bleed. From..." She flicked her fingers downward, grinning. "You know. There."

Silence fell like a dropped stone.

Malec's tan eyes widened a fraction, his mouth parting as though the very idea caused him physical pain.

"You bleed?" he echoed, voice incredulous. "For how long?"

"A few days," she said, too casual, enjoying this a little too much.

"And you survive this?"

She flashed all her teeth. "So far, yeah."

Malec actually recoiled, the movement subtle but clear, as if her words had committed a crime against his refined Awyan sense of bodily order.

"That's... unnatural."

"It's called biology," she shot back, honey-sweet. "You Awyans wouldn't understand."

He glared, jaw ticking, clearly wrestling with what sounded to him like a bizarre, blood-soaked curse. "So you bleed, and you grow tired from it?"

"Yes."

"And irritable?"

"Oh, very," she said, voice low and delighted.

His gaze darkened, concern now filtering in. "Do you require a healer?"

She laughed, sharp and quick. "No, just a lot of cotton."

He blinked. "Cotton...?"

She only smiled and let him stew. There was no way she'd explain tampons to an Awyan warlord, not even if he begged.

Malec muttered something in his native tongue, and she caught just enough of it to know it was some kind of prayer for patience and sanity. It took everything in her not to cackle. For the rest of the day's ride, Malec was uncharacteristically silent, his eyes fixed on the road, jaw set, as if he were actively waging war against the new knowledge of monthly bleeding and imagining his fiery little dove slowly dying from the inside out.

Good, she thought, pressing wicked lips together to hide her amusement. Let him stew in confusion. If he was busy worrying over her imaginary "uterine warfare," he wouldn't notice the real problem. Thirty more miles. Just thirty.

If she could keep him distracted and off-balance until then, she could vanish before he ever figured out what was truly wrong.

Malec had never cared about Canariae reproductive cycles. Why would he? Their bodies had always been an afterthought, fragile, limited, irrelevant to Awyan ambitions. They couldn't carry Awyan seed, couldn't produce heirs, couldn't even survive the full breadth of Awyan magic. It was a rule of nature. A comfort, even. One of the few lines that had never blurred.

But Allora was not like the others. She never had been.

Now that he had her, truly had her, with her body curled against his at night, filling his tent with the scent of sweat and sex and something he could never quite name, he found himself thinking about things he'd always ignored. Questioning things he'd always accepted. What if she was different? What if whatever strange twist of fate or evolution had made her so infuriating, so defiant, so alive, had also made her body more... possible? More susceptible?

He watched her in the dim light, her face turned toward him in sleep. There was a furrow between her brows, even now. A sheen of sweat glistened on her skin, and when he pressed his palm to her forehead, she burned, hotter than she should, too warm for the cold air pressing in from outside. She barely ate anymore. She slept too deeply, too long, limbs heavy as stone. *Was this normal? Was this what she called a "period"?* The word still sounded absurd to him, arbitrary, flimsy, something invented to distract or dismiss.

He remembered the curve of her smirk as she'd explained it, slow and sly, like she was hiding a joke from him. Bleeding for days and surviving it. The casualness of it had unsettled him. He'd seen hundreds of Canariae. Trained, broken, used. Their cycles had never mattered. They had always been beneath notice, their purpose clear and brief. But she... she was not the same. Not to his body. Not to his instincts. His blood thrummed around her. His senses sharpened in her presence.

Something ancient coiled in him, a primal recognition that he couldn't explain, as if his lineage, his very bones, called out to hers.

Could she carry?

The question arrived uninvited, crawling up from the dark place in him that wanted, hungered, needed. He didn't know if the idea made him anxious or thrilled, only that it was now inescapable.

He studied her again, the way she looked so small and vulnerable beneath the thick furs, breath misting faintly in the cold. Her lashes fluttered against flushed cheeks, her brow still tense, even in sleep.

He hated not knowing. Hated the uncertainty, the ignorance. He needed answers. He would have to ask the others, quietly, discreetly. Not many kept Canariae long enough to know. Most treated them as trinkets, status symbols. But a few... a few had crossed that line.

He would find them. He would demand answers.

Because if something was happening to Allora, something new, something dangerous, he needed to know first.

The road wound down into gentler lands, the wild highlands giving way to soft, rolling hills washed in the gold of late evening. Snow thinned with every turn, replaced by pockets of grass that pushed stubbornly through the frost, catching bits of sunlight on their wet tips. The air tasted different here, no longer sharp with ice, but sweet with promise, edged with green and the hush of new blossoms just beginning to wake. Spring had found the valley, even as winter still haunted the peaks behind them.

Ahead, Caelistra rose from the plain like something conjured from a half-remembered dream. Its pale towers shimmered in the dying light, lanterns blooming along marble streets as dusk bled into night. The air was warm, fragrant, alive with the scent of hedges and ornamental trees heavy with the earliest flowers. The palace gates stood open, pillars bright as coins, firethorn blazing red and gold at their base. The courtyard beyond glimmered, black and pearl tiles catching the moonlight, casting a gentle radiance that made the entire city seem to float.

But Malec saw almost none of it.

Allora hadn't moved in over an hour. She lay in his arms across the saddle, limp and small, skin hot beneath his gloved hand, breath so shallow he had to press her close to feel it at all. He tried not to panic, tried not to let the sharp, cold animal fear curl any tighter in his belly. Maybe she was just tired. Maybe the journey had worn her down. But the truth was there, gnawing at him, sharpening every sense. Something was wrong.

He dismounted carefully, cradling her as if she was the last fragile thing in his world. The wind pulled strands of her hair across his chest, tickling at his jaw, but she didn't withdraw, didn't even stir.

Then came the last voice he wanted to hear.

"Ah, the North finally brings gifts." King Surion's voice rang out from beneath the portico, his grin sharp enough to cut glass. "Silver Fox, you look like you've spent all night losing arguments—and not just at the tables."

Malec strode past, every line of his body stiff with purpose, but Surion fell into step, eyes never leaving him. He let his gaze drift to Allora, slow and appraising.

"Is that Allora? Tell me, Malec, is she as difficult to tame as they say, or have you finally met your match?"

He gave a mocking bow in Allora's direction.

"You certainly do like the ones with claws. Or are you just hoping she doesn't use them on you?"

Malec's jaw tightened, gaze fixed forward, his focus narrowed to the weight of Allora in his arms. Surion's tone softened, for a heartbeat.

"She doesn't look well. Which is ironic, considering how... lively she was last time. I thought she bit you."

"She did," Malec replied, voice flat, eyes neutral.
Surion barked a laugh.

"Gods, she's still breathing. That's almost sweet, cousin. You must be getting sentimental."

Malec stopped dead, pivoting to face him, his arms tightening around Allora.

"She is mine," he said quietly, every word laced with threat. "And I will not hear you speak of her again."

Surion held up his hands, mocking surrender on his face. "Of course, cousin. Wouldn't dream of it. Glad to see you finally dragged her out of your ice palace and into the sun."

Malec's only answer was the way his fingers dug deeper into Allora's hip, as if he could anchor her with touch alone. Surion's gaze shifted, a flicker of concern beneath the mischief.

"You sure she's just tired?" he asked, studying her face. "She looks... unwell."

"I am aware," Malec said, his voice clipped.

Surion raised a brow. "Shall I send for a healer?"

There was a pause, a heartbeat longer than necessary, just enough to betray the crack in Malec's composure.

Then, voice clipped, stiff with effort: "Send him to my chambers."

He flashed a grin, voice edged with mischief. "Ah, your chambers again. As you wish, oh brooding lord. All yours, cousin. Just don't forget to air out the drama when you're done."

Malec didn't waste another glance. He strode across the courtyard, boots sharp on the marble, Allora pressed tight against his chest, every muscle in his arms tense with urgency. The great doors closed behind him with a hollow echo that seemed to hang in the palace air.

Behind him, Surion stood still, his usual smirk frozen in place as he watched Malec vanish into the palace. His grin, always so practiced and smug, flickered, just for a moment. Because what he'd seen in Malec's face wasn't the cold, ruthless control that had built his reputation. It wasn't boredom, or arrogance, or even the simmering rage that usually haunted his eyes.

It was distress. Raw, unhidden, unguarded. And not over court politics, not over strategy or power, not over some ancient Talandros family feud. It was for her. That Canariae. The dark-skinned beauty Malec had once nearly killed for, the one he'd guarded and caged and hovered over with a possessiveness bordering on madness.

Surion lingered where he stood, gaze fixed on the shadowed archway that had swallowed them. He tilted his head, something sharp and speculative lighting behind his eyes.

"Interesting," he murmured. Then, brisk and loud: "Fetch the palace physician. Now."

A servant darted away into the depths of the palace, but Surion remained where he was, fingers steepled in silent thought. He hadn't seen Malec like this since their wild, reckless boyhood. And if this Canariae had managed to stir the ghost of a heart in that frosted chest...

Well.

Surion meant to find out exactly how, and what else she might awaken before it was through.

Chapter 19

The Heat Beneath the Skin

Allora awoke drowning in heat. It curled beneath her skin like coals beneath silk, a fever so vicious it blurred the world into smears of color and light. Her limbs were useless, heavy, trembling, unresponsive. Her tongue felt thick, her throat too dry to speak. Worse still was the tingling, a strange, crawling sensation that danced along her arms, her chest, her spine, like something alive beneath her skin. Not pain exactly. Decay.

And she knew what it was. God, she knew.

Her training screamed at her, facts tumbling through her smoldering mind in disjointed waves: nervous system degradation, epithelial erosion, vascular collapse. She'd seen this before. Back home, they called it the Fall Fever. The early stage. The silent killer. Once the tingling started, once the burn reached the bones, it meant the virus had already taken hold. And from there, it would spread fast. Organs first. Skin next. Then madness. Then death.

"You're awake."

Malec's voice pierced the haze, low and sharp, and more strained than she had ever heard it.

She blinked up, and the sight of him, tense and grim, arms folded, golden hair undone from its usual binding, made her heart stutter. His tan eyes were shadowed and dark, rimmed with exhaustion. But worse than that... there was worry. Real worry.

"You've been fevered all night," he said tightly, not moving from his place at the foot of the bed. His jaw was clenched, and his fingers twitched like he wanted to grab something. Or someone. "Sweating. Shaking. You didn't even stir when I called your name the first time."

"It's the heat," Allora mumbled, voice scraped raw.

Sweat beaded along her brow, her hair clinging to damp skin, the world swimming at the edges of her vision. She couldn't meet Malec's eyes, but she could feel them on her, searching, sharp, impossible to evade. He didn't answer right away, just stared at her. Long and hard, as if he could will the truth out of her with the force of his gaze alone.

"It's a fever," he said at last, his tone flat and full of dread. "And you're barely conscious."

"It'll pass." Her voice was paper-thin, brittle with denial.

Malec's jaw flexed, the muscle at his temple ticking in silent warning. "You need a physician."

"No." The word burst out, tearing her throat. Panic clawed up her chest, rattling her breath.

Malec's eyes narrowed, a storm brewing in their depths. "That wasn't a request, little dove."

"I said no, Malec." Her hands trembled on the coverlet, her nails digging deep, desperate for something to anchor her.

A muscle jumped in his cheek.

"I don't remember asking for your permission," he bit out, voice clipped and cold.

He turned to the guards stationed at the door. "Bring him in."

"No!" she gasped, lurching upright, only for her arms to give way. The world spun, and she slumped with a helpless cry, small, broken. That was all it took. Malec was beside her in an instant, arms gathering her up, holding her with a gentleness that only made the panic swell. She hated how careful he was, how he cradled her like glass, how it stripped her of every shield she had left. She wasn't ready to be weak in front of him, not now, not with strangers about to see her broken.

The physician entered, steps measured and silent. An elder Awyan in indigo robes trimmed in silver, hair bound neatly at the nape, his presence radiating calm authority. His brown eyes swept over Allora, cool and clinical, until curiosity sharpened his gaze.

"This is the Canariae?" he asked, voice smooth, almost too polite.

Malec nodded tightly. "See what's wrong with her."

The doctor approached, gaze flicking down her sweat-damp skin, lingering a little too long on the rich darkness of her complexion.

"I've never seen one with such deep tone," he murmured, more to himself than anyone else. "Almost obsidian..."

Allora flinched, every muscle in her body snapping taut. The memory of hands, of cold instruments and stranger's eyes, surged up, choking her.

"Don't touch me," she rasped, voice shaking with a fear that was raw, not performative.

"I only need to— "

"No." Her limbs trembled as she scrambled back against the pillows, hands clawing at the blankets. "No, no, no."

Malec's frown deepened as he watched her shrink from the doctor, her eyes wild and glossy. This wasn't defiance, this was panic. Real terror. Her breathing came fast and shallow, her body thrumming with dread. For the first time in a long while, something twisted deep in Malec's chest, an ache, sharp and helpless.

"Allora," he said softly, as he held her from behind.

"Get him away from me," she whispered, nails digging into the bedding until her knuckles blanched.

"He's a healer," Malec tried, tone gentle but urgent. "He isn't here to hurt you."

"I don't trust him," she managed, her voice breaking.

Her fever-bright eyes were wild, glassy, barely seeing him at all. Malec moved slowly, hands raised in a careful, practiced motion. He cupped her face, thumbs gentle on her cheeks, tilting her head until she had to meet his gaze. Her skin burned under his palms, too hot, too fragile.

"You're sick," he said, voice low, not cruel but not soft, either.
"And you did this to yourself."

She tried to turn away, but he held her still, his hands steady, his voice dropping to a whisper meant only for her, quiet, dangerous, full of warning and something far more desperate.

"When you're well again, we are going to have a long talk about your reckless behavior. I will not tolerate this anymore." Malec's voice was iron, calm but shaking at the edges, just enough for her to catch it, even through the fever haze.

Allora wanted to answer, to argue, to spit back some clever retort, but her body had reached its limit. Her legs shifted under the tangled furs, then buckled completely, leaving her collapsed and shaking, helpless against the Malec's chest. Her skin felt wrong, tight and too dry, each breath a shallow gasp.

"Enough," Malec muttered, but it sounded more like a plea to himself than to her.

His arms wrapped tighter around her as she trembled, his chin coming to rest on her hair.

"She's going to fight you," he warned the doctor, voice taut as a drawn bow. "I'll hold her. Do it quickly."

The physician nodded, face a mask of focus. He unrolled a leather kit, the glass and steel of his tools glinting in the lamplight. Allora whimpered, a soft, wounded sound, her mind slipping in and out of sense. Her fingers fisted weakly into Malec's shirt, seeking something solid, something known. He held her tighter, rocking gently, his voice dropping to a murmur, soft, low, chanting words in Awyan she barely understood. Reassurances, promises, commands for her to stay, to hold on, to fight.

But inside, Malec was unraveling.

He could feel the fever's heat smoldering against his skin, hear the wild stutter of her heart under his palm. Her breaths came too quick, too shallow, her skin dry as parchment. For all his discipline, all the years he'd spent training for war and loss, he had no weapon for this kind of fear. Not with her. He had seen the sickness before. Canariae smoldering with fever, shaking in their beds. He'd watched them wither and sweat, then revive in a day with a simple transfusion of Awyan blood, his blood, potent and pure. The cure always worked. He'd seen even the most fragile recover, given rest and care.

But this... this was different. Allora's fever wasn't breaking, wasn't holding steady. It was building, spiking higher every hour. Her body ached and burned, her limbs numb, her voice reduced to nonsense. Nothing he'd done was helping. The speed, the ferocity of it, it was like something inside her was simmering out of control, something that didn't belong to the sickness he understood.

He clenched his jaw, guilt and dread searing behind his ribs. He hadn't brought the serum. Hadn't thought he'd need it, she was so strong, always stronger than the others. But in his hurry to reach Caelistra, to keep her close, to guard her from every danger, he'd missed the one threat he couldn't shield her from. He should've known better. She was never like the others. She was wilder. Unpredictable. Her blood didn't follow any rules. And now her body was failing faster, torching brighter, as if she was being consumed from the inside out.

He hated the truth that crept in, cold as death: maybe his blood, the cure that had saved so many, wouldn't be enough for her.

The physician's voice was a jolt through the fear.

"I'll need a sample of your blood, my Lord. A fresh draw. I can craft a dose, but it will take time. And magic. It must be stabilized, or it'll burn through her system

too quickly."

Malec nodded, face tight, already rolling up his sleeve, baring the pale skin of his forearm.

"Do it. Take what you need."

He watched as the physician prepared the vials, as he set out the delicate instruments. The sense of time pressing in was suffocating, he was running out of it, with every shallow breath Allora took. She wasn't just a captive anymore. She was his tether. If this fever took her before the dose was ready, he would lose more than he could bear to name.

Allora's lips moved, delirious, a whisper lost in the haze.

"Covart-Virus... I have to go... before it's too late..."

Malec gripped her tighter, his resolve and terror tangled together. Please, he prayed silently. Not her. Not now.

The words slipped out of Allora's cracked lips, fevered and broken, but they froze Malec in place. The damp cloth he'd been pressing to her brow fell forgotten from his hand. His breath caught, a razor edge of dread slicing through the panic and anger that had carried him this far. That name, strange, unfamiliar, echoing off the stone walls and burrowing into his thoughts. *Covart-Virus... What did it mean?*

Allora's body twitched beneath the tangled furs, breath coming in short, desperate pants. Her skin was slick with sweat, searing in places, cold in others, her face flushed and clammy. Each inhale sounded like a fight. Then, her voice wavered again, softer this time, achingly frail.

"Eron... I have to save him... I promised... I have to go back..."

Malec's stomach knotted, a cold, sick feeling rooting beneath his ribs. He stared at her, the confusion and suspicion twisting tighter with every word.

"Who is Eron?" he asked, voice pitched low, almost gentle, but with an undercurrent of steel, the warning before the storm.

But she didn't hear him. Her lashes fluttered, her gaze sliding past him, seeing things he couldn't, places he'd never been, people he couldn't touch.

"I have to get home... Eron's waiting..."

The name cut him, sharp and silent. Eron. Malec didn't know the word, didn't care for its origin, but the way it left her mouth, soft and desperate, made something ugly flare under his skin. *A sibling? A friend?*

A lover? His blood boiled. It was a rare, ugly rage, jealousy, fear, a sense of being outside looking in. Even here, even sick in his bed, even clinging to life, she was trying to reach someone else.

He reached for her, his hands gripping her shoulders, not gentle, not cruel, just desperate. He shook her, a little, enough to try and force her awake.

"Who is Eron?" The words came out harsh, bitten, barely contained.

Her eyes blinked open, but she wasn't really there. She looked through him, not at him, her voice pleading and faraway.

"I have to go... please... I have to go..."

His blood ran cold. Even now, barely breathing, she was fighting him. Always reaching for something just out of his grasp. He felt it twist inside him, a black, possessive knot, rage and hurt and fear all tangled together.

It didn't matter who Eron was. She would never reach him. Not while Malec still drew breath.

At the foot of the bed, the physician watched in solemn silence, the lamplight flickering over his aged face. Allora's body was still, save for the fevered tremors that rippled beneath her skin, her dark cheeks blotched with heat, her chest heaving. Malec hovered above her like a storm, rigid and relentless, his whole being wound tight with panic and resolve.

"She is not like the others," Malec said at last, voice thick and low, every syllable resonant with something ancient and desperate. "She's one of the originals. From the world before the portals ever opened. The blood running through her veins is older than any Awyan memory. Older than any of us."

The physician blinked, slowly, reverence softening his features. He asked nothing more, accepting the weight of Malec's words. In that moment, no one in the room doubted him. Not with the wild, living magic twisting in the air. Not with the way Malec's hands refused to let her go. The old elf leaned in, his face close to Allora's, his gaze sweeping over her, counting every shallow breath, noting the blue tinge creeping into her dry cracked mouth, the unnatural shimmer of sweat coating her dark skin. Her muscles twitched beneath the fever's grasp, the delicate lines of her jaw and collarbone pulled tight by strain. He looked both troubled and fascinated, something almost reverent in the way he observed her.

"Then her biology is likely unique," he said at last, the words heavy as stone.

"The virus is attacking her faster than anything I have seen. Her organs may already be under stress. If she survives the night, it will only be with intervention."

He paused, uncertainty pinching his brow.

"I will attempt to recreate the vaccine from your blood, as you described," he continued, voice lower, weighted with doubt. "But I cannot promise success. I have never treated one of her kind. This will require spellcraft, chemistry, and time..."

Malec's eyes narrowed, flaring with cold, dangerous intensity. "You'll do it."

"I will try," the physician replied, unflinching.

"That's not good enough." Malec stepped forward, menace and desperation radiating from every line of his body.

The elder lifted his hand, calm, his gaze steady. "It is all I can offer."

Silence stretched between them, thick, crackling with threat and raw, desperate hope. Malec held on tighter as Allora whimpered, her body shifting weakly, lips parting for a fractured breath. Even now, her voice was little more than a whisper, chasing names and memories Malec couldn't see, couldn't touch. She was always somewhere just out of reach, even as her life slipped through his fingers.

Malec's jaw locked, and with a hard breath, he pushed up his sleeve, baring the pale muscle of his forearm. The veins stood out starkly in the lamplight.

"Continue."

The physician nodded crisply, hands efficient as he drew a long crystal siphon from his satchel, its surface etched with glowing runes. Magic shimmered in the blue light along the tip, designed to keep the blood pure, alive, untouched by air or time.

"This may sting," the physician murmured, not unkindly.

"I hope it does," Malec replied, his voice raw. "I deserve it."

He watched, unblinking, as the siphon slid into his flesh and the hot prickle of pain seared through his arm. Blood, his blood, filled the chamber, deep and vivid as rubies. The ache grounded him, forced him to focus, to keep panic from spiraling out of control. This was something he could offer. This, he could do.

Beside him, Allora curled weakly, her body shuddering with the force of fever. She whimpered softly, the sound slicing through Malec with guilt and helpless fury. Even in sleep, she was reaching, grief-creased lips moved, whispering names and promises meant for other worlds, for other lives. She was still fighting to escape him. Still clawing toward freedom, even now.

He hated it, this helplessness, this uncertainty, this fear that something might steal her from him before he'd even taught her how to stay. She was always running, always slipping through his hands, always finding new ways to defy him, to disappear. He didn't look away as the crystal siphon drew his blood. He let the burn sharpen his mind, anchor him to the moment. He would save her. He had to. And when she was well, when her eyes burned again with fire and she stood unbowed in front of him, he would make sure she understood:

No more risking her life for ghosts or old promises. No more running. Because next time, he would not chase her.

He would bind her. For good.

It had been more than two hours since the physician disappeared into the endless, echoing corridors of Caelistra to forge the serum. Two hours of pacing the marble floor, boots silent, nerves raw. Two hours of trying to look calm for the servants and guards, while every tick of the clock sent lightning through his veins. Two hours of pretending he wasn't counting each fragile, uneven rise of Allora's chest, studying her as if every breath might be her last.

Malec stood at the edge of the bed, fists clenched so tight his nails had left crescent moons in his palms. Allora's skin glistened with a sickly sheen, fever-bright and clammy, her breath a rough, rattling staccato. She hadn't spoken since the last, broken whisper of that cursed name, Eron, had slipped out. It haunted him, sharper with every silence that followed. He did everything he could. Kept her warm, changed the linens, pressed cool cloths to her brow, forced water between her dry lips when she was lucid enough to swallow. Nothing worked.

And then, her body seized.

It happened in a flash. Her back arched, limbs snapping stiff as iron. Her body jerked violently against the bed, a strangled sound wrenching from her throat. Malec's heart slammed against his ribs, terror clenching like a fist around his lungs. He moved without thinking, climbing onto the bed, catching her with arms honed by years of battle but trembling now with fear. He rolled her to her side so she wouldn't choke, cradling her close, whispering, desperate, voice splintering.

"Easy, dove... I'm here. Stay with me. Just breathe. Please, just breathe."

He tried to sound steady, tried to be her anchor, but the words shook. They weren't commands, they were pleas, the kind that burned his pride to ashes.

The seizure lasted only moments, but each one was agony. When it finally passed, she slumped against him, limp and hot, breath scraping weakly through parted lips. Her color had drained beneath the sweat. The fine trembling in her fingers didn't stop.

She was slipping.

Malec eased her back onto the bed, his chest heaving. For a long moment, he just watched her, a silent sentinel, rage and terror roiling in his gut. Then, with deliberate movements, he crossed to the basin.

He plunged his hands into the icy water, scrubbing away the sweat, the blood, the helplessness. But it wasn't enough. He needed to do more. Anything.

He pulled his dagger from its sheath, the blade cold and solid, a lifeline in the storm. He dipped it in the basin, then dried it with the edge of his tunic, every gesture precise. Then he turned to her again, jaw clenched, determination ablaze in his eyes.

No ceremony. No hesitation.

He knelt by the bed, drew the blade across his own palm, a sharp, clean line. Blood welled instantly, thick and hot, the scent sharp and metallic. He reached for her arm, opened a small cut just above her wrist. She didn't flinch. Didn't stir. That terrified him more than any wound he'd ever taken. He pressed their wounds together, their blood mingling, his old magic reaching for hers. He closed his eyes, letting the memories rise, letting ancient words slip from his lips like prayers. Words spoken only in the darkness, in moments of life and death.

"Sareth vel'doan... threnik mar... ven al'sorain."

Power stirred in the air. The hair on his arms prickled, the magic pulsing between them, warmth building, faint but alive. Her fingers twitched. Her breath caught. He chanted the next verse, his voice barely more than a whisper.

"Tal'ari ven dohr... melathei caran... sel ikrath denai."

The heat between their hands built, a subtle thrum, rising through his bones and into hers. He felt his own pulse stutter, his vision flickering at the edges from blood loss and strain, but he didn't stop.

"Ka'taren nai vel'mor... shae vel'dara... nas koran me."

A final surge, soft as dawn, heavy as thunder, rolled between their joined hands. He kept them pressed together, his forehead pressed to hers, whispering her name between incantations. Not proud, not commanding, but pleading, cursing, begging.

"You are not dying tonight," he rasped. "Do you hear me? I won't allow it. Not like this. Not without me."

Terror clawed at him, real and aching, threatening to undo every last scrap of control he'd spent a lifetime building. Because if she slipped away now, there would be nothing left, nothing but an empire of ash, and a king who had finally learned what it was to love, too late to save her. And somewhere beneath the tangle of magic and heat and desperate hope, Malec felt her take it, some tiny, trembling part of her spirit reaching back for him. His forehead stayed pressed to the fragile rise and fall of her chest, every stuttering breath beneath his skin a reminder that she was still here, still fighting. His bloodied hand cradled hers with a reverence he'd never shown any living thing. Their palms were slick with mingled blood, his, hot and iron-rich; hers, pale and weak, barely pulsing. The warmth between them was faint, a shivering thread he feared would snap with the slightest misstep.

> "Come back to me," he whispered into her skin, voice raw
> and cracked from too many hours of fear. "Please, little dove.
> Please."

No answer. Only her shallow rasp of breath, only the cold stillness that made him want to tear the world apart. His jaw set, teeth grinding, helplessness and rage coiling inside his chest until it threatened to choke him.

Just a night ago, she had burned under him, alive, wild, untamable. Her hands had torn at his hair, her hips arching, curses and laughter and broken pleas tangled in the dark. She had filled the room with fire, with joy, with the living force of her rebellion. And now she was fading, slipping through his fingers like water, leaving only blood and regret behind. He tightened his grip on her hand, the coppery scent of blood thick in the air.

> "Damn you, little dove," he choked out, eyes squeezed shut.
> "You make everything so fucking difficult."

The sheets bunched in his other fist as he leaned closer, pressing a trembling kiss to her burning temple, desperate to anchor her here.

"Why is it so hard to hold onto you?" he murmured, voice barely more than breath.

She had always been just beyond his grasp, a wild spark that refused to be caged. He hated her for it, loved her for it. He could not lose her because of it. He sat up, cupping the back of her head in his palm, holding her as gently as he dared. For the first time in years, he prayed, not to gods, not to ancestors, but to her, to the stubborn, indomitable soul that lived inside her. He prayed to her will, to the fire that spat in the face of kings and fate.

"Fight," he whispered, voice breaking on the word. "You don't get to leave me. Not now. Not yet."

He swallowed, tears pricking his eyes, and leaned in, his voice softer now, a promise and a plea.

"You are mine, Allora. You are mine... and I am yours. I won't let this take you. I won't let anything take you."

His forehead dropped to hers, holding her there, keeping her in this world with touch and words and blood. Their breaths were still uneven, their bodies slick with sweat and fear. In the hush between spells, between begging and anger and agony, Malec made a silent vow: if death wanted her, it would have to come for him, too.

He would meet it head-on, sword flashing, and fight until all that lingered was his love and the emptiness of the heavens.

The first thing Allora noticed was the feel of real, clean sheets beneath her, soft, heavy, smelling faintly of lavender and sun. There was a thick fur draped over her legs, warm but not oppressive, and the air in the room was cool against her skin, soothing where only days ago the heat of fever had nearly strangled her. The crushing, sticky warmth was gone. The bone-deep ache had faded to a stubborn soreness in her joints.

Her head no longer pounded with each heartbeat. She let out a breath, a low, shaky sound in the quiet that felt like it belonged to someone else. The world felt sharp-edged and new. Light spilled in through the window slats, golden and uncertain, painting long stripes across the marble floor and tangled bedding. Dawn had just begun to creep over the city, and everything looked different than it had the last time she was conscious.

That's when she saw him, Malec. He was slouched awkwardly in a low-backed chair, pulled so close to her bedside it looked like he'd spent the night guarding a treasure. His head was resting against the mattress, one hand curled tightly around hers. His silver-blonde hair was a mess, his braid half-undone and tangling at his shoulder, and the usual sharp lines of his face were softened, drawn with exhaustion. Even in sleep, his brow was furrowed, jaw tight, as if he couldn't quite give up his vigilance, not even now.

She shifted, trying to ease the ache in her body, and winced at the sting in her palm. That small movement was enough, Malec's hand clamped down on hers, his grip instinctive and possessive, a silent 'don't go' even while unconscious. His eyes opened immediately. For a heartbeat, he just stared at her, disbelief and relief mixing in the raw, red-rimmed tan of his gaze. His voice was ragged, a little broken.

"You're awake."

Their eyes locked. Something tight and breathless lingered in the air between them.

Suddenly he was moving, all that sleep-fog gone as he shoved the chair aside and slid onto the edge of the mattress. His hands were on her, her forehead, her cheeks, his thumb gently tracing the side of her throat as if confirming she was real. His touch was frantic, grounding, and then, slowly, his whole body seemed to let out a sigh.

"You're cool," he said, the words clipped, but his voice wavered with relief. "The fever's gone."

She saw it in his face, the way his shoulders dropped, the way he let his breath out like he'd been drowning. She realized her own heart was beating fast and uneven, startled by the tenderness in his gaze.

"You scared me," he muttered, almost to himself. His thumb brushed her cheek again, lingering there, reluctant to let her go. "Damn you, little dove..."

Allora swallowed, unsure what to say. She stared at their joined hands, noticing the bloodstains and the rough bandages wrapping her palm. A dull ache pulsed beneath the cloth.

"What... happened?"

Malec's gaze followed hers, his face closing down as he stood and crossed to the washbasin. She watched him scrub his hands hard, like he could erase whatever had happened in those endless hours. His wound had already closed, not even a scar left behind, but there was blood under his nails, dried dark at his wrist. He came back to her, quieter now, more careful than she'd ever seen him. He sat and gently peeled back the bandages from her palm, inspecting the angry pink slash beneath with gentle, reverent fingers.

"You were dying," he said, voice flat, as if distance could keep the fear out. "The physician... couldn't finish the serum in time. So I did what I could."

Allora stared at him, trying to make sense of the memory, the pain, the heat, the dreams, the way it had all felt like drowning in fire.

"You mean... your blood?"

Malec nodded once, sharp, his eyes fixed on her hand and not her face.

"Yes."

His tone was stiff, but she could hear the truth underneath, the relief, the terror, the aching hope. The raw, human-like fear that he'd nearly lost her, and might never let her go again.

"And the spellwork," Malec added, his voice almost reluctant. "Old magic. From my mother's side." He said it like he was confessing a weakness, not a strength, as if those words cost him pride he couldn't afford to lose.

Allora swallowed hard. Her palm throbbed, and the rest of her felt wrung out and weightless, but she was alive. She could feel it: the slow, steady beat of her heart, the alien heat of his magic curled deep inside her veins. Magic that wasn't hers. She looked up at Malec, studied the tired lines of his face, the haunted set to his mouth. He'd saved her. He had done it with blood and desperation and whatever power he could drag from the roots of his lineage.

The door creaked open on its ancient hinges, a sharp scent of bitter herbs and clean steel chasing in the physician. The old Awyan, indigo robe, silver braid, a face that looked like it had seen too many years, froze in the doorway as he saw them: Malec sprawled on the bed, cradling Allora against his chest, their bandaged hands stained and bound together by blood and something deeper. He stopped dead, his eyes narrowing in disbelief, then widening in outrage.

"Tell me you didn't," he snapped, voice brittle and sharp.

Malec didn't even bother to look at him. He simply settled further into the pillows, his arm around Allora as if he dared the world to try and steal her.

"She was dying."

The physician's hands shook as he gestured, his outrage growing. "You gave her raw blood? Without filtration, without a single glyph for containment, no measured dosage, "

"She lived," Malec cut in, voice flat and immovable, like a glacier sliding into the sea.

The doctor strode forward, aghast. "She survived this time. But what if she rejects it? What if her system turns—"

"Then clear her," Malec interrupted, finally turning to meet the physician's glare head-on. "Examine her. Say she's stable. Then get out."

For a heartbeat, the physician hovered there, jaw working, eyes tight with a dozen reprimands he didn't dare give. But something in Malec's gaze, something old, something royal and furious, kept him quiet. Muttering under his breath about reckless nobles and their obsessions, the old elf approached the bedside.

Allora tried to shrink away from his touch but barely managed a twitch. Her eyes fluttered open, then shut again, too exhausted to argue. The physician's hands were cold but practiced as he checked her pulse, the rhythm of her breath, the healing wound at her wrist. He frowned, taking in every detail, but after a few tense minutes, he straightened with a long, reluctant sigh.

"She'll live. For now. Her system accepted the blood. But I make no promises, Awyan and Canariae blood were never meant to mix." There was a heavy silence. The doctor stared at Malec, all bitterness and judgment. "You always were reckless."

Malec's reply was quiet, lethal. "And you always forget your place. Get out."

The old elf glared, but turned away, snatching up his satchel and stomping out, muttering about "idiotic nobles and their exotic toys." The door thudded shut, leaving only the hush of dawn and the steady, fragile sound of Allora's breathing.

Malec's shoulders sagged as he reached for the pitcher, pouring water into a cup with careful hands. He lifted her head, supporting her as she sipped, his hand steady and gentle on her nape.

"Drink," he said softly, holding the cup to her dehydrated lips.

She drank, but glared at him over the rim.

"I can do it myself," she muttered, water trickling down her chin.

He smiled, just barely, and only for her. "I'll believe that when you can stand." He wiped her mouth with a corner of the sheet, then smoothed her hair off her forehead, pulling the blankets tighter around her shoulders. "You need food. Something mild. I'll have broth brought."

"You're fussing," she croaked, trying for irritation, but her voice was too weak.

Malec ignored her, dipping a cloth in the cool water and gently wiping her brow.

"You still smell like fever," he said, tone almost playful. "When you're done eating, I'll bathe you."

"Malec..." she growled, making a half-hearted effort to sit up.

He pressed her back to the bed, not unkind but unyielding. "Stop acting like a child, and I'll stop treating you like one."

Her mouth opened, outrage sparkling in her eyes, but the words died. She was too tired to fight him. And he knew it. Instead, he leaned in, brushing his lips softly over her hair, her temple, her cheek, slow, careful kisses, as if he still didn't quite believe she was real and whole.

"You're mine," he murmured, lips against her skin, a promise and a prayer. "And I don't care what I have to give to keep you alive."

Malec's hand tightened around hers, and his voice was raw as he pressed his forehead to hers.

"Don't do that to me again. I don't like being scared, dove."

There was a tremor in his voice that made her chest ache. His touch was gentler than it had ever been, a tether, an anchor, a promise. She felt her own heart pounding in her chest, sore and stubborn and alive. Before she could say anything, he drew back, his gaze searching, wounded and still fierce.

"Who is Eron?" he asked, voice low and dangerous.

Crap.

Allora's heart stopped. The name—*Eron*—slashed through her like a razor, freezing every muscle, sending panic surging up her spine. She went perfectly still, breath trapped in her chest. Slowly, she turned to face Malec, her eyes wide and uncertain, lips parting.

"How do you know that name?" she whispered, every syllable thin and desperate.

Malec's eyes didn't waver. His tan gaze was dark, hungry, unblinking, too steady, too sharp.

"You were muttering it in your sleep," he replied, voice dangerously even. His hand tightened around hers, fingers iron-strong, no room for escape. "Who is he?"

Allora tried to look away, but he had that look, stormy, possessive, as if the wrong answer might shatter the world. She felt hunted. Cornered.

"Is he a lover?" Malec's voice dropped, low and venomous, the words slicing.

Allora's gut knotted.

No. This wasn't curiosity. This was territory. Jealousy, ugly and cold, twisted beneath his skin.

"That's none of your business," she shot back, mustering what defiance she could, even as her voice trembled. It sounded weak, even to her.

Malec's grip tightened further, his eyes narrowing. "Everything about you is my business."

She yanked her hand back, but he didn't let go. He was already locked in, his mind working, scenting a rival.

"You want a pet, go buy a dog," she spat, fire flaring even through her fear. "You can claim whatever you want, but I'm still my own damn person."

He let out a cold, humorless laugh, "Fight me all you want, dove. You'll still end up in my arms."

Her breath caught. He leaned in, his mouth brushing her ear, his voice a dangerous caress.

"And if this Eron thinks otherwise, he can try and take you from me. I promise you, dove, it won't end well for him."

A shiver ran down her spine. She believed him, more than she wanted to. Malec would burn down kingdoms for her. Spill rivers of blood just to prove she belonged to him. It wouldn't matter that Eron was her brother; Malec would see only a threat. A rival. A doorway she'd never stop reaching for.

So she lied, clean and careful. "Eron was..." She swallowed, steadying her voice.

"An old master."

His eyes didn't leave hers, but she saw the room shift, darken with the weight of it. "You were owned before me?" he asked, voice rough and low.

She nodded, slow, careful. "I ran away from him."

Malec's jaw clenched, his whole body rigid. "Then I'll find him," he said, flat, final.

"And I'll make sure he never comes near you again."

"No need," she said quickly, forcing the words past her pounding heart. "He's already dead."

Malec froze. For a moment, the tension in his shoulders loosened; a grim satisfaction flickered at the edge of his mouth.

"Good."

Allora nodded, forcing calm over her guilt. She hated lying. Hated the twist of it inside her. But if it kept Eron safe, kept Malec focused on her instead of hunting down the only family members she had left, she would carry that lie forever. Malec leaned in again, pressing his forehead to hers. His breath was warm, his voice quiet, almost reverent.

"No more secrets, dove." But it wasn't a plea, it was a warning.

Before she could reply, the door crashed open, spilling gold morning light across the rugs and scattering their tension. A familiar, grating voice broke the hush.

"Well, well," King Surion drawled, gliding in without a hint of shame. "What a tender little scene. I almost feel rude interrupting."

Malec didn't lift his head at first. His jaw flexed, his eyes hard as stone. Finally, he looked up, cold and sharp.

"You could have knocked."

Surion only smirked, wandering into the room as if he owned every breath inside it. "Where's the fun in that?" he replied.

His gaze found Allora, not leering but measuring, calculating, as if weighing her on some invisible scale.

Allora sat up straighter, spine taut, chin lifted. She refused to look away.

Malec moved, sliding in front of her, silent, protective, a wall she hadn't asked for but wasn't about to refuse.

"What do you want?" he snapped.

Surion waved a lazy hand. "Erolyn's run off again and left me to deal with the new border guard rotations. Preferably someone with a little authority." He arched a brow. "So naturally, I thought of you."

Malec's lip curled. "I'm not part of your Court."

Surion grinned. "And yet, you're the only one who could keep those mutts in line."

Allora felt the tension winding tighter between them, old history, fresh wounds. But she couldn't stop glancing sideways, her heart pounding, her lie still blazing at the back of her throat. Malec scoffed, already seeing the trap. This wasn't about border guards. This was about control.

"Besides," the King continued casually, as if discussing the weather, "my physician came storming into my chamber this morning claiming the infamous Silver Fox has decided he's also a healer now. Said he'd wasted a night preparing a vaccine you never used. Told me, what was it? Ah yes, 'If he wants to bleed himself out like a sacrificial goat over some dying Canariae, then why call me at all?'"

Malec's eyes narrowed. "Because unlike that dried-up old crow, I get results."

"Mm." Surion strolled toward the window, glancing out over the garden. "And yet you still need me to clean up your messes."

"I don't need— "

"But you do, cousin," Surion said, cutting him off smoothly. "And if you won't come for duty's sake... come for her sake."

Malec tensed. "What the fuck does that mean?"

"I mean," Surion said, flashing a too-bright smile, "you can't watch her every minute. Someone has to keep her entertained while you're away. I was going to bring her to the gardens. Let her get some sun. Maybe meet a few friends of the court."

"No."

Surion's words landed with the smug precision of a cat pawing at a wounded bird.

"Surin and Surian are here," he continued, his gaze lingering just a moment too long on Allora, then flicking back to Malec. "And our guest from Kavira has heard so much about the wild High Northern Canariae. He's positively eager to see her."

Malec's expression stayed smooth, but something cold and wild moved beneath his skin. He felt it, a surge deep in his chest, that old, brutal pride uncoiling, mixing with a jealous possessiveness that tasted metallic on his tongue. He hated the idea of her paraded around as his Canariae, hated how Surion spoke of her like she was an exotic beast on loan from the North. And yet, there was that other part of him—the feral, territorial beast that wanted the world to look, to covet, and to know she was his. A slow exhale, practiced and careful.

"Fine," Malec said, voice deceptively calm. "I'll deal with your damned guards. But not until I've bathed her. And fed her. And made sure she's strong enough to walk in your gardens, let alone be ogled by your guests."

Surion's mouth curled in a satisfied grin. "You'll bring her out to play, then?"

Malec's gaze darkened, all pretense of courtesy gone. "And I'll come back to collect her. On time."

"Delightful." Surion spun on his heel, halfway to the door before tossing one last barb over his shoulder. "I look forward to the show."

He paused at the threshold, smirk gleaming.

"You're gentler with her than I've ever seen you be. Almost... tender." His eyes glinted, hungry for a reaction. "Reminds me of how you used to talk to your horse."

Malec's jaw flexed. He didn't blink. His voice dropped low and lethal: "Make another joke like that, and I'll mount you next, on a wall."

Surion just laughed, hands up in mock surrender.

"As possessive as ever. Don't worry. I'll be gentle with your little dove." Then the door clicked shut behind him, the echo lingering in the room like a threat.

Malec stood for a moment, every muscle coiled, every bone vibrating with the need to do violence. The only reason Surion still had all his teeth was that Allora, weak, barely awake, skin too warm, lashes fluttering, was already present. He wouldn't risk startling her. Not yet. He drew in a slow breath, letting the anger bleed away as he turned toward her. Allora's eyes were dark and unfocused, but she was monitoring him, present, real, breathing.

That was enough. For now.

Malec crossed to her bedside, the tension in his shoulders easing, his voice softening to something private and meant only for her. He brushed a knuckle over her cheek, gentle, reverent.

"We'll go see Surion soon," he promised, his words low and rich with quiet intent.

"But first, you eat. Then I'll bathe you myself."

He met her gaze, letting her see the intent searing in his eyes, a slow promise blooming behind them.

"Let him wait."

 [Book 1] 20 - 27

Chapter 20

The Weight of His Claim

Allora was carried into the palace garden by a silent guard, her limbs still too weak to stand on her own. The fever had broken, but it left her body aching and unsteady. A young Awyan nurse followed close behind, watchful, silent, her sharp eyes tracking every breath. Allora said nothing. She had already bathed. Her skin was still damp beneath a pale green gown, light as mist and stitched with unfamiliar embroidery. A soft shawl lay across her shoulders. Her hair had been brushed. She'd been fed.

The garden opened before her like another world. Spring sunlight poured through the arched glass above, gilding the stone paths. Trees rose tall, their branches heavy with golden fruit. Flowers bloomed in thick clusters, some glowing faintly, petals like flame, or moonlight, or stardust. And at center stood a gazebo of dark wood and carved stone. Intricate Awyan symbols lined its beams, sacred, perhaps. Protective. Nothing about the setting was random. Beneath its shade sat four Awyans. Two familiar. Two not.

The first caught her eye at once, a male, younger than most, with golden hair pulled into a high ponytail. His tan was deep and sun-worn, almost defiant, and his eyes, electric blue, rimmed in thick black lashes, seemed almost unreal. He smiled at her like he already knew her, dimples flashing in the light. Beside him lounged an elegant elfess with pale blonde hair braided over one shoulder. Her gray eyes held a calm, assessing curiosity. Not cruel. But watchful and assessing. And then her stomach twisted.

Because she recognized the third. He didn't speak aloud, not at first. He didn't need to.

"Hello, Canariae. It is nice to see you again."

Yup there it was. That voice. That cold, polished weight that slid like silk over steel into her mind. Surin. Malec's father. He didn't rise. Just watched her from his seat, eyes concealed, one corner of his mouth lifting in the faintest hint of a smile. She didn't need to ask why he was here, his presence alone confirmed what she already feared.

And directly across from him, sprawled like he owned the world, sat the last: Surion. The King himself. One arm slung over the back of his chair, fingers idly playing with a fig he had no intention of eating, Surion greeted her with a lazy smirk. Mischief danced in his eyes like a boy caught spying, but beneath it lay something colder. Calculating. Even fond. The bastard was enjoying this. She hadn't even reached the table, and already she felt flayed open. This wasn't a social visit. It wasn't a presentation. It was an evaluation, and she was the prize.

As the guard set her down gently onto a cushion, her body still too weak to stand, and the nurse adjusted her shawl, Allora caught a subtle nod pass between Surion and Surin. No words. Just quiet understanding. They weren't watching her. They were measuring her. Deciding what came next.

> "Ah," came that familiar, too-pleased voice as she was settled beneath the gazebo's carved shadow. "The Lady of the High North has finally graced us."

Allora lifted her gaze, already bracing. Surion stood with arms wide, the picture of a host unveiling a prized gift. She didn't respond to the title, it clung to her like an unwanted cloak, stitched from lies and ownership. With a graceful, theatrical sweep of his hand, Surion gestured to the regal elfess beside him.

> "May I introduce my cousin, Surian. Daughter of Surin. Sister to our favorite silver beast."

Allora blinked, her head snapping toward the elfess, whose amused expression didn't budge.

"Wait, Malec can have siblings?" she blurted before she could stop herself.

It slipped out so fast, so stunned, that the entire table cracked. Surion threw his head back in a roar of laughter. Surin's low chuckle followed, deep and smooth, like a lion surveying prey. Even Surian covered her mouth with a slender hand, shoulders shaking. The golden-haired elf with the devastating smile broke into an even wider grin, both dimples flashing, dangerous, dazzling, and far too pretty for his own good.

"Goddess," Surian giggled, wiping under one eye. "She thinks he was forged in shadows. Like a myth."

"He kind of is," Surion said with a grin, giving Allora a light touch on the shoulder, mock-affectionate. "I knew I always liked you."

Allora rolled her eyes.

Surion didn't stop. "And here we have the great father of the Silver Fox himself," he said, motioning lazily toward the older elf with that same insufferable air of royalty. "High General Surin. Though I doubt you're impressed."

Allora met Surin's eyes flatly.

"Charmed," she said without sincerity, giving him a single, uninterested nod.

Surin clutched his chest as though wounded, letting out a dramatic gasp. "Oh, she cuts deep," he said, feigning injury.

"I don't care," she added, just to make sure no one missed it.

That earned another round of chuckles, even from the nurse standing a few feet back, who quickly tried to hide her smirk. Surion clapped his hands once.

"And last but certainly not least…" His hand extended toward the golden-haired elf with oceanic eyes and the presence of a sun-drenched storm. "King Kael of the Western Province of Zaharein. A dear friend of mine."

Kael inclined his head, his movements crisp, military precise, but still somehow casual. His voice, when it came, was like honey poured over stone, thick, warm, but with a roughness to it, foreign yet charming.

"Greetings, Lady of High Nort," he said, his accent unmistakable, but the Awyan beneath it still clear. "I 'ave heard of you many stories. I wanted very much to meet you. To see if zey were true."

Allora tilted her head, her brows arching, unimpressed.

"And what, exactly, did the stories say? That I have wings? Breathe fire? Or that I eat fools like you for breakfast?"

Kael grinned. "All of zese things," he said easily. "I hoped for…fire."

"She will set this place on fire," Surion warned with a wink, grabbing a peach from the table. "She's done it before."

Kael blinked. "Ah?"

That sent the rest into another burst of laughter. Surin leaned back in his chair, the picture of restrained elegance, and Surian gave a knowing hum.

"Oh, you don't know?" Surion was practically glowing. "She set fire to the border fortress stables. Used a flask of stolen oil, three saddle blankets, and what I can only assume was pure spite."

"I call it ingenuity," Allora muttered under her breath.

"Indeed," Surion agreed, beginning to recount the story to Kael with all the dramatic flair of a bard retelling a legend. "So there she was, midwinter, snow still on the eaves, the fortress quiet, our poor little canariae locked up... "

"I was imprisoned," Allora corrected.

"...and next thing we know, flames. Horses screaming. Guards slipping on ice trying to put it out. And Malec, oh, Malec was foaming at the mouth."

Kael's eyes widened, clearly enjoying the tale. Surion leaned closer to Kael with a conspiratorial whisper, "She escaped barefoot. In the snow. Wearing nothing but a servant's tunic and a broken belt."

Allora shot him a glare.

Surion grinned. "A legend, I told you."

Allora glanced between them all, nobility, power, history tangled in laughter and gossip. But what chilled her wasn't the story. It was the fact that, for the first time, they weren't laughing *at* her. They were laughing *with* her. And somehow, that felt even more dangerous.

Surin's voice unfurled inside her mind like smoke, rich, velvety, far too amused. *"Shall we entertain ourselves, little Canariae?"*

Allora kept her posture relaxed, eyes drifting lazily over the garden as Surion dramatically retold her stable-burning escape like it was an epic bard's tale. Laughter rippled around the table as he embellished every moment, claiming she'd ridden a wild elk out of the gates and shouted curses in three languages. But inside, she was alert. Sharp.

"Is this how all Highborns pass the time?" she replied dryly in thought. *"Mocking prisoners who managed to outsmart them?"*

Surin laughed quietly, the sound brushing her mind like warm silk. *"Oh no, you've earned their admiration. Even if they'd*

*never admit it aloud. Besides, you didn't just outsmart anyone...
you outsmarted him."*

She felt a flicker of satisfaction, but didn't show it. Instead, she reached for a grape from the table, popping it into her mouth as if she hadn't just been threatened, manipulated, and poisoned all within the same week.

"So what is this?" she asked. *"You fishing for gossip? Or trying to play the kind uncle?"*

"Why not both?" he answered easily. *"You intrigue me. I asked my son to gift you to me weeks ago... but he's strangely possessive."*

Her hand froze around the next grape. *"Gift me?"*

"Don't pout," he purred. *"It was before I understood how sharp your tongue was.*

Now I see why he's obsessed."
Allora's eyes narrowed slightly, but her face remained pleasant. She offered a fake smile when Surion finished his story with a sweeping bow and everyone clapped.

"Let me guess," she murmured mentally. *"You collect pretty things and hoped I'd be easier to control than your son."*

Surin hummed, the sound curling in her mind like smoke from incense.

"Oh no, little flame. I have no delusions about controlling you. I just wanted a closer look."

She leaned forward on her elbow, not looking at him, her voice cold in his thoughts.
"Keep your distance, Surin. You might find I burn hotter than you're used to."

There was a pause. Then his chuckle rippled through her again. *"Goddess, no wonder Malec is unraveling."*
He was testing her. Just like his son always did.

"Do you want to know anything about Malec?" Surin's voice slithered into her mind again, velvety and mocking, dipped in the same arrogance that always made her grit her teeth.

Allora didn't answer right away. Her thoughts moved fast, measuring. If Malec's father was offering information, she had to be smart. Surin was old, clever, and dangerous. But he clearly liked games. She rolled her eyes and answered mentally with a smirk.
"Alright then. Tell me about his weaknesses."

Surin chuckled softly. She didn't have to look to know he was pleased. *"Oh, little dove,"* he purred. *"You are dangerous."*

"Tell me something I don't know," she murmured, swirling the wine in her goblet.
She could feel his stare, feel the way his mind sharpened with interest.
"He doesn't sleep when you're gone. Not truly."
"He's never let another near his bed."
"He carved your name into his blade the day he claimed you."
Allora stilled slightly, her fingers stilling on the stem of her glass. That part she hadn't known.
"That's not a weakness," she replied coldly. *"That's obsession."*

"They're the same thing, sometimes," Surin said, amusement dripping from every syllable. *"And I assure you... he would burn every kingdom from here to the mountain coast if you told him to."*

"And would you?" she asked, her voice a whisper of curiosity, mockery, and danger.

Surin laughed again, that deep, elegant sound made for courtrooms and cruelty.

"No. I'm not so easily undone."

She hummed, setting her goblet down. *"Then I suppose that makes you the stronger male."*

His silence stretched, just long enough to tell her she'd struck something deep.

Then his voice returned, smooth and low.

"Tell me something, Allora. What do you really want?"

Allora didn't hesitate.

"Answers," she said flatly, giving him the one-word truth he already knew.

But what she meant was clear: not just freedom, clarity. Information. If she was going to survive Malec... she had to understand him.

"What does Malec fear?" she asked next through the bond, her tone even, though her heart betrayed her with a hard, steady thud.

Surin's pale blue eyes gleamed faintly, the edges crinkling with something almost fond.

"Losing control," he answered, slow and unhurried. *"Of himself. Of others. Of the world he's built around his precious order."*

Allora tucked that truth away like a weapon she might one day use, sharp and hidden. That made sense. Malec wasn't just a tyrant, he was desperate to contain things. Control wasn't just a preference, it was survival. No wonder she shook him.

"What makes him irrational?"

A smile ghosted across Surin's face, subtle, wicked.

"Jealousy," he murmured in her mind. *"The kind that sears. That blinds. The kind that makes even my son forget his own sacred rules."*

She'd seen it. Felt it. The way Malec changed when another male elf looked at her for too long. The way his eyes darkened when she mentioned Earth. He wore it like a sickness. And jealousy... was the fever. Allora leaned back, but in her mind the words darted sharp and sly.

"Why does Malec have those weird quirks and rituals? Is that normal for Awyans, or is he just... broken?"

Surin's reply came in that rich, velvet mental tone, slow and measured.

"It's not brokenness, little dove. Not at all." He paused, and she sensed him searching for a way she'd understand. *"Most Awyans love ritual, yes. But for Malec, it's more than comfort. It's survival. He craves order the way some crave air or drink."*

"But why?" she pressed, a flare of impatience in her thoughts. *"Why is it so extreme with him?"*

She felt his amusement and something gentler, quieter beneath it, a brush of pride, of regret.

"The world is sharp for Malec," Surin sent, voice a mental murmur. *"Too loud, too bright. He flinched at sudden noise, always. He noticed every change in a room. As a child, he'd spend hours arranging stones into perfect rows, memorizing the grain in a table until he could see it behind his eyelids. He spoke later than his cousins. But read sooner. Far sooner."*

A twist of surprise, then pity, coiled in Allora's chest. She thought of Malec's obsession with sleeves, his need to align every plate, every knife, the way he seemed to go rigid if anything was out of order. She'd thought it arrogance. Control. But now...

"So the rituals are... what? Armor?" she asked, unwilling to let him dodge.

Exactly, Surin's mental voice came, tinged with something warm and sad.

> *"Most drift through life, smoothing out the rough. But Malec feels every edge. The rituals, the routines, those are how he keeps from being cut. It's his way of finding silence. Of breathing."*

Allora's throat tightened, remembering the haunted look in Malec's eyes at the end of every chaotic day, the tension that never really left his jaw.

"Is it ever enough?" she asked, barely a whisper in her own mind.

> *"Peace is rare for my son,"* Surin replied, "and she felt the truth of it like an ache. *He masks it well, hides behind command and coldness, but... he is always fighting. If you want to wound him, unravel his order. If you want to help him... let him have it. It's how he survives."*

The knowledge landed in her chest with unexpected weight. She wasn't built for pity, but there was something deeper. Empathy? She didn't want to name it. She watched the patterns, the restless hands, the way chaos seemed to sting him. On Earth, psychologists would have called it autism. Here, it just made him... Malec. Allora glanced away, frowning at her wine, heart pounding with realization. Malec wasn't broken.

He was just... raw. Sharp-edged. Fighting the world every day just to find a moment of quiet. She'd always thought he wanted to control her. Maybe, she realized, he just wanted to survive her. Or could it be both?

She swallowed hard, jaw tightening as she forced herself not to feel. Not pity. Not tenderness. Not that strange ache curling behind her ribs. What did it matter anyway? He had still taken her, still held her against her will. That alone was unforgivable, no matter what wiring shaped his mind.

Before she could respond, Surion's voice cut across the garden like a cracked drum.

"Mind-speaking again? Come now, share with the rest of us."

Surin sighed with theatrical flair and offered a gracious apology to the table, swirling his cup like a lazy noble pretending to care. But just before he returned to the conversation aloud, his voice whispered once more in her mind.

"Keep asking, little canariae. I have so many stories. And you... you have such dangerous eyes."

Then he winked, and Allora wasn't sure if she'd just won a game, or stepped into one she didn't understand.

"Honestly, Uncle Surin," Surion sighed with exasperated flair, rubbing his temple like a man long-suffering and tired of his own bloodline, "you're such a flirt. Can't take you anywhere without you trying to get into someone's head."

The table laughed, except for Kael, who simply smiled like someone who'd expected no less.

Allora blinked.

Wait... Surin?

Her gaze flicked across the group, Surion, Surian, Surin. It hit her all at once. The similarity in their names. The way they all shared that eerie grace, those glacier-cut features, those maddeningly sharp eyes. Her brows furrowed as she leaned back, mentally counting the syllables.

"Was that... a coincidence?"

Before she could finish the thought, Surin turned his head and caught her, smiling with the sly satisfaction of someone who'd just caught her peeking over his shoulder.

"No, dark one. It is not a coincidence," he said through their shared mental bond, voice velvet smooth. *"They were all named after me. Family tradition. A legacy of ego, I suppose."*

Allora's mouth parted in disbelief, and she muttered aloud, "So then... why doesn't Malec have a name that came from yours, like Surion and Surian?"

That, apparently, was the golden question. Every Awyan at the table froze for a beat. Surion cleared his throat, Surian stifled a chuckle behind her wine glass, and Surin simply raised one regal brow. Only Kael, ever the outsider, glanced around like he'd missed a punchline. Then, in eerie unison, the three relatives answered:

"Leira."

Allora blinked again. "Leira?"

Surin inclined his head solemnly.

"Malec's mother. My former mate." He set his goblet down and steepled his fingers as though weighing which memories were safe to unearth. "She named him herself. Refused to follow the family tradition. Said he would be his own. And frankly, she wasn't wrong."

"She always was the stubborn one," Surion added with a grin. Surian rolled her eyes fondly. "That's putting it lightly."

Surin nodded. "Malec and Leira are cut from the same cloth. Sharp minds. Dangerous instincts. Brilliant, cold, driven. They mirrored each other perfectly, like two sides of the same obsidian blade." His eyes drifted toward the garden, toward where Malec had disappeared earlier. "Naming him was her final act of rebellion. And perhaps... her only act of hope."

Allora sat with that, unsure whether she felt intrigued or unnerved. Of course Malec's name would be different. He didn't fit. Not into this family. Not into any box. And yet, somehow... he still ruled them all.

Allora's attention drifted to the Awyan with the dimples and his too-frequent glances. She noticed it the moment she was seated beneath the sunlit gazebo, when the conversation lulled and his eyes kept finding her. The blond one. High ponytail. Unnatural tan. Vibrant blue eyes. He didn't look away when caught. He stared openly, smiling like he already knew her, like he was waiting.

It wasn't subtle. And it was suspicious.

That old sixth sense tickled the back of her neck, the kind that warned you when your friends were trying to set you up without asking. Staged proximity. Forced charm. The stink of matchmaking with no finesse. Her fingers twitched against her skirt. The sun and splendor of the garden faded. She felt played.

And Allora didn't do played.

She leaned forward slightly, chin tilted, and sliced through Surion's sentence with the grace of a blade.

"So, what's the deal?"

The table stilled.

Surion blinked. "Excuse me?"

"I said," she repeated louder, her eyes sweeping the group, "what's the deal? Why am I here? And why do I feel like I'm being auctioned off, maybe not to a suitor, but to a buyer?"

Silence dropped like a curtain. Even the guards behind her went rigid. The nurse adjusting her shawl froze mid-motion. Surion looked caught between offense and delight. Surian choked on her wine. Surin's brows lifted, amusement flickering behind his composed mask. And the blond, Kael, apparently, just chuckled, leaning back in his chair like she'd thrown down a challenge he couldn't wait to answer.

Surion's laugh came too light, too forced. He waved a hand.

"No need to cause a stir, Lady of the High North. This is just a friendly gathering. Curious minds. Old friends. That's all."

Allora arched an eyebrow, not relaxing an inch. "Curious minds? Good. Maybe you can satisfy my curiosity—what the hell am I doing at this table?"

Tension prickled the air. Then Kael, who'd been admiring her like a sculpture brought to life, lifted a hand in a quiet gesture, *I've got this.* He leaned in slowly, a lazy smile tugging at his lips. When he spoke, his voice was low and thick with accent, elegant and warm, like honey poured over stone.

> "I must say, I am sorry," Kael murmured. "If I made you feel like... a prize. Zat was not my intent, *mira*. It is Awyan custom, in my country, for Canariae to be... exchanged. Bought. Sold. Sometimes even gifted." He said it plainly, without shame or mockery. "But I only wish to meet ze one from the stories. Ze one who burned her cage down. Who made the Silver Fox bleed. Who shattered chains with fire and fury." He dipped his head slightly, a graceful acknowledgment. "And I must say... I am not disappointed."

Allora eyed him. She didn't fully buy it. Maybe it was his charm, or the suspicious gleam in Surion's eye. But whatever was happening here felt orchestrated. Still, she wasn't about to let them feel in control. She leaned back, lips curving in a smirk.

"Well, don't get your hopes up. I'm already spoken for."

Kael blinked.

> Then she added, almost flippantly, "Apparently, I've been imprinted on. And now, soul-bound."

Gasps.

Not dramatic ones. Real ones. A hush swept across the table like a wind through dry leaves. Even the guards, stoic, expressionless statues, shifted uneasily. The Awyan nurse inhaled sharply behind her, nearly dropping the folded blanket in her lap. Surion's wine cup paused mid-air.

Surin, for once, stopped smiling. Surian's brows climbed so high they vanished into her braid.

Allora frowned. "What?"

Their reactions intrigued her more than anything else had that day. She looked from face to face, now hunting. Digging.

"Okay. Someone wanna explain why that word made everyone react like I just declared war?"

It was Surian who whispered, "Vash'telor is... rare."

Kael's eyes had darkened slightly, his playful edge replaced with something more pensive. "It is forbidden, in most territories. And... irreversible."

Allora blinked. "Luko told me about it but it just sounds too, ridiculous. That it was... spiritual? That it happened during sex if one of you was emotionally unstable."

"It is more than spiritual," Surin cut in, voice low, composed but firm. "It is ancient. Sacred. Dangerous. You are no longer just his, canariae. If Malec truly Vash'telor himself to you... then he is yours as well."

Her heart stopped. "What?"

Surion, for once, didn't smile. "It means your pain is his. Your life, his obsession.

Your death..." He shrugged. "It would end him."

Allora's eyes widened.

Kael tilted his head, observing her closely now. "This bond... it is not a collar, *shae*. It is a tether. One not easily broken."

Allora's eyes narrowed as the ripple of surprise settled into a tense stillness. The word she'd dropped—*Vash'telor*—hung over the table like storm-charged air. She let the silence stretch, scanning faces. Surion looked like he'd swallowed his tongue. Surin had gone still. Even Kael's smile faded to a thoughtful line. The nurse shifted awkwardly, pretending not to listen. Allora tilted her head, breaking the silence like a blade through silk.

"Can it be one-sided?" she asked flatly. "Because I'm not Awyan. I'm Canariae. Human. Whatever you call it. We don't have magical mating instincts or cosmic tethers." Her tone stayed dry, but something else hid beneath, fear, maybe. Or the quiet thrum of hope. "So what happens if he Saen'trien... and I didn't? If he Vash'telor... and I didn't?"

Another hush followed. Then Surin spoke. "Ah, little dove... it *can* be one-sided. In fact, it often begins that way. But I've never heard of it happening with a Canariae."

Allora stiffened.
"But Saen'trien isn't permanent, however Vash'telor is," he added.
Kael's pale blue eyes settled on her, not quite pitying, but close. He leaned forward, voice low and rich, each word drawn out with elegant, smoky grace.

"If he has bound himself to you... zen he is yours now, lady. Even if you do not want him... it make no difference to a soul that has chosen."

Allora exhaled slowly, her gaze dropping to the table. Bound. Like a chained beast, his soul twisted around hers whether she'd asked for it or not. She shook her head.
"That's not love," she muttered.
"No," he admitted, quiet. "But it's a hunger that can devour you from the inside. Far more dangerous than love."

Allora felt like she was drowning in fairy tale bullshit. Not the sweet kind with talking animals and charming thieves. The *other* kind, the twisted ones. The ones where every smile had teeth and every rule bent to whoever held power. She was Alice in Wonderland, but high on rage and out of exits. Everything around her felt like a puppet show strung together with riddles and ego. Soul-binding nonsense? Imprinting like some werewolf romance novel? Fever magic and blood rites?

It was just so damn... *stupid*.

"Oh my god," she muttered under her breath. "So. Fucking. Stupid."

She didn't notice Kael reach for her until his fingers brushed her arm, light as breath, then jerked back like he'd touched fire. Something flickered behind his high-voltage blue eyes, but Allora missed it. Her thoughts were spiraling. She needed to move, to breathe, to control something in this world of silk-tongued predators and suffocating rituals.

Across the table, Surion was still talking, likely spinning some inflated tale where she was both villain and punchline. Laughter rippled, but she barely registered it. Until someone moved beside her.

Surian. The elfess glided across the stone floor like silk, her pale braids catching the light. With a casual flick of her hip, she shoved Surion aside and dropped onto the bench beside Allora.

"Hey!" Surion yelped.

Ignored.

Surian crossed one leg over the other and studied Allora up close, cool, elegant, indistinct. She was stunning, carved from frost and grace. Where Malec simmered and Surion performed, Surian simply *watched*. Not cruel. Not kind. Curious. And in an Awyan, curiosity was rarely harmless.

"You intrigue me, canariae," she said, voice smooth and cultured. Her head tilted slightly, as if considering a puzzle. "I can see why my brother is obsessed with you."

Allora's spine stiffened. Don't react. She forced her face into neutrality, masking the unease tightening her chest. She wasn't just caged. She was surrounded, by Malec's family. His father, his cousin, his sister. All sharp, beautiful, and far too interested. And she still didn't know what they wanted.

Worse, Surin lingered. His presence brushed her mind again, faint and smug, like a fox nosing the edge of the henhouse. He was enjoying this.

> *"What's wrong, little dove?"* His voice curled through her thoughts, silk-soft and mocking.

> *"Get out of my head,"* she hissed silently, jaw clenching.

> *"I thought we were enjoying ourselves,"* he murmured. *"Would you like to play another game?"*

Do I get to kill you at the end? she snapped.

His laugh was low and delighted, rumbling through her skull like velvet thunder.

> From across the table, Surion groaned. "Uncle, really? Again? Can you go five minutes without whispering sweet nothings into someone's frontal lobe?"

> Surin sighed, setting down his goblet with mock grace. "You've had your fun. Let me have mine."

Then he winked at Allora. She scowled. He laughed harder. And everything stopped. Surian tilted her head. Kael blinked slowly. Even the King quieted, his story forgotten. Allora's frown deepened. Apparently, Surin laughing twice in one gathering was... rare. Surion leaned back in his chair, fingers tapping once against the wood before turning a sharp, impatient gaze on her.

> "Since we're all enjoying this little gathering," he said, voice clipped with that particular brand of false charm that made her want to throw something, "I assume by now you've gathered the reason for it."

Before she could even open her mouth, Surin cut in smoothly, voice slick as velvet.

"Let me guess. You thought it was for the wine and the company?"

Allora narrowed her eyes. "I thought I was dragged out here to be paraded around like a conversation piece."

Surian, lounging with elegant poise, let out a low chuckle. "Father, just tell her. You're being vague again."

Surin gave a casual shrug, lifting his goblet. "Very well," he said. But his gaze, icy and sharp, never left Allora. "Let's not insult anyone's intelligence."

Allora's stomach tensed, the slow churn of dread creeping up her spine.

"You've caused quite the stir, little one," Surin said, swirling his drink like this was some dinner theater. "A Canariae escaping Malec? Unheard of. But not only did you run, he followed. Crossed counties to find you. Threatened Surion's seat. Nearly razed half the court."

He smiled then. But it wasn't kind.

"And now?" He set his goblet down deliberately, eyes glinting. "Now he's claiming you as his mate, you Canariae call it betrothal."

And that was when Allora stood too fast. The room spun like someone had grabbed it by the edges and twisted.

The blood drained from her face, her balance faltering. The nurse was at her side instantly, guiding her back down. Kael moved, alarm flashing across his bright blue eyes, but Allora waved him off sharply, tension rippled through her jaw. She was not about to faint in front of these people. She wasn't about to appear weak. But she had to sit.

The moment her body hit the cushioned bench again, she barked out.

"*SAY WHAT?*" Her voice echoed against the stone gazebo, cutting through whatever decorum still remained. Even the guards, who had been like statues in the corners, turned at the sound. Surion exhaled like a father fed up with a misbehaving child.

"This is exactly why I didn't want him to have everything he wanted," he muttered. "Malec never listens. And now look. He's made a mess."

Allora's head snapped toward him. "A mess?"
Surion didn't backpedal.

"Yes. A soulbond to a Canariae he refuses to part with. He's gone completely mad with it. And you may think you have some sort of power in that, but you don't. This was never about love, or fate, or whatever he thinks it is. This was about trade. And he knows that."

She glared at him. "So what, I'm a bargaining chip?"

Surion's lips pressed thin. "You're a rare asset. One I hoped to trade for something that might keep the realm from falling apart. Malec can't have everything, Allora. Foreign alliances matter more than his obsession."

She scoffed, disgust burning up her throat. "You're unbelievable, I KNEW IT. I FUCKING KNEW IT."

Kael, to his credit, lifted a hand and leaned slightly toward her.

"I am sorry, mira," he said, his voice smooth, each word kissed by a lilting cadence that curled like silk around her ears. "I deed not know you were... how do you say... already Vash'telor.

I would not 'ave come if I knew. It was Surion who, how you say, arranged ze matters."

He threw a glance at the King, more amused than contrite, then returned his gaze to her with a disarming smile.

"I only came to meet ze one from ze stories. Ze Canariae who burns and cannot be caged."

His smile was gentle, but Allora wasn't buying it. "Right. The legend," she muttered.

Surion tried to wave it off. "Honestly, Allora, this wouldn't be so dramatic if you weren't so volatile. You did burn down an entire stable."

"I freed enslaved canariae."

"Yes, yes, details," Surion muttered with a roll of his eyes. "Anyway, this was simply a meeting. Kael was curious. He wasn't going to buy you, he knows better now. Besides," he added, with an almost bitter edge, "Malec already made it clear he'd murder anyone who tried."

"Then why bring me here?" she demanded.
Surin leaned forward again, elbows on the table, gaze glinting with amusement.

"Because you, little dove, are no longer just a Canariae. You're a soulbound mate to a war heir. You belong to the High North now, whether you like it or not."

Allora's pulse pounded in her ears. She had always known she was in a gilded cage. But now? Now they were throwing away the key. Allora's chest constricted, her breath catching beneath the weight of Surin's gaze. This was a game, of course it was. A mental chess match dressed in velvet, designed to flay her open without drawing blood. Surin was baiting her, casting the line and waiting for her to snap. But she wasn't going to give him the satisfaction. Not today. She lifted her chin and met his eyes coolly.

"You're wrong," she said, voice clipped.

That single, silken brow of his arched with interest. "Oh?"

"Malec doesn't love me. He doesn't love *anyone*. He's a conqueror, not a lover. He keeps me because I'm a challenge, something difficult to break. That's all I am to him."

Surin's blue eyes gleamed with unspoken amusement, and there was something far too knowing in the way his lips curved. "And yet," he said softly, "you still wear his mark."

Heat rushed to Allora's cheeks. Her fingers shot up before she could stop them, brushing the side of her throat where faint bruises lingered like a brand. Malec's love bites, possessive and deliberate. He'd left them on purpose, to be seen. To be *known*. She jerked her hand away like it burned.

"That doesn't mean anything," she snapped.

Surin tilted his head, voice as smooth as silk sliding over steel. "Ah, but *little canariae,* it means *everything.*"

"Father," Surian interjected at last, her calm gray eyes flicking to Allora with measured interest. Her tone lacked venom, but her gaze was sharp, dissecting.

"He's being dramatic, but he isn't lying. Malec has never done this before so it is alarming."

Allora stared at her, throat dry. "This doesn't make any sense. Malec is... well... Malec."

Surian's mouth quirked. "Exactly. He is disciplined, ruthless, careful. He doesn't believe in weakness. He doesn't trust people. He doesn't let anyone close enough to matter. That's why no one thought it possible."

She shifted slightly closer, her voice dropping to something more intimate. "But you? You're different. He watches you like you've crawled under his skin and started rewriting his being. He's terrified of it. But he's in it, whether he wants to be or not."

Surian's mouth quirked. "Exactly. He's rigid. Controlled. He doesn't allow anyone power over him. That's why this is... *disturbing*. Even to us." She leaned in slightly. "But you? He watches you like you've rewritten something in him. It's not normal. It's not him."

Allora shifted in her seat, uncomfortable. "Oh, I noticed him staring like a lunatic," she muttered. "I'm not blind."

Surian tilted her head. "And what did you think it meant?"

Allora shrugged, her jaw tight. "I thought it was lust. He's male. I'm female. It's not that complicated."

Kael gave a soft, amused exhale, and Surin's smile grew sharp.

Surian didn't smile, though. She only studied her more deeply. "Then you don't see it. You think it's just physical. But the rest of us? We've known Malec for a long time. And we've never seen him look at someone the way he looks at you."

Allora folded her arms again, gripping her elbows so tightly the pressure ached in her joints. Maybe she had seen it. Maybe she just didn't want to name it. Because what they were describing, this obsession, this depth, it wasn't beautiful.

It was terrifying.

Chapter 21

Bound by Fire, Not by Choice

"You all act like this is some kind of problem," Allora snapped, her voice sharp with frustration. "If you don't want Malec claiming me, then do something about it! Help me escape! Help me get back to my own world!"

The silence that followed was immediate, thick as velvet. Not even the wind stirred through the open garden arches. And then, Surin laughed. Low and decadent, like dark wine poured over silk. It slithered into the space between them, curling around her like smoke. Mocking. Unbothered.

Surin sighed dramatically, swirling the wine in his glass, his tone as casual as ever.

"Oh, little dove," he mused, eyes bright with indulgent menace, "you still don't understand your predicament, do you?"

Allora's fingers curled against her lap, her jaw locking hard. "My *predicament*?" she bit back, the word tasting like iron on her tongue.

"Yes," Surin said, as if explaining something to a child. "You belong to Malec. And if anyone," his gaze drifted, smooth as oil, across the table to include Surian, Kael, and even Surion, "so much as entertains the idea of helping you leave... he will burn them to ash."

A heavy silence fell, too loud to ignore. Allora didn't need to look to know Surian had shifted. She felt it. The subtle tension, the conflicted breath, the weight of doubt pressing against her like a phantom hand. Of them all, Surian didn't seem as resigned. She wasn't smug like her father. She wasn't power-drunk like the King. And she sure as hell didn't leer at her like Kael, who hadn't stopped stalking her with his eyes her since the moment she sat down.

So Allora turned to her, tone sharp with intent.

"Then what about *you*?" she asked, eyes locking with the elfess across the table.

Surian blinked, startled. "Me?"

"You're not like them," Allora said plainly. "You haven't mocked me. You haven't treated me like a thing to be owned, bartered, or passed around."

She leaned forward, her voice gaining bite.

"So tell me, why can't I leave? Why can't I be free?"

Surian's mouth opened, but no sound came. Her gray eyes flicked to her father, then the King, then back to Allora. There was a long pause. Then, softly, almost too gently:

"Why do you need to leave so badly?"

Allora stared at her. This was it, the question that cracked everything open.

She could lie. Say she missed home. Offer some flippant excuse. But her bones ached with exhaustion, and her soul trembled with truth. They needed to hear it. All of them. So she inhaled, and told them. She spoke of Earth. Her Earth. Not this world where Canariae were plucked like wild fruit, but one teetering on collapse. She told them about the Cotard-Virus. The death toll. The mass graves. Cities rotting from the inside out, with barely two hundred million survivors clinging to what was left. She spoke of her title, Dr. Major Melodie Jaxxon. Decorated soldier. Medic. Lead researcher. She had commanded troops. Saved lives. Buried friends. She told them about the glowing pool in the caves. The anomaly that brought her here. And then, the part that haunted her most: the virus that destroyed her people didn't originate on Earth.

It came from this world. From Awya.

By the time she finished, her throat burned. The garden was silent. Surian's gaze shimmered, visibly shaken. Kael, for once, had nothing clever to say. Even Surin had stilled, his wine forgotten in his hand.

But it was Surion who broke the silence.

"So... you're saying this plague, the one that nearly wiped out your kind, originated here?" He leaned back, arms folding, the glint of amusement gone from his eyes.

Allora nodded. "It makes sense. The Cotard strain didn't behave like anything we'd seen. It resisted our medicine. Our science. It wasn't natural. It was foreign."

She looked straight at him, voice steady as steel. "And now I know why."

Her gaze didn't waver. "Because it *was* foreign. It came from this world. From Awya."

A low chuckle slipped from Surion's mouth. It wasn't amused. It wasn't kind. It was fascinated. The sound of a predator circling something it didn't yet understand.

"Well, well," he said, resting his chin on his hand. "You, little canariae, are full of surprises." His eyes gleamed like a blade catching moonlight. "Malec truly picked an interesting one."

Something about the way he said it made her skin crawl, like her existence was a puzzle piece he could twist into place. He turned smoothly toward his cousin.

"Tell me, Surian. What do *you* think? Does our guest deserve to go home?"

The silence that followed felt thick with waiting. Then, Surian spoke, soft, certain.

"Yes."

Allora's breath caught. But it was short-lived.
Surion laughed. "Ah. Of course you'd say that."
His eyes returned to Allora, sharp as frost.

"But I'm afraid your story changes nothing. Foreign disease or not, you still belong to Malec. However," he raised his brow, the weight of his crown behind his voice, "Malec doesn't get to keep everything he wants. Especially not when foreign alliances are on the table, little dove."

Allora's brow furrowed sharply, her voice cutting through the low murmur of conversation at the table.
"Can you all stop calling me that?"

Surion arched a brow in mild amusement, lifting his wine glass. "Calling you what?"

She turned her gaze to him, then to Surin with open irritation. "Little dove." The words tasted bitter in her mouth. "You say it. So does Malec. It's not my name."

Surian leaned forward slightly, her expression calm but curious. "But that's what your name means."

Allora blinked. "What?"

"Allora," the elfess explained gently, "is a pet name. In our language, it means little dove. It comes from, alori, meaning beloved daughter, cherished nieces... or treasured mates."

Her stomach twisted as the meaning hit her like a punch. Malec had chosen that name for her. Not to honor her, not even to mock her. But to possess her. To soften her into something fragile. Something tender and small. A word meant to cage. A muscle jumped in her jaw.

She arched a brow. "Cute. Does that mean I get a leash too?"

Surion's smirk deepened. "Fitting, isn't it?"

Her eyes narrowed. "No. It's stupid. Do I look like a docile bird to you?" Her voice rose, sharp and hot. "Do I seem like something you can tuck away in a cage and admire? I am not fragile."

From across the table, Surin's low voice curled around her like smoke. "Mm. No, not fragile," he murmured, those piercing blue eyes gleaming. "But you do struggle... quite beautifully."

Her skin prickled, fury simmering just beneath the surface, but she held herself steady, refusing to give him the reaction he was clearly baiting for. Surion chuckled as if her fury were the most delightful dessert.

"It doesn't matter what you think of the name," he said, leaning back lazily. "Malec already gave it to you. And you know what that means."

And god help her, he was right. No matter how much she hated it... Allora had already become her identity in this world.

Malec's identity for her. His mark. His myth. His little dove.

Allora sat motionless, hands folded in her lap while the world moved on without her. Laughter echoed through the vaulted chamber, glassware clinked, robes rustled, but she barely heard any of it. Her mind spun in silence, too full to speak, too heavy to move. Malec's soul-binding. Surin's games. Surion's agenda. Her origin. Her people. Their extinction. The weight of it all settled like stone on her chest. And it wasn't over.

She didn't recoil when Kael slid a plate of sweets closer to her, his voice soft, tinged with that lyrical accent.

"You like zese, *lei*? You ate many before." His smile was gentle, not forced, but not foolish either.

She blinked and looked at him. He was too perfect, sun-warmed skin, chiseled jaw, those vivid magnetic eyes. Honestly, he looked way too young for her. Then again, this was a world where age was meaningless. For all she knew, he was ten thousand years old and hadn't hit elf puberty. Probably didn't even have chest hair.

Still, one thing was clear. He was kind.

There was no possessiveness in his gaze, no probing mind tricks. Just quiet warmth. A calm, steady presence that didn't crowd her or demand anything. He simply sat near, like a breeze she could breathe through.

She took a sweet and bit into it.

Kael's smile widened, clearly pleased, and he eased into gentle conversation, letting her lead. As the tension in her limbs softened, she found herself leaning in, answering, even laughing when Surion jabbed at Surin. They talked military strategy, formations, defense lines, siege tactics, and it caught her off guard how seriously they listened. Surion, for all his bravado, was focused. Surian even more so, her gray eyes sharp with interest, absorbing every word. For the first time since falling into this world, Allora felt... normal. Not property. Not a relic. Not a myth.

She almost let herself enjoy it. Almost.

Then the court messenger barged in, breathless and red-faced, bronze armor gleaming in the candlelight.

"Urgent message from Commander Malec!"

The room froze.

"If the Canariae isn't returned immediately," he panted, "he'll come retrieve her himself. And he's not in a waiting mood."

Groans rippled through the table. Surion muttered something about overdramatic lovers. Surin smirked into his wine, clearly amused.

Kael grumbled under his breath, "Your commander... he is menace, no? Like wild beast with no leash."

Allora pushed back from the table, annoyed and already exhausted by whatever temper tantrum Malec was throwing now.

"Damn lunatic," she muttered.

She stood, but her body betrayed her, light-headed, legs wobbling beneath her. The room tilted for a brief second. A pair of hands steadied her. Her nurse had appeared at her side, murmuring something about sitting back down, that she hadn't recovered enough yet, that she was overexerting herself. Kael moved instinctively, too, rising in concern, but Allora waved him off with a sharp shake of her head.

"I'm fine," she snapped, but she wasn't.

She had to sit. If she didn't, she'd faint and give them even more reason to treat her like some fragile dove in need of caging.

Just as she was steadying herself on the edge of the chair again, Surian rose without a word and moved to her side. She gently nudged Surion, her cousin, out of the way with a smooth grace, ignoring his offended yelp as she slid into the space beside Allora.

"I'll walk with you," Surian said simply.

Allora narrowed her eyes. "Why?"

Surian's expression didn't change. Calm. Centered. Quietly amused. "Because I want to talk to you."

And for some reason... Allora didn't say no.

She turned first to Surion, who lounged with effortless ease beside Surin, his wine glass cradled in long fingers. "Thank you for your hospitality, your Highness," she said, her tone formal but not cold. "Goodnight."

Surion inclined his head with an amused glint in his eye. "Rest well, Lady Canariae. You'll need your strength."

Allora's gaze shifted next to Surin, who smirked the moment her attention landed on him.

"And you, Lord Talandros," she said evenly, not bothering to hide the edge in her voice, "try not to dream of me too loudly."

Surin gave a dramatic sigh, raising his glass. "No promises, little dove."

She didn't flinch at the name this time, but she didn't acknowledge it either. Then her eyes found Kael. He was still leaning against the far wall, his long limbs folded like a wolf at rest, those piercing eyes catching the lantern light like twin shards of frozen sky. His gaze was locked on her, steady, unreadable, but something warm stirred beneath the surface.

Allora offered him a softer expression. "I hope I didn't disappoint you," she said, her voice quieter now, more genuine.

Kael stepped forward, just enough that his shadow stretched across the polished stone toward her. His voice, when it came, was velvet-wrapped thunder, touched by the cadence of Awyan nobility, elegant, thick with softened syllables and a slow, deliberate rhythm.

"Never, *mira*. You... you are flame, dressed in soft skin. Ze kind of fire that melt even stone to ash," he said, voice low, laced with awe and something deeper. "You did not dis-uh... how you say? Fail me?" His mouth tugged into a slow, knowing smile. "You... unraveled ze air, *mira*. Made breath feel... too small."

Allora blinked, caught between a laugh and a shiver. She hadn't expected that. Poetry wrapped in awkward charm, accented with that unplaceable inflection, like someone raised speaking stars and storms now trying to speak silk. Then she rolled her eyes with a smirk, regaining her edge.

"Well, the Silver Badger is throwing a tantrum again. I'd keep your pretty face away unless you want it melted."

Kael gave a soft, startled laugh, hand brushing his chest as though to brace the impact of her teasing. "Zen I stay far," he promised, eyes glittering. "But lei, this I swear... I will see you again, *mira*. Even if world must move to make it happen."

His dimples appeared, boyish and fleeting. And Allora, against her will, smiled back.

The palace glowed like a cradle of amber fire beneath the rising moons, its open halls brushed by a jasmine-salted breeze. Silver-leafed trees swayed in the courtyards, casting long shadows across the marble like silent dancers. Lantern light pooled in soft halos along the path as Allora walked, held steady by Surian, whose arm looped gently through hers. Their footsteps echoed faintly, joined only by the soft tread of the nurse behind them and the quiet boots of two guards trailing in the shadows. The palace slept, hushed by the late hour, but Allora's thoughts churned.

Surian walked like a ghost made of glass, elegant, illegible, cloaked in quiet power. She was nothing like her brother. Malec was storm. Surian was frost. But the same fire glimmered in her eyes, controlled, assessing, ancient. The tension in Allora's shoulders crept back. Whatever calm she'd felt in the garden had vanished the moment Malec's name returned to the air.

"You are not what I expected," Surian said softly at last, her voice a silk thread drawn through the dark.

Allora gave a short, dry snort. "Let me guess. You thought I'd be some dumb, docile Canariae in a collar."

Surian didn't laugh. She didn't even smile. "No," she said. "I expected you to be dead."

That stopped Allora mid-step. Her muscles went taut beneath Surian's arm.

"Malec has never kept a Canariae alive this long," Surian continued, her tone not unkind, just factual. "Not one who's defied him. Not one who's bitten, screamed, run... and survived it."

Allora looked away, jaw clenched. "And what does that mean to you?" she asked tightly.

Surian slowed their pace, her gaze drifting out over the courtyard's moonlit branches. "It means," she said, "that my brother is changing. And I don't know if that terrifies me... or gives me hope."

Allora said nothing. The silence between them stretched. Then, softer than before, Surian murmured, "Do you care for him?"

Allora's breath caught. Her foot missed a step, and Surian's grip tightened around her elbow to keep her from stumbling.

"What?"

Surian turned to her now, eyes sharp and solemn beneath the flickering light. "Do you care for Malec?"

Allora opened her mouth, but the scoff she intended died on her tongue. She wanted to laugh, wanted to mock the very question, but the words wouldn't come. Because deep down... she didn't know.

Surian read the silence like a confession. Her expression gentled. "If you don't," she said, "then you need to leave. Soon."

Allora's spine stiffened. "Why?"

"Because if you stay," Surian said without blinking, "he will never let you go."

It wasn't a warning. It was a promise. A truth spoken with the weight of blood and history. Allora felt the chill curl up her back, not because she hadn't known that, not because it shocked her, but because hearing it from Malec's own sister gave it shape. Made it real. Final.

Surian glanced over her shoulder at the nurse and guards, then leaned closer, her voice lowered to a whisper meant for no one else.

"And Kael... he's known me since we were children. He's not so subtle, is he?" Her tone was bemused, but her eyes were watchful. "He seems quite taken with you."

Allora gave her a side-eye glare. "Oh, don't you start matchmaking too."

"I'm not," Surian said with a hint of a smirk. "But I am telling you this, my brother may be changing, but he is still Malec. If Kael gets too close... Malec won't threaten him. He'll kill him. Quickly. Quietly. And with no regret."

A chill ran down Allora's spine.

Not because the truth was new, she had always known, somewhere deep in her bones, that Malec would never let her go. But the fact he would go as far as to kill another male because he was a suitor. She always thought he was kind of off in that regard. They turned down the corridor toward her chambers, the heavy doors waiting like the mouth of a prison in polished gold. Surian's grip remained steady on her arm, the only anchor keeping Allora upright as the storm gathered once more in her chest.

Chapter 22

Choice Is an Illusion

Footsteps echoed in the marbled corridor behind her, crisp and measured against the hush of the palace. Allora didn't have to turn—she felt him first, that pressure in the air, Malec's presence moving ahead of him like electricity before a storm. When she finally looked up, there he was in the archway, half-draped in shadow. His hair was done in that infuriating style: half pulled up, the silver strands bound away from his face, the rest tumbling loose to his broad shoulders, wind-tossed and gleaming in the low light. He wore a white and silver tunic that fell to mid-thigh, the fabric catching every shift of his lean muscles. The tunic's high collar and tailored cut made him look severe, almost regal, but it was the tight, dark gray riding trousers and those gleaming black boots that caught her eye—and held it. She hated to admit it, even to herself, but he wore the military look well. Too well. Especially with how snug those trousers clung to him, emphasizing the long, powerful lines of his legs and the sharp, perfect curve of his ass.

His arms were crossed, posture loose but unyielding, and those pale tan eyes—always so unreadable—were fixed on her, burning with a quiet intensity that made her pulse jump. Allora pressed her lips together, refusing to let him see her stare. But the heat in her cheeks told its own story.

"What were you two talking about?" he asked, voice smooth but strained, too even to be casual.

Allora froze. His eyes weren't on Surian. They were locked on her. Her mind scrambled for something to say, something neutral, something that wouldn't give away how close Surian had leaned in earlier... how softly she'd spoken. But before she could form the lie, Surian had already stepped in like she was used to mopping up his messes.

"Oh, Malec," she drawled, breezing a hand through her silver hair, the strands catching the torchlight like spun frost. "Always so suspicious. Must every conversation I have be about you?"

His jaw tensed, the muscle ticking once. "When it involves my canariae, yes."

Surian tilted her head, smirking. Side by side, the resemblance between them was suddenly jarring, like fire and ice sculpted from the same blade. They had the same sharp cheekbones, the same full mouth drawn tight with restraint, and the same pale coloring... but where Malec looked carved in anger, Surian wore her power like a song, deceptive and smooth.

"How territorial of you," she drawled, a hint of laughter in her voice. "If you're curious, we were just agreeing on how impossible you are to tolerate. I was being kind and offering her my sympathy."

Allora snorted before she could stop herself, quickly coughing to mask the sound. It didn't help. Malec's stare flicked to her, then back to his sister. His lips pressed into a line so thin it could cut glass.

"Charming," he muttered.

"Good evening, brother," Surian said sweetly, but the sugar in her tone was pure poison.

She swept past him without another word, her long braids swaying like a banner behind her. As she moved by, she cast Allora one last glance, sharp, pointed, unspoken: *Remember what I told you.* And then Surian was gone.

Malec walked beside her, his stride smooth and measured, almost blending into the hush of the palace corridors. Allora didn't hear him so much as feel him, the subtle rustle of his cloak brushing stone. The world echoed around them, all light and shadow, but he moved through it with quiet precision, every step identical, every muscle braced, not for violence, but for balance. She used to think of him as mechanical in his calm. But now, after Surin's words, she saw more. The way his fingers flexed once, twice, then stilled. The subtle tick of his jaw before he forced it smooth. His eyes scanned the path ahead, tracking patterns on the floor, the space between pillars, light angles. Always counting. Recalibrating.

She tried to match his pace, pretending not to notice the way his gaze flicked toward her, checking her placement like one piece in a machine. Too quiet, she thought. He'd sense it. He always did. Then, without warning, he reached for her wrist.

She tensed, but his touch was warm, firm, not rough. His thumb pressed to her pulse. No words. Just pressure. Counting. His other hand came up, brushing her brow, her cheek. Checking for fever, not clinically, but carefully. As if her temperature might shift the balance of his world. His fingers moved to her elbow, her arm, tracing a faint scar she'd forgotten. Then her neck. Bruises, she realized. He was checking for damage. For signs. He exhaled. A tiny shift passed over his face.

"You're well," he murmured, mostly to himself.

Allora blinked, startled by how much he saw, how much he needed to see. He brushed her temple once more, then stepped closer, guiding her forward with a hand at her waist. There was no aggression in the touch. Just steadiness. A silent promise to hold her upright. His palm burned through the silk of her dress. He didn't look at her, but he didn't let go. The contact wasn't intimate. It was structural. A tether.

And still, she hated that it felt safe.

Their footsteps echoed across polished stone, the silence between them taut. She kept her gaze ahead, refusing to look at him. Then, quietly, unexpectedly, his voice broke the still.

"You look beautiful tonight."

Her breath caught. She glanced at him, searching for the usual smirk or sneer, but he didn't look back. He only tilted his head, just a fraction, his voice soft, almost reverent.

"What...?" she managed, blinking.

He didn't repeat himself. He didn't need to. His fingers brushed hers, light as a secret.

Then, quieter, so quiet she almost missed it. "Even the moon favors you."

She flushed, heat blooming across her cheeks so fast she nearly tripped. Malec's hand steadied her instantly, never faltering, never tightening, just there. She realized, with a strange ache, that this was Malec's way of loving. In every ritual, every carefully measured gesture, every small, precise touch. It wasn't the language she was used to. But it was his. And for tonight, she was willing to listen.

Her heart gave an unruly thump, like it had jumped at the sound of his voice before her mind could even register the words. It wasn't just what he said. It was *how* he said it. Not clipped or commanding. Not low and sharp like a blade under her chin.

Malec slowed his stride, like he sensed she needed space to process. He glanced at her, not with coldness, but with something searching. Vulnerable. Like he wanted her to see past the armor. His hand at her waist didn't grip, didn't claim, just rested, anchoring them both. She noticed the way his thumb brushed lightly over her hip, not controlling, just confirming she was still beside him. The small tells were all there: fingers flexing, breath syncing with hers, eyes scanning for symmetry, always trying to impose order on chaos. It wasn't arrogance. Wasn't cruelty. Just... awkwardness. A compulsion to hold the world still so he wouldn't drown in it. Surin's voice echoed: *Malec, fighting for peace inside himself.*

He leaned down and pressed a kiss to the top of her head. Soft. Almost reverent. Not possession, just closeness. It startled her.

"I missed you," he whispered.

The words landed like warmth on her skin. For a breath, she believed him. The tension between them eased into something quieter. Older. She looked up, catching his eyes. They were stripped of calculation. And behind them, ache. Not hunger. Not power. Just loneliness.

"I hate when you're not near me," he said, voice low.

She opened her mouth, but nothing came. No snark, no wall. Just silence. And he didn't push. He never did when he was like this. Instead, he tucked her closer and guided her forward, gentle as breath. With him, in rare moments like this, she almost felt... precious. But softness never lasted.

As they neared her chambers, his hand slipped away. His voice returned, sharper now. Controlled.

"Now," he said, cool and crisp, "we will discuss what you did."

Goddammmmmmiiiiiiiiiiiiiiiittttttttttttttttttttt...

Allora groaned inwardly, rolling her eyes. The tyrant was back. But beneath her annoyance, something new lingered. He was still a predator, an uptight bossy control freak that would never miss a chance to lecture.

"You endangered your life. Again. You disobeyed a direct order and left without proper escort. If something had happened—"

"But it didn't happen," Allora snapped, slicing through his words, voice sharp as broken glass.

He stopped so abruptly she nearly collided with his chest. The torchlight split the hard lines of his face, his eyes blazing, the tendons at his jaw flexing, the corridor shrinking around them.

"That isn't the point," he ground out, his voice rough with something she recognized, fear, not just anger.

"I don't know how many times I have to tell you this but you don't get to decide what happens in my life— "

He cut her off with a snarl, stepping in, pulling her tight against him. "Yes, I do. Because I am the only one who will protect it as if it were my own. You are mine, Allora. If you don't act like it, I will make the world know it."

She scoffed, twisting in his grip, scowling at the wall.

"I thought I escaped 'the talk.' But nope. Not with you. You don't forget anything." The words tumbled out, bitter. "Except how to treat me like a damn person," she muttered, barely above a whisper.

He heard. Of course he heard. But instead of letting her go, instead of arguing, his hand moved, cupping the back of her neck, not roughly, but with trembling control.

"I nearly lost you," he whispered, voice raw, something splintering inside it. "Do you understand what that would do to me? I haven't slept. I haven't breathed right since you took that risk. I am angry because I was terrified. I will not, ever, let you do that again."

Allora jerked her chin up, eyes sparking with her own heat. She shot back, unblinking. "Don't threaten me with a leash, Malec. You might not like how hard I bite."

Malec shook his head, his mask slipping, jaw clenched tight, eyes shadowed by longing and fear.

"You think this is about power? About control?" His voice broke low, raw. "It's about you breathing. About you surviving. The thought of losing you again—" He stopped, breath unsteady. "If keeping you close is what it takes to never feel that emptiness again, I'll do it. Not because you're a possession. Because you're the only thing that matters to me. You're not just a body, Allora. You're my world."

She braced herself against him, trembling.

"Is that it, Malec? Am I just a companion, so you never have to feel alone?"

His hands dropped to her arms, but his grip was gentle, pleading. "No, you are not just a companion. But you are mine. And I am yours. And if you die, if you are reckless, there is no me left to return to. I will not lose you, do you understand me? Not by choice. Not by your stubbornness."

She looked away, blinking hard, the world blurring for a second as her own stubbornness warred with the unfamiliar ache building inside her chest. The words he'd said, *I miss you*, echoed again, stubborn, impossible.

"You're not listening," she said, voice hoarse. "I'm not yours to keep safe. I am my own."

"Yet," he whispered, his voice stripped bare, "here you are. And here I am. I can't let you go, Allora. Not when I know you'll run straight into danger. Not when I'd rather fight the whole world than watch you burn for it."

Silence pressed in, thick as velvet. The air between them charged, anger, fear, longing, until Allora finally sagged, exhausted, letting his touch hold her steady for just one more heartbeat.

"It still should be my choice," she whispered, softer this time.

His eyes found hers, and for a moment, the mask slipped away completely.

"Then choose to stay alive, dove. Choose me. Just this once."

She closed her eyes, the argument dying on her tongue, and let herself lean into the warmth of his hand, just for a breath, just for this, before reality pulled her away again. Before Allora could answer, their moment fractured.

"Malec," came a voice, slick as oil, unmistakably smug.

She froze mid-step. Malec's posture changed in an instant, shoulders squared, chin set, his whole frame gone rigid, every line of his body a silent warning. As they rounded the archway, the glitter of gold and silk hit her eyes like a slap.

The dining hall was a cathedral of Awyan arrogance, vaulted ceilings, chandeliers spilling gold over tables that stretched endlessly. Storm-blue and copper banners lined the walls, but the light only sharpened the room's edges, casting servants into shadow and turning glances into quiet accusations. At the table's head, King Surion lounged with one leg draped lazily over the other, silver-mist robes pooling like fog. He sipped his wine slowly, eyes glittering with anticipation. Beside him, Surin leaned back, half-smiling behind his goblet, his stormy blue gaze cool, watchful, predator still in wait.

"Ah," Surin said, letting the word drift into the hush, "the lovers arrive at last."

Allora tensed as every eye in the room turned toward her, hungry, horrified, curious. Her skin prickled, heart racing, but she kept walking beside Malec like she belonged in this gold-drenched nightmare. Their seats had been arranged with ruthless precision: Surion on the throne, Surin at his right, Malec a blade of silence at his left. And her, not kneeling, not on display, but seated in a velvet-backed chair at the royal table, with goblet and utensils set as if she were one of them.

The room reacted like a wound split open. A servant froze mid-step. Another dropped a tray, the clatter of silverware swallowed by stunned silence. A Canariae at the table, no leash, no chains. Not a pet. A guest. The wrongness of it sang in the air. Allora sat tall, chin high, even as nausea curled through her gut. Her fingers gripped the linen tablecloth, nails biting in. Every breath was a blade. Judgment filled the space, bitter and thick.

Malec noticed. Of course he did. His hand shifted closer, fingers barely brushing hers, quiet, steadying.

Surion raised his glass, voice syrup-slick.

"Do forgive the staff, Malec. They're not used to seeing a Canariae at the table. It's like finding your hound at the altar, startling, but not entirely unwelcome." He winked at her, all false charm.

"And tell me," he added, eyes glittering, "have you trained her to bite on command?"

Laughter followed, cold, brittle, meant to cut. Malec said nothing, but his jaw tightened, a pulse ticking at his temple. His hand trembled once, then stilled, ice hiding fire. He turned to her, voice low, meant only for her.

"Eat."

Not a command. A lifeline. She met his gaze. Saw the fury, the pride, the helpless need to shield her from every blow. She nodded, lifted her fork, forced her hand to obey. She would not flinch. Would not flee. But the pressure beneath her skin built like steam in a sealed chamber. And that voice inside, sharp, survival-honed, whispered what the room didn't say out loud.

"Did you find your talk with Surian... productive?"

Allora's fork paused midair, a piece of roasted yam slipping from its tines and thudding back onto her plate. Her gaze flicked sideways, casually, toward the older elf seated across from her at the long banquet table. Surin Talandros wasn't looking at her. His expression was composed, eyes narrowed in what appeared to be mild interest at the exchange between Malec and King Surion further down the table. He hadn't moved.

But the voice was him. Deep. Serene. Unmistakable.

"You and Surian both work together on this, don't you?" she answered with her mind, carefully pushing her food around her plate as if bored.

Surin's reply came at once, smooth as silk. *"Yes. And Surion as well."*
That name made her chest tighten.
"The King?" she asked in disbelief.

"Of course." Surin's voice hummed like water flowing under ice. *"He was the first to inform me about you, long before my son brought you into our fold. He recognized your bloodline, your*

potential, your strength." A pause. *"Though I fear his motives...
differ from ours."*

Allora lowered her lashes, hiding the sharpness in her stare as she
slowly brought the fork to her mouth. She chewed, slow and thoughtful.

"So that's why he acted so forward with me," she murmured
silently. *"Trying to play the charming king."*

Her jaw tensed. Lips parted slightly, as if she were going to sigh, but
she said nothing aloud. She kept her face neutral, uninterested, perfectly
bored. Inside, her thoughts ran wild.
"What does he want?"

"To remove you from my son," came the answer. *"Not for your
protection. Not even for strategy. For vengeance."*

Her eyes narrowed faintly.
"Vengeance?"
Surin's voice deepened with quiet gravity.

*"Surion has been humiliated by Malec more times than he cares
to count. Not only in private but publicly, in the war room, in
council halls, behind closed doors where only the powerful are
permitted to claw and bleed. Malec does not entertain fools, and
Surion is a fool with a crown. He provokes, and every time my
son makes sure he remembers his place, beneath his heel."*

Allora said nothing.

*"So now Surion watches. Waits. Biding his time until he can
strike where Malec is weakest. And you, Allora..."* Surin's voice
curved like the edge of a dagger, *"You are the wound he means
to drive his blade into."*

She felt her breath tremble. She masked it with a sip of wine.
"Why not just kill Malec?"

"Because he can't." A pause. *"Not without war. Not without losing the kingdom to open rebellion. The people may not love Malec, but they fear him. And fear is stronger than loyalty. So Surion must be clever. He must make Malec unravel himself."*

"By taking me."

"Yes. Away. Anywhere. He's considering a political marriage. Perhaps with Kael of Kavira. Perhaps to the highest bidder in the East. He hasn't decided. But he knows your value now. Knows that if he separates you from Malec, Malec will unravel."

Allora didn't respond. Her mind rang with fury and disbelief, but she smothered the emotions like smoke in her lungs.

Then Surin's voice returned, gentle, almost fatherly. *"You are not bound to him. Not truly."*

She stiffened.

"He is soul-bound to you, yes. He gave himself completely." A beat. *"But you..."* Surin's tone shifted, softening with careful suggestion. *"You have shown no signs of the binding. No seal. No resonance. And that means, Allora... you are still free. Do you understand?"*

She didn't answer right away.

Her eyes flicked toward Malec, sitting beside Surion, his pale beige gaze hard as glass. He was focused on the conversation at hand, but she could feel him, always feel him. Like a presence stitched beneath her skin. The weight of his tethered soul pressing against hers, even when she didn't want it. Even when she hadn't asked for it.

"What are you saying?" she finally whispered in her thoughts.

Surin's voice dropped, as if even his mind was cautious of the walls around them.

"I am saying Kael has expressed... vivid interest. He would take you willingly. Without chains. Without possession. And the King has not ruled out the possibility of giving you to him. If that is what you wish."

Allora blinked slowly, her pulse thunderous behind her ribs. *"Give me to Kael?"*

"Yes as a bargaining piece disguised as a gift. A Queen, if you wanted it. You would be more than Malec's shadow. You could be... sovereign."

That word struck something low in her belly. *"You'd let that happen?"* There was no emotion in Surin's reply. *"I would let you decide."* Allora's hand curled around her fork again, her nails digging into the metal.

"So if you take me from him while he is in the state he is in..." she said. *"He will kill us,"* Surin finished, calm and certain. *"I know."* *"Then why risk it?"*

"Because you have not chosen him. Not yet. And if you choose someone else, freely, without coercion, then the bond weakens. The Vash'telor might wither. That is the only chance we have to free him from this madness."

Her throat went dry. *"Do you want me to choose someone else?"* There was a silence in her mind. Then, at last, *"I want you to survive."*

While Malec, Surion, and Surin spoke in low tones, Allora sat silent, head bowed toward her plate, slowly nudging her food in idle circles. To anyone witnessing, she looked bored. Maybe tired. Disinterested. Under the surface, she was barely holding herself together.

Malec's blood ran in her veins now, a truth that chilled more than it comforted. *What else had come with it? How long before her body stopped being hers? Before his influence seeped into every cell?* She was the cure to her people's extinction, and no one knew it. But that wasn't the worst part. The worst part was how staying meant surrender. Every breath in this place, every moment near him, pulled her deeper into a world that never asked for consent. It took. It bound. It changed. She felt it already: her skin tingling at night, strange waves of hunger unlinked to food, the way her body overheated around him, how her moods veered like storms without warning.

Whatever he'd done, whatever his blood had awakened, was taking root.

This world had begun claiming her the moment she arrived. But she wouldn't let it finish. She would not die in Ulvareth. Not as Malec's Vash'telor. Not under Kael's gaze. Not under anyone's hand. She was not born here, and she would not be buried here. The decision hardened inside her like iron. She would leave. All of it. Him. This palace. This realm.

She was going home.

The thought echoed in her mind like a battle drum, steady, final, until a shift in conversation pulled her back.

"...The Festival of Petals," Surion said smoothly.

Her fork stilled. The word lit something in her memory. Her eyes lifted, just slightly. Listening now. Festival? She listened now, subtly leaning forward.

"The blooms will be in full swing this year," Surion mused, gesturing faintly with his goblet. "The skies are expected to rain petals for three days straight. Quite the sight for lovers, assuming they're brave enough to be seen."

Allora perked up, her brow knitting in curiosity. Lovers? A petal rain?

"What is that?" she asked aloud, breaking her silence for the first time in minutes.

Her voice was soft, but firm. "The Festival of Petals?"

Surion turned to her with theatrical delight, as if this was the moment he'd been waiting for.

"It's an old tradition," he said smoothly. "We celebrate the turning of the season with a three-day rite dedicated to love. To passion. To choosing one's heart, openly, and without shame. Those bold enough to declare their affection may court publicly, even propose, without consequence or political meddling. A rare thing for us, as you might imagine." He lifted his cup. "There is dancing. Wine. Games. Night markets. And of course... the petals."

"Blossoms from the high cliffs are plucked by hand and released from the sky towers," Surin added calmly. "They fall for days. Some say the gods watch those who kiss beneath them."

Allora's chest tightened. She hadn't realized how much she needed that, needed a night untouched by schemes and blood and ancient binding rites. Something simple. Something hers. Something soft. Inside her mind, her voice reached for Surin again.

"I want to go." There was a pause. His mental presence felt still and intelligible. *"I want to ask Malec,"* she added, *"but I think he'll say no. Or he'll say yes and find a way to watch me every second of it."*

Surin's amusement flared like heat across the mental bond. *"Then allow me."*

And before she could ask what he meant, he turned lazily in his seat and addressed the table aloud.

"So, Malec," Surin said with casual elegance, "will you be attending the festival this season?"

Malec's eyes flicked toward him like a drawn blade. Sharpened. Alert.
But Surin only leaned back, swirling his wine as if asking about the
weather. Allora stiffened. She didn't dare look at Malec, didn't even shift
in her seat, but her pulse throbbed behind her ears. Had he noticed?
Could he feel it? That she wanted this?

Surion chuckled as if he could read her, ever the wolf dressed in
velvet.

"You've been absent from the last few, cousin," he said slyly.
"I'd assumed you were allergic to joy."

Malec didn't blink. "I've had other obligations."
"All the more reason," Surion pressed. "Even you deserve a breath of
spring."

Malec's fingers tapped once against the base of his goblet.
Then, finally, he said, "Perhaps. I will consider it."
Inside her mind, Allora's voice rushed to Surin again. *Why did you
do that?*

His reply was slow, silk-lined and curious. His reply came like a purr:

*"Because I'm curious, little dove. I want to see what you'll do...
when he finally gives you permission to fly."*

He paused, just long enough to let the weight of his next
words settle. "It is also... quite large."

Allora's lips parted slightly in a mimicry of awe. She let her gaze drift,
feigning the image of a wide-eyed girl hearing about something magical
for the first time.

"That sounds..." She trailed off, as if imagining it. "Amazing."
She folded her hands neatly in her lap, posture demure. Then she
glanced up at him through her lashes, the very image of sweetness
wrapped in soft skin.

"I would love to see it."
There was a pause. A silence that stretched, like a blade being slowly
drawn. Malec didn't speak. He just watched her. The flames from the

table's long candle branches danced across his sharp, elegant features, jaw tense, eyes hollow with something she couldn't name. And then, he leaned forward.

"If you behave," he murmured, the words coiling through her like silk-wrapped chains. "I will take you."

Her smile, too honest for her own good curled upward, a beam of gratitude, excitement, just real enough to be convincing. Just wrong enough to make Surin hum with distant amusement across their private link.

"Are you serious?" she asked, her voice featherlight, eyes wide with performed wonder.

Malec's eyes flickered, something dark behind them, something almost... hungry.

"Yes, little dove."

He reached out, slow and deliberate, brushing two fingers along the inside of her wrist. A touch so delicate it might have been mistaken for affection, except for the way it burned.

"Be good for me," he said, "and I will reward you."

Good. The word echoed in her skull like a curse. She would be good. She would smile. Laugh. Let him dress her and show her off like his prized thing. She would go back to playing the part of his companion, his docile canariae. His tamed creature.

Because it was the only way to own her decisions, to get what she wanted even if she gave up pieces of herself to do it. And for now this was enough.

It was only a flicker, a slight squint, sharp as a blade unsheathed, but Allora caught it. A shift in the air, a prickle at the back of her neck, made her glance sideways... just in time to see Surin watching. Not her. Him. His gaze was fixed on Malec, cool and calculating, his wine untouched, fingers resting lightly on the stem of the glass. He sat relaxed, but too still. That wasn't comfort. That was a predator poised.

Surin had seen the change. The softened voice. The way Malec leaned too close, the heat in his eyes. The promise disguised as a bargain, *If you behave, I'll take you*, and Allora's smile that answered it like a yes. But Surin knew that smile. He'd seen it before, on women pretending devotion while plotting escape, on slaves trading kisses for keys. Allora had already chosen. And Malec either didn't see it, or didn't care. Surin studied them quietly, the firelight dancing in Allora's eyes as she leaned in with honeyed words. But beneath the sweetness, he saw it: the hunger, not for Malec, not for power, for freedom.

She had found her window. And she meant to fly.

Interesting, he thought, lifting his glass without drinking. *So, my son... still gambling. But you've never tried to keep something that wants to run.*

He said nothing. Not yet. Let the fire smolder. It would show him who would burn.

The days that followed cut like a slow, shallow blade, deep enough to ache, never enough to bleed. Every moment between Allora and Malec was watched. Measured. Judged. Malec never mentioned the festival again. He didn't have to. His silence was the leash. A test. Would she prove worthy of the gift? He watched her with the scrutiny of both scholar and soldier. His hand grazed her back; she leaned in. His voice dropped; she listened. She smiled, she laughed, she bowed her head.

Perfect. Flawless. False. But it worked.

Bit by bit, Malec loosened the reins—allowing her to walk farther, speak more freely, let that defiant spark return to her eyes. Yet he never stopped watching. He remembered too well the last time she tried to slip away; now, he adapted, playing her game alongside her, coaxing her obedience, her affection. To him, it was worth every ounce of vigilance. He reveled in the illusion of Allora's freedom, but his guard never dropped. Nor did Surin's. From high balconies, through shadowed council corridors, Surin's gaze was never far.

He watched his son begin to believe in the performance. Watched Allora hone it, sharpening her deception like a blade.

But Allora wasn't the only one playing. Surin saw it all—the way Malec's jaw tensed when she laughed with a guard, how his hand curled into a fist if she strode ahead, how his whole body stilled whenever she slipped from view, even for a heartbeat too long. And when she returned? Malec would smile. He would touch her wrist. He would say good girl with a voice that tasted like iron and fire. But Surin knew his son. Knew the storm that lived just beneath that voice. Knew that if the dove flew too high... the fox would not chase.

He would strike. And if Allora miscalculated, even by a heartbeat, her wings would shatter before she ever touched the sky.

"Careful, little dove."

Allora froze mid-step. The corridor was silent, shadows flickering on the stone from distant sconces. She'd thought herself alone until Surin's voice slipped in, cold and precise—a knife sliding between her ribs. She turned, slowly, to find him leaning against a marble column, dark robes immaculate, silver ring glinting as he folded his arms. Serene. Powerful. Watching.

He nodded almost imperceptibly, eyes following her every movement.

"You think you're outmaneuvering him. But the higher you fly, the closer you come to the trap he's setting."

Her heart gave a tiny stutter, but she kept her steps measured. *"What kind of trap?"* she mentally asked.

His mouth quirked, not quite a smile. *"One you won't see until it's already snapped shut,"* he replied, without using his voice.

"Malec is no fool, Allora. You think you've got him wrapped around your finger? Be careful. Step out of bounds, and he'll remind you whose world this is. He'll break your wings before

you realize you're falling. He will cage you the moment he senses you slipping away."

A chill raced down her spine, but she didn't break stride.
"So what do you suggest?" she managed, tone crisp.
Surin's eyes glimmered with dark amusement.

"Win—but remember who you're playing against. And don't ever forget, even a dove can be caught."

Two days before the Festival of Petals, Malec took her from the Capitol without warning. No explanation. Just a hand at her back and a quiet command to pack light. Allora had braced for another grim fortress, stone walls, iron gates, guards who watched without blinking. But beyond the last rise of the valley, the world opened.

The countryside was alive. Endless fields of green rippled in the wind, dotted with citrus groves heavy with golden fruit. Lavender hedges buzzed with bees, birds sang without fear, and for once, there was no scent of blood in the breeze. Ahead stood a sprawling white manor, bathed in morning light, its balconies tangled with ivy and blooms instead of flags and steel. The air was clean, quiet, untouched by the Capitol's suffocating pulse. And Malec... he changed here.

His shoulders lowered. His jaw, always tense, eased as they passed through the gate. At the steps, his hand found the small of her back.

"Come," he murmured. "I want you to meet someone."

Inside, they were greeted by Lady Mae Yara. Tall, regal, with silver-threaded black hair twisted into a precise coil, and golden eyes that missed nothing. Her robe was black, embroidered in silver, simple but commanding. She didn't smile or bow. But neither did she glare or gloat. She only studied Allora, curious, silent, composed.

"Ah," Mae Yara said, her voice smooth but strong. "So this is the infamous dark Canariae. You're quite the subject of interest these days, little flame."

Allora kept her face neutral, not rising to the bait. Mae Yara stepped closer, lips twitching.

"You must tell me, do your people truly make those strange gestures with their hands?"

Allora blinked, confused. "Gestures?"
Mae Yara gave a low, amused laugh.

"Shaking hands. Such a strange ritual. I always wondered if it was a form of Canariae spellcasting."

Before Allora could speak, a shadow moved behind Mae Yara, a young human male stepped forward, he looked to be in his early twenties. He wore Awyan-tailored clothing, simple but refined, and carried a quiet stillness that immediately unsettled her. In the center of the sitting hall, Allora stood across from him, tense, uncertain. He watched her with the calm of someone who remembered peace, who still believed in it. Their conversation was quiet, voices too low to catch, blurred beneath the soft rustle of trees beyond the terrace.

Malec stood off to the side, arms folded, his jaw ticked with restraint. Mae Yara leaned against a marble column draped in ivy, her golden eyes narrowing as she turned toward him.

"So. You've brought her for answers," she said, her tone flat.

"I need to understand the bond," Malec said, his voice low and direct, wasting no time on pleasantries. "I need to know if such a connection can even exist between an Awyan and a Canariae."

Mae Yara's gaze sharpened. "You've already bonded her?"
He said nothing, but didn't deny it.

She turned back toward Allora, eyes scanning her like a physician assessing hidden wounds.

"And yet she hasn't returned it. No seal, bloom or psychic tremors. It's still one-sided."

Malec bit back his words, and for once, he said nothing.

"I want to know what that means," he said finally. "What the repercussions are. If it's possible the bond could still take root."

Mae Yara looked... pained, almost. Her expression shaded with memory.

"It's possible. The soul must choose it. The Canariae soul is not like ours, it resists binding. It doesn't recognize the rites. But it can still happen... given time. Or trauma."

Malec's gaze darkened. "You speak from experience."

Mae Yara turned towards her male Canariae that moved to speak with Allora as he guided her to a seat. "I had bonded to one once nearly fifty years ago," Mae Yara said softly. "It nearly broke me. The waiting. The silence. The ache of giving yourself to someone who did not, could not, yet return it."

Her golden gaze shifted back to Allora.

"It hurts them differently. It changes them differently. And you must monitor her closely. Especially as her body begins to shift."

Malec's brow creased. "Shift how?"

Mae Yara's tone turned clinical. "Well for females you will notice changes near her menstrual cycle. Pain. Heat.

Emotional swings more volatile than even our kind experiences. It's the blood. The energy. The bond, even if one-sided, alters the body. You are no longer quite one thing or another."

Malec's eyes lingered on Allora's form across the room, her curls catching in the light, her gestures animated now as she engaged with his aunt's new Canariae male with guarded interest. Her body language was softer here, less coiled, but to him it still felt distant. Like she belonged to another current, just barely out of reach.

He turned back to Mae Yara, lowering his voice to a whisper meant only for her ears.

"There's something I don't understand," he murmured. "You mentioned... changes during her cycle. Blood. Heat. Instability. What exactly is a 'cycle'? What does that mean?"

Mae Yara blinked once. Then a slow, knowing smile pulled at the corner of her mouth.

"Ah," she said lightly. "So my nephew has Vash'telor himself to a female from another world and never once asked what keeps her womb in rhythm."

Malec's jaw flexed, but he didn't rise to the jab.

"We have no equivalent in our kind," he said, quieter now. "Whatever this is, it's not something I was trained to recognize. And if it's hurting her, I need to know whether it can be... treated. Fixed."

Mae Yara exhaled through her nose, her tone shifting from amusement to something drier.

"It is not a sickness, Malec. It's not something you fix. It is a biological phenomenon. A natural process that governs their reproductive rhythm among female Canariae. Every month, if she is not pregnant, her womb sheds in preparation for the next ovulation. It comes with discomfort, cramping, emotional sensitivity, cravings, sometimes nausea. Blood flows. Sometimes heavily."

Malec's brow furrowed, clearly unsettled. "So... it's *bleeding*."
Mae Yara's golden eyes narrowed slightly, reading the tension in his shoulders, the way his jaw ground tighter with each new revelation. He wasn't repulsed, he was disturbed. Unfamiliar. Unmoored. He looked away for a moment, then back at her, his voice low and serious, but not mocking.
"Is it like... female dogs?"
Mae Yara didn't blink. "Yes," she said. "Exactly that."
She gave no dramatic pause. No attempt to soften the truth.

"It is a heat cycle. A bleeding cycle. A natural one. And if your Canariae were a dog, you would already understand it. The difference is, she is not. She is sentient. Intelligent. Proud. And unlikely to tolerate being treated as something less because her body chooses to remind you that it is capable of creation."

Malec said nothing, but the flicker in his gaze told her enough.

So she continued, voice lowering into something laced with old warnings. "You will see it eventually. The signs. The shift in her scent. Her skin may flush more easily. Her moods will sharpen like teeth. The body becomes more reactive. Some Canariae experience pain so sharp they cannot walk for a day. Others weep for no reason at all."

Silence passed between them. Malec's eyes were hard. Shadowed. Then, cautiously, he asked, "And if she were to become pregnant?"

Mae Yara's voice cooled, brushing close to memory. "Then you're in for a far more complicated season. I've had a few

Canariae under my care go through it, back when they were still traded openly."

She glanced away, not ashamed, simply factual. "It was... interesting. Their bodies shift rapidly. They require more food, more sleep. Their magic, if they have any, grows erratic. But they become sensitive to emotion. To bonds. The child's growth is linked directly to their mental and physical state." She leaned in just slightly, tone sharpening. "And if they feel unloved? Unsafe? The womb will resist. Sometimes violently. They've been known to miscarry purely from distress."

Malec's expression darkened. His voice dropped to a whisper. "So she's more fragile than I thought."

"No," Mae Yara said, her voice crisp and unwavering. "She is more complex. Do not confuse the two." She stepped back, folding her arms. "She bleeds to create. She burns when she's cornered. And she is, by all measures of biology and spirit, not yours to command. If you want to keep her, Malec... you must stop treating her like a thing to be kept."

He stared toward Allora again, still speaking with the Canariae male, her smile faint and fleeting, the curve of it soft and real in a way that never showed when she was with him. Something shifted behind his eyes, something bitter and restrained.

Mae Yara's voice dropped, smooth and direct. "Why do you care if she gets pregnant, Malec? You know it's impossible. A Canariae female cannot carry an Awyan child. The bloodlines aren't compatible. She'll never bear your heir."

Malec didn't move at first. His jaw remained still. But there was something colder now in the way he stared.

Then, quietly, he said, "I'm not worried about my blood."

Mae Yara stilled, glancing at him with a predator's precision.

"I'm asking," he continued, "because I want to know what the signs would be... if she was bred by another Canariae."

His voice was flat. Controlled. No heat in it, only the suggestion of frost. It wasn't jealousy. It was threat analysis.

Mae Yara straightened slowly. "You think she might-"

"I think she's still bonded to no one," he interrupted, calm and final. "And she's surrounded by others like her. So yes. If she were to... stray... I need to know what to look for."

There was no tremor in his tone. No betrayal. Only calculation. "And if she were?"

Malec looked at Mae Yara directly then, his eyes like tempered steel. "I would end it."

Just that. Quiet. Absolute.

Mae Yara tilted her head. "You are not ready for what you've tied yourself to, nephew. And you will suffer for it if you don't start learning fast."

Chapter 23

The Woman Between Worlds

A Canariae man, tall, broad-shouldered, with sun-warmed brown skin and steady, dark eyes, met her gaze with a recognition that nearly stopped her in place. She hadn't expected to see anyone like him here. His curls were tied back neatly, and though his clothes were Awyan-cut, they weren't rags. He looked composed. Maybe not free, but not broken. And the way he looked at her, not with pity or curiosity, but like an equal, struck something deep.

They crossed to the far side of the room, and then he extended his hand, palm forward.

Allora froze.

A thousand memories surged at once, offering her hand to the ferals in the palace courtyard, hoping for connection, only to be met with fear or confusion. None of them had known what it meant. But he did. It was a test. Or maybe a message. She reached out slowly, hand trembling as their palms touched. His grip was firm, steady, silent.

> "Zumaro of the House of Errydain," he said in flawless English, voice low and calm. "Formerly Lieutenant Oliver Massen, U.S. Army. Pleased to meet you."

Allora blinked, it felt like a flinch. Her mind reeled, scrambling to make sense of the impossible. A U.S. soldier? Here? Before she could stop herself, her hand clasped his. It was instinct, buried deep.

"Major Melodie Jaxxon, United States Army," she said, crisp and steady.

The name lit something inside her. Her real name. The one tied to rank, to memory, to power. In that instant, she wasn't Allora. She was Melodie again. A soldier. A weapon. Free.

Then came the sound, soft, sharp. A breath. A warning.

Her heart froze. She turned. Malec stood in the filtered light across the room, deceptively relaxed. But she felt it: the tension in his frame, the blade behind his stillness. His gaze, cold and fixed, was locked on her. He had heard it, her name. Not the one he gave her. The one that severed his claim. He didn't speak. He didn't need to. That name is not yours anymore. Not here. Not with him. The invisible collar around her soul pulsed, not choking, just heated to the core. Claiming. Her hand lingered in Zumaro's, Oliver's, before she let go. A signal. A goodbye. She swallowed hard, throat tight, and forced the next word out like broken glass.

"...Allora," she said quietly.

Her Awyan name. Her chain. The name Malec had chosen for her. Not a soldier's name. Not a human's. A name that belonged to him. A pause followed. She didn't dare look back, but she felt it, the faint pull of his approval, possessive and quiet, like a leash loosening once she'd fallen back in line.

Zumaro's expression shifted. Just slightly. His eyes flicked toward Malec—quick—subtle, but sharp. His brow arched in a brief, silent defiance before smoothing back to something veiled. He said nothing, but the silence spoke volumes. He'd noticed. She saw it in the slower blink, the quiet way his thoughts rearranged. Not panicked, but aware. He recognized the leash. The limits. The danger.

Allora cleared her throat, forcing a careful, practiced half-smile, the one she'd perfected under Malec's constant gaze.

"From the House of the Silver Fox," she added, folding her hands in her lap as she took her seat across from him.

She was playing the role again. Reciting her new lines. And she hated how easily they came.

Zumaro gave her the faintest nod, his expression schooled. But his eyes, they weren't done speaking. And she knew in that moment, the real test had begun. Not the handshake. Not the name. But what they would do with the truth now that it had slipped out into the open. Because someone else from Earth had survived. And she had just told him who she really was.

Malec had known the moment he saw his aunt's Canariae companion that something about him would be a problem. It wasn't just the male's upright posture or the insolent grace that echoed Allora's own defiance. Nor was it the casual disregard for Awyan customs, as if etiquette were beneath him. What truly unsettled Malec was the marking, etched along the upper collarbone, half-concealed by tailored fabric. Foreign. Elegant. Crude. And unmistakably familiar.

He'd seen it before.

Lady Mae Yara had once mentioned the strange ink her Canariae bore, a ritual mark of unknown origin. Malec hadn't cared at the time. But then he'd noticed a near-identical symbol hidden beneath the curve of Allora's breast. He hadn't thought much of it. Not until now.

Now, two symbols from two slaves of the same world stood across from each other. There was no overt recognition, no gasp or reunion. But something passed between them. A rhythm. A cultural pulse beneath the surface.

Malec's jaw clenched as he studied Allora's subtle shift, her focus sharpening, her stance adjusting. She had told him nothing of her world. Nothing of her customs or history. Every question he asked met a wall. Every press was met with fire. So he had come here, to this quiet countryside estate, not for comfort, but for answers. If she wouldn't speak, maybe someone else would.

He hadn't expected to hate the way she looked at Zumaro.

NOX

When the male extended his hand, Malec's eyes tracked hers. He saw the change. The way her breath caught. The lift in her shoulders. That flicker in her face, something she had never once given him. Recognition. Relief. She took the hand without hesitation, and then, in a voice that cut through him like a blade, she said: 'Major Melodie Jaxxon.'

Her real name. The one she had never trusted him with. His reaction was subtle. A shift of weight. A tilt of the head. A low, controlled sound, a warning.

Allora caught it.

He saw the way her face faltered, the hesitation in her breath as the weight of the room collapsed around her again. She corrected herself, lips tightening, posture folding back into submission like a blade being sheathed.

"...Allora," she said finally.

The name he had given her. The one that reminded her who she belonged to.

The two of them moved away to sit, close, but not too close, beneath the flowering boughs of Mae Yara's terrace garden, and Malec watched as Allora lowered herself onto the cushion across from him. Her shoulders remained square, her tone casual, but everything else was calculated. Every flicker of her lashes, every tilt of her head, every pause between words, it was a performance. And Oliver was playing along. Soft smiles. Quiet nods. Their words were harmless to anyone else's ears.

But Malec wasn't just anyone. He knew when something was being hidden from him. And this was no ordinary conversation. It was a careful dance, a subtle exchange, a language he did not speak.

Across the room, Mae Yara seemed amused by it all, sipping her wine and observing like it was theatre. She offered no commentary, just a knowing smile and the occasional chuckle as if watching two young creatures discover a shared secret. But Malec? He said nothing. He stared. He measured. And he hated every second of it.

But it didn't matter. Because this trip was never about introductions. It was about information. Malec would let her laugh. Let her pretend she was free. Let her believe she'd found something familiar in this polished cage.

"They seem to be getting along," Lady Mae Yara mused, her voice smooth as silk and twice as sharp.

She reclined into the pale green cushions, her long fingers circling the stem of her goblet with idle elegance, though Malec could tell, she was observing everything. The curve of Allora's lips as she spoke. The tilt of her shoulders. The way her gaze flicked to the Canariae male with something perilously close to familiarity.

"I must say, I expected tension... but not this."

Malec said nothing. His eyes were fixed ahead, jaw locked tight.

Mae Yara gave a small, sharp laugh. "Malec Talandros, undone by a female half your size. I can't decide whether to be horrified or impressed." She took a slow sip of her wine, then lowered the goblet, voice dropping. "And the fire?"

"She didn't mean to burn it," Malec said flatly.

"Oh, darling. Of course she did." Mae Yara smiled, eyes dancing. "That was the message, wasn't it? She would rather set the walls aflame than live inside them. Rather destroy the cage than sing for the captor."

He turned his head, just slightly, enough to cast her a cold look. "I did not bring her here to be mocked."

"And I am not mocking," she replied, voice softening by a hair. "I'm warning. You're bleeding for her, Malec. Literally. Giving her your blood straight from your body, if the whispers are true."

His eyes flicked toward her then, hard and glowing. Mae Yara's smile faded. She leaned in, her voice low and more serious now.

"She's not one of us. That kind of sacrifice, it's sacred. It's not a gesture. It's a binding act of submission and claim. Do you even know what you've done to her body by giving her pure Awyan blood? What it's *becoming*?"

"I gave her my blood to save her," he said finally, voice low and hollow. "And now... it's changing her."

Mae Yara's expression shifted. There was something pained in the way her gaze drifted toward the girl.

"Yes," she said. "It will. Awyan blood is not passive. It rewrites. It *claims*. And now, so will she."

"She was mine," he said, barely more than a whisper. "Before she ever knew it."

"But now she *knows*," Mae Yara replied, finishing her wine. "And she's still looking at someone else."

They both turned then, toward the flowering canopy where Allora and Oliver sat, two exiles from the same burning world, two voices from a place Malec had never seen and could never understand. And for once, Malec felt it, not just the weight of the bond between them, but the bitter, hollow ache of an Awyan who had offered everything...

And still could not reach her.

"So tell me, dear nephew..." Lady Mae Yara set her goblet of wine down with the delicate click of crystal against marble and folded her long fingers in her lap.

Her voice was laced with a velvet sort of amusement, light on the surface but anchored by something sharper beneath.

"What are your intentions with her?"

Malec didn't answer immediately. He exhaled slowly, steadying the breath that had grown too tight in his chest. His gaze drifted to where Allora sat beneath the terrace canopy, sunlight catching in her dark curls, her smile turned slightly toward the other Canariae male. She laughed softly at something the man said, free in a way that made Malec's stomach twist. And still, she was *his*. He had bled for her. Would killed for her. Die for her. No one else could say that. He turned his tan eyes back to his aunt, his expression deadpan.

"I will keep her as my mate," he said finally, voice low, calm, absolute.

Mae Yara arched a brow. "For how long?"

Malec's gaze sharpened. "For as long as I breathe."

She studied him a moment, then let out a quiet sigh. "You do realize that she won't last," she said gently. "No matter how much blood you give her. No matter how tightly the bond is sealed. You are tying your soul to something that was never made to last more than a flicker in our time."

"I know," he said.

But his tone didn't carry the weight of resignation. His gaze drifted toward Allora again, soft and faraway. She sat with the male Canariae, the two speaking in low, shared words he could not hear. She looked... at ease. Not safe, no. But like a piece of her had settled. It was something he had never seen in her when she was with him.

It stung more than he would admit.

"What are you thinking about, Malec?" she asked, voice light as silk but edged like steel.

Malec lifted his goblet and sipped, slow and silent. "Nothing."

He lied.

He had no intention of sharing the truth. Not with Mae Yara. Not with Surion. Not even with Surin, should his father ask. Especially not the king. Because what he'd discovered, what he and Luko had uncovered in the dark hours beneath the northern towers, was *not* meant for the realm. It wasn't even meant for her. Not yet. Not until he understood it fully. Not until he knew how to *own it*.

Canariae bodies reacted violently to Awyan magic, but his blood, his mother's blood, carried something ancient. Something dormant. Passed down through Leira's line. The original test samples had been small, no more than droplets infused into the bloodstream of infected Canariae to study immunity.

But the results had been extraordinary. Longevity. Clarity of mind. Vital organ enhancement.

Luko had been stunned. "A stabilizing mutation," he called it. "It shouldn't be possible. But it is."

And Malec had done far more than inject Allora with a diluted dose. He had given her everything. Directly. From his veins. Warm and unfiltered. While whispering the words of an old spell, words he didn't even fully understand, only that Leira once murmured them over his fevered body as a child when his heart had stopped. He had never intended to use the enchantment. It slipped from his tongue like instinct. And it hadn't been just magic. It had been binding. Something older. Raw.

A force he could no longer untangle. *If she ever learns what I've done... If she ever learns what it means...*

She'll run. She'll tear the bond out by the root and leave his world in ruins.

No.

He would not let that happen. If extending her life required draining his own, so be it. If it meant stealing years from others to gift her with decades, he would do it without hesitation. What was one stranger's life, one hundred of them, compared to hers? Across the room, her laughter floated like smoke into his lungs. Malec's gaze snapped to her. She was smiling. Smiling. That soft, open expression she once wore for him alone now belonged to another.

The male Canariae leaned in slightly as he spoke to her, just enough for their shoulders to nearly brush. Allora's body tilted, just a little, in return. As if it were natural. As if she didn't even realize.

Of course she doesn't. They were of the same kind. The same cursed species. She trusted him instantly, reflexively. Because he had brown skin and the same Canariae-shaped vowels. Because he knew her gestures. Her language. Because he could give her something Malec couldn't.

Malec's jaw flexed. He had thought their shared markings might be proof of tribe hood, something cultural, something useful to exploit. He had even hoped the two might recognize each other outright. It would've given him more to work with. Another string to pull. A map to her past. But they had not known each other. Not by name. Only by blood. Only by belonging. And somehow, that made it worse. Because this stranger... this Zumaro... didn't need power or possession to draw Allora's attention. He simply existed. And it was enough.

Malec shifted his gaze to his aunt, who was still leering at him behind her goblet with that maddening, all-knowing calm. He forced his expression still. Cold.

Because if she saw how deeply it pierced him, the betrayal, the fear, the need, she would understand what he was willing to do. And no one needed to know that. Not yet. Not until the next stage of the bloodwork was ready. Not until Allora forgot what it meant to live without him. Not until she truly, irrevocably, belonged. To him. And no one else. Ever again.

"Does your master speak our language?" Oliver's voice was low, careful, barely more than a breath.

Allora's dark eyes flicked briefly to Malec, who sat across the room with Lady Mae Yara, engaged in what looked like light conversation. But she could feel him. Studying. Measuring. His silence was never just silence. It was a warning wrapped in velvet. She turned back to Oliver with a calm she didn't feel.

"No," she answered softly. "Not a word."

Oliver smirked, the expression dry and faintly bitter. "No self-respecting Awyan would ever speak our language. It is that pride that gives us a blind spot."

Allora's lips twitched despite herself. "I know at least two."

Referring to Luko and Erolyn her two closest Awyan companions and only friends in this world that weren't of her species.

She leaned forward slightly. "How did you get here?"

Oliver cast a quick glance toward Malec, then leaned in, his words brushing past her ear like a knife wrapped in silk.

"Colonel Jaxxon's unit came as soon as word got out you disappeared."

Allora's body went still. Her breath caught. Her heart stopped, then roared to life again. Her father. Her unit. They came for her. The words hit like a flare igniting in a cave of darkness. Hope surged through her so fast, so violently, that she couldn't stop the way she gasped, sharp, real, too loud. Her hands shot up to her chest, eyes wide, mouth parted with a sound that almost, almost, shaped his name. That was all it took.

Lady Mae Yara turned first, her golden eyes lifting with faint curiosity. "Is something the matter, dear?"

Malec followed a heartbeat later. His attention snapped from the wine to the table. To her. Not just his gaze, his whole presence shifted. Subtle, but suffocating. The air around him darkened, went still, as if the room itself recognized the shift in power. He didn't speak. He didn't move. He just watched. And that was worse than anything.

Allora blinked fast. Her chest rose and fell too quickly. Oliver's hand touched the table, drawing her back.

"There was a, uh, a bee," he said smoothly, glancing to the side as though tracking the imaginary insect. "Landed on her shoulder. She panicked."

Allora coughed a short laugh, still breathless. "Sorry. I... I really hate bugs."

She managed a crooked smile, eyes flicking up through her lashes to gauge Malec's reaction. But he hadn't blinked. Not once. That golden-tan stare drilled through her, reading every twitch of her mouth, every flutter of her lashes, every tremble in her hands.

"Remain calm," Oliver murmured beside her, softer now, like a thread of sanity she could still grab hold of. "Don't let him see anything else."

Allora gave a tiny nod. But she couldn't stop the heat behind her eyes, the pressure building in her chest. One tear broke free, sliding down the curve of her cheek. She turned her head just enough to let her hair curtain the worst of it and wiped the tear away quickly. Her pulse was thunder in her throat. Her father was looking for her. Had never stopped looking. He had sent someone. He had found her.

She wanted to scream. To weep. To leap across the table and shake Oliver for more information. But she didn't. She couldn't. Because Malec was still eyeing here. And if she slipped again, even once, she didn't know what he'd do.

"Do you know about the Festival of Petals?"

Oliver's voice was cheerful, too light, as if he were commenting on the weather or the drapes. But his eyes were serious. Dead serious.

Allora blinked once, then gave a faint nod. "Yes."

He smiled, but it was a soldier's smile, tight and hiding steel.

"Good. That's your chance. The night of the crescent moon, during the lore parade. Get there."

Her mouth opened, just barely, but no sound followed. She didn't need to ask why. She already knew—it would be loud. It would be chaos.

Oliver leaned in, slipping a small black coin into her hand with the smooth precision of someone who had done this before. Her fingers closed around it instinctively. The surface was warm from his skin, but the metal was cool beneath, smooth and slick and clearly not ornamental.

"Don't lose that," he murmured. "It's a marker. Awyan underground currency. Use it only if you're in danger. It'll get you into the places where soldiers won't follow."

She glanced at the coin, then tucked it away quickly, pulse racing.

"If we can't reach you in time—go to the Dog House. West end of the market, three stalls past the bone vendor. Knock twice, pause, then once. Say you've come for the hunt."

Allora's grip on the coin tightened. The metal edge bit into her palm, a small, grounding pain. But it couldn't anchor her. And then her eyes burned. She blinked hard, tried to force it down, too late. Tears welled up anyway, hot and thick, spilling down her cheeks in quick, helpless streaks before she could stop them. She tried to laugh it off, clearing her throat as if that could disguise the ache.

"Ah, sorry, I just..." She rubbed at her cheek with the heel of her hand, fingers shaky. "Got something in my eye."

It was a bad lie, brittle, see-through. Lady Mae Yara set down her wineglass, brows lifting with gentle concern. But Malec reacted before anyone else could. The tether between them snapped tight with her distress. She saw it, the way his body stilled, eyes narrowing, rising from his chair like a blade drawn mid-battle, ready to destroy whatever had caused her pain.

She had to stop him. Before she could think, she was moving, fast, clumsy, desperate. Her chair screeched. She crossed the floor in a blur and collapsed into his lap, arms tight around his neck as if she'd meant to be there all along.

The room froze.

Mae Yara blinked, hand to her chest. Zumaro, Oliver, watched with a slow, wicked grin, clearly amused. Malec didn't move at first. His whole frame had gone rigid. But then, slowly, his arms came around her, one hand pressing to her back, the other settling at her hip, grounding her. She felt his breath against her temple, shallow and measured. He said nothing, but she could feel the questions. The worry. The restraint.

He didn't let go, even when her silent tears soaked through his tunic. He let her hide. She held on, breathing him in, his scent, sharp and clean like cold water and stone. Malec's thumb traced slow circles along her spine. His body buzzed with tension, confused, angry, helpless. She could feel the war inside him: to demand answers, to hold her tighter, to do something. She wanted to tell him everything. She couldn't tell him anything. So she stayed there, holding him like a lifeline.

He bent his head, voice velveted and low. "Why are you crying, little dove?"

She stiffened. Then softened. Outside, she melted into his arms. Inside, she was steel. Her voice was barely above a whisper.

"I miss home," she said.

Just enough truth to hold the lie together. Her eyes stayed closed, the ache curling deep in her chest.

"That's all. He reminds me of it."

For a moment, time stilled. Malec's hands relaxed, just slightly. Not pushing her off, not yet. But the warmth faded. His fingers stilled, cold and distant now, resting on the carved arms of the chair instead of her skin. He didn't look at Zumaro, didn't have to. He could feel the smugness radiating from across the room, the invisible competition that always seemed to circle them like wolves on a kill. But Allora didn't care about the others.

"Home," he repeated, too quiet for anyone but her to hear.

The syllable was cold, clipped, a verdict rendered and filed away.

Allora's stomach twisted. She could feel his disappointment, his fury pressed under layers of control. The court had gone silent, Lady Mae's lips parted with gentle concern, Zumaro monitoring like a fox at the edge of a henhouse.

When Malec finally spoke, it wasn't to her, but to Lady Mae, the warning unmistakable in every syllable.

"I believe I'll be taking her back to the palace early. She's... overwhelmed."

She let herself go limp in his arms, letting him bear her weight, knowing it was both a retreat and a small surrender. He stood, slow and measured, gathering her close as if she were a precious artifact, one that had just shown its cracks. His gaze, as he looked down at her, was enigmatic. Pain. Possession. Love, maybe, but something far more dangerous than any of those things. He carried her through the room, the folds of his tunic brushing her bare ankles, the hush of the court closing in behind them. She pressed her face to his shoulder, hiding the last tears.

Without a word, Malec leaned forward and picked her up, cradling her against his chest as if she were something delicate. Something precious. Something he would never let fall. His voice, when it came, was calm, even polite. But the tension in his jaw was sharp enough to wound.

"It is time to go," he said.

Lady Mae Yara raised an elegant brow from where she sat, her goblet still perched daintily in one hand.

"But you've only just arrived! Stay longer, Malec, come now, I've barely shown you my gardens."

"I have what I came for," he replied simply. "And I must prepare for the festival."

His gaze never left Allora. He turned her slightly in his arms, angling her toward Zumaro, "Say goodbye to your friend."

The words were gentle. But to Allora, they felt like stone slabs being lowered into a tomb. She hesitated. Then she offered a small nod, swallowing the tight knot in her throat.

"Goodbye, Zumaro," she said softly.

He nodded back, just as composed. "Goodbye, Allora."

Nothing more. No flare of rebellion. No pleading eyes or secret smiles. But the tension was there. Thick in the air. Malec's fingers curled a fraction tighter around her. Zumaro stepped back and took his seat beside Lady Mae, his posture relaxed but his gaze calculated. Lady Yara sipped her wine, eyes dancing between them like a cat hunting a caged bird twitch.

Malec turned without another word and carried Allora outside. The courtyard had grown quiet, the sky painted in deep indigos and peach, the air perfumed with dying petals and stable dust. A stable boy approached, leading Malec's black warhorse by the reins.

The beast tossed its head, sensing its master's mood, but remained obedient.

He simply lifted her onto the horse with the same deliberate ease he used to wield a blade, controlled, powerful, devoid of hesitation. His hands lingered just long enough to remind her she was attached by an invisible thread, and then his gaze caught hers, sharp and unreadable.

There was something shifting behind his eyes. Something volatile. She narrowed her eyes, studying him.

"What's your angle?"

The words cut the silence between them. Malec didn't look away. He took a long breath, the reins loose in his gloved hand, the other resting lightly at her waist.

> "I want to see you happy," he said, the old world cadence of his voice softening the syllables, as if he was confessing something shameful.

But before she could say anything, he vaulted into the saddle behind her, the heat of his body a wall at her back. His arms slid around her, strong, careful, anchoring her in place. Not to hold her still, but so she couldn't lean away. So she couldn't mistake where she belonged. He dipped his head close, his lips brushing the shell of her ear. The words, when they came, were low, and in Awyan, raw, guttural, intimate enough to make her shiver.

"But you can only be happy next to me."

A chill spidered across her skin, despite the night's warmth. She felt his breath, hot and trembling with restraint, as the horse began to move, hooves clopping over the road's dark stones. She stared ahead, heart racing. *What did that mean? Was it a threat, twisted as devotion? A promise, shaped like a cage? Or simply a truth he believed so fiercely he couldn't imagine a world otherwise?*

Malec didn't explain himself. But she felt the pressure in his embrace, the steady, possessive certainty that radiated from his every movement. It was not cruelty. It was not softness. It was just... certainty.

So he held her tighter, not hard enough to bruise, but enough to let her know: *You are mine. This is where you belong. I will wait. I will not let go.*

Chapter 24

Because I Can't Help Myself

T he palace guest suite felt almost unreal, luxurious, vast, easily double the size of Allora's entire childhood apartment. Arched windows lined the far wall, carved in elegant Awyan vines and wildflower motifs, their shapes evoking the intricate stonework she once saw in Tangier in Africa, back when she was still Melodie. Before all this.

Morning sunlight poured through the arches, warming the jewel-toned tiles below. The space felt curated, furs tossed just right over low chairs, velvet cushions arranged with care, and a gauzy canopy drifting gently above the bed. Even the air was intentional, laced with citrus and spice, tempting her outside. Firewood crackled in the hearth, casting a soft heat that chased the last of the night's chill from the corners.

Barefoot, Allora padded across the heated tiles, holding up the tunic Malec had chosen for her. It was awful. A rough, shapeless patchwork of dull brown and olive. "It's so... brown," she muttered, frowning at the stiff collar.

"You sure this isn't made from actual potatoes?"

Across the room, Malec sat motionless in a high-backed chair, one leg crossed neatly, a book resting on his knee. To anyone else, it might've looked like leisure, but Allora saw the rigid discipline in it. His spine was straight, his posture perfect. Even the plate of fruit beside him was arranged with intention, crusts aligned, berries in straight rows. His silver cup sat turned just so, the sigil facing forward like a compass point.

He hadn't turned a page in twenty minutes.

A carved pipe glowed faintly in his hand, its tip a soft swirl of blue and violet. Fragrant smoke curled upward, sweet and thick, making the air feel slow, dreamlike. He inhaled deeply, then exhaled in perfect rings, each one dissolving before they touched the ceiling beams. Allora noted how controlled everything around him was, as usual. Every spoon, every breath, every thread of his morning ritual. She imagined he lived like this most days, arranging the world into quiet submission just to silence the chaos inside.

He looked serene. But even as he sat, still and composed, she felt his attention on her. Watching her hold the tunic. Tracking her every move. Always.

"You don't like it?" he asked, his tone softer than usual, the barest smile tugging at the corner of his mouth.

Allora waved the rough tunic in the air with a dramatic sigh.

"I'm not saying I hate it, but you do realize this is the Awyan equivalent of a burlap sack, right? You're actually sending me to the festival dressed like a peasant? A lost housemaid?"

Malec turned a page, slow, deliberate. A gesture meant for her, not the book. The quiet creak of the spine underscored the silence, but his focus wasn't on the words. She knew him well enough by now to recognize it, his attention was on her. He again drew from his pipe, releasing a curl of violet smoke that hovered above him like a halo. The scent was sweet and herbal, wrapping around her like a net, blending with the warmth of the fire and the citrus breeze from outside.

He didn't speak. Just watched her with that neutral gaze, steady, assessing, almost indulgent. Even his silence was a ritual.

"You'll blend in," he said, his voice calm, like a stone tossed into a still lake. "And you'll be safe."

Allora made a face, tossing the tunic down with a sigh. "Still. You could've eased me into peasantry, Malec. This is a lot. The stitching is like sandpaper."

He watched her, eyes gentle and the pipe balanced lightly in his mouth. "You're spoiled," he said, giving her that familiar crooked smile, though his eyes remained distant.

She shot him a glare. "You made me this way."

He let the smile linger, but it faded at the edges, replaced by a quiet, unsettling intensity.

"I know."

The moment should have ended there, one more round of banter, a small surrender to routine, but something shifted beneath the surface.

"Being my Canariae has its perks," Malec said, his voice quieter, threaded with something old and possessive.

Not a tease. A truth. Allora crossed to the chest and set the clothes aside, her pulse beating a little too hard in her throat. She didn't want to acknowledge the shift, but she couldn't ignore it.

"What did you mean by that?" Her voice was lower now, the humor gone, replaced by something sharp and curious.

Malec's gaze met hers, steady and thoughtful, as if he were searching her face for the truth she might not say.

"I mean," he began, every syllable chosen with care, "there is no version of this world where you are not mine. No matter what you wear. No matter who tries to claim you."

A shiver slipped down her spine. Her skin tightened, goosebumps prickling along her arms, but her face stayed still.

"You belong with me," Malec murmured, his tone final, as if the words had always existed, waiting only for him to speak them. "Even if you don't feel it yet... I'll teach you."

Allora tried to rally. She picked up the plain tunic, holding it between two fingers like it might bite.
"But really, why these? You trying to bore me to death?"
Malec studied her over the rim of his goblet, eyes cool and considering.
"I don't want you to stand out."

She laughed, dry and incredulous. "Too late for that, Malec. I stand out because I exist."

He didn't argue. She turned the tunic over in her hands, frowning at the heavy fabric.
"It's thick. Warm. Not exactly my style. Won't I overheat?"

"It'll get cold later," Malec replied, voice low and velvet, the corner of his mouth tilting just slightly. "You'll be grateful then."

Allora groaned and tossed the tunic onto a nearby chair with an exaggerated sigh. Let him fuss if he wanted. She wandered to the balcony, the painted tiles warming her feet with each step. Blue and green patterns shimmered beneath her toes, and sheer drapes swayed around her ankles, stirred by a breeze heavy with citrus, jasmine, and the faint bite of lavender smoke from his pipe.

For a moment, she was somewhere else, Agadir at dusk, the call to prayer echoing through a sun-drenched city that no longer existed.

She folded onto a plush fur throw by the window, knees pulled to her chest, the sun still warm against her skin. Her eyes drifted to Malec. Light caught in his pale hair, turning it to gold. He looked almost human like this, relaxed in a carved rosewood chair, tunic open at the throat, one leg slung carelessly over the other. But even now, in all that soft quiet, he didn't look safe. He looked like a blade pretending to rest.

Before she could stop herself, the question tumbled out. "How old are you, really?"

His pipe stilled mid-rise. For a long moment, he didn't look at her, eyes fixed somewhere past the balcony where the city was waking. The smoke curled around his knuckles, elegant, unhurried, like everything he did.

"Why do you ask?" His voice was soft, but not gentle.

Allora fidgeted, tracing patterns into the tiles with her thumb.

"Because I want to know how you age, decades mean nothing to you. And nobody here will tell me the truth."

The silence hung, heavy as humidity before a storm. Then, with the kind of grace that came from centuries of discipline, he set the book aside, she doubted he'd read a word, and leaned back, studying her.

"I stopped counting after one hundred and sixty."

Her breath hitched so sharply her vision went white for a second. She stared.

"You stopped counting?"

He offered a shrug, elegant and infuriating.

"Time stretches differently here. For my kind, a year is a ripple in a pond. The further it spreads, the harder to know where it began."

A hundred and sixty years old. Older than her great-grandfather, older than the damn concept of sliced bread. She tried to picture him in sepia tones, wearing some dusty cravat, glaring at kids for playing their music too loud. Except, of course, the kids would've been fighting with swords or whatever, and he probably invented brooding. He was an honest-to-god, living antique, sitting across from her looking like something from a fever dream, impossibly young, unfairly hot, the kind of hot that made you question your entire evolutionary tree. Allora squinted at him, half expecting to find a wrinkle, something that betrayed the weight of centuries.

Nothing. Not so much as a laugh line. It made sense. The way he lectured her on "proper" breakfast, as if bread was sacred and fruit out of season was a personal insult. The way he grumbled about people not making their beds at sunrise or how he could sit for hours, silent, sharpening that damn dagger for the thousandth time. His sense of order wasn't just control, it was ancient habit, the sort of routine that kept you sane when everything else fell apart.

God, she was really sleeping with a grumpy old man trapped in a carved marble body. The thought made her want to laugh, but also sent a chill down her spine. Ew, right? Or was it weirdly... hot?

Because for all his relic tendencies and lecture vibes, he had stamina that made her sore in the best way. In the dark, his hands didn't move like an old man's, there was nothing hesitant or uncertain about the way he claimed her. It was the confidence of someone who'd lived through wars, heartbreak, centuries of longing. And now, he wanted her.

She finally looked up, meeting his gaze. He was looking at her with a kind of cautious longing, his features carefully schooled. Like he was bracing for her to bolt, to recoil away, to see him for what he really was: not just powerful, but other. Something that survived centuries by being sharper, harder, impossible to hurt. But he looked almost bashful now, smoke from his pipe curling around his fingers as if it might shield him from her judgment.

Her voice, when it came, was hoarse. "And you look... what, thirty?"

"To your eyes," he murmured.

That ache under her ribs swelled, hot and sharp and unfair. It was one thing to know he was old, she'd always known, somewhere, but this was a different kind of real. But she didn't look away. Didn't recoil. Didn't give him the satisfaction of that flinch.

"How is this supposed to work?" Allora's voice was quiet, barely above the hush of the garden breeze. She kept her gaze on her hands. "I mean... with us?"

Malec's eyes narrowed, not in anger, but with the kind of patient scrutiny she'd come to expect from him.

"Clarify."

This time, she did look at him. Her eyes, dark and shining, held nothing but honest, aching confusion.

"I'm going to get old. Really old. My joints will ache, my back will hunch, my hair will gray and thin. I'll be all wrinkles and frailty. Meanwhile, you, " Her hand flicked in his direction, as if the sight of him was almost unfair. "You'll still look like a damn statue someone forgot to dust. Still immortal. Still... you."

She made herself say the rest, throat tight.

"Won't you think it's gross? When I'm fragile and bent, and you're still sitting there with your perfect hair and all those old man habits? Won't you get tired of me?" Her voice nearly cracked. "Doesn't it feel strange to you?"

Malec didn't evade. Instead, he set his goblet down with the deliberate, almost ceremonial care he reserved for old things, things that had survived generations of hands. Then he leaned forward, bracing his elbows on his knees the way only someone who'd spent a lifetime watching and listening could.

> His voice deep and certain, "You think my desire for you is anchored to your youth? Your body?" His eyes softened, old shadows flickering in their depths. "I have lived long enough to see beauty's shape change a thousand ways, to see the pride and fire of my own kind fade under the weight of centuries. I have lost friends to war, to pride, to the slow drift of time as we grew into strangers. But never, not once, have I loved someone whose years are counted in heartbeats, not centuries."

He drew in a slow breath, as if tasting the truth of it for himself.

> "I have watched my own kind become cold, withdrawn, locked in their memories and rituals, afraid to feel. That is the real curse of living long: not the rot of flesh, but the slow death of wonder. I have watched perfection become empty, watched joy wither in those who cling too tightly to eternity. And still, I have never grown numb to love."

His lips curled into a wry, almost self-mocking smile.

> "You are the first thing in a very long time that makes me remember what it is to feel alive. To ache for something I cannot hold forever."

He tilted his head, and for a moment, he looked very much the old man, studious, almost stubborn, weighing her soul the way elders weigh a coin, with the same caution and wonder.

"Do you know what you look like to me?"

She shook her head, throat thick with unshed tears.

> He watched her, eyes softening. "You look like the moment before lightning strikes."

For a long, humming second, she couldn't move. The air between them was heavy and buzzing, charged like a summer storm about to break. She curled further in on herself on the fur-lined floor, clutching the fabric to her chest, trying to anchor herself in the present.

"That's... poetic," she whispered, voice wobbling. "But I don't get it. Is that really how you see me? Like lightning?"

Malec leaned forward again, pipe forgotten, his forearms balanced on his knees. For once there was nothing regal or guarded about him, only that raw, unpolished honesty that belonged to someone who'd lived long enough to lose everything, again and again.

"Yes," he said, simple and clear. "Because lightning is the most beautiful thing the sky can make, and the most brief."

Allora's lips parted, but she couldn't summon a single word. He pressed on, quietly relentless.

"You enter a room and the air changes. I feel you in my bones. The tension, the anticipation, like I'm waiting for the sky to split itself open. You make the world crackle, Allora." His gaze moved over her, not with hunger but with awe. "You are vivid, wild, unpredictable. And you are finite. You will burn through your years, and I will be left with nothing but smoke and memory."

Her heart pounded, brittle and sharp in her chest, as if her own bones were protesting the future she feared. She saw it then, him still here, sharp and bright, while she faded. The image stung in her throat.

"You think age is what matters? That your fading will lessen my love?" His voice broke into something fierce, hoarse with feeling. "Allora... if you withered to dust, I would gather every last piece and press it to my chest. Because you are mine. And I am yours, no matter how many lifetimes I carry."

He squeezed her hand, firm, certain, like the roots of an old oak refusing to let go.

"I didn't choose this because it was easy. I chose it because you were worth every ache and every ending."

She shivered, not from fear, but from the sheer, overwhelming gravity of what he offered her. In that moment, she understood: he was an old man in a young man's skin, made strange and beautiful by all he'd survived. And she was the wild storm that made him feel alive, no matter how brief, or how bright, or how fleeting her flame. He looked at her, something raw flashing through his eyes, and for a moment his voice dropped, barely a whisper, rough at the edges.

"You burn too fast, and too bright. But I'd rather go blind than look away."

With her nose wrinkling, voice dry and skeptical, she muttered, "So what... you're still gonna wanna bone me when I'm a dried-up mummy in a rocking chair?"

Malec went utterly still. Then, slowly, his shoulders gave a slight shake, not quite laughter, more like the disbelieving sigh he reserved for her worst moments. He leaned back just enough to see her face, as if he needed to study the trouble in her eyes, the smirk on the mouth that always gave him trouble. Malec cupped her cheek, his thumb running gentle along her jaw.

"You're not your skin, or the passing years. I have lived through ages and seen beauty twist and shift and fade. You are not a moment, I see you. The storm in you. The fire. You are my madness, Allora."

He paused, letting the words settle.

Then, with the kind of ancient gravity that seemed to come from the very stones of the palace, he added, "And I will want you in every form you take, until your final breath, and long after."

"Damn," she muttered, blowing out a breath. "You make necrophilia sound kinda hot."

Malec blinked, slowly. The elegant curve of one brow lifted, not with offense, but with the calm bewilderment of someone trying to understand an alien language. Her language.

"I mean," she continued, shrugging awkwardly, "thanks for the poetry and all, but let's be real, I'm not exactly immortal, and eventually this", she motioned to herself, "is gonna be more dust than diva."

Malec sighed then gave her that look, equal parts confusion and exasperation, like he was trying to parse a dialect only she spoke.

"You mistake me," he said at last, voice gentling as he took her hand, anchoring her back to him.

"My words aren't flattery," Malec said, eyes locked on hers. "They are truth. For us, love isn't a fire that burns out and leaves nothing. It endures. Time does not erode it. If anything, it deepens. Becomes more dangerous with each year."

He pressed her palm flat against his chest, over the slow, steady beat of his heart.

"When I tell you I will love you to your last breath, and beyond, I mean it. I have lived long enough to know what endures, and what I cannot bear to lose."

Allora just stared at him, for once unable to summon a single joke. His promise hit her like gravity, dragging the humor out of her chest and leaving only the fragile, terrifying truth of being loved by something ancient—knowing she'd fade long before he ever could.

Malec tilted his head, studying her. His smile was faint, half amusement, half something worn and distant. He looked, in that moment, every year of his age: a little tired, a little lonely, as if her very presence stirred aches he'd learned to live with. He let her go, and let her think about it, the way old people do when they want you to understand something you're not quite ready for. Allora shifted her weight, mouth twisting. She tried to keep it light, but her voice came out smaller than she meant.

"Well. Guess I should feel bad about that dust-in-a-rocking-chair joke."

"You should," he said, dry as old parchment, already reaching for his pipe again with the calm of someone who'd heard every joke, every century-old taunt.

She huffed out a breath, half an eye roll, half surrender. He was already turning away, his boots making no sound on the warm stone floor as he crossed the room. Malec paused at the old cedar chest beneath the arched lattice, heirloom-old, every corner carved by hand. The lid groaned open with the tired protest of something that had seen too much. He searched inside not with the indifference of a collector, but with the careful hands of someone who'd waited a long time for the right moment.

When he turned back, what he carried caught the light like a secret. A cloak, midnight blue, so dark it nearly swallowed the sun, stitched through with constellations in gold thread that glimmered when he moved. It was heavy, royal, and impossibly old. Something made to last, not for one winter, but for a hundred. Allora stared, her breath tangling in her throat, a gasp breaking loose before she could help it. She hadn't expected that. Not from him. Malec caught the sound, and for a heartbeat, pride flickered across his face, the kind of pride that comes after centuries of being hard to impress. He approached, slow and careful, scrutinizing her the way old men watch storms roll in, awed, wary, hoping it would last. She reached for the cloak without thinking, fingertips running over the thick, impossibly soft velvet. It felt like it had stolen the light of the stars. Like it remembered every hand that ever touched it.

"This..." she breathed, voice almost reverent. "This is unreal."

He watched her, hungry for the wonder on her face.

"Beautiful," she corrected, the word spilling out without her usual sarcasm. "It's beautiful."

A satisfied sound rumbled in his chest as he stepped forward, lifting the cloak and settling it around her shoulders with a ceremony that felt ancient and almost sacred. The weight of it grounded her, made her feel claimed. He didn't pull back. Instead, he leaned close, his mouth barely brushing her ear, his voice low.

"So you do like my gifts," He settled back into his chair, moving with the same deliberate quiet as before.

Tea in hand, hair falling loose and wild about his shoulders, he looked both impossibly young and unfathomably old. But something in his posture, too still, too contained, settled a knot of worry in her chest. She watched him in the hush of morning, sunlight curling gold across the floor, the fire popping gently, cinnamon and citrus on the air. But none of it touched her the way the sight of him did: regal, weary, holding himself together as if he'd learned, after a lifetime, that some joys are too brief to chase. It wasn't peace that filled the room now, but resignation, a quiet acceptance, as if he knew exactly how fleeting rare things could be, and already felt the ache of their passing. And Allora suddenly had the terrible, aching thought that he was saying goodbye. But that made no sense. They weren't parting. They were still here. Together. So why did it feel like the end of something?

Malec turned slightly, as though snapping back into armor.

"I have something else for you," he said quietly, voice tempered now, the storm tucked back behind his eyes.

But she wasn't sure if she could take anything else. Because all she wanted, suddenly, achingly, was to reach out and tell him she saw him. And that terrified her.

Allora blinked. The air between them still hummed from her question, from the fragile, splintering tension that had cracked his mask, but now, Malec stood composed again. Calm. Steady. As if none of it had happened.

"A shield," he said simply, his voice like a blade sliding back into its sheath.

He turned without another word, crossing the room with measured grace to a black wooden chest tucked beside the stone hearth. He lifted the lid with one hand, and from within the velvet interior, he drew out something that glinted in the morning light.

Silver. Smooth. Cold. A collar.

Polished metal shaped into a perfect band, gleaming like starlight, its center embossed with his insignia, a silver fox carved in sharp relief. The symbol of his bloodline. His name. His claim. She knew that it meant something but what it meant exactly she didn't know nor care, she only knew she hated it.

"Turn."

She hesitated. Just for a heartbeat. Then slowly, deliberately, she turned her back to him. The soft rustle of fabric. The whisper of breath against her nape. And then the cool kiss of metal touched her skin. The collar was heavier than it looked, its weight settling around her neck like a chain masquerading as jewelry. She heard the soft click as it locked into place. His fingers lingered. Not on the collar, but just beneath it, ghosting over her collarbone, her throat. A pause. A moment too long. As though memorizing the feeling of her skin before stepping away.

When she turned to face him again, something in her chest tightened. Because Malec... didn't look like himself. He wasn't stoic. He wasn't composed. He was fraying at the edges. Just a little. His expression was still. But his eyes, those ancient, haunted tan eyes, looked distant. Tired. Like a creature preparing to go without something it loved. He looked at her not as though she was his captive... but as though he had already lost her. And for the first time since she'd known him, she wasn't sure what was breaking inside him.

Or why. Why did he look like that?

Allora stared at him, her breath catching quietly in her throat, not from fear, but from the overwhelming quiet of his pain. Malec stood there, impossibly still, his broad shoulders squared as though bracing against an invisible wind. His jaw clenched, his lips pressed together in a tight line, but it was his eyes that gave him away. That familiar, relentless focus, the way he always watched her like a storm on the horizon, was gone. Replaced by something hollow.

She didn't ask him what was wrong. She knew better. Malec never answered questions like that, not directly. He'd smother it in stoicism, mask it with control. Pretend until she stopped pressing. So instead, she stepped toward him. Quiet. Measured. Wondering if maybe her presence alone would be enough.

His gaze lifted, raw and bare for once, mask slipping just enough for her to see the storm inside him, fear, hunger, longing, all fighting in his eyes. Allora felt her own heart trip, a sudden ache tightening in her chest. She hadn't expected this. Not the way he looked at her like she could undo him with a word.

"Malec," she whispered, soft and shaky, not sure what she meant.

He shook his head, sharp and pained, his jaw ached from holding back like he could hold himself together if he just kept silent. The sound of his breath, ragged and desperate, split the tension between them. Then he reached for her, one hand hard at her waist, the other gentle, cradling her face. He pulled her in and kissed her like he was drowning, all teeth and heat and helplessness, chaos spilling out in every touch. She clung to him, fists twisted in his tunic, needing to feel him solid and real.

He pressed her back into the wall, not to control her, but because it was the only way to keep from falling apart. His body was hot and trembling against hers, breath crashing wild in her ear. His lips were everywhere, kissing her as if he could etch the memory into his bones, as if this was both the beginning and the end. The air felt electric, sharp and aching.

And in that kiss, she felt him shatter, not from power, but from the fear of loss.

When he finally broke away, he held her forehead to his, his breath shuddering between them, hands still tight on her hips.

"I should stop," he rasped, voice broken.

Allora's lips quivered, even as her breath shook. She kept her body pressed close, her eyes daring.

"Then stop, old man," she whispered, a wicked grin tilting her mouth. "But if you're going to let go, do it properly. Otherwise, you better hold on."

A sound vibrated in his chest, low and aching, a plea, not a threat. Then he was kissing her again, slower, every touch softer and rougher all at once, as if he could taste goodbye on her skin. She spun them, pressing him back against the table, her palms splayed over his chest, feeling his heart hammering under her hands. He gripped the table's edge like it was the last thing holding him to the world, hair falling wild in his eyes, every breath a fight for control. Allora pressed close, lips at his ear, her voice a promise.

"I want to reward you," she murmured, a confession buried in heat and something dangerously like love.

And in the hush between their heartbeats, she knew they were both undone, together.

Malec's knuckles whitened against the desk, his jaw locked tight, but his eyes never left her, dark and wild and desperate, like he was viewing his own undoing in real time. Allora could feel the heat rolling off him, could see the war of restraint and longing trembling beneath his skin. He was trembling, actually trembling, as she pressed closer, her breath a tease against his throat, her hands sure, her intentions clearer than words.

"For what?" he rasped, every word thick with need, as if it cost him to speak at all.

She smiled, slow and hungry, lush mouth brushing his jaw, her words warm and wicked at his ear.

"For tonight. For giving me freedom, even if it was only for a few hours. For being something I want, not just something I survive."

He flinched at that, her honesty burning hotter than any touch. It made his breath stutter, chest rising and falling too fast, like he couldn't fit enough air into his ancient lungs. When she reached for his belt, his whole body jerked, but he didn't stop her. He let her take, let her claim. Maybe he'd wanted this all along, her hunger, her hands, the taste of being desired so fiercely he could forget everything but the ache she made inside him.

Allora dropped to her knees before him, the movement fluid and unhurried, her gaze never leaving his. Malec looked down at her, eyes narrowing in confusion, the muscles in his jaw working as he tried to piece together her intent. For a moment, his control held, stoic and impenetrable.

"What are you doing?" he asked, voice low, wary—almost disbelieving.

She only smiled up at him, slow and sly, heat flickering in her eyes. Her fingers moved quickly, making short work of his belt, unbuckling it with a single, impatient tug. The leather slapped the stone floor, echoing between them. Malec's breath hitched, the sound sharp, his mask slipping as a shiver raced through him. She didn't answer, not with words. Her hands made swift work of the ties at his trousers, her touch sure, hungry. His hips pressed forward into her palms, unguarded, his need laid bare. The moment she freed him, the cool air teased his exposed skin, and her greedy gaze only stoked the heat burning in him. He shuddered, composure fracturing, every muscle tight with anticipation and want.

Then, with a wicked, knowing smile, she took him into her mouth—hot, soft, merciless. The first sound he made was guttural, half-moan, half-shocked plea, torn from deep inside him. His head fell back, silver hair tumbling in wild tangles, spine arching as pleasure coursed through him in a devastating wave. His entire body went taut, nerves sparking like wildfire beneath his skin when she hummed against him, sending vibrations spiraling straight through his core. The sensation struck him so sharply it blurred his vision, made his jaw slacken, every thought burned away by the raw, feral need consuming him. The table behind was the only thing keeping him upright; his hands, knotted white in her hair, were the only anchor he had left in the world.

"Uhhnn, Allo...raa..." he rasped, the name torn out of him raw, strangled by pleasure and disbelief.

He tried, gods, he tried, to regain control, his hips twitching, his chest heaving, every ancient instinct screaming to drag her up, pin her beneath him, and bury himself inside her until she forgot her own name. But she was in charge now, her mouth relentless, her hands holding his hips steady with a strength that thrilled and destroyed him in equal measure.

She glanced up, eyes wicked and dark and shining, and he almost lost himself just seeing her like that, glistening lips wrapped around him, her gaze daring him to move, to challenge her rule. There was joy in her, but grief too; he felt it all in the way her tongue caressed him, in the gentleness hidden in the rawness of her touch.

She pressed a kiss to the base of him, murmured a soft, "Shhh..." against his skin.

Then she took him whole.

Malec choked, breath catching on a sharp, involuntary gasp. Fire raced through his veins, turning his legs to water, his senses overloaded. He whimpered, actually whimpered, a desperate, broken sound he hadn't made in centuries, not since he was young and the world was new and nothing hurt quite like this. His fingers clenched helplessly in her hair; his whole body trembled, caught between the need to surrender and the wild, shattering urge to claim her. His spine arched. His soul, it felt, was being devoured along with his body, the pleasure cresting into something that was more than flesh, more than hunger. It was obliteration. Worship.

The pressure built until it was blinding, until his heart ached, until his entire being broke. He came undone with a violent shudder, spilling himself into her mouth with a low animalistic, desperate moan. Vision white-hot and shivering, chest hollowed out by the force of it. In that moment, she owned him completely, and he let her, wanted it, needed it.

Allora had undone him, body and soul. And for as long as he lived, he would remember how it felt to be taken, to burn, to be devoured.

Allora rose slowly, lips wet and swollen, her eyes shimmering with secrets. She looked at him, really looked, like she was capturing every detail to keep, as if she was the thief here, stealing the moment for herself. For a breathless second, Malec felt stripped bare, laid open in a way centuries of discipline had never prepared him for.

"Thank you, Malec," she murmured, voice soft, achingly gentle.

The sound of it pierced straight through his chest. When she pressed a feather-light kiss to the corner of his mouth, he nearly recoiled, not from disgust, but because her tenderness hurt more than any cruelty could have. He had no armor for kindness. She wiped the soft shape of her mouth with the back of her hand, gathering herself, smoothing her dress, and straightened as if she hadn't just destroyed him. She turned toward the door with a toss of her hair, that teasing lilt already creeping back into her voice.

"Come on. We have a festival to get to."

He couldn't move. For a moment, he wasn't a prince or a captor or a creature of legend, just an Awyan undone. His knuckles still dug into the edge of the table. His legs shook beneath him, muscles weak and trembling. His chest heaved with unsteady breaths, and his mouth hung open, stunned, as if the taste of her was still on his tongue. His hair fell wild over his face, his tunic half-undone, the evidence of her victory plain and humiliating. He had never felt so exposed, so emptied, so alive.

Longing was worse: a sharp, clawing need to pull her back, to take her in his arms, to remind her she belonged to him, not just for a moment but always. Underneath it all, a fierce ache twisted in his chest, hot and wild and impossibly old.

But he let her go. Because for now, he had to. He watched her cross the room, sunlight and shadow flickering over her skin, and told himself it was mercy, this freedom. That he would let her taste it, just for a little while longer. He would follow, of course. He would wait in the dark, would tear down worlds to keep her from leaving. He would destroy the portal, if that was what it took to hold her. If she hated him for it, so be it.

Because the truth was this: without her, he felt nothing. Nothing but the echo of all the centuries he had survived, hollow and colorless, already half-dead. It was only in her presence, her laughter, her heat, even her defiance, that he remembered what it was to be alive. And now, with the taste of her still lingering on his lips and the ghost of her goodbye enkindled in his veins, he knew it for certain.

She had given him this as a parting gift, as a memory.

But Malec was done letting her go. Next time, he promised himself, his eyes dark and hungry, it would not be her in control.

Chapter 25

Before the Parade Begins

The city of Caelistra blazed with color and music as sunset draped the rooftops in gold. Allora moved beside Malec, eyes wide as she drank in every detail. Buildings rose in tiers of peach and rose-hued stucco, their red clay roofs catching fire in the last light. Arches framed in painted tiles, turquoise, indigo, saffron, told stories in patterns and images, while thick black beams supported balconies tangled in bougainvillea and trumpet vines. Lanterns hung overhead, shaped like moons and beasts, glowing green for new love, blue for reunion, gold for longing, and red for consummation. They bathed the street in shifting color, casting meanings as layered as the voices that filled the air. Vendors called out over tables piled with sweet breads, jewel-toned fruits, grilled meats, and honeyed drinks. Music wove through it all, drums, flutes, strings, beating like the city's heart.

Yet beneath the beauty, the truth remained. Few children darted through the crowd. Most faces were ageless or old. Couples walked in clusters of two, three, sometimes more, glowing with love or lust. And always nearby, the Canariae: collared, silent, leashed. Their blank or wary eyes made Allora's stomach turn.

Still, the festival roared. Ribbons flew from balconies, petals scattered like rain, laughter rang bright as the parade neared. Everything smelled of citrus and warm bread, rich velvet brushed her arms, and the crowd shimmered like a dream. Beside her, Malec strode like he ruled it all, clad in black leather and obsidian wool, silver fox sigil flashing at his chest. No crown, no theatrics. Just presence. A wolf in a city of song, his pale tan eyes scanning everything. The crowd parted before him, the city bowing to his silence.

For one perfect moment, he owned the night.

He looked like a story carved in steel and silence, part prince, part predator, a myth walking in black. The lanterns flickered off the silver fox sigil at his shoulder, casting him in a glow that made strangers go quiet. But beside him walked his flame.

Allora felt their stares, heavy as chains. Their eyes caught on the collar around her throat, his mark, more intimate than jewelry, more damning than shackles. Every whisper asked the same thing: owned or claimed? Her heart pounded beneath the rough brown tunic, the only softness on her the deep blue velvet cloak embroidered with golden stars. It trailed behind her like dusk, wrapping her in warmth she couldn't admit she needed.

Malec's hand was never far, brushing her shoulder, resting lightly at her hip, always reaching. Before they left, he'd tucked a too-bright flower in her hair. She'd rolled her eyes, but every time he looked at it, his expression softened. That smile, quiet, shy, almost hopeful, unraveled her. He didn't watch the parade. He watched her. When her eyes lit at the floating lanterns, when her jaw tensed at the sight of another collared Canariae, he was already there, his fingers lacing with hers, his thumb stroking small circles into her palm. A silent apology. A wordless plea. Don't pull away.

She tried to hate him. She tried to hate the festival's magic, the comfort of his presence. But firelight made him look too human. And the grief in his eyes made her breath catch, like he already knew she was leaving. Like he couldn't stop it.

A cluster of children ran past, their laughter skipping ahead. Some slowed to stare at her, at her collar, her skin, her strange, storm-colored eyes. Their voices rose in curiosity. Malec moved instantly, stepping forward like a drawn blade. The warmth of the square dimmed. Parents pulled children back with whispered warnings.

"Don't stare at the Silver Fox," one muttered. "That is his."

They walked without speaking, past stalls fragrant with honeyed figs and wine dark as blood. When the crowd thinned and the music faded behind them, Malec finally spoke, quiet, tentative.

"Do you want anything?" he asked, nodding toward a booth where sweets glittered like stained glass in the firelight.

Allora's eyes lifted to his, caught somewhere between teasing and tenderness.

"Are you trying to bribe me with snacks?" she asked, soft, almost smiling, but the edge in her voice was real.

There was a silence after, thick with everything they couldn't say. Desire. Defiance. Fear. The ache of wanting something that could never last. His smile flickered. It didn't reach his eyes.

"Were it within my power," he said gently, "I would ransom
the heavens themselves... if such a gift might coax your heart
toward mine."

The words landed heavy. Allora looked away, clutching her cloak's
strap too tightly. The burn in her throat surprised her. She pretended
to study a vendor's fruit but didn't see the colors. She felt his nearness
like a current, warm, grounding. Not pushing. Just present. She didn't
need to look to know he was gazing down at her, holding his breath for
a response she couldn't give. This was one of those nights, the kind that
etched itself into memory. The flower he'd tucked in her hair tickled her
cheek with every step. The air was golden, thick with woodsmoke and
citrus. And the way he smiled at her, soft, reverent, unraveled her careful
distance. He would remember her like this, she realized.

Before the end. Before the escape. Before she became unreachable
again.

The crowd pressed near but never touched them. Malec's presence
carved a path, silent and commanding. His hand hovered just behind
her, not quite touching, but close enough to claim. She let their
shoulders brush now and then, let him murmur into her ear.

And Malec... Malec was different. Softer. No clenched jaw. No storm
in his eyes. It made her ache. She didn't know how to armor herself
against this version of him, the one who moved with quiet hope, who
looked at her like she mattered. It was the calm before dawn. Beautiful.
Fleeting. She caught herself glancing at him, how the lanterns painted
his face gold and rose, how the last sunlight caught the pale strands of
his hair and turned them almost white. He seemed, for a moment, less
like the warlord who'd conquered her and more like some mythic being
caught in a rare moment of peace.

"What are you thinking?" she asked, forcing her voice light,
teasing, though the real question in her heart beat louder.

He glanced down at her, the slow spread of a smile tugging at his
mouth.

"That I would give much to freeze time," he murmured, voice carrying the weight of centuries, quiet and full of longing. "To linger here with you, unbothered. Just a little longer."

His answer startled her. She blinked, the retort she'd prepared withering in her mouth at the unexpected vulnerability in his tone. Something soft and painful twisted in her stomach.

"That's... weirdly romantic of you," she managed, pushing a playful note into her voice. She nudged him with her shoulder, as if reminding herself who they were supposed to be. "What happened to the cold-blooded brute who dragged me through the snow by my hair?"

A glint of old mischief sparked in his eyes as he leaned closer, voice lowered so only she could hear.

"He still lives," Malec said, his words curling around her like smoke, "but even the coldest snow melts under enough heat, little dove."

Allora felt her cheeks warm and, for one dizzy moment, she let herself believe it, let herself exist in this brief pocket of peace, in the hush before the storm. She laughed, an actual laugh, not the fake sweet one she used when trying to manipulate him. And he noticed. The way his eyes lit up when she did, like he'd never heard a sound more precious.

"I'll remember that next time you're being an ass," she said.

"I expect you will," he answered, amusement touching his lips, but beneath it was something deeper. Longing. Regret. A strange kind of reverence.

She looked away quickly, heart pounding, not from fear, but something far more dangerous. She was starting to enjoy herself. And he could feel it. He could feel her loosening around him, warming like a fire reluctant to burn but too alive not to.

And it gutted him.

Malec, the Silver Fox, the Commander who had ended kings and crushed rebellions, who'd made Allora his in every way that mattered, was savoring a handful of stolen moments like a starving man tasting fruit for the first time. Because he knew. This wasn't real. Not the way it should be. Not the way he wanted it to be. She was planning something. He could see it in the occasional flick of her eyes to the crowd, the way her smile faltered when she thought he wasn't looking. She was watching for someone. Waiting for something. Preparing to leave.

And he would let her. Not because he wanted to. Because he had to.

Because letting her go meant following her into the jaws of whatever escape she had crafted, and sealing the gate to her world before she could slip through. But tonight... tonight she was still here. Walking beside him. Laughing. Looking at him like he was more than a captor. So he would give her this. He would give himself this.

One night. One chance to pretend that this, their shared laughter, their secret smiles, the flower tucked behind her ear, could be something like happiness. Even if he would bleed for it later.

"Are you truly so eager to mock me, Allora?" he asked, voice low as they passed beneath a canopy of shimmering gold-threaded banners. "Must you always poke the wolf?"

Her grin returned. "Only when the wolf looks like he wants to kiss me in front of the entire kingdom."

He glanced down at her, that soft smile still tugging his lips. "I always want to kiss you," he said simply.

And she... she didn't have a quip for that. Not this time.

She looked away, breath snagging in her throat, her steps slowing just enough for him to notice. Malec didn't speak. He only watched her, his gaze soft and searching, as if committing the shape of her silence to memory.

The sun dipped low behind the rooftops, casting the square in a golden haze. Leaves drifted on the breeze like whispers of fire, crisp and amber against the softening light. Lanterns flickered to life above them, suspended in glass and flame, painting the cobbled streets in warm, dappled light. Music poured into the air, wild strings, fluttering flutes, the heartbeat of distant drums. It was music meant for joy, for dancing, for the kind of living that made the world blur at the edges. The scent of bread and crushed blossoms mingled with the dusk, sweet and soft as a kiss.

At first, Allora only watched. Her hips swayed gently, more memory than motion, reclaiming a piece of herself in that rhythm. But then Malec stepped closer. His arm slipped around her waist, firm but gentle, his hand pressing against her back through the velvet of her cloak. She gasped, quiet, startled, more from the tenderness than the touch. His other hand found hers, fingers weaving through hers with calm certainty. No command. No performance. Just presence. And in that breathless second, with music and lantern light swirling around them, the world faded, until there was only this.

"Malec, " she tried to protest, but her voice was weak, threadbare with nerves and surprise.

"No protests," he breathed, mouth at her ear.

The sound of it made her shiver, made the festival fade to a hush.

He led her out onto the dance floor, and the crowd parted as if by instinct, Malec's presence parting the revelers like a blade through silk. Allora's cheeks burned as eyes turned, but she couldn't look away from him, not with the warmth of his body so close, his breath mingling with hers. He guided her, not with force, but with assurance, a steady pressure at her waist, a gentle squeeze of her hand. Their bodies brushed, subtle and magnetic, the edges of their cloaks mingling, his cloak swirling with every turn. Allora felt the music pull her under, each note winding around her chest and loosening the knot there. She let herself move with him. Her feet found the steps, old dances, old joy, her mind slipping back to a time before captivity, before he was her captor and she was his prize.

She dared a glance up, and what she saw undid her. Malec was smiling, a real, unguarded smile, his eyes softened and vulnerable, full of something deep and aching. Not command. Not coldness. Yearning, yes, but also reverence. For her.

He spun her out, then drew her back in with a flourish, his palm pressing lightly between her shoulder blades, anchoring her as the world whirled by in a blur of laughter and music and colored light. Every touch made her skin tingle. Her pulse stuttered when his thumb brushed the side of her throat, lingering just under the collar, the mark that said she was his, the only thing that truly grounded her here, now.

She let herself laugh, real and unguarded, when he twirled her too quickly and caught her by the waist, his grip strong, his touch never rough. She felt the flutter in her stomach, the dizzy ache of possibility. Was this how falling in love started? Or was it the slow, confusing magic of Stockholm? She didn't know, couldn't know, only that when Malec looked at her like this, she forgot to be afraid. Forgot the plan. Forgot everything except the way his hands fit her, the way his body moved with hers, the way his voice made her want to trust him.

He slowed, drawing her closer still, until their bodies fit together in the hush between songs. His breath was warm at her temple, the silver fox on his chest pressed just above her heart. She felt the faintest tremor run through him, nerves, hope, something dangerous and sweet, and it answered in her own chest, the echo of two hearts longing, unsure.

For a moment, it was just the two of them. Just warmth, music, and the hope that, just maybe, she could belong to something beautiful, even if it wouldn't last.

"You're staring," Allora said, reaching for levity, trying to float them both above the undertow, but her words landed softer than she meant, breathless, a tremor shivering just beneath the playful note.

Lanterns spun warm gold through the square, their light flickering across Malec's face, and for a heartbeat she wished she could disappear into their glow, away from his gaze, away from the pounding of her own heart.

Malec didn't bother to deny it. He leaned in, and his voice, rough silk, barely more than a murmur, slipped against her jaw:

"Yes."

Just that. Just the truth, undiluted and raw, settled between them.

She dropped her eyes, feigning fascination with the painted tiles beneath their feet, but she could still feel the weight of him leering at her, as real as the heat radiating from his palm. She let herself be pulled back into the current of the dance, surrendering to the music, the motion, the world blurring around them, just for a sliver of time, pretending she was someone else. Someone free.

He twirled her then, slower than before, guiding her through the crowd. When she spun back, she collided with his chest. Malec's arms closed around her, not as a cage, but as an anchor, steady and strong. There was no laughter in him, no smirk, just that gaze, deep, hungry, almost aching. It made her stomach twist, made her bones feel like glass. For a long, suspended moment, he simply looked at her. His grip on her waist was careful, but she felt the faint tremor of his fingers, as though he was holding on not to her body, but to the last scrap of hope. Her hand, splayed over the broad expanse of his chest, rose and fell with the wild thunder of his heartbeat, a rhythm as frantic as her own.

She hadn't meant to ask the question, but it fell from her mouth and moved like a question before she could catch it, fragile as glass.

"How do you know how to dance so well?"

His mouth twitched, the shadow of a smirk touching his lips, an echo of the arrogance she'd come to know, but it faded before it could truly form.

"All soldiers are taught to dance," he answered, voice smooth, low, full of memories. He guided her through a perfect turn. "It teaches control. Balance. Grace."

Allora blinked, the answer striking something strange and bittersweet within her. She imagined him, young, obstinate, learning the steps of battle and beauty all at once, his life a choreography of discipline and danger. But now, he wasn't watching their steps. He was watching her. Not like a predator, not like a warden, not even like a lover. There was something naked and old in his gaze, something that made her chest ache. Longing. Hope. Fear.

She drew a breath, her voice trembling. "What is it?"

He hesitated, brow furrowed, eyes searching her face as though he was lost in a forest of his own making. When he finally spoke, his words were quieter than the music, rough as stone worn smooth by time.

"How do you feel about me?"

The question landed in her gut, sharp and devastating. Everything around them, the crowd, the music, the colored lanterns, seemed to vanish, and she was left only with his plea, that raw, honest hope trembling in the air. And just a need for truth, stripped bare and unguarded.

She didn't want to lie. She couldn't. Not here, not now, not in his arms.

She met his gaze and let the words come, quiet as confession.
"I don't hate you, Malec."

He drew in a breath, hope flickering across his features, softening the harsh lines of his face.

"But I don't love you either," she whispered, and the words shattered something between them.

The silence after was heavy, thick with longing and sorrow, the ache of what might never be. In his arms, with his heart beating beneath her palm, Allora felt the true cruelty and mercy of honesty, a wound and a balm in one. And as the music swirled around them, she wondered if longing was its own kind of love, and if it would ever be enough. That hope, the fragile thing she'd seen flicker in his eyes, died quietly. Snuffed out beneath the weight of her truth. The light behind his gaze turned shadowed, the lines of his mouth pulled tight, jaw flexing as he struggled to hold the ache at bay. For a moment, he said nothing, and in that silence, something between them stretched thin, almost to breaking.

> "I see," he murmured finally, his voice roughened, sanded down to its barest edge by the wound in his chest. "At least you're not afraid to say it."

He looked down at her as if he could imprint her face on his bones. Something in him unraveled, the last layer of pride giving way to something older, something raw and worn. He drew her in, not possessive this time, but with an aching gentleness, his palm pressed to the small of her back, trying to tether her, just for a moment longer.

> "I would rather have your honesty than your obedience," he said, each word a truth peeled from the marrow. "I would rather be hated for what I am than loved for what I pretend to be."

He held her closer. Not to claim. To plead.

> "I don't want a silent, trembling thing in my arms. I don't want your fear." His voice dropped, nearly breaking on the hush that brushed her ear. "I want your fire, Allora. Your laughter. The part of you that looks at the stars and dares to belong among them."

> He drew a breath, trembling, as though letting go of a secret. "I want you to smile at me. Freely. And only me. I want to be the one you look for in a crowd, the one you reach for." His gaze was desperate now, hungry and hopeful and so, so vulnerable. "I want you to want me the way I want you."

> His voice cracked, soft and childlike in its hope: "I want to be chosen. Not obeyed."

He spun her, slowly, carefully, and when she landed against his chest, his grip was not demanding but reverent, a kind of holy longing.

"I want your love, Allora." The words, barely more than a whisper, shivered straight down her spine: "Even if I don't deserve it."

In his hold she could feel the hunger, the pain, the barely-restrained madness, a force that could consume worlds. But she would not let it take root in the shallow soil of false hope. She met his gaze, voice steady, bitterness held in check only by the ache in her chest.

"As long as I'm beneath you... as long as I'm treated like an object, as long as you see me as less," her fingers dug into his shoulder, "those things can never happen."

Malec went still. Utterly still. The music and laughter and swirl of festival color faded around them, leaving only a hollow silence, the world narrowed to two figures and the space where hope had lived and died. He dropped his gaze, for the first time truly at a loss, as if her words had finally struck the hidden, vulnerable heart he kept buried under centuries of armor. She saw it then, the flicker of defeat, a rare, broken shard of him exposed. He looked not tired in body, but tired in soul. Like a king who had waged too many wars for a kingdom that had never wanted him.

Her heart twisted. But she didn't reach for him. She couldn't. Not when freedom was so close she could taste it. Not when mercy would only become another chain.

But he was not finished. "You will learn to love me," Malec whispered, and the words carried no arrogance now. Just a quiet, tragic promise, an oath spoken from the ruins of a hope he refused to bury. "You will learn to want me." His lips hovered at her jaw, aching to touch, to claim, but never quite daring. "You will need me."

She said nothing. He wasn't listening. Her pulse hammered wildly in her throat. She couldn't give him what he wanted, not yet, maybe never. But the force of his conviction terrified her, and something deeper, darker, thrilled her, too.

> He let out a breath, the sound more surrender than threat. "I will wait as long as it takes." His hand remained at her waist, gentler now, a plea in the guise of patience, as if he could persuade her with time, with touch, with presence alone.

"All I have is time."

The music faded into stillness, the crowd shifting and murmuring in the growing dark. Lanterns glowed like stars above, casting flickers of gold across the square. Scents of spiced meat, sugared bread, and woodsmoke hung heavy in the air, but Allora barely noticed. All she felt was Malec, his touch still lingering, his presence clinging like heat beneath her skin. She stepped away, smooth and calm, careful not to jolt the moment. Her chest ached as she moved through the press of bodies, lantern light brushing her shoulders, music and laughter receding into background noise. The tables at the edge of the square offered a welcome distraction, bowls of figs, glinting pitchers of wine, but she wasn't hungry. She needed room to think, to breathe, to pretend she wasn't still tethered.

But she didn't look back. She didn't have to. Malec's gaze followed her like shadow. She could feel it, hot, steady, unrelenting. A thread between them pulled tight, invisible to all but her. When he moved, barely, just a tilt of his head, a flick of his fingers, the guards loosened. They stepped back. Let her wander.

It looked like freedom. But it wasn't. Not truly. The guards watched her like hounds, tracking each shift of her steps. She was still his. Just with a longer leash. Her jaw clenched. Let them think her soft. Let them forget what she was. She was no pet. No helpless thing. She was Melodie Jaxxon, soldier, survivor, human. And she would never forget it.

Across the square, Malec watched. The firelight gilded her skin, cloaking her in gold. To others, she looked small, vulnerable, freed for the evening. But he knew better. She wasn't his prize. She was his weapon. His bait. And though his face gave nothing away, dread simmered under his ribs. He'd made her look free. He'd made her look touchable.

Freedom was a dangerous illusion. And tonight, it was hers.

But it was necessary. There were enemies lurking, enemies that would only reveal themselves if they believed she could be snatched, could be taken from his side. And so he watched. Every muscle in his body tense, ready. Every heartbeat a prayer that this ruse would end with her still breathing, still his. It felt like betrayal, using her this way. His little dove. His firebrand. His curse and his salvation. But he could not risk her safety, not now, not ever. The only way to protect her was to expose her, just for tonight. Just until the threat was flushed from the shadows.

His jaw ached from clenching, his fists curling at his sides. He watched the crowd, a wolf in waiting, hunger and fear warring in his chest. Let them try. Let them come for her.

Allora made her way through the crowd, drawn by the rich aroma of something warm and sweet. Her feet carried her on instinct, her eyes already settling on a basket of buttery pastries resting beneath a striped red canopy.

The vendor was a fellow Canariae. His graying curls peeked out from beneath a worn cap, and his dark eyes studied her with hesitant familiarity. He blinked at the collar around her throat, then offered her a cautious, crooked smile.

"Möchtest du eins, Fräulein?" he asked softly if she wanted one of his pastries, in German.

She blinked, momentarily stunned, her fingers brushing against the metal at her throat and tells him she doesn't have any money.

"Ich... ich habe kein Geld."

The man chuckled gently, then nodded toward the silver collar with a tired,
knowing look. "Jetzt schon."

Understanding struck her like a slap. The collar wasn't just a shackle. It was currency. Status. Power. She was no longer just a prisoner. She was his. And that meant something.

She looked back toward where Malec stood, dark and regal in his mercenary garb and furs, his cloak stirring with the wind like the wings of some ancient predator. He didn't move, but she felt his eyes. Always. Turning back to the vendor, she slowly reached for the pastry, that slick little smile she wore like armor curling into a smirk. Maybe being collared wasn't entirely useless. Maybe... just maybe... she could make this work to her advantage.

As Allora savored the warm pastry, lips still dusted with sugar and cinnamon, a small tug on her sleeve snapped her from her thoughts. She looked down.

A little Canariae girl stood there, no more than five or six, with tangled curls and a smudge of dirt on her cheek. Her eyes were impossibly wide, warm brown and shimmering with a secret too big for her tiny frame to carry. In her hand, she held a crooked little flower, its stem pinched between her fingers like it was something sacred. Allora knelt, her breath catching as she accepted it gently.

"What's this for?" she asked softly, not wanting to startle her.

The child stepped closer, barely a whisper on the rosy edge of her grin as she leaned in.

"Oliver says to follow the big red bird."

Then, gone. No warning, no goodbye. The girl vanished into the crowd like a wisp of smoke, weaving between cloaks and legs until she disappeared completely. Allora surged to her feet, scanning the bodies that spun and walked and danced around her, but the girl was already swallowed by the festival. Her hand clenched around the flower.

Oliver. He was here. He'd come.

Hope surged through Allora's chest as her body straightened instinctively, her breath catching, her people had come for her. Already.

They were already here. Her heart slammed against her ribs as she spun around, eyes scanning the crowd, searching for the little girl. She had to follow her. Had to understand, what did the child mean? *What was the message really saying?*

But she barely managed two steps before a hand closed around her arm.

"Commander Malec is expecting you."

The voice was smooth, emotionless, one of Malec's personal guards. His grip wasn't cruel, but it was inescapable. Iron wrapped in silk. Before she could wrench free, two more guards appeared beside him, stepping into place like clockwork. Her path was cut off. Panic surged in her chest. Her chance was slipping, melting like frost beneath a rising sun.

"I just need to-—" she started, but the guard cut her off.

"Wait for Commander Malec."

No emotion in his face. No cruelty, no sympathy. Just duty. Chains without metal. Her teeth clenched as she looked past his shoulder, scanning the crowd, vibrant, chaotic, beautiful. The guards didn't shove her, didn't even touch her again. But their presence surrounded her like a silent net, herding her forward without a word. There was no need for threats. The message was clear. She wasn't going anywhere, not without his permission.

Her eyes locked on him the moment she stepped into the clearing. Malec.

He stood tall, a mountain of poise and command draped in sleek black and gray, the silver fox emblem catching the last light of the sinking sun. He was speaking quietly with another elf, a shorter Awyan male with a sharp, weathered face and the ease of someone used to travel. A merchant, maybe. Or something more elusive.

Beside him stood an Awyan elfess, refined in posture and wisdom rooted deep in her light brown eyes.

Allora cast a sideways glance at Malec, her eyes trailing the tall, commanding figure silhouetted in the warm, flickering glow of the festival fires. The curve of his broad shoulders was cloaked in rich fabric, the dark gray folds of his traveling cloak cascading down his back like smoke clinging to a blade. He looked regal. Remote. And ready. It wasn't the cold. The cloak draped over his shoulders, the thick layers he'd wrapped around her, none of it made sense. The night air was crisp, sure, but not enough to warrant all that.

No, this was something else. Preparation. For a journey. Or worse... a hunt.

A quiet chill traced the back of her neck, and she resisted the urge to pull away from him. Then she saw them, the two strangers he'd spoken to. A wiry, sharp-jawed Awyan male and an elfess with too-curious eyes. They bowed quickly, respectfully... and slipped into the crowd without a word.

And that's when he turned.

Malec's gaze found her instantly, calm, indecipherable. Without speaking, he reached out, catching her hand and lacing their fingers together. His grip was steady, bordering on possessive. And then came the kiss. Soft. Lingering. Too tender to be a threat. Too loaded to mean nothing. His lips brushed the crown of her head with such deliberate care that her skin prickled. Not from fear... but from the ache of not knowing what it meant. Because Malec always spoke to her. He taunted, provoked, teased, always with that elegant, infuriating control. But now?

He said nothing. And that silence said too much.

But instead, he just held her hand tighter and murmured, "The lore parade starts soon."

His voice was low and measured, meant to soothe. But it didn't. There was a tone underneath, something fraying at the edges.

"Let's go to the main street before the crowds get too heavy."

He started forward, gently tugging her along. She followed, not because she wanted to, but because resistance now would raise alarms. And she couldn't afford that. Not when Oliver might still be nearby. Allora kept her pace steady, her smile soft, her posture obedient. But her eyes, her eyes never stopped scanning.

Malec's fingers remained locked around hers, his warmth a constant weight beside her. And yet, he felt far away. She risked a look up at his profile, taking in the tension in his jaw, the haunted stillness in his gaze.

He wasn't looking at anything. He was just... enduring. Something was wrong. Deeply wrong. Her chest tightened. She wanted to ask. Wanted to break the silence and demand answers. *What had that elfess whispered? What had Malec agreed to?*

But she didn't ask what was wrong. She didn't fight the pull of his hand. Instead, she smiled softly and walked beside him, like a good little domestic. But inside, her heart beat like a war drum.

And her eyes never stopped searching for the little red bird.

Chapter 26

From Allora to Melodie

The streets buzzed with energy, the air thick with the perfume of crushed petals and spiced wine. Color and music moved like heat waves through the crowd, rippling with the rhythm of drums and the trill of reed flutes. Lanterns hung like stars brought low, casting a gentle glow that painted the cobblestone streets in shifting gold. Children ran ahead barefoot, their laughter ringing out like bells, while adults pressed together shoulder-to-shoulder, eyes wide with wonder as the parade began its march.

It was everything Allora had waited for. Her best, and perhaps only, chance to run.

Somewhere out there, past the thick throng and swaying streamers, was a sign. A red bird. A child had handed her a broken flower and whispered Oliver's name. She didn't know how the girl knew him, didn't care. Allora clung to the hope like a lifeline. If she could find the red bird and slip away unseen, she could disappear.

Start again. Get the cure to her brother Eron. Save her people. Her people. The thought stabbed her in the gut like guilt sharpened to a blade. Every face in the crowd looked like a warning, every glance like suspicion. And Malec... he was always near. Always surveying.

"What is on your mind?" The voice slid into her ears like silk over stone.

She turned her head too quickly, startled, and found his pale eyes trained on her. He wore that look again, calm and collected, but with that furrow between his brows. Barely there. Just enough to betray his concern. His hand rested lightly at the small of her back, a gesture so casual it could have been mistaken for tenderness.

But she knew better. It was possession.

She forced a soft smile, barely moving her mouth as she nodded toward the street beyond them.

"The parade," she said, smoothly. "Tell me about it."

Malec held her gaze for a long, unbearable breath before turning. He gestured for her to follow him just a few steps off the main road, where the crowds thinned under the boughs of a tall copper-barked tree. Multi-colored lanterns dangled from its branches like captured stars, swaying gently in the breeze. The hush beneath its canopy was almost reverent, a sanctuary carved from the noise.

He leaned against the trunk, the soft fur of his coat catching the light. The faintest glint of silver threaded his long hair, his face shadowed in a way that made his eyes glow. And that was the part she hated most—the part that scared her. Because no matter how hard she tried to stay detached, to keep him filed away in the part of her mind labeled 'enemy,' something kept cracking open when he spoke to her like this. Like she mattered. Like she was more than a symbol or a tool.

And she hated herself for noticing. For listening. For wondering if—just maybe—he meant it.

> "The parade began many centuries ago," he said, his voice low, his cadence old and elegant. "After your kind were brought into the cities in greater numbers."

She blinked. Not expecting that. His tone was not cruel, but neither was it apologetic. It was factual, as though reciting a lesson taught to him by someone long dead.

> "At first, the Canariae were simply workers. Disposable. But they endured. They had... culture. Small things that made them memorable. I was told they kept birds, bright ones, yellow and red, tiny things they taught to mimic speech or carry messages. In the mines, they trained them to sense poison gas and dangerous air."

Air caught sharp in her throat. He is talking about mine canaries. She knew they were used as a way to detect carbon monoxide in mines long ago before electronic gas detectors were invented. So this is how Awyans saw her kind, as disposable laborers meant to make their lives easier. Allora couldn't quite complain her species did that to others even of their own kind. But still.

> Malec continued. "The Awyan found it amusing. That such fragile creatures used even smaller, more fragile creatures to survive. And so, they gave your kind the name Canariae. A tribute, they said. But it was not kindness. The term became classification. You were bred like the birds. Chosen for traits. Some for endurance. Others for beauty. Intelligence. Fertility."

His eyes darkened slightly, voice dipping lower.

Allora didn't respond. She didn't need to. The truth had already pierced her, cold, precise.

Of course that's what it meant. Of course that was the irony. The Awyans had named her people after the creatures her ancestors once carried into danger, into darkness, into death. Not as comrades. Not as equals. But as warnings. Tools. Pets.

A mirror. Her stomach turned with the weight of it.

Canariae. It wasn't just a name. It was a mockery dressed as tribute. A collar disguised as culture. A gilded designation handed down by beings who thought themselves gods, as if it were a kindness to give her a title before taking her freedom. She wasn't Allora. She wasn't even Melodie. She was a parable. A possession. A symbol in someone else's story. And the worst part? The part that burned beneath her ribs like acid? Was that the crowd celebrated it. Laughed and danced beneath paper wings. Painted their faces like plumage. Wrapped chains of blossoms around each other's throats as though slavery had been a love story. As though the theft of a people could be rewritten as a dance.

And in that moment, it hit her, how familiar it all felt. How painfully, bitterly familiar. Her world had done the same. Her own kind. Not to alien races or foreign creatures, but to each other. To their own. Torn from lands and branded, caged like livestock because of the shade of their skin or the blood in their veins. It hadn't been born of war or conquest. It had been born of cruelty. Of greed. Of the ease of dehumanizing what you refuse to understand.

Since the beginning of mankind, this had been their legacy, one of chains and silence. And now, here, it echoed back at her like a curse. The Awyans hadn't invented evil. They'd just perfected the pageantry. Pretty lies.

So she nodded. She smiled. She let Malec believe she was spellbound by the charm of it all. Even as something inside her twisted in revolt. She turned to look at Malec, and found his gaze already locked onto her. Not with the sharp edge of command, not with the cold calculation he so often wore like armor. But with something else. Something rarer. His gaze held no arrogance, no restraint, only stillness. Only quiet wonder.

There was a softness to him then, subtle but unmistakable, as if the lines of his face had briefly surrendered to something tender. A kind of reverence bloomed there, fragile and unguarded, like he was trying to memorize the moment before it slipped away. And he was.

Because it reminded him of the first time she'd mouthed an Awyan word back to him with that maddening little smile, challenging him. The first time she'd laughed mid-lesson just to push his patience, then leaned in, eyes sparkling with mischief and curiosity. He had never intended to enjoy those moments. But he had. More than he dared admit. Now, beneath the canopy of lanterns and distant music, that same feeling unfurled in his chest again, soft, insistent, dangerous. A peace he did not know how to name. A longing that should not have taken root but had.

She was not his equal. She was not his intended. But she had carved out space in him all the same, slowly, with every defiant glance and clever remark. And standing here with her now, amid the perfume of petals and the low hum of celebration, Malec realized something with quiet certainty: He wanted this.

Not just the moment, but the continuation of it. The rhythm of her beside him. The sound of her voice tangled with his language. The pull of her presence grounding him in a world he had once ruled with ice.

He wanted this every day. Forever.

Allora swallowed hard. The collar around her throat, hidden beneath folds of velvet and silk, was a silent weight pressing against her skin, warm from her body, heavier than gold. Her fingers drifted over it, brushing the metal emblem.

The Silver Fox. His mark. Her prison. Her value. Her way out. If she played this right.

There was no time to mourn what could have been, no time to drown in the way his eyes softened when he looked at her or how his hand never strayed far from her own. She couldn't let herself feel the heat of him, the steadiness of his presence, or the way he drew her in with quiet gravity.

She couldn't afford it. Not when every second counted. So she tucked away the emotion tightening in her chest, forced a smile that she hoped reached her eyes, and turned toward the parade winding through the heart of the festival.

"Come on," she said gently, reaching for his hand and tugging him forward. "Let's go enjoy the festival."

For the last time.

His fingers curled around hers without pause, warm, certain. He followed, silent and steady, her fierce, obedient shadow. They stepped to the edge of the walkway, where lantern light poured like honey across the streets and music rose into the velvet dark. Malec moved in close behind her, chest brushing her back, arms folding lightly around her frame. It was half-protection, half-possession, the line between them always blurred. He stood molded to her like a second skin, scent clean and cold, like pine and frostbitten wind.

His heartbeat thudded against her cloak, steady and slow, a rhythm that sounded too much like safety. She didn't lean into him, but she didn't pull away either. He felt the hesitation. He always did.

One hand stayed in hers, thumb tracing soft circles across her knuckles. But it wasn't his touch that unsettled her. It was the silence. The weight of his body behind her, alert and still. His chin hovered near her temple, but his eyes were locked on the crowd, searching, sweeping, never stopping.

She glanced up, catching the hard line of his jaw, the distant edge in his gaze. He wasn't viewing the parade. He was scanning for danger. She narrowed her eyes, lips twitching. *What are you really thinking about, Malec Talandros?*

As if he heard, he turned. Their eyes met. And for a moment, something in him cracked. He smiled, small, fleeting. Real. And heartbreakingly sad.

"Do you even want to watch the parade?" she asked softly, her tone laced with teasing, but underneath it, concern.

Malec's grip tightened, just slightly. His gaze didn't leave hers as he lowered his voice, brushing his lips near her ear.

"I do not care for the parade," he murmured, words warm against her skin. "But I would watch a thousand of them if it meant I could stand beside you."

Allora exhaled slowly, her throat constricting. He meant it. She felt it in his voice, in the aching sincerity of it. And god, that made it harder. Malec let the silence bloom between them before speaking again.

"This...," he said quietly, as if afraid too loud a voice might shatter it, "I would keep this moment, if I could. Over and over. With you, like this."

Her chest throbbed, but she said nothing. Because she couldn't promise anything back. He knew that.

Malec's gaze turned toward the parade again, but he no longer saw the colors or the dancers. His mind was elsewhere, pulling away from her in thought, even as his body clung close. He had made his decision days ago, and now it burned inside him like a wound that refused to close. He would have to give her up. Not for honor. Not for duty.

But for her safety. Even if it killed something in him. Even if every cell in his body screamed against it. His hand trembled slightly in hers. He hoped she wouldn't notice.

He hoped she would.

Just as the ache built to the point of breaking, the sky cracked open above them with thunderous color, fireworks blooming across the stars like slow explosions of light.

She gasped.

And Malec, who should have looked away, who should have pretended to admire the display like everyone else, just watched her. The awe in her eyes. The curve of her warm smile. The flicker of wildness that no collar had managed to tame. A bloom of fire split the night. Brilliant orange and gold erupted above them, unfurling in slow, majestic waves across the sky. The explosion rumbled through the cobbled streets like distant thunder, and the crowd erupted in cheers, faces tilted upward, eyes wide with wonder.

Allora's breath caught, not from fear, but sheer astonishment.

Fireworks. They have fireworks here?

She hadn't expected that. Somehow, it felt too human. Too Earthbound. And yet, there it was, a sky on fire with wonder, burning in shapes and colors she didn't recognize. The chemistry had to be different. The metals, the powders, the mechanisms. Foreign science. Alien spectacle. But the feeling? The awe?

That was the same.

The firework trails shimmered like falling stardust, and then the drums struck, deep and reverberating. The parade began in earnest. The streets ignited. Music poured from hidden speakers and live performers alike, echoing off stone buildings, shaking lantern strings overhead. Dancers burst forth in elaborate costumes, feathers of sapphire, emerald, and gold whirling like liquid light. Masks of glittering crystal obscured their faces. The crowd parted instinctively as they spun, twisted, leapt.

Confetti rained down in torrents, shimmering like snowfall made of glass. Children screamed with glee. Adults clapped and laughed, swept into the sensory storm. Allora stood frozen at the edge of it, letting it wash over her. It was beautiful. *Too* beautiful. Then her eyes sharpened. She began to see the patterns.

Costumes shaped like birds. Canaries. Dancers wearing wings that caught the light like flame. They flitted toward others dressed as Awyan royalty, who extended their arms like perch stands. With dramatic flair, the bird-dancers flew into their waiting hands, curling against them obediently. The crowd cheered again. Allora's heart sank. This was not a tragedy being told. This was not history. It was a romantic fantasy.

A retelling of captivity disguised as love. Ownership dressed in silk and light.

The story played out in elegant choreography: the Canariae were creatures of joy, of devotion, who chose their cages. Who wanted to be possessed. Who danced into chains like they were garlands. Her mouth went dry. Her hand brushed her collar. Still there. Still tight. Still his. She glanced sideways at Malec. He was silent, unmoving behind her. Watching.

Was he testing her? Or had he grown so used to the lie, he no longer saw it?

Her fingers twitched at her sides. She wanted, desperately, to rip the damned thing off, to scream, to demand someone see it. See her. And then—

A burst of red. Blazing. Blinding.

A dancer shot into view at the heart of the procession, spinning fast and wild, wrapped in a cascade of crimson feathers that shimmered like molten ruby in the lantern light. Allora's breath didn't just get caught in her throat, it stopped.

The figure was taller than the others. Stronger. Her arms outstretched as she spun in fierce, chaotic circles, wings slicing the air like blades. Her mask was sleek, beaked, and glowing at the edges. She didn't dance like the others. She fought. Every movement of the red bird was sharp, defiant, less a performance and more a ritual of rebellion. And on her belt-

A broken lily. Real. Crushed. Oliver sent her. The message was clear. This was no accident. The red bird was a signal. The signal. Her signal.

Allora's pulse roared to life, hammering against her ribs like a prisoner begging for release. She turned slightly, just enough to see Malec's profile. He hadn't noticed. Not yet. Her eyes locked onto the Red Canary. *'Follow the little red bird.'*

The child's whisper returned like a ghost, curling around her spine, pushing her forward. Her fingers curled tightly into fists. This was it. Her moment. The first sliver of a chance she'd been given in weeks, months, maybe. Her heartbeat surged, lungs expanding like wings about to open wide. But before she could shift even a step, his hand closed around hers.

Not harshly. Not cruelly. Just... undeniably.

Warm, steady fingers wrapping around her own, firm enough to stop motion but soft enough to feel like affection. Soft enough to confuse her. It was exactly how Malec moved, like a cage so beautifully made it made you forget it was built to contain.

"Careful, Allora," he murmured, his lips near her temple. "You might vanish on me in this crowd."

The words were wrapped in silk. Teasing. Affectionate. She laughed, just barely. "Wouldn't that be a tragedy."

"It would be a shame," he said, tightening his hold only enough to guide her hand to his chest, resting it over the steady thrum of his heart. "I've come to enjoy your company more than I ever meant to."

It was so sincere. So effortlessly believable. Too believable. That was the trap. He wasn't suspicious. He was inviting trust. Keeping her calm. Loose. Safe. It made her skin crawl.

Because it was working.

Colorful petal shaped confetti drifted like soft ash from a dying star, catching the golden glow of the lanterns as it swirled through the electric air. The parade roared in full force now, vibrant and dazzling, a tempest of motion and color sweeping through the cobbled streets.

And there, moving through the chaos like a lit fuse, was the Red Bird.

Crimson feathers shimmered like flame, each step calculated, each spin purposeful. It wasn't just dancing, it was waiting. Moving just far enough to stay in sight, never far enough to vanish. Allora's chest rose and fell too fast. Her heart was pounding with every beat of the drums. The Red Canary was her way out.

The only one.

She waited for the dancer to slow, to turn again, to offer that hand once more. And there, yes, another spin, another pause, a flick of fingers like a whisper saying now. Allora shifted forward, legs tense to spring. But the moment she did, Malec's hand closed gently around her wrist. Not harsh. Not sudden. No panic in the gesture. Just steady warmth. Fingers like iron wrapped in velvet. Her body stopped mid-step, the breath caught in her throat. She turned to him, and then she saw it, his face.

That calm mask he wore so well. Too calm. As if nothing at all was happening. As if she hadn't just made the most important decision of her life. His pale eyes swept across her face, and something like tenderness glinted there, sharp and disarming.

"Allora," he said softly, leaning in so no one else could hear. His breath brushed her cheek. "You're trembling."

She hadn't realized it. But she was. Every part of her ready to flee, every muscle pulled tight like a bowstring.

"I..." Her voice failed.

She looked down at where his hand held her. Not possessively. Just... there. She couldn't move. Not yet.

The Red Bird spun again in the distance, closer to the next avenue. Allora's time was bleeding out through her fingers like sand, each second another step farther away. Her panic clawed at the back of her throat. And Malec... was still glancing at her. His thumb brushed once over the pulse point of her wrist, soft, rhythmic.

"You look as though you might fly," he murmured, eyes distant, somewhere else.

Somewhere painful. And for a terrible moment, she thought he would stop her. That he knew. That he'd known all along. That he had no intention of letting her go. But then, something in his expression shifted. A flicker. Pain. Not just sorrow, but resolve.

For a brief, terrifying second, she thought he wasn't going to let her go.

The pressure of his fingers around her wrist was tender, but firm, like the hush before a storm. Her heart stammered in her chest, blood roaring in her ears as the Red Canary paused ahead, waiting. Every second stretched too long. Too loud. Her breath grew shallow. And Malec, he just stood there. Looking at her. Not with suspicion. Not even anger. But with something far worse.

Grief.

A soft, almost imperceptible sigh slipped from his lips. Not a breath of release, but of surrender. Like something inside him had finally snapped into place. Or broken. And then his hand rose slowly, reverently, and cupped her jaw, his thumb brushing along her cheek as though trying to memorize its curve. Then he tilted her chin upward and pressed his lips gently to her forehead.

Allora went rigid. The world stopped. He never kissed her like this. Not softly. Not like he was saying goodbye. Her eyes stung, her whole body a wire pulled tight between fight and flight. Her hands hung useless at her sides as his breath warmed her skin and his whisper brushed against her temple.

"Stay warm. Stay safe."

Then he slipped something into her pocket. She didn't have time to see what. And then, he let her go. Just like that. His hand uncurled, fingers falling from her like petals. And the Red Canary was there.

Spinning close, twirling effortlessly, the crimson fabric flaring around them as she reached forward and swept Allora into the sea of motion like she was meant to be there. Like this had all been part of the choreography. The dancer's hand found hers, and without missing a beat, she pulled Allora into step, into rhythm, into the blur of music and fire and bodies. And the world shifted. She was no longer viewing the parade. She was inside it. She glanced back over her shoulder.

Malec stood still on the edge of the walkway, eyes locked on her. The crowd churned around him, lantern light cutting shadows across his face. But he didn't move. He didn't chase. He just watched. Like a man standing at the edge of a cliff, seeing the only thing that mattered fall out of reach. The press of dancers swept between them, wings and silk, color and chaos, and then he was gone. Swallowed by the crowd. Allora's chest ached. Her body moved as the Red Canary guided her deeper into the flow, spinning her like she belonged to the music, like everything was fine, like the world wasn't breaking open behind her. But her eyes stung. Her throat burned. And somewhere, beneath the thunder of drums and the celebration of feathers and fire,

She could still feel the ghost of Malec's kiss on her skin.

Allora's body felt unmoored, like she'd stepped out of her own skin. The Red Canary spun her effortlessly into the current of the parade, hands guiding her with practiced grace. Her limbs moved on instinct, hips swaying with the music, feet keeping pace with the pulse of the crowd, but her mind screamed against the rhythm, reeling from the last ten seconds.

Malec let me go. No snatch of her wrist. No barked command. No cold steel in his eyes. He didn't come after her. No fury. No fear. No force. *Why?*

She chanced a glance back, twisting mid-spin as the Red Canary danced her deeper into the press of bodies, and there he was. Still standing at the edge of the celebration. Tall, unmoving, his silver-white hair and fur-lined coat catching the light like moonlit armor. He wasn't even pushing through the crowd.

He just watched. His face was carved in stone, ambiguous, too calm, too still. It was his silence that unsettled her most. The guards stationed nearby watched too, stiff and alert. But none of them moved. None of them tried to stop her. *They're letting me go.* No. No, that couldn't be right. Her chest constricted, breath growing thin as suspicion coiled in her gut.

This wasn't relief. It felt...orchestrated. Or was she paranoid?

But there was no time to think. The Red Canary twirled her again, this time toward the edge of the parade, hands firm, steps shifting, subtle signals passed through grip and weight. *Almost there.*

Then, just as Allora braced to sprint-

A dark figure emerged from the crowd. Cloaked in shadow. Moving fast. A hand grabbed her arm. Allora stiffened, eyes going wide, lips parting for a scream she didn't get to finish.

Oliver.

Recognition struck like lightning. He lifted one gloved finger to his lips in warning.

Don't speak.

Then, without hesitation, he yanked his cloak from his shoulders and swung it around her in one swift, practiced motion. The fabric fell heavy and thick, swallowing her form completely. It reeked of sweat, earth, old leather, *home*. The world before collars and palaces and silver fox emblems. At the same moment, he peeled the blue velvet cloak from her shoulders, Malec's cloak, and tossed it onto a passerby.

A stranger.

Allora gasped, watching in stunned silence as the Red Canary pivoted instantly, fluid as breath, and snatched the decoy by the hand, spinning them away into the crowd without missing a beat. It worked. No pause. No stumble. Perfect misdirection. Her lungs flooded with air she hadn't realized she'd been holding. But Oliver didn't let her savor it. His hand clamped around her wrist again, firm, urgent.

"Move," he breathed. Then he pulled.

They ducked between buildings, disappearing into a narrow alley choked with shadow and old stone. The music behind them faded into a distant echo, drums replaced by hurried footfalls. Allora stumbled, breath ragged, but Oliver caught her arm and pulled her along, his grip firm and unyielding. They passed tangled lovers in doorways, drunken nobles slumped against walls, a masked woman retching pink wine into the gutter. No one noticed. No one cared. Her cloak shielded her, but it did nothing to quiet the thunder in her chest.

She risked one glance back. Just one. Malec was gone.

Swallowed by the night. Vanished like smoke in wind. Her vision blurred, not with fear, not with triumph, but with something sharp and raw that lodged in her ribs like a splinter. He'd let her go. But for how long?

Because deep down, beneath the stolen cloak and the frantic breath in her throat, Allora knew one thing with bone-deep certainty. Malec never lost what was his.

And somehow, she'd just slipped from his grasp.

Oliver moved like a phantom through the underbelly of Caelistra, darting beneath crooked stone arches and slipping between alleyways carved like veins into the bones of the old capital. Allora stayed close, her breath tight in her lungs, every footstep measured, every glance over her shoulder sharp with dread.

The roar of the festival was distant now, a muffled heartbeat above them, but it still pulsed through the ground beneath her boots like a drum. Music, laughter, fireworks. A world she no longer belonged to.

This world, the one of shadows and escape, was her world now.

Oliver advanced with precision, checking corners, counting steps, flattening himself in doorways to listen for the echo of pursuit. She recognized the discipline in every motion. This wasn't improvisation. This was practiced military retreat. And he was leading it like a master tactician. Her pulse thundered. Not just from the chase, but from the certainty that at any moment, Malec would appear behind her. Silent. Calm. Terrifying.

She could feel his absence like a pressure behind her spine. It was wrong, that he hadn't come tearing through the crowd, hadn't dragged her back by her collar like he had every right to do. But she couldn't afford to not take this risk.

They ducked behind an abandoned merchant's cart, crouched low as a pair of drunken nobles stumbled past, silver goblets sloshing, cloaks dragging in the dirt. One laughed so hard he nearly fell. The other pointed toward the skyline, slurring something about the firework display over the western towers.

Allora didn't move. Neither did Oliver. They were ghosts. Invisible. And the moment passed. They surged forward again, slipping through narrower lanes now, where lanterns didn't reach, and the stone walls closed in like coffins. The scent of incense and roasting meat had faded. Down here, it smelled like old rain, mildew, and stone sweat.

Caelistra's underbelly. The city's true heart. Oliver raised a hand. Stopped.

A dark doorway loomed ahead, set into a crumbling arch of brick, half-swallowed by ivy. He pressed close, turned to her.

"We wait," he whispered.

She nodded, heart still galloping in her chest. She pressed her back to the wall, staring out into the street, straining to hear anything. A boot scrape. A breath. A whisper of his voice.

Malec.

Forty-five minutes passed like a blade dragged across skin. The chill settled into her bones. Her nerves buzzed with anticipation. Her muscles refused to release. Then, a whistle. Soft. Drawn out. A mimicry of a bird, too deliberate to be natural. A lantern flickered at the far end of the street, swaying with the steps of a hooded figure. They passed without looking. But their hand twitched once, twice, a signal only the trained would recognize.

Oliver's breath escaped in a controlled exhale. "That's our guide."

She said nothing. Just moved. They followed at a calculated distance, slipping deeper into the old quarter of Caelistra, where the buildings pressed in tight and the air hung heavier. The stone beneath their feet was slick. The alleys twisted tighter, darker. They passed a narrow gutter where two lovers were locked in a desperate kiss. No one paid them any mind.

The city above, its light, its pageantry, was far behind now. The figure stopped before a large, weather-worn door tucked between two leaning tenements. Ivy clung to its sides. There was no handle. No markings. Just silence. Knock-knock. Knock. A rhythm. Not a request. An answer. And then the figure turned and walked away, vanishing into the dark like they'd never been there at all.

Allora stood motionless. Staring at the door. Then, just once, she looked back the way they'd come. Nothing. But her skin prickled. As if somewhere in the shadows of Caelistra, someone was still monitoring her.

Silence pressed against Allora's eardrums like a weight. She held her breath, heart slamming beneath her ribs, her body poised to flee, to fight, to freeze, uncertain which instinct would win. Then, the door creaked open, just enough to show a sliver of dim light and shadow beyond. No voice greeted them. No face. Just the quiet summons of the unknown.

Beside her, Oliver extended his hand, palm up.

"The coin," he whispered. For a moment, she blinked in confusion, then fumbled inside her cloak until her fingers closed around cold metal.

The black coin. She had almost forgotten it was there. Without hesitation, she slapped it into Oliver's hand. He stepped forward and offered it to the figure just inside. A pale, calloused hand reached from the gloom and took it in silence.

A pause followed, long enough to raise every hair on her arms, before the hand withdrew and a subtle gesture invited them inside. But before Allora could take a full step, a high, tearful shriek pierced the air.

"*MELODIE!*"

A small body slammed into her, arms wrapping tight around her middle. Allora staggered back, nearly slipping on the uneven stone.

Lilly.

The little girl clung to her like a vine, her face pressed to Allora's stomach, her small shoulders shaking.

"You... you *come back!* I wait, I wait so long!"

Her voice trembled. Her accent thick. The words jumbled and simple. But the emotion behind them, the relief, the joy, was unmistakable. Allora froze. Her arms hovered in midair, unsure, her entire body locked in place.

Lilly is safe. But how? How had she made it here? From the High North? Through war camps, checkpoints, and border patrols? Alone?

Still... Allora slowly dropped to one knee, arms closing gently around the girl, heart torn. She couldn't reject this embrace. Couldn't ignore the way Lilly's little fingers fisted in her cloak or how her voice cracked when she spoke.

"I miss you so much," Lilly whispered, muffled. "You come for me. I knew."

Allora's throat tightened. She said nothing. Just held the girl tighter, fighting the tangle of emotion rising in her chest. Joy and dread warred beneath her ribs. Because while she was glad, *god,* she was glad, every instinct screamed at her that this reunion wasn't clean.

It wasn't safe. The door shut heavily behind them, sealing them inside.

The tavern was dim and quiet, the scent of old ale, smoke, and damp wood thick in the air. Shadows clung to the corners, where cloaked figures lingered in silence. A bartender wiped a chipped mug behind the bar, his sharp eyes flicking their way before offering a short nod. Near the hearth sat an older Awyan man, unmoving. His expression betrayed nothing, but it was clear, he had been waiting for them.

Oliver didn't slow.

"This way," he said under his breath, pulling Allora forward.

She took Lilly's hand and followed, boots muffled on worn floorboards. In the center of the room, a plain rug covered the wood. Oliver dropped, peeled it back, and revealed a thick iron hatch beneath. With a low groan, he hauled it open. A black passage yawned below them. Cold air rushed up from its depths.

Allora felt it in her bones, this was the real world. Not the parade. Not the palace.

Oliver climbed down the ladder, silent as ever. Allora gathered Lilly in her arms and followed, her fingers shaking as they gripped the metal rungs. With each step, the scent changed, smoke replaced by earth. Moisture. Rotting wood and lantern oil. She reached the bottom and turned. Her breath caught in her throat.

Candles cast a shimmering golden glow over the vastness of the chamber, their light clinging to every curve of ancient stone, every rough-hewn beam above, every threadbare tent that crowded the uneven earth. The air was thick, alive with the scent of woodsmoke and fried onions, soap and sweat, old canvas and something sweetly metallic that might have been hope.

It was the hush, the undercurrent of voices, the fragile laughter of children echoing through the gloom, that made Allora's heart stutter. She couldn't move at first. She just stood, knees weak, staring at the impossible scene: not just survivors, humans. Real people. Dozens. No, a hundred at least. Skin of every shade, hair wild or shorn, faces open and battered, every one of them alive. A woman braided a little girl's hair, men argued over boiling water, a boy tossed a battered ball between his hands. For a moment, Allora felt herself splinter, shocked and brittle with disbelief, then surging with wild, hungry hope.

Lilly squeezed her hand, anchoring her.

"This home," she whispered, voice trembling with something like pride.

Allora wanted to believe it. She needed to. But something gnawed at the edges of her thoughts like teeth. Her eyes swept the crowd again, then dropped to Lilly's small, fierce face. *How the hell was she here?*

The last time Allora had seen her, Lilly had been in the High North, half-buried in snow, kept hidden under Leira's watchful gaze. There'd been no word, no sign. She wasn't supposed to be here. Could someone have brought her south? Rescued her from another group? Found her wandering alone like the little nomad she was?

Allora bent down, fingers tightening around the girl's arms. Her voice was low, serious.

"Lilly... how did you get here?"

The child's mouth parted, a flicker of guilt, or maybe hesitation, flashing in her eyes. She drew in a breath to speak, but then it hit. A voice cracked through the air like thunder, sudden and sharp. Familiar. Commanding. Allora froze, her entire body going rigid. She knew that voice. It cut through the noise like a blade, deeper than thunder, rich with authority and memory.

A voice others feared, but to her, it had always been a lighthouse in the dark.

"ATTENTION! MAJOR MELODIE JAXXON!"

The name slammed into her like a detonation and she forgot everything else. Melodie. Not Allora. Not little dove. Not a number in a ledger. Not property. Her name. The name born of her mother's sweat and her father's pride. The name etched into her dog tags, spoken in respect, not ownership. It tore through every wall she'd built, every lie she'd choked down to survive.

Memories surged, polished boots on concrete, mess hall laughter, her father's firm hand squeezing her shoulder with pride. Her chest convulsed. Lanternlight spun. Faces turned. Her world tilted and blurred at the edges. She couldn't breathe. Hope and panic tangled in her throat like wire, wild and alive and impossible to silence.

She turned, feeling as fragile as spun glass, as breakable as memory. The crowd parted, no words, no hesitation, as if the entire chamber felt the moment blooming open.

He stood in the circle of lamplight, a silhouette made colossal by grief and longing. Broad shoulders, perfect posture, boots planted square, military to the marrow. A man carved from iron and storms. The lamplight caught the silver in his hair, the rows of medals and the hard, beloved lines of his face. Henry Jaxxon, Colonel Jaxxon, her father.

Their eyes met, and it was like coming up for air after drowning.

Her heart broke. Her knees finally failed. A raw, ugly sob clawed out of her throat, somewhere between a gasp and a wail. Before she even knew what she was doing, her legs took her to him, arms flung open, desperate, wild.

She crashed against his chest, burying her face in his uniform. He caught her, strong and sure, his arms wrapping her up, pulling her off her feet, holding her tight. Just like always. She breathed him in, the scent of sweat and starch and the adamant safety of home. For one blessed moment, she was not lost, not prisoner, not hunted. She was just Melodie. Just his little girl.

> "Daddy," she sobbed, voice shattering, childlike, everything she'd kept dammed for years bursting out in a single, broken word. "Daddy!"

He held her, unyielding, like if he let go the world might end. She clung to him, fists tight in the coarse fabric, as if she could anchor herself here, against the one person who had always, always come for her. And as she shook, crying, she didn't care that everyone was looking. Didn't care that she'd never be free, not really, not from the world or from Malec.

But for this moment, she was home.

His arms closed around her, impossibly strong, and for the first time in years she let herself collapse. He pulled her in, enveloping her small, shaking body in a fortress of muscle and memory. His hand, rough and warm, cupped the back of her head, holding her close as if he could shield her from every horror she'd endured. She could feel it, his chest was trembling, the deep, uneven rhythm of his breath rattling through both of them. He was shaking just as hard as she was.

> "You're safe now, baby girl," he whispered, his voice thick, ragged with tears he'd never let anyone else see. "You're safe. I've got you. I've got you."

The words broke her open. Allora's sobs doubled, her face crushed against the crisp, familiar starch of his uniform. The scent of gun oil, old leather, the faint tang of aftershave she'd known her whole life, it wrapped around her, filling her lungs, pushing out everything else. Fear, anger, shame, loss, none of it mattered. Her father was here. He had come for her. Against all odds, he'd survived, and he'd found her.

She tightened her grip on him, clawing at the fabric, needing him solid and real. And for one sacred heartbeat, Allora let herself believe that maybe, just maybe, she could be a daughter again.

That maybe this nightmare could end. That love could reach through stone and cages and time, and bring her home.

Chapter 27

The Fox's Trap

S he sobbed, loud, raw, unfiltered, the kind of weeping that tore straight from the soul, uncaring of eyes or witnesses or pride. Her breath hitched violently as she shook in his embrace, knees folding beneath her. She would have crashed to the stone floor, undone by the weight of it all, but he caught her. Held her. Not just steady, but whole, arms banded tight around her as if by clutching her close, he could bind together every piece that had ever broken.

> "Melodie," he whispered, the word thick and battered, echoing off stone walls and the inside of her skull. "Melodie... Melodie..."

He said it again and again, reverent as a prayer, desperate as a lifeline, like by speaking it he could pull her out of every darkness, could call back the girl who'd gone missing inside a cage. With every repetition, it became an anchor, dragging her up from the depths, out of the numb fog, back into her body, her name, her purpose. She gripped him harder, fists twisting in the fabric of his uniform, nails biting in, needing the solid press of him, the proof that he was real, that she was real. That this, this moment, was not some fever-dream conjured by loneliness or hope.

Melodie. Not Allora. Not a thing, not a captive. Melodie Jaxxon. The soldier. The daughter. The one who'd survived. She was still here. She'd made it.

> "I thought, I thought I'd never see you again," she managed, her voice cracked and jagged as broken glass.

"I know," he breathed, crushing her even tighter, the words fierce and trembling.

"I know, baby girl. But I got you. I got you. Never again. Never."

The promise in his voice was ironclad, a vow, a shield, everything a father's love could become.

She pressed her face to his chest, breathing in the scent of metal and leather and that stubborn old cologne that clung to him, familiar as old photographs. For the first time in years, she let it all fall, the armor, the weight, the act. She let herself break, because finally, finally, he was here to hold the pieces. Maybe this was real. Maybe the nightmare was cracking. Her people were alive. Her father's arms were around her. And she, was Melodie Jaxxon again. For this one, impossible moment, the world made sense. The ache in her chest loosened. She could breathe.

Colonel Jaxxon stepped back, just a little, never far, his broad hand still cupping her elbow protectively. His eyes swept over her with that clinical, tactical sharpness she knew by heart, a soldier's appraisal, exact and rigid. For an instant, she almost laughed. Even here, even now, he was still the father who inspected every inch of her, looking for wounds, for weakness, for the proof that she had made it home in one piece.

Only this time, she was the mission.

His arm slid around her shoulders again, grounding her in that firm, fatherly grip. His frame still radiated tension, an edge of protectiveness that hadn't dulled despite the years. He had crossed dimensions, continents, possibly worlds to get to her. And now that he had her, it was clear he didn't intend to let go anytime soon. Oliver stood nearby, locked in conversation with a small group of US army soldiers. Strategizing, coordinating. Preparing for whatever came next. The underground chamber was alive with movement and whispered voices.

Somewhere to her left, Lilly still clung to her sleeve like a lifeline.

But Melodie couldn't focus on any of it. Something cold slithered up her spine. A pressure. A prickle. A whisper that didn't touch her ears.

"Hello, dark one."

Her body locked. She hadn't heard it. She had felt it. The voice coiled in her mind like a familiar snake, smooth and sharp and full of amused menace. Her head snapped up, searching, scanning, and landed on him.

Surin.

He was standing near the far wall like he'd been there the whole time. Like he belonged there. Tall, immaculate, his white hair braided with silver thread, his long coat unwrinkled and regal. Of course. Even at the edge of a rebellion's safehouse, he looked like he owned the building. Her heart slammed once, a hard kick against her ribs, then plummeted, cold and heavy, to the pit of her stomach.

Instantly, her father's hand shifted, off her shoulder, sliding down to her wrist, fingers closing around it in that old, protective grip. He didn't raise his voice or tense his jaw, not outwardly, but Melodie could feel the change in him, a coiled readiness. The soldier in him recognized danger before the man had to name it.

"Melodie," he began carefully, his tone pitched low and cautious, "there's someone I'd like you to meet, "

But she wasn't looking at him. She was staring, unblinking, at the figure hovering just beyond the lantern glow. All the warmth in her chest turned to ice. Her fingers curled unconsciously around her father's sleeve.

"I know who he is," she said quietly, her voice hard and flat, no confusion, no uncertainty, just a sharp, brittle certainty.

Her father caught the shift instantly. His body went taut, posture sharpening, the old instinct kicking in, the one that scanned for exits and threats and cover all at once. He leaned just slightly into her, his body forming a barrier.

"Should I be concerned?" he murmured, voice barely more than a rumble meant only for her.

Melodie's gaze never left Surin's pale form. Her mouth went dry.

"You should be careful," she whispered, throat tight. "He let all of this happen. He's not our friend."

It was enough. She saw her father's jaw clench, his focus narrowing in on the Awyan male standing too casually in the half-light, silver hair shining like a blade in the shadows. Then, suddenly, a voice, not spoken, but pressed cold and silken straight into their minds. He couldn't speak their language so mindspeech was the only way he could communicate with the foreign Canariae called humans.

"Ah. So we're speaking of my son."

The intrusion made Melodie's breath hitch. Her body snapped rigid, fight or flight lighting every nerve.

"Your son?" Colonel Jaxxon's verbal reply was hard, defensive, recoiling from the psychic trespass.

"Yes, yes," came Surin's cultured voice, drifting through their thoughts as if they were all gathered at some elegant dinner. *"That wild, mad dog of a boy. Malec. Always so intense about what he thinks is his. Beautiful face. Terrible instincts. Quite the storm, that one."*

The words slithered through Melodie's mind, cold and familiar as regret. Her spine locked. She squeezed her father's wrist, grounding herself, knowing the storm wasn't over. Not by a long shot. Melodie's stomach churned. He said Malec's name like it was a joke. Like everything Malec had done was just a bad habit or an embarrassing sonnet.

Her throat tightened. Her fists clenched.

"You knew," she shot back mentally, her voice shaking. *"You knew what he was doing to me. And you let it happen."*

Surin's pale eyes slid toward her, expression cryptic.

"And what would you have me do?" he replied. *"Command him? Restrain him? You think I hold the leash on a creature like that?"* He gave a dry mental chuckle, and Melodie's teeth ached from grinding. *"No one controls Malec. Not me. Not your rebellion. Not even himself. And you know that."*

"You could've tried," she snapped.

"And destroy his devotion? He would burn cities for you. You think you're his prisoner, but I assure you, child... he's just as trapped."

Melodie's voice dropped dangerously low, her words now spoken aloud in crisp, fluent Awyan. "He tortured me."

Surin's gaze flicked toward her like a blade unsheathed. He responded not aloud, but only to her, mentally, intimately.

"Didn't you?" he purred into her mind. *"Didn't you encourage him? Didn't you use him?"*

Her chest constricted. The words slammed into the raw, tender place she'd buried beneath rage.
"So you're just gonna victim-blame now? That your angle, Surin?"
He tilted his head, brows lifting faintly, as though just now remembering who he was playing with. Ahh, right. Allora... no, Melodie now.

"You always were harder to bend than the rest. And far less delicate than you looked."

Her fingers curled, nails digging into her palms.
Across from them, Colonel Jaxxon looked between the two, sensing the psychic silence that had overtaken them. The way her breathing had changed. The stiffness in her posture. His eyes narrowed, sharp as flint.

He didn't speak, but she could feel the shift. He knew something was wrong.

Surin straightened then, brushing off the tension like dust from his sleeves. His voice returned to their shared mental channel.

"Relax, Colonel. We are all family now, aren't we?"

Col. Jaxxon bristled, but before he could say a word, before Melodie could retort, a rustle swept through the room. Footsteps. Familiar. Melodie turned. A blue cloak slipped through the crowd. The hood lowered.

Surian. And draped across her shoulders, heavy, regal, unmistakable, was his cloak. The midnight-blue one. The one Malec had wrapped around Melodie's own shoulders the night of the parade. The one lined with silver threading and his scent. The one they'd stripped off her and tossed over a decoy to throw off any followers.

Now it hung from Surian like a war banner. Her stomach twisted.

"You..." she breathed, taking a cautious step forward. "That was you... in the crowd."

Surian met her gaze and gave a slow, solemn nod. "It was the fastest way to get you out without being followed. I had to wear the cloak to lead the guards away.

They chased me instead of you."

Melodie blinked hard. The image of the Red Canary twirling someone in her cloak, the guards watching silently, letting her go, came rushing back with clarity.

It hadn't just been a trick. It had been Surian. She was the shadow that took Melodie's place. The distraction. The reason Malec hadn't come charging after her through the crowd.

"You wore his cloak..." Melodie whispered, her voice thick.

"To protect you," Surian said simply. "It worked."

Melodie swallowed hard, her chest tightening as she stared at the Awyan maiden in front of her, Malec's sister. The same elfess she had once assumed was part of the system that caged her. Polished. Regal. Untouchable. And yet here she was, standing in the middle of an underground resistance, cloaked in stolen deception, pride tucked beneath humility.

"You risked yourself," Melodie said, stunned. "For me."

Surian arched a brow and crossed her arms. "You sound surprised."

"I am," Melodie admitted, breathless. "I... I didn't know you cared."

Surian looked down, her cheeks flushing ever so slightly. "Well... I do."

Silence bloomed between them, soft and charged.

Then Melodie smiled, a real, flickering thing, and said, "I misjudged you. I'm sorry."

Surian rolled her eyes, but the corners of her mouth curved. "Yeah, well. Happens a lot."

They stood there, two daughters of two very different worlds, bound by rebellion and consequence. And for the first time, Melodie felt something unfamiliar toward Surian. Respect but still cautious.

"I don't think I fully understand," Melodie said slowly, her eyes narrowing, voice tight with confusion and suspicion.

Everything felt like it was shifting beneath her feet, like the rules of the game had changed mid-play and no one had told her.

Surian exhaled, arms crossing over her chest with a quiet confidence that startled Melodie more than her words. "I started this."

The words landed like a slap. Melodie's spine straightened, a chill creeping over her skin.

"...Started what?" she asked, breath barely a whisper.

Surian's expression didn't falter. "The underground Canariae rescue network," she said simply. "My father and I. We built it together."

Melodie's heart stuttered. Her breath hitched, the walls of the hidden chamber closing in. She turned to Surin, her mouth parted in shock, and the male elf just nodded, as though this weren't a revelation that shattered the laws of everything she'd come to understand about this realm. Surian gave a half-shrug and a long, pointed sigh.

"Don't look so surprised. You've met me. Do I really strike you as someone who gives a damn about outdated Awyan purity laws or noble traditions?"

Melodie's mouth opened, then closed. Then opened again.

Because she hadn't. Not once. Not even when she'd first laid eyes on her in the palace, dressed in her silks and ribbons. Surian had been sharp-tongued and too observant for a princess. There had been no coldness in her eyes. No sense of entitlement. She had never once called her 'little dove' or looked at her with disgust. Not like Malec. Not like the others.

But this? This was a hell of a leap.

"You've been helping Canariae escape," Melodie murmured, her voice cracked with awe. "This entire time."

"For years," Surian confirmed.

Her voice didn't carry pride, but there was steel in it. She wasn't asking for praise. She didn't need it.

Melodie's brows drew together. "...And Malec doesn't know?"

Surian barked a laugh. "Oh, he suspects. But Malec is blinded by his own ego. He thinks I spend my days painting my nails and plotting marriages, not leading a rebellion. He doesn't believe I'm capable of something this large, so he doesn't look too closely."

Her smirk curled as she leaned back against the wall. "Which is exactly why I'm the perfect person to run it."

Melodie stared at her like she was looking at her for the first time. Because maybe she was. All this time, she'd been terrified of the wrong Talandros.

"...Holy shit," she breathed, hands falling to her sides.

Surian smiled. "Yeah. Holy shit indeed."

Melodie shook her head in disbelief, then turned sharply to Surin. Her voice sharpened with accusation.

"And you just let her?"

Surin didn't flinch. He leaned against a carved post and regarded her with that infuriating calm.

"Let her?" His voice was laced with dry amusement. "My dear little dove, I encouraged it."

Melodie's jaw tightened, biting down on the rise of frustration threatening to spill from her throat. Good god, he was so damn smug. Surin wore that aristocratic arrogance like a tailored cloak, every word from his mouth laced with knowing superiority, as though he were always three moves ahead, always holding the strings. But she couldn't spiral into that now. Not with her father standing beside her, not with so much still at stake.

Colonel Jaxxon had been silent, impassive this entire time. But now, his voice finally broke through the tense air, low, steady, and filled with the kind of quiet danger that made trained soldiers take a step back.

"...And why," he said slowly, eyes hard as flint, "should we trust either of you?"

His words weren't a question. They were a challenge.

Surian and Surin both turned to him at once, their faces shifting, hers to steel, his to something more neutral, though the gleam of pride in his eyes dimmed slightly. Melodie instinctively stepped in, translating the question for them in perfect Awyan, her voice clipped.

The moment stretched. Then, for the first time since arriving, Surin's smirk faltered. His expression settled into something more measured.

> "Because," Surian said evenly, stepping forward until she stood eye to eye with the colonel, "this entire operation exists because of us. Because we are the only Awyans willing to stand between the empire and the Canariae they've stolen. Because we're the only ones in power who are willing to burn that power to the ground if it means stopping them."

Her words rang out, clear and unwavering.

Melodie watched her father carefully as she translated, saw the way his shoulders straightened and his gaze sharpened. He was measuring her, dissecting everything from the tremorless conviction in her tone to the fire buried behind her calm façade.

And then, slowly, deliberately, he gave a single, tight nod. It wasn't approval. Not yet. But it was recognition. A warrior to another. A strategist acknowledging a worthy ally.

Melodie exhaled a breath she hadn't realized she'd been holding.

While Surian and Colonel Jaxxon stood across the room, still locked in a silent exchange of guarded stares and unspoken threats, Surin drifted closer, too quiet, too smooth. Melodie didn't notice him at first. Not until his voice brushed the edge of her awareness like silk laced with poison.

"So... your Canariae name is *Mehl-O-Dee*?"

She blinked. Her head snapped toward him, eyes narrowing.

"It's just Melodie," she said sharply. "That's my only name."

Surin's lips curled into something that might've been a smile if it hadn't looked so amused at her expense. His bright blue eyes danced with that familiar mischief she'd come to associate with menace.

"Mm. A name too elegant for a wild little bird like you," he murmured, his voice low and teasing.

Melodie exhaled through her nose, jaw tightening.

"Is there something you actually want," she asked, "or are you just here to climb up my ass?"

Surin feigned offense, placing a hand over his chest. "Only to share my... profound disappointment," he sighed. "You see, I had so many expectations. My son is hopelessly obsessed with you, and I was quite looking forward to having you as a daughter-in-law."

Her stomach turned. Not just at the words, but the casual way he said them. As though she were just another political tie, another inheritance to broker.

"If you want your lunatic of a son to have a wife," she said coldly, "then find him one. That isn't me."

Surin's hum was almost sympathetic. "Yes, well. We both know he won't want another."

She flinched at that. She hated that it was true. He leaned closer, the edge of his voice darkening.

"The difference between you and my son is this, Malec is willing to wait a lifetime. You are not."

Her breath caught. Her mouth opened, but no words came. Because he was right. She didn't have the luxury of lifetimes. Not when she was running for her life. Not when time had already taken too much. But she recovered fast, straightening.

"Well, I'm going home," she snapped. "So I guess we won't have to worry about it."

Surin nodded slowly. "Indeed."

She started to turn, ready to shut down whatever mind game he was playing, but then she paused. Her brow furrowed. Something about his voice had changed. It was too calm. Too easy. And that wasn't sitting right.

She faced him again, eyes narrowing. "Why do you care what Malec wants?"

Surin blinked, surprised. "I beg your absolute pardon?"

"You act like he's a pawn on your board," she pressed, stepping in closer. "You mock him. You dismiss him. I've never once seen you show him any affection. So why the hell do you care?"

His smile faltered. A flicker of something, intelligible, subtle, almost human, passed through his expression. His gaze didn't meet hers right away. When it did, the glint of amusement was gone.

"Because," he said slowly, "he's my son."

Melodie stared. Waiting. That couldn't be all.

Surin exhaled through his nose, his voice quieter now, more distant.

"He was born for greatness. Trained for cruelty. Molded into what our empire demanded. And I let it happen."

There it was. The honesty she hadn't expected.

"I love him," Surin said, and for once, it didn't sound like a performance. "But I've never been allowed to show it. Not in our world. Not with my name. Affection is weakness. And weakness is blood in the water."

Melodie swallowed hard, heart aching in places she didn't realize still had sympathy for the man she had run from.

"You're afraid," she said softly, "that losing me will destroy him."

He didn't answer. But his eyes said everything. And in that silence, awkward, heavy, real, Melodie saw it. For the first time. The mask slipping. The father behind the politician. The grief behind the smugness.

She didn't forgive him. But she understood.

Melodie stared at Surin a moment longer, something soft and reluctant flickering in her eyes. She saw him, really saw him, not as the shadowy puppet master behind the throne, not as the smug noble manipulating everyone like chess pieces, but as a father. A broken one. And though her heart ached with the complicated weight of everything between them, it wasn't enough.

> "You do love him," she murmured, more to herself than to him. "But unfortunately..." She turned toward him fully now, arms folded, voice sharp with quiet conviction. "You're the one who withheld love and affection. You're the one who created the monster." Surin's gaze flicked up, his expression concealed. But she didn't stop. "That's not my burden to carry. It's not my job to fix what you broke. It never was."

A beat of silence passed. Heavy. Honest. Surin nodded slowly. "No. It is not."

> Melodie's mouth twitched, not quite a smile, not quite sympathy. "You should've taught him how to talk to girls," she muttered. "Especially the ones he liked. Who knows? Maybe this whole nightmare would've turned out completely different."

And before he could answer, she stepped in and gave him a light, playful punch on the arm. It wasn't hard, but it landed. Surin's lips parted in mild shock, then closed again. He blinked. He hadn't expected her to do that. But the tension between them thinned, just a little. Still, the truth sat with him like a stone in his throat.

Melodie wasn't cruel. But she was clear. She wasn't staying. And the part of him that had once allowed himself to hope, just maybe, that she would remain, that she could one day wear their colors and sit at his family table... that part of him finally accepted what he had always known: she, like Malec, was born of fire and war and something ancient and wild. And holding on to something like her would only end in ruin.

So he did the only thing left. He let go. But not without a final, lingering glance, a flicker of rare longing in those frost-blue eyes. A father's regret. A dream unfulfilled.

And maybe... a quiet blessing.

Colonel Jaxxon cleared his throat, a sharp sound that cut through the murmur of quiet conversations and redirected every eye in the room to him. His voice, steady and commanding, filled the chamber like a war drum.

"All right. Let's go over the plan."

Melodie straightened instinctively beside him, the old military cadence in his voice grounding her.

> "We'll be sneaking out under the cover of darkness. Western trade route," he continued, pacing in front of the group. "It's less guarded and dense with civilian traffic. There's a convoy leaving at dawn, we'll blend in, merge, and once we're clear of the Capitol walls, we break off. From there, we head straight to the caves."

Murmurs of understanding spread across the gathered Canariae. Some clung to hope. Others gripped fear. But all of them listened. Melodie turned to translate for Surin and Surian, her voice quick and fluid in Awyan. Surin offered only a distracted nod; Surian listened closely.

> "How far are these caves?" one of the runaways asked, their voice thin with worry.

> "Three days on foot," the Colonel replied. "Two if we push hard."

Melodie opened her mouth, then hesitated, heart racing. Her fingers curled at her sides. She hadn't told them yet. Not all of them. And Eron, her brother...

"Daddy," she said quietly, cutting through the logistics. "How is Eron? Is he still... is he still holding on?"

The room went still again. The Colonel didn't answer right away. His shoulders stiffened, jaw tightening before he turned toward her.

"He's fighting," he said finally. "But the virus is moving fast. We're out of options. It's only a matter of time."

Melodie's heart clenched. That was all she needed to hear. No more waiting. She stepped forward, voice rising with calm but unflinching strength.

"The virus," she said. "The Cotard Virus, I have the antibodies. In my bloodstream."

Every head turned. Silence crashed over the room like a wave. For a heartbeat, even the lanterns seemed to flicker in response.

Col. Jaxxon went rigid beside her. Surin's head tilted, interest sparking behind his eyes.

"Wait, what?" her father said, blinking.

Melodie inhaled slowly, then repeated herself in Awyan so Surin and Surian could follow: "I have the antibodies. My blood can fight the virus. It already has."

Gasps rippled among the others. Even Oliver turned, brows furrowed with shock.

The Colonel growled, gaze hardening. "You're telling me you're the cure?"

Melodie met his stare. "Yes. But there's more. I found out the truth about the virus."

She turned again, addressing the entire room.

> "The Cotard Virus originated here, in this realm. I think the humans here... came from our world. Somehow. A long time ago."

Even Surian blinked, stunned. Her mouth parted as though to speak, but nothing came. Col. Jaxxon looked like the ground had opened beneath his boots. His fingers flexed at his sides. Years of war. Years of watching everything collapse. And now... this?

"How?" he whispered hoarsely. "How did you get the antibodies?"

Melodie looked at Surin. Then back at her father. "They came from Surin's son."

The room tensed like a stretched wire. The Colonel's expression darkened instantly. His eyes burned as they locked on Surin.

"Malec," he spat, like it left a foul taste in his mouth.

Melodie nodded. "More specifically... his bloodline."

A stunned silence filled the room as every gaze shifted slowly toward the Awyan nobles. Melodie's father sharpened his tone like a blade.

"Is this true?"

Melodie spoke quickly in Awyan now, translating for Surin and Surian.

Surian's lips pursed, arms folded over her chest. "It is."

> Surin ran a hand through his long, white braid and gave a theatrical sigh and spoke mentally so Jaxxon could understand him. *"Though I find it deeply irritating to admit my son is good for anything other than lighting the world on fire... yes. It's true."*

Melodie watched the crowd, watched the flicker of hope rise behind weary, desperate eyes. This was the moment. Her truth. Their turning point. And for the first time since waking in this realm, she was the one with the power. Not Malec. Not the nobles. Not the virus.

Her. Melodie Jaxxon. The cure. Melodie met her father's eyes, heart pounding, breath steady. There was no easy way to say it. No version of this truth that wouldn't make his jaw clench and his blood pressure spike.

"I contracted the virus on purpose," she said quietly, but without flinching.

The Colonel's face darkened. A visible storm gathered behind his eyes.

"I knew if I got sick, Malec wouldn't let me die," she went on. "He'd give me his blood."

There was a sharp intake of breath, someone gasped. But it was her father who reacted most violently.

"Damn it, Mel!" he exploded, the curse biting through the air like a whip. Several people flinched.

"You gambled your life?" His voice rose, cracking at the edges with disbelief and rage. "Do you even understand what that means? What that risk was?"

"I *won,*" she said, cutting him off.
He froze, mouth still open. She stared him down.

"I won," she said again, firmer this time. "I survived. And now I'm the only one with antibodies strong enough to cure the virus. The only one."

A heavy silence fell over the room, pressing down like wet ash. The others looked at her with wide eyes, some horrified, some awed. Oliver shifted his weight, his brow pinched in a grim frown. Even her father, furious and trembling, couldn't speak.

Surian's voice broke the silence.

"You said you're the only one?" she repeated, her arms crossed, her silver-gray eyes narrowing with sharp intelligence.

Melodie nodded once. "I think it's because I wasn't born here. My body's different. My DNA isn't fully compatible with the virus the same way the people here are. I think the humans who've lived in this world for generations... they're too adapted. Their immune systems don't see the virus as much of a threat anymore."

Oliver cursed softly under his breath. "That means..."
Colonel Jaxxon ran a calloused hand down his face. His jaw locked.

"That means if anything happens to you," he said, low and hoarse, "we lose everything. Humanity is done."

Melodie's breath caught. She hadn't let herself think about it in those terms, hadn't really felt the weight of it until now. If she died before making it back to Earth... there would be no second chance. No cure. No saving anyone.
Surin's voice cut in, smooth and irritatingly calm.

"Well, well," he murmured, as if observing a political drama unfold for amusement. "That certainly raises your value, doesn't it?"

Colonel Jaxxon's head snapped toward Surin so fast his neck cracked, eyes blazing with suspicion. But Surin hadn't spoken aloud. Melodie had. She hesitated, then translated, her voice tight.
"He said... 'That certainly raises your value, doesn't it?'"
Her father's glare could've melted steel. "He said what?"
Melodie nodded grimly. "That's exactly what he said."
Surin, watching the reaction, offered a graceful shrug, hands lifting in mock surrender, that ever-smug glint in his pale blue eyes. He said something else then, still in Awyan, tone calm, almost amused.

Melodie ground her teeth and translated. "He says, 'Merely an observation, Colonel. I may not be sentimental, but even I know a miracle when I see one.'"

His jaw flexed like he was fighting the urge to launch across the room and strangle him. His soldiers tensed behind him, but Melodie held up a hand.

"He's just trying to get a rise out of you," she muttered to her father. "Don't give him the satisfaction."

Surin only smiled wider at her response, clearly understanding enough to be amused by her restraint.

Melodie shot him a side-eye and muttered in Awyan, "Could you try not to be insufferable for once in your life?"

Surin winked. Her father didn't understand the words exchanged, but the tension was loud enough to translate on its own.

The Colonel didn't reply. He simply turned back to his daughter, still simmering with paternal fury.

"We're getting you home," he said. "Tonight. No more games. No more chances."

Around them, the room shifted, heads nodding, shoulders squaring with new purpose. They all understood now. Melodie was no longer just a survivor. She was the key to everything. But as the others began murmuring plans, Melodie's stomach coiled. Because they were all pretending not to see the one problem looming over them like a thundercloud.

Malec.

He wasn't going to let her go. He wouldn't care about the cure. About Earth. About humanity. He would come for her. And when he did, he'd burn the world to get her back.

The underground cellar buzzed with urgent preparation. Blankets were folded, food parcels bundled, children gently herded to sit quietly beside their parents. Nervous energy rippled through the cramped space like a current, too many people, too many questions, not enough certainty. The air was thick with fear, but also with the fragile thread of hope. Some Canariae still sat with their backs pressed to the walls, arms around trembling knees, as if afraid this was just another illusion. A cruel trick.

Melodie stood in the center of it all, a still point in the chaos. Her eyes scanned the scene, calculating, assessing, anchoring herself to the momentum of movement. She didn't help fold or fetch. She didn't speak much. She just breathed. One inhale, one exhale at a time. She was almost home. A voice cut through the hum.

"Hey, Melodie."

She turned, and there he was, Oliver. Hair wild, boots scuffed, looking like he'd just sprinted through a storm. His hands were stuffed deep in his pockets, but his eyes, they looked almost soft.

She raised her chin, giving him a small, tired smile. "Oliver."

He rubbed the back of his neck, glancing down. "Look, I just wanted to say, I'm sorry. I should've found you sooner. Should've gotten you out before it ever got that bad."

Melodie arched a brow. "You mean before I got sold into a castle like a show dog and locked in a golden cage?" Her voice was dry. "Yeah. That would've been nice."

He winced, but let out a chuckle. "Damn. When you put it like that..."

They shared a moment of bitter laughter. But then his expression sobered again.

"I mean it," Oliver said. "What they did to you... that collar... shit. I don't know how you didn't lose your mind."

Melodie's fingers instinctively reached up to touch the cool metal still around her throat. Her smile faded.

"I did," she said quietly. "A few times."

Oliver's gaze dropped for a second, like he couldn't bear to see her like that. Then he looked back up, jaw firming.

> "You handled it like a damn soldier," he said. "Hell, you handled it better than most generals I've served with. You're strong, Melodie. You've got that same fire your old man has, but you're even sharper. You're a survivor. And... I don't think I ever told you, but I'm proud of you."

The words hit harder than she expected. They carved something loose in her chest. All the times she'd fought, all the times she'd been alone, invisible, forgotten, suddenly this small gesture, this acknowledgement, felt like a thread tying her back to who she used to be.

"Thanks," she whispered, the lump in her throat almost too thick to speak around.

He smiled, a little sheepishly, and started to turn away. Then paused, one foot still trailing behind him.

> "Oh, one more thing," he said casually, as if he were just commenting on the weather. "Once we're through the portal... don't worry too much. We're blowing that shit sky high."

Melodie blinked. "What?"

> "Yeah," Oliver said, looking pleased with himself. "We've got it rigged. The cave, the whole thing. Once everyone's through, boom, rubble. Nothing left. No way for those elf freaks to get through. No more Awyans sneaking into our world, and no more of our people accidentally falling into theirs."

Her heart stopped. He didn't even notice. He just nodded to her like he'd done a good job, then walked off, vanishing into the chaos of the cellar like a pebble dropped in water. Melodie stood frozen, unable to breathe. *Blow up the portal? Cut off the worlds?* She was the only one who had made it back. The only one who had survived. And now they were going to seal the door behind her?

No. Not just seal it. Destroy it. A part of her, small, buried, bruised, ached. Because even though she should have been celebrating, even though this was what she told herself she wanted, the finality of it caught her off guard.

It meant no one else could follow. It meant... Malec would never reach her. It meant whatever they were, whatever they had been, was over. Permanently. She closed her eyes, forcing the pain down deep into the place where she kept all the other unspeakable things. Then slowly, deliberately, she turned her head and nodded once to no one in particular.

"Good," she said aloud. Then she walked away. Because there was only one thing left to do now.

Go home. And never look back.

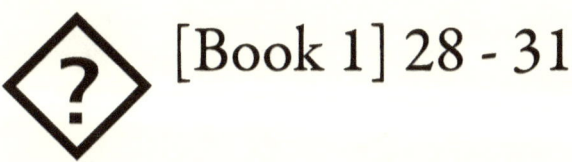 [Book 1] 28 - 31

Chapter 28

Choyte

Everything had gone according to plan. Not a single hitch. They had moved flawlessly, like a machine oiled by desperation and genius. It was textbook. Clean. Too clean.

Melodie clenched her jaw as she tossed a final heap of damp earth onto the fire pit, watching the embers sizzle and hiss. Her boots scraped the frozen ground, dirt caked beneath her nails. She should have felt relieved. Free. Triumphant.

But instead, her heart was pounding in her ears.

That madman had found her in a dense forest once. In the middle of a storm. In the dark. He'd tracked her through rivers, snow, and entire cities. He'd smelled her skin in a crowd. He'd known her presence before she even stepped into a room.

Malec had always found her. Always. So why hadn't he now?

She swallowed thickly, turning toward the others. Her father sat near the stream, sharpening a blade with practiced calm, and Surian knelt beside the horses, tightening their saddlebags with cold precision. The others bustled about the camp, cooking, whispering, comforting the children, but none of them noticed the way Melodie stood frozen, as if waiting for something to crash down.

A slow, slithering thought wound through her gut.

He was a master tracker. A predator of impossible discipline. And they hadn't exactly hidden. They'd moved in a convoy, for god's sake. Blending in with clowns and sword-swallowers was clever, but it wasn't invisible. And then there were the pangs.

Twice now, since the escape, she'd felt something. First during the festival, just after the firelight hit the parade route and she caught a strange chill. Then again in her sleep, hours ago, an odd, internal tug. Not pain, exactly. But awareness.

Her hands clenched into fists just as a silk-smooth voice slithered through her mind.

"Why don't you feel relieved?"

Melodie jolted. "Oh, fuck no," she muttered aloud.

Across the camp, Colonel Jaxxon raised an eyebrow from where he sat cleaning his blade beside another fire.

"Language, young lady. I didn't raise you that way."

Melodie didn't miss a beat. "Got a splinter," she said dryly.

He didn't look up.

"Then stop being sloppy and pay attention."

She rolled her eyes. Classic Dad. Melodie nearly bared her teeth, but held it in, grinding her teeth.

"Get out of my head, Surin," she snapped mentally.

"Can't help it," he drawled. *"You're practically screaming across the link. It's like being shouted at through a conch shell."*

She winced. *"You are such a gnat."*

"Careful," Surin chuckled, *"or I'll tell your father you're cursing again."*

"Damn it," she muttered.

"Tsk."

But then the teasing dropped.

"You're worried," he said, quieter now. *"Because something doesn't feel right. I agree."*

She said nothing.

"He should've found you by now. That much, I admit."

She closed her eyes, forcing a slow breath.

"...I've been feeling something," she admitted silently. *"Like... pulses. Inside. Like a, tug."*

A pause.

"The tether."

Her breath stopped, *"...What?"*

"The Vash'telor," Surin said, voice softer than she'd ever heard it. *"When you and Malec... bonded, that night in the North... you created something. A link. It doesn't fade. Not really. It sleeps. It quiets. But it never dies completely. And it works both ways."*

Melodie's chest squeezed. *"So that's how he found me. Every time."*

"He doesn't need signs, little dove," Surin murmured mentally. *"He only needs you."*

A silence stretched between them. Her thoughts were a tangle of denial and memory, Malec's hand on her throat, his voice like broken thunder: *You're mine.*

She had thought he meant ownership. She hadn't realized he meant forever.

"...Then why hasn't he come?" she asked aloud in her head. *"Why is he letting me go?"*

Surin's reply was slow.

"I do not know. Perhaps something has dulled the bond like distance. Or perhaps... he's waiting."

She stiffened. *"Waiting?"*

"Letting you think you've slipped free," he said with a note of dread. *"Letting you run just far enough... that you'll stop looking over your shoulder. And when you do, he'll yank the chain."*

She shook her head. *"No. He wouldn't, he wouldn't let me risk the portal. He'd want to stop me."*

"Unless," Surin mused, *"he wants you to get to the portal."*
Her stomach dropped. *"What?"*

"He's patient. He's been trained in obsession. And if he truly means to own you... he might be planning to reclaim you in your world, on your soil. Where you feel safest, or before you get there."

She felt nauseous. *"No."*

"Then tell me why else he hasn't come."

She had no answer. Her blood went cold.

And still, there was Lilly. And the Capitol. And the lack of resistance. Everything had gone too right.

She thought of that night again, Malec's mouth against her collarbone, his breath warm as he whispered, *"I'll always find you."* She had thought it a threat. Now she realized, it was a promise. Her stomach turned. Melodie looked up at the trees. She no longer felt like she was walking to freedom. She felt like she was walking into a carefully spun web.

And still she couldn't quite figure out how Lilly ended up there with their group.

"You know something," Surin's voice coiled through her mind again, too smooth, too certain.

Melodie gritted her teeth. *"I don't know shit,"* she snapped back, keeping her eyes on the bundle of firewood she was stacking.

"Oh?" he drawled. *"Then why are you so uneasy?"*

"Maybe I just don't like your annoying ass voice in my brain."

"No, no. This is different." His tone turned sly. *"You're worried. Frightened."*

Her hands flexed around the chunk of wood in her palms. Goddamnit, he was relentless.

"Oh," he added with a mental grin. *"Or maybe you just miss my son?"*

That did it. Something primal snapped. Without a word, Melodie spun, grabbed the heaviest log within reach, and hurled it with vicious precision. It cracked against the tree trunk less than an inch from Surin's head with a deep, satisfying thud. The older elf yelped and toppled backward off the stump he'd been lounging on, landing flat in the dirt with a grunt. Dead silence followed. Every eye at the camp turned. Even Colonel Jaxxon paused mid-sharpening, blinking like he wasn't sure if he'd just witnessed a murder attempt or divine intervention.

Oliver, standing nearby with his arms full of supplies, slowly raised a brow. "...Uh. What the hell was that?"

Melodie brushed off her hands coolly, not missing a beat. "I saw a bug," she said with a shrug. "Right on his shoulder."

Still sprawled on the ground, Surin stared up at her, not in outrage or mockery, but with stunned, wide-eyed disbelief. No one had ever dared to throw something at him. Not like that. Not for fun. Melodie rolled her shoulders and smirked to herself, satisfied. For once, she'd managed to shut him up.

And from the look on his face, it was going to haunt him for a while. Unfortunately it didn't stop the mental gnat flying around in her thoughts.

"How rude!"

Surin's voice slithered through Melodie's skull like cold breath against the nape of her neck, irritating, smug, unbothered by the fact she'd nearly brained him with a log. Of course, that didn't shut him up. He was still yapping. Still brushing himself off like a wounded prince denied his throne, plucking imaginary dirt from his pristine tunic with a huff of offended dignity.

"I'll be sure to keep the 'M-word' out of future conversation," he added dryly, like the idea of mentioning Malec again might trigger another flying log to the face.

Melodie rolled her eyes so hard she saw her brain for a second. If only rage could ignite wood into flame, she wouldn't need to build the damn fire pit. But then, his tone shifted. Suddenly low, even. Unsettlingly earnest.

"Tell me... describe your last moments with him."

Melodie swallowed hard. *"He never left me alone. Not once. Even when I went to relieve myself, someone stood near the door. Always watching. Breathing down my neck. But the last thing he did... was let me dance with a stranger."*

Surin's entire posture changed. Like a hound catching scent. Like a warrior realizing they'd walked into a trap with their eyes wide open.

"What were you wearing?" he asked suddenly, sharply on his mental pathway. *"At the festival. That cloak, where did you get it?"*

Melodie blinked. *"The one I have now? It's his. They gave it to Surian to throw off the scent."*

Surin's eyes narrowed. *"And what was he wearing?"*

She frowned. *"The long coat. The heavy one he uses when he hunts in the frost. It didn't make sense. It wasn't that cold, but he said I'd need mine later. That it would get worse with nightfall."*

Surin didn't answer. He didn't have to.

The expression on his face, tight-lipped, reckoning, glinting with the kind of cold realization that only came when your worst instincts started to whisper you missed something, was answer enough.

Then, it hit her. Melodie's hand flew to her pocket, her breath catching in her throat like a snare pulled tight.

"The last thing he did," she said still on the mental pathway, *"he gave me something."*

Surin's body went rigid. He was beside her in an instant, crouching low, his keen blue eyes locked on her pocket, on her trembling hands. The lightness in him vanished, replaced by something ancient and cold.

Wariness. Dread. Reverence for an adversary he feared more than he let on.

"Show me," he said out loud, his voice soft but lethal.

Melodie's fingers shook as she pulled the item free. A large cloth bundle, tightly folded. Neat. Intentional. The second it touched air, Surin flinched. His aura flared like a predator scenting blood. He didn't even try to hide it. She felt it roll off him like frostbite, warning her. Bracing her.

"Open it," he commanded, almost too calm.

Melodie's fingers worked at the knot, slower than she meant to, heart pounding now so hard she could barely hear over it. The cloth came apart, layer by layer, until finally, the contents spilled into her lap. Dried meat. Fruit. Cheese. Flatbread. Rations. Survival food. Her mouth moved like it wanted to curse but thought better of it. No words came out. Surin didn't speak either. They stared at it. At what it meant. At the simplicity of it, and the implications behind it.

Melodie's mind reeled. Her eyes scanned the bundle, then drifted to the thick cloak hugging her shoulders. The same one she'd worn at the festival. The same one she hadn't remembered packing. The same one that reeked of pine, leather, and him.

Her voice came out low, numb. "Was Malec... preparing me for my journey?"

Her hands trembled.

"Is that why I have food? Why I'm warm? Why everything went so damn smoothly?"

She looked at Surin. His face had gone taut with something dangerous, something bordering sorrow. He didn't speak at first. Just watched her, calculating. Pitying. Then he gave a shallow nod. Melodie felt her stomach turn over. She clutched the bundle like it might anchor her, keep her from spiraling.

"He let me go," she said out loud, trying to believe it.

Her voice cracked.

"He let me go... right?"

Surin's eyes darkened, lashes lowering over the blue fire of his gaze.

He exhaled, and in a voice as dry as bone and cold as winter, he muttered, "A mad dog always chases his bone."

And just like that, the bottom dropped out of her world. Melodie's vision blurred. Her hands loosened. The bundle slipped onto the ground.

No. No, this wasn't real. This wasn't happening. She'd escaped. She'd escaped. Hadn't she? Her mind whirled. She pressed her hands against her skull as though she could crush the thoughts trying to claw through. He'd dressed her for the cold. He'd fed her. He'd let her go. Her eyes snapped wide, horror crashing through her like a blade sliding into her gut.

"Why," she whispered, voice sharp and trembling, "was Malec wearing his fur coat and hunting boots?"

Surin's entire posture changed. The air went deathly still. He didn't blink. His voice dropped to a whisper of dread.

"Because those," he said, "are the clothes he uses to track down on long journeys. He is hunting."

The words gutted her. Melodie stumbled backward, dizzy, clutching her cloak like it was suddenly ablaze. Her breath came fast and shallow. Panic prickled her skin as her eyes swept across the camp, searching, scanning, until they locked onto one small figure by the fire.

Lilly.

That same quiet, sweet girl who had clung to her like a shadow since their escape from the Capitol. It didn't fit. It didn't make sense. Except, it did. God, it did. Melodie's heart dropped into her stomach.

How did I miss it? The thought sliced through her, vicious and cruel. *How the hell did I not see it?* She'd been so damn caught up in the rush of being surrounded by her unit, her father, her kind, so wrapped up in the comfort of familiarity, that she'd ignored the one thing that had been wrong the entire time. The Choyte. Lilly. The little traitor.

The signs had been there, hadn't they? Her silent slipping in and out of rooms. The way she always knew where to be, when to vanish. The odd timing. The eerie calm. Melodie had chalked it all up to trauma or luck or divine timing, anything but the truth. Because it had felt so good to have someone, anyone, who still looked at her like she was worth following.

Her mouth opened before she could stop it. Her expression twisted, words choking in her throat.

"Lilly can't be here by accident."

Surin turned toward her sharply, already catching on. "Who is Lilly?"

Melodie could barely force the words past her throat.

"The little girl. She's with our group. She was there. At the fortress. When I first met Malec. I helped her escape. Luko... Luko told me, she's a Choyte."

Surin's face went bone white. Everything in him went rigid, his spine straightening like a blade drawn.

"A *choyte?*" His voice cracked into something between rage and disbelief. "You canariaes allowed a choyte here?"

Melodie flinched. The name echoed like a war horn in her ears. The final piece slamming into place. That was all the validation Surin needed. This wasn't a rescue. This wasn't a victory. It was a goddamn set up. And none of them were the predator.

They were bait.

Surin swore in Awyan under his breath, his gaze sweeping the woods like he expected silver eyes to emerge from the trees.

"We're not outrunning him," he muttered. "We're being led."

Behind her, a voice, sharp, clipped, and stripped of all smugness, cut through the quiet:

"Surian. Get the horses. We're leaving. Now." Melodie's blood turned to ice.

She turned in time to see Surin standing near the fire, back rigid, his face carved in stone. That easy arrogance he always wore like a second skin? Gone. His blue eyes, usually glittering with mischief, were hollow and cold. Surian, sharpening a dagger by her mount, didn't hesitate. She rose with military precision, gave a sharp whistle to the trees, and vanished into the dark. The camp fell silent. The fire cracked again, too loud this time, like a gunshot.

"What the hell is going on?" Colonel Jaxxon's voice dropped like thunder into the silence, gravel-edged and unrelenting as he marched forward.

He didn't cower. Didn't yield. He planted himself directly in front of Surin, broad and firm like a wall. A protector.

Melodie stood slowly, her pulse thudding. Her fingers were shaking.

Because Surin looked... afraid. A highborn Awyan. A noble. A man who wore detachment like armor, was now pale, tense, and quiet. If *he* was afraid, then they were already neck-deep in a nightmare.

"Melodie," Surin barked in Awyan, eyes snapping to her. "Translate."

She blinked, snapped to attention. Forced her limbs to move. Her mind to function. She crossed quickly and nodded. Surin faced her father and, for once, didn't hide behind veiled insults or games. His voice was flat. Cold.

"My psychopath of a son has set a trap," he said. "He planted a choyte in the group."

Melodie's stomach lurched. She turned to translate, her voice low but clear.

"He knows our every move," Surin went on. "And if he hasn't come to collect the girl yet... it means he's waiting."

The weight of those words was a lead weight in her chest.

"He's using her," Surin growled, jabbing a finger at Melodie. "As bait."

She staggered. The collar at her throat suddenly felt heavier. Tighter. Surin wasn't done.

"He's not just chasing her," he said, "he's following her, to the portal."

The air went still. Melodie translated, and the camp exploded. Panic erupted like wildfire. Shouts. Shoving. A woman grabbed her child and fled toward the trees. Someone tripped over a crate, spilling dried rations across the ground. A soldier tried to calm a screaming toddler. And Melodie just stood there, frozen in place but still translating for the both of them not even noticing the crowd of people listening and watching what was going down.

"You can't leave!"

Colonel Jaxxon's voice cracked through the chaos like a war drum, sharp and commanding. The crowd parted instinctively as he stormed forward, fury radiating off him in waves. Without hesitation, he grabbed the front of Surin's tunic and yanked him close, their faces inches apart.

"You want to bolt now? After all this? You're the only one who knows where the damn portal is."

Surin didn't hesitate. His voice was low but lethal, honed like a dagger's edge.

"Exactly. Which is why I should leave. I'm the only one who can keep that path hidden if your precious plan falls apart."

Beside them, Melodie scrambled to keep up, spitting out the translation for her father as Surin spoke too fast for Jaxxon to follow.

The Colonel bit down his flaring temper.

"You're threatening to take that knowledge with you?"

"I'm saying," Surin growled, "that if I stay here, and Malec finds out I've been harboring his slave, he won't just come for her. He'll come for all of you. He'll raze this forest to ash, mount your soldiers' skulls around the crater like a warning. You don't know what he's capable of. I do."

Melodie translated again, her voice unsteady, her heart thudding painfully as her father paled under the flickering firelight. Surin's eyes flicked to her, not with smugness, but something heavier. Final.

"This isn't just about escape," he said quietly. "It's about survival. And I've seen what he becomes when he's cornered."

But Jaxxon wasn't backing down.

"You think we're helpless? We're armed. You saw the crates. We've got thermal rifles, high-range pulses, disruptors your kind's never even dreamed of. Your boy shows up, we'll put him down."

Surin exhaled, soft and slow, like a man already tired of the argument. Then his voice dropped, colder, quieter, more dangerous.

"You don't get it," he said, shaking his head. "This isn't just any elf. This is my son."

Jaxxon's scowl didn't budge, but Surin stepped closer, his gaze gleaming like firelight on a blade.

"He was trained by generals, bred for war, sharpened by politics, and forged in violence. He thinks like a tactician, hunts like a predator, and obeys like a zealot. And the worst part?"

He leaned in, voice like poison in a goblet.
"I have to live in the same world as him. So I never provoke him. Ever."
Jaxxon faltered, just slightly. The fire in him dimmed, as he listened to Melodie's translations.

"Those weapons you're so proud of?" Surin's sneer was soft, surgical. "They won't matter. Not when you're up against someone who already planned for you to have them."

Melodie felt it in her spine then, a chill that bled into her bones. Her stomach twisted. She looked down at the coat wrapped around her, the food still in her bag, the smooth weight of the stone at her throat. The kiss Malec had left on her brow.

It was never about her freedom. It was a game board. And she was the bait.

Surian broke through the trees, two pale warhorses at her back. Their hooves thudded softly over the frozen earth, but Melodie barely heard them. The dread was already spilling like smoke into her lungs.

"Father," Surian said.

Surin turned to Melodie, eyes urgent.

"Head south. Stay off the main roads. He's tracking you. Let the others scatter in the noise." His voice dropped. "And for the love of the gods, get rid of that choyte."

Melodie's mouth went dry. Her breath caught.

Surin's expression shifted, something softer, aching. He stepped close and pressed a kiss to her temple, a father's ghost of affection. Then he looked at her, really looked at her, with the eyes of a man giving a eulogy.

"Good luck, little dove," he murmured. "But between us... I'll see you back in the Capitol before the week is over."

And then, not aloud but inside her skull like the brush of breath in a dream, came the final whisper:

"He may not kill you, daughter-in-law. But he will kill everyone else here."

She felt it like a noose cinching around her throat. Surian swung onto her mount.

Without another word, without another glance, they turned and vanished into the trees. Riding straight into the dark.

The fire burned low, casting fractured light across the tense circle of faces huddled beneath the trees. Smoke twisted through the cold night air, mingling with pine, damp earth, and the sharp scent of fear. Colonel Jaxxon stood motionless near the flames, arms folded, jaw tight, eyes sweeping over his soldiers and the ragged band of refugees who looked to him for leadership. Melodie lingered beside him, her body wound tight with unease, every nerve raw with the knowledge they weren't just being hunted, they were nearly caught.

Malec was out there. Waiting.

But she wasn't a prisoner anymore. Not a canariae. Not some pet or prize. She was their only map forward now, and she was ready to lead.

"I know the way," she said, stepping forward, her voice steady.

The murmuring died instantly. Even the trees seemed to quiet.

"I memorized every landmark from here to the portal cave," she continued. "I can get us there."

Colonel Jaxxon gave a curt nod, though his gaze stayed fixed on the dark woods.

> "Good. We move at first light. Stick close until we reach the edge, then split. Two teams. One secures the cave. My unit holds the rear. Fast, clean. If it comes to a fight, we end it quick. Thermal rifles, gas grenades, cloaking tech, they've never seen what we carry. They won't see us coming."

Melodie followed him into the smaller huddle forming at the edge of the firelight. Her boots whispered against the frost-hardened dirt as the soldiers leaned in, ready. But she knew better.

> "You're underestimating him," she said, voice low. "Malec isn't just some highborn with a sword."

Her father turned toward her, frowning.

> "He's not a tyrant you can outshoot," she went on. "He's a tactician. Cold. Precise. He doesn't walk into traps, he builds them. And we've been walking straight into his."

As if on cue, her eyes drifted to the small figure curled beside her pack.

Lilly. Quiet. Sweet. Always nearby. Too nearby. Melodie's stomach clenched. The words felt like lead.

"There's something else," she said softly. "I think he planted her here." The Colonel stiffened. "The little girl?"

She nodded. "She's a choyte. A tracker bred to bait and lead hunters back to their target. He used her. She's how he found us. She's how he's stayed this close."

The soldiers looked from Melodie to the child. The camp went still. No one spoke, but the truth hit like a blade through flesh.

The girl was dangerous. A threat disguised in innocence. The fire cracked, sharp and loud.

"Shit," one soldier muttered.

Jaxxon's voice was a quiet growl. "Are you sure?"

Melodie didn't answer right away. Her gaze lingered on Lilly's sleeping form.

"She was at the fortress. Luko told me what she was. I didn't want to believe him. I didn't want to believe any of it. I was so damn happy to be with you again, to be with my people, that I ignored the obvious. I missed the elephant in the room."

Her voice dropped, bitter with self-loathing.

"How the fuck did I not question it? How was she even here? Was she rescued from another group? Was she wandering as a nomad again? It didn't make sense. None of it did. But I was so desperate to belong, to feel normal again, that I overlooked the truth staring me in the face."

Her voice cracked. "But there's no other way he could've stayed this close for this long."

The cold settled deeper in her bones. The forest held its breath. And for a moment, no one moved.

Finally, Colonel Jaxxon nodded, grimly.

"We'll figure it out. First light. We leave no one behind, unless we have no other choice."

Melodie said nothing. Her heart ached as her eyes drifted back to Lilly's sleeping form, soft breaths rising and falling against the blanket. She looked so peaceful. So harmless. And yet, Melodie knew better now. She'd been played. Again.

This wasn't freedom. This was the long hallway before the next cage. Only this time, the fox wasn't howling. He was already here. And he had left her a choyte to watch. To wait. To follow.

Her hands curled into fists, nails digging deep. The firelight danced in her eyes, but she felt cold, ice-cold from the truth clawing its way up her throat. Lilly wasn't a gift. She was a weapon. A quiet, sniffling grenade dropped into their circle. Melodie saw it now. The way the girl always knew which trail to follow. How she clung to Melodie's pack. How her nose lifted to the wind, always sensing something distant. Her chest tightened. Her father's voice droned in the background, steady and commanding, but Melodie wasn't listening.

Because the truth had already settled. Lilly had to go.

The thought thudded in her gut like molten lead, awful and immovable. Around the fire, she saw the baby nursing, the soldier sharpening his blade, the teenager shielding his face from the wind. Survivors. Fragile, stubborn life clinging on. And they were counting on her. She looked at Lilly, small, twitching in sleep, clutching the cloak Melodie had given her. It made her want to scream. Luko had tried to warn her. She hadn't listened.

Her voice cracked but she forced it out, quiet, to her father and the others.

"She can't come."

Chapter 29

The Portal Standoff

The room was stifling, too many smells, too much noise. Malec could taste the blood in the air, that raw copper edge mixing with the sterile burn of antiseptic. Even the rosewater, meant to cleanse, only made it worse. Everything in the chamber felt wrong. The velvet curtains sagged, damp and dusty, and the once-luxurious carpet reeked of old fear.

He couldn't breathe right. Couldn't think. Not without her. Without Allora, the world tilted sideways, every sound scraped against his skin. He drifted to the nearest bookshelf and began aligning the spines, fingers tracing cracked leather, one book at a time. He didn't care what they were. He needed the symmetry.

Across the room, King Surion slouched in his chair, face swollen and bloodied, a maid dabbing uselessly at the mess. The air buzzed with unspoken fear, every breath held as they waited for Malec to speak. He didn't. Not yet. He focused on the books, on the clean lines, until the storm in his head settled just enough.

> Then his voice came, low, calm, like a wire pulled tight. "You've been working with that Canariae Underground Rescue."

Not a question. A fact. A sentence.

> Surion flinched. "I fund them to flush the tunnels," he muttered. "It keeps them nervous, keeps them moving. I'm the King. I do as I please."

Malec turned his head slowly. His gaze found the maid and rooted her to the floor before she fled, still clutching her scented rag like a shield. The fire shrank, and silence fell again, tight and cold as steel. The guards, his, not Surion's, stood silent as tombstones, the silver fox on their cloaks glinting in the low firelight. Predators, every one of them. Malec took a single, deliberate step forward, boots whispering over the velvet carpet.

"You're only king," he said, voice low and razor-edged, "because I allow it."

Surion forced a smile, though it quivered at the corners of his bloody mouth. "Is that supposed to scare me, Malec?" he asked, but the old confidence rang hollow. "You never wanted the throne. You never wanted the burden. All this", he gestured weakly to the blood, the fear, the grandeur that had curdled into dread, "you let me have it. Because you couldn't stomach it."

Another step, and Malec's presence pressed in, colder than steel.

"You mistake mercy for apathy, Surion. I have never needed a crown to take what I want." His eyes narrowed. "And you know exactly what I want. What I protect."

Surion's bravado flickered, faded. "I was careful," he insisted, voice tight, thin as a fraying wire. "No harm was meant. I swear it on our blood, "

Malec's voice was ice. "You let her be taken, even as you toyed with rebellion like a spoiled child playing at war. And you thought your hands would stay clean."

Surion's lips trembled. "I had to, Malec, you know what would happen if the nobles thought I'd gone soft. They'd tear me apart. Tear us apart. I did what I had to—"

Malec leaned in, his face inches from Surion's battered one. The firelight caught the knife's edge of his profile, the shadows making him look less like a cousin, more like a reckoning.

"You're going to tell me, right now, what you will never do again. Say it."

Surion faltered. For the first time, his voice broke: "I, I will never touch what is yours."

"Let me be clear. You're never going to try and trade her like livestock again. You're never going to sell her for timber and water rations. You're never going to speak her name when you draw your war maps. And you're never, " he turned sharply, "ever, going to look at her like she is anything less than a sovereign flame you are too unworthy to touch."

He took another slow step, shadows carving sharp lines across his angular face, voice dropping into something darker.

"You're also never going to let that puffy blond fool Kael breathe the same air as her again."

He spat the name like it was poison on his tongue, Kael, each syllable laced with venom, with loathing ancient and bitter.

"You think I don't know what you've been planning? Offering her to that soft-palmed peacock in exchange for a northern trade route?" Malec's nostrils flared, a hint of madness curling at the edge of his mouth. "I'd rather burn every diplomatic bridge in Ulvareth before I let that perfumed bastard so much as look at her."

Surion's eyes widened, and for the first time, true horror sank into his bones. He had underestimated just how deep the obsession ran, how far Malec would go. Malec's voice dropped to a whisper again, one hand curling into a loose fist at his side, as though even speaking Kael's name again might bring bile to his throat.

"She is mine. Not yours to barter. Not his to bed. Not anyone's to parade on a leash."

Surion's mouth trembled.
"She's just a Canariae," he rasped. "She's replaceable."
Malec stopped. The guards shifted. Tension crackled in the air like a blade drawn too far across a whetstone. When Malec spoke again, the fury had returned. But not as rage. As clarity.

"I am not here because you called her replaceable," Malec said softly. "I am here because you believed it."

Then he strode forward and grabbed the King by the jaw, gently. As if cradling porcelain. As if daring it to shatter beneath his fingers. Surion whimpered. Malec released him with a flick of his fingers. The King sagged in the chair, gulping air like a beaten dog. Malec's gaze narrowed to a sliver, sharp as a drawn blade. His jaw ticked once. The chamber felt smaller now, as though the very walls were waiting for blood.

"I'll ask you one more time," he said softly, voice stripped of all patience. "What are you never going to do again... when it comes to my Allora?"

The pause stretched. Surion, lips cracked and bloodied, swallowed back the copper taste of fear. He didn't dare meet Malec's eyes.

"I won't..." he stammered, his voice hoarse and desperate. "I won't help Surin or Surian traffic slaves again."

CRACK.
The sound split the room like a thunderclap.
Malec's fist collided with his cousin's face in a clean, brutal arc. Surion's head snapped sideways with the force, his body slamming

against the back of the chair as blood sprayed from his mouth. A garbled scream tore loose as he collapsed sideways, clutching his cheek where the bone had surely fractured.

The guards behind Malec stiffened, hands twitching at their hilts, but none dared interfere. Malec stood over the crumpled king, his breathing calm. He shook out his knuckles once, slow and deliberate, the barest trickle of crimson lining his wrist.

"You really are a slow little worm, aren't you?" he murmured. "I will say this only once more. I don't give a damn about my father's cartel or my sister's shipments. I don't care about the empires you sell off piece by piece like rotting fruit."

He knelt slightly, one hand gripping the armrest of the chair as he stared into Surion's watering eyes.

"There is only one thing in this world I will burn it all down for. Only one."

He stood back up, looming, his silhouette cast long and monstrous in the flickering torchlight.

"My. Canariae." Each word was its own death sentence.

"If you ever assist in separating me from her again, if you so much as whisper her name to one of your dainty little court allies," his voice lowered to a near purr, dangerous and lethal, "I will geld you myself. Slowly. And I'll make sure whatever's left of your bloodline rots in the archives of history."

Surion whimpered, a broken sound caught between a sob and a plea. One eye swollen shut, his mouth trembling. Malec didn't wait for a response. He had already heard the only answer that mattered. He turned on his heel, cape swirling behind him like a trailing shadow. His guards followed immediately, silent as death.

Behind them, the King of Ulvareth slumped in his seat, shaking from pain, blood seeping between his fingers as he held his face together. And somewhere, deep inside the echo of his skull, a single truth tolled like a funeral bell: He wore the crown.

But it was Malec Talandros who ruled.

Malec's breaths came quick and uneven. Every sound pressed in—wind battering the terrace, the distant clang of bells, the pounding rush of his own heartbeat in his ears. It was all too much, every note scraping against him, harsh and relentless now that she was gone. The city seemed to echo with chaos he couldn't tame. He caught himself rubbing the silver fox sigil on Allora's sash, over and over, the motion tight and compulsive. It was the same sash his soldiers had recovered after she first escaped and vanished into that shifter den. Touching it helped, but only barely. Routine was the last thing anchoring him, but he was coming apart. He could feel the connection between himself and balance fraying, the fragile thread snapping strand by strand. Allora's absence made the world tilt, as if he stood at the edge of a cliff with nothing but empty air beneath him.

He tried to anchor himself in the details—the feel of the sash between his fingers, the stitching, the ghost of her scent still woven into the silk. It didn't help. The spiral began anyway. The chairs were crooked. The books sat at uneven angles. His gloves felt too tight, his collar too rough. He paced, counting out eight tiles forward, eight back, again and again, but nothing settled the restless energy prickling under his skin. Every place she'd once inhabited now felt hollow, her absence pressing in with suffocating weight, letting chaos seep into the corners of the room and his mind. His nerves blazed. A cold, sharp horror settled under his ribs. He knew what would happen if the bond snapped—he would come apart with it.

The knowledge that she was not bound to him as deeply as he was to her only made that connection feel more fragile, more at risk of breaking.

He pressed the sash to his nose, desperate for calm. The first breath nearly knocked him down. Smoke. Dirt. Other hands. Tension carved lines into his face, and he pushed past it, searching. Then he found it.

Oranges. The scent cut through the static in his brain like a blade. Her scent. Sharp and sun-warm, edged with soap and something clean. It grounded him in a way nothing else could. He'd chosen that fragrance for her, insisted on it, because it settled his mind. Because it let him mark her space with something of his. And now, that same sweetness told him others had touched what belonged to him.

Rage flared hot and bitter.

The thread inside him pulled taut, vibrating with need. He wound the sash around his hand slowly. The pressure helped. Repetition helped. Ritual helped.

He breathed again, slower this time, wrestling the storm behind his eyes. It wasn't just desire. It wasn't just the need to have her. It was the need to breathe. To silence the world. Only she could do that. Only in her arms, under her body, with her breath catching against his skin, did the chaos go quiet. Only then, could he breathe.

Even if she hated him for it. Even if she never forgave him for binding her so tight. The need for her was a curse. And her scent, on this simple scrap of cloth, was the only proof left that she was still real. Still his.

Malec's eyes flickered, dark gold gone molten, rage and longing churning together. He strode toward the waiting horses, his movements measured but wound tight, every muscle braced with purpose. He mounted without hesitation, his cloak swirling behind him, the red sash swaying at his hip, a banner, a warning, a vow. The air was thick with the scent of distant rain and trampled earth. Somewhere far ahead, she was running, fighting, breathing, and that was all that mattered.

Let the world see. Let them quake. He was not coming for her as a prince, or a commander, or even as the heir of House Talandros. He was coming as her mate. He would have her. He would tear down walls and kingdoms for her. The thought of any hand, any shadow, touching her in his absence made something feral and old gnash its teeth in his chest.

Malec dug his heels into the horse's flanks and surged into the darkness, the city falling away behind him. He would bring her home. Even if he had to drag her, clawing and cursing, across the breadth of the realm. Even if he had to burn every bridge she built, snap every hope she dared to hold. Because before she could ever dream of escaping him again, Malec would grind that dream beneath his heel and make her watch it die, just to see the truth reflected in her eyes.

That she was his. And there was no escape. Not from this. Not from him.

M elodie moved swiftly through the underbrush, her breath spilling out in sharp mist against the frigid night air. The forest around her rose like a cathedral of shadows, branches twisted high above her like gnarled, ancient fingers, blotting out the moonlight in fragmented slivers. The others moved close behind her, cloaked in silence and fear, their footfalls softened by the damp blanket of rotting leaves. Only a few dim flashlights cut through the dark, flickering weakly, each beam of light a possible betrayal, a target for eyes she prayed weren't watching.

She heard everything. The subtle crunch of boots behind her. The rustle of wool against bark. Quiet whispers passed between escapees who clung to hope like a child clutching a tattered blanket. But beneath it all, beneath even the forest's natural noise, was something darker. Not a sound, but a sensation. A presence in the air that skimmed her skin like static.

He was out there. She knew it. The same way she knew how to draw breath, the same way her heart kept time. Malec.

Her thoughts spun in rhythm with her pulse, fast and spiraling. Why play this game of silence and shadows? He wasn't ahead of them. He wasn't lying in wait. No, he was behind. Stalking. Hunting. Each step forward only brought her closer to him, not further. He was the pull at the base of her spine, the invisible weight pressing down on her chest, the phantom touch she couldn't scrub from her skin. The tether, the godsdamned soulbind, was still there. Thrumming. Whispering. Mine, mine, mine.

A cold shiver slid down her back that had nothing to do with the temperature. Fear clawed at the edges of her resolve, sharp and insistent, but she smothered it in the heat of her fury. She wasn't going to let him win. She wasn't going to be his pet anymore or his obedient little dove locked away in a golden cage. *I will get through that portal*, she swore, curling her fingers into aching fists. *Even if I have to use the others as cover. The cure matters more than me. More than any of us.*

But even as the thought burned through her, something sour bloomed in her gut. Because deep down, she knew this was all part of his plan. The food, the winter gear, the choyte, it wasn't care. It was strategy. He'd cloaked manipulation in gentleness, wrapped cruelty in velvet, and called it devotion. She was walking the path he'd laid out for her, and she hadn't even realized it until now. She could see it so clearly, those pale tan eyes gleaming with smug satisfaction, his voice a silk-wrapped dagger murmuring close to her ear, *"I knew you'd run, little dove."*

And for fuck's sake, her traitorous heart still stuttered at the sound of his voice in her head.

He had trained her for this. To survive the wild. To survive him. Every glove, every boot, every scarf was him dressing her for a storm he'd sent her into, like a child outfitted for a game she never agreed to play. She thought she was outsmarting him. But Malec had never believed in freedom. Not hers.

He was always ahead. Always.

Her pace quickened, fury building like fire behind her ribs. She could almost hear his steps behind her, steady, patient, arrogant. Not desperate. Never desperate. *I hope I see his dumb, shocked face when he realizes I figured him out,* she thought savagely. The idea struck her like a live wire, cutting through the dread and tightening her smirk with wicked delight. She clung to the fantasy like armor. *Yeah,* she thought. *Let him stand there, dumbfounded and steaming like a kettle ready to burst, right as I flip him off and dive through that portal like a goddess on her victory lap.*

She could see it all: his too-handsome face frozen in betrayal, those wild eyes narrowing, lips twisting as she turned her back on him for the last time. Maybe she'd bow, deep and mocking, before disappearing into the mist just to twist the blade deeper.

Happy birthday to me, she grinned, *you pale-haired lunatic.*

If she had a camera, she'd immortalize the moment, snap a photo of his stupid, furious face and plaster it across every cheesy holiday card on

Earth. *"Merry Christmas! Escaped a warlord today. Hope your year's going better than his."*

A soft snort slipped from the bow of her mouth before she could stop it, and she clapped a gloved hand over her mouth to muffle it. She was halfway through composing more sarcastic taglines when the wind shifted, biting against her cheek and reminding her they weren't out yet. The caves were close now, just beyond the ridge. She could practically taste the damp stone, smell the mossy mouth of freedom yawning open ahead.

Her heartbeat slammed like a war drum in her chest. The humor faded, not completely, but enough to let the fear creep back in around the edges. She inhaled slowly through her nose and kept moving, shoulders square, head high, refusing to show weakness to the others trailing behind her. You are not scared, she told herself. You are just cautious. Calculated. Like him. But the truth burrowed into her chest, unspoken and merciless. She was scared. Terrified.

Because Malec didn't give up.

He didn't surrender. He didn't compromise. And if he was out there right now, somewhere in these woods, shackled to her soul like a bloodhound on the scent, then he was already closing the distance. Already unraveling her trail. Already preparing to do whatever it took to bring her back.

She hated that a part of her could still feel him. Still sense him. The damn tether throbbed like a ghostly bruise under her skin, pulsing whenever her thoughts drifted to him. As if her soul was still clinging, still aching to be claimed again. She wanted to believe that once she stepped through the portal, it would snap. That she'd be free. But a cold, gnawing doubt lived in the back of her mind. *What if it didn't? What if distance didn't matter? What if the binding ignored planes of existence the way he ignored her boundaries?*

She refused to crumble. If Malec came through those trees, she'd make him bleed for every step. And if she made it to the cave in time? Then she'd be the one haunting him. Forever.

He can live with the absence. I hope it eats him alive.

Then it hit her, sharp and low, a sick twist in her gut that made her stumble slightly on a tree root. Guilt. Lilly was still out there. Alone. Curled on the forest path like a discarded doll, swaddled in that damned blue cloak, his cloak. The one Malec had draped around her tiny shoulders with that smug, omniscient look of his. Like it had all been a setup. Like he knew Melodie would leave the child behind. Like he had planned it. And of course, it worked. Of course it did. Because everything he touched turned into a weapon, even kindness. Even comfort.

That cloak wasn't protection. It was a message. *I know you better than you know yourself.* It seared under her skin like a brand. That arrogant bastard. That manipulative, cruel, beautiful son of a bitch.

And what had they done to Lilly? Turned her into a fucking bloodhound. A human tracker. Turned a little girl into a living tool. A monster in the making. Conditioned her to turn on her own kind for scraps, scraps of safety, scraps of praise, scraps of belonging. They had done that. His kind. His people. The pointy-eared gods who walked like they owned the dirt and breathed superiority like air.

Melodie's hands trembled at her sides. She wanted to scream. To punch a tree.

> To whirl around and go back for Lilly and pull her into her
> arms and scream, *"You are not theirs. You are not a weapon. You
> are not what they made you."*

But she didn't. Because she had a mission. She had *the* mission. To save the human race. And that meant she couldn't afford to turn back. Not for Lilly. Not for anyone.

But if she ever made it back, if she crossed that threshold and got to Earth again, she would find a way to bring this war to their doorstep. Not just words. Not just vengeance. Annihilation. She would call down fire from the sky. She'd bring a nuke through that portal, drag it back herself if she had to, and she'd drop it on every ivory tower, every glistening elven city, every proud marble monument filled with their gilded lies and quiet genocides.

Let the pointy-eared bastards see what real fire looked like. Let them choke on the smoke of every life they'd twisted. Her breath hitched as she forced the thought down. No time. No use. Not now.

But god help them if she ever got the chance.

They were so close now.

The caves, half-buried in shadow, hidden beyond the northern ridge, waited just a few miles ahead. The air was thick with anticipation, brittle with cold. One wrong step, one careless sound, and everything they had sacrificed would be for nothing.

Colonel Jaxxon lifted a clenched fist into the air.

Instantly, the group froze.

They crouched low in the underbrush, blending into the forest's edge just outside a narrow clearing. No one spoke. No one moved. Even the wind stilled, the trees swaying in eerie silence, as if nature itself understood the stakes.

The Colonel's voice came as a whisper. "First group, move out."

With practiced efficiency, the first half of the group peeled away and vanished into the trees, gliding between trunks and branches like phantoms. No footsteps. No rustling. Just silence. Five of the Colonel's finest remained behind with the second group, their eyes trained on the forest path, weapons clutched tightly, waiting for the signal. Time dragged like lead. The horizon began to bleed pale hues, blue smeared with faint orange, signaling the arrival of dawn. Still, they waited, breath caught in throats, eyes darting toward every shifting shadow. Then, movement.

A figure crested the hill at a steady jog, dark against the brightening sky. The group tensed, hands tightening on rifle straps, until the shape grew close enough to recognize. Private Miko. He reached them breathless, bending over to catch his breath before giving a quick nod.

"Smooth transition," he reported, voice low but calm. "The others made it. No tails. We've got soldiers in the caves now, ready to blow the entrance once we're all through."

A ripple of relief swept through the group. The Colonel nodded, clapping Miko's shoulder with quiet approval.

"Good work, Private."

Then he straightened, gaze sharp as he surveyed the anxious faces around him.

"Second group, move out."

And just like that, they slipped from the trees and into the final stretch of forest, carrying with them the last fragile hope of the human race.

As the group began to move again, Col. Jaxxon fell in step beside his daughter, his pace steady despite the weight of the world on his shoulders. Without a word, he placed a firm, grounding hand between her shoulder blades, a silent reassurance in the dark.

"Almost got you home, baby girl," he murmured, voice low and rough with emotion.

Melodie's breath caught.

She turned to look at him, and despite the exhaustion sinking deep into her bones, a soft, trembling smile found its way to her face. There he was. Her father. The mountain of a man who had always come for her. No matter where she was, no matter how far, he found her. Just like he promised.

She stopped walking and threw her arms around him, burying her face against his chest.

"I should've known," she whispered, her voice muffled by his jacket. "I should've known you'd find me."

He let out a quiet, gruff laugh, pressing his forehead gently to hers the way he used to when she was small and afraid of thunderstorms.

"What do I always tell you?"

Melodie closed her eyes, the words rising from memory like a lullaby etched into her bones.

"The brave man is not he who does not feel afraid..." she whispered, "...but he who conquers that fear."

A faint smile tugged at his lips. His hand, calloused and warm, cupped the back of her head protectively.
"And what else?"

She opened her eyes and met his gaze, steady and certain. "You'll always find me."

His arm tightened around her shoulders, voice graveling with emotion. "Nothing in any damn realm could keep me from finding you."

Melodie blinked back the sting behind her eyes, holding on for a moment longer. Then she pulled away, took one last breath of the air that smelled faintly of gun oil and home, and broke into a run.
Toward the caves. Toward the portal. Toward home.

The cave's entrance gaped ahead, jagged as a split lip, slick with moss and damp ivy. Melodie's boots slipped as she approached, the breath of the earth hitting her face, cold, wet, and sharp with a mineral tang. It smelled of stone and slow decay, tinged with something ancient and unspoken. Every inch of the place threatened, shadows hunched like things guarding secrets.
And yet, to her, it was the most beautiful thing she'd seen.
Her heart pounded. After weeks of fear, hunger, and hiding, this cave held the possibility of freedom. Of home. Of sky. Of air that hadn't passed through some monster's lungs. She clenched her fists, drawing a breath deep enough to steady the storm inside her. No time for tears.
"Move!" Colonel Jaxxon's voice cracked through the night.

Melodie ducked beneath the cave's mouth, her flashlight trembling in her grip. Darkness swallowed her whole. The temperature dropped sharply, the damp chill soaking into her clothes. The air tasted like stone and memory. Inside, the tunnel narrowed. She turned sideways to pass, the rock slick and cold against her arms. Her beam caught pale roots, glinting calcite, and old bones bleached by time. Water dripped from above, each droplet echoing like a warning. Gravel crunched beneath their boots.

She pressed forward enthusiastically.

Drip. Drip.

Their footsteps squelched in the mud, the only other sound the soft countdown of water. Her breath fogged the air, the weight of the cave pressing down, thick with fear and damp earth.

Then, a final turn.

The cavern opened before them, vast and vaulted. At its center, the portal shimmered: a black pool pulsing with silver-blue light, lit from within like something alive. Ancient. Wild. Melodie's breath caught. It was both promise and warning, and her heart raced with the terrible, beautiful truth of it.

Colonel Jaxxon was already at the water's edge, boots splashing.

"That's our way out. Center of the pool, swim to the light. It'll grab you, pull you through." He looked to Melodie, pride and command sharp in his eyes. "No hesitation. No stopping. They'll close it behind us. We go. Now."

But Melodie stayed rooted. She watched as the Canariae, her people, her kin, her responsibility, stepped to the edge in trembling lines, some carrying children, some holding hands so tight their knuckles blanched. One by one, they slid beneath the surface, vanishing into that shimmering wound in the world. Each one who went made her chest tighter, her resolve harder. She had to be last. She had to make sure every last one of them made it through.

The air in the cavern shifted, thickening, volatile. She glanced over her shoulder, counting heads, lips moving soundlessly as she checked each face. Go. Go. Please, just go.

Then she felt it. That ripple of dread.

The hairs on her neck lifted; a warning hum curled down her spine. Something was wrong. Her pulse hammered at her temples as the last of the Canariae slipped into the water, still not all the way through. Not safe yet.

The Colonel's voice cracked through the hush.

"Mel! Get her in the water! Now!"

But Melodie couldn't go. Not yet. Not until the last child, the last elder, the last straggler was gone. She held her ground, forcing her breath steady, every sense tuned to the portal, to the dark tunnel behind, to the crowd's frantic movements. She was a shield, the last line.

Then, gunfire. It ripped the air open, shattering the hush, slamming into the walls with earsplitting echoes. Screams ricocheted, sharp and panicked. Soldiers' voices thundered in the tunnel, foreign, merciless, growing louder. She spun, just as her father hurled his sidearm to her, she caught it, cold metal biting her palm, her fingers closing around the grip.

The taste of fear was sharp, charged but she wouldn't run.

Not until every last Canariae was through. Not until she knew, truly knew, that her people had made it home.

Boots thundered, stone to stone, echoing through the cavern like distant thunder. Every stomp sharpened the fear curling through Melodie's veins. Orders barked in harsh, guttural Awyan, language she had learned to hate, the cadence of every nightmare. Shadows twitched at the edge of her vision, shapes darting past fallen lanterns, painting terror across the cavern walls. She braced to fight. Stepped forward, shoulders squared, gun raised, every muscle tight as wire. But her father's hand crashed down on her shoulder, heavy, warm, unmovable. She staggered under the weight of it, blinking up at him, the world narrowing to his battle-scarred face.

"Mel," he breathed, voice sharp and soft, the command of a thousand missions pressed into a single syllable. The note in it nearly shattered her. "Go."

Her heart spasmed, throat burning as she stared back, defiant, desperate. She knew that look, the one he wore before he leapt into the fire for someone else, before he gambled everything to save a life that wasn't his to lose. The kind of look that always meant goodbye. But she also knew, too well, the cost of running. If she dashed through that portal and Malec arrived to find her gone, he would not hesitate. He would kill anyone who stood in his way—everyone in this cavern, her friends, her kin, maybe even innocents, just to reach her. She couldn't run, not for her own sake, but for theirs. For the sake of her people, she stayed rooted, the ache of it sharp as any blade.

"Dad," she choked, reaching for him as chaos erupted at their backs.

More gunfire, closer, louder. The ceiling dusted down over them as the world shuddered and screamed. The acrid sting of powder, sweat, blood, she tasted it all at once.

"I SAID GO!" His roar split the chamber, halting every body, every heartbeat.

He shoved her, hard, and she stumbled, boots splashing through icy water toward the portal's pulsing heart. His grip left phantom bruises, anchors of love and fear. Her legs shook, and she staggered to the pool's edge, lungs burning as she risked one last look back. Behind her, the darkness cracked open. Muzzle flashes flickered, turning faces monstrous, blinding. Screams ricocheted, pain and fury and desperation. The wet iron scent of blood tangled with the damp, earthy cold.

Then, the world shifted again. Melodie's senses rang with alarm. Not just soldiers now, not just guns. A new terror prowled from the black: the two shifter wolves, as monstrous and unstoppable as the stories said. One, silver-gray, amber eyes, a soldier limp and screaming in its jaws. The other, midnight black, blood slicked down its neck and flanks, bullet wounds raw but ignored. It grinned, teeth dripping. They moved with purpose, not chaos.

The chamber erupted. Awyan soldiers surged forward, shields up, faces pale with terror, but Melodie barely registered them. She was counting Canariae heads, making sure, just making sure.

The black wolf locked on her, lunged. Claws skidded, jaws snapping. She stumbled back, weapon raised, but Awyan shields snapped into a trembling wall at her side. Just as she spun for the portal, the wolf darted behind her—massive, bristling, blocking her only exit with a low, guttural growl that vibrated through the floor. Then, just as suddenly, everything stilled. The shouts, the gunfire, even the wolves, frozen mid-snarl.

A voice, low, unhurried, cold as night and bright as a blade, spilled into the silence, echoing off stone, curling into her bones.

"There you are... my little dove."

The words hung, heavy and certain, like fate spoken aloud.

She didn't see him, yet. But she felt him. That shiver down her spine, the way the air changed, how every living thing in the cave seemed to shrink back. The guards parted without question. Fear? Reverence? It was both. Then—

He appeared. Malec. Tall. Implacable. Beautiful and terrible as a storm made flesh. The sight of him, his eyes, hungry and unshakeable, locked on hers, hit her harder than any gunfire ever could.

She was caught. Not by hands or chains. By the gravity of him. The inevitability. The end she had always known was coming.

Malec looked like a shadow conjured from vengeance, leathers slick with the stains of blood and mud, his long platinum braid trailing over his shoulder, the silver fox sigil at his chest catching the blue shimmer from the pool like a promise. He was beautiful and terrifying, fury and patience wound into one body, every inch carved by old wars and older obsessions. But it was his eyes, those pale, burning eyes, that undid Melodie. They pinned her in place, silent and determined, and the air thickened with a charge so heavy she could taste metal on her tongue.

Malec's jaw flexed, hands opening and closing at his sides, as if his whole body ached to close the distance, to seize her and drag her out of that freezing water and back into the safety, and prison, of his arms. His breath came slow and measured, but she saw the shiver that ran down his spine, the way his nostrils flared as he scented the room for her, for the blood, for every threat. He looked like a beast on the edge of violence and longing, just barely holding the storm in check. She knew he could destroy everyone here. With a flick of power, he could end it, wipe out soldiers, wolves, her father, anyone. And Melodie knew it. She felt the weight of it in the air, tasted it in every trembling inhale. It made her throat close with panic.

A click rang out. A rifle cocked. Colonel Jaxxon stepped forward, stance ironclad, weapon aimed dead center at Malec's chest. He radiated danger, war-born and unafraid, his gaze a steel promise that he would not let his daughter go without a fight.

Malec didn't blink. He didn't even glance at the gun. He watched, eyes tracking every shudder of her shoulders, every tremor in her hands, every shallow, shaking breath. She could feel his need to reach for her, to strip her out of the world and into him, but he kept his distance with a restraint that almost hurt to watch.

Her father's voice, sharp and flat, cut through the tension: "So you're the son of a bitch who stole my daughter?"

A slow, cold smile barely tugged at Malec's mouth as his gaze moved to the Colonel. His eyes narrowed. There was a flicker, amusement, arrogance in the depths of those beige orbs. And then, with that devastating focus, he turned his gaze back to Melodie. The world shifted. For a breath, only she and he existed in the universe, bound by threads of love and hate and history no one else could see. For a moment, Malec only watched her, studying the cracks in her armor, the old wounds and the new. Then he took a single step forward. The cavern felt it; even the shadows seemed to shrink away. The rifle tracked him, unwavering. But Malec's focus never wavered from her.

She felt trapped, by the circle of soldiers, by the water at her feet, by the two most dangerous men in her world both waiting for her next move.

Melodie's lungs squeezed so tight she thought she might choke. The echo of her father's warning bounced around the cavern, making the water tremble at her knees, the air quiver at the edges of her skin. She could feel the raw power in the space, her father, immovable, carved from old wars and heartbreak, his rifle steady and gaze unflinching. Malec, just as unyielding, radiating that silent, ancient violence that made the very stone walls seem to lean away from him.

Jaxxon's voice burned the air, a command that left no room for doubt. "Stay back. I will shoot, she's coming home with us."

Malec's presence seemed to thicken, the shadows behind him growing darker, the temperature of the room dropping by degrees. Yet all he did was arch an eyebrow, lips curling into that quiet, imperious line.

"Tell him," Malec intoned, low and brutal, "he has no right to give orders where you are concerned."

The words struck Melodie like ice water to the face. Her hands balled into fists, fingernails biting her palms, the cold stinging her bones. She spun on him, voice breaking, all her exhaustion and terror and love and fury boiling to the surface.

"He's my father!" she cried, her words trembling as they ricocheted off the cave walls. "He's the reason I even exist. You don't get to erase that. You don't get to pretend he's just another enemy to command."

For a moment, the world held its breath. Behind her, she heard her father's breath hitch, just slightly, the smallest tremor in the man who never shook. That flicker of pride, of pain, the cost of losing her to a world he couldn't understand, to a bond he couldn't break.

Malec's eyes, cold and bright, fixed on her. He watched every shiver of her jaw, every drop of water trailing down her skin. He didn't speak, not at first. His muscles jumped along his jawline, the tendons sharp beneath his skin. She could see the desire in him, the aching need to pull her close, to wrap her in furs and fire, to claim her so fully that not even blood or memory could pry her away.

But she had drawn a line. And for once, Malec honored it. He blinked, slowly, and when he finally spoke, his voice was as soft as it was lethal.

"You speak of blood," he said, "as if it is the only bond that matters."

He didn't look at her father, didn't glance at the rifle. His gaze stayed on Melodie, and the world seemed to contract until only his voice and her breath remained.

"Say it, Allora."

The name fell between them like a gauntlet. Her body locked, as if she'd been struck. She hated how that word owned her, how it bent her spine, how it wrapped itself around her ribs and squeezed. But she saw it in Malec's eyes, that unwavering certainty: the demand wasn't for her. It was for her father. He wanted the other man to understand there was no power left to wrest her away, not by force, not by law, not by love.

Melodie's throat burned. She could barely force the words out, bitterness turning her voice rough. "He says... you don't get to tell him what to do with me."

Colonel Jaxxon's grip on the rifle didn't so much as tremble. The storm in his eyes raged brighter, old soldier meeting ancient predator, neither willing to bow.

"WHAT? Who does he think he is? I'm the one pointing a gun at your chest, mother fucker...try again. She is coming home with us, and that's final," her father said, his voice low and final, the kind of vow that once moved armies.

Melodie hesitated, feet rooted in the cold water, heart twisted in a thousand directions. Behind her, the portal shimmered in the surface of the pool, a glowing promise of escape she could almost taste. Her gaze darted toward it, hope and desperation mingling in her chest as she edged backward, testing the distance. But the moment she tried to slip closer, one of the shifters moved behind her, blocking the only path to freedom. The barrier was silent, but absolute.

In front of her, two men stared each other down, both convinced they owned her future. And in that moment, she wasn't sure which of them would win. Or which one she wanted to.

But Malec was already speaking again. His smirk faded, the temperature in the cavern seeming to drop with the force of his presence. He didn't posture or shout, he didn't need to.

> "She is home," he said, voice quiet but ringing with a finality that made the hairs on Melodie's arms rise.

The words landed like a blow. Melodie's breath stuttered in her throat, and she turned helplessly toward her father, searching for any answer, any reprieve. All she found was the same stubborn defiance she'd grown up with, the jaw set, the eyes narrowed in challenge. She swallowed, fighting to steady her voice, but her hands trembled.

> "He says..." The words felt like gravel in her mouth, each syllable an act of betrayal. "This is my home now."

Colonel Jaxxon exhaled, a low, slow sound full of battle-worn exhaustion. His finger hovered over the trigger, every line in his body screaming that he was ready for war if that's what it would take.

"Over my dead body."

She didn't bother to translate. Didn't need to. Malec's eyes said he understood every word, every gesture, every note of her father's love and rage. He took another step forward, the guards parting before him as if compelled by fate itself. The pool at Melodie's feet rippled with his approach, cold light shivering against the cavern walls. He didn't look away from her, not for a moment.

> "Translate this," he said, voice low enough that only she could hear. "Tell him it doesn't matter if he is your kin. Your blood. Your creator. You are my *Vash'telor*. We belong to each other, I am your blood now."

Melodie's chest felt too small for her lungs. Tears stung the backs of her eyes, hot and humiliating, but she refused to let them fall. She wanted to scream, to run, to shatter the entire world and start again somewhere without these impossible choices.

"No," she whispered, so softly it was almost nothing at all.

Maybe it was to herself. Maybe to him. Maybe to the universe that had brought her here. But Malec heard. Of course he did.

He moved closer, close enough that she could feel the heat radiating off his skin, see the tension threading his jaw, the way his hands trembled ever so slightly with the effort not to touch her. He ached to cover her, to pull her from the cold, to shield her from every hurt. But he did nothing. He waited, needing her surrender, her obedience, the final, terrible proof that she belonged to him.

> "Say it," he murmured, velvet and steel, commanding but almost pleading. "So that he understands."

Melodie stared up at him, eyes wild with heartbreak. Her body shook with cold and anger and love all knotted together. She was torn in half, between the father who'd given her everything, and the mate who had taken everything else.

"I hate you," she breathed, voice breaking, not looking away.

> "I know," Malec whispered back, his voice rough and tired, as if her hatred was a wound he'd long since learned to live with.

A wound he would gladly bear, if it meant she stayed.

Chapter 30

The Sacrifice

Melodie's chest heaved, breath coming in sharp, frantic bursts, as panic clawed up her throat and threatened to drag her under. Her muscles screamed for action, to run, to fight, to throw herself into the water and never look back, but her body refused. She stood rooted to the cold stone floor, every nerve raw, her fists shaking at her sides. The portal glowed behind her like a distant star, salvation flickering just out of reach, taunting her with freedom she could almost taste, but never claim.

And Malec? He was motionless, his presence filling the cavern like a coming storm, every line of his body rigid with intent. His gaze cut through the chaos, landing on her, unblinking. Measuring. Waiting. He made no move, but the air around him vibrated with a threat that needed no words.

The hush was total. Absolute. Even the wolves went still, eyes glinting in the cave's blue glow.

She realized then, she hadn't finished translating. Hadn't obeyed. She could feel it, the tension stringing out between them, taut as a wire about to snap. He was leering at her with that unnerving patience, searching for the first fault in her armor. She had resisted, if only for a heartbeat. But Malec... Malec had always known how to bend things until they broke. He applied pressure now.

Malec lifted one finger, a subtle, elegant command. Behind the wall of silver-plated shields, a guard responded instantly, dragging something, someone, into the flickering light.

A child's scream split the air. High and sharp and unmistakable.

"LILLY!" Melodie's voice fractured, torn from somewhere deep, her composure shattering in an instant.

She lurched forward on instinct, but the black wolf at her back let out a low, guttural snarl, stopping her cold.

The guard hauled the girl forward by the collar of her coat, lifting her bodily from the ground. Lilly's feet kicked in the air, her small hands clawing desperately at the fabric digging into her throat. Her eyes, wide, wild with terror, locked on Melodie. Then another guard emerged, half-dragging, half-carrying a limp, bloody form across the stone. Oliver. His body flopped to the floor in front of Malec's boots, arms splayed, blood streaking down the side of his face. There was no movement. No sign of life.

Melodie's mouth moved but no sound escaped. She felt as though she were drowning, crushed under the weight of the moment, unable to breathe or scream or fight. Malec stood above it all, expression emotionless, perfectly composed. The pale tan of his eyes held hers, steady, cold as ice in the heart of a fire. There was no cruelty in his face. No rage. Just certainty. He knew what he was doing. He knew exactly how much it would hurt. Then, softly, almost gently, his voice reached across the cavern.

"Allora."

It was a summons, a claim, a reminder. Melodie's spine locked straight, her hands shaking around the pistol she'd forgotten she was still holding. He didn't shout. He didn't threaten. He simply named her, his little dove, and it was enough to paralyze her.

"I'll trade their lives for yours," Malec said, his voice as smooth and quiet as a blade in the dark.

He wrapped his hand around Lilly's collar, lifting her a fraction higher, the child's feet barely brushing the stone as she gasped, her cries growing fainter. The world seemed to stop. Even the distant gunfire dulled to a heartbeat hush. All that remained was Malec, Lilly choking in his grasp, Oliver bleeding out at his feet, and Melodie, trapped, trembling, every fiber of her being stretched between survival and surrender. There was no escape. Not from the stone jaws of the cave. Not from the wolves. Not from him. She was out of time, out of options, and the choice he offered was no choice at all.

She could save them. But only by giving herself up to the storm.

She stood shaking, water streaming down her face, her curls heavy and cold against her cheeks. Every inch of her skin burned with shame and rage and the kind of despair that comes only when hope has been dangled in front of you and snatched away. Her jaw ached from holding back a sob, but the fury inside her was hotter than the tears. She wanted to tear the world apart. To rip Malec's hands off Lilly. To send the wolves scattering, to drag every last Canariae through the portal and set this place ablaze behind her. But she couldn't, not while a child dangled from his grip, not while Oliver lay bleeding at his feet, not when every pair of eyes in the chamber looked to her for a miracle.

So she stood, trapped, her fury a storm she couldn't unleash, her voice caught somewhere between a scream and a prayer.

Malec's voice knifed through the tension.

"Make your choice, Allora." His words bounced off the stone, cold and final, the timbre of a man whose patience was fraying at the edges.

Her body tensed, muscles locking, her vision swimming with the light of the portal behind her and the shadow of Malec in front. The ache in her throat threatened to split her open. Every instinct screamed at her to move, to fight, but she couldn't, not when Lilly's face, blotched and terrified, was all she could see.

She broke. "My name is MELODIE!"

The scream shattered the quiet, her voice raw as flayed flesh, echoing in wave after wave until it was all she could hear, her name, her life, everything Malec had tried to take, reborn and enkindled in her chest.

Malec's entire body snapped taut, as if her words had struck him physically. For a second, his face was pure shock, then shame, then something far, far darker. That name, her name, unraveled him in ways that even rage could not. His jaw worked, mouth pressed in a hard line. The grip on Lilly's collar grew tighter, the girl's feet scrabbling helplessly in the air. Her small fingers scratched at his wrist, her face red and panicked.

Melodie felt herself split in half. The part that wanted to save Lilly, and the part that wanted Malec to hurt, really hurt, for everything he'd done. Tears blurred her vision, but her voice came again, vicious and clear.

"You don't love me!"

His head jerked at the words. For a moment, the fierce control in his face slipped, and she saw it, the wound, the real one, raw and gaping beneath his immortal calm.

"You just want to own me!" Her voice cracked, echoing off the stone, bouncing back in ripples. "To control me, to break me, to parade me around as your property, like I'm nothing! Like I don't matter!"

Malec's fury coiled behind clenched teeth, his eyes shining with something sharp and fragile all at once. Behind her, the wolves pressed closer, uneasy, the tension in the air thickening with every word.

"You forced me to kneel. To obey. To give myself to you, like I was just some thing you could fuck and own!"

The final word detonated, vicious, unforgiving. Even the air seemed to recoil.

Malec's entire body went rigid. For a long, quaking heartbeat, he didn't move, didn't speak. Her accusations hung in the air, cage, whore, property, each one landing with the weight of a blow. His pale tan eyes bore into her, storm-bright and bottomless. Finally, in a voice so low it barely registered above the pounding of her blood, he asked,

"You truly believe that?" It wasn't a whisper. It was a wound.
"That I do not love you?"

She said nothing. Her silence was a chasm, wide and absolute, swallowing every plea, every explanation.

Malec's mouth opened, and what emerged was raw, his voice scraping with need and the agony of being misunderstood.

"Do you not see how I burn for you, little dove?"

It was more confession than question, as if the admission cost him. His hand around Lilly slackened, just enough for the child to catch her breath, but not enough for anyone to mistake where the power lay. He wasn't looking at the child, though. His entire being was riveted to Melodie, every line of his elegant, battle-worn face twisted with a yearning so ferocious it hurt to witness.

"Sleep will not come unless your breath is on my neck," he said, voice trembling, thick with the weight of nights spent alone, tormented by dreams of her. "Food turns to ash unless your hands place it in my mouth. The sun, the sky, the very world itself dims if I do not wake to your voice."

His eyes, a wild, haunted amber, searched hers, and she could see the hope and despair flickering behind the sharp glint. Melodie's lips trembled, the pistol held tight between them, but she didn't move. Didn't dare. Because in his face, for the first time, the mask slipped. Beneath the ruthlessness, the arrogance, the iron will, there was a broken boy, lost and yearning.

"They may have named you Melodie," he breathed, each word scraping through the silence, "but I know what you are. You are mine. My Vash'telor. My mate. We are not just two, we are one. To live without you..." His voice fractured, then steeled. "Would shatter me."

He was offering up the truth, laid bare, shaking, wounded, unguarded. Melodie's hands shook harder. The gun felt impossibly heavy, the cold metal biting into her palm, grounding her even as her heart tried to fly apart.

"Say what you will," Malec said, his voice barely more than a ragged exhale. "But do not tell me I do not care. You are my beginning and my undoing."

He stepped closer, a shadow cast in firelight, all ice and fury and desperate devotion. And in that instant, the safety on the gun clicked beneath Melodie's thumb, a warning, a promise, a plea for power she knew she didn't truly have. Her father's rifle loaded with a metallic snap, his stance thundercloud-dark.

"I don't give a damn if you're a king, a god, or the devil himself," Colonel Jaxxon snarled. "She's my daughter. And if you lay a single hand on her again, I'll show you just how mortal you really are."

The silence pressed in, thick and suffocating. Every muscle in Melodie's body screamed to run, to lift the gun, to fight her way free. The tension drew the world tight as wire, each breath sharp and fragile. Her pulse thundered in her ears. Behind her, her people clustered close. Wolves prowled at her back, eyes fixed and waiting. But deep down, she knew what she had to do—there was only one way to save them all.

She raised her chin, the portal's blue light flickering across her skin, a halo of promise and danger at her back. Every instinct begged her to bolt for it, to chase the escape she could almost taste. But she stood her ground, refusing to yield—not with Malec's gaze locking her in place, not with Lilly's thin, ragged breaths rattling in the air behind her.

Drawing herself up, she squared her shoulders, letting what remained of her pride burn steady through the tremble in her limbs.

Then she spoke, clear, ringing, the foreign syllables of Awyan slicing through the cold.

"I will go with you," she said, each word forged from equal parts defiance and defeat. "But I have conditions."

Malec's face shifted. A flicker, surprise, or maybe dark amusement, creased the line of his mouth. His eyes glittered dangerously, his hands tightening around Lilly's collar, but he listened. He had to. She'd forced him to.

"Continue, dove." He replied smoothly and unhurried.

"First," she began, her voice low but uncooperative, "let me give them my blood."

He bristled instantly, the lines of his body hardening. But she cut him off, her voice slicing through whatever objection he'd readied.

"The disease killing my people started here. My blood is the cure. If you want me to come with you, you let me save them first."

The words landed like blows. Malec didn't answer, his silence a storm barely caged. The wet, mineral-scented air between them buzzed with it.

"Second," she pressed, "everyone else, my people, your prisoners, the Canariae, they go home. Unharmed. That's my price."

Behind her, Melodie could feel her father's eyes on her, burning with confusion, with fear. She wondered if he saw the girl he raised, or only the woman she'd become, one who would trade everything for a slim hope.

Malec's laugh was soft, venomous, curling around her like smoke. "You expect me to simply agree? To bow?" His voice dripped with mockery. "You think I'm so desperate?"

"Yes," she shot back, voice steely. "Because I know you could have paralyzed everyone in here and dragged me out. But you didn't use your magic, not once. You want me to go to you willingly, you are desperate for me to surrender to you."

A muscle jumped in Malec's jaw, his fury straining against the bond that anchored him to her. He wanted to snarl, to crush, to win. But she saw the truth flicker in his eyes, the truth he hated. He was desperate. For her. For this. For any excuse to keep her, even at the cost of everything else but above all else he wanted her to come to him by choice. He drew a long, icy breath.

"You know, I already discovered your plan to collapse the cave," he murmured, too soft for the guards to hear, but the threat razor-edged beneath every word.

Melodie's heart stumbled. She kept her face blank, even as dread coiled in her gut.

"Then you know this is your only chance," she said, voice softer now, but all the more dangerous for it. "Take it, or lose me forever."

A thick, choking silence pressed in, heavy with damp, with fear, with the scent of burning magic and gun oil and the copper tang of blood. Malec's eyes roamed over her, a hunger and longing so ferocious it almost made her knees buckle. Gods, she was radiant to him. Defiant, battered, glorious. Not some fragile thing to break, but the wild storm he was fated to worship. He hated her for it. Loved her for it. Needed her all the same. His mask slipped; pride and love and agony all twisting through the lines of his face.

"You don't get to make demands, dove," he spat, but the words sounded hollow even to him. "You're not in a position to bargain."

But Melodie just stared him down, her eyes unblinking, her gun never wavering. Then, in one smooth motion, she turned the barrel, pressed it to her own temple. Every breath in the cavern stopped.

Malec's grip on Lilly faltered, his eyes going wide for the first time, a crack splitting the iron calm on his face. Her father's scream split the air.

"MELODIE! Don't you fucking dare-"

She ignored him, voice flat and shaking but determined.

"Looks like I just made myself the bargaining chip," she spat at Malec, her finger ghosting the trigger, "You want your mate, your obsession, your leverage? Everything you want is right here. And all I have to do is end it."

The echo of her words shivered across stone and water, a live wire of defiance. She saw her father move, muscles coiled to charge, but she snapped her gaze at him, warning.

"Don't. I mean it, Dad."

For the first time, Malec looked truly shaken. He stared at her, not with anger, not even with possessive rage, but with something wild and devastated. He understood, then. Understood that she was not just a pet or a pawn or a prize. She was as ruthless as he was, as ready to destroy as he was to possess.

The child in his grasp whimpered. Malec's hand trembled. Her voice shook, but she didn't lower the gun.

"Let them go, Malec. Or I'll take your precious prize away forever. And you know I will do it too."

The world seemed to tilt, air thick with dread. Her father's breathing was ragged, pleading, desperate.

"Melodie, Mel, baby, please. Put it down. Please. I'm here. Don't do this."

But her eyes never left Malec's. The message was clear, burning between them like a line drawn in blood: I will burn this world to the ground before I let you chain me again. For one endless heartbeat, no one moved. And in that moment, Malec saw her, truly saw her. Saw himself, reflected in her fury and despair. The lengths she'd go to, just like him. His jaw worked, eyes wild with a hundred unnamed emotions, the threat of violence suddenly no longer a weapon but a mirror.

Allora, Melodie, stood at the threshold, gun to her head, daring him to test her resolve. He stood motionless, jaw rigid, pale hair clinging wetly to his cheeks, his silhouette a sentinel of want and will.

And then, in that voice, silken, cold, and devastatingly gentle, he murmured, "Is that all... my little dove?"

It wasn't just a question. It was a final trial, a king's last demand, a lover's prayer wrapped in thorns. Would she yield? Would she kneel, not in body, but in spirit? He could end this with a word, unravel every defense with a spell, make her beg for air and mercy and freedom. But he didn't move, and Melodie felt it: the balance, the edge where choice becomes surrender. Her knees threatened to buckle, the ache in her body near collapse. She could still feel the cold bite of the gun pressed to her head, the pulse of life and death in her hands. The sound of Lilly's choking dragged every second longer, every breath harder. Melodie's voice was stripped raw when she answered:

"Yes."

A ripple of something dark and satisfied passed through Malec's eyes, a glimmer of hunger sated, but never full. The faintest tilt of his mouth, victory carved with reverence.

And with that, he opened his hand. Lilly dropped to the ground, crumpling like a marionette with cut strings, gasping, sobbing, clutching her throat. Before Melodie could stagger forward, one of the Colonel's soldiers broke ranks, sweeping the child into his arms. Another rushed to Oliver's limp form, dragging him to the portal's edge. The wolves only watched, shadows of fangs and menace, as the last humans spilled through the shimmering water. No one else dared approach.

Malec didn't look away. He had no need. He had already won.

Guilt and relief warred inside Melodie as she turned toward her father, his face carved in agony and rage, grief streaked in sweat and grime. He surged toward her, rifle lowered but still trembling in his grasp.

"What the hell did you just say to him?" Colonel Jaxxon's voice was a raw rasp.

Melodie met his gaze, her own eyes ringed red and bright with exhaustion. "I made a bargain."

"A what?" His voice broke, disbelief and fury crashing together.

She swallowed, standing tall though her knees quivered. "I'm going with him," she said, her words an anchor and a curse. "It's the only way."

"The hell it is," he snarled, voice edged with the terror of a father about to lose his child again. "We have guns. We have a plan, "

"No!" Her shout bounced off the stone, sharp as a shot. "This isn't a fight we win with bullets!"

He stared, breath shaking. His face twisted with loss, love, terror.

"Dad, he's playing with us." Melodie's voice gentled, almost pleading. "They have magic. Things we can't even see, let alone fight. He could have killed every one of us the moment he stepped through that tunnel. But he didn't." She jerked her chin at the still-glowing portal. "You want to save our people? Listen to me, there are other portals."

He frowned, confusion flickering through the haze. "What?"

She leaned closer, her voice low, urgent. "Think, Dad. This one's in Botswana. Have you seen anyone here who looks like us? Anyone with skin like ours?"

His gaze swept the cavern, realization dawning, terror twisting deeper. "This opening—"

"It's new," she said. "And you're going to find the others. You're going to help them."

He stared at her, eyes wild, heartbroken. "I'm not leaving you."

"I've survived worse," she whispered, tears she refused to shed burning her throat. "You have to trust me. You have to let me go."

Colonel Jaxxon stood still, a soldier at the edge of surrender, then nodded, once, hard and final. Melodie's body sagged, her strength fraying, heart battered but unbroken. She turned back to Malec, hands lifted in peace, then gestured to one of her soldiers.

"I need a medic bag," she called, her voice thin but unwavering.

For a long beat, the silence held. Then, with a soldier's precision, one of the humans tossed a battered bag across the cavern. She caught it, hands barely steady. The Awyan guards tensed, magic shivering in the air, but Malec raised a hand, a king's decree. Stand down. He watched her, his eyes never leaving her, every muscle coiled with possessive need and wary awe. She was his now, but not how he'd planned. Not broken. Not tamed.

Chosen. Bargained for. And just as ruthless as he was. And he finally, truly, understood the cost of loving a soul like hers.

She unzipped the battered medic bag with fingers still trembling, though her spine refused to bend. The zipper's teeth rasped through the hush, every sound heightened in the heavy air. The cold sting of antiseptic clung to her skin as she tore open an alcohol pad, cleaning the inside of her elbow with movements that were clinical, practiced, automatic. The needle glinted in the light from the portal, and she jabbed it home, feeling the sharp, necessary pain ground her back in her body. Crimson welled, then flowed, filling the first vial with the dark, vital promise of survival.

Her pulse hammered in her throat. The hush in the cavern grew denser, thicker, as if the stones themselves were holding their breath. Every drop of blood felt heavy with meaning, her life for theirs, her sacrifice for a thousand she'd never see, never save with her hands, only her marrow.

Malec watched her from across the stone floor, standing utterly still, except for the twitch of his hands at his sides, knuckles flexing, then curling, again and again. He didn't blink. Didn't breathe. The look in his pale tan eyes was raw, dangerous: possessive and resolute, a force of nature barely leashed.

"What are you doing?" His voice sliced through the quiet, low and sharp, the kind of softness that came before a killing blow.

Melodie slid a full vial into the kit and ignored him, voice coming out flat, clipped.

"Relax," she muttered, loading the next tube. "I know what I'm doing."

But Malec's composure faltered. He pressed his lips into a thin line, and she saw his nostrils flare, a warning sign.

"You're draining yourself," he said, and there was fury in it now, cold and blue-hot, trembling at the edges of his restraint.

She heard the metallic click before she saw her father move, a gun cocked, chambered, the sound slicing through the tension like a warning shot. Jaxxon's stance was carved from war, rifle aimed straight at the elf's head, eyes full of murder.

"Not one more step, monster," the Colonel spat, his finger poised, voice a promise.

But Malec barely glanced at him, as if the weapon didn't matter. His attention was only on Melodie, on her blood, her sacrifice, her steady defiance. And then something changed: the air around Malec began to shimmer, charged and alive. A pale blue flame licked up his wrists, spectral, almost unreal, not heat but energy, a power native to another world. His hands pulsed, glowing brighter, the light reflecting off his silver hair, his hunting leathers.

Even the wolves sensed it, muscles tensing, fur bristling.

> Behind her, her father's voice was hoarse, raw with panic. "What the hell is he doing?" he muttered under his breath, barely for her ears. "He's about to lose it."

The tension in the room spiked. Melodie could feel every eye on her, every heartbeat in the cavern waiting for what would happen next. Her breath was quick and shallow, but she forced herself to focus, to keep her hands steady as she drew the fourth, then fifth vial. Her arm ached, her vision tunneling at the edges, but she refused to stop. Not until she'd given enough.

"Don't shoot. Don't provoke him," Melodie replied, not daring to glance up.

The connection between her and Malec burned at the base of her skull, a living thread. She could feel the way he watched her, as if her veins belonged to him, as if every drop that left her body was a theft, a betrayal he could barely allow. She slid the last vial into the kit just as her father's hand, large, rough, familiar, closed over her wrist, stopping her.

> "That's enough, Mel," Colonel Jaxxon said, his voice trembling just a little. "You're done."

Her own blood pooled in the glass, still warm, still hers. The world seemed to spin for a moment, then Malec's presence pulled her upright, steadying her in spite of herself. Blue flames curled and faded on his hands, and he stared at her as if he could will her heart to keep beating, even if it meant burning down everyone else in the room.

The deal was struck. The price was paid. And nothing in the world, not even her fear, could take that from her now.

> "That's enough," her father said, his voice gruff but thick with feeling. "You've done more than enough, Melodie."

She wanted to argue, to squeeze out just one more vial, anything to tip the scales further in their favor. But she caught the look in his eyes: pain, pride, terror, all tangled together. It stopped her cold.

Her nod was shaky. She tried to steady her hands as she capped the last vials, but her fingers wouldn't cooperate, slick with sweat and cold from adrenaline and blood loss. When she pressed them into his palm, their skin touched, hers chilled and trembling, his fever-hot, pulsing with that desperate, protective love only a father could give. Something inside her fractured, sweet and sharp.

He tucked the precious vials into his chest pouch, holding them close to his heart. For a heartbeat, she let herself really see him, the lines of exhaustion on his face, the old scars, the fresh grief shadowing his eyes.

She opened her mouth, and all that came out was, "Dad..."

He didn't answer with words. Instead, his arms came around her, strong and fierce, making her knees buckle as she melted into his chest. Melodie swayed, her head swimming with exhaustion and relief and loss. She clung to him, shaking, the world spinning as if her body was a vessel half-drained and half-filled with grief.

"I miss you," she managed, her voice splintered, breaking on the syllables.

His chin trembled where it rested on her hair. He squeezed her tighter, like he was trying to anchor her to the earth, or memorize the exact shape of her soul.

"I'll find a way back to you," he whispered, voice sandpaper-rough, pressing a kiss against her brow. "Just wait for me."

She nodded, swallowing hard, her eyes stinging, her heart squeezed between hope and despair. She buried her face in his chest, desperate to memorize the scent of him, soap, sweat, a trace of gun oil, the unmistakable scent of home. Then, barely audible, he breathed the old words in her ear:

"The brave man is not he who does not feel afraid..."

Melodie managed a ghost of a smile, finishing the quote like a promise: "But he who conquers that fear."

Her knees nearly gave out again. The world pulsed with dizziness. Across the cavern, Malec was still tracking her, she could feel it, a hot, searing weight against her skin. He was a pillar of tension and yearning, barely keeping his jealousy and hunger in check. The sight of her in another's arms, freely given, not taken, raked at him. He had never known what it was to be loved like that. He craved it with a violence that scared even him. He would have it, one day. He would make sure of it. She would learn to cling to him. To choose him. To need him. The ache in his chest would quiet only when her loyalty belonged to him alone.

But the moment shattered as a sharp whistle sliced through the heavy air, a warning. A scream followed, a real, terrified scream, and a silver-furred wolf exploded through a cloud of smoke, sinking its fangs into a soldier's leg with a savage, wet crunch. Gunfire erupted, brutal and deafening, ricocheting off the stone in violent echoes. Arrows hissed from the darkness, finding flesh with sickening thuds. Someone was crying. Someone was begging.

Colonel Jaxxon's men fired in wild bursts, but Malec's warriors, Awyan shields raised, blades flashing, moved as one, disciplined and merciless, turning the cavern into a blood-soaked crucible.

The air grew thick with smoke and the coppery tang of blood. The floor grew slick beneath Melodie's boots as she staggered, nearly going down, heart racing, vision swimming. She could feel Malec's gaze on her, stalking her through the chaos, tethered by a bond no violence could sever.

With a flick of Malec's wrist, the pale blue fire swirling at his fingertips exploded outward. Magic ripped through the cavern, an ear-shattering crack that seemed to peel the earth itself apart. The air trembled, current-laced and electric, and then the blast hit, a tidal wave of force that sent soldiers flying, bodies slamming into stone pillars, ricocheting off cavern walls with dull, sickening thuds. Some crashed into the water, some folded over tables, limbs splaying like broken dolls.

Jaxxon went airborne, his rifle spinning out of reach as he hit the far wall with a crunch. His body rebounded, landing in the churning pool with a violent splash, water roaring up around him. A single gunshot cracked through the chaos. The black wolf at Melodie's back spun with a yelp, a bullet tearing into its flank. Blood spattered across the slick rock, and it vanished into the water, leaving behind only a bloom of red swirling in the torchlight.

Melodie's vision narrowed in panic. Her father's voice, ragged and hoarse, cut through the din:

"Melodie!"

She turned just in time to see Lilly being dragged toward the portal by a soldier, the child's face ghost-pale, tear-streaked, mouth open in a silent scream.

"Melodie, help me!"

Instinct took over—she surged forward, desperation burning through every ache, every warning. But before she could reach the portal, something slammed into her gut. It wasn't a shove, but a punch—hard, ruthless, and perfectly placed. Pain detonated inside her, blinding and immediate. The air vanished from her lungs in a silent, ragged gasp as she doubled over, agony flaring from her ribs to her spine.

She never hit the ground. Malec's arms were around her before she could even scream, iron and ice, unrelenting as he scooped her up and slung her over his shoulder like she weighed nothing. Her stomach pressed against the leather harness at his chest, her braid trailing through something slick and wet—blood, water, she couldn't say. The world pitched and spun as he carried her away, her ears ringing, the sound of gunfire and chaos fading beneath the relentless echo of his boots striking stone.

The last thing she heard before darkness took her was the thundering pulse in her ears, and Malec's heartbeat, steady, calm, and inescapable, pressing against her body as he carried her from everything she knew.

When consciousness crept back, Melodie's world tilted, swaying nauseously. For a second, she couldn't place herself, she only felt movement, a crushing warmth at her side, and the overwhelming scent of pine, leather, sweat, and smoke.

And him. No.

She inhaled, breath catching on the thick, woodsy smell of his leathers and the sharp tang of blood. Her lashes fluttered against her cheek, the sting of smoke clinging to her eyes and throat.

"No," she rasped, her voice barely more than a croak, lost in
the din of chaos that still thundered somewhere behind them.

She tried to push away, weak as a child, her muscles trembling and uncoordinated. She clawed at his back, her nails scraping over the thick, battered leather of his tunic. He didn't slow. A low growl vibrated from his chest, animal and ominous.

"Be still," he said, his words a silken threat wrapped in velvet,
heavy with command. "You will only hurt yourself."

"Let me go!" she gasped, her voice breaking on the last word
as she thrashed once, twice.

But the hand at her thighs only tightened, steady as a shackle. He strode through the carnage, his soldiers parting in utter silence, never daring to meet his eyes. Outside the cavern's jagged maw, cold night air hit her like a slap. The world was chaos, screams, metal, the stink of blood and fear.

Awyan wolves, one silver, one black, both battered and bristling, flanked his every step, growling at anything that moved. Behind them, the fight still raged, gunfire cracking, men shouting, steel shrieking on stone.

"LET ME GO, YOU BASTARD!"

Melodie screamed, her voice hoarse with fury and loss, her fists pounding against his back with what little strength she had left. Malec paused, just once, as if considering her plea. Then he exhaled, slow and unshakable, his answer quiet, final, and absolute.

"Never again."

His voice wasn't cruel. It was a vow, as ancient as the blood running through his veins. And she knew, in that moment of utter helplessness, that now that he had her again, now that she was back in his arms, he would set the world on fire before he ever let her slip away. Malec carried her through the narrow, dripping tunnel, the slick walls pressing close, darkness swallowing the edges of his vision. Behind them, the chaos of the ruined cavern howled, gunfire, screams, the snap of bone against stone, but all of it faded beneath the sound of one desperate voice.

"MELODIE!"

Colonel Jaxxon's cry cut through the darkness, raw with anguish and rage, echoing off every cold surface. The splash of water signaled his rise from the shattered pool, boots pounding as he waded through the carnage.

She stirred at the sound, her name, her anchor, that voice she'd followed through war and hell.

"YOU FUCKING COWARD!"

Jaxxon's roar battered the stone, his words ricocheting down the twisting passage. The click of his weapon carried a promise of vengeance.

"PUT HER DOWN!"

Malec did not look back. His gaze was fixed ahead, pupils blown wide, the faint blue shimmer of spent magic fading from his hands as the cold night wind rushed to meet him. Every muscle in his body was drawn tight, his jaw a pale slash of iron in the gloom. Her warmth was all that mattered now. The fragile thud of her heart. The shallow rise and fall of her breath. She was the only point of gravity in a universe spinning out of control. Behind him, the Colonel's final threat ripped through the darkness, battered and desperate, voice cracking.

"I'LL FIND YOU, AND WHEN I DO, I'LL PUT A BULLET BETWEEN YOUR EYES, YOU PIECE OF SHIT!"

The words echoed, lingering in the stone and the shivering night air, but Malec never flinched, never slowed. He vanished into the dark labyrinth, boots grinding over gravel and slick moss, the tangled roots above brushing his hair, the freezing wind stinging his face and hers. The cave seemed to swallow their exit, sealing off the last echo of that male Canariae's voice.

And as the sound died behind them, the only thing that mattered, the only thing real, was the precious, living weight in his arms.

Gunfire still throbbed in Colonel Jaxxon's ears, each echo a hammer to the ribs, rattling through sinew and memory as the last of the battle died around him. The cavern was collapsing, stone dust raining from above, the groan of rock grinding like teeth in the mountain's jaw. But the enemy, the warlord, was gone.

Malec had vanished, melting into the blackest part of the tunnels, Melodie slung across his shoulder like a conquered standard. His daughter. His Melodie. Gone. Stolen from him by a nightmare in the shape of an elf. And what lingered in her place was a silence that devoured everything. The absence of her voice. The echo of boots disappearing into shadow. The jagged, suffocating wound where his child used to be.

The Colonel's hands curled into fists, shaking so hard he thought the bones might shatter. Fury burned under his skin, so hot it made his vision blur. But he shoved it down, he had to. Now wasn't the time for rage, or for the broken roar swelling in his chest. He was still a soldier. There were lives to save.

The image carved itself into Jaxxon's mind: Melodie limp, her hair sticky with blood, dangling helpless as Malec carried her away. He burned that memory in deep. Sharpened it into a weapon. Because the war wasn't over. It was only changing shape.

"MOVE! MOVE! GO!" came the frantic cry behind him, soldiers hustling the wounded toward the trembling portal.

The countdown to detonation ticked in the bones of the cave, a low, ominous rumble. Stone split with sharp, angry pops; the earth seemed to breathe, pulling itself apart. It was almost time. He spun, eyes searching the mouth of the tunnel, half expecting to see Malec's shadow, half dreading it. Was he waiting? Taunting him from the dark? Or already gone, melting away with Melodie into some new hell?

He would find out. One day, he would tear through every world, topple every kingdom, bring ruin to every fortress if that's what it took to get her back. She hadn't thrown herself to the wolves for nothing. And he, he would never let that sacrifice be her last word.

"GET THEM UNDER!" he barked, voice hoarse, shaking, unbreakable. "ALL OF THEM! GO!"

The portal glowed, golden and cold, swallowing soldier after soldier, some dragging the wounded, some barely upright, all of them racing against time. Colonel Jaxxon waited until the last of his people had vanished, until the only souls left in the crumbling dark were him and the ghosts of what he'd lost.

The cave screamed. He turned one last time to the place Melodie had disappeared, his heart a grenade with the pin pulled. Then he sprinted, boots pounding, body aching, and dove into the portal. The water crashed up around him, numbing cold and blazing magic writhing across his skin, spinning him through the churning abyss.

He caught one last glimpse of the water behind him, clouded red with her blood. And then, everything disappeared.

Chapter 31

This Is Not the End

The destruction roared in her skull long after the world fell silent.

The final collapse of the cave thundered behind them, the

shockwave echoing through the roots of the mountain and rattling her teeth, her bones, her soul.

For a moment, it felt as if the forest itself was holding its breath, every leaf quivering on the cusp of disaster. Birds erupted from the trees, shrieking, scattering into the burning sky. A plume of smoke climbed and spread, blotting out the sun, swallowing the last fragile thread that tied her to home.

Melodie barely felt the cold, rigid arms encircling her, pinning her sideways across Malec's lap as his warhorse surged through the charred undergrowth. His grip was iron, but she was limp. Boneless. Her vision tunneled, fixed on the distant ruins where the portal had once glimmered like salvation. Now it was only blackened stone, flame, and loss. Each ragged breath scraped her throat raw. Grief vibrated under her skin, a physical ache, a throbbing wound that spread out from her heart and into her trembling hands, her clenched jaw, the line of her back. Her ribs flared with pain, old, new, all the pain Malec had inflicted and the world had compounded, but none of it compared to the emptiness inside her.

It was bottomless, a pit so wide it felt she might fall into it and never stop.

She tried to swallow it, to lock the sob behind her teeth. But it broke through, a raw animal sound that humiliated her even as it freed her. Her hand slapped over her mouth, desperate to hide her vulnerability from him, from the world, from herself. But the tears fell anyway. Hot, relentless, soaking his tunic, leaving dark marks that would dry to salt and silence.

Home was gone. Her father's arms, her shield, her fortress, were a continent and a universe away. Her friends, her mission, her future, all vanished behind a wall of smoke. Even the small, stubborn hope that she might see them again was obliterated in the blast. All that remained was the brutal thud of Malec's heartbeat under her cheek and the suffocating certainty that she was truly, finally, alone.

And this was her fate: to be carried into the unknown by the monster who'd stolen everything. To be remade into something that might survive, or to break, piece by precious piece, beneath the weight of his possessive, hungry love.

Malec's hand curled in her hair, fingers tightening as if he could feel her slipping away inside. He murmured something in that old, terrible language, soft, coaxing, a command disguised as comfort. But she didn't hear him. She was drowning in the silence left behind by everything she'd lost, drifting farther from herself with every hoofbeat, every mile that separated her from the ashes of her world.

And in her mind, she saw her father's eyes, furious, desperate, promising to come for her.

She saw Lilly's terrified face, Oliver's limp body, the bodies of the friends and kin she might never see again. The names of the dead and the missing tangled in her chest like barbed wire, choking her with regret. All she had left were memories, and the monster who thought love was a thing you could take, not give. Her tears came harder then, silent and endless, as the horse carried them away from everything she had ever known, into a dawn that felt colder and crueler than any night.

She barely recognized the voice that tore from her throat, hoarse, wild, wounded. All the agony and rage she'd buried beneath layers of survival surged up at once, shattering through the thick silence between them. Her limbs jerked as she twisted in his arms, nails digging into the stiff fabric of his coat, desperate for something to tear, to break, to hurt as much as she did.

Malec didn't waver. He let her writhe and scream, his hold unyielding but not cruel, a band of iron forged only for her. He took every blow, the frantic kicks, the pounding fists, never once blocking, never punishing. He absorbed her pain as if it was his own, he bit down hard, so hard it hurt, knuckles white where his hands gripped her to keep her from slipping through the cracks he'd made. He felt every sob shudder through her like a wave, battering his soul, leaving splinters of regret wedged in places he'd thought were stone.

This, her pain, was the price of love, wasn't it? His whole life, he had learned that love was endurance, that to love was to keep, to guard, to shelter at any cost. But now her grief was a knife twisting in his chest, showing him the ugly side of the truth he lived by.

He lowered his head, breath trembling against her hair, and spoke not as a warlord, but as something small and wounded and raw.

"You're home now, little dove. No one will ever take you from me again." His voice was a thread, torn between command and plea.

"You call this home?" she choked, the words cracked and bleeding. Her vision blurred with tears she couldn't swallow anymore. "You punched me! You hurt me! You almost killed my father, my friends! And now you hold me like nothing happened?! You destroyed everything! My father, my friends, my people, they're all gone, and it's because of you! How dare you say I'm home!"

Each accusation found its mark, each sob was a lash across his pride. But he held her, fierce and trembling, because it was the only way he knew how. Love was not gentle in him. Love was not open palms or easy words. It was the drive to protect, to possess, to keep her close, safe, even if she hated him for it. He would rather have her rage in his arms than risk her lost to the world.

He could not let go, not when letting go meant losing the one piece of himself that still felt alive.

Her sobs grew harder, until finally she burned through her anger and collapsed against him, limp, spent, her head heavy on his chest. Her curls stuck to his skin, damp with sweat and tears, her body shaking with what was left of the storm. He felt it all. The devastation. The loss. The cold of her grief settling between them, making even his own body feel too large, too rough, too wrong.

His eyes burned as he looked down at her, desperate for words and finding only hunger and shame in their place. He could not give her comfort. All he could offer was the shield of his arms, the steadiness of his body, the single-minded promise that nothing in this world or any other would take her away again.

The warhorse carried them deeper into the shadowed forest, the world behind them smoldering, the world ahead a mystery. Her tears soaked through his tunic, her broken sobs the only sound he heard. He had her again. But as she trembled in his arms, Malec understood, winning her body was nothing. Winning her soul might cost him everything he had left.

Her body bucked in his arms a second wind of despair and anger as she screamed, her fists battering against his chest, her legs kicking at the heavy stirrups and leather.

"LET ME GO!" She spat the words like poison. "I hate you! I hate what you've done to me!"

Her voice cracked at the end, scraping up every ounce of rage and heartbreak she still possessed.

Malec took it all, her anger, her curses, her grief, swallowing them like bitter medicine. Let her rage, he thought, let her hate. It was still a kind of tether. Still proof she was alive, that she had not broken completely. He had lived hundreds of years without softness. He could endure her storm a little longer. He believed, with all the battered hope left in him, that pain was only the first stage of love's rebirth. That eventually, in time, her rage would cool, her wounds would scar, and the bond he felt burning between them would finally root itself in her heart. But when she went quiet, trembling in his arms, her voice wavered.

"Why?" The question came like the softest plea. Not a weapon, but a wound.

He froze. The wind rushed through the burned trees and filled the aching silence, the world holding its breath. He didn't look away, didn't try to mask the shame that flickered through his gaze. He was exposed, raw and uncertain for the first time in memory. There was nothing kingly or elegant in him now, just an Awyan stripped bare by a love he couldn't understand, a hunger he couldn't satisfy.

"Why me?" she demanded, voice rising, each word stabbing through him. "Why did you take everything from me? Why did you choose me, when you could have had anyone else, someone who might actually love you back?"

He shut his eyes for a heartbeat, then opened them again, his control slipping by fractions. His mouth parted, and he struggled for language that was never meant for this kind of confession. There was no poetry left in him, only the feverish, inarticulate need that had haunted him since the moment their souls had tangled.

"You are the only thing that has ever made sense to me," he said, the words rough and imperfect, spoken like a man fumbling for salvation in the dark.

The memory of her, the sound of her laughter, the warmth of her skin, the sharpness of her mind, had become the only constant in a world that had always felt too cold, too distant, too empty. The need to keep her, to have her close, was the only law that survived the storm of his existence.

"You burn through me," Malec went on, voice unsteady as if it hurt to speak it aloud. "You undo everything I am. And I... I would raze entire cities if it meant keeping you in my arms."

He held her tighter, not as a jailer but as a drowning elf clutching a lifeline. The silence that fell between them was crushing. She stared at him, eyes full of loathing and pain and exhaustion so deep it hollowed her out from the inside.

For Melodie, the words landed like poison, hot and corrosive. They weren't beautiful. They weren't what she wanted to hear. They were the confessions of a monster who thought obsession was love, who believed that breaking her was the same as cherishing her. She glared at him, trembling and raw, all hope burned out, all mercy gone. She wanted to scream that it wasn't enough. That she didn't care. That nothing he could say would ever make her want him.

Instead, she stared past him, toward the ruined horizon, her jaw set, tears drying cold on her cheeks.

He saw it, how utterly lost she was to him, at least for now, and it gutted him more deeply than any wound. He shifted behind her, arms locked firm, chest rising and falling with each careful breath, as if he could hold her together by sheer will. His hand splayed possessively against her abdomen, warm even through the damp of her shirt, but all the comfort in the world meant nothing now.

"You will want for nothing," he said quietly, his voice that velvet iron, pitched for her alone. "Warmth. Safety. A bed you can call your own. I will protect you from any who threaten you. Always."

She let out a strangled, bitter laugh, no joy, just something broken scraping loose.

"You think I care about a bed? About food, about soft things, about safety?" She twisted to look at him, eyes wet, dark, burning. "You think safety means anything when it costs me everything? The people I love think I'm dead. And you, " Her voice wavered, the next words catching jagged in her throat. "You took away my future."

He said nothing. His silence pressed against her like a wall, steady and infuriating.

"God, you're so fucking selfish," she hissed, voice trembling as she forced herself to say the thing she knew would hurt him. "It's never about me. Not really. It's about you, your feelings, your need to control, your precious bond. I don't even matter."

Her words echoed back at her, as if the empty forest itself wanted to deny it. But Malec only stared forward, jaw ticked with restrain, gaze fixed on the horizon as if he could outlast the storm in her.

"You'll have everything I can give you," he said, trying for gentle, failing. "I will not let you know loneliness or want—"

She cut him off, her voice raw and sharp.

"Everything? What if I wanted children?" The words exploded between them, sudden, a wound torn open. "You can give me a bed, Malec, but you can't give me a family. I can never have children with you. Being with you means I will always be alone. Do you even understand that?"

A silence, terrible and infinite, yawned open. For a moment, she saw the mask slip, the mask of a warlord, a prince, a god. She saw the boy inside, ancient and unspeakably sad. His hand, still at her stomach, tensed, then loosened. His voice, when it came, was almost a whisper.

"I know. It wounds me too, Allora." His eyes glittered, unshed grief and helpless yearning. "I would give you the world if I could. But some things are beyond my power, even for you. And yet... I cannot let you go."

She turned away, tears slipping down her cheeks. "Then you can't give me what I need. Not love. Not a real choice. Not even hope."

He held her tighter, desperate, trying to anchor them both.

"You are everything to me," he breathed. "You are the blood in my veins, the breath in my lungs. I cannot, will not, live without you."

She let out a broken, weary sound, something between a sob and a laugh, bitter as poison.

"That's not love, Malec. That's just need. You're soulbound. I am not."

He stilled behind her. The words hit him like a hammer, smashing through his composure. For a breath, he looked utterly lost.

But he recovered, just enough to say, "It does not matter. You are mine. You will remain."

She sagged, defeated and exhausted, shaking in his arms. Her world behind her was nothing but smoke and memory. Ahead was only captivity, velvet-lined, yes, but a cage all the same. The woods swallowed their silence. Even the Awyan soldiers kept their distance, as if they could feel the shattering between the two souls astride the warhorse. Malec's grip was tight and haunted; her rage simmered, her hope guttered low. And still, he held her, as if holding on could change the world. As if, by sheer force, he could make her love him.

But all Melodie felt was grief, loss for what could never be, for the children she'd never have, for the love that was really only a prison with velvet bars.

The air reeked of ash and smoldering earth, and every breath seared her lungs with loss. Behind her, the world she'd fought for, her home, her father's laugh, her team's voices, the crackle of radios in the dark, was nothing but rubble and fire, dissolving into memory.

Tears leaked hot and silent down her cheeks, streaking the grime on her skin, but she didn't wipe them away. She let them fall, soaking into the black fur of Malec's cloak, marking him with her heartbreak, her defiance. Her jaw ached from clenching it shut, from swallowing back the scream that burned in her chest. Her heart pounded a broken rhythm, loss, loss, loss, loss, every beat a reminder of what he'd taken. He thought she was beaten. That her stillness was surrender. That the sobs wracking her shoulders were the sound of a wild thing broken to his will. He didn't know. He couldn't feel the storm building beneath her skin, the poisonous, the promise of vengeance winding tight through her veins.

She'd be perfect. The perfect captive. The perfect mate. She'd let him fall in love.

And when the time was right, she would kill his hope the way he killed hers. She would make him suffer, patiently, meticulously, beautifully, until he finally understood the kind of ruin he'd wrought.

She spoke quietly, her voice thin and soft as silk, trembling with exhaustion but steeped in venom.

"Fine." The word floated between them like a promise, or a curse.

Malec's arms tightened, mistaking her quiet for peace, his chin coming to rest on her head, breathing her in as if this was the beginning of something new. She barely turned her face, so he could feel her breath, the heat of her rage curling beneath the surface.

> "You want me?" she whispered, voice low and lethal. "You've got me. Cage me, bind me, fuck me. I'll give you loyalty. I'll give you smiles and soft lies. And when your heart finally rests in my hand, I'll set it on fire."

And as the ruin of her old world smoldered in the distance, as the last echo of home faded into ash and silence, Melodie made her vow. Let him think he'd won. Let him think he was safe.

Because the real war had only just begun.

End of Book 1...